CUTTING EDGE

CUTTING EDGE

WARD LARSEN

A TOM DOHERTY ASSOCIATES BOOK NEW YORK

This is a work of fiction. All of the characters, organizations, and events portrayed in this novel are either products of the author's imagination or are used fictitiously.

CUTTING EDGE

Copyright © 2018 by Ward Larsen

A Forge Book
Published by Tom Doherty Associates
175 Fifth Avenue
New York, NY 10010

www.tor-forge.com

Forge® is a registered trademark of Macmillan Publishing Group, LLC.

Library of Congress Cataloging-in-Publication Data

Names: Larsen, Ward, author.
Title: Cutting edge / Ward Larsen.
Description: New York : Tom Doherty Associates, [2018]
Identifiers: LCCN 2017039663 (print) | LCCN 2017044103 (ebook) |
    ISBN 9780765393425 (ebook) | ISBN 9780765393418 (hardcover)
Subjects: | GSAFD: Suspense fiction. | Mystery fiction.
Classification: LCC PS3612.A7734 (ebook) | LCC PS3612.A7734 C88 2018 (print) |
    DDC 813/.6—dc23
LC record available at https://lccn.loc.gov/2017039663

Our books may be purchased in bulk for promotional, educational, or business use. Please contact your local bookseller or the Macmillan Corporate and Premium Sales Department at 1-800-221-7945, extension 5442, or by email at MacmillanSpecialMarkets@macmillan.com.

First Edition: January 2018

Printed in the United States of America

0 9 8 7 6 5 4 3 2 1

TO KARA,

for giving me so many stories to tell

The first step is to establish that
something is possible.

–ELON MUSK,
technology innovator and founder of
the pioneering Neuralink Corporation

1

The second time he died was more difficult than the first. More difficult because he saw it coming.

He stirred to consciousness between the two events, twin sources of light above him seeming like a pair of struggling midday suns behind thick layers of cloud. He was flat on his back, that much he knew, and beneath him were sheets that had been washed too many times and stretched tight over a thin mattress.

The voices were every bit as opaque as the light, a man and a woman, neither familiar. He could make out most of their words, a disjointed back-and-forth that seemed to arrive through a soup can.

How long had he been awake? A minute? Two? Long enough.

A shadow blocked out the suns, and again he willed his eyes to open. There was no response. All voluntary movement had ceased. Then a brush of warm breath came across his face, moist and without scent.

And somewhere, he was sure, a needle. His first hint, moments ago, had been the smell of alcohol. Not the beery scent of a pub or anything from a crystalline decanter, but the biting, antiseptic variety. His hand was pulled outward, and two fingers probed the flesh of his useless right arm in that time-honored way. *Tap tap. Tap tap.* Searching for a fat, well-formed vein. Then, apparently, success. A cool wet swab rubbed the flesh of his inner arm.

"What's the point of that?" said the man.

"Oh, right," the woman replied. "Force of habit, I guess."

The patient was not prone to panic—no man of his background could be—yet a sense of desperation began to settle. *Move an arm, a hand! A finger, for God's sake!* He tried mightily, yet every muscle in his body seemed detached, like a machine whose gears had disconnected. The pain in his head was excruciating, unyielding, as if his skull might explode. But at least it told him he was alive. *What had happened?*

"Want me to do it?" the man asked.

"No, I'm okay."

"It bothered you last time."

"I said I'm okay," she countered tersely.

Open your eyes! Move! No response.

The jab came quick and sharp, but was over in an instant. Nothing compared to the constant throb in his head. What followed, however, was worse than anything he'd ever experienced. A terrible sensation of cold. No, not cold. Frost coursing through his veins. It crawled into his arm, toward his shoulder, numbing everything in its path. Leaving no more than twitching, frozen nerves in its wake. He battled for alertness, fought to think logically as the glacier inside him flowed toward his neck and chest. When it reached his heart, piercing like an ice pick, the first flutter of oblivion arrived.

He felt a cool circle of metal clamp to his chest. A stethoscope.

"Almost," she said. "This one's going fast."

"I'll get the bag."

The lights above began to fade, a gathering overcast. The voices fell to no more than unintelligible mutterings. His only remaining sense was that of touch. He could still feel the sheets, the needle. The cold within.

But why can't I move?

His ending thoughts were oddly lucid and vivid. The needle being pulled. Adhesive sensor pads getting plucked from his chest. His body was rocked from side to side as they worked cool plastic under him. A zipper closing, beginning at his toes, then a long, practiced pull up over his knees and waist. Over his chest and face.

And finally, all at once, the darkness was absolute.

———

The nurse watched her coworker wriggle the sealed gray bag back and forth, adjusting it to the center of the gurney.

"Why no autopsy on this one?" he asked.

"Those were the doctor's instructions. He said he already knew what went wrong with the procedure." The nurse clicked off the brake and began wheeling the gurney toward the door. "I can take it from here. Why don't you get a head start on the cleanup."

"Yeah . . . I guess you're right. We won't be using this room again for at least a few months. Can you believe they're going to pay us to just sit at home until the next phase?"

Neither commented on that thought, which only added to the nurse's discomfort.

"Wait!" he said. "I don't see the last syringe we used. We have to account for that."

"Crap!" she muttered. "I must have dropped it into the sharps container."

He frowned at her. "Force of habit again?"

She said nothing, but paused at the door, watched him peer into a red plastic box full of spent needles.

"Okay," he said. "I think maybe I see it. I'll just get rid of the whole box."

"Good," she said. "And do me a favor, don't tell the doctor about that— you know how he can be."

"No problem," he said. Then as an apparent afterthought, "Maybe we could get together for dinner tonight."

Having worked with the man for six months, she was accustomed to his clumsy come-ons. Even so, being delivered from behind a surgical mask, by a man wearing a gown and fabric booties—the proposition seemed inane by even his standards. He was nearly sixty, with a big belly and a bad comb-over, and as far as she knew had never been married. She was matronly, on the high side of forty, and over the whole damned dating thing. If that wasn't enough, his timing couldn't have been worse. She said without flinching, "I have plans."

Before he could respond, she pushed through the swinging doors and turned left down the hall. She wondered how the man had ended up here. Aside from the doctor, there were only four of them—carefully selected to be sure, and competent, but each with some strike that had left them outcasts in their professions. Men and women who were happy to have a job at the price of discretion. At the elevator she hit the call button and set the brake on the gurney. The incinerator in the basement was already fired up.

The cab arrived, and she pushed the gurney inside and took a last look down the hall. When the doors sucked closed, she ignored the button labeled B and instead pushed 1.

2

One week later

It is a shoreline that begs for words like "desolate" and "austere." On a map
it forms a ragged line between Maine and the North Atlantic, a whipsaw
collection of coves and promontories that defy any compass, and whose nameless breaks and repetitive tree lines seem designed by God himself to confuse mariners. The ribbon of shore muddles its way north out of the affluent
landings of Cape Elizabeth and Kennebunk, only to be swallowed hundreds
of miles later by the indifferent wilds of Canada. Standing helpless in the
middle is the place called Cape Split, a waypoint to nothingness more ignored
than forgotten.

If there is a beach it is in name only, a place where rock coexists with sand,
and where great tidal shelves lounge belligerently on the threshold of a cold
and tireless sea. Stout stands of pine and spruce shoulder straight to the shore,
towering over the shattered skeletons of ancestors washed up at their feet,
and leaning ever so slightly seaward as if anticipating the next big blow. Just
offshore, islands of submerged rocks rise and fall with the tide, and deep in
the valleys between them rest the remains of innumerable boats whose hardy
survivors find their names echoed generations later in the nearby villages.

Shorebirds by the thousands build nests in the low cliffs, and thick-pelted
animals teem through the forest. Indeed, if there is an underrepresented species on Cape Split it is the humans, well outnumbered in summer by moose,

and on the leading edge of winter, after the annual outward migration, a population that cannot even keep numbers with the resident black bears. Those unreliable souls who depart Cape Split after the fair and brief summer for the most part leave behind sprawling seaside mansions, whereas the year-round residents, a more hearty and practical bunch, tend toward cottages, these also by the sea, but far enough back in the pines to cut the lashings from the inevitable nor'easters. It was in one of these small lodgings, coyly south-facing and near the Eastern Pitch, that the nurse had taken up residence.

She had come to the coast nine years ago—nine years exactly, because people here tracked such things as a matter of pride. She was not a local, but to her credit not from the city, and she kept to herself a bit more than she should have. There were rumors of a bad divorce, others of an inheritance pirated by siblings. It was all quite dramatic, and likely no more than gossip. But she *was* a nurse. There had been no mistaking the proper bandage she'd put on the young boy who cut himself on the rocks two summers ago, nor the dutiful CPR she'd performed, to no avail, on old man Ferguson the winter before. At least one year-round resident had seen her car parked behind an urgent care clinic in Bangor, although he couldn't say whether she'd been there as a patient or an employee. She was polite to the clerk at the grocery in Columbia, and equally so when gassing her old Honda every Sunday at the Circle K on Route 1. Her only defined shortfall, if it could be characterized as such, was laid bare by the garbageman, who swore by all that was distilled that the nurse's recycle bucket was invariably filled with enough wine bottles to maintain three thirsty men. Still, as with her social reticence, that was her business. There were two types of year-rounders in Cape Split—those whose ancestors swam onto its rocks, and the rest who came to escape the dispensed ills of life.

Her weathered cottage—because no place with such a view could be called a shack—was little more than four walls of shaker siding, once a happy blue, and a roof that didn't leak. One path led to the road, another to the sea. The nearest neighbor was half a mile in either direction. It was a small place, and private, which here was saying something. And by one reliable account, for the last three weeks the recycle bucket had been empty.

Joan Chandler rose early that morning, not much after the sun, and stepped onto the small porch that overlooked the sea. She stretched gingerly, thinking the light seemed unusually intense. Her heart was racing even before her morning coffee, and she steadied one trembling hand on the rail. The trees were silent in a slack wind, the sea serene. Other than a few gulls wheeling in the distance, the world outside was uncommonly still. *How fitting,* she thought.

Her patient hadn't stirred in the week since she'd brought him here. Or for that matter, in the week before, not that anyone was counting. He had stabilized, as far as she could tell, although her equipment was laughably rudimentary. The portable heart monitor she had stolen from work—it would never be missed because it had been closeted for dodgy leads. There were scads of redundant equipment in the small place where she worked—lab, clinic, she'd never known what to call it—and she'd reasoned that one fault-prone monitor wouldn't be missed. God, what a budget they had. Everything was new, full digital suites suitable for surgery fitted into each of the four rooms. Most outlandish of all were the imaging machines: functional magnetic resonance imaging, gamma knife, helical X-ray CT, all brand-new and perfectly calibrated.

Chandler knew little about any of that—she'd been recruited for the operating room. Her baseline clinical experience had been years ago, right after nursing school, and like so many in her profession she had gravitated to a more lucrative specialty: perioperative nursing. She'd made a good living before her troubles—an abusive husband, two miscarriages, and a financially ruinous divorce. Her drinking had gotten the better of her, costing her a good job—a career, in truth, or so she'd thought. Then she'd been granted one last chance, the most peculiar of job offers.

She pulled open the weather door, which creaked heavily, and stepped back inside to check on her patient. There was no chart at the foot of his bed. For that matter, there wasn't really a bed, her little used trundle substituting for a proper high-low setup. Aside from the heart monitor, there was little else. An IV pole, now empty, and a few supplies on a shelf: bandages mostly, and an assortment of medications to ward off infection and manage pain. Like the rest, all pilfered from the clinic since the patient had arrived. Since she'd made her decision.

She took a pulse and a blood pressure reading. Much better than last week. His color was improving, and respiration seemed normal, not the shallow rasps of the day when she'd wheeled him up the porch in the collapsible wheelchair that had barely fit into the trunk of her Honda.

He was a good-looking young man. Short brown hair with streaks of blond from the distant summer, regular features, and a swimmer's build. She checked his eyes now and again for pupil dilation, and found them vacant and clear, and, she couldn't deny, a storybook blue. Chandler wondered how different they would look with life behind them. Aside from the legend behind his injuries, which might or might not be true, she had little background information on patient B—that was how he was referred to at the clinic, and of course she knew why. But she *had* learned his name. Against regulations, she'd rifled through the doctor's files and found it. She had wanted that much. If there was a date of birth in the record she hadn't been able to find it, but she guessed him to be thirty, maybe a bit younger. Fifteen years her junior, more or less. Almost young enough to be the son she'd never had.

Chandler sighed. She went to the kitchen and put the coffeepot on the stove.

He woke just before noon, while she was changing the bandage on his head. His eyes cracked open, only slightly at first, then suddenly came wide. Even in that startled state, vacant and imprecise, the eyes were as blue as any she'd seen.

"Well, hello," she said in her best nurse's singsong.

He responded by blinking once.

"Take it easy. You've had an accident."

He looked around the place, trying to get his bearings. His lips began to quiver as he tried to build a word.

"Go slow, it's all right. You'll have all the time you need to recover."

"Wa . . . water," he rasped.

For the first time in two months, the nurse smiled.

3

By the third day the patient was sitting up in bed and eating solid food. As he downed a second plate of pasta, he asked, "What can you tell me about the accident I was in—I don't remember anything."

"That's often the case, Trey." They had settled that much the first day. Trey DeBolt, originally from Colorado Springs, twenty-seven years old and single. He was a Coast Guard rescue swimmer, one of the most physically demanding specialties in all the services—and probably the only reason he was still alive. "You took a beating when your helicopter went down. Your right shoulder was damaged, and there were a number of cuts and contusions. The most significant injuries were to your head."

"No kidding. How about another Percocet?"

"No."

"I need something."

"Only on schedule." Chandler said it firmly, no mention that stock was running low.

"I remember a hospital . . . at least I think I do. Now I'm in a beach house?"

He had heard the surf yesterday, and she'd admitted that much. "I told you, it's complicated. I'll explain everything when you're stronger. For now you're safe, you're recovering. What's the last thing you do remember?"

"You're changing the subject."

"Obviously."

Trey DeBolt smiled, another first. "I remember reporting for work at the station . . . Kodiak, Alaska." His eyes went far away, something new recollected. "Then we got scrambled for a mission. There was a rescue." After a lengthy pause, he shook his head. "I can't remember where we went, or what we were after. A foundering ship, a lost crewman. It was a dire situation, I know that much. The weather was awful, but . . . no, I can't remember anything else."

"Parts are coming back—that's good. I can't tell you any details of the accident. I only know that when they brought you into surgery you were in bad shape."

"What about my crew, Lieutenant Morgan and Adams? Mikey?"

"You were the only survivor, Trey—I'm sorry."

He was silent for a time. "That's a Class-A mishap. There will be an investigation. Has anyone come to interview me?"

"I'm sure they will. In time."

"When?" he demanded. His first touch of impatience.

"I don't know."

He looked out the window. "This isn't Alaska."

"You're in Maine."

"Maine?"

"You were brought here because you needed our doctors. They specialize in head trauma, the best in the world. Tell me—who will be wondering about you?"

"Wondering? What do you mean—like my commander?"

"No, he's been notified."

DeBolt's eyes narrowed. "She."

"Sorry—I was only told it had been done. I was thinking more along the lines of family."

"It's all in my personnel file."

She waited.

"My father is dead. Mom is in Colorado Springs, but she's got early-onset Alzheimer's, so I doubt she's been told anything."

"Brothers or sisters?"

"None."

"Significant other?"

"I'm between relationships—isn't that what everyone says these days? I've been stationed on an island in the Aleutians for a year, and the guy-to-girl ratio is pretty bleak."

"All right."

"I'm taking classes, an online program. At some point my professor will wonder what became of me."

"What are you studying?"

"I'm halfway to my bachelor's degree in biology. I like the Coast Guard, but I'm not sure I'll last twenty years."

She stood abruptly. "Your appetite is improving. I should go for provisions. Is there anything you'd like?"

"Drugs."

She frowned.

"Maybe an omelet. And some OJ."

"That I can manage." She was out the door.

The room fell quiet. DeBolt looked all around. He tried to remember more about what had happened in Alaska. A small engine kick to life, followed by tires crunching over gravel.

He fell fast asleep.

It was sleep in only the roughest sense, troubled dreams jolting him in and out of consciousness. Shooting images, angular shapes, letters and numbers, all colliding in his battered brain as he drifted just beyond the grip of consciousness. He was rescued by a noise, a sharp wooden creak. DeBolt opened his eyes and looked around the room. He saw no one.

"Joan?"

No reply.

He wondered how long he'd been out, but there was no way to tell. Not a clock anywhere. He turned his head gingerly, examining the place in detail, and found every limit of movement a new adventure in pain.

What was it about this room?

Then it struck him. It was completely devoid of anything electronic. No television, no computer, not even a microwave in the tiny kitchen. He had yet to see Joan use a cell phone, which in this day and age was striking. Was the place that remote, completely beyond cell coverage? Or was his nurse an antitechnology type, a back-to-basics pioneer with a vegetable garden and two chickens out back, a wind generator on the chimney?

Whatever.

He sat up straight, fighting a stab of pain in his skull. Never one to sit still, DeBolt began moving his arms, up and down, rotating in expanding circles. Not bad. He graduated to leg lifts, but that somehow involved the muscles in his upper back, and a bolt of lightning struck the base of his neck. He lay back down.

A car crunched closer on gravel outside. DeBolt heard the engine die, a door open and close. Then an unfamiliar voice as Joan Chandler began conversing with someone—apparently a neighbor. Most of it he didn't catch. But he heard enough.

Soon she was inside with an armload of groceries, the visitor having been sent packing.

"Who was that?" he asked.

She busied herself unloading two paper sacks. DeBolt would have thought her a reusable-bag sort.

"Bob Denton, lives in town. He does a bit of handiwork for me now and again. Said he was in the neighborhood, and he wondered how my weather stripping was holding up."

"You told him my name was Michael."

A lengthy pause. "I have a nephew by that name."

"You have a patient named Trey."

She slammed a can of beans on the counter, her face tightening as she fought . . . what? Anger?

"Look," said DeBolt, "I don't mean to be ungracious. I appreciate all you've done me. But this is no hospital. I've seen no doctors, and haven't been allowed to contact anyone I know. What the hell is going on?"

She came to his bed and sat down on the edge. Instead of answering, she began unwrapping the wide bandage on his head. Once done, she took the old gauze to the bathroom and returned with two hand mirrors. She held them so he could see the wounds on the back of his skull. What he saw took his breath away. Two deep scars formed a V, joining near the base of his scalp, and three smaller wounds were evident elsewhere. There had to be a hundred stitches, but it all seemed to be healing; hair was beginning to grow back where his head had been shaved, covering the damage.

She turned the mirrors away.

After a long silence, he asked, "Will there be any long-term effects?"

"Some scarring of course, but the damage to your scalp was minimal. As long as you keep your hair a certain length, your appearance will be unchanged."

"That's not what I mean."

She met his gaze. "The trauma to your brain was significant, but so far I see no evidence of cognitive impairment. Your speech and movement seem normal, which is a very good sign. But then, I'm no expert."

"But I *will* see them at some point—the experts."

"Of course you will. Tell me, do you notice anything different?"

"In what way?"

"Mental processes, I suppose. Have you had any unusual thoughts or sensations?"

"I'm hungry, but that's hardly unusual."

She waited.

"No," he finally said, "although I'm really not sure what you're asking. There is something when I sleep, I suppose. I see things—angular shapes, light on dark."

The nurse almost said something, but instead launched into a series of cognitive exams. She made him calculate a tip for a restaurant bill, spell a given word forward then backward, arrange historical events in chronological order. When she asked him to draw a picture of his childhood home, an increasingly irritated DeBolt said, "If I earn a passing grade, will I be allowed out of the house?"

"You're lucky to be alive right now, Petty Officer DeBolt."

"And you're lucky I'm not well enough to get up and walk away."

"You will be soon. For your own sake, I hope you don't. I hope you'll stay a bit longer."

"How caring," he said, his sarcasm falling to crassness. Realizing he'd crossed a line, he sighed and rubbed his forehead. "I'm sorry."

"It's all right. When you've been a nurse as long as I have, you avoid taking things personally—force of habit."

Those last words, the tone and intonation, clicked in DeBolt's dented brain like a light switch. *Force of habit.* "You . . . ," he said tentatively, "you were there in the hospital. You put the needle in my arm." He shivered inwardly, remembering the glacial sensation of the drug crawling through his body.

She didn't answer right away. "Yes, I administered a special narcotic—it's what saved you, Trey. There are other things that must remain unsaid for now, until your recovery is more complete. But please . . . *please* trust me when I say that I only want what's best for you."

DeBolt searched her open gaze, her earnest expression. And he did trust her.

4

DeBolt was soon walking with confidence around the cottage and porch, and days later he set out toward the rocky beachhead. The next weeks were full of rehabilitation, the intensity increasing and pain lessening until it was something near exercise. The nurse performed rudimentary tests: an eye chart on the far wall, whispered hearing evaluations, all of which DeBolt passed, or so he guessed because they were not repeated. She brought him clothes, ill fitting and—he was sure—purchased from a secondhand store. He thanked her for all of it.

The quandary of time was settled when she bought him a watch, a cheap Timex that promised but failed to glow in the dark. It was accurate enough, though, and DeBolt found strange exhilaration in keeping a schedule. Wake at 6:00 A.M. Soft run on the beach, three miles back and forth over the same quarter-mile stretch of rock-strewn sand. Breakfast at 7:10 A.M. Rest until 8:15 A.M. The running he hated—always had—and with obvious reluctance she allowed him to swim. He took to the water gratefully, but complained the cold was intolerable, and she managed to procure a used neoprene wet suit, two sizes too large, that made the daily plunge bearable. Each day brought advances and, rare setbacks aside, DeBolt progressed in but one direction. The headaches lessened, and so correspondingly did his need for pain medication. New examinations were introduced—memory games, mathematical puzzles, cognitive exercises. She assured him in every case that he performed well.

Yet as the patient was improving, he sensed a notable decline in his caregiver. She seemed increasingly withdrawn and distant, more so each time he pressed her for an explanation of how he'd ended up in a beach house in New England after the frozen Bering Sea. Her descending mood was more apparent each day, relentless and foreboding. One morning, as she counted his push-ups on the beach, he spotted a young girl far in the distance. She was eight, perhaps ten years old, prancing barefoot through tide pools with a net and a bucket. As she neared the edge of the rock outcropping where she was gathering creatures, DeBolt recognized a shift in the sea beyond—a strong rip current funneling offshore. He said they should warn the girl to stay clear of the water. Chandler responded by immediately ushering him shoreward.

DeBolt complied at first, but then stopped halfway to the cottage, fixed and immovable—his first resistance to any of her instructions.

"Tell me one thing," he said. "Besides you, does anyone know where I am?"

"No."

"I'm in the service. A soldier who doesn't report his whereabouts is considered AWOL. That's a crime under military law."

"I understand. Soon I'll explain everything . . . I promise."

After considering it for some time, he turned and went inside.

That night she sat on the porch with a glass and a full bottle. She emptied both in silence, and sometime near midnight went unsteadily to her room. He heard her bed creak once, then nothing.

The weather was taking its first turn to winter. Before sunset, DeBolt had watched banks of slate-gray cloud whipping in fast and low, and he noticed that the ubiquitous flocks of seagulls had disappeared. The forest began to groan under a pulsating wind, and waves thundered ashore in a continuous pronouncement, absent the punctuating gaps of receding stillness.

Unable to sleep, DeBolt pulled a dog-eared novel from a bookshelf and went to the trundle bed, more inviting now that the monitors and IV pole had been pushed aside. As he crossed the room he looked through the open bedroom door and saw Chandler splayed awkwardly across her bed. He paused, studied her for a moment, then entered the room hesitantly. Her hair was stiff and matted, folded to one side, and her nightdress crumpled—

completely still, she looked like a long-forgotten doll on a child's closet shelf. He doubted she had moved since passing out. DeBolt guessed she might be attractive if she wanted to be, yet her focus on his recovery was so absolute, so single-minded, it seemed to preclude even her own upkeep. Not for the first time, he wondered what was driving her.

Her blanket had slipped to the floor, and he retrieved it and covered her. Other than a slight tremor in one hand, she didn't move. He turned back to the main room, and near the doorway his eye was caught by a file folder on the highboy dresser. It was plain manila stock, and on the title tag DeBolt saw his own name written in pencil, sloppy block letters that were unsettlingly familiar. It was his copy of his Coast Guard medical records—a folder that should have been in his apartment in Alaska.

How the hell did that get here?

It occurred to DeBolt then that for all the diagnostic tests Chandler had performed, she'd never once taken a note. When he'd last seen the folder it had held perhaps fifty pages of military-grade paperwork. Now it looked exceedingly thin, and one page edged out from a corner. The positioning of the file on the dresser could not have been more obvious. He also noted that beneath his name someone had added in black ink, *META PROJECT,* and below that, *OPTION BRAVO.*

His eyes went to Chandler, then back to the folder. He picked it up and found but two sheets of paper inside. He had never seen either. On top was a printout of a news article from the *Alaska Dispatch News,* a four-paragraph summary of the crash of a Coast Guard MH-60 in the Bering Sea six weeks earlier. Again he saw *META PROJECT* and *OPTION BRAVO* scrawled in a hurried hand that was not his own. He read the article once, took a deep breath, then read it again. His eyes settled on one sentence in the second paragraph.

> *Confirmed to be killed in the accident were aircraft commander Lt. Anthony Morgan, copilot LTJG Thomas Adams, AN Michael Schull, and rescue swimmer PO2 Trey DeBolt.*

He stared at it for a full minute. *Confirmed to be killed . . .*

With gauged caution, he lifted the printed page to see what was beneath. The second paper was of thicker bond, and carried a stamp and signatures, everything about it implying official weight. It was a death certificate issued by the state of Alaska. There were a few lines of legalese, and in the center two fields of information that finalized the shock:

Name of Deceased: Trey Adam DeBolt
Cause of death: blunt trauma to head/aircraft accident

5

DeBolt did not sleep like the dead man he supposedly was. In recent nights he'd stirred frequently as bolts of light and dark, post-traumatic he was sure, coursed through his beaten head. Now he lay awake trying only for control, some logic to replace the encroaching madness. The accident, the severe injuries, a hospital stay he barely remembered. Chandler bringing him here, caring for him, isolating him. Her self-destructive behavior. There was simply no solution—every way DeBolt painted the facts, something seemed wrong, a wayward stroke of color that clashed with the rest. In the end, he drew but one conclusion. His time here was drawing to an end.

But what would take its place? Return to Alaska and the Coast Guard? A cheery hello to friends and coworkers who'd already attended his funeral? He wondered if he could walk into his station and claim amnesia. He had the head wounds to back it up. *I have no idea what happened, but here I am . . .*

The full truth, he decided, was not an option, because he saw no way to present it without harming Joan Chandler. She had brought him here, put him into hiding. Anyone taking those actions on face value could accuse her of endangering a gravely ill patient by keeping him outside a proper hospital environment. Yet DeBolt knew otherwise. He was convinced she'd saved his life, and put herself at professional risk by doing so. So he would protect Chandler, in turn, by taking the most difficult path—that of patience.

He was sure there was more to the story, circumstances his nurse had not yet explained. Details that would cause everything to make sense. A file, perhaps, he had not yet seen.

He rose at his customary hour of 6:00 A.M., and dressed quietly so as not to disturb Chandler—even though she hadn't moved since last night. DeBolt was on the beach before the sun lifted, ready for his morning run. The storm was building, and in the predawn darkness he stood at the water's edge and watched a rising sea. An intemperate wind whipped his hair, which was growing fast and increasingly out of regulation. Rain appeared imminent, and he briefly weighed it as an excuse to postpone his run. DeBolt looked up and down the beach. He'd seen no one since the young girl at the tide pools, and today was no different, only brown rock and sea and walls of evergreen forest. Staring at the desolate scene, he was reminded that Joan Chandler was the only person on earth who knew he was still alive. It seemed simultaneously comforting and troubling.

The sun cracked the horizon, a brilliant arc of red, and DeBolt realized he had not put on his Timex. Without actually speaking, and for no particular reason, he formed a very deliberate mental question: *What time does the sun rise today?*

He was debating whether to go back for his watch—in order to time his run, and the swim he would also not forego—when an odd sensation swept over him. It came like a strobe in his head, a tiny flash amid darkness. DeBolt blinked and closed his eyes, fearing he was suffering some manifestation of the injuries to his brain. An omen of complications.

Then, suddenly, he acquired a strange manner of focus. Ghosting behind tightly closed eyes he saw a perfectly clear set of numbers.

6:37 A.M.

DeBolt snapped his eyes open.

The sea and the rocks were there, steady and ever present. The sky was unerring, coming alive in subtle colors. The apparition disappeared as abruptly as it had come. With a thumb and forefinger he rubbed the orbits of his eyes, pressing and massaging until the last glimmer was gone. *Christ,* he thought, *now I'm seeing things.*

He took a single step back, turned, and struck out east on a determined sprint.

"I got a hit," said a young man from his basement workstation.

The woman at the computer next to him said, "What?"

They were located sixteen miles outside Washington, D.C., in a remote outpost run by DARPA, the Defense Advanced Research Projects Agency. The building in which they worked was as new as it was unremarkable. Indeed, should the word "nondescript" ever be translated into an architectural style, the place could be held as a masterpiece. It was rectangular in shape, although not perfectly so, one gentle portico at the front entrance, and a slightly larger blister behind at the supply dock. What lay inside, however, was anything but ordinary. The first floor was dedicated to electronics and cooling, and twin diesel generators allowed independence from the local power grid. The second floor consisted of a few offices and conference rooms, all rarely occupied, and three banks of supercomputers that churned without rest. The roof was banded by a high concrete wall, inside of which lay over a dozen antennae, all sealed in radomes to give protection from the elements and, more to the point, from unwanted prying eyes. There was a road and a parking lot, both new, and enough surrounding acreage to put the nearest neighbor a comfortable two miles away. There had been one man, old and cantankerous, who'd lived less than a mile to the east, and who had held out for a ridiculous price during construction. In the end, he got it.

It was all built for what was in the basement.

"Really . . . I got a hit," the young man repeated. "A primary response on node Bravo 7."

She set down her Coke. "No, Chris, you did *not* get a hit. How could you?"

He leaned back and invited her to check his screen. She did, and saw the tiny warning flag and data bubble.

"Has to be a bug in the software," she said.

"Could it be a test?" he ventured. "Do you think the general might input something like that to validate the system?" He was referring to the project director, Brigadier General Karl Benefield.

"Could be," she said. "That's pretty much all we're doing at this point, making sure everything works. You know our status—three months minimum before phase two is active. There won't be a valid warning like that until phase five goes live, which is years away."

"Should I report it?"

"Normally, I'd say yeah. But the general isn't even around this week—I hear he's buried in meetings to address software issues."

"So what should I do?"

With no small degree of irritation, she leaned over and began typing on his keyboard. "There," she said with finality, "all node interface alerts are disabled. We can bring it up at the next project integration meeting, but for now just forget it."

The young man looked at her questioningly, a *Can we do that?* expression.

The woman, who had been here for two years, since the project's very beginning, ignored him and went back to her screen.

The two technicians had no way of knowing that the warning had also lit on a second computer thirteen miles away, in a much larger five-sided building. The reaction there was very different.

6

Over the course of that day, DeBolt said nothing about having seen the folder. Nurse Chandler didn't ask if he had. The storm arrived in full gale, rain sheeting against the clapboard outer walls in what sounded like thousand-bullet volleys. Patient and caregiver hunkered down in the cottage, and shortly after dusk, as he cleaned up the remains of dinner, she caught him by surprise with, "You should go soon. You're well enough."

He weighed his response carefully, reflecting on what he'd learned last night. "Go where?"

"That's up to you. But physically you're ready—you're getting stronger every day." She was sitting at the counter, her nightly opener in hand.

"And what will you do? Stay here? Do that?"

She fell encased in a profound silence, and DeBolt let it run. The walls seemed to pull outward with each gust, then bend back in place—as though the house itself were breathing, gasping as it fought the storm. Both were startled by what sounded like a gunshot, then a clatter as something struck the house. Moments later subdued scraping noises kept time with the wind.

"A big tree branch," DeBolt said. "I should go outside and pull it away from the wall."

She didn't argue, which he took as agreement. DeBolt went to the door, ignoring an oversized slicker on the coatrack. As he reached for the handle, she said, "The surgery you had, Trey . . . it wasn't only to make you well. It was to make you different."

He paused where he was, staring at the door handle and waiting for more.

Nothing came. He heard the empty glass hit the counter and the bottle slide. Heard the tree limb clawing at a windowpane. DeBolt went outside.

The wind hit him like a wall, and he leaned forward to make headway. Rain slapped his face and pelted his body. He found it at the southeast corner, a pine branch with a base as thick as his leg leaning against the cabin's outer wall. He looked at the roof and a nearby window, saw no obvious damage, and began dragging the limb clear. DeBolt struggled mightily, the weight of the branch and the incessant wind conspiring against him. Feeling a stab of pain in his injured shoulder, he adjusted to a different grip until he had the limb far enough away. Out of breath from the exertion, he leaned against a tree and stared out at the sea. The night was black, no moon visible through the thick cloud cover, yet there was just enough ambient light to see whitecaps troweling the surface all the way to the horizon. Closer to shore he saw rows of massive breakers, and he watched them rise to height, poise in anticipation, and smash onto the beach, each stroke rearranging the shore in a maelstrom of sand and foam.

DeBolt stood mesmerized. He'd been outside no more than five minutes, yet he was soaked to the core, his shirt sodden, hair matted to his head. He shouldered into the wind and walked toward the shoreline, drawn by some primal urge to witness nature's fury up close. He was more familiar than most with the compulsion—that irrational human urge to test oneself, to step close to the edge and look fate in the eye. How many times had he seen it in Alaska? Fishermen and sailors who crossed the boundary of common sense, trying to lay one last longline or arrive home a day early. A few got lucky and beat the odds. The rest ended in one of three groups: those who were rescued, those whose bodies were recovered, and the rest who were never seen again.

His bare feet reached the surf, and the Atlantic swept in cold, gripping him up to his calves and then releasing in cycles. DeBolt looked up and down the beach, and in the faint light he saw nothing but the storm doing its work. Then suddenly, in his periphery, something else registered. Movement shoreward, near the cottage.

It was another talent DeBolt had acquired in the course of so many search and rescue missions—the ability to separate the natural from the man-made. For thousands of hours his eyes had swept over open ocean searching for life rafts and boats, desolate shorelines for telltale wreckage. Objects made by man were more angular and symmetric than those occurring in nature. They moved against flows, with irregular motion, and created by-products of smoke and light. And that was what he saw at that moment—the smallest of lights, green and diffuse, moving counter to the wind near the cabin.

In a spill of illumination from the window he saw a dark figure rush onto the porch, followed by two more. Then a strobe of lightning captured everything momentarily, a frozen image DeBolt could barely comprehend: five men now, all wearing battle gear and carrying machine pistols, the barrels bulked by silencers. They worked without hesitation.

Two men battered through the cabin door. Chandler cried out. DeBolt heard shouting, a slammed door, followed by an explosion of crashing glass. He saw Chandler leap from the seaside bedroom window, glass shards bursting all around her. She landed in a heap, then scrambled to her feet and began to run. Within three steps she was cut down, muzzle flashes blinking from the window behind her, a matching clatter of mechanical pops. She dropped, a terrible leaden fall, and went completely still.

Seconds of silence followed, an agonizing stillness.

Without realizing it, DeBolt had sunk to one knee in the surf. He stared in horror, willing Chandler to move. Knowing she never would again. There was no time to wonder what was happening, or who they were. Three dark figures burst out of the house, weapons sweeping outward. DeBolt remained frozen, chill water sweeping over his legs. It was hopeless. The man in front, wearing some kind of night-vision gear, looked directly at him.

DeBolt jumped to his feet and broke into a sprint. Only it wasn't a sprint at all—the beach gripped him like quicksand, each footstep sucking in, holding him back. He heard a second volley of muffled pops, and the surf around him exploded. He was sixty yards from the cabin, but barely moving. It occurred to him that the men behind him were wearing heavy gear. If he were fit, in prime condition, if he had a hard surface on which to run, he might be able to get away. As it was, wallowing through sodden sand, still recovering from severe injuries—DeBolt knew he didn't have a chance. He angled higher up the beach, zigzagging as he went, and found more stable footing. He ran for his life.

The clatter behind him turned nearly constant, rounds striking left and right, chiseling rock and spraying sand. He glanced once over his shoulder and saw Chandler still there, unmoving, the squad of killers giving chase.

DeBolt realized he had but one chance—the water. Long his adversary, it would have to become his refuge. He nearly turned toward it, but the idea of fighting the waves and the wind seemed overwhelming. Then he remembered— just a bit farther, in the lee of the natural jetty near the tide pools. The rip current.

He squinted against the rain and darkness, his bare feet flying over sand. He was trying to make out the flat outcropping when something struck his right leg. The pain was searing, but he didn't slow down. DeBolt heard shouting behind him—they realized he was heading for the sea. Soon the voices were lost, drowned by the thunder of tons of water slamming ashore, enveloping him, stalling his progress. With his last stride he dove headlong into an oncoming monster.

The cold was paralyzing, but he kept moving, trying to keep his orientation in utter blackness. He had to stay submerged for as long as possible, pull himself seaward, but it felt as though he were tumbling in some massive agitator with no sense of up or down. Waves lifted him high, and then sent him crashing to the bottom. There was no way to tell if the rip even remained—DeBolt knew currents often altered during storm conditions. He rose for a breath of air, but didn't chance a look back, and the instant he submerged again the sea was torn into a froth by arriving bullets. He dove for the bottom, found it with his hands, and felt that he was moving quickly. In which direction he had no idea.

DeBolt rose for his second breath on the back side of a wave. On the third, finally, he ventured a look shoreward. In the black night he could make out none of the assailants. He was at least fifty yards offshore now, and he knew they wouldn't follow him. Swimming in conditions like this bordered on insanity. Yet it seemed to be working. He was escaping . . . *but to where?*

A hundred yards to sea he no longer bothered to stay submerged. The shore was only visible in glimpses on the rise of each wave. He could tell he was being pulled north by the current, away from the cabin, but he was also being dragged out to sea. Sooner or later, he would have to swim clear of the rip and return to shore. Probably sooner. In recent days, even when he was wearing the wet suit, his swims had been getting shorter, the water temperature having dropped markedly. Now, with no protection, no sun for warmth, the beginnings of hypothermia were already evident. Shivering, a racing heartbeat, his muscles becoming sluggish. Soon the most dangerous element would take hold: his decision-making would become impaired. The upside for DeBolt was that he was an expert, not only in the clinical presentations of hypothermia, but knowing from experience the sequence in which his own body would shut down.

He reached down and felt his right calf. There was definitely damage of some kind, but for now adrenaline overrode the pain. He drifted around a bend and the shoreline was barely visible. The cabin lights disappeared. Had it been five minutes? Ten? Would the attackers organize a search up and down the beach? How far would he have to drift to get clear? Soon, he knew, it wouldn't matter. The cold would kill him just as surely.

A rogue breaker caught him in the face, and he sucked down a lungful of the frigid brine. He coughed and spewed, and sensed he was moving faster than ever. Then, in an awful moment, he lost sight of shore. DeBolt spun his head left and right. He pulled himself up in the water, yet saw nothing but black sea and foam. He had no moon or stars for reference, the storm blotting out the sky.

Safety lay to the west. *But which way is west?*

The question looped in his head, again and again.

Which way is west?

And then suddenly, incredibly, an answer arrived. It displayed clearly amid the blackness, like some divine vision—a tiny compass rose and arrow. West was on his left shoulder. Could it be true? Or was he hallucinating, his mind playing tricks due to the cold?

Apparition or not, it was all he had. Without understanding, without caring how or why the answer had come, DeBolt used the last of his energy to pull in that direction. His arms lost any sense of a rhythmic stroke, more clutching at the water than a means of propulsion. Time lost all meaning, and there was only one thing . . . *Stay up, keep moving!* The waves began to lift him, and it was all he could do to keep his head above water, keep his lungs charged with buoyant air. Finally, salvation—in a bolt of lightning, he caught a glimpse of the shoreline. It gave him a reference, a thread of hope.

His feet touched sand and he was elated, then a tremendous breaker threw him into a cartwheel and his head struck the bottom. Tumbling and churning, he fought back to the surface and gasped when he got there, sucking in as much water as air. He glimpsed the shadowed outline of the beach. There was no sign of his attackers, although at this point it hardly mattered—he would go wherever the sea threw him.

The muscles in his arms burned, and his good leg began to cramp. He tumbled beneath another breaker, and the water became shallow. Under his knees he felt a change in the bottom, not sand or bedrock, but a field of loose stone—the foreshore shelf that existed on every beach. DeBolt half rolled, half crawled the last yards, merciless waves pushing him on like a wayward piece of driftwood. With his knees on the rocks he coughed up seawater, and dragged himself higher up the slope. He only relaxed when his hands found the trunk of the first tree.

He leaned against it and searched the night. There was no sign of the assault team. *Assault team*. It was the only name that fit. In that moment, as he lay frozen and spent, a disquieting notion came to DeBolt's cold-soaked mind—whoever they were, they had not come here tonight with the aim of killing a nurse.

They had come to kill him.

7

That the mountain rises out of the sea into one of the bleakest climates on earth ought to instill caution. That it is called Mount Barometer is all but an omen. Unfortunately, some people never listen.

Shannon Lund climbed the rise carefully, having left the proper hiking trail a hundred yards back to reach the burnt-orange marker flag. The November ice was ahead of schedule, taking root in the gullies and fusing with last night's snow, and causing her to slip repeatedly on the steep gravel slope. Farther up the mountain, white predominated. In a few more weeks there would be little else.

Lund wished she had a good pair of climbing boots. The ones she'd been issued had met their end last March after an unusually punishing Alaskan winter. She had applied for a replacement pair, but probably wouldn't see them until next spring. That was the thing about being a civilian employee of the Coast Guard, particularly in times of tight budgets—your requests always went to the bottom of the pile, beneath those of active-duty members who did the "real" work.

She grabbed a thick branch and hauled herself up the last incline, ending at a stone landing of sorts. She decided then and there that the climb would replace her thirty-minute treadmill session tonight. It was a good excuse—at least better than most she came up with. An exhausted Lund plodded the last few steps to reach the scene, a twenty-foot patch of level rock and brown grass, all of it dusted with an inch of fresh powder. Two familiar figures were waiting. Frank Detorie was one of two full-time detectives with the Kodiak police, Matt Doran an EMT with the local fire department. Both were young and fit, seasoned climbers who preferred duty like this to being cooped up in an office. Lund herself might have seen it that way a few years ago.

"You okay?" Detorie asked.

Lund was panting as if she'd run a marathon, which she'd done once a long time ago. "Yeah, I'm good." She was only thirty-one, but had gotten out of shape—far enough that she no longer pretended to be able to keep up. She reached into her parka for a pack of cigarettes, and lit up without offering to share. Both men were lean, outdoorsy types, and presumably not inclined to tobacco.

"Okay, what do we have?"

The men led to a stand of brush that shouldered to a sheer granite face where the mountain again went vertical. Nestled tight against the rock wall was the crumpled body of a man. His legs were bent at dreadful angles, and he was wearing a plastic helmet that had split open like an egg. A climbing rope had landed mockingly in loose loops over his torso, like the string of a dropped yo-yo.

Detorie said, "His name is William Simmons. We got a cell call a few hours ago from his climbing partner." The policeman pointed up the mountain. "They were four, maybe five hundred feet up. Had some gear, but didn't know how to use it—I could tell right away from the partner's description of what happened."

Doran pointed upward. "I climbed part of the way up. Found his ice ax and a bunch of skid marks."

"You sure he's a Coastie?" Lund asked. This was the reason she'd been called in—she was one of two employees of the Coast Guard Investigative Service, Air Station Kodiak detachment.

Detorie handed over the mort's wallet. Lund flipped it open to find his military ID front and center. Petty Officer Third Class William Simmons. She tried to correlate the picture on the ID to the face inside the crushed helmet. It wasn't pretty, but probably a match.

"Where's the other guy?"

"He was Coast Guard too, pretty broken up," said Doran. "Simmons had climbed up higher, but the guy didn't want to go along—said it looked too dangerous."

"Best call of the day."

"My partner took him down to the station. We told him he'd have to talk to you later. It all looks pretty straightforward, but we're taking plenty of pictures."

"The ax and the marks?"

"Done."

"The spot where it all went wrong?"

"I haven't been that high yet," said Detorie, "but I might get there today . . . assuming the weather holds." They all looked up at a darkening sky.

"Has anybody informed his commander?"

"I figured that'd be up to you."

"Yeah, I guess so." Lund turned and looked out over the city. It had been a murky day, even by the dubious standards of November in the Aleutians, and late afternoon was gripping the landscape hard as gunmetal clouds rolled in from the sea. Dusk would go on for hours, drowsy and restless in equal parts—a land suffering from insomnia. Having been raised in the Arizona desert, Lund was accustomed to extremes, and so she embraced Kodiak in spite of its severity. Or perhaps because of it. Seven years ago, mired in a sinking relationship with a naval officer in San Diego, she'd jumped at a temporary posting to Kodiak to cover for another CGIS civilian who'd gone on maternity leave. The mother had ended up having three kids, one after the other. Lund was still here.

She went to the body, bent down, and studied things more closely. The climbing rope appeared worn, and had broken at a point that looked particularly frayed. The victim wore a belt with carabiners and quickdraws and anchors, no two pieces of hardware seeming to match. His climbing backpack was what a middle-schooler might use to haul textbooks. She looked up the ice-shrouded mountain and saw challenges everywhere. Nothing seemed wrong with the greater picture. It happened every year or two—a hiker or would-be adventurer went careening off the eastern face. The western trail was more forgiving, but it didn't have the same view of the city, a dramatic panorama that begged for an Instagram moment.

Lund stood. "Can you get him down?"

"I've got some help on the way with a basket," said Doran. "We'll manage."

"Okay, do it. And thanks for the heads-up."

"No problem," said Detorie.

Relationships between permanent Kodiak residents and Coasties, who generally rotated in for three-year tours, were not always founded in warmth. Lund, however, by virtue of her longevity—she *could* have left four years ago—was more accepted than most. She dropped her spent cigarette on the ground and twisted it out with her toe. Then, suspecting the two men were watching, she picked up the butt and stuffed it in her pocket.

Doran said, "Too bad about that rescue swimmer we evac-ed out last month."

Lund paused a beat. "Yeah, I know . . . I heard he didn't make it."

"Those guys are in great shape," he said respectfully. "He was really banged up, but when he lasted two days in the hospital here, I thought he might pull through."

"You saw him?"

Doran chuckled. "Not much choice. They called me in the middle of the damned night—I helped transport him to the Lear."

"Oh, right." She thought back, and remembered what she'd heard about it. "I was told he went out on the daily eastbound Herc." The air station ran a regular C-130 Hercules flight to Anchorage.

"Nope. Definitely a Lear, civilian model, geared-up for med-evacs."

Lund tipped her head to say it wasn't important. She started back down the hill at a cautious pace—as the body behind her proved, down was the dangerous part. She gripped the same sturdy branch where the plateau dropped away, and took one last look at the scene. She was at a point in her career where she was getting reliable instincts, and the accident in front of her seemed nothing more than that. Too much youthful vigor, too little caution. All the same, something clawed in the back of her mind.

She turned her attention to the terrain, setting a careful course, and as she took her first steps down the slope a chill rain began to fall.

8

DeBolt had never been so cold in his life, a grave statement for an Alaska-based Coast Guard rescue swimmer. The temperature had dropped precipitously, and he was lurching through the forest with leaden legs, ricocheting from tree trunk to rock like a human pinball. He'd seen nothing more of the assailants, but that was hardly a relief given the utter darkness. He doubted he would hear them either, the noise around him like an oncoming train as the forest canopy was whipsawed by gusts and pelted with rain.

He wondered how much ground he'd covered since leaving the beach. A mile? Two? It would have to be enough. In both training and operations, DeBolt had faced some of the harshest conditions on earth with considerable tenacity. Now, for the first time ever, his legs defied his commands. He twice ended on his knees in wet moss and muck. When he got up the second time he nearly ran into the building.

He stood back at first and tried to make sense of the shadow. It looked different from the nurse's place, larger and more rustic, a Lincoln Log beater. There were no lights inside, no signs of life at all, and by the time he'd staggered around two corners to reach what had to be the front door, he didn't care if anyone was home. He gripped the door handle with two frozen hands and found it locked. Not having the strength to curse, DeBolt reared back, put his shoulder down, and threw himself at the door, more a guided collapse than a controlled strike. There was a sharp wooden crack as something gave way, and the door swung open. He stumbled inside, bringing the wind with him. It stirred stagnant, mold-infused air. The place was completely dark. DeBolt felt the wall for a light switch, found one, and flicked it up. Nothing happened.

He tried to shut the door, but the frame and latch were ruined, and the wind won another battle, slamming it back decisively against the inside wall. DeBolt ignored it, turned into a pitch-black room, and began feeling his way through the place with outstretched hands. His shin struck a table and he maneuvered around it. A floor lamp went over with a muffled crash, and he ended up on his knees. Then, finally, he found what he wanted—a six-foot length of fabric that could only be a couch. He crawled onto it and stretched to his full length, aching and depleted. There were no more visions. Nothing at all but an inexorable blackness.

The assault team commander, a former Green Beret, called off the search after an hour. The team assembled at the targeted cabin. He immediately assigned a two-man detail to deal with the woman's body, and sent a third outside to monitor the perimeter. Only then did he turn on the lights in the cottage. The leader set his weapon down, pulled the earbud from his ear, and surveyed the damage. A few overturned pieces of furniture, some holes in the woodwork. It wasn't bad, definitely containable. But they'd sprayed over a hundred rounds into the beach and surrounding sea. *Messy,* he thought. *Very messy.*

The storm outside had peaked, but conditions would be extreme until daybreak. That was in their favor. Maybe the only thing that had gone right all night.

"*Dammit!*" he said. "I can't believe he wasn't inside! Who goes to the beach on a night like this?"

He was venting to his second in command, a crew-cut man with a cinder-block build, who responded, "He made the perfect move to go for the water. It was dumb luck—we know this guy's not an operator."

That much was true. They'd never been given their target's name, which seemed peculiar. But the mission briefing *had* included the fact that he was a rescue swimmer in the Coast Guard. "We knew he was a swimmer. We should have planned for that contingency."

"I say the ocean did the job for us."

The commander stared at his second, weighing it.

"He took at least one hit," said the crew-cut man, trying to make his case. "We found a trail of blood. Swimmer or not . . . Michael Phelps couldn't have survived the riptide and those waves."

"Maybe not. But carry that idea forward. If he washes up on a beach tomorrow, what happens? It would be a suspicious death, which means an autopsy. The briefing was *very* specific about the male target—get rid of his body with no traces."

"Why do you think that was?"

"I don't know, but it seemed important."

The crew-cut man cursed like the Army grunt he'd once been.

The commander acquired a faraway look. "Dead or alive, we have to find him. Obviously, there's no way the five of us can cover the entire shoreline. We'll have to ask the front office to put out feelers with local law enforcement. If somebody finds him washed up, we go in fast with our provisional federal IDs, claim jurisdiction. Then we get the body out of sight before anybody figures out what's going on."

"Okay. And if the guy is half fish and actually survived?"

"Then we track him down."

"How?" asked the second in command.

"We put ourselves in his shoes. If you made it back to shore, what would you do? Would you go to the authorities?"

The subordinate thought about it. "Not a chance—not based on what we know."

"Exactly."

The crew-cut man frowned. "There's something else we should consider."

"What's that?"

"What if someone saw him here, saw the two of them together? Our target might get blamed for the nurse's death . . . at the very least he'd be a person of interest."

The commander's brow furrowed as he considered it. "True. Every law enforcement agency in the state would start looking for him. We can't let that happen—far too much attention." He looked around the room, contemplating how to handle it. "All right, so if he didn't make it our hands are tied. We recover the body as fast as we can. But on the off chance that he did survive . . . it might be in our interest to help him avoid the authorities."

"How?"

"By covering his tracks for him." He explained what he wanted done.

"Okay. Then what?"

"Then *we* find him and provide some long overdue closure."

"If he did survive, and if he could move, where do you think he'd go?"

The commander only looked at his protégé, implying he should answer his own question.

The crew-cut man thought it through, then said, "True. It's the only place that makes sense."

The explosion came forty minutes later. Manufactured by an artfully designed gas leak, closed windows, and a precisely governed ignition source, it could be heard miles away. Yet because there was still thunder in the distance, only one neighbor, an elderly woman who lived halfway to the main road, recognized the blast as something unnatural. When her 911 call was logged, at 12:07 A.M., a beleaguered dispatcher explained that due to the severe nor'easter, first responders were at a premium. Unless loss of life or severe injury was impending, or already proven, there was no one available to investigate a report of an explosion in a remote area. Someone would look into it tomorrow, the dispatcher promised. Possibly in the morning. Afternoon was more likely.

9

It was nine that evening when Lund tracked down PO3 William Simmons' commander. Lieutenant Commander Reggie Walsh was nursing a beer at the Golden Anchor, the on-base sports bar. The bad news about the accident on Mount Barometer had already reached him by way of the wives' network—in all branches of the service, there was no more lightning-paced intelligence organization.

"I'm sorry," said Lund from the stool next to him. She already had a dark beer in hand thanks to a bartender with a quick wrist and an infallible memory.

"Me too, he was a good kid," said Walsh. "Never gave me a lick of trouble."

"How long has he been here in Kodiak?"

"A little over a year. Will was an aviation maintenance technician—worked mostly in the spares and expendables section, issuing and ordering parts."

Lund inquired about the other young man who was involved, Simmons' climbing partner, and Walsh had nothing bad to say about him. "They were just a couple of kids, indestructible and looking forward to life." He explained that both young men seemed adventurous, constantly hiking and borrowing kayaks, and that Simmons had inquired about attending rescue swimmer training.

"I was going to recommend him too. He was friends with a couple of the ASTs on station, guys who'd been through the program. But now . . ." He took a long draw on his beer. "At least I won't have to make the notification—had to do that once, and it's lousy duty. Will wasn't married, and his family hails from Georgia. I'll make some phone calls tonight, find out who's going to knock on the door. They need to have everything straight going in."

Lund spun her mug by its handle. "So tell me something—were you around a few weeks back when we lost that helo?"

The lieutenant commander stiffened. "That investigation is hot and heavy right now, so I can't say much about it. It was one of our birds, and the place has been crawling with investigators. I can tell you they looked at our maintenance records long and hard last week, but found no evidence of mechanical issues. That crew was trying to pull a guy out of a raft in twenty-foot seas with wind gusts over eighty knots. I guess that's why the flyers get paid the big bucks." He looked at her warily. "Why do you ask?"

"I'm not involved in the safety investigation. I was just wondering about the young man they brought back—the AST who almost survived. I'd heard he was flown out to Anchorage on one of our C-130s, but then today somebody told me he was airlifted out on a civilian Lear."

Walsh seemed to stand down. "I wasn't there, but one of my mechanics was doing an inspection that night. She told me a small jet came to pick him up."

"Isn't that strange?" she asked. "I mean, doesn't the Coast Guard usually handle their own med-evacs?"

"Usually, yeah. But it's not my end of the operation."

Out of nowhere, a third voice entered the conversation. "You knew him, didn't you, Shannon?"

Lund looked up and saw the bartender addressing her. She hadn't been to the Golden Anchor in months, but the guy remembered her beer *and* her name—which put him two up on her. He was stout, in his mid-forties, obviously nosy and with a bear-trap memory. He'd probably make a good detective, she thought.

"You knew DeBolt," he pressed. "I remember you being here with him once or twice."

"Once," she said. "It's a small base."

It had been six months ago, a strictly professional encounter in which Lund had tracked DeBolt here, finding him in the middle of a unit hail-and-farewell party. She'd needed to interview him regarding a rescue in which a trawler captain had been plucked from a rocky beach—even four hours after his boat had sunk, the man was stone drunk, so much so that he'd fallen out of the helo when they arrived back at Kodiak. Someone had decided to build criminal charges against the captain, although it hadn't been Lund's section. After filing her report, she'd never tracked the disposition of the case. But she definitely remembered DeBolt, with his sharp blue eyes and cool confidence. He was one of the elite: well trained, exceptionally fit, and, she was sure, very intelligent. His death was the kind of thing that frightened people in the service, in the sense that if it had happened to him, it could happen to anyone.

Lund tipped back the last of her beer, and regarded the two men in turn. "So tell me, do either of you gentlemen know where Simmons lived?"

Not surprisingly, it was the barman who said, "Apartment house just outside the gate. A lot of the enlisted guys end up there. Do you need to take a look at his place?"

"I probably should."

"I can get you in."

Lund raised an eyebrow. She looked at the cash register receipt on the bar in front of her and saw her server's name printed near the top: *Tom*.

"It's a small town," said Tom the bartender. "My wife keeps the books for the guy who owns the building, does some sales work on the weekends. She has keys for all the units. I'll tell her you'll be by in the morning."

"Right," she said. "A real small town."

DeBolt opened his eyes to light that was blinding. He squinted severely, trying to make sense of things. An open doorway, beyond that swathes of blue sky and trees. Remnants of last night came hurtling back. The storm, the killers, fighting for his life in the surf. He remembered Joan Chandler sprawled motionless on the ground. In the air and on the sea, DeBolt had faced more than his share of trials, and he took pride in his ability to stay calm under pressure. But after last night—jumping into the Arctic Ocean from a helicopter seemed like child's play.

He struggled up to a sitting position, and the couch creaked beneath him. DeBolt felt a host of new pains. Looking at his bare feet, he saw cuts and bruises. A new gash on the outside of his calf was very possibly a gunshot wound—a personal first. His head ached in the vicinity of new scrapes and contusions, which was at least different from the generalized pain he'd been battling for weeks. The soreness in his shoulder was more familiar, an aggravation of the injury from the crash. After allowing a few moments to get his bearings, DeBolt looked around the room, seeing it for the first time. It was similar to the cottage where he'd spent the last month, only more dated and worn. He guessed the place hadn't been lived in since summer. Maybe the summer before.

He stood and felt the grit of sand under his feet. DeBolt searched out the bathroom. He avoided the mirror at the washbasin, and turned on the tap. The faucet spit a stream of brown muck, but eventually ran clear—cold only. He cupped his hands under the faucet, girded himself, and plunged his face into the icy water.

DeBolt braved a quick shower, the cold reminding him of the Atlantic. In a cabinet he found shaving supplies and even a new toothbrush in its packaging. He cleaned his wounds, found bandages for a few, and then began foraging through the largest bedroom. At least one of the cabin's owners was male, and roughly his size. A pair of boat shoes were two sizes too small and bit into his heels, but they were better than nothing at all. In a bedside table he found a twenty-dollar bill, and scrounged a few more dollars in loose change from a kitchen drawer. DeBolt kept a mental log of everything he took, in vague hope that he might someday repay the owner.

His stomach reminded him that he was due a meal, but the kitchen had been cleaned out save for a box of sugar packets and an old can of asparagus. As he drew a glass of water from the tap, DeBolt decided there were issues far more critical than breakfast.

Last night he had witnessed a murder, the only person he knew in Maine having been killed by a squad of armed men. He didn't know who they were, but he recognized a military operation when he saw one. He'd worked regularly with components of the DOD and DEA on missions involving smuggling and drug interdiction, and DeBolt himself had been trained by the Coast Guard on small-unit boarding and assault tactics. Yet there was one glaring disconnect with what he'd witnessed last night: those men had killed without hesitation. There had been no warnings to their targets to stop or surrender. No rules of engagement or abiding of laws. They had only wanted him and Chandler dead. That wasn't how legitimate military units operated.

His previous conclusion was more persistent than ever. They *had* come for him. Joan Chandler's last words came back in a particularly haunting echo. *The surgery you had . . . it wasn't only to make you well. It was to make you different.*

Different.

He remembered how he'd been saved last night, when he'd lost sight of land and was being swept seaward. The odd vision that had guided him to shore, a tiny arrow pointing west. Any connection seemed inconceivable, and DeBolt shook the idea away.

Of all the tragedies to find him in recent weeks, last night was singular in its cruelty. The crime had taken place only hours ago, and it occurred to him, given the remoteness of Chandler's cabin, that it might not yet have been discovered. A pang of doubt set in. Could Joan Chandler possibly have survived? He recalled the agonizing scene, watching her collapse and fall still. Even so, no matter how slight the chance, DeBolt knew he would second-guess himself for the rest of his life if he didn't put in a call for help. He searched the cottage. No phone, no radio, no computer. It left only one option.

He hurried outside into a cold wind, pulled the collar up on a jacket that wasn't his, and set out to find a road.

Joan Chandler's leveled cottage was discovered at 9:24 that morning. A reserve deputy, called into action under the auspices of the Washington County Emergency Preparedness Plan, drove his truck to within a hundred yards of the cabin before breaking clear of the trees and seeing the problem.

He instantly realized that the storm, severe as it had been, could in no way be responsible for the catastrophe in front of him. The cabin, which the deputy had seen often from the sea while fishing in nearby coves, was essentially gone. The only markers of where it had been were a charred slab of concrete, one section of wall, and a few pipes and conduit sleeves that rose up like the stumps of cut saplings. Even now, hours after the initial report of an explosion, a few wisps of smoke remained, and bits of debris dressed the nearby pines, turning them into so many postapocalyptic Christmas trees.

The deputy knew better than to get any closer. He suspected—correctly it would soon be proven—that he was looking at the aftermath of a gas explosion. There could be no survivors, and he wondered ruefully if the nurse, whom he'd once met but whose name escaped him, had been home last night. He put in a radio call to dispatch, requesting both sheriff's department backup and a fire department response. As an afterthought, he mentioned to the duty officer that there was no particular hurry.

10

DeBolt set a brisk pace along the shoulder of the first road he came across. It was twenty minutes before he saw a sign announcing the nearest town: Jonesport, Maine, lay two miles ahead. He thought the name sounded familiar, although the reason escaped him. He kept a good pace along the two-lane road, and his body loosened up. At that point his main impediment became caution. Twice he scrambled into the woods to avoid being seen by oncoming vehicles. After the chaos of last night, at least some degree of paranoia seemed in order.

He tried to come up with a plan, and decided his first priority was to alert the authorities to what had happened at the cottage. Even if Chandler hadn't survived, the sooner the police reached the scene, the sooner they would begin searching for the men responsible. DeBolt assumed the attackers were still in the area, and might be looking for him—the reason he dodged out of sight whenever a car appeared in the distance. As a secondary matter, he considered his AWOL status, and the madness of being declared dead weeks ago. He strongly suspected it was all connected. Unfortunately, the idea of walking into a police station with such a story was problematic to say the least.

A distant growl brought his eyes up, and he saw an eighteen-wheeler approaching from the opposite direction. He looked to his right and saw a broad ditch filled with water. Across the road, more of the same. DeBolt simply kept going, thinking it doubtful that such an obviously commercial vehicle could pose a threat. As if to validate his thinking, the truck thundered past, never slowing, and kicked up a swirl of dust in its wake.

He slowed and turned away from the cloud, but not before his face was misted with particles. He came to a stop, and rubbed his irritated left eye with a knuckle. As he did so, DeBolt noticed a distinct blank spot in his vision. When the irritant cleared, he kept his left eye closed and looked into the distance. It was definitely there—not dark, not light, but simply an off-center void in his field of view. He moved his head left and right, and distant objects vanished. He opened both eyes and the problem abated, bilateral vision compensating for the loss. Was it another complication from his head injury?

Great. First I'm seeing things, and now I have holes in my vision. What next?

He set out again, and soon the township of Jonesport came into view. It was a small place, so small that he wondered if there would even *be* a police station. He considered borrowing a phone from someone to call 911, but didn't like the complications involved. His face would be remembered, his position pinpointed. Ridiculous as it seemed, DeBolt felt a compelling urge to remain anonymous.

He reached the center of town in no time, and walking briskly along Main Street he took in homes, businesses, and the rocky shoreline bordering the bay. Across the water in the distance he saw a collection of islands, most dotted with what looked like vacation homes. He saw a few people out in town, most of them cleaning up after the storm—collecting downed branches and tending to boats. He passed a boatyard that looked full, all manner of craft having been lifted to dry storage for the winter. Then, at the base of a distant bridge, a revelation—DeBolt saw why the town's name had seemed familiar. He also saw an answer to his problem. He knew exactly how to alert the authorities while remaining anonymous.

In that moment, DeBolt realized that his former way of life, a once orderly and purposeful existence, was being amended into something else. He found himself detouring, ever so slightly, into darker disciplines.

DeBolt moved quickly. He was so engaged in his plan that he never noticed the white Chevy Tahoe parked on the opposite side of Main Street.

"Mayday! Mayday! Mayday!"

Seaman Apprentice Jacob Wilhelm bolted upright in his chair and reached for the volume control on the number three VHF radio. The receiver was always tuned to channel sixteen, the emergency maritime frequency, and for that reason it was seldom used. Coast Guard Station Jonesport was a small boat station, home to three utility and response boats and the eighty-seven-foot patrol vessel *Moray*. On this particular morning, CGS Jonesport was unusually quiet. *Moray* was at sea, along with her crew of ten, and two of the rescue boats had run to Bar Harbor where the storm had hit hardest. It left Wilhelm alone in the communications center, with only two other enlisted personnel on station. Both were on the far side of the building.

"Calling mayday, say your vessel name," Wilhelm instructed.

"Mayday! This is the sailboat Spar*! I am in southern Wohoa Bay and need information relayed to local law enforcement agencies!"*

"Is your vessel in distress?" Wilhelm responded.

"Negative, negative. I've just witnessed a shooting onshore. I'm familiar with the area—immediate police response is required at the southern end of Cape Circle Road."

It was a highly irregular call, Wilhelm thought, but at least one that wouldn't require a Coast Guard response. That was good, because they were acutely short staffed today. He initiated a phone connection to the Washington County sheriff's department, and while it ran, he said, "I need your name, and can you tell me anything else about the situation?"

Wilhelm waited. The radio remained silent.

A woman answered the phone line with, "Washington County Sheriff."

Wilhelm identified himself and explained the situation.

"Cape Circle Road?" the dispatcher replied. "We've had people out there all morning."

"So there *was* a shooting?"

"More of an explosion, from what I heard. One of those little cabins blew sky high from a gas leak last night. The fire department is finding pieces over a mile away."

"Okay," Wilhelm said hesitantly. This was getting stranger by the second. "So if anything *was* happening out there, I'm guessing you guys have it covered."

"Been there for hours."

"Great. If I hear anything else, I'll let you know."

The phone connection was broken. Wilhelm went back to VHF number three, and again tried to raise the sailboat *Spar*. There was no response, but all the same, he kept the volume up on channel sixteen. It was probably a hoax of some kind—Lord knows, they got their share. He heard nothing but static for the rest of his shift.

The sheriff's department had indeed been crawling over the remains of 302 Cape Circle Road for the best part of an hour, ever since the fire department had given the all clear to approach the place. They quickly found traces of human remains, but the condition of that evidence—indeed, the condition of everything—suggested a long and arduous inquiry. An investigator from the fire department, who was responsible for determining whether the blast was accidental, said her answer would take at least a few days. Unaccustomed to such devastated scenes, the sheriff's department requested help from the regional FBI office, who replied tentatively that they might be able to send someone by in a day or two.

While the local specialists went about their work, the sheriff department's lone detective, a dour and long-faced man named LaSalle—tenth-generation Washington County—saw right away that there was little useful evidence at the scene. That being the case, he began interviewing neighbors—a simple enough process, as there were only two, and one of them had not been in residence for nearly a year.

At the threshold of the only door he knocked on that day, LaSalle asked an elderly couple if they had seen anything unusual at the cabin to the south. They said they hadn't. That was when LaSalle got his only break of the day, or as it would turn out, of the week. The couple's young granddaughter, who'd been staying with them for a month, and who spoke with one cheek pressed to her grandmother's apron, said she had seen a young man exercising on the beach near the cabin. Her fifth-grade narrative was painfully lacking in de-tails. Her eyesight, however, was excellent. She placed the man at the cottage on three consecutive days that week. He was rather tall with sandy hair, and seemed a very good swimmer. Pressed on this last point, the girl insisted she'd seen the man walk from the cottage to the beach each day, and swim until he was out of sight.

When LaSalle could think of nothing more to ask, he thanked them all, and warned them to stay clear of the adjacent property for the next few days.

He left wondering who had been visiting the nurse. And perhaps more troublingly: Whose DNA had exploded across half his jurisdiction?

DeBolt turned off the battery switch to power down the VHF radio. He was thankful to have selected a boat that had been pulled from the harbor only recently—in a few months the ship's batteries would likely be dead in the middle of a cold and hard winter. Before leaving the radio panel, he re-engaged the red DSC switch on the VHF control head. Had he not disengaged it earlier, his exact GPS position would have been automatically transmitted with his distress call.

The boat was a Grand Banks trawler, forty-two feet of polished brass and hardwood set high on a hard stand. Her bottom was not yet scraped clean, and her left prop was missing. More of interest to DeBolt, the cabin had high sidewalls and a salon door that had been left wide open. She was at the back of a large storage yard, and the only person in sight was a single listless mechanic—he was presently drinking coffee near the main shed fifty yards away. It had been simplicity itself to round the perimeter fence unnoticed, climb aboard, and power up the radio. With his mission complete, DeBolt did it all in reverse, and was soon back on Main Street.

He began walking north, covering new ground. The skies were clearing fast, the storm having moved east, and a strong wind filled the void, pulling in Arctic air from the north and raking whitecaps across the bay. DeBolt looked cautiously up and down the street. Nothing seemed out of place. He passed a playground where a toddler climbed a ladder under the watchful eye of his mother, and at the end of a jetty an old man with a walrus mustache stood contentedly with a slack fishing pole. Normal people resuming their normal lives after the passing of a storm.

But how can I? he wondered.

He was thousands of miles from Alaska. Men were hunting him. He had twenty stolen dollars in his pocket, and no way to get more. DeBolt had no identity documents to prove who he was—indeed, nothing to prove he had ever existed, save for a copy of his death certificate, and that was back in the cottage, a place to which he could not return without risking another deadly encounter.

And then there was the other problem: the odd visions he'd experienced twice now. Hallucinations? His battered brain playing tricks? He wanted desperately to reclaim his life, but the obstacles seemed overwhelming. So DeBolt went back to basics. He decided it was time to eat.

He reached into his pocket and fingered the twenty-dollar bill. He looked up the street and saw a restaurant, then a second farther on. Roy's Diner was the closer of the two, and something called The Harbor House a block beyond. Both looked open.

A gust of wind sent leaves cartwheeling across the street, and DeBolt stood on the sidewalk making the most basic of decisions. *Roy's Diner,* he thought. *I wonder what's on the menu.*

Seconds later the answer arrived, posted in absolute clarity. In the blind spot in his right eye, he saw a high-definition image of the breakfast menu for Roy's Diner.

11

DeBolt sat alone in a booth at Roy's Diner. He stared at the menu the hostess had given him with a level of interest likely never before seen in the establishment. Word for word, price for price, it was an exact duplicate of the image fixed in his head.

Shaken to the core, DeBolt tried to delete the thought, tried to force the image away. At one point it did disappear, but by some inescapable urge he called it up again—or perhaps more accurately, he conjured it, like a magician pulling a card out of thin air. The result was the same. Somehow he had an ability to acquire images, displayed perfectly on the tiny screen in his right eye. He remembered seeing the time of the sunrise, and the compass heading that had saved him as he'd foundered in the sea. Both had appeared in a similar fashion, but he'd written off those events as curiosities, as fleeting apparitions. This time there could be no doubt.

". . . I said, coffee?"

He looked up and saw a waitress with a metal pot in her hand. "Uh . . . yeah, please."

She turned over the upside-down coffee cup on the table and began filling it. "You were a million miles away," she said. "Never seen anybody so taken with Roy's breakfast menu." She was a smiling woman, fortyish, manufactured blond hair, and the beginnings of a stoop in her shoulders.

"Sorry, I've been a little distracted lately."

"Cream?"

"No, black is good."

"Want me to come back, or have you made up your mind?"

He looked at the menu—the one on the table—and saw a boxed entry on top: Everyday special—two eggs, bacon, and all-you-can-eat pancakes for $9.99. "I'll take the special, over easy."

She smiled and reached for the menu. He almost asked her to leave it, but decided it would seem strange and let it go. DeBolt looked around the place, and with some trepidation thought, *So what other tricks can I do?* A television mounted on the wall nearby was tuned to a cable news channel. The volume had been muted, but in a corner of the screen he saw numbers. DeBolt cleared his head of everything else, and thought: *Dow Jones Industrial Average . . . current value.*

A number lit to view in his blind spot. It was fractionally different from what he saw on the television, but soon that number changed to match the one he'd grasped out of nowhere. DeBolt tensed, and a sudden burning sensation caused him to look down. Both his hands were around the coffee cup, and he saw a few drops of brown liquid on one thumb. He dried it using his napkin, then discreetly reached back and fingered the scars at the base of his skull, now hidden beneath hair that was longer than it had been in years. And there, he knew, was his answer. How had Chandler put it? *. . . to make you different.* An operation? Had something been surgically implanted? Was his brain now wired to the internet, some kind of biological routing device?

His waitress scurried past and he noted her nametag: SAM.

DeBolt pondered how to phrase a request, and settled on: *Roy's Diner, employees, Sam.*

It took only seconds.

SAM VICTORIA TREMAIN
AGE: 41
ADDRESS: 1201 CRISP BAY ROAD, APARTMENT 3B

DeBolt then noticed a scroll bar at the bottom of his visual field. He concentrated on it, and after some awkward interactions, more information rolled into view.

MARITAL STATUS: DIVORCED 12/03/2014
2015 AGI: $24,435

AGI? he thought incredulously. *Adjusted gross income?*

He sat motionless for a very long time, pondering the imponderable, until Sam Victoria Tremain arrived with a mountainous plate of food, four pancakes sided by eggs and bacon. In her other hand was the ever-present coffeepot, and she began topping him off.

"Your name," he said, looking deliberately at the oval tag on her blouse, "I was wondering—is it short for Samantha?"

She chuckled good-naturedly. "I'm afraid not. I was the youngest of five girls, and my dad was Sam Tremain the fourth. Mom insisted on getting her tubes tied after me, so it was the only way to keep the family name going."

He did his best to mirror her smile, and then she was gone to another table. He briefly stared at his plate, his appetite gone. DeBolt forced himself to eat, and all throughout the meal his eyes wandered the room, seeing countless ways to test his newfound abilities. The potential was all at once frightening, exhilarating, and intoxicating. The cook was named Rusty Gellar, a guy with two cars, one child-support payment, and three minor drug convictions, all over ten years ago. The owner of the place was not named Roy, but Dave. He owed back taxes to the state of Maine for the last two years, and headed up the local VFW. A dozen tables were occupied behind DeBolt, twenty people with backgrounds and stories. All there for the taking.

He sat frozen in his seat, unsure what to do. He stared out the plate-glass window on his right shoulder, and saw a crisp and glorious day. He also saw a world fraught with unthinkable complications. Unthinkable opportunities. It was as though he'd been given the keys to some perilous kingdom. DeBolt was already facing a mountain of problems, life as he knew it having ended weeks ago. And now this.

What the hell do I do with it?

To that question, the high-definition screen in his head remained maddeningly blank.

Lund rose early, and by seven thirty was at the apartment building where William Simmons had lived. She'd arranged to meet the bartender's wife in front of the unit marked OFFICE, and she was there waiting, a pale-skinned woman with lively green eyes and an eager manner.

"Hi, I'm Natalie. You must be Shannon—Tom told me you needed some help."

The woman was animated and cheerful, more than Lund could match at that hour. "Yes, thanks for your cooperation." She pulled out her credentials and showed them to the woman, wanting to keep things official. "How long had William lived here?"

"Since he arrived, about a year ago. I rented the unit to him." She lost a bit of her buoyancy as she said, "What a terrible tragedy. He was such a nice young man."

"Yes, that's what everyone tells me."

Natalie led to an apartment on the first floor of a three-story affair. She pulled a key and opened the door, then said, "I know the drill—you'd rather I wasn't here looking over your shoulder. I'll be in the office. Just let me know when you're done, and I'll close up."

Lund said that she would, and went inside. It was a charmless place consisting of one bedroom, one bath, and a small kitchen, all done up in bachelor modern: a big couch facing a flat screen TV that looked wired for gaming, novelty beer bottles lining a window ledge, and a wall-sized banner with the Denver Broncos logo. No surprises so far.

Lund began in the bedroom. The carpet could have used cleaning, and the bed wasn't made—reminding her of her own place. She saw some climbing hardware and a poster of a guy free-climbing a sheer wall of granite. All aspirational, but nothing to suggest that Simmons was any kind of seasoned mountaineer. Lund went through the closet and dresser, then spun one last circle. She saw nothing of interest. After another ten minutes in the main room and kitchen, she relented. She had found exactly what she'd expected—the crash pad of an adventurous young man who'd slipped and fallen off a mountain.

As promised, the effervescent Natalie was waiting in the office.

"I think I'm done," said Lund. "Thanks for letting me in."

"No problem."

"I do have one question . . . earlier, when you said you 'knew the drill.' What did you mean by that?"

"Well, it was just last month. Your cohorts came by to see Trey DeBolt's place. It's so sad . . . two boys gone before their time in just a few weeks. Trey in particular I liked—he always seemed so purposeful. That boy was going places, I tell you."

Lund felt a stab as she recalled her own last vision of DeBolt. "My cohorts?" she repeated.

"Yes, two men."

"And they said they were with the Coast Guard Investigative Service, here in Kodiak?"

"Yes. At least, I think that's what they said. They had badges of some kind."

Lund pondered this. The staff of CGIS Kodiak could not have been more straightforward. It consisted of her and one active-duty chief petty officer. CPO James Kalata rarely worked outside the confines of their office—or for that matter, inside. "Do you remember their names?"

"Well . . . no, I'm afraid not."

"Can you describe them?"

"Is there a problem?"

"No, not at all. I was just wondering who they sent out."

After some concentration, Natalie gave a description of two average-looking young men with short haircuts. That narrowed things down to roughly half the Coast Guard.

"Were they in uniform?"

"No," she said. "Civilian clothes, like you."

"Okay. Before I go, would you mind if I looked at that place too?"

"Trey's apartment? I don't see why not. Today is actually your last chance."

"Why is that?"

"There's a crew with a truck coming later to take his things—it's all been approved, and he only paid through the end of last month."

"I see. Where is it all going?"

"Salvation Army—everything will be put to good use, I'm sure."

"I'm sure."

They went through the same drill, and soon Lund was alone at the threshold of Trey DeBolt's apartment. After Natalie was gone, she drew a deep breath. For weeks she'd been trying to ignore the memory—unfortunately, it was the kind of vision that didn't fade. The interview at the Golden Anchor hadn't been the only time she'd crossed paths with DeBolt. There had been one other encounter, in a setting so strained and intimate, it would be forever cemented in her mind.

Lund forced her attention to the room.

On first glance it looked very much like the room she'd just seen. There was a surfboard leaning against the wall in a corner, another next to it that was broken in half. *Got to be a story there,* she thought. A set of scuba gear lay near the closet. On the wall was a framed picture of DeBolt riding a monstrous wave, taken from the tail of his board, a whitewater lip curling ominously over his head. Another of a skydiving DeBolt in free fall, his smiling face warped by the wind and a set of goggles. It took Lund a moment to realize she was focusing on the man and not the room. When she made that shift, her outlook began to alter.

DeBolt's room was different from Simmons' in one very troubling way. It had nothing to do with his standards of tidiness or anything he owned. Dresser drawers had been pulled, the contents of the closet upturned. Lund might have written it off as the lousy housekeeping of a twenty-something male, yet she saw neatness elsewhere: shoes paired precisely in line, dishes stacked, books on a shelf perfectly squared. Her concerns were made complete when she found a Walmart-grade security box that had been pried open, and a file cabinet drawer left ajar. Either might suggest a burglary, but she saw three twenty-dollar bills in plain sight on the dresser, and a nice iPad on the kitchen table. Taken together, Lund saw but one possible interpretation. Somebody had beaten her here.

She was looking at the aftermath of a search. One performed by two men confident enough not to care if they left tracks, yet undertaken in a targeted manner. That implied a government agency, but one other than CGIS, because that would have necessitated her involvement. Lund performed a search of her own, and after twenty minutes determined that three things she would like to have found were missing. There was no passport, which virtually any Alaska-based serviceman would have. There was no last will and testament—a requirement for those assigned hazardous duty. Of course, either of those items could have been gathered by someone else with good intentions—DeBolt's commander or a fellow Coastie—at a time when Natalie hadn't been present. But the last one bothered her. At the file cabinet, which was nicely arranged in alphabetical order, she saw a distinct gap among the Ms: right between MASTERCRAFT BOATS and MOM'S PAPERS. In a modest leap of speculation, Lund guessed someone had removed Trey DeBolt's medical records.

She closed the place up and headed back to the office where she dropped off the key and thanked Natalie. Minutes later Lund was in the parking lot. She walked past a fresh-faced young enlisted man in uniform who was probably on his way back to his apartment after a night shift. She found herself hoping the building's bad karma didn't run in threes. A Salvation Army truck was just pulling up. Lund considered telling them they'd have to come back another day, but decided against it.

None of the items missing from DeBolt's place were of singular importance, and their unexplained absence did not constitute a crime, or for that matter, a problem. On the other hand, a pair of men had presented themselves as CGIS officials, and searched the residence of a crewman who'd recently died in the course of duty.

And that? Lund reflected. That was definitely a problem.

12

DeBolt managed to clean his plate, and declined Sam's offer of a second serving of pancakes. The coffee, however, kept coming, and when he finally waved her off Sam put a check on the table. He paired it with his twenty-dollar bill, and it was swept up and change quickly delivered. He left Sam five dollars, which he thought a generous tip given that it was, in that moment, precisely half his personal fortune.

He was ready to leave, but hesitated realizing he had no destination, nor any means of transportation. His eyes drifted outside to the road and the windswept bay. He watched a white Chevy Tahoe ease into the parking lot. The truck pulled into a spot fifty feet from where he sat. DeBolt, still on edge after last night, watched cautiously. The Tahoe was parked facing the restaurant, and he could make out two men in front. The backseats remained in shadow. Neither man moved—they simply stared at Roy's Diner from behind dark sunglasses. No, not the restaurant.

They were staring at him.

DeBolt hurriedly looked around the diner. He saw a red EXIT sign over the doorless passageway to the kitchen. The Tahoe remained still. The two men inside didn't move or seem to be talking. They weren't coming inside for breakfast. It all seemed wrong, out of character for Jonesport. He noticed the front license plate on the Tahoe—a Maine plate, but different from others he'd seen, more generic. In a burst of inspiration, he whispered to himself, "Maine license plate 864B34."

It took longer this time, the seconds seeming like hours as he tried not to stare at the men in the truck. Finally, a response:

864B34, MAINE
CHEVY TAHOE, WHITE, VIN 1GCGDMA8A9KR07327
REGISTERED U.S. DOD
VEHICLE POSITION 44° 31'59.5"N 67° 63' 02.5"W
JONESPORT, MAINE

DeBolt sat stunned. His senses went on high alert. Department of Defense? It made no sense at all. And the lat-long position—he knew vehicles could be tracked, but to have near-instantaneous *access* to that kind of information? Where was it coming from? He saw but one certainty—the information he was getting was so accurate, so detailed, that it could only be true. More ominous, but equally certain—the men in the Tahoe were part of the squad from the beach last night.

The EXIT sign beckoned, pulling him as if by some sidelong gravitational force. But why weren't they moving? he wondered. Of course he knew the answer. Last night there had been five of them. So where were the others? Might there be another truck out back, someone covering the perimeter? He had no idea. They were the professionals, he was the amateur. DeBolt knew he was trapped. Then it dawned on him why they hadn't made a move—they needed to do this quietly. He was cornered, but they couldn't simply walk up and shoot him in a public place.

That gave him time. Not much, but time all the same.

With all the self-control he could gather, DeBolt sat where he was and tried to think it through. He looked all around the restaurant, but short of throwing a chair through a window there were only two ways out: the front door and the back. Might there be a weapon inside the restaurant? A handgun under the cash drawer or a patron with a concealed weapon? Yes, he decided, it was possible, but that kind of firepower wouldn't give him any chance against five heavily armed commandos. *DOD.* The acronym looped through his head until he forced it away. He looked out across the parking lot and saw a half-dozen cars. Could he steal someone's keys and make a run for it? Not without raising a commotion inside that would give away the idea. Forewarned, the Tahoe could easily reposition to block in any car on the lot. The street beyond had light traffic, so a carjacking seemed impractical. *Is that what I've been reduced to,* he thought, *a common thug?* Joan Chandler had already paid the ultimate price at the hands of these men. He vowed to not endanger anyone else.

DeBolt methodically studied each vehicle in the parking lot, and his gaze settled on a late-model Cadillac. It was a sporty model, a CTS. He wondered who owned it, thought *What the hell,* and mentally ran the plate number. The response was almost instantaneous:

> *HFJ098, MAINE*
> *CADILLAC CTS, VIN 1G6KS17S5Y8104122*
> *REGISTERED PAUL SCHROEDER*
> *VEHICLE POSITION 44° 31' 59.4"N 67° 63' 02.4"W*
> *JONESPORT, MAINE*
> *ONSTAR*

DeBolt looked over his shoulder. He saw at least five men who could be Paul Schroeder. Or had Mrs. Paul Schroeder borrowed her husband's car? No way to tell without asking.

Then his thoughts snagged on the last line of the response—something different from his search on the Tahoe. OnStar. He knew what it was—an emergency communications system built into General Motors cars as an option. He recalled a salesman's pitch for a Chevy he hadn't bought some years ago: automatic crash notification, theft protection, and a wide variety of other functions. But why had it been included in the response? Why indeed . . .

DeBolt concentrated mightily: *OnStar, HFJ098.*

Nothing came.

One of the men got out of the Tahoe, passenger side, and stared directly at him. DeBolt gripped the table, forcing himself to stay put. Everything around him seemed to constrict; he felt like a fish watching a net close around him. He saw the man's lips moving ever so slightly, no doubt coordinating with others who remained unseen. His right hand hovered just above his belt line, near the open zipper of an all-weather jacket.

Then, finally, a response flashed into view:

ONSTAR CAPTURE HFJ098
KEY BYPASS ENABLED THIS VEHICLE

DeBolt sat stunned, his attention alternating between near and far vision. *Capture?* he almost said aloud. What the hell did that mean? His next command seemed more like a prayer. He waited, transfixed, and seconds later the parking lights blinked twice on the unoccupied Cadillac and he heard two muted chirps.

The doors had unlocked.

Another sent message brought the smallest of tremors from the car. A puff of blue smoke from the exhaust.

The engine had started.

Sweet Jesus . . .

Without another thought, DeBolt leapt out of his seat and ran for the back door.

13

"He's moving! Back door!"

The warning arrived in the commander's earpiece as he was backed hard against a spalled concrete wall near the diner's rear entrance. He readied himself and nodded to the man on the other side of the doorway who was ready with a Taser.

"Remember, quick and quiet, immediate egress!" he whispered into his mic.

He listened intently, waiting for the hard footfalls. He heard only the roar of the Tahoe's engine out front. Three seconds passed since the last transmission.

Five.

Ten.

Too long. The Tahoe skidded into view, swimming in a beige cloud of dust.

"Five, report!"

Five was now the only man still in front. He was sitting on a park bench across the street, ignoring the stray dog he'd been petting until moments ago—a nice touch of improvisation they'd all agreed. His primary task was to watch for threats—in particular, law enforcement—while the grab went down.

Five responded, "I don't see him in the . . . wait . . ." An excruciating pause. "Target is out the front door! I repeat, *front* door! He's getting in a car, late-model Caddy, blue!"

Nothing more had to be said as the team shifted their tactical focus. The commander ran for the Tahoe, his partner right behind. Both bundled into the backseat, and the leader ordered Five to retrieve their second vehicle, a Toyota SUV parked nearby. Their chase had gone mobile.

"There!" said the driver.

They all saw the dark blue sedan fishtailing through gravel, heard rubber squeal when its tires met asphalt. The Tahoe's driver did well, taking a good angle across the parking lot, but they couldn't cut him off. The Tahoe bounded onto Main Street and found its footing, but the Caddy was fast. They all watched the car round a bend and briefly disappear from sight. When they reacquired a visual, the Caddy was in the left lane passing a delivery truck.

The Tahoe's driver tried to mirror the move, but an oncoming car caused him to brake hard. Well-trained in both offensive and defensive maneuvering, he steered onto the gravel shoulder, which was suitably wide, accelerated, and soon had the Tahoe back on the road with the truck behind them, its horn blaring. The Caddy was still in front, moving fast, its brake lights flickering on the next curve. All eyes went to the dash-mounted GPS map—the road led north, away from town, and connected to a number of secondary roads.

"Dammit!" the commander shouted.

The problem was obvious, a simple equation of weight and horsepower. The Caddy was half a mile in front and accelerating like a rocket. Unless their target kept to the speed limit—which he'd blatantly disregarded so far—they could never keep up.

"Did anybody get the plate number?"

Silence was the answer. The man who still had a Taser in his hand said weakly, "It was parked in front of us, and we have the dash cam—the head office can figure it out in time."

When they next saw the blue car it was barely a dot, almost a mile out front. The town was falling away, the terrain going to countryside and freshly plowed fields. Another distant blink of red as the Caddy approached a curve at breakneck speed.

"Maybe he'll do the job for us," the driver said, only half in jest.

The car disappeared from sight around the curve.

"Call it off!" the commander ordered.

The driver pulled smoothly to the gravel and grass shoulder. For a time there was silence, only the weary rumble of the Tahoe's overstressed V8 and the rub of shifting bodies on leather upholstery.

"What could we have done?" said the man with the Taser. "It wasn't practical to tag all the cars in the lot with transmitters. We watched him from the minute he went in—he never went to another table, never talked to anybody." And there it was, they all knew—in a few unconvincing sentences, the after-action report of a failed mission. "How the hell did he get the keys?"

The driver said, "I lost sight of him when he went in back. Maybe it was the cook's car."

They all looked at him dumbly. Fry cooks didn't drive new top-end Cadillacs.

The commander slammed his palm against the door in frustration. "This guy is smart," he said. "We didn't give him enough credit."

"And he's lucky," said the man with the Taser.

The commander thought about it. "Maybe . . . but something about this bugs me. There's something we're not seeing."

The Toyota caught up and pulled smoothly into formation behind them.

"Where to?" said the Tahoe's driver.

"Not much choice. Back to square one."

"The field of play just got a lot bigger."

"I know," said the commander. "Which means we're going to need some help."

DeBolt didn't let his foot off the gas for nearly ten minutes. He saw no sign of the Tahoe behind him, and after a series of turns he slowed to nearly the speed limit on an empty rural road. The car seemed to relax, acquiring a spongy ride and a more civilized tone from the engine.

He looked at the dash-mounted GPS navigation display, which showed his position on a map in bright LEDs. Feeling cocky, he tried for his own personal map, thinking, *Map, present position.*

Nothing happened.

He tried again, still got nothing. He input the Cadillac's license plate number, and then concentrated intently on the menu for Roy's Diner.

No information arrived.

On a straightaway he closed his left eye and saw the blind spot—it was every bit as empty as when he'd first noticed it. What was he doing wrong? He felt a tremor of unease, which seemed absurd—having recognized his new talent barely an hour ago, he could hardly have become reliant on it. He felt as if his mind were under attack, some kind of cognitive Pearl Harbor. DeBolt felt confused, paranoid. He checked the mirror for the hundredth time.

Ten miles later he was sure he was in the clear. All the same, his death grip on the wheel was unrelenting. He felt an overwhelming urge to get out of sight, to stop and assert control over the anarchy in his head.

He veered onto what looked like a logging road, a barely groomed dirt and gravel path, and began churning up an incline—something between a large hill and a minor mountain. When the road deteriorated and he could go no farther, DeBolt put the car in park and instinctively reached for an ignition switch that was empty of any key or electronic fob. He closed his eyes. Was there even a way to turn the car off? The gas gauge showed half a tank, but every ounce of fuel spent idling cut the distance he could put between himself and Cape Split. Where was he even going? What was the use of running without a destination in mind?

He got out of the idling car.

He'd been in the driver's seat no more than thirty minutes, but it felt good to move and stretch. He breathed in the cool, evergreen-scented air. DeBolt left the car where it was and hiked to the top of the hill, the softly rumbling engine heavy in the background, a gasoline-driven stopwatch to remind him that time equated to distance. After a three-minute trek over God's hardscape, hidden in the shadows of stunted pines and leafless maples, he crested the hill and looked out across a bucolic scene. The engine noise had faded, and the stillness before him was stark—surely made more so by the events of the last day. He saw a small town perhaps a mile away, a second at the base of a sister mountain in the distance.

He wondered idly what the name of the town was, and to his surprise the answer was immediately furnished:

BAILEYVILLE, MAINE

DeBolt's head drooped in disbelief. *What the hell?*

He rubbed the back of his neck and looked up at a faultless midday sky. He had the beginnings of a headache. For most people a mere annoyance, but for him . . . what? A concern? A system malfunction? DeBolt found himself in a new and unimaginable realm. In the Coast Guard, when he'd encountered difficult situations he had always had his training to fall back on. But how could anyone prepare for something like this?

On a hill adjacent to the town he noticed a small antennae farm. *Is that the answer?* he wondered. *Do I need a connection of some kind, a cell tower or a Wi-Fi portal? Are there mobile circuits wired inside my head?* As incredible as it sounded, DeBolt knew there had to be at least a grain of truth in the idea. Somehow he was gathering information, linking to a network. He shuddered to imagine the long-term health consequences of such a transformation. But then, "long-term" had little place in his recent thinking.

The concept was as unnerving as it was frightening. *I can find out anything. But how much does anybody* really *want to know?*

Whatever this new faculty was, whatever *he* was, he had to learn its functionality, understand how it operated and what limitations existed. DeBolt decided he could test the antenna theory simply enough when he began driving again. The greater question, however, remained moored in the back of his mind. "Now what?" he said to no one. "Where do I go?"

He began with the most simple of inquiries: *Trey Adam DeBolt.*

After a considerable delay, he saw:

UNAUTHORIZED ACCESS

DeBolt expelled a sharp breath, part laugh and part exasperation. "You can't be serious . . ."

He sank to his haunches, sat back on a rocky ledge. It would be comical were it not so demoralizing. Sam the waitress, a cook named Rusty, and Dave who owned Roy's—he could get information on anyone in the world. Anyone except himself.

He wished desperately that he could talk to Joan. She had asked him if he'd had any unusual sensations, and promised to explain everything soon. Joan had known. She understood what had been done to him. Perhaps she'd even been part of it. After considerable reflection, he realized this was where he had to begin. The best way to find out what had been done to him? Find out where Joan had worked. Find the hospital where it had begun, the place that floated through his mind like a fractured dream.

There was little to go on. He remembered everything before the accident, before the rescue mission that had killed his crew and put him on the brink.

Call sign—Neptune 11. But that was where his past ended. Since that day he had known only Joan Chandler and a cottage on the shores of Maine. Now five men were hunting him. DeBolt feared those men, but—in a response he'd never before had—he hated them even more. Then something else came to mind. Words he'd seen scrawled on his medical file: *META Project, Option Bravo*. What did they mean?

He was desperate for answers.

But how? How do I find them?

A soft uphill gust brought the murmur of the Cadillac's engine—the clock was running. No longer a stopwatch, but an alarm. It was time to go. Time to learn what he had become.

14

Lund was at her desk talking on the phone, an unrequited stack of papers pushed to one side. It wasn't much of a conversation.

"Permian Air Ambulance," she repeated.

"Don't know. Don't know that one," said the woman, who sounded distinctly Asian. She assured Lund for a second time that she ran a dry-cleaning service in Fresno, not an air ambulance company.

"All right, thanks anyway," said Lund.

"We run half-off special Wednesdays," said the woman. "You come in, bring your—"

Lund clicked off. She double-checked the number, and saw she'd dialed it correctly. She had found the phone number for Permian Air Ambulance in the air station flight logs. It was right there on the flight plan: the operator of the jet and contact information. On the night in question, N381TT, a Learjet 35, had collected Trey DeBolt and airlifted him to Anchorage International.

Only it hadn't.

She was trapped in a classic backpedal. Her first calls had been to the Air Force hospital at Elmendorf and the Anchorage VA hospital, but neither had any record of a patient named Trey DeBolt. She tried all spelling variants of the name, and even asked record-keepers at both facilities go through the admission logs for the date in question, plus or minus one day. Still nothing. So Lund had tracked down information on the med-evac flight, hoping the company that ran it could shed light on where DeBolt had ended up. Now that appeared to be a dead end. *Fresno, for God's sake.* It could have been a mistake, a pilot inputting a phone number that was off by one digit. Or . . . it could have been an intentional error.

She went to her computer and performed a search on Permian Air Ambulance. Lund found no such company. She decided to go back one more step— an inquiry she knew would at least get honest results. It took two calls to find the right number, and on the third ring Matt Doran, EMT, picked up.

"Hi, Matt, it's Shannon Lund."

"Hey, Shannon." Doran sounded sleepy.

"Did I get you at a bad time?"

"No, I'm good. Just got off a twenty-four–hour shift, but it was a quiet night. You make any headway on that climbing accident?"

"Yeah, it's coming along. But I was calling about something else. You mentioned that you helped transport Trey DeBolt to a med-evac jet a few weeks back."

"Yeah, what about it?"

"Well, do you remember anything else? Did the crew actually say they were going to Anchorage?"

"I never saw the pilots. There was a doctor and a nurse in back, but they were pretty busy prepping Trey for the flight."

"A doctor . . . like an MD? Isn't that unusual on a med-evac?"

"Yeah, I guess it is. I only talked to the nurse, and that was how she referred to him—'the doctor.' She did mention Anchorage, come to think of it—said they were going to perform surgery there, something about relieving the pressure on his brain."

"Do you remember their names?"

"I don't think I ever heard his. Her first name was Joan or Jean, something like that."

"What did they look like?"

"The nurse was maybe mid-forties, average build, a little round at the edges. Brown hair cut short—kind of frumpy, I guess you could say."

Me in fifteen years, Lund thought. "What about the doctor?"

"Had to be sixty, hair going silver, frameless glasses. I don't remember much else. He seemed real busy, focused on Trey."

She pumped him for a few more minutes, but got nothing notable. After hanging up, Lund sat back in her chair. She wondered who had searched

DeBolt's apartment and why. Wondered where besides Anchorage he had been taken in a private jet. When Doran had asked her about the climbing accident, she realized she'd been neglecting that case. Not that there *was* a case—the death of William Simmons was cut-and-dry compared to the klaxons going off around Trey DeBolt's disappearance.

She pulled open her desk drawer and retrieved a bottle of pills, a ten-week regimen of iron supplements the doctor had insisted she take. She took it most days, but the bottle was more full than it should have been. She decided to go outside for a cigarette.

At the second-floor landing she waited for the elevator. On the wall next to her was a full-length mirror, and above it a sign that read: WEAR THE UNIFORM PROUDLY. Every building on station had a mirror like it, credit to an old commander, twice replaced, who apparently thought his troops weren't looking snappy enough. There was a dress code, of course, for civilian employees of the service. Lund had been issued a copy when she'd first arrived, and while she reckoned it had probably changed over the years, nothing in her closet was going to raise anyone's hackles. In truth, her wardrobe was so consistent it was practically a uniform in its own right: plain pants, loose-fitting shirt, therapeutic shoes. There were a few colors among the earth tones, none particularly bright, and not a single dress that she could remember. As she stood looking in the mirror, she realized her pageboy was overdue for a trim.

Lund sighed. She'd become a shadow of what she might be. Worse yet, she didn't much care. *Is that wrong?* she asked herself. Before an answer came, the elevator rumbled to a stop and the door opened, interrupting her little sulk.

Lund turned away, opted for the stairs, and soon was outside walking into a chill fall breeze.

He had an incredible new gift.

People were trying to kill him.

Which seemed rather redundant, since he was officially dead.

That was the sorry state of PO2 Trey DeBolt's life as he drove north toward Calais. It was a small township nestled between Canada and the Bay of Fundy. He had never been there before, but he'd heard of the bay, which was famous for its extreme tidal surges. DeBolt held the Caddy to the speed limit, but tensed all the same when a state trooper passed in the opposite direction—it was, after all, a stolen car. The trooper kept going.

He felt a compulsion to experiment with his abilities, and he wasn't surprised to learn that there were indeed limitations. In certain rural stretches he drew blanks, but now, nearing Calais, all the world's information was once again there for the asking. Some of it was downright disturbing. He passed a tanker truck carrying a load of hazardous material. Within a minute DeBolt knew that the placarded warning diamond signified the eighteen-wheeler was full of ammonium nitrate—with a reactivity hazard rating of three, a load that was extremely combustible under shock. The truck was destined for a fertilizer manufacturer in Presque Isle.

He also made mistakes. When he tried for information on Calais, DeBolt wound up on the seaside in France. It was just like any computer—garbage in, garbage out. A mile farther on, stopping at a red light, he pulled next to a small Audi whose female driver, a very attractive blonde, glanced his way and locked eyes for a moment. But only for a moment. He began with the license plate number, and by the time they reached the next light he knew her name: Christina Fontaine. He also knew that she was a recent graduate of Brown, cum laude, newly employed by a local accounting firm, and quite active in various green-leaning movements. She was single, active on at least one online dating service, and had $6,503.26 in her Bank of America Preferred Awards account.

What some guys would give for this, he thought.

It was like being a voyeur, peeking into the lives of others at will. It was also profoundly distressing. The internet offered information to everyone, but only to a point. DeBolt's new faculties went far beyond that. It was more akin being a hacker, he imagined, only without the days and nights spent cracking passwords, and without constantly looking over one's electronic shoulder for a cyber-crimes task force. As far as he could tell, he'd somehow acquired a pass—unlimited access without the attribution or headaches. At least not the metaphorical kind.

There were noticeable quirks to whatever network had found him. Most obvious—the length of time for responses varied. Some information came almost immediately, while other inquiries took minutes to fulfill. He was not surprised that Christina Fontaine's bank balance had been particularly slow in coming—in truth, he was heartened. His secret server had worked overtime for that one. He watched her pull away from the stoplight in a flourish of blond hair and gleaming metallic paint. As she did so, that final thought remained lodged in DeBolt's head. A bank account. Everybody had one, unless they were penniless . . . or dead.

He fell back and hooked a turn into a pleasant-looking neighborhood, less a conscious decision than an impulse to get out of sight. With the gas tank running low and five dollars in his pocket, his immediate need was obvious. He needed money, and while he'd never before sunk to thievery, DeBolt saw little recourse but to leverage his newfound abilities in that direction. He had to find a way.

He regarded the homes on a quiet suburban street in ways he never had before. Front doors, coach lights, newspapers in driveways. A canopy of trees formed an archway above the road, filtering light and expanding shadows. When performing rescues DeBolt had always preferred the light of day, yet being hunted brought a new perspective. He edged the car toward darkened curbs and coasted behind stands of foliage. The neighborhood was tony, large and elegant residences on one-acre lots, towers of brick and mortar that seemed more statements than homes. Unlike so many developments where the land was first clear-cut, the houses here had been trenched into the surrounding forest. Which made for good cover.

At an intersection he paused to check the road name, then continued slowly and combined that with the numbers on mailboxes. It was difficult at first, certain requests denied, formats not recognized. After much trial and error, however, responses began to flow.

87 MILL STREET: OWNERS OF RECORD, MR. AND MRS. JAMES REDIFER.

DeBolt saw two cars in the driveway. He kept going.

90 MILL STREET: OWNERS OF RECORD, DON AND LINDA BRUNS.

No cars in the driveway. DeBolt paused, until he discovered that Linda was a local veterinarian whose office was closed today.

After five inquiries, DeBolt touched the brake pedal for the first time at

98 Mill Street: Owners, Paul and Lori Thompson. No cars in the driveway. More pertinently, Paul Thompson was the principal registered owner of a defunct hedge fund. He had recently been arrested and charged with embezzlement, and was currently awaiting arraignment in a New York City federal detention facility. He was also fighting tax-evasion charges from the IRS. DeBolt pursued the legal trail and, by means he could not envision, discovered that a warrant was pending judicial approval for a search of Thompson's homes in New York, Key West, and Maine.

Also unearthed: Lori Thompson, apparently unfazed by her husband's professional exertions, had used her credit card this morning at Saks Fifth Avenue, Macy's, and a Starbucks in Manhattan. DeBolt also learned the couple had no children, presumably increasing the odds that no one was presently in the house. He weighed other methods to confirm that the home was unoccupied, and targeted the Eastern Main Electric Cooperative. After a ninety-second delay, he was looking at the previous month's electric bill: $42.12. This for a home of at least five thousand square feet. He was satisfied. Nobody was home at 98 Mill Street.

He pulled the Caddy a block down the street and parked in front of a vacant lot. DeBolt got out and looked all around. Once again, he left the engine running.

15

It was midmorning when Lund put in a call to Fred McDermott, the Coast Guard's FAA liaison for Alaska. McDermott worked out of Anchorage, and when he didn't pick up, she left a message explaining what she needed. He called back at two that afternoon.

"Well, I found that jet you were looking for," he said in his gravel-edged voice. The same voice Lund would have someday if she didn't stop smoking.

"Did it land in Anchorage?"

"Actually, no. They changed their destination once they got airborne—said they were diverting."

"Diverting? Is that common?"

"Not common," he said, "but it happens. Sometimes you have to land at a different airport because the weather at your original destination goes bad, or maybe due to a mechanical problem. As far as I could tell, it wasn't any of that. No record of an emergency, and the weather that night was fine."

"So why would they have gone elsewhere?"

"Business jets do it now and again, generally for corporate reasons—maybe a meeting schedule changes. Private owners might change their minds about which vacation home they want to visit. There aren't any rules against altering a destination."

"So where did they go?"

"They refiled their flight plan for Minneapolis."

"Minneapolis?"

"That was the first change. You piqued my curiosity, so I tracked the jet as far as I could. Bear in mind, this requires transiting a foreign country. Canada is more inviting than most—they charge for air traffic services, so every time an airplane goes through their airspace it's money in the bank. This jet flew southeast through British Columbia all the way to Manitoba. Reentered U.S. airspace in northern Minnesota, and at that point they canceled and went VFR."

"VFR? What's that?"

"Visual flight rules. Basically, they said bye-bye to air traffic control. Below eighteen thousand feet you can do that, go anywhere you want without being tracked."

"So there's no way to tell where this jet ended up?"

"Not really. But there is one way you could get an idea of their intentions."

"How?" asked Lund.

"I do a little flying myself, and I happen to know that aviation fuel is outrageously expensive in Kodiak. The government wouldn't care, mind you, but no private jet operator is going to buy an ounce of fuel more than necessary."

Seeing where he was going, Lund scrounged through the pile of papers on her desk for the servicing records she'd printed out earlier. "How much gas would a jet like that need to get to Anchorage?"

"Well, it's not the sort of airplane I fly," said McDermott, "but Anchorage is about three hundred miles. A Lear might need two, maybe three hundred gallons."

"And to Minnesota?"

"That's gotta be a couple thousand miles more. The jet could do it, no problem, but you'd need full tanks."

Lund found the paper she wanted. "They paid for eight hundred gallons."

"I'd say that's full. Which implies to me that they never intended to go to Anchorage in the first place. More to the point . . ." His coarse voice drifted off, allowing Lund to finish the thought.

"They were trying to hide where they *were* going."

DeBolt was casing a neighborhood for a home to burgle. There was simply no other way to think about it.

He approached on foot, looking up and down the street. He watched the homes adjacent to 98 Mill Street closely, but saw no activity, although the house diagonally across the street had an open garage door and a minivan parked inside. The tasteful stone path that led up to 98 meandered through tight landscaping, and near the front steps he encountered a plastic sign shaped like a shield. It warned that trespassing was inadvisable, courtesy of AHM, a home security company so commonplace that even a lifelong renter like De-Bolt had heard of it.

He went straight to the front door like any visitor would, and paused in a portico twenty feet tall. There DeBolt turned three hundred and sixty degrees, taking in everything around him. He wondered if there might be a key under the doormat, or behind the terra-cotta planter that held the remains of last spring's annuals. He was dismissing that hopeful thought when he looked again at the sign. AHM. Having never been a home owner, he was unfamiliar with how such systems worked. All the same, two questions arose. Did the Thompsons really have an active security contract with AHM, or was it only a sign meant to frighten away shady people like him? And if there was a system—what could AHM do for him?

He looked up and saw a security camera. A tiny red light glowed steady, the lens pointing directly at him.

DeBolt composed his thoughts in the way that was becoming second nature: *98 Mill Street, AHM, front door camera.*

He waited, thinking, *Surely not.* For almost a minute there was nothing.

Then, all at once, DeBolt was looking at himself. It streamed in near real time on the tiny screen in his visual field. He shook his head in disbelief, which actually registered in the feed, although not right away. Curious about the delay involved, he put it to a test—he waved and began counting Mississippis. Four and a half seconds later, he saw the wave in his right eye. He supposed the interval might be different for another camera, or another system. All technologies had variables and electronic quirks, the likes of which he had no hope of comprehending. In this case it was a four-and-a-half-second relay gap. He was learning.

DeBolt suddenly felt vulnerable, wondering who else might be watching the feed—it *was* a monitoring system after all, and not intended for his private use. He suspected the Thompsons in New York could, if they wished, see his image on their phones or tablet computers with the same four-and-a-half-second delay. Fortunately, both were probably too busy to bother, he in meetings with well-starched attorneys, she engaged with smiling sales associates in front of changing-room mirrors.

He thought: *98 Mill Street, AHM, front door camera, disable.*

This took ten seconds. Then the image disappeared from the screen in his eye.

16

He was on a roll and, on the same principle as the OnStar system he'd used to steal a Cadillac, DeBolt wondered if AHM might unlock someone's front door for him. It seemed a logical feature, useful for an owner who'd lost their key, or to let in a neighbor to feed the dog. His question was answered by the clunk of an electronic dead bolt sliding free.

This is utterly insane.

He cast one glance toward the street, then stepped inside. DeBolt closed the door behind him and immediately encountered a keypad. Should he have sought a code to disarm the system before entering? There was a backlit number pad, along with a tiny TV screen, currently blank—the dead camera on the front steps? A system status field assured him the system was armed, and next to it were two comforting green lights. Both remained steady. Satisfied, DeBolt turned into the home.

What he saw was not unexpected. Over-the-top furnishings, a living room with an old-world theme, fusty and manufactured, all of it incongruous against an open kitchen that was a veritable sea of stainless steel. Wood inlays did little to soften marble floors, and the walls were crammed with knockoff copies of Renaissance masters. At least, he thought they were knockoffs.

The air was stale and musty, and diffuse light came from transom windows over the closed curtains. Constellations of dust floated in the air. The place had clearly not been occupied for some time, instilling a funeral home pallor that compelled DeBolt to move quickly. In the back of his mind he imagined a judge reviewing a search warrant in New York—how quickly could such an order be acted upon?

A hardwood staircase beckoned, and DeBolt climbed to the second floor. On the upper landing he steered toward a room whose entrance was sided by two massive faux Roman columns. Predictably, he encountered the master suite. Far less expected was what he saw on the bed.

"I'm so sorry," said General Karl Benefield, "I wish I had better news."

He was addressing the complete staff of the Metadata Transfer and Analysis Project, thirteen somber faces, many of whom had been here for the entire first two years of what was to have been a five-year campaign. Each of them Benefield had cherry-picked from government and private industry—some of the best minds in computing and cyberspace. The general struck an imposing figure. He'd worn his Army combat uniform, with its digital camouflage pattern, thinking it would give him the most gravitas amid a herd of civilian techies. He spoke smoothly, and his swept silver hair—just within regulations—suggested a post-retirement corporate scion in the making.

"DARPA is facing devastating budget cuts, and META, in spite of its far-reaching potential, simply didn't make the cut. All of you, of course, will be given priority in finding jobs within the agency, or assistance in returning to private industry. A few offers have already come across my desk, so rest assured, the talent in this room will find a home—I will see to it personally.

"In the coming days I'll be meeting with each of you, one on one, to discuss specific opportunities and your desired career paths. That said, I must also impress upon you the continued need for secrecy, and remind you of the strict confidentiality agreements we all signed."

This point, Benefield knew, was less important than he made it out to be. He had gone to extreme lengths to compartmentalize the project. The technicians here were only partially aware of META's greater aims, having seen the same vague and sanitized PowerPoint briefing he'd given to their DOD and congressional overseers. Besides himself, only two people were aware of META's more ambitious goal. And there, he knew, lay his greater problem.

One was the neurosurgeon, Dr. Abel Badenhorst, who led the clinical team in Maine. The other was the chief programmer, Atif Patel, PhD, who was currently attending a conference in Austria. Benefield knew he could never end those relationships so easily—both men were fully vested in the more complex mission. Each was also a brilliant scientist in his own right. But perhaps *too* brilliant.

There were a few questions from the crowd, which the general fielded ably and with as much compassion as he could manufacture. He then instructed everyone to remain in the building, explaining that a team would soon arrive to begin the out-processing paperwork. Benefield departed the building virtually unnoticed.

In his wake, the gossip began in earnest. Programmers and analysts milled about the place, and there were traces of grumbling, but more optimism— the general had been convincing, and most took the favorable view that their follow-on work would be every bit as groundbreaking and lucrative as what they'd found in the META Project. Someone discovered that a table with sandwiches and drinks had been set up in the break room, and the gathering that ensued was something between a going-away party and a wake.

It was a female programmer, part of the original cadre, who noticed it first.

"I smell smoke."

A Caltech grad, one of the world's leading experts on signal compression, said, "Look at the vent."

All eyes went to a ceiling ventilation panel where wisps of white drifted through like amorphous hands.

The most clear-thinking person in the room was a female encryption specialist who pulled the fire alarm handle near the refrigerator. Nothing happened. No bells, no red lights. The smoke thickened and turned black, belching from ventilation grates and rolling through the hallway in a surging ebony wave.

"Everybody out!" someone yelled.

All thirteen ran to the nearest door, the front entrance at the portico. The double doors were made of high-tensile steel and fitted with sturdy electronic dead bolts, standard issue for a highly classified facility. The doors were firmly locked, and the emergency release handle seemed disconnected. In the ensuing panic the group split, half going to the rear loading dock, and the rest coughing and wheezing their way up to the stairwell roof access. Neither door could be budged.

It was then that the screaming began.

Flames licked in from the ductwork, and began climbing the eastern wall. By some unseen consensus, or perhaps through survival instinct, everyone ended back at the front door, the last few arriving on hands and knees as the smoke began to prevail. Soon thirteen panicked sets of fists were banging on the vaultlike steel doors.

Five minutes later the banging went to silence.

By that time Benefield was over a mile away, driving slowly through the front gate. He could see the smoke from where he was, yet there was no sign of first responders. The place was remote by design, and with all lines of communication either cut or jammed, the fire department wouldn't arrive any time soon.

He disliked what he'd had to do, but there was the crux—he'd *had* to do it. Like successful commanders throughout history, he had no misgivings about sacrificing good men and women. Not when the military objective was so vital. Early in his career, during the First Gulf War, senior officers had put his life at risk. Against serious odds, and through some combination of training, tenacity, and good soldiering, Lieutenant Benefield had survived to become General Benefield. He doubted any of those behind him would be so obstinate.

So lost in thought was Benefield that the phone call didn't register until the third ring.

He saw who it was, and answered by saying, "Any luck?"

"We have a location on the car."

"Where?"

"Northern Maine, right on the Canadian border."

"Do you think he's trying to get out of the country?"

"I have no idea," said the commander of the tactical team.

He was a good man, Benefield knew. The small Special Forces unit included operators from three different services, and was unique in its anonymity, as well as its charter—it was the only unit authorized to work domestically. That legal footing had never been tested, but as long as they did their job cleanly, without mistake, it wouldn't have to be.

"How soon can you get there?" Benefield asked.

"Twenty-eight minutes."

The general smiled. He liked that kind of precision.

"And the other mission?"

A hesitation—the first from the colonel. Then, "Yeah, we took care of it."

"Trust me, Colonel. What you are doing is imperative for the security of our nation. It will change the future of warfare itself."

"How can one guy be so important?"

Benefield let silence be his answer.

"Right," said the team leader. "We'll let you know when it's all wrapped up."

17

The man they were looking for was, at that moment, staring at two suitcases. They were lying on the bed in the master suite, their flaps unzipped and contents exposed. DeBolt's first impression was that the bags had been packed in a hurry: clothing folded haphazardly, toiletries thrown on top. One suitcase overflowed with women's blouses and bathing suits, everything light and airy, meant for the sun. The other held men's shorts and shirts, a pair of sandals, and—the eye-opener—three bricks of cash that would fill a large shoe box.

Between the suitcases were two passports and a printout of the confirmation number for an airline reservation—Cayman Brac, tomorrow night. He thought again of a courtroom in New York where an arraignment was playing out. A defense attorney pleading for bail, explaining to the judge that his client was not a flight risk. DeBolt wished the judge could see this picture. He idly wondered if there was some way to provide it. *Can I send information out as well as I can acquire it?* He discarded the idea. This wasn't his battle.

He looked around the bedroom and wondered if there was a camera somewhere. Perhaps counterintuitively, he hoped there was. Aside from a team of killers, no one on earth knew that Petty Officer Second Class Trey DeBolt was still alive. A few pictures would at least validate his survival to this point. He picked up one of the stacks of cash and fanned through it. The bills were all hundreds, crisp and neatly bundled in fresh bank wrappers that belied their undoubtedly soiled provenance. In the closet he found an old backpack high on a shelf, and he requisitioned it and stuffed the money inside.

All of it.

He spent a few minutes rifling through drawers, no real idea what he was looking for. At some point, DeBolt knew he would need identification, yet Paul Thompson, as evidenced by his passport, was six inches shorter than DeBolt, dark haired, and balding severely. He looked at the other passport on the bed and was surprised to see not Lori Thompson's document, but that of a young blond woman named Eva Markova.

Christ.

He was back in the Cadillac minutes later, the backpack on the seat beside him. He had considered locking the front door after leaving the house, but it occurred to him that his requests for information, so diligently answered, were likely getting logged somewhere. He knew enough about cyberspace to understand that flows of information could be tracked, and he wondered if he was leaving some kind of digital footprint. Did someone know where he was right now, what he was doing? Even what he was thinking? This last concept was particularly disturbing—the simple nakedness of having the window of one's thoughts open to strangers.

Perhaps even recorded by them.

And kept forever.

He drove away from the scene of his most recent crime, and at the main road DeBolt turned toward the Calais Lodge. There was nothing left of the sun, only a lingering burn on the western horizon. He went through town once on the main drag, which didn't take long, before settling on a destination and backtracking. He parked in the side lot of a chain pharmacy, hit the button near the steering column, and for the first time in seven hours the engine went silent. If it became necessary, DeBolt reckoned he could start the car as he had before. He was, however, increasingly worried that it might be used to track him—he wasn't the only one in the world with access to information.

With a backpack full of cash in hand, he crossed the street and entered the office of the Calais Lodge. It was a small place, designed decades ago in the image of an Alpine lodge, three stories of siding that had once probably been white, and an A-frame roof capped by weathered shingles. He found a neat front desk, and behind it a woman in her fifties who wasn't wearing any kind of uniform. She smiled in a familiar small-town way.

"Do you have any vacancies?" he asked, having already seen the empty parking lot.

"Nothing but vacancies," she said. "How many nights?"

"Two," he replied.

She situated herself behind a keyboard and screen. "It'll be ninety a night."

DeBolt was naturally frugal, having grown up in a home with limited means, and later making ends meet on an enlisted-ranks paycheck in the service. That being the case, there was a brief hesitation, belying the fact that his pocket was stuffed with hundred-dollar bills. "That'll be fine," he finally said.

"I'll need a credit card and driver's license," she said, her fingers hovering over the keyboard.

"That could be a problem," he said. "My girlfriend has my wallet, so I don't have any ID right now. She was supposed to meet me here, but her car broke down and she won't arrive until later." The woman looked crestfallen until DeBolt added, "But I can give you cash up front."

She eyed him more closely, a clear risk-benefit analysis. DeBolt had not shaved in forty-eight hours, and after a long day on the run he probably looked as weary as he felt. He apparently passed the inspection. "Name?" she asked.

DeBolt was prepared. He gave her the name Trent Hall, an old high school friend, along with a fictional Colorado address. He followed that with two hundred-dollar bills. She faltered in providing change, and was forced to go to her purse for a twenty to complete the transaction—who paid cash for hotel rooms anymore? Minutes later DeBolt had a key in hand.

"We don't serve dinner this time of year, but the Melodee next door is good. We offer breakfast from seven to nine, a buffet if we have enough guests."

"Thanks."

DeBolt found the room near the second-floor landing. Outside his door was a knee wall in need of paint, and on the abutting stair rail he saw a loose post that had fallen free. Happily, things inside the room seemed in better shape. The first thing he did was look out the window. He saw the Caddy across the street, and had a good view of the pharmacy and the Melodee restaurant. There was little traffic, and the few cars he did see moved at a distinctly local pace. On the distant river a small boat plowed seaward leaving a chevron wake behind. The extended dusk reminded him of Alaska, and he wondered how much farther south Calais was than Kodiak. Unnervingly, DeBolt realized an answer might come, and he pushed the question away. There were advantages to having all the world's information for the asking, but at that moment it seemed heavy and onerous.

This is going to take some getting used to.

Feeling dog-tired, he closed the curtains, which brought the room to near darkness. He lay down on the bed and closed his eyes. The last twenty-four hours began rewinding in his mind. He fell distracted by the empty screen in his vision—blank now, but waiting with unending patience, ready to blink to life with facts and figures. Was there any way to ignore it? Would it ever go away? He hoped there was some command he had not yet imagined, a mental switch he could throw to suspend operations.

He thought: *Power off. Disable.*

Nothing changed.

He wondered what would happen while he slept. There was a fine line between sleep and consciousness: who hadn't startled awake with arms outstretched to avoid an imaginary fall, or talked in their sleep? In that limbo would his dreams interact with his personal supercomputer? Network into his nightmares?

Or was none of it real at all?

For the first time DeBolt considered an alternate scenario: Was he simply going mad, his "connection" no more than the psychotic imaginings of a brain-damaged crash survivor? No, he decided. Part of him wished it *was* so simple, but the evidence was incontrovertible: the car outside, the money in the backpack, all made possible by his strange new aptitudes.

A few weeks ago DeBolt had been at the crest of life, no worry beyond the next mission, the next round of Natty Light at the Golden Anchor. He'd had friends and college and a job with a mission. Now he was hunted, wandering, alone. He had all the world's information in his head, but no idea what to do with it.

Minutes later DeBolt was fast asleep.

As he drifted off, not fifty yards from where he lay, a dark blue Toyota SUV cruised slowly past in the long New England dusk. Its brake lights blinked once in front of the pharmacy parking lot.

Lund hit a wall trying to find out where the Learjet had gone. She had no FAA contacts in the upper Midwest, and didn't feel like there was enough evidence to launch a formal inquiry on the issue of where Trey DeBolt had been taken. She simply needed more.

She was at her desk, contemplating how to proceed, when her work cell rang. The number didn't register as a contact.

"Hello?"

"Hello, is this Agent Lund?" The voice was male, bass-toned, and made her think of New England.

"Yes, this is Shannon Lund."

"My name is LaSalle. I work for the sheriff's department in Washington County, Maine. Something has come up in an investigation, and I was hoping you might be able to help."

"I'd be happy to try, but you realize I'm in Kodiak, Alaska—not exactly your neck of the woods."

"Yes, I know. But you're with the Coast Guard there, right?"

"Coast Guard Investigative Service—I'm a civilian employee." There was a pause, and she imagined LaSalle trying to wrap his mind around the idea of a civilian serving as a detective in a branch of the service. If the man had ever served, it must have been before the age of outsourcing. "What can I do for you?" she prompted.

"Well, we had an accident out here recently—although we're beginning to think it wasn't actually an accident. A cottage in a remote corner of the county blew sky high from a gas leak. It was owned by a local woman, and she was killed, but we've found a few signs of tampering and multiple ignition sources."

"So you think the blast was an intentional act?"

"Could be—the FBI is looking into it."

"Okay, but what does that have to do with Air Station Kodiak?"

"Ever heard the name Trey DeBolt?"

Lund went rigid in her chair. "Yes . . . I have. He was a Coast Guardsman who died recently in the line of duty."

"Right—I found out that much from the official records. But the thing is, we found a doorknob about two hundred yards from ground zero here, and we were able to pull two solid prints from it, right-hand thumb and index.

Mr. DeBolt, being a service member and all, had his prints on file in the national database—we made a match right away."

"Are you *sure* about this? The match?"

"As sure as you can be about that kind of thing. Now since Mr. DeBolt predeceased this accident, we know he wasn't involved, but the prints are fairly recent—we know because they overlay some others. What's bothering me is that I can't make any connection. DeBolt is originally from Colorado, and nobody around here seems to know him. I'm trying to figure out what he was doing out our way."

"Well . . . I really couldn't tell you. But I'd be happy to look into it."

"That would be great. We do have a witness who saw a man near the cabin in the days before the blast. I figured if I knew a little more about DeBolt and why he'd been here, there might be some connection to help me identify this other fellow."

"Do you have a description of the man who was seen?" Lund asked.

LaSalle hesitated. "You think he might have been from Kodiak too?"

Lund knew she wasn't thinking clearly. "DeBolt was tight with a lot of the guys on station. Maybe someone else here had an aunt or a girlfriend in Washington County."

"Yeah," said the detective, "I guess I see your point. The witness is a little girl, so her description is sketchy. She said the guy was maybe on the tall side, light hair." LaSalle chuckled, and said, "Oh yeah, and he likes to swim."

"Swim?" she managed.

"Yep. Jumped into the ocean every day and went for miles."

Lund sat transfixed, the phone clamped to her ear. The next thing she heard was, "Miss Lund? Are you still there?"

"Yeah, sorry. I'll look into this and get back to you."

"Thanks. I know it's a long shot, but I'm spinning my wheels over here."

"I know the feeling. Tell me one more thing, Detective."

"What's that?"

"The owner of the home—what was her name?"

"I'm afraid I can't release that yet; we haven't reached her next of kin. I can tell you she was a quiet type, kept to herself. Apparently she was a nurse."

"That's it—that's definitely the car!" said the man driving. They were on their second pass, and he slowed but didn't stop.

They all looked at the Cadillac, and then the pharmacy. The second in command said, "Do we wait and see if he comes out?"

The commander thought about it. "No. When we first got the signal it was moving, but it's been parked there for almost an hour."

"If this car has GPS tracking, why didn't we get a location sooner?"

"We're not Delta Force, okay—things like that need approval. Approvals take time."

"I'm betting he ditched it," said the driver.

The commander considered it. "Maybe." He looked all around and saw a bus stop shelter, a restaurant, and a lodge across the street. Plenty of options. He looked at his men. They were tired, none having gotten more than a combat nap in the last twenty-four hours. A tired unit made mistakes. *He* had made mistakes.

"All right," he said. "We give it two hours, split up three and two. Let's cover the area discreetly. Every bar and restaurant and transit point." He went over the action plan in detail, including contingencies in case they found DeBolt.

"And if we don't find him?" someone asked.

"Ask me in two hours."

18

Since taking over the front desk from his wife thirty minutes earlier, Demetri Karounos had found plenty of time to ruminate—the front door of the Calais Lodge had not opened once.

They'd owned the place for two years now, and their dream of running a B&B in a small town—one whose tourist base was heavily seasonal—was fading with each utility bill. They'd done their best to make things right— the rooms had been refurbished, the lobby floor replaced, and they'd even found a Filipina maid who doubled as a cook, filling both squares admirably. Unfortunately, the roof was another matter, as was the crumbling parking lot, and their website was notorious for crashing on anyone who tried to book a room.

So it was, when three men walked in wearing heavy boots and work clothes, Karounos beamed a smile that could not have been more heartfelt. It was after eleven o'clock, the hour at which walk-in traffic normally went dead.

"Good evening!" he said.

"Hi," said the man in front, a rangy sort with close-cropped hair. "We're in town for a little survey work—the power company's relocating some electric lines. Need a place for my crew to stay tonight."

The other two men wandered into the lobby and gravitated toward the television, which was tuned to a West Coast college football game.

"How many rooms?"

"Only one. We'd prefer the one in front, on the third floor—it might actually help with our survey. How many beds in that room?"

"Well, that unit has two doubles. But I'm sure you'd be more comfortable with two—"

"That'll be fine. Like I said, we like the view."

Karounos stared dumbly at the man, then at his two burly compatriots who were glued to the game—they'd each taken an apple from a welcome bowl on the coffee table. The view from 306 was decent, looking out across the river, but nobody had ever asked for it with that in mind.

"Are you sure I can't—"

"I'm sure," said the man, this time insistently.

"Of course," Karounos agreed.

He was sure these men were private contractors—or consultants, or freelancers, or whatever they called themselves these days. Karounos was familiar with the type, and they were not his favorite. They didn't have the backing of corporate expense accounts, which meant they did everything on the cheap. He was sure all three would show up at the free breakfast—it was advertised on the marquis outside, so he had to provide it—and eat everything in sight.

"There are two other guys who might come later with some equipment," the front man said.

Here Karounos laid down the law. "Sir, fire regulations do not allow more than four to a room."

"And we won't ever have more than three."

The guest handed over a credit card, and out of ideas, a defeated Karounos took it. While he ran the card, the man asked, "Looks quiet around here. You have any other guests tonight?"

"Only one other room," Karounos said, trying not to sound embarrassed.

"It's not a young guy with light hair, is it? We were expecting a power company rep to meet us."

Karounos repeated what his wife had told him, "I only know it is a young couple."

The man nodded. "Well, then . . . that wouldn't be our rep."

When the men disappeared minutes later, a resolute Karounos thought, *If all five raid the buffet tomorrow, I am going to charge them extra.*

———

DeBolt was awakened by a herd of buffalo. That was what it sounded like, anyway, heavy boots stomping around the room above him. He looked at the bedside clock. 11:21 P.M.

He pulled a pillow over his head.

They began rearranging the furniture.

"You've gotta be kidding!" he muttered to no one.

He had an urge to bang on the ceiling. Or he could pick up the phone, call the room, and tell whomever it was that people were trying to sleep. Better yet, he could call the front desk and complain, let them deal with it. Any of that would feel good. But he knew better. The last thing he needed was to get caught up in a shouting match with strangers. Or worse yet, have the night manager, or even a sheriff's deputy, come knocking on his door.

So DeBolt rolled over.

The noise kept coming.

He distracted himself by imagining less conventional responses. A year ago he'd taken an online class on network systems, an elective overview course for nonmajors. Among the subjects covered was SCADA—supervisory control and data acquisition. SCADA was an operating structure, both software and hardware, used to control complex industrial and commercial systems. As an academic subject it had been dry and tedious, but now, given his new talents, DeBolt saw SCADA in an all new light. It seemed a veritable playground of possibility. Of course, he doubted that a small bed-and-breakfast in Maine would have such a network in place. All the same, he imagined commanding the doors on the room above to lock. Imagined cranking the heater full blast and lighting the gas fireplace. He could turn out the lights . . . or better yet, cause them to blink on and off at some seizure-inducing hertz.

His mind began to drift, and the noise above lessened. Soon DeBolt was asleep again, a scant trace of amusement on the margins of his lips.

So energized was Lund, she stayed at the office until nearly midnight. As a civilian, she was expected to be on duty no more than eights hour a day. Unfortunately, the demands of law enforcement rarely meshed with any kind of civilized nine-to-five schedule. In truth, she hadn't looked at a clock since getting off the phone with LaSalle.

Washington County, Maine.

She'd looked on a map to see where it was, and had no trouble finding the place. Unfortunately, that added nothing to her understanding. Trey De-Bolt? Was he really still alive? Swimming at a beach on the other side of the lower forty-eight?

Late that afternoon she'd gone into town, and reached the credit union as the manager was locking the door. He made the mistake of letting her in, and she made an inquiry about DeBolt's account. Lund said she was on official business, which wasn't quite true, but the branch manager, a suit-clad bastion of procedure named Norm Peterson, had surprisingly shown her the records. He probably shouldn't have, since she didn't have a specific warrant, but she knew Norm from previous investigations, and anyway, Kodiak was Kodiak. In the end it had amounted to nothing. DeBolt's last outflow had been the day before he'd died, a charge for $12.61 at the Safeway on Mill Bay Road. There had been no mysterious withdrawals since, say from an ATM in Maine. The truth was never so easy.

AT&T was more troublesome—the phone company declined to give up DeBolt's records without official authorization. Not sure if she could get it, Lund took a more direct course, going straight to his unit and meeting with his skipper, Commander Erin Urlacker. Urlacker was happy to help: DeBolt had left his phone in his locker, she said, and it was still there waiting to be claimed. After a month the handset was dead, of course, but it used a universal charger, and within minutes Lund was able to access the call log. The last time the phone had been used was on the morning of the accident, and there had never been a call placed to a Maine area code. A look through the contact list was equally unproductive—no connections to Washington County.

At that point, Lund had thanked Urlacker and gone back to her office. She'd trolled social media sites, and found a handful of accounts, but De-Bolt had never been very active, and there was no usage whatsoever since his alleged passing. She did get hung up briefly on his Facebook profile picture: a rescue swimmer in midair jumping out of a helicopter, the sea below a maelstrom of white in the rotor wash. She thought it might be a stock photo, dramatic as it was, but then she discerned DeBolt's name stenciled on the back of his survival suit.

In the end, her hours of work went for naught. She could find no evidence to support the idea that DeBolt was still alive. The only things she had to work with: an apartment that had been searched, fingerprints on a door-knob thousands of miles away, and a young girl who'd seen a swimmer. Perhaps most mysterious of all, a Learjet flown to parts unknown.

It gnawed at Lund late into that evening, until she finally told herself it was nothing more than false hope. She rarely let cases get to her, but this one was an exception. Exhausted, she decided to go home. Before she did, however, one last thought flickered to mind. She pulled out her phone, added a new contact, and left a brief voice mail.

It was, without doubt, the most ridiculous thing she'd done in her investigative career.

19

Atif Patel rose in a pestilent mood. He pulled open the curtains and was greeted by a depressing Viennese morning, the sun powerless against espresso clouds and a dense mist. He could barely see the adjacent Stadtpark, and the few people braving its paths looked hunched and hurried. Altogether, a world far removed from the California sun he so enjoyed.

He ordered room service, and thirty minutes later Patel was drinking tea that had gone cold and suffering a stale croissant. This from the Hilton Vienna, a reputed five-star establishment. By eight he had succumbed to the inevitable, and thrust his knobby arms into the sleeves of his winter coat. He patted his pockets methodically: room key, glasses, wallet, and the flash drive containing his PowerPoint presentation. All there. He struck outside and became one of the wretched figures in the park.

With his head down into a stout November wind, Patel hurried along without noticing the statue of Schubert, and gave but a passing glance to the Kursalon, the pavilion where Johann Strauss had performed his first concert. Patel was a slightly built man with distinctly Indian features: dark skin and olive eyes, a nose like the prow of a ship. His mother was from Bangalore, his father Mumbai, but their only son had been born in Palo Alto, in the shadows of Silicon Valley and the Vietnam War. Indeed, if there was any providence at all in Patel's life it was that he'd been born a U.S. citizen—without that he would never have gotten the security clearances necessary to be where he was today.

As he put the park behind him a drizzle began to fall, and with quickened steps Patel navigated the busy Tuesday streets until the Hofburg appeared. The palace façade was grand as ever, its wide arcing entrance topped by a magnificent golden eagle. Contained within the endless halls and colonnades were the official residence of the president of Austria, the Imperial Library, and the famed Winter Riding School. Inspiring as that might be, what had begun in the thirteenth century as a palace destined for kings and emperors had inevitably diversified in scope and digressed in grandeur, now putting on offer banquet facilities, exhibition space, and an array of tawdry gift shops. And this week only: the World Conference on Cyber Security.

Patel had hoped the long walk would have a tranquilizing effect, yet as he climbed the final set of stairs a statue of Hercules slaying Hydra with a club did nothing to soothe his frayed nerves. Of course, it was neither the coldness of his tea nor the inclemency of the weather that had soured his day so early. At 3:00 A.M. he had gotten a call from the general, and been told to expect a visit.

He thought the timing might have been intentional, meant to ruin a good night's sleep. Patel tolerated the man, yet even after two years he did not completely trust him, this in spite of the most intimate professional association he'd ever joined. His future and the general's had become forever intertwined, and he supposed it was the permanency of that bond that bothered him. Patel was a software designer, and the swirl in his gut today was not unlike what he felt during the beta testing of a critical new version of code— the fear of failure, the excitement of new possibilities, and always that back-of-the-mind certainty that more work lay ahead. But then, Patel had never been afraid of work.

He walked into the conference center and found a schedule of the day's events on a pedestal. He dragged a finger down the program to find his name. Hofburg Galerie: Dr. Atif Patel, "Protocols and Architecture in Highly Secure Systems."

He sighed mightily. There had been no getting around it—he'd committed to the presentation nearly a year ago. It was the kind of thing that was expected from professors at Cal Berkeley, and in spite of the poor timing, Patel knew that great minds across history had endured worse. Among these was his personal hero, J. Robert Oppenheimer, who'd also taught at Cal, and who had published groundbreaking work regarding wave functions, approximation, and quantum mechanics. Yet in spite of his technical brilliance, Oppenheimer was today known for but one thing, the government project he had so capably managed—the Manhattan Project. Oppenheimer was universally regarded as the father of the atomic bomb.

It was curious, Patel had always thought, how history unfailingly distilled the life of any scientist to a single prominent work. Einstein and his special theory of relativity, Schrödinger and the paradox of his cat. He supposed authors and filmmakers and musicians were likewise doomed: a relevance of singularity. Still, the important thing was to have that one masterpiece. To have a Manhattan Project. Patel thought he might have found his—if he could make it work, it would be every bit as revolutionary. The surgeon, Dr. Abel Badenhorst, was capable enough, but Patel was without question the innovator, the driving force. And Badenhorst knew it. General Benefield, unfortunately, was another matter. His unmatched ego and aggressive nature were likely bred of education. Patel had attended Caltech, the general West Point, which meant they were trained to different standards, and dispatched into the world with markedly different missions. Now, by some tease of fate, those missions had intersected in an undertaking with mind-bending potential: the META Project.

With a few minutes to spare, Patel diverted to a washroom. At the mirror he removed his glasses and used a wad of paper towels to wipe the mist from his thin face. Strangely, it seemed to reappear after a few moments. He knew it wasn't the presentation—with a lectern in front of him, he was always at home, firmly in command of his subject matter. *It is the critical juncture of the project,* he thought.

Patel wiped his face dry a second time. He then straightened his lapel, snugged his tie, and walked resolutely to the Hofburg Galerie.

DeBolt woke late and ill rested, but a shower improved his outlook considerably. The wound on his calf was sore, and he decided it would require a bandage and something to ward off infection. He had other aches and pains, but most were improving. He went to the window where light was streaming in, and the first thing he saw was the pharmacy. *That'll be the first stop,* he decided.

The Cadillac was still in the parking lot, which seemed reassuring. Even so, DeBolt was reluctant to use the car again, and for the same reason he discarded the idea of stealing a different vehicle using OnStar or a system like it—convenient as it was, such thefts could be tracked. Anyway, the issue of transportation seemed pointless with no destination in mind. That would be his priority today.

He had to find out what had been done to him, and his only lead was Joan Chandler. He referenced the mainframe in his head, performed a search on her name, and was soon faced with choosing the correct Joan Chandler out of sixty-three on offer. It turned out to be a simple problem. He cross-referenced inputs of *nurse*, *Maine*, and, finally, *property records for Washington County*. There was only one Joan Chandler who met those narrow criteria.

He was getting more proficient.

She had been born in Virginia, educated at the University of North Carolina, and was an RN with a certified specialty in perioperative nursing—in essence, a surgical assistant. This gave DeBolt pause. She had admitted to putting a needle in his arm. *It's what saved you, Trey.* But had she also been present during his surgery? He thought it likely until the next bit of information arrived. Chandler's nursing license had been revoked last year. The reason: substance abuse.

He recalled her nightly bouts, the drinking that seemed to accelerate each day at the cottage. DeBolt steeled himself, then requested recent news about Joan Chandler. He expected an obituary, an investigation into her violent death. What he saw was incomprehensible. Her cottage had been destroyed in an explosion, the origins of which were suspicious and under investigation.

DeBolt, of course, knew the truth. Five men. Five professionals who would never be held to account. Not unless he could do something about it. He suppressed a surge of something new—anger—and began plodding through Chandler's work history and tax records. He discovered that for the last nineteen months she'd been employed by RTM Services, an ambiguous name for a company whose digital footprint turned out to be equally opaque. The only grain of useful information—RTM was incorporated in the state of Maine.

DeBolt stared out the window, past his heisted car to the river beyond. Soon a new option came to mind. He input Chandler's name, her address on Cape Split, and performed a search for her phone number. The wait was longer than usual, but he got a result, courtesy, apparently, of AT&T. He wondered if the company was aware that its data was being shared. If not, could he somehow be held accountable for the breach? That question was easily replaced by another: *What can AT&T do for me?*

DeBolt input the number, then added: *Location track, last two months.*

He waited a full five minutes, but there was no response, not even "REQUEST INVALID," or "NULL." Nothing at all. He had presumably found a new boundary, and took it with grudging acceptance. Certainly there were limits to what he could acquire.

Still at the window, a defeated DeBolt focused on the Cadillac. More than ever, he was bothered by it. It seemed like a marker, a beacon that could only attract trouble. He should have parked farther away. Last night he'd been tired, not thinking clearly. Now he felt a compulsion to get clear, even if he didn't have a destination in mind. He turned away from the window and grabbed the backpack full of cash—he had yet to count it, or even estimate how much was inside. DeBolt decided to set out on foot, and once he was safely away from the car he would concentrate on the basics—food, fresh clothing, a bandage for his leg—before trying to discover more about Joan Chandler and her mysterious employer.

He'd just gripped the door handle when he heard heavy boots on the stairs. DeBolt froze. He'd heard a similar clatter last night, but now it struck him differently. Then it had seemed an annoyance. Now it came as a warning.

I'm too close to the car.

Five men.

DeBolt put his eye to the peephole and saw a man on the staircase landing outside. He only got a glimpse, but it was all he needed—a face he would never forget, last seen in the parking lot of Roy's Diner in Jonesport.

DeBolt let go of the door handle like it was on fire.

20

The room above DeBolt's own was the only other with a view of the Cadillac. Multiple sets of boots stomped across the floor. *How did I not see it?*

He quickly crossed the room, keeping to the shadows, and looked out the window with a new suspicion. On the sidewalk he saw two old men walking side by side, one with a dog on a leash. A woman maneuvered a stroller around a puddle. A UPS driver was delivering packages to the pharmacy. With rising paranoia he mistrusted them all.

DeBolt tried to settle his thoughts.

The Tahoe—he tried to recall the license plate number, but drew a blank. *Maine, 846 . . . no . . .*

"Dammit!"

How could he recover it? He sent: *Archive searches.*

INVALID CRITERIA

History.

NULL INPUT

DeBolt pressed his eyes shut, tried to concentrate. *How does it work?* he wondered.

Very deliberately, he input: *Search history, November 19, Chevy Tahoe, Jonesport, Maine.*

864B34, MAINE
CHEVY TAHOE, WHITE, VIN 1GCGDMA8A9KR07327
REGISTERED U.S. DOD
VEHICLE POSITION 44°31'59.5"N 67°63'02.5"W
JONESPORT, MAINE

"Yes!" he whispered.

DeBolt focused on the first two lines, trying to highlight them. The image faltered and blinked, his frustration mounting. Then success—the VIN went bold: *Present position this VIN.*

He waited. His heart missed a beat when another set of boots shook the staircase outside, then faded. Climbing or descending? He couldn't tell.

The result flashed into view.

CHEVY TAHOE, WHITE, VIN 1GCGDMA8A9KR07327
REGISTERED U.S. DOD
VEHICLE POSITION 45°11'02.5"N 67°16'07.3"W
CALAIS, MAINE

And there it was—confirmation. In an increasingly common theme, DeBolt was encouraged to have gotten a result, but shaken by another disquieting truth.

Input: *Plot lat-long on map.*

Seconds later a perfectly scaled map of Calais, Maine, appeared—there were also two dots, one blue and one red. What could be more intuitive, he thought. Blue Force and Red Force, just like a military exercise. The Tahoe was two blocks south of the Calais Lodge. They had tracked him here, likely through the Cadillac.

But DeBolt had one advantage. They had no idea he was nearly in their grasp.

He listened for five minutes, watched the street from the window. DeBolt felt like an animal in a sprung trap, waiting for the hunter to arrive and collect him. He saw the occasional passing car, a few pedestrians who looked harmless. A state wildlife officer drove by in an SUV, and it made him think of calling the police. But the men chasing him were driving a government vehicle, which meant they were official at some level. Going to the police would be akin to surrender.

The conservative option would be to sit tight and watch. They had followed him to Calais, but obviously didn't realize he was literally under their noses. How long would that last? DeBolt had never been patient by nature— not when there was a more dynamic option.

He decided to leave.

All too late, he wondered if there was a back door in the hotel. Fire escapes? Emergency exits? He should have researched it all last night. Yet there might be a way to find out—DeBolt was aware of it because as a Coast Guard rescue swimmer he was also an EMT, and had trained and worked with firemen. He went to the phone by the bed and saw the hotel's street address typed neatly on the cover plate. He entered this into his request field, along with: *fire department building plan.*

After some delay, a computerized diagram came to the frame in his vision. It was a layout of the hotel, and he moved and magnified the image until he had what he wanted—clear markings for all the building's exits. Fire departments had something like it on file for every public building: a floor plan with emergency exits and stairwells and fire axes marked. DeBolt was disappointed to see only two options—the front door, and a lone exit to the rear, the latter down a short hallway from the base of the main staircase. Either way, he would be exposed for a short time.

He searched the room for a weapon. A clothes iron he thought too cumbersome, and even more so a heavy table lamp. There was nothing—until he remembered the loose balustrade post outside his door. Crude certainly, but his best option.

He shouldered the backpack momentarily, but then reconsidered and opened it. He stuffed wads of folded hundreds into each of his four pockets, then reloaded the backpack by a single strap onto his left shoulder. He listened intently, checked the viewing port. He stepped outside with his senses on high alert. He heard a television below, the vaguely familiar baritone of an over-the-hill actor giving a pitch for reverse mortgages. DeBolt saw the loose post, wrenched it free, and was heartened by its weight. A door rattled open on the floor above. DeBolt was about to rush down the staircase when he heard voices below.

The first had to be the manager. "There have been five of you—that is too many! You must pay for breakfast!"

A smart-ass reply, "Yeah, right. Here's twenty, and we'll call it even."

Footfalls on the staircase above.

DeBolt saw an alcove on his right. Inside was a square shadow on the lino-leum where a Coke machine had probably once been. He ducked inside, but realized too late that it wouldn't work—he could still be seen from the landing. He rushed back out to the stairwell and was instantly eye to eye with a man he'd never seen before. But based on his reaction, a man who clearly recognized him.

The man reached behind his back, at the belt line.

DeBolt already had his wooden post swinging. His first strike landed a glancing blow, one that stunned the man and sent him stumbling against the rail. The second was a backhand swing, less powerful, but one that con-nected cleanly with the man's temple. He crumpled in a heap. DeBolt rolled him and found the gun under the tail of his shirt. He didn't know the make or model, but saw a safety and made sure it was off. He shifted the club to his left hand, then quick-stepped down the stairs, betting with his life that the gun was loaded and had a round in the chamber.

He'd gone three steps when a second man he'd never seen appeared. He looked legitimately stunned, and went statuelike when he realized DeBolt was pointing a gun at his head.

"Hang on," he said in a calm voice. He was older than the others DeBolt had seen, concerned but collected. A soldier who'd been in tense situations before. DeBolt was no expert, but he had enough training to know where the threat was—the man's hands remained still at his sides.

"You killed her," DeBolt said. "You killed the nurse. Why?"

"Listen, buddy, you're confused if you think—"

"*Why?*" he shouted. "Because of me? *What they did to me?*"

The man remained silent.

But he knew . . . he *had* to know. With the gun steady in his right hand, DeBolt swung the club with his left like he was chasing an outside fastball. The man leaned away, but the club connected with his right shoulder. He staggered to one side.

"What the hell!"

Something dark and unfamiliar took hold of DeBolt. He brandished the post high and said, "Why . . . why did you kill her?"

"It was by the book—a kill order. You're a confirmed threat!"

A threat? DeBolt's thoughts went into free fall. He felt as though he were jumping from a helo into a cloud, unalterably committed but with no idea what was below. "A threat to what?" he managed.

This time the man didn't answer.

"Who do you work for?" he demanded.

Again no response.

DeBolt sensed a shuffle of motion from around the corner, near the front desk. The manager? He stepped to his right, trying to see who it was. The instant his eyes shifted, it happened—a foot lashed out, sweeping his legs from under him. DeBolt went down hard and the gun clattered away. The man was closer, and made a dive for it. DeBolt realized he still had the post, and from his knees he brought it down like an ax, catching the man's arm just before it reached the gun. He screamed in pain, and the gun skittered away across the polished wood floor.

DeBolt scrambled to his feet.

The man shouted, *"Thunder! Thunder!"*

Words that made no sense. Not until DeBolt noticed the wire looping into his adversary's ear. Soon he would be facing five men. Still brandishing the post, DeBolt saw his backpack and the gun on the floor. He wanted both, and they were only five steps away. But he would have to get past the man to reach them. With a glance over his shoulder, DeBolt ran toward the back door and disappeared.

The deputy sheriff arrived in less than five minutes. Even with such an admirable response time, there was little to see. A broken rail on the staircase, some blood on the carpet of the second-floor landing. One very distraught innkeeper.

Karounos said, "They are violent, I tell you. One of them had a gun!"

"Any shots fired?"

"No, I don't think so. But I haven't checked the rooms."

"Where did they all go?" the deputy asked.

"The one from the second floor, the crazy one—he ran toward the back door. The other two staggered out front together and got into a truck."

"Can you describe the vehicle?"

Demetri Karounos tried. Something white or perhaps gray, he said. A big SUV.

The deputy frowned and stepped outside, ostensibly to see if any of the perpetrators were loitering in the parking lot. He keyed the microphone mounted on his chest, and began talking to the dispatcher.

When Karounos came outside a minute later, what he heard was, "I dunno, some kind of altercation. Doesn't sound too serious. I'll see if I can get the owner to avoid an official complaint . . ."

The Tahoe sped south on a secondary road, the Toyota locked in trail. No one had spoken since leaving the Calais town limits.

The commander was in back, bruised but functional. His second in command was next to him—he'd regained consciousness, but his bloody head lolled against the window and his eyes remained glassy. The man in the front passenger seat turned and looked at the backpack their target had dropped—the commander had snatched it up in the course of a rushed egress.

The man in front exchanged a look with his commander, then pulled the backpack onto the center console and yanked the zipper open. Everyone gaped at the wads of cash.

"What the hell?" he exclaimed, rifling through the stacks. "There's gotta be close to a million bucks here. Where did he get that?"

Of the four men in the car, three still had their wits about them. The driver spoke for everyone when he said, "I don't know who this guy is . . . but I'm done thinking he's some ordinary Coastie."

21

UBER REQUEST SENT
INTERSECTION LINCOLN AVENUE/SPRING STREET
CALAIS, MAINE
DESTINATION MACHIAS, MAINE

DeBolt stood away from the curb as he waited for his ride. He'd seen a small-town cab in the distance, and that set the idea of an Uber call into his head. He'd made the request on the fly, thinking it wouldn't work—Uber only dispatched cars for people with active accounts. He had barely caught his breath when the response came:

UBER CONFIRMATION
PRESENT LOCATION TO MACHIAS, MAINE
FARE ESTIMATE $35 USD
DRIVER 2 MINUTES AWAY

So apparently he did have an account. Somewhere, in some name.

He was hopeful the immediate threat was gone, but all the same DeBolt kept in the shadow of a large maple tree. He'd kept tracking the Tahoe, and minutes ago had actually seen it speed past on Route 1 in the distance, no more than a white flash from where he stood—and precisely where the map in his head said it would be. It was an overwhelming tactical advantage—

knowing your enemy's position in real time. Comforting as that was, he kept out of sight as best he could until a Volkswagen Golf arrived three minutes later. A young woman with purple hair was at the wheel.

"Going to Machias?" she asked as he got into the backseat.

"Yeah, that's right."

Machias, Maine, was thirty miles south. DeBolt had plucked the town from the map in his head because the most direct route there looked isolated, and because it looked big enough to offer transportation options going forward. He would have preferred Bangor, but that was nearly a hundred miles south. He had no idea if Uber would take him that far, but more critically, it would mean uploading a destination two hours before his arrival. His greatest advantage, DeBolt reasoned, was unpredictability.

The driver kept to herself, and he was happy to do the same. They followed a narrow road through a tunnel of leafless trees that had probably been stunning a month ago, but now appeared lifeless and gray, their branches shivering under chill autumn gusts. The road was virtually devoid of traffic, and other than an occasional farmhouse he saw few signs of life. He'd made a good choice, in both using Uber and selecting a route. Any sense of victory, however, was dimmed by the uncertainty that lay ahead.

DeBolt massaged a new bruise on his shin—acquired when his legs had been chopped out from under him. In that same moment he'd dropped the backpack. He felt no remorse about losing the money. He'd never even bothered to count it, and it was dirty in the first place. The cash was no more than a tool, a necessity to keep moving forward.

Ensuring the driver's eyes were on the road, he pulled out the wads of bills he'd stuffed into his pockets, and took the time to count a more manageable sum. Fourteen thousand five hundred dollars. He folded the bills, more carefully this time, and put them back, thankful he'd had the foresight to separate a stash. *Maybe I do have a talent other than jumping out of helicopters,* he thought.

He sat back and closed his eyes. The window next to him was cracked open and fresh air buffeted in through the gap, an evergreen scent that belied the forest's lifeless appearance. He was somewhere in a remote bend of eastern Maine, and predictably he'd lost his connection. The Tahoe had long ago dropped from his private radar. DeBolt didn't want to put too much trust in that anyway—his pursuers would at some point acquire a new vehicle, something he couldn't track. The road was smooth, the air cool, and with his eyes still closed his thoughts drifted.

His makeshift meditation lasted ten minutes, at which point, without even a request, a map flashed into view. It startled DeBolt—would he ever get used to this?—and for a time he didn't understand what he was seeing. The map was full of red dots, the majority concentrated in two clusters. Only when he discerned that one group was centered on Cape Split did he realize what he was looking at: the results of his search last night for a track on Joan Chandler's phone. Arriving ten hours after his request.

Why the delay? he wondered in frustration. For all his capabilities, he had little understanding of how things worked, how the information was being acquired and fed. But he had what he wanted—a record of the movements of Joan Chandler's cell phone.

He had requested two months of data, but the result framed in his vision was clearly labeled as covering the last thirty days. No matter. He had a pictorial display of where she'd been in the weeks before he had ended up at her cottage. Not for the first time, it struck DeBolt that the data he was receiving was eminently user-friendly. Unlike some interfaces, it came presented in a format that was easily deciphered and direct, implying that the system was designed with a certain type of user in mind. A distinctly tactical approach.

As expected, the largest concentration of hits on Chandler's phone had occurred near the cabin on Cape Split, with a few scattered nearby—travel for groceries, clothing, undoubtedly a liquor store. A secondhand wetsuit. Of more interest to DeBolt was a second cluster of dots, these twenty-five miles west near a place called Beddington. Oddly, this group appeared to be in a remote district, a place where lakes and forest predominated. With some trial and error he was able to focus on individual hits, and he acquired what appeared to be time and date stamps for a few. Each predated October eighteenth, the day he had awakened in the cottage by the sea.

There could be no doubt. This second grouping identified the place where she had worked. But was it also where his nightmare had begun? Where his surgery had been performed? It seemed an implausible setting. What kind of clinic was situated in the middle of nowhere? What kind indeed.

"You okay?"

DeBolt blinked, the words breaking his spell. The driver was looking at him in the mirror, concern on her face.

"Yeah," he said. "I'm fine."

"You looked really worried—seemed a million miles away."

"Not quite a million . . . but yeah, I had a rough night." For the first time DeBolt recognized what would be an ongoing problem—how distracted he must look when discoursing with the computer in his head.

"We're almost to Machias. Where exactly did you want to go?"

"I'll let you know when we get there."

In the mirror the driver's expression turned doubtful.

"Don't worry," he said. "I don't think it's a big place."

The Gulfstream III business jet was gliding high over the Atlantic, seven hundred miles northeast of the Azores, the water below going dark in the late afternoon light. Benefield had never before warranted a GIII, but the secretary of state had upgraded at the last minute to a Boeing 757 for her trip to Israel, leaving the GIII, with its superior range and speed, empty for a repositioning flight to Europe. The general had not hesitated.

It was the kind of perk some men relished for prestige, and others for the accoutrements: a bed in the aft compartment, a plush conference area, and a communications suite that was on par with Air Force One. Benefield only cared about speed. He was desperate to shut down his fast-disintegrating operation.

And there it was. No denying it.

The META Project *was* his, a bond as intimate as any marriage. His name was stamped on every concept briefing, every equipment order, every funding request. In the end, he saw but one salvation—the project was so radical, so intrinsically risk-laden, that no one above him had dared attach themselves to its precarious coattails. META wasn't a black project—it was a black *hole* project, a place where money went in but no light escaped. Not unless success was stumbled upon. In the arcane world of DARPA, the defense department's laboratory for speculative technologies, there were many such ventures. A handful even succeeded, some spectacularly. New stealth coatings for aircraft, software algorithms to distinguish Bedouin SUVs from those of terrorists. The majority of the agency's efforts were expected to end in failure. Some rattled to slow deaths when the scientific premises upon which they were based proved to be flawed, while others flamed out in shocking budgetary fireballs. In Benefield's view, however, META was different from any other DARPA project ever envisioned—different because it assumed a new level of risk. META wasn't a gamble on advanced polymers or encryption methods—it directly leveraged human life in order to achieve its miracle.

"Message, General."

Benefield was sitting in a leather swivel chair, and he looked up to see the attendant, an Air Force master sergeant. He was a strongly built black man, with a starched uniform and impeccable deportment. He handed over a printout from the cockpit as if it were some kind of holy scripture. The general unfolded the paper.

MAINE STILL INCOMPLETE. UNABLE REPOSITION TO VIENNA.

Benefield sat stunned. He knew how very capable the colonel and his team were. So why couldn't they finish this one thing?

"Do we have an ETA?" Benefield asked the sergeant.

"Three hours and ten minutes remaining to Vienna," he replied, clearly having anticipated the question.

"All right. And have you heard if I'll be allowed to keep the jet for a second day?"

"I'm sorry, but we did get a ruling on that, sir. The assistant secretary of defense is in Germany, and he needs to go downrange tonight."

"Downrange," Benefield knew, meant somewhere in the Middle East. It also meant he would be flying commercial home. He supposed it didn't matter. By that time, if all went well, he would no longer be in a hurry.

Machias, Maine, was perfectly predictable. You could buy a brand-name tool at a mom-and-pop hardware store, or a used one at the thrift shop. Within fifty paces you could visit a lawyer, a health insurance office, and the doctor situated anxiously in between. A big fireworks outlet was positioned strategically across town from the fire department. Machias was like any of a hundred other New England towns: small, cozy, and centered around the spire of a Gothic revival church. It would be a simple and unsurprising place. Which was exactly what DeBolt wanted.

He decided to eat while he worked through his next steps, which put him in a seat at the counter of a diner called The Granary. The chair was a high-backed circular stool with worn upholstery, and it groaned every time he leaned to the right. The man seated next to him was easily in his seventies, gray haired and engrossed in a half-eaten plate of pancakes. DeBolt caught the man's eye and nodded.

A waitress dropped a laminated menu in front of him without missing a step. As he began to study it, the man next to him leaned in and whispered conspiratorially, "Don't worry, they got real food here too." He pointed to the wall and DeBolt saw a chalkboard DAILY SPECIALS menu. It was colorful and cluttered with things he'd heard of but never tasted: tofu, kale, and a wide array of gluten-free options.

"I recommend the cheeseburger," his seatmate said with a chuckle, then added, "medium rare."

DeBolt gave in and smiled.

"Now the whole wheat bun, that's not half bad. And the sea salt on the fries is a step in the right direction."

"Thanks for the advice—sounds like just what I need." DeBolt held out a hand. "My name's Trey."

"Ed Murch."

The two shook.

"You live nearby?" DeBolt asked.

"Two blocks from here," Ed replied, dropping his R like the locals did.

The waitress arrived in a flurry, her pencil poised over a pad. DeBolt said, "Cheeseburger . . . medium rare."

She stared at him for an instant, then fixed an accusing glare on his seatmate. "Ed Murch, you're at it again." DeBolt could see a smart-ass reply brewing, but she was gone before Murch could deliver it.

"Her name's Florence," Ed said, "but whatever you do, don't call her Flo, in spite of what her nametag says."

DeBolt realized he hadn't even looked at her nametag. He also hadn't checked the menu before arriving, and didn't know the cook's name or the owner's, or if either of them had tax problems. He had ignored an entire parking lot full of cars. It felt good.

"You're not from around here," Ed surmised.

"Colorado originally. I'm only passing through. But I'm guessing you've been here a long time."

Ed told him all about it, starting with high school and the Vietnam War. DeBolt responded in kind, telling Ed about Colorado and Alaska, although he only admitted to being "in the service," and didn't mention what his job entailed. The two didn't stop talking for nearly an hour, and by the time De-Bolt was down to his last cold, sea-salted fry, Murch seemed like an old friend. Murch finished by explaining that his wife had passed a few years back.

"Sorry to hear that," said DeBolt.

"Yeah, it was a damn shame. But you have to keep going, you know what I mean?"

"I do."

Ed settled his bill, and said, "Well, it's been nice chatting with you, Trey. You can learn a lot about people by just talking."

A slight smile creased DeBolt's face. "I was thinking the same thing."

Ed got up from his stool. "I've got to go see my sister. She's a good bit older than I am, and I finally convinced her to give up her driver's license. I need to sell her car before she changes her mind."

"What kind of car?" DeBolt asked.

"Oh, it ain't much, a twelve-year-old Buick sedan. Real cream puff, though."

"How much you asking?"

22

The Buick was a peach, or so said Agnes Murch Reynolds. They settled on four thousand cash, and according to Ed the license plate was good for thirty days. *With any luck,* DeBolt thought, *twenty-eight more than I'll need.*

He got a handshake from Ed, a hug from Agnes, and after best wishes were exchanged DeBolt set out south along Route 1. He estimated that his journey to the lake district south of Beddington, Joan Chandler's presumed place of employment, would take roughly an hour. The Buick handled differently from the Cadillac, the suspension stiff and the steering loose, but it was at least his own car, legally if not morally.

Having not requested information for over an hour, he tried for a map in his head, but the image drifted in and out of view, and he finally gave up. It hardly mattered—he needed only to identify one turn to reach the general area. It felt good to be making headway, to have seized the initiative. For too long he'd been reacting. DeBolt would find the place where Joan Chandler had worked, and confront anyone he saw there. He would ask and plead and demand, in that order, until someone gave him answers. Until someone told him what had been installed in his jury-rigged head.

Meeting Ed Murch and his sister had been a pleasant diversion, and acquiring a car under such simple circumstances was a godsend. He had ample cash to see him through the coming days, and a vehicle that could not be traced to him. DeBolt suspected things were about to get more difficult.

When he passed through a place called Columbia Falls, his connection strengthened, and a new idea came to mind. He had requested a locator history on Joan Chandler's phone, and gotten it, albeit a day late. *Why not check my own phone?* Voice mail, email, messages—perhaps there was something to advance his cause. At the very least, he might hear a familiar voice. He uploaded the request, and it seemed to process. The delay this time was only sixty seconds:

3 NEW VOICE MAILS

He tried to select them, and got the response:

AUDIO DISABLED
STANDBY

What on earth did that mean? DeBolt was wondering if there was some kind of audio capability in his new cranial system when the voice mails arrived in transcript format. The first two were anticlimactic—his mother's nursing home thanking him for a donation he'd made, and a reminder for a dental appointment he'd missed because he was dead.

The last one caused his heart to miss a beat:

TREY, IT'S SHANNON LUND, KODIAK CGIS. I KNOW YOU'RE STILL OUT THERE. CALL ME.

"Another, monsieur?" said the sommelier.

"Yes," said Atif Patel, "but no more until my guest arrives." His glass came full with the rich Rhône garnacha, and without so much as a sniff he sucked down a great gulp.

Restaurant Ville was ten miles west of Vienna, along the A1 West Autobahn near Pressbaum. Patel had chosen it for his meeting with General Benefield because it was one of the few things he could control. The place was small, with a subdued atmosphere and, more relevantly, served some of the most varied and exotic cuisine in Austria. Not that the general was a connoisseur of fine dining. To the contrary, he was, as they said in America, a meat-and-potatoes guy. Restaurant Ville would do its small part to keep the man off kilter.

Patel had arrived thirty minutes early, but was shown to a table in spite of it. The general was now thirty minutes late. In that time Patel had kept the sommelier busy—only, he told himself, to appease the staff in light of his protracted use of the table. He turned his glass by its base, spinning an endless circle. His eyes bounced between his Timex and the room around him. The place was busy. He saw staunch business meetings where profits were being toasted, and other tables where happy couples celebrated . . . whatever happy couples celebrated. Patel had never found the time to marry, much to his mother's despair, but he thought he might manage it someday. Perhaps even a child or two. He was still young, having only recently eclipsed thirty. The problem was that in his field, youth was reserved for making one's professional mark. The good news—success was imminent. This Patel knew with absolute conviction.

He had just emptied his third glass when the general appeared. He wasn't in uniform, of course. Benefield unfailingly dressed in what he called "civvies" when he traveled overseas. He'd once explained that it was actually a higher headquarters directive—in too many foreign countries, terrorists, kidnappers, and political protestors would salivate at the sight of a flag officer of the United States military in full regalia.

Benefield saw him right away, and he ignored the maître d' and charged across the room as if assaulting a pillbox. Patel rose and took a bricklayer's handshake.

"My flight was late," said Benefield. It was as close to an apology as Patel had ever gotten. As soon as they were seated, the waiter appeared—one of his best tables had been occupied for an hour with but three drinks to show for it. Benefield didn't even look at the menu—a disappointment for Patel—but simply told the man to bring him the biggest steak in the house, medium rare. That was exactly how he said it, in blunt American English, and Patel thought he might have heard a *tsk* from the waiter. He himself ordered the six-course special, and the waiter was gone.

"There's been an accident," Benefield said, never one to bog down in pleasantries when business was at hand.

Patel hesitated before replying. "What kind of accident?"

"A fire in the operations center—it was catastrophic. We lost the entire team."

"*What?*" Patel went ashen. "Lost as in—"

"Yes," said the general impatiently. "Everyone was inside during a shift change. There were no survivors." Benefield said nothing for a time, letting it sink in.

"Howard? And Ann Dorsett?"

"I'm sorry. I wanted to tell you personally—I know you were close to many of them."

"Dear God . . . when did this happen?"

"Yesterday. I don't have many details yet, but apparently everyone was overtaken by some kind of toxic smoke. The facility is a total loss."

Patel set his fingers very deliberately on his silverware. He stared at the empty bread plate in front of him.

"I'm afraid there's more," said the general. "This will cast everything in a very bright light—something you and I knew from the beginning that the META Project could never survive. Not without putting both our careers at risk. That being the case, I've decided to shut it down."

"You can't be serious!" said Patel incredulously. "Not after so much work!"

"I'm sorry, but my decision is final. I've already informed our overseers at DARPA. Aside from a wind-down account, funding has been zeroed."

The diminutive programmer stared pleadingly at the soldier, and got a predictably iron gaze in return.

"I'll carve out a good severance for you from the budget," said Benefield. "A man of your talents will have no trouble finding new research."

"It's not that," said Patel. "What we've put into place is so . . . so unique, so groundbreaking. META is a visionary concept. The government access you worked so hard to attain might never be repeated. Who can say when such an opportunity will come again?"

"I understand your frustration. If one of the subjects had survived the neural implantations, even *without* achieving a network . . . maybe we could have made a case."

"None of the original subjects were *expected* to survive—all were terminal cases from the outset. Phase two might bring success."

"Atif, you know we've put ourselves on extremely delicate ground. Terminal or not, we subjected live human beings—service members, for God's sake—to extremely invasive surgery. In my opinion, META is as much a breakthrough in ethics as it is in technology, but the risks going forward were simply too great. Which leads me to something else. You said there would be a way to wipe the servers clean of your control architecture—some kind of abort code to erase the highest level software. We can't just leave something like that lying around like an unexploded bomb."

"We didn't get past phase one, so the software never activated. I don't see any harm in leaving it in place."

"*That*," Benefield said decisively, "is out of the question. We have to be very careful in shutting things down. The software code you inserted must disappear—it's the only way to be sure the more delicate aspects of META can never be traced back to us."

"All right," Patel relented, "I will take care of it."

"No, Atif—*I* need to take care of it. I worked very hard to get unprecedented access. The host agency only agreed, only gave us that autonomy, because I guaranteed that I would have a kill switch. Since we never reached phase three, I never bothered to ask you for it. But now we're aborting, and only I have the security clearances necessary to initiate the termination."

Patel sighed. "Yes, there is a special sequence of commands. It requires a series of codes."

"Do you have them memorized?"

Patel might have laughed if the situation weren't so delicate. Those who were not brilliant gave great credit to those who were. Sometimes too much. "I will return from the conference next week. When I get back to Washington—"

"No!" Benefield said, chopping his hand down on the table like a blade. He whispered in a venomous tone, "I need them *now!*"

"All right. But I would never keep anything so critical on my laptop—it will take time for me to retrieve the codes securely. Even then, I'll need help from my liaison on the server end."

The general seemed to look right through him. Or perhaps *into* him. Patel held steady.

"All right," said Benefield. "We'll meet again tomorrow evening. Have them by then."

Dinner was an afterthought for both men. Benefield seemed content, devouring a massive slab of beef. Patel mostly spun his fork, nibbling at three of his six courses. In the end, the general paid and they walked outside.

"Where are you staying?" Patel asked.

"The Grand Hotel Vienna—it's not far from the Hilton. I took a cab here."

"I have a rental," said Patel. "Can I give you a lift back to town?" There was little invitation in his voice.

Benefield smiled congenially.

23

Lund was on a private mission to cook more at home, shunning the caloric content of restaurant food. To that end, she created time each day for a trip to the grocery store in search of something fresh. Today it was a halibut fillet that would carry her through two nights. She'd just dropped the fish into her cart, and was turning toward the produce department, when her mobile rang.

The number didn't register as known, but she picked up all the same. "Hello?"

"Hi, Shannon . . . it's Trey DeBolt."

Lund froze in the middle of the seafood aisle. "Trey . . . well, hi. I'm really glad you called." She heard him expel a long breath. "Are you okay? Last time I saw you . . . I mean, when you left here, you weren't doing so hot."

"Still kicking," he said.

Lund had heard that one before—a rescue swimmer's response. "Look, I know we only met once, but do you remember me?"

"Sure I remember. You interviewed me at the Golden Anchor about that drunk skipper who lost his boat."

"That's right."

"There was almost one other time," he added. "You were at Monk's Rock Coffee House . . . I saw you talking to another guy, so I didn't want to bother you."

Lund racked her brain, trying to remember. "Okay, right, a couple of months ago. I was with Jim Kalata, the petty officer who works in my office. He and I make up CGIS Kodiak. I wish you had come over."

DeBolt said nothing for a time. The small talk was clearly awkward for them both. "Anyway," he finally said, "it's good to hear a familiar voice. When I got your message it surprised me. I guess it means you've been looking for me."

"I have."

A hesitation. "Can you tell me why?"

"Trey—"

"The reason I ask," he interrupted, "is because some other people are looking for me. They've already tried to kill me twice."

"*What?*"

"I watched them gun down a woman in cold blood. Now they're after me."

Lund wasn't sure how to respond.

"Look, I know this sounds crazy . . . like I'm some paranoid lunatic. But there's a lot going on, and . . . and I don't know who to trust."

Lund sensed an edge in his voice, and she tried to place it. Fear? Anxiety? Whatever it was, he sounded nothing like the easygoing, confident young man she'd had a beer with at the Golden Anchor. Lund was deliberately calm with her response. "Who are they, Trey?" she asked, caring less about his answer than his reaction.

"I don't know. I'm pretty sure they're under DOD, but I have no idea which branch."

"DOD?" Lund struggled for another calm reply, something logical and full of assurance. Nothing came to mind.

"Sounds delusional, doesn't it? The government is out to get me. I don't know how to make you understand what's happened. I wish I could, Shannon. I wish someone could explain everything to me and . . ." His voice went hollow and trailed off.

"Maine," she said. "I can come to Maine."

"*What?* Christ, you're triangulating this call! You're tracking it to tell them where I am! I'm outta here—"

"No, I swear I'm not, Trey! Please don't hang up! I got a call from a detective, a place called Washington County. He called me because he'd discovered you were stationed at Kodiak—he said you were implicated in a case he was investigating there." Lund waited, not breathing. The disconnecting click didn't come.

"Implicated in what?"

"There was an explosion—a cottage along the coast blew up from a gas leak. They found fingerprints in the wreckage and got a match to yours, what the Coast Guard has on file. This detective saw right away that you were listed as deceased, but he was trying to figure out why you'd been to the cottage. He seemed to think the blast was suspicious."

"Suspicious? That's putting it mildly. I know exactly who was responsible—the same men who are trying to kill me. They did it to destroy any traces of their murder."

For the first time Lund sensed a thread of reason, slim as it might be. That was good, because otherwise DeBolt was right—what he was telling her sounded delusional.

"But you left a voice mail I could access," he said. "You didn't believe I was dead. Why?"

She explained that she'd gone to his apartment and seen things that didn't add up. She told him about the med-evac flight that never went to Anchorage.

"So that's how I got here," he said, "a private jet. I never even knew. I have a hazy recollection of being in a hospital, but the first thing I remember for sure is waking up in Joan's cottage. That was her name, Joan Chandler—she was a nurse. Look it up. Now she and her house are both gone."

"Excuse me!"

Lund turned and realized she was blocking the aisle, a stern-faced woman trying to get by. She steered her cart to one side, then leaned forward on the push handle.

"Trey, I'd really like to help you. But whatever else is happening, I can't ignore the fact that you're AWOL right now. For God's sake, think about it . . . the Coast Guard, your commander, your friends. They all think you're dead."

Another silence. "Maybe I am."

"Trey, I *want* to help you."

"Let me guess—I should proceed to the nearest Coast Guard facility and turn myself in? Look, I know it's part of your job to track down AWOLs, but I'm not some E-3 who's running from a child support payment or who got caught in a drug deal. You know the condition I was in after that accident—I did *not* leave Kodiak of my own free will."

"I understand that."

"My life was *taken* from me! And . . . and there's something else, Shannon. Something that overshadows the very fact that I'm alive. I don't know how to explain it, but believe me when I say I can never go back to Kodiak or the Coast Guard. I can never be what I was. In that hospital—they changed me."

"Who changed you? How?"

Silence.

"Trey, I only want to help!"

"They gave me an ability to do things, Shannon. Things you could never imagine. A few days ago I wouldn't have thought what's happened to me is possible. It's a curse more than anything. The whole world is mine for the taking, yet at the same time I feel . . . I feel so damned isolated."

Lund didn't know how to respond. She felt like a crisis counselor. He wasn't making sense, sounding more unbalanced by the moment. Was it the damage to his brain? she wondered. The ensuing silence stretched too long, and she felt him slipping away. "Trey, I'm coming to help you. I'll be on the next flight. I want you to go to Boston, meet me there tomorrow."

No response.

"Trey, I won't ask where you are, and I won't tell anyone I'm coming."

"No."

"I will be in Boston, whether you like it or not. You have my number, call me tomorrow."

Silence.

"Trey, please! Sooner or later you *have* to trust someone."

A click, followed by silence. Lund stood still, but only for a moment. She left her cart and her fish where they were. By the time she reached the parking lot Lund was already talking to Alaska Airlines.

24

DeBolt turned off the burner phone and set it on the Buick's passenger seat. The car was parked on a dirt pad along the remote road he'd been navigating. Straight lines had gradually surrendered to casual curves, and the forest had gone thick. The hills here were more demanding, the air still and noticeably cooler. Sharply angled shafts of light cut through a high canopy of maple and aspen, accentuating shadows on the road before him.

The hospital where Joan Chandler had worked, according to the tracking data on her phone, was half a mile in front of him. It had been ten minutes since he'd left Route 9, and in that time DeBolt had seen only one other vehicle, an official-looking sedan with a state-issued license plate—a plate he should have run, he realized only after the car was gone. Would his abilities ever become second nature?

He looked up and down the road, and tried to imagine why anyone would put a hospital in such a remote location. There wasn't a town within miles. The only answer he could think of was reinforced by the government car he'd seen leaving. Was this a DOD facility of some kind? Intentionally remote to be out of public view?

DOD.

In spite of the remoteness, his prepaid phone had a good signal here, and he had parked the car wanting to give full attention to his call to Lund. It felt good to hear a familiar voice, and while he couldn't say she was on his side, DeBolt felt reasonably sure Lund wasn't part of the threat. He supposed he could research her later, find out everything possible about Shannon Lund of

Kodiak, Alaska. And if he saw no red flags? Would he do as she asked and go to Boston? His mood took a downswing when he remembered what happened to the last person he'd trusted—Joan Chandler.

Wary about what he might find at the end of the road, DeBolt decided to go the rest of the way on foot. He left the Buick where it was, and set out climbing a slight incline. He soon encountered a dirt side road, and curious, he followed it. A hundred feet into the woods he saw what it was—an access path for an electrical substation, a quarter acre of transformers and capacitors and whatever else such a facility was made of. It was all surrounded by a tall concertina-topped fence. As DeBolt walked nearer, he felt an unusual sensation. It began as a tingle in his head, and then the screen in his right eye went to static, like a television that had lost its signal. He heard a buzzing sound in one ear that he'd never noticed before.

Unnerved, he moved back in the direction of the road, and the symptoms immediately abated. He studied the substation, and the high-voltage wires that ran outward on easements north and south. DeBolt walked slowly back toward the fence and the symptoms returned. *High voltage*, he thought. *Electrical interference. It interrupts the signal, or scrambles . . . whatever is in my brain.* It made a certain sense, and he logged it as a curiosity, wishing once again someone had given him a damned owner's manual.

With November's long dusk falling, DeBolt set out again along the main road, riding a carpet of fallen leaves over what looked like new pavement. The leaves were wet and soft beneath his feet, cushioning every step and muting the sound of his progress. He'd never before cared about silence, but now it seemed comforting. Even important. Yet another revision brought by his new and grave existence.

DeBolt soon saw a second fortified fence in the distance, this one marking a larger perimeter. He slowed as he approached it and saw signs at regular intervals.

U.S. DEPARTMENT OF DEFENSE FACILITY
NO ADMITTANCE WITHOUT AUTHORIZATION

There was an access camera and card scanner at the entrance—both made nonsensical by the fact that the sturdy double gate stood wide open. He neared the access point, then came to a halting stop. DeBolt had been expecting some kind of hospital or clinic. What he saw was unidentifiable. It was hard to say how big the place had been, but the word "hospital" seemed generous. What was left standing would fit in a single dump truck. Everything was charred, and while three of the four walls remained partially intact, everything between them had been incinerated to ground level. Gray ash predominated, and what little remained vertical was stroked with slashes of black attesting to the ferocity of the inferno. A singular wisp of smoke trailed upward like the remains of a dying campfire, and an acrid chemical stench replaced the fresh forest air.

DeBolt saw two vehicles nearby, one a red SUV emblazoned with the words FIRE CHIEF and the other a Crown Victoria, government plates similar to those on the car he'd seen leaving. He recalled what Lund had told him: Joan Chandler's cottage had exploded. DeBolt recognized that disaster for what it was—a blunt attempt to hide and corrupt evidence. Was that what he was looking at here? The aftermath of another slash-and-burn cover-up?

He started walking again, and noticed someone in the Crown Vic, a hunched figure highlighted by the glow of a laptop screen. A large man in a fire department uniform was picking through the wreckage with an iron bar. The guy with the iron bar saw him coming, and quickly came to intercept him. His tone wasn't welcoming. "Sir, can I ask what you're doing out here?"

DeBolt already knew what to say—he'd been rehearsing his story since he'd spotted a sign for a hiking trail two miles back. He was perfectly dressed for the part—at the Walmart where he'd bought the prepaid phone, he had also purchased two changes of clothing. He now wore Levi's, a warm long-sleeved shirt, and a set of hiking boots.

"Man, I'm really sorry. I got lost hiking the Lead Mountain Pond Trail. It's getting dark, and when I saw you guys I thought you could steer me straight."

The fireman seemed to soften.

"Okay, buddy. You must've got turned around. Go back down that road; the parking lot for the trailhead is about a mile and a half on your right."

"Okay, great." DeBolt then looked over the scene. "What happened here? It looks like a war zone."

There was a slight hesitation, then, "Bad fire . . . really bad. The five people who worked here were all trapped inside. None made it out."

DeBolt held steady, remaining in character. "God, how awful. I never even knew this place was out here. What is it?"

The fireman's gaze hardened. "Can't say. Maybe you should get back."

From fifty feet away, DeBolt studied the building's wreckage in the fast-dimming light. He saw what looked like an X-ray machine, the support arm melted and misshapen. An IV pole loomed over the charred remains of a bed, the mattress and sheets of which had gone to dust, and a few blackened steel springs poked upward like some kind of junkyard-inspired flora. He said, "It looks like a clinic or something."

"Sir, I—"

"Hey!" shouted a man from the Crown Vic. "This is a crime scene!" He got out and strode over. He was short and stocky, and wore an FBI windbreaker. "You need to leave!"

DeBolt raised a hand apologetically. "Okay, sorry. I'm on my way." He turned away and began walking, feeling two sets of eyes on his back. It didn't matter. He knew what he needed to know.

His steps were steady and methodical, belying his staggering thoughts. *Five people . . . none made it out.* A mysterious fire. There could be no doubt—what had happened here was no different from Joan Chandler's cottage. Evidence destroyed and innocent people killed. He wanted to tell the poor fire inspector it was hopeless. *Don't waste your time; you'll never find out who's responsible.* Then DeBolt felt a connection on an even deeper level. This was the place he remembered. The muted lights, the needle. The cold that had seized him from within and crawled into his heart. This was where he had been zipped into a plastic body bag.

The place where life as he knew it had ended.

"Look, I'm sorry about your dad, but you can't just leave!" said Petty Officer James Kalata from across their utilitarian office.

"I can, and I will," said Lund calmly.

Their desks were arranged to oppose one another, a functional reflection of their strained relationship. One uniform and one civilian, they were both attached to CGIS Northwest Region, and reported to the same person: Special Agent in Charge Jonathan Wheeley in the Seattle district office. Having a boss fourteen hundred miles away was a considerably long leash. Not helping the situation was that when Kalata had first arrived a year ago, he'd immediately started hitting on her. Lund was less than receptive, particularly since Kalata had a wife and three kids less than a mile outside the main gate.

"You need to get approval from Seattle," he told her.

"I'll send an email, Jon will understand. My flight is already booked." Lund had considered making her trip to Boston official business, but for that she would have had to go through channels. The paperwork would take days to process, and given that her evidence was minimal, the request could very possibly be turned down. Something told her Trey DeBolt didn't have that kind of time. So she'd opted for an emergency leave ploy, explaining that her father in Arizona was ill—a man who was in truth as robust as the Prescott hills he hiked daily.

Kalata finally quit arguing, and he sarcastically wished her a pleasant journey. As Lund was rifling over her desk for documents to take on the flight, her phone rang. She looked at the number guardedly. It wasn't the one DeBolt had used an hour ago. It was Matt Doran.

"What's up, Matt?"

"Hi, Shannon. You got a minute?"

"Barely." Lund heard wind rushing across the microphone of Doran's phone, a bass static that told her he was outside. "Where are you? You sound like Jim Cantore in a cat five."

"Yeah, well, that's why I'm calling. I finally got up the mountain. I'm standing near the top, the spot where William Simmons fell off. I thought you should know there are actually two sets of footprints up here."

Lund stopped rifling through papers. "Okay."

"I'm no detective, but I do a little hunting, so I can track pretty well. One set of footprints is definitely Simmons'—when we recovered him I took a picture of the soles of his climbing boots, figuring I'd get a match up higher. I see his prints near the edge, and I think I can even make out where he slid over the side."

"Can you get pictures of that?"

"Yeah, I'm working on it now. The thing is, all this happened a few days ago and it's rained a couple of times since. The other set of footprints I'm looking at have the same distortions from the rain. I'm convinced they were made at nearly the same time. His climbing partner told me he never got up this far."

"Yeah, he told me the same thing—he didn't think it was safe to go up where Simmons had gone. But even if there *is* a second set of footprints, Matt, is it a big deal? I mean, other people climb the mountain, right?"

A big rush of wind, then, "This time of year . . . not so much. And the ledge Simmons was on is pretty tough to reach. I mean, not impossible, but you'd have to know what you're doing. With that in mind I took a detour south, which is the only other passage up. I picked up the same second set of tracks, and even found a climbing anchor in a crevice—looks like it jammed in place and they couldn't get it out. I took a picture of that too."

Lund was silent in thought.

"I dunno, Shannon. This is bugging me. I really think there was somebody else up here that day, somebody who knew how to climb."

"Okay, I'll look into it. And send me those pictures when you can."

"Sure thing." Another gust of wind.

"And for God's sake, Matt, be careful up there."

The call ended, and Lund looked out her office window. It wasn't much of a view—the side of a hangar and an out-of-service boat sitting on a trailer. Doran's suspicions might be nothing. There were any number of explanations for what he'd found. But one awkward truth settled in—she *hadn't* looked very hard into William Simmons' death. She'd found out that he had a steady girlfriend named Ashley Routledge, also a Coastie, and Lund had been meaning to talk to her. Then something else registered. The day after the accident she remembered talking to Lieutenant Commander Reggie Walsh, Simmons' supervising officer, and he'd mentioned that Simmons had inquired about applying for rescue swimmer training. *I was going to recommend him too. He was friends with a couple of the ASTs on station, guys who'd been through the program.*

Walsh's words . . . *ASTs on station.*

Like Trey DeBolt.

Lund didn't like the coincidences brewing in her head. In the window's reflection she caught Kalata staring at her ass. She was as repulsed as ever, but there was a part of her—a *very* small part—that was encouraged. She'd actually used the treadmill twice this week, and was picking up her pace. Feeling more confident.

Before turning around, Lund unhooked the top button on her boring brown blouse. She walked near Kalata's desk and leaned over at a file cabinet to put a little cleavage on display. Not really a provocative move. More . . . informational. The man might be a desk-potted philanderer, but he was a decent investigator when he wanted to be.

She stood straight, and said, "Jim, I need you to look into something while I'm gone . . ."

25

The Alaska Airlines 737 touched down at Boston Logan International Airport at 10:33 the next morning. It was a firm landing, and the thump of the main wheels on concrete jolted Lund out of a sound sleep. The jet cleared the runway, and as soon as the flight attendant made an announcement that phones could be turned back on, Lund did so and saw a message from Kalata: Call me.

She did, and he answered right away, even though it was four hours earlier in Kodiak. Picking up calls at zero dark thirty came with the job. So, correspondingly, did sleepy voices.

"Damn, Shannon. You know what time it is?"

"My plane just landed—I got your message."

"You're just now landing? I didn't think it took so long to fly to Arizona."

"Flight delays," she said, not knowing or caring if he knew where she'd really gone. "Did you get in touch with Ashley Routledge?"

A yawn, then, "Who?"

"Simmons' girlfriend."

"Oh, right. Yeah, I found her. Works over in the education office, a real cute brunette."

Lund rolled her eyes. "I'm insanely jealous. What did she say about Simmons? Was there anything strange going on in his life?"

"She did mention one thing—like you guessed, it had to do with Trey DeBolt."

Lund felt a clench in her gut like a tightening fist. She'd asked Kalata to look for any relationship between Simmons and DeBolt.

"Apparently the two were pretty tight," Kalata continued. "Turns out, the day after DeBolt was evac-ed out, Simmons was scheduled to be in Anchorage for a two-day training session of some kind. As soon as he arrived he tried to track down DeBolt. He went to both hospitals but couldn't find him. About that same time we got official word here on station that DeBolt hadn't survived his injuries. Ashley called Simmons and told him. She said he got really upset. He went back to the Air Force hospital in Anchorage and raised a ruckus— nearly got himself arrested. Nobody there seemed to know anything about DeBolt or where his body might be. When he got back to Kodiak, he started making phone calls and sending emails—the hospitals, the mortuary section. Routledge showed me a few, and they were pretty accusative. She said he was frustrated that nobody would listen to him, and making noise about contacting CGIS. Then he fell off Mount Barometer. That's about it—I hope it helps."

Lund tried to think of something to say. "Okay, Jim, thanks for looking into it."

"Anything else I can do for you? Anything at all?"

"I'll be in touch."

"I hope your dad is—" Kalata's words were cut short by the end button.

She looked out the window as the jet pulled into the gate. She combined the new information with what Doran had discovered on the mountain, and what Fred McDermott had told her about a Learjet trying to cover its tracks with false flight plans. Her suspicions only deepened. What had happened to DeBolt after he was evac-ed out of Kodiak? How had he survived his injuries and ended up in Maine of all places? Then Lund came to a more disturbing realization.

William Simmons, who was no investigator, had been the first to start asking questions. He'd seen inconsistencies in the story of what had happened to a gravely injured Trey DeBolt. Many of his questions were the same ones Lund herself was now asking.

And today William Simmons was dead.

When Benefield got the message that DeBolt was still at large, he took it poorly. The general sent an invective-laden response to his team suggesting, in colorful terms, that they ought to do better. He surfed news outlets to assess the investigations into a pair of fires, one at a small clinic in Maine and another at a DARPA research facility in rural Virginia. Neither inquiry seemed to be making headway, although as generals knew better than anyone, what was fed to the media was rarely the full story.

More encouragingly, Benefield's phone had rung only once since last night. To an FBI investigator he expressed a commander's regret over the loss of life in Virginia, and commented in passing that he had only recently visited the troops there. That was what he called them—*troops*. As if they'd all taken the oath of service and been inducted into active duty. Nothing was mentioned about the tragedy in Maine, and he was sure it never would be. That venue had been established very carefully via a series of shell companies, each a dead end in its own right. It had been the riskiest part of the entire project, and illegal on any number of levels. But of course it had been essential.

More than ever, he hoped Patel would have the abort codes for him tonight. And if he didn't? Then Benefield would have to find another way to sever META's remaining loose ends.

Less than a mile away, Atif Patel began his morning with matters unrelated to META. He had long ago decided that his pursuit of the project, secretive as it was, would only succeed if he could maintain the veneer of a normal professional life. So from his hotel desk he corresponded by email with a Cal professor regarding a paper they were co-publishing, and had a lengthy phone conversation with a graduate student who was preparing to defend her doctoral thesis.

Absent from his schedule that day was any attempt to retrieve the codes General Benefield wanted to activate META's kill switch. The reason was eminently simple—they didn't exist. Patel viewed it as an insurance policy of sorts. Without his drive and vision, the gains from the META would never have been realized. His integration software was installed deep in the bedrock of some of the most highly classified and complex mainframes on earth, and he wasn't going to let so much work be put at risk by the whims his careerist overseer. Simply put, he had lost faith in General Benefield, and by extension DARPA. When the general had insisted at the outset that an abort code be included in the software—his words, as if it were a ballistic missile or something—Patel had agreed with the conviction of a child with his fingers crossed behind his back. The agency's sudden removal of funding was a surprise to Patel, and certainly a setback, yet he had months ago sensed in Benefield a lack of enthusiasm for the project. Timing aside, none of it was unexpected. Patel had been working with various DOD entities since graduate school, and so he knew all too well the sad truth: invariably, generals fixated on nothing beyond putting the next star on their shoulders. It was scientists like himself who reached for the galaxies.

All the same, he would have to give Benefield something tonight. He found a pad of hotel stationery on the desk, and on it he scrawled an impressive-looking series of commands, followed by a ridiculous thirty-character alphanumeric sequence—special characters included—that might someday be decoded for what it was: a simple anagram of "3decimal-141GOCALTECHBEAVERS!!!." Scrambled randomly, it looked convoluted and imposing, but of course was completely useless. Yet it *would* buy Patel just a little more time.

Enough time to finalize the true core of the META Project.

26

Lund was exhausted after the red-eye flight, and realizing she could do nothing but wait for DeBolt's call—if he called at all—she decided to find a hotel room and get some sleep. Her only baggage was a small roller bag she'd carried on, so from the gate area she followed signs to the only on-property hotel, the airport Hilton. She wandered into the expansive lobby, went to the front desk, and secured a room for one night at an exorbitant price. Lund hoped DeBolt called soon, because this wasn't the vacation she'd been saving for.

After she received a key, her attention was drawn to an exercise room at the far end of the lobby. Behind a set of glass doors she saw rows of treadmills and elliptical machines, and she walked closer to get a better look. Lund thought, *Maybe later,* and turned around to find the elevators. She nearly ran into Trey DeBolt.

"Hi, Shannon."

Lund took an involuntary step back and tried to right her capsized thoughts. "Trey . . . it's good to see you." She looked him up and down, and thought he seemed in decent shape. Far better, at least, than when he'd left Kodiak.

"How are you?" he asked.

"Tired. How are you?"

"Given my circumstances . . . could be a lot worse."

"I'm glad you decided to come—but I never called. How did you find me so fast?"

"That," he said, casting his eyes around the lobby, "is something we should talk about. Can I buy you a cup of coffee?"

They went for a walk, ending at a Dunkin' Donuts in Terminal E. DeBolt ordered two large coffees, and Lund noticed that he paid with a fresh hundred-dollar bill. At the cream and sugar stand she took a splash of half-and-half and shunned her usual two packets of sugar. They found a table and settled in while travelers rushed through the corridors behind them.

Sitting across from the not-so-late Trey DeBolt, Lund amended her standing assessment. He seemed in good shape physically, but there was something different about him now. This wasn't the DeBolt she knew from the Golden Anchor, a carefree young man with an easy manner and an engaging smile. She sensed some great weight on his shoulders now, a burden that subdued his affable nature and made him seem older.

"I need to convince you of something, Shannon, but I can't just come out and say it. You'd never believe me—nobody in their right mind would. I think a demonstration would be better."

Lund's eyes narrowed as if she was expecting some kind of magic trick.

"You came in on Alaska Airlines Flight 435, sat in row fourteen, seat C."

She nodded. "That's right."

"The middle seat was empty, but the guy on the window was named Garland Travis, sixty-one years old. He's from Texas, recruits people to work on oil rigs up in Alaska."

She took a deliberate sip of her coffee, enjoying the rich scent as much as the taste, and tried to guess where he was going with this little game. Lund was good at what she did, a professional when it came to managing interviews so that witnesses and suspects ended up in the arenas where she wanted them. She knew how to mete out facts, while retaining enough information to verify responses. It was the game all law enforcement officers played. Yet DeBolt had no such background, and the tenor of his voice, the urgency in his gaze, convinced her that whatever he was up to, it was no attempt to manipulate. She felt more like a priest holding confessional.

She said, "We didn't talk much. But yes, his name was Garland, and anybody with a name like that has got to be from Texas. He never told me what he did because he slept most of the flight. What are you getting at, Trey?"

"Bear with me. You were born in . . . no, that's too easy. You were born at

7:47 in the morning. Your mom's name was Beth, your dad's Charles. The name on your birth certificate is Ruth Shannon Lund, but Ruth never stuck, and in 2001 you had the order of the first and middle names legally reversed."

"Look," she said, "you're right, but anybody could find out—"

"Your adjusted gross income last year was $82,612, twelve thousand of that from an annuity. You canceled your Netflix account last week, and your most recent phone bill was $109.63." Lund went very still. Her phone was on the table, and he picked it up and selected the calculator app, then gave it to her. "Give me a random number, something over a thousand."

"Trey, this is—"

"Please."

She sighed with forced patience, or perhaps to hide the trace of unease that was building. "Five thousand six hundred and seven."

In an instant, he said, "The square root is 74.879903. Check it."

He repeated his answer and Lund multiplied it out. He was dead-on—six places to the right of the decimal. "So . . . what are you telling me? That you're a savant of some kind?"

He chuckled humorlessly, then gave her an appraising look. "When I called you yesterday you were at the Safeway in Kodiak. You didn't buy anything when you left."

That did it. Lund felt a chill go down her spine. "What the hell? How could you know that?"

"Look at the street behind me. Pick out a car or a van, any vehicle. Give me a license plate number and the state."

She almost protested, but the resolute look on DeBolt's face didn't allow it. She supposed it was the same expression he wore when he jumped into the Bering Sea to rescue foundering shipwreck victims. Sheer determination. She looked outside and saw a road packed with options. There was no way he could see the cars given how he was positioned.

"Maine plate 4TC788."

A distinct hesitation, then, "Yellow cab, Dodge minivan."

"Guess that was too easy."

"Cab number is AY3R."

An increasingly unnerved Lund checked the numbers on the roof. AY3R. She didn't tell him he was right, but the expression on her face must have done it. Her hands were beginning to fidget, and she fought back by stirring her coffee with a plastic stick.

"Here's an even better one," he said, "I figured out I could do this while I was waiting for you this morning." He pointed toward the crowds. "Pick out a person, anybody except a kid."

"Why?" she said tautly.

"Oh, you're gonna like this. But you will have to check my work."

There were more than a hundred people in sight. She pointed out a man standing in a nearby line with a briefcase in his hand. DeBolt seemed to study him for a time, then thirty seconds later, he said, "His name is Roger Pendergast. He works for an accounting firm in Chicago—Smyth, Carling, and Waters. Forty-one years old, wife and two kids. His address is 1789 Townsend Hill Road in Elmhurst."

Lund stared at him as if he were crazy.

"Go and ask him. Smyth, Carling, and Waters." There was not a trace of humor in DeBolt's voice. Only conviction.

She got up tentatively and walked toward the man. Lund was a few steps away when she saw a tag on his roller bag. Roger Pendergast. 1789 Townsend Hill Road. Elmhurst, IL. Her mind began to reel. She turned toward DeBolt, looked at him, and wondered what he saw in her expression. Confusion? Fear? He made a shooing motion for her to carry on.

"Excuse me," she said.

The man turned.

"I think we might have met. Do you work for an accounting firm?"

A rather plain-looking man, Roger Pendergast beamed. He was clearly not used to being recognized in a crowd. "That's right—Smyth, Carling in Chicago. And you?"

"Oh . . . no, I . . . I'm from up in Alaska."

He gave her an odd look, and Lund retreated to the table. Not knowing what to say, she sat in silence.

DeBolt said, "Facial recognition, I guess. I'm not sure how it works—but so far it's been dead-on. I can—"

"Stop it!" she insisted. Lund groped for an argument of some kind. "I don't know what kind of parlor tricks you're playing, but I *don't* like them."

DeBolt was quiet for a moment, introspective. "I wish it were a trick,

Shannon. Really I do." He pulled his chair around the table, closer to hers, and said, "Let me show you one last thing—I think it will convince you." He turned his head, and with a hand he raked his hair upward. She saw terrible scars on the base of his skull.

"My God! Trey . . . is that from the accident?"

"No. I had a severe concussion, some internal bleeding. My shoulder was messed up, and there were a few lacerations. But I had only minor cuts on my scalp from the accident. The scars you're looking at are from the surgery that came later. The surgery that enabled me to do all these crazy things."

He pulled away and sipped his coffee, his eyes going distant. He was giving her time to think it through. Hurried travelers swept past, purposeful and quick, oblivious to the distracted young couple drinking coffee. A recorded announcement looped on the public-address system, something about security and having a nice day.

She finally said, "I don't understand. What exactly have they done to you?"

"That's the problem," he said. "I don't know. But I need to find out . . . and it would be really nice to have some help."

27

They began their quest from Lund's room, which was more comfortable, and certainly more secure, than an airport donut shop. It was standard-issue: two beds, one television, and a desk near a tiny sitting area. Everything was clean and gray and soulless—a road warrior's bunker. It was exactly what they both needed.

He spent nearly an hour explaining what he'd been through since leaving Cape Split. Lund allowed him to talk with minimal interruption, holding her questions until the end.

She said, "Tell me how this thing works. How do you manage it?"

"There's a screen in my right eye, embedded in my field of vision. I concentrate on words, phrases, and they appear on the screen. It's hard to explain, but I'm getting better at it."

"The facial recognition—how did you do that?"

"I can capture images, almost like snapshots, and upload them. I don't always get an answer, and it doesn't work on kids, probably because their faces aren't in whatever database I'm drawing from."

"Where do you think this is all sourced?"

"I have no idea—that's one of the things I've been trying to figure out. I have noticed that I lose my connection every now and again—in rural areas mostly, just like a cell phone. Even when I have a good connection, certain responses come more quickly than others. Sometimes I get no information at all. I managed to get a plot on where Joan Chandler's phone had been in recent weeks, but it took half a day to arrive. It all makes sense, I guess. Every information source has its limitations, and plowing through data takes time."

"But you can get information on license plates and income taxes—that could only come from our government."

"Probably."

"FBI, DOD, CIA," she said, thinking out loud. "It has to be some three-letter agency."

"Maybe all of them. Right now, the most frustrating thing is that I don't even know what I'm capable of. I'm constantly stumbling onto new ways to use it, angles I'd never thought of."

"This is mind-numbing, Trey." She strolled to the fifth-floor window and looked outside blankly, trying to grasp the scope of what he was telling her. "Imagine the things you could do. Access to *any* electronic file. Do you realize how powerful that could be?"

"Gets you thinking, doesn't it? But honestly, at the moment . . . it doesn't feel powerful at all. It seems like a burden. And I'm sure it's the reason I've been targeted."

"The clinic you told me about, the one that burned down—do you think that's where the surgery was performed?"

"It's a only a guess, but Joan Chandler *was* a surgical nurse. And like I said, I got a track on her phone. She went to that clinic almost every day in the weeks before and after my accident."

"But then she took you to her cabin after the surgery. Why would she do that?"

"She never said, but I don't think anyone else knew I was there. I think I was given up for dead at the clinic. Joan might even have made it look that way. One of the few things I recall from the hospital was her administering a shot. I've never felt so cold . . ." His voice drifted away for a time. Lund said nothing, and he eventually finished the thought. "She somehow transferred me to her place to recover. I think she did it all secretly, without anyone else at the clinic realizing I was still alive."

"So she rescued you."

"I think so."

Lund pondered it all. "When this clinic burned down, were there any casualties?"

"Five fatalities according to the fire chief I talked to."

"Then there must be an ongoing investigation. That's something I can work with."

"How? I mean, no offense, but why would CGIS Kodiak be interested in an arson in Maine?"

"I've already talked to a detective in Washington County about you. I have contacts in the other Washington as well."

He sat on the bed, and she eyed the wound on his leg. "I should have a look at that. It's a gunshot wound?"

"I can't say for sure, but yeah, probably. It happened that night on the beach . . . there were a lot of bullets flying."

She kneeled for a closer look. "It seems to be healing, but it's pretty deep. I could take you to a clinic or a hospital."

"Out of the question. If it *is* a gunshot wound it would have to be reported to the police, right?"

Lund nodded.

"Until I know who's after me, I can't take that risk. And besides, just to sign in at a hospital you need insurance information and an ID. I don't have any of that . . . not anymore."

DeBolt retrieved bandages and antibiotic ointment from the pocket of a light jacket, all bought at Walmart yesterday. She cleaned and dressed the wound, and as she did, he said, "Now that you know my situation, I have to ask—are you sure you're up for this? There are people hunting me. They've found me twice, and there's a good chance they'll find me again."

"I'm up for it," she said without hesitation. "You really have no idea who they are?"

"All I can say for sure is that they were driving a Chevy Tahoe with DOD plates."

"I don't get that," she said. "The Department of Defense doesn't send out kill squads, and certainly not on home field. Maybe if you were a terrorist, and they thought an attack was imminent . . . but you don't fit that bill."

"Neither did Joan Chandler, but they gunned her down in cold blood. I saw it with my own eyes. And if our government *is* involved, then going to the police or the FBI isn't an option. All I could tell them is what I'm telling you. Chances are, they'd put me in a straitjacket and hand me over to the very people I'm worried about."

She finished the dressing and stood. "All right . . . if there's DOD involvement, then that's where we start looking."

"How?"

"You do whatever it is you do, and I'll search the old-fashioned way—my laptop, maybe a few phone calls."

Lund saw him smile for the first time since the Golden Anchor. "Old-fashioned?" he said. "Cell phones and laptops?"

"In light of what you can do," she said, smiling in return, "I think maybe so. Think about it, Trey. Where was the world with connectivity when you and I were kids? Dial-up modems have gone to smartphones and beyond. What you can do now—it's the next logical step. Miniaturize, create a direct interface to the brain. I never thought I'd see anything like it in my lifetime . . . but here you are."

"I suppose you're right. Technically, it's not that far beyond what already exists."

"Not far at all."

"I feel like some kind of science experiment—only I wasn't exactly a volunteer." His humor dissipated as quickly as it had come.

"What's wrong?" she asked.

"I remembered something else. When I saw my medical records there were annotations next to my name in two places. It said 'META Project,' and below that, 'Option Bravo.'"

"Next to your name?"

"Yeah. Like . . . like *I* was Option Bravo in some kind of experimental project."

She blew out a humorless laugh. "Right. Trey DeBolt . . . Plan B."

Dinner the second night was earlier, Benefield choosing on the very un-Continental hour of half past six. The general insisted on driving, and he arrived at the Hilton behind the wheel of a rented Land Rover. The two exchanged a perfunctory greeting, and Patel was happy when Benefield did not ask immediately for the codes. He had far more weighty issues on his mind.

With a distinct tremor in his voice, he said, "I saw a news article today about our facility in Virginia burning to the ground. It was difficult to see the names of the victims. So many of them were my friends."

Benefield looked somberly at Patel and nodded. "A terrible tragedy. One of the FBI investigators called me this morning. He asked for information about the project."

"What did you tell him?"

"What we tell everyone—that it is a highly classified effort to achieve breakthroughs in information technology. He'll spin his wheels for a time, but given the level of secrecy we enjoy, not to mention the ambiguous nature of our stated goals—he'll only hit a brick wall. I should have given him your number, let you inflict your briefing on META's system architecture—the man would have fallen sound asleep, just like that senator from the Select Committee on Intelligence."

A humorless Patel looked out the window. "What about the surgical unit in Maine?"

"The facility has been shut down," Benefield said. "Everything was removed."

"And the team?"

"They're all aware of META's termination, and everyone will get a well-deserved severance package."

They arrived at the restaurant fifteen minutes later. It was no surprise to Patel that the general had shunned Restaurant Ville in favor of something called Brandeis Schlossbräu, a beer house in the Baumgarten district. In spite of the chill evening air, Benefield asked to sit outside in the garden. Patel sat in a wooden chair beneath rows of carriage lamps that had been strung on wires. He didn't complain when Benefield ordered beers for them both, and they arrived tall and frothing in the hands of a buxom waitress. Dinner was two slabs of beef that came on platters, sizzling with the smell of fat, and a heavy carving knife protruded from each like some medieval invitation.

Only then did Benefield finally get around to business. "You have the abort commands?"

Patel had his carving knife in hand, hovering over the set of ribs as if planning an assault. He set down the knife, pulled the hotel notepad from his pocket, and handed it over. The general flipped through, glancing at all three pages, then put them carefully in his pocket. More food arrived, the same waitress delivering a plate of sausage and sauerkraut to be shared. The two men suffered through challenged conversation for the course of the meal, Patel doing his best to deflect Benefield's ill-informed technical questions. There was more beer, but thankfully no coffee or dessert, and at the end Benefield again picked up the check. Soon they were back in the Land Rover, Patel gorged with meat and beer, and sulking in the passenger seat.

"Have you seen much of Austria since you arrived?" Benefield asked.

"Hardly."

"That's too bad. It's a beautiful country, and who knows when you might come here again."

Patel saw a sign indicating that the A1, which would take them back to town, was one kilometer ahead. A bridge in front of them was backlit by moonlight, the high span arching gracefully between twin buttresses. Benefield suddenly veered the Rover off the road. He steered onto a gravel path but kept his speed up, and soon they were enveloped by darkness, the headlights flickering white over the forest ahead.

"What are you doing?" asked Patel.

"There's something I want you to see, Atif."

Patel looked outside, and the forest fell away. To one side he saw the fast-moving waters of a river. The only lights he saw were upstream, a row of streetlights at least a mile distant. Benefield pulled the Rover to a crunching stop on the gravel path. Patel looked squarely at a grinning Benefield, and was about to say something when the general interrupted with, "I'm sorry, Atif. This is not the end I envisioned for our mission, but it's the only way."

The window at Patel's shoulder lowered, and he instinctively turned. A man appeared out of nowhere, a hulking figure dressed in a dark greatcoat. His arm swung up, and Patel instantly saw the long barrel of a silenced handgun. He shrank back into his seat.

It took only one shot from such close range, but of course there was a second for insurance. The killer was, after all, a professional. In no more than thirty seconds the body was in the water, carrying downstream and bounding off the occasional rock. The Rover began its steady climb back toward the A1 with the assassin in the passenger seat.

28

They worked through that afternoon, searching their respective databases. Lund took a law enforcement slant, but the hotel's open internet connection was useless for accessing the secure networks she typically relied upon. That being the case, she began making phone calls to friends. DeBolt dove into the black pool of his mind, the depth and breadth of which was still undefined. He continued to make adjustments, organizing his thoughts for concise requests. For all its utility, META gave nothing on itself, which seemed a paradox of sorts. It was like a Google search on the word "Google" coming up empty.

Lund hung up after a lengthy phone conversation.

"So who was that?" he asked.

"A Coast Guard friend at the Pentagon."

"The Coast Guard is under Homeland Security—since when do we keep an office in the Pentagon?"

"It hasn't happened since World War II, but in times of war the DOD can assume control of the Coast Guard. So yes, we have a presence in the Pentagon."

"Okay—so what did your friend say?"

"I had her look into the META Project. She actually found a listing for it under DARPA, the DOD's research arm."

"I've heard of DARPA."

"Yeah, so have I. They work on cutting edge stuff. But my friend hit a roadblock after that. There were no details at all on the project, it's totally black. Did you have any luck?"

"On META? No. In fact, I think I've only done one search that got me *less* information."

"What was that?"

"Me—I input my name and discovered I wasn't authorized access to myself."

DeBolt was sitting on one of the beds, and she stared at him from across the room. "How weird is that—you can get intel on anybody in the world except yourself?"

"Apparently."

Lund got up and stretched. "So how long do we stay bunkered up here?"

"Until we have something to go on, something that gives us direction. At least one night, I guess. After that we should probably move."

"Move? How?"

"I bought a Buick."

"A Buick." Lund stared at him. She seemed about to ask for an explanation, but instead only sighed. "I need some fresh air. I think I'll go outside."

"Need a cigarette?"

"How did you know that? Checking my credit card purchases, or maybe what my doctor wrote in my medical records?"

"There's a pack of Marlboros on the table—it fell out of your purse."

She looked and saw them. "Oh, right. Well, the thing is, they ding you two hundred dollars if you smoke in your room."

"Only if they catch you. But I get it. I'm feeling a little caged up too. Want some company?"

"Sure."

Five minutes later they were walking a winding path across the commons in front of the hotel. The wind was coming from the east, steady and brisk, and the heavy scent of the sea mocked their urban surroundings. It reminded Lund of Kodiak, only on a far larger scale. She lit up a cigarette, then held out the pack to DeBolt. To her surprise, he took one.

"You smoke?"

"Can't stand it. But I light up once a year to remind myself why. Usually in a bar somewhere after a few beers."

She handed over her lighter, and DeBolt lit up with the deftness of a middle-schooler in a bathroom stall.

Lund said, "This system you have to get information—do you realize how many laws it must break? Not to mention the ethical and privacy issues."

"If I've learned anything in the last few days it's that there is no privacy—not in today's world."

They walked in silence for a time, until he pulled to a stop under an elm whose leaves had gone yellow. "Tell me something. Did you talk to any of the guys in my unit . . . I mean, after the helo accident?"

"About you?"

He took an awkward pull on the cigarette. "Actually, I was thinking more about Tony, Tom, Mikey—the rest of my crew. The guys who didn't make it."

"No, not really. But then, I don't mix a lot with operational types. Why do you ask?"

"I guess I just wonder what everyone was saying. We were tight, and that's a lot for a small unit to handle."

"Yeah, I'm sure it was hard. But don't forget, as far as anybody in Kodiak knows, there were four fatalities."

He said nothing.

"There was a memorial service at the chapel. Pretty much everybody on the station came. Even me, and I stopped having conversations with God a long time ago."

"Me too. But times like that . . . they make you wish you were better, don't they?"

"You mean more religious?"

He didn't give an answer, but instead looked at her squarely, and said, "Why are you here, Shannon?"

"Because you convinced me over a cup of coffee this morning that you're in trouble. And given the nature of it—that took some *serious* convincing."

"That's not what I mean. Why did you come in the first place? I'm an enlisted guy who's technically AWOL. You should probably have me in custody right now. What made you drop everything, buy a ticket to fly across the country, and try to rescue somebody you'd only met once?"

She tried to think of a good answer. "That day, when we talked at the Golden Anchor . . . I don't know. I guess I liked you." She took a deep draw on her cigarette, then said, "No, it was more than that—I *believed* in you, Trey. I'd heard a lot about rescue swimmers, but you were the first one I got to know. I liked the way you talked about your job, as if it was no big deal. You put your life at risk for others. That's a noble thing. Honestly, on the day that helo went down . . . I prayed it wasn't you."

"See? There it is again. Praying, but only when you need it."

"Actually . . . ," she hesitated mightily, "there was something else. I did a little more than pray."

He turned to face her, and she saw the unspoken question.

Lund pulled to a stop, but found herself looking at the ground as she explained. "You see . . . they put out the word at the station that you'd survived the crash, but were in desperate need of a blood transfusion. You weren't going to make it without one, and they didn't have any stock of—"

"O-negative," he said, finally seeing it. "A pretty rare blood type."

"So I've been told."

DeBolt stood looking at her.

"They took me into your room to do it. You were unconscious, really beat up. You looked so different from the first time I saw you, and . . ." Lund's words trailed off there.

He turned away and seemed to study an airplane taking off in the distance. After the roar of its engines died down, he said, "Thanks, Shannon."

Lund grinned, then contemplated her Marlboro. It was only half gone, but all the same she dropped it on the sidewalk and twisted her toe over the remainder. "You're welcome."

Found early the next morning by a man walking his schnauzer, the body was stuck in a stand of aquatic weeds behind a small private school along a minor tributary of Vienna's Wien River. The police were quick to arrive and cordon off the scene, and quicker yet to realize that the two bullet holes in the victim's forehead were an assured marker of foul play.

The medical examiner was equally prompt, and he went about his responsibilities with the utmost of care. He recorded the scene meticulously, took DNA samples, and ascertained that aside from the two bullets, all remaining damage to the victim, which was considerable, was likely attributable to the body colliding with rocks in the river since the time of death—between nine o'clock and midnight yesterday evening. Everyone's work was procedurally sound, and undertaken with the highest degree of professionalism. In truth, quietly more so than in most investigations, this due to the fact that the victim's identity had been ascertained in the opening minutes. The responding officer had found a passport and wallet in the victim's pockets. Four photo IDs, three government issued, left no room for doubt.

By ten that morning, the body of General Karl Benefield, United States Army, had been placed securely in the provincial morgue. The United States embassy was discreetly notified.

29

The killer sitting in front of Patel spilled out of a chair that was much too small for his bulk. He was an enormous man, tall and broad-shouldered, a feral counterpoint to Patel's own stature. He was presently seated behind a desk, his arms crossed over each other like fireplace logs as he concentrated on the lesson Patel had given him today. He was a notoriously slow reader, yet absorbed a surprisingly high percentage of the material. At the very least, his concentration never ebbed. He was perhaps the only man Patel had ever known whose will was greater than his own.

Until three months ago he had been assigned to the First Marine Raider Battalion, the Marine Corps' lesser-known counterpart to the Navy's SEAL program. He was thoroughly trained in irregular warfare, and within his tactical squad he was—no surprise to anyone who knew him—a close-quarters combat specialist. Or as his commander had put it so succinctly in a training report, *This is the last man on earth you want to make angry inside a closet.*

He'd had a sterling military record before his misfortunes—plural because there had been two. The first was three years ago in Iraq. The small reconnaissance team he'd been leading had uncovered a cache of artillery shells in a shed outside Fallujah, and when the unit's EOD specialist extracted one for inspection it began to leak gas. Of the three members of the squad exposed to the vapor, two were dead within a year. Patel's killer, however, had survived, albeit with one aberration: he no longer had a hair on his body, every single follicle having dropped off-line. No eyebrows, no whiskers, nothing on his head or chest or arms. Complete alopecia, and something the doctors had never been able to explain. Not that it really mattered—shaved heads were all the rage. For its part, the Marine Corps was delighted to have such a lethal individual back, and they deployed him straight back into the field, rather like a howitzer with a new wheel.

The more serious setback had occurred the previous January when the dirt bike he was riding, somewhere near the Iraq–Syria border, struck a concealed IED. By witness accounts he was thrown thirty feet into the air, and the mere fact that he'd survived was a testament to recent advances in battlefield medicine. Survival, however, is not an outcome in itself. He spent two months in a coma before his family authorized the machines to be turned off. It was then, during that narrow window of administrative limbo when paperwork was being run and final arrangements made, that the gunnery sergeant was paid a visit by Dr. Abel Badenhorst. After a review of the case—in particular, an extensive series of brain MRI's—Badenhorst thought the patient an ideal candidate for META's experiments.

And indeed he had been.

The huge man turned around, his face as expressionless as ever. He handed Patel a yellow Post-it note on which he'd scrawled: *I understand all of this except the satellite link.*

Patel said, "You don't have enough effective radiated power to connect to a satellite, but certain GSM repeaters may work."

He thought about it, scribbled again, and handed over a second Post-it: *How can I find these repeaters?*

"Do a standard search for available signals. They should show up on the map with a red R."

More scribbling: *Can I get more power?*

"No, you can't," said Patel. "The human brain runs on twelve watts of power, roughly one-third the requirement of a refrigerator lightbulb. Your power sources are nanowire fuel cells, catalyzed from enzymes that occur naturally in your body. Transmissions are the most demanding, so they're compiled and sent in a burst format. You'll always have modest limitations, but if you manage your requests with care, in particular by staggering the outbound caches, power should never be a problem."

He seemed to absorb it all, then nodded and turned back to his studies, his anvil-like head bowing over the notes.

Like an amputee learning how to manipulate an artificial limb, Delta was making good progress. His brain was adapting, translating thoughts into electrical impulses and thereby connecting to META. As far as Patel knew, the man had but one limitation—he'd completely lost his capacity for speech. There was the occasional grunt to get attention, a few mumbled consonants now and again, but any aptitude to form words had simply left him.

Atypically, he displayed no concurrent language problems. He expressed ideas in writing as concisely as ever, and had no trouble understanding what Patel told him—all, at least, within preexisting limitations. Patel and Badenhorst had performed dozens of cognitive evaluations on their subject, who'd been META's first survivor. He had above average intellect, particularly—as Badenhorst was fond of jesting—for a Marine. The two of them had tried diligently to determine the source of the speech impairment, thinking it critical to distinguish whether the loss was a consequence of the explosion or something gone wrong in the implantation process. They'd sent the results of their tests to a number of specialists, necessarily holding back any images that displayed the neural implants, and without fail keeping secret their patient's identity. As it turned out, Badenhorst had not lived long enough to see the responses to those inquiries. Patel had. And they suited him perfectly.

He watched the man study his notes, concentration evident in his hunched posture. He'd spent most of the morning in the hotel fitness center, which given his build was presumably a lifelong pursuit. He was slightly over six feet tall, but twice the width of a normal man, raw power in every pink, hairless limb. He reminded Patel of some great pelagic fish, a creature that spent its whole life moving and hunting in an endless blue void, never seeing the sky above or the bottom below—the place where it would inevitably come to rest.

Patel tried to recall his name. He'd seen it once, months ago, shortly after the first surgery. Gunnery Sergeant Thomas Something-or-other. It hardly mattered. Gunny Something-or-other would never use that name again. From this point forward, there would be only false identities, and those would change on a regular basis. Patel never bothered to keep up with them, and the reason was clear. The two of them had embarked on a journey together, one that had no return ticket. So intertwined, Patel had taken to referring to the former Marine by the only constant—his identifier from the META Project.

Of course, even that was a bit of a misnomer, as the sequencing of their test subjects had fast gone astray. The Marine had been the third subject operated on, but the first trail of Badenhorst's novel implantation techniques. The first two procedures had been complete failures, Charley not surviving the surgery, and Alpha never recovering brain activity. But then, finally, success.

His name was Delta.

30

DeBolt woke shortly after sunrise the next morning, and the first thing he saw was Lund. She was sleeping peacefully on the other double bed, curled on her side under the cover. He couldn't see her face, but he found himself imagining it. It was a good face, regular features and clear eyes. Not a woman who endured life, but one who reveled in it. DeBolt was glad for that, because he knew it might have been different.

He'd discovered it yesterday, in the course of researching Lund. He'd been looking for ammunition, details on her background to convince her of his new aptitudes—on the face of it, no different from Googling a prospective employer or a blind date. Unfortunately, his newfound methods were unavoidably invasive, and in the course of his search DeBolt had come across something unexpected. The kind of thing that, once learned, could never be unlearned. Old court records from an incident in California. Was that the reason she'd spent seven years in Kodiak? Had she been trying to run away from her troubles?

Isn't that what I'm doing right now?

His chain of thoughts was broken when Lund rolled over. She stirred, but didn't wake. Shafts of light leaned in through gaps in the curtains, and De-Bolt wished he could flick some kind of switch and take back the darkness. He had again slept roughly, and felt fatigue setting in. Not wanting to disturb Lund, not wanting to alter her stillness in any way, he closed his eyes.

It was no use—rest was impossible as one inexorable thought presided.

He tried for the hundredth time to upload the question: *Information on META Project.*

A minute passed.

Two.

Nothing came.

He remembered the delay when he'd run Joan Chandler's phone record—that information had come after ten hours. Might some river of answers regarding META eventually cascade into his head? He thought not. He had tried every variation he could think of: *META, DARPA. META, DOD. META Project, research.* Every time he drew a blank. Information on the project, whoever and whatever it involved, seemed sequestered in some impenetrable place, a cyber lockbox of sorts. As he lay still the room's heater kicked off, and in the heightened silence DeBolt again noticed a slight buzzing sensation in one ear.

Did it mean something? Or was it only the beginning of tinnitus or some other common malady? He imagined that would become a recurring question. *Is this new pain the beginning of a simple headache, or has a capacitor detached in my cerebral cortex?*

It was the kind of question endured by no other person on earth.

"Good morning." Lund's voice, relaxed and drowsy.

DeBolt blinked his eyes open. He looked at her and grinned.

"You didn't sleep well," she said.

"The fact that you know tells me you didn't either. I guess we both have a lot on our minds."

"I'm trying to figure out if that's a pun," she said, adding a smile of her own.

"Only in my case."

They ordered room service, two full breakfast plates and a pot of coffee. They ate at the tiny coffee table, Lund in a cotton pullover, DeBolt in the clothes he'd arrived in. They talked about Kodiak and the Coast Guard until the pot went dry.

Lund picked up the phone and ordered a refill. She hung up, and said,

"Tell me more about how you make this thing work. How do you interface with META?"

"It's hard to describe. There was some awkwardness at first—still is, I suppose. Each day I learn new things, new functions. This visual display in my field of view, I guess it's something like Google Glass, the optic device, only embedded in my right eye. The rest, the circuits and wiring—judging by my scars, I'd say it was all surgically implanted."

She looked at him with concern. "That's got to be unnerving, knowing you were put through such extensive surgery. But it raises some good questions. First of all, I see profound ethical and legal issues in what was done to you. That makes META an exceedingly risky proposition for whoever's behind it. Then there are more practical matters—someone spent a lot of time and money to make this happen. There must have been research done beforehand, a surgical team with equipment and support. The flight that took you from Maine to Alaska. None of that comes cheap."

DeBolt watched her face contort as she hashed through it.

"Yet if somebody went to all that trouble," Lund continued, "it seems strange that you could end up alone in the cottage with that nurse."

Two words rose in DeBolt's mind. *Option Bravo.* He pushed it away, and said, "I've been giving that some thought. What if I was never expected to survive the surgery, but by some miracle I did? Maybe there was no contingency plan for that. It's possible they told Joan Chandler to pull the plug on me, and she decided she couldn't do it. Like you said—there are some serious moral dilemmas involved. I think maybe she took it upon herself to rescue me."

"Did she ever imply anything like that?"

"Not directly. But I can tell you she had issues of her own. She had her demons."

Lund seemed to consider it, then moved on by saying, "All right. So where do we go from here?"

"I have to ask again, Shannon—are you sure you want to get involved? Those men are still out there. I wouldn't think less of you if you took the next flight back to Alaska."

She met his gaze.

"Okay . . . maybe a little less. But I'd understand."

"You know I'm not going anywhere."

He nodded.

Lund said, "There has to be a record of META somewhere. We're just not looking in the right places."

He pulled back the curtain and, much as he'd done in Calais, studied the scene outside. Bigger parking lot, busier road, a bustling port in the distance. The hotel's row of flags—United States, Massachusetts, and Hilton in rank order—all snapped sharply in an unyielding autumn breeze. The sky had gone to gray, the next storm approaching.

"Fresh air?" he suggested.

"Fresh air."

Lund dressed quickly, warmly, and they passed through the lobby entrance to take up the same path they'd walked last night. The morning air was cool and clean. A small crowd was gathered at a nearby municipal bus stop, and a pair of groundskeepers were trimming back the hotel's sculpted hedges for the winter. In the distance DeBolt saw the same air and road traffic they'd seen yesterday, as hurried and raucous as ever. He ignored it all and set his eyes on Lund.

She caught him looking. "What?"

"I was thinking you're attractive."

"No I'm not. I'm plain."

He burst out in an easy laugh. "Not for you to say."

"Honestly—I've let myself go a little."

"Why?"

"I don't know. People do sometimes."

"Have you given up on men?"

"Is it that ob—" She stopped in midsentence. Lund grabbed DeBolt's arm and twisted him to a stop. She pinned him with an accusing stare. "You know, don't you?"

He frowned, knowing exactly what she meant. After a long and uncomfortable silence, he said, "I didn't go looking for it, Shannon . . . but yes. I know you filed a restraining order against the guy you were living with in San Diego. Domestic battery charges were filed against him at about the same time, but they were eventually dropped because the anonymous victim left town and refused to pursue it."

Her gaze dropped to the gravel path.

"I'm sorry," he said.

"I made a lousy choice—he was a loser."

"Definitely. But . . . I mean, I'm sorry I found out. It was none of my business. I search for information on people without knowing what I'm going to get. I don't understand how this thing in my head works. I've never had any kind of class or tutorial—everything is trial and error."

They began walking again, and both were quiet. A cool gust brought a clatter of cords clapping against the nearby flagpoles. She finally asked, "Are you doing it now?"

"What?"

"Getting information on me?"

He saw a slight grin, so he knew she'd gotten past his transgression. "No." Then he laughed, and said, "Damn—it's gonna be impossible to date again with this thing."

"Is this your idea of a date?"

He cocked his head to one side. "I see your point. Running from a squad of assassins isn't exactly dinner and a movie. But for the time being . . . let's just say I'm practicing. How am I doing so far?"

"Terrible."

"Would it help if I mentioned that I liked you the first time we met in Kodiak?"

"You never asked for my number," she said.

"I gave you mine," he countered.

"I was interviewing you as a witness. I had to be able to get back in touch for follow-ups."

"See? You had an easy excuse to call me, but you never did." He studied her more closely. The breeze caught strands of her short brown hair and swept them across her face. DeBolt thought she seemed a contradiction, delicate features that were somehow serious and resolute. Fragile yet unbreakable. He wondered if her defenses were still in place, a drawn-out response to what had happened in San Diego.

Lund said, "I think I mentioned it, but a couple of days ago I went to your apartment in Kodiak."

"Why?"

"I was investigating."

"Did I leave anything embarrassing laying around?"

"Yes."

He looked at her, more curious than worried. She was grinning again.

"You have a wicked sense of humor."

"Sometimes."

"I'll bet you're a good detective."

"Usually."

"I'm glad you didn't see my first apartment in Kodiak—it was a room above a crabber's garage."

"Sound lovely. Sorry I missed it." She pulled out her Marlboros, offered him one.

He shook his head. "Ask me again in a year."

"Over a few beers?"

"Maybe so."

She seemed to reconsider, then put the cigarettes back in her pocket without taking one herself.

"Am I a good influence?" he asked.

"Hardly."

So engaged were DeBolt and Lund in one another, they never noticed the two groundskeepers. Both had edged considerably closer in the last sixty seconds. Nor did they realize that their work van, with its rakes and ladders on the roof, had moved nearer on the service road.

The two men closed the final few yards with lightning speed.

Lund shrieked in surprise when one of them seized her from behind.

DeBolt had barely raised his arms to resist when two electrodes penetrated his shirt, followed milliseconds later by two thousand volts.

31

DeBolt woke with a start. His body convulsed once, then settled to an aching stillness. He opened his eyes but saw nothing. His senses came back, seemingly one at a time, like a bank of light switches flipped on one after another. Sight . . . sound . . . smell . . . touch. It was the touch that explained why the others were impaired—a hood over his head. It was made from a material that was coarse and scratchy, probably tailored with the very intent of being an irritant.

Lying on a cold floor, he writhed up to a sitting position. It was no simple feat—his hands and ankles were bound, probably tighter than necessary. A virtual silence told DeBolt he was inside, no traffic noise or seagulls crying. The smell was correspondingly indoors, stale and musty, the air unmoving. He soon discerned voices—not far away, but muted as if coming through a wall. A discussion in the next room. No, an argument, but absent any bladed tones of anger. A measured disagreement. DeBolt strained to extract words, but only a few registered.

General.

Headquarters.

Abort.

Then long minutes of silence intervened until a nearby door opened, never-lubricated hinges squealing in protest. Heavy footsteps came close, then paused in front of him.

"Get up."

DeBolt twisted, found a wall behind him for balance. He wrenched himself up through aches and stiffened joints until he was standing tall. "Who are you?" he asked.

No reply.

DeBolt saw nothing to lose in trying again. "Where is my friend?"

"You have no friends. Not anymore."

All at once DeBolt recognized the voice. The Calais Lodge, the man whose arm he'd clubbed as he reached for a gun.

DeBolt stumbled over this thought, sensing an odd disconnect. What was it? He had recognized the man's voice. But why did that seem so important? There was no accent to speak of. The tone was rough edged. Educated, but not in a private school way. Then he understood—the voice itself. It was something he could use and leverage. Something to concentrate on. He framed his next thought carefully, in the way that was becoming second nature: *Voice recognition.*

No response. He racked his altered brain, then: *Voiceprint capability.*

STANDBY
VOICEPRINT ENABLED
CUE ON COMMAND "START"

"What do you want from me?" DeBolt asked.

"You can begin with your name."

DeBolt nearly did, but instead said, "If you tell me why you've been chasing me it might help us both make sense of things." He gave the command: *Start!*

VOICEPRINT INITIATED

"You made some good moves, I'll give you that. First on the beach, then later in Calais. We weren't going to lose you a third time."

"I don't understand. Who do you work for?" DeBolt asked.

"Not germane—not for you anyway."

"My friend?"

"We have her as well. She's safe. But how did Miss Lund get involved in this? I really need to know that. Is she your girlfriend?"

"No."

"Then what is she doing here?"

DeBolt was working up a reply, something to keep the man talking, when the door squeaked open a second time. A new voice said, "Important call, sir."

DeBolt said, "Let's talk about how she—" A slap on his cheek surprised him, cutting off his words. "Hold that thought," the man said. "I'll be right back."

The man with the sore arm walked away. The door closed.

DeBolt stood in silence, wondering if he had enough. Wondering if it would even work. If not, he would simply have to find another way. He closed his eyes inside the black hood and saw:

VOICEPRINT VALIDATED AND QUEUED. AWAITING CONNECTION.

No connection? No . . . not now.

DeBolt tried the most basic command he could think of: *Own location.*

No response.

His frustration mounted. He had actually captured a sample of the man's voice. But he couldn't do anything with it.

The call had come two hours ago to the late General Benefield's cell phone. Patel only saw it when he returned to his room from the conference—he had decided not to take the phone with him. The message was succinct, in the way military men preferred their communications.

BRAVO IN CUSTODY. WOMAN OBSERVED WITH HIM IS LEO—COAST GUARD INVESTIGATOR SHANNON LUND FROM KODIAK. NO INFORMATION ON ANY CURRENT COAST GUARD INVESTIGATION. POSSIBLE PERSONAL RELATIONSHIP. BOTH BEING HELD U.S. CUSTOMS DETENTION FACILITY BOSTON. ADVISE HOW TO PROCEED.

Patel sat on the bed, stunned. *Bravo? Bravo was reported to have succumbed to his surgery.* Patel knew Benefield had organized a tactical team—they had been tasked to eliminate every trace of META. He'd feigned surprise when the general had brought it all up at dinner: the facilities in Maine and Virginia, whisperings of a nurse who'd disappeared. Patel knew full well the general was cleaning house—it was why he himself had been on guard.

But Bravo still alive?

He tried to make sense of the rest of the message. *LEO.* Law enforcement officer? Yes, that had to be it. The team had her in custody, and suspected that Bravo might be involved with her. A Coast Guard investigator from Kodiak. *Why couldn't he have hit on a nice preschool teacher?* Patel thought sourly.

The officer in charge of the tactical team was still sending messages, so obviously he had not yet been informed of his commander's demise. That would change soon. Probably very soon. Patel weighed sending a response in Benefield's stead, but saw a host of problems with the idea. Indeed, he admonished himself for even bringing the phone to his room—he of all people knew how dangerous that could be. That settled, he knew what had to be done.

Patel removed the SIM card from the phone, then the battery. Taking the elevator downstairs, he walked to the river on a casual stroll, and at intervals sent each of the three pieces spinning into a Donaukanal whose surface was speckled with rain. *Is it ever pleasant here?*

He kept walking, and eventually found shelter beneath a concert pavilion that looked like it hadn't been used since the distant summer. Patel took out his own phone and saw two new emails, one from China and another from Russia. He ignored them for the moment, and dialed a number from memory.

Delta answered. Which was no answer at all. Patel could hear his breathing on the microphone, and in the background a boarding announcement for a departing flight. But of course it was him. That was an equation of logic Patel had long ago derived—when Delta answered there was never a greeting. And if the man's phone was ever lost or stolen? Any other person would say "hello," or its equivalent in another language. By his very silence, Delta's greeting was unique.

His exhalations were steady, controlled as ever. Awaiting instructions.

"I have an amendment to your mission." Patel explained what he wanted done. Of course there was no argument. "If you have questions, text me, either now or after you land."

Patel rang off, then watched his screen.

A text: Who are these extras?

Patel: Involved in META Project. They will be the last—then we are in the clear.

Delta: And when I am done?

Patel: Return to Austria. I will contact you.

Patel waited. There was nothing else.

He wondered if he had done the right thing. He'd vacillated over dispatching Delta to begin with, the risk being considerable. He thought the man would prevail, but it wasn't a certainty. And if he failed? Patel would then be forced to reboot his dream. Not at square one—in fact, considerably to the right. Badenhorst might be dead, but Patel had the surgeon's notes. His work had been exquisite, this made clear by the results. But there were other competent surgeons in the world. Certainly other patients.

He decided he would order a good Napa Valley red tonight and raise a glass to the doctor's memory. Who would have imagined it—*two* had survived the implantation surgery. Bravo *and* Delta. It spoke volumes about the efficacy of Badenhorst's new technique. And even without those successes, the most important component of META was established—the software had gone active and, barring Patel's intervention, would soon worm its way home, embedding as a permanent fixture in its host.

Patel was increasingly sure he'd made the right decision. It would be the ultimate test. And if Delta *did* survive? The very thought was intoxicating. The man was a force of nature. Atif Patel's surrogate assassin. He remembered as a teenager playing Mortal Kombat and Call of Duty. First-person shooter games in which a nearly invincible killer wreaked havoc across the battlegrounds of the world. Patel had now taken things to the next step—a second-person shooter. Or was it third-person? Either way, this reality was not virtual. He controlled the ultimate weapon, as surely as if he had a joystick in his hand. All he had to do was sweep away the vestiges of its birth, make everything look as it had before META's genesis. Patel would remove all the creators save for one.

He pocketed his phone and walked back out into the rain. He looked up at a sky that was gray and brooding, and once again longed for the California sun.

32

The colonel relayed the improbable news. His team was assembled in a conference room inside the massive federal building at 10 Causeway Street in
downtown Boston, barely a mile removed from their double snatch on the
lawn of the Logan Hilton.

"So there it is," the commander said.

His second in command, an Army major, spoke for the others. "This whole
mission had been an abortion from the beginning! Now Benefield, our commanding officer, gets murdered halfway around the world? Does this not
bother you?"

The colonel nodded. "No doubt about it—he was executed. The State Department is up in arms, but so far they haven't attached Benefield to us. Chances
are, they never will. So the question becomes, where do we go from here?"

"We reported solely to Benefield, and none of us know what unit or command he was responsible to. With the general gone? No question—we chop
back to SOCOM." He was referring to Special Operations Command, the
joint overseer of U.S. Special Forces.

Everyone looked at the colonel.

"Look," he said, "I know how you all feel about this mission. The general
assured us this op was targeting a domestic terrorist cell, a group who were
an extreme and immediate threat. That's the reason our unit was created—
we are the no-questions-asked response to verified domestic threats. But
we've all seen this mission play out. That woman we killed at the cabin, the
clinic we hit. I'm having the same doubts you guys are—this whole thing

has stunk from the get-go. Now we're sitting here with two people in custody and no guidance on what to do with them. We've been chasing this guy for days on a 'kill quietly' order, but the officer who issued it is suddenly out of the picture . . . and, I should add, under highly suspicious circumstances."

The major spoke up, thumbing toward the hallway behind them. "You talked to this guy. What do you make of him?"

"Gut feeling . . . I can't picture him as a threat. As for the woman, she's a Coast Guard investigator, and *definitely* not on our target list. So that's our situation, gentlemen. The way I see it, it's our decision as to how we clean this mess up."

One of the two Navy SEALs, a lean, angular man, spoke up. "None of it adds up, boss. I think we have to consider the possibility that Benefield went rogue. If so, then none of our orders were legal to begin with."

"If that's true, we didn't know it," the other SEAL argued. "We can't be held accountable."

"Probably not," said the colonel. "But if this goes public—that SOCOM has put together a black unit whose purpose is to strike terrorism suspects domestically, and with limited oversight—it'll blow up big-time. Every two-bit congressman on Capitol Hill will be throwing knives at SOCOM, and heads *will* roll. I probably don't have to tell you which five careers will be the first ones down the crapper—assuming we can stay out of Leavenworth."

"Everything has been clean so far," said the major, a man who never drifted from his tactical nature. "The nurse's death, the op at the clinic—none of that can be tied to us. The only two loose ends are right here in this house." He chinned toward the adjacent holding rooms.

"We can't just waste 'em," argued the colonel.

"No, I'm not saying that. But maybe we can impart on them the importance of keeping everything quiet."

"Impart?" the second SEAL queried. "I can do some imparting."

The colonel said, "No, it isn't gonna be that easy. This guy saw what we did on Cape Split—he said as much at the hotel two days ago. He knows we've been hunting him. He's probably wondering right now how the hell he's still alive. He's also seen at least two of our faces, including mine."

"The girl hasn't," chimed in the second SEAL. "I got her clean today. I'm sure she didn't get a look at either of us during the takedown."

The colonel considered it, looking at each man in turn. "Okay, maybe we *can* talk our way out of this. I need to find out more about this guy—we don't even know his name, for Christ's sake. I want to know why he's so important. Problem is, we can't go about it in a damned Border Patrol lockup." He looked around the room, and got four nods. "Okay, Trigger and Fry, I want a safe house. We need to move soon, so not too far away."

"Duration?" said the Air Force master sergeant whose call sign was Trigger.

"Three days is plenty."

"Can we borrow one from somebody?"

The colonel thought about it. "Yeah, might as well. Speed is life." He turned to the second SEAL. "Knocker, transportation. Same goes—if you can requisition something from Homeland or Border Patrol, I don't care. We'll only need it for a few days."

The three men got up and left the room, leaving the colonel with his second in command.

"I'm thinking we ditch the girl," said the major. "Drop her somewhere outside town."

"My thoughts exactly. But we wait until tonight. In the meantime, let's keep her wrapped tight—the less she sees and hears, the better for everyone." The commander looked at his subordinate and saw him wrestling with something. "What is it?"

"The guy . . . there's still something about him I don't like, something under the radar. He's been *way* too lucky."

The colonel nodded—the same thing had been gnawing at him. "He's a survivor, I'll give him that. But yeah . . . I know what you mean. Benefield didn't tell us everything. This guy is getting information from somebody. He's seen us coming more than once. After we get safe, I'm going to have another talk with him. We need to find out who the hell he is, and why Benefield wanted him dead."

"Okay, boss, but does the irony of what you just said not strike you? Right now—look at who's dead and who's not."

33

"Passport," said the immigration officer.

Arrivals at JFK International Airport had been streaming in all after-noon, the European rush heavier than usual, and the officer inside the booth was nearing the end of her shift. She reached out and took a document from the next person in line. Her head was down as she did so, and after finaliz-ing the keyboard inputs for the previous traveler, she looked up and was doubly surprised.

The first thing to get her attention was the massive bald head. It was pink and cylindrical, reminding her of a gallon paint can. The body supporting it was built like a blockhouse. The second surprise was what came with the passport—a small wallet-sized card on which was printed: I HAVE NO VOICE AS A RESULT OF COMBAT-RELATED INJURIES. Beneath that was the emblem of the United States Marine Corps.

The immigration officer gave a tentative smile that was not returned. But then, the face in front of her looked barely capable of it. There were no crinkles at the edges of his mouth or eyes, and his features seemed swollen, the way she remembered her uncle when he'd gone on corticosteroids. Con-versely, the man didn't appear angry or taciturn. His face was simply a blank—as expressionless, apparently, as his voice.

She scanned the passport into her reader and his information lit to her screen. Douglas Wilson from Missoula, Montana. Departed JFK October twentieth, arrived in Vienna, Austria, the next day. Departed Vienna on the return trip nine hours ago. There were no flags, no warrants, no notices for special handling. Everything was in order.

She handed back his passport, and said, "Welcome home, Mr. Wilson. You can go."

He turned away, and as he did she saw the scars on the back of his scalp. She called out, "Oh . . . one more thing, sir."

He paused and looked back at her.

"Thank you for your service."

He seemed to consider this for a moment, the look on his meaty face something near confusion. Then he turned toward the exit and was gone.

DeBolt's circumstances went unchanged for most of that day. He sat in a holding room, hearing only the occasional muted voice through thick walls. The restraints on his arms and legs remained in place—he'd moved about the room to explore, but there was little of interest. Twelve feet by twelve. Linoleum on the floor, solid painted walls, a door that was all business. One simple table, no chairs. Most dispiriting of all, he still had no access to information—the screen in his vision remained a blank other than the "voiceprint queued" notification.

It was late in the afternoon, or so he guessed, when DeBolt got his first useful nugget of information—acquired by old-fashioned listening. He heard a male voice outside the door use the term "SCIF." Taken with his surroundings, he knew what the man was referring to, as would anyone who'd spent time in the military in the last decade. SCIF. Sensitive compartmented information facility.

The building he was in, save for one anteroom near the entrance where mobile devices could be checked, was highly secure, designed specifically for the dissemination of classified information. Everything around him had been hardened to defeat electronic eavesdropping, which explained why he had no connection. Thick walls and shielding allowed no radio frequency signals in or out. The very fact that he was in a SCIF suggested he'd been brought to some kind of government facility. Military most likely, but possibly the regional office of some law enforcement or intelligence agency.

This much DeBolt found encouraging. These killers who at one point had tried to shoot him on sight seemed to have taken a new tack. He'd been placed into custody in a government building. There his logic faltered. De-Bolt thought it contradictory that the man who had begun questioning him, and who'd recently tried to kill him, didn't seem to know his name. Yet he did know Lund's. Perhaps it was only an interrogation technique.

DeBolt arrived at two conclusions. He was secure for the moment. And whoever these people were, whatever they wanted, it *had* to be linked to his new abilities. Had to be linked to META. Nothing else made sense.

He was pondering it all, imagining where things might go from here, when, as if in answer, two men burst into the room. Without a word, they hauled him up and frog-marched him down a hallway. He stumbled twice in his shackles, but didn't fall, the hands under his elbows not allowing it. Soon a door opened, and DeBolt felt a rush of clean night air.

34

DeBolt was pushed and shoved into the backseat of a car. Two doors closed, and the car shot forward like a racehorse out of a gate.

Still cuffed and hooded, DeBolt was thrown left, then right, before the car's accelerations dampened and fell in with the hum of steady traffic. Realizing he was finally outside the confines of the SCIF, he tried for a connection. His first request was simple: *Own location.*

The answer arrived instantly, a crisp map in vivid color. His blue dot was at the edge of something called the Thomas P. O'Neill Jr. Federal Building in central Boston. DeBolt was barely a mile from Logan International Airport, where he and Lund had been captured—the only word that fit. He searched for information on the building, and learned that among its tenants were the Department of Homeland Security, which encompassed Customs and Border Protection, and also the departments of State and Justice. The Secret Service was there as well, as was an administrative outpost of the Peace Corps. Even discarding the latter, it made for a long list of suspects who could be responsible for his abduction.

More ominous was the fact that he was leaving. The man who'd begun interviewing him—whom DeBolt had last seen on the floor of the Calais Lodge, and whose arm he'd nearly broken—had been interrupted by an important phone call. Had something in that call altered the situation? He didn't like the trajectory of things. For a few hours a semblance of order and reason had taken hold. Now he was suddenly being hauled off to the notorious "undisclosed location." He sensed someone in the seat to his left, and decided engagement was worth a try.

"Where is Shannon?" he asked. They already knew her name.

No reply. DeBolt used his knees and arms to explore. To his right was a door, and he could feel the buttons for the window and a recessed handle. There was no way to tell if the door was locked. Didn't police cars have doors that could only be opened from the outside? It was yet another question he'd never before asked.

He decided to try again.

"I want to speak to an attorney. I have a right to—"

The blow struck DeBolt in the rib cage, an elbow probably, compact and heavier than it needed to be. It completely winded him, a nonverbal message that couldn't have been clearer. DeBolt said nothing more.

He did not, however, give up on communication. There was a chance he was being transferred to a different federal facility, which meant he might end up in another SCIF where he wouldn't have a signal. Sensing the car bogging down in traffic, DeBolt put META into high gear.

The first thing he did was call up the voiceprint of his interrogator, already recorded and saved—somehow—but never sent. DeBolt launched it into cyberspace. The reply took nearly five minutes, but was worth the wait. He received the identity of his interrogator with: "99.8% certainty." Under present circumstances, good enough for DeBolt.

That name led to more requests, and soon the information floodgates opened. He approached his research from every conceivable angle. Some of the answers came right away, others more slowly. A handful never came at all. Certain information altered his course, new vectors taken and gaps filled in. His thoughts fell to a rush. Data in and queries out. He logged certain details as important, discarded others as irrelevant. With the greatest possible speed, DeBolt amassed a trove of information on the men who had been hunting him.

The results were nothing short of spectacular.

The colonel was happy. The transfer of their captives from the federal building to the safe house had gone smoothly.

Moving prisoners was never an easy thing. It combined the logistics of travel, always awkward, with any number of complications. Prisoners rightfully saw it as their best chance for an escape. Cars could break down and police could get involved. The last time the colonel had transferred a captive was three months ago: he and a Mossad assassin had hauled a much sought militant out of Yemen's Empty Quarter, the man bound by his own bootlaces and strapped to the back of a donkey—or more precisely, he'd later been told, a Nubian wild ass. A bar story and a punch line all in one. That they'd succeeded was nothing less than an act of divine providence. This time the commander of Unit 9 had everything in his favor. Two borrowed federal vehicles—solid and serviced, and staffed by his own team of operators—to move a pair of well-shackled prisoners to a suburb of West Boston. No ass involved.

During the journey to the safe house, he'd ordered that Lund and their mystery man were to have no contact whatsoever. Not yet anyway. They arrived in separate cars, and were taken to rooms on opposite sides of the house, one in the basement and the other on the second floor. The place was a two-story colonial, an FBI retreat established six months ago but rarely used since, situated in an agreeable neighborhood west of town. If the community had a theme it was acreage, the homes spaced widely apart. Mature trees and hedgerows gave further privacy to residents who clearly craved it—and none more so than the temporary occupants of 3443 Saddle Lane.

Once their charges were secured behind locked doors, the colonel assembled his team and went over the plan. "I've heard nothing new about what happened to the general, but honestly, I don't expect to. It's time to put this op to bed. We'll dump the girl soon, but first I want to interrogate our man, and I need her as leverage—he seems to care about her safety."

"Time frame?" the major asked.

"We unload the girl tonight. Then we'll egress clean first thing in the morning."

"And the Coastie?"

The commander hesitated. "That depends on what I find out about him."

A watch schedule was posted, and two men were allowed to rack out in what was done up as a kid's bedroom—there were *Star Wars* posters on the walls, and the bunk beds were dressed in sheets printed with fire engines.

The colonel went to the room where their man was locked up—it had been hardened by the FBI for just that purpose. He went inside without knocking, but before he could say anything, their captive greeted him with, "It's about time, Colonel Freeman."

35

Freeman stood stunned. It was a gross breach of protocol for a detainee to know his interrogator's name. A damned bad thing in a lot of ways. "How the hell—"

"In five minutes I can tell you everything you need to know. And it won't be what you expect. Agreed?"

The colonel said nothing.

The man in the hood began.

"You are Colonel Brian Freeman, United States Army. Green Beret, and six years on Delta Force. Your team is Unit 9, a highly selective squad embedded in SOCOM. In the rooms behind you are Major Randy Piasecki, United States Army. Petty Officer Second Class Jack Stevens, and Petty Officer First Class Patrick Baumann, both Navy SEALs. Air Force Master Sergeant Jeffrey Chambliss is your unit comm specialist."

"How . . . no . . . nobody knows that."

"Right now we're in a safe house at 3443 Saddle Lane in Watertown, Massachusetts. I was brought here from the O'Neill Federal Building in downtown Boston." The man paused, as if to let the burn in Freeman's gut etch deeper. "You attended West Point and deployed for three tours, Iraq and Afghanistan, before being selected for the Green Berets." Another pause. "Last night you went to your bank's website and transferred eight hundred dollars from savings to checking. You were married on December 26, 2000, to the former Marie Angleton. You have two daughters, Bethany and Jackie."

Freeman went rigid. He took two steps toward the man, and hissed, "Are you making idle threats against my family, Coastie?"

"Idle? Is that an assumption you can afford to make right now?"

Freeman felt something rise inside him, imminent like thunder after lightning. "What are you implying?"

"At this minute your wife is pulling into the driveway of a house in Fredericksburg . . . her parents' place. She's dropping off the girls so she can go to her book club, which meets once a month, rotating between the houses of the nine women who take part."

Freeman lunged and took the man by the collar, constricting the fabric around his throat. There was a momentary gag, and he said, "Listen, you mother—"

The Coastie showed a sudden strength. He dropped a shoulder, loosening Freeman's grip but not breaking it. It was enough to allow a breath, and he said, "Colonel . . . I think it's time for you to join me in the darkness."

Seconds later, every light in the room went dark. The blackness was absolute.

Then the Coastie said, "Your phone is about to ring."

On that cue, Freeman felt the familiar vibration in his breast pocket—he'd set the ringer volume to mute.

"It's your wife, answer it."

In the darkness, a disbelieving Freeman let go with one hand and retrieved his phone. He saw a call from his wife. An electric jolt went down his spine. He swiped to take the call. "Marie! Are you okay?"

"Yes, I'm fine . . . but what about you? I got your text to call right away, you said it was something urgent."

Freeman's thoughts began to spin out of control. He enforced order on his military mind, the same as when he was under fire on a battlefield. "Where are you?"

A stutter from his wife, who was typically rock-solid, then, "I'm at Mom and Dad's. My book club is tonight and—"

"*Marie*, listen very closely! I want you to take the girls inside and stay there. Lock the doors and don't let *anybody* in the house! I will call you back in ten minutes."

"Brian . . . you're scaring me."

"It's okay, don't worry. Ten minutes."

He ended the call, but before he could speak again the man behind the hood said, "Lights back on now."

There was a pause, and Freeman stood silent and stunned. Five seconds later the lights flickered to life.

The door behind him suddenly opened, and Piasecki said, "Power outage, boss. No explanation, but we're looking into it. You okay in here?"

Freeman hesitated and, without turning to face the major, said, "Yeah, I'm good. Stand up the watch outside."

"Will do."

The door closed.

One of Freeman's hands was still on the Coastie's collar, but his grip had loosened considerably. No longer throttling, but keeping a distance, in the way a snake handler might hold a pit viper. Then Freeman did something he hadn't done since he was a lieutenant. He completely lost his cool.

He ripped the hood off the man's head, and his free hand balled into a fist. Ready to go. He watched the blue eyes blink in surprise, adjusting to the light. Then they met Freeman's gaze.

As a Green Beret, Freeman had seen his share of terrorists and lowlifes. He'd seen well-trained officers and raw recruits. The man in front of him was none of those things. For reasons he couldn't quantify, he felt like he was staring at an alien. He said nothing for a time, and managed to keep his fists in check. He searched the strong young face, the steady gaze for . . . *For what?*

A threat?

An explanation?

"Who?" Freeman finally growled. "Who the *hell* are you?"

When DeBolt finally saw his interrogator's face, it confirmed the voice association he'd made—in front of him was the man he'd last seen on the floor of the lodge in Calais. Same square jaw, same military haircut. The primary difference now was in the eyes. In Calais, DeBolt had seen a soldier's steady gaze. The man had been on the defensive then, but continuously acquiring information, searching for a tactical advantage. The man he was looking at now was positively befuddled, as if the sun had risen in the west. DeBolt thought he might have overplayed his hand.

"Your family is in no danger," he said. "I was only making a point."

The officer's eyes went narrow and tilted upward. He was wondering about the lights.

"This home has a computerized system to manage everything electrical," DeBolt explained. "Heating, lights, CO_2 sensors, ceiling fans. All of it can be monitored and controlled remotely—good for saving energy. All you need is the right codes and a connection."

"Connection? You don't have a phone—no way. You've been thoroughly searched three times, once by me personally."

Once again, DeBolt considered how to say the unsayable.

He knew that at least one dynamic had changed—this team was no longer trying to kill him. With reaching optimism, he thought the colonel might even be persuaded to help him. But first he would have to earn the man's trust. In measured words he presented it much as he had yesterday to Lund. As he talked, DeBolt saw a range of emotions play across Freeman's face. Disinterest was not among them. On finishing his story, he turned and showed Freeman the scars on his scalp, exactly as he'd done with Lund. The physical badge to reinforce his otherwise wildly implausible story.

"At this point, I'm sure I at least have your attention," said DeBolt. "So let's clear up a few things. Before today, you wanted me dead. Now we're standing here talking. What changed?"

"My wife," the colonel said, as if not hearing the question, "how did you know about her?"

"It was simple phone play. Call logs, a triangulated location. I sent her a text in your name. It's not hard to do—not if you have the right backing."

"You can do all that with . . ."—he hesitated and pointed to DeBolt's head—"with whatever you've got in there?"

DeBolt nodded. "And a lot more."

Freeman was still skeptical. "No—you'd need more than a connection to the internet. Information like that, following someone's phone and hijacking call logs? That requires access. Some people might even call it hacking. I know because my unit gets exactly that kind of help, only we have a dedicated tech team, dozens of specialists who make it happen."

"Exactly—so you know it's operationally feasible. Now take the next step. Allow that I have access to something similar."

"Who does it go through?" Freeman asked, order slowly returning to his upended world. "Who's the provider?"

"That's the million-dollar question. I really don't know. A couple of months ago I had a pretty normal life. Then I was injured in a helicopter accident—the rest of my crew didn't make it, and I almost died. I woke up at a beach house having no idea how I got there, or what had been done to me. I spent weeks rehabbing, getting back on my feet—until you and your team came in with guns blazing. That's all I know. I'm figuring out what I can do, day by day, but if you ask me who's behind it? I have no idea. I'd really like to find out though." DeBolt held his breath, then added, "Maybe you can help me."

"Help you? Yesterday I was trying to kill you."

"But not today. Why?"

Freeman almost said something, then shook his head. "I need to bring the rest of my team in on this."

"No problem," said DeBolt. "I'll take all the help I can get."

36

The house was nicely furnished, from top to bottom a cut above any place De-Bolt had ever lived. There were wood floors, burnt brown and rich, and a smooth stone fireplace the color of an iron winter sky. High-end steel dominated the kitchen, marble the bathrooms. More telling was what was missing. He saw no pictures on the walls, no travel keepsakes, no letters on the kitchen counter. Altogether, a scrupulously warm place, but without the soul of a home.

The shackles came off, and DeBolt rubbed his wrists and ankles as he sat on the plush living room couch. He was unbound, but it was hardly freedom. *Not when I'm surrounded by five of the world's most thoroughly trained killers.*

He'd already downloaded their names and service affiliations, but now, with Unit 9 presented in person, DeBolt could make a more palpable study. There were slight variations in height and build, but the similarities were more pronounced. The sinewy necks and athletic postures, the way they stretched to unwind coiled muscles. Their shared facial expression must have been standard issue: a stare that was in equal measure resolute and impassive. As individual soldiers they were intelligent and capable. As a unit they exuded bravado. At that moment every bit of it was directed at the lone newcomer. A pack of alpha dogs working together, deciding how to deal with an encircled quarry.

They denied his request to see Lund, but assured him she was reasonably comfortable in the basement. For the sake of the others, DeBolt repeated what he'd told Freeman. His description of META was met by a sea of blank faces, suggesting none of them knew their recent missions were derived from a deep-black DARPA project. He then performed an abbreviated version of the act he'd been using to demonstrate his abilities. Any remaining skepticism was soon crushed.

In turn, Freeman gave DeBolt a condensed briefing on his team, enough for him to understand their unit mission, along with a measured description of the orders they'd received to hunt him down. With all the facts laid bare, it was this final point, the kill order against DeBolt, that clearly perplexed everyone. The central lie was apparent, but not the reasons behind it, and confusion reigned on both sides of the room.

DeBolt was sure Freeman was holding back certain elements, gaps and details left unsaid. Possibly because they were classified, but more likely because they were incriminating. He didn't care—he was desperate for anything to help him understand his situation. At the end, Freeman explained that Unit 9's provisional commander, a brigadier general, had been murdered the day before in Austria. It was another unimaginable complication. And far too much of a coincidence to ignore.

Freeman cleared his team in hot to ask questions of DeBolt.

Major Piasecki was first in line. "The woman we killed at the cabin . . . you're sure she was only a nurse?"

DeBolt said, "I can tell you she had medical training, and I found records of her job history. She also had personal issues, drank more than she should have. But in my personal opinion—there's no way on God's earth she was any kind of terrorist."

"The place where she worked—we were ordered to take that out as well. It was supposedly a lab set up by a terrorist cell for manufacturing biological agents."

Here DeBolt was less sure. "I don't know anything about that. I remember being in a hospital of some kind, and that could have been the building. I did find evidence that Joan Chandler spent a lot of time there in the weeks before I ended up at her cabin. The few details I have suggest my surgery was performed there, but it's all circumstantial—I don't have any evidence to prove it. I also can't tell you what else might have gone on in the place." As they all chewed on it, DeBolt asked, "Was I supposedly part of this terrorist cell? Was that the justification for the kill order on me?"

Freeman nodded. "No questions asked. You were to be eliminated at any cost, made to disappear and all evidence destroyed. Benefield's rationale was clear—everything had to be kept quiet. In a way it made sense. A biological attack, the components of which were already in place on home soil—the mere mention of it could instigate a nationwide panic. Apparently that was all just eyewash."

The weight of so many new facts brought silence to the room.

Eventually DeBolt spoke, almost at a whisper. "What could I have done?"

"What do you mean?" Freeman asked.

"That night on the beach, at the cabin. I've run it through my mind a hundred times. I lie awake thinking about it. Was there anything I could have done to save her? Could I have . . . I don't know, distracted you? Split you up and fought somehow?"

Freeman shook his head. "Look . . . I've been where you are. Don't waste time beating yourself up. You were unarmed, outnumbered, and had no means of communication." He looked at his team one by one. "There's not a man in this room who could have done more than you did. You survived."

DeBolt didn't reply for a time. Then he nodded, and said, "Okay. So where do we go from here?"

Freeman spoke for his squad. "I'm convinced the general was bent—I only wish I'd seen it sooner. There were a lot of red flags, but I missed every one. We didn't get enough background on you or what was happening at the clinic—not enough to justify what we did. I take the blame for that." He looked around the room before announcing, "As far as I'm concerned, this mission is over."

One by one, DeBolt saw the other four nod in agreement.

Piasecki said, "We're all to blame. I wish we could take back what happened, both at the cottage and the clinic. And for what it's worth, I'm glad we couldn't shoot straight on that beach."

Freeman said to DeBolt, "For the sake of my team, I have to ask—are you going to pursue this? We made mistakes, bad ones, but in the strictest sense my men were only following orders. If there's any culpability it shouldn't go beyond me."

DeBolt considered it, and said, "I have access to a lot of information. I can probably verify everything you've told me, for better or worse. If it all happened as you say, then the general who issued your orders is responsible—and it sounds like he's already found his justice."

"That's something I will personally verify," said Freeman.

"But I'm stuck with one big problem," said DeBolt. "Aside from me, it seems that everyone associated with this META Project is dead. If that's the case, I'll never find out what I've got in my head."

"I'm not so sure," said Piasecki. "If everybody associated with the project is dead—then who killed General Benefield? And why?"

Everyone pondered it, and Freeman said, "He's right. We may be missing something. Someone. And I'd say we *all* have a vested interest in making sure every loose end is cleared up."

The five men looked at DeBolt, who nodded agreement. "Like I said, I could use some help. But there's one thing I want done before we go any further."

DeBolt explained what it was, and Freeman said, "You don't trust us?"

"Actually, I do—about ninety-nine percent, anyway."

The colonel grinned. "Well, that's considerably above our approval rating for you . . . but okay. We'll do it your way."

37

Lund heard a door open, then footsteps across the concrete floor. She tensed unavoidably, and startled when the hood was pulled off her head. The first thing she saw was Trey DeBolt's eyes. She looked past him and saw no one else. The room's only door was ajar.

She opened her mouth to speak, but it was cut short when he pulled her in and held her. After so many hours of isolation and, she had to admit, fear, the warmth of his gesture brought a wave of relief.

"It's okay," he said quietly, keeping her close. "It's going to be okay." When DeBolt finally backed away, she saw that he was holding a pair of wire cutters. He reached down and cut the flex cuffs from her wrists and ankles.

"You're all right," she said breathlessly. "I was so worried about . . . what they might have done to you."

"I'm fine. We're going to get you out of here."

Lund heard footsteps outside the door. For the first time she studied her surroundings. The floor was broomed concrete, the walls painted cement. The door led to a set of stairs that disappeared upward, and one of the walls was topped by three transom windows. The windows were water-spotted and opaque, almost no light filtering in. A basement, obviously, probably beneath a house. She could see no one at the door but sensed a presence outside.

"Where are we?" she asked.

"They say it's a safe house."

"They?"

"The guys who brought us here—I've been talking to them."

"Okay, that's good. But you said there was a group of men who'd been trying to kill you, and I thought—"

"Yeah, it's them. But we're good now."

Her eyes narrowed, suspicion pleating her face. "A gang of killers abduct us off a sidewalk, hold us hostage? But we're *good* now?"

"Things have changed, Shannon. It's a long story, one that none of us completely understands. I'm convinced these guys are not a threat anymore. At least not to me or you."

"Do you know who they are?"

"I was right to a point. They're soldiers, a special unit."

"Like a SEAL team?"

"Yes, something like that. But I promised not to say too much. You have to understand that this may not be over. The people who created the META Project are fast becoming an endangered species. Truth is, they may *all* be dead. Right now, my only concern is to get you safe. These men are going to let you go."

"What about you?"

"I have to find out what's been done to me, Shannon. Can you understand that?"

She nodded.

"The only way I'll get my life back is to learn what's happened, to understand META and how it affects me. These men can help me do that."

"And if you figure it out . . . then you'll come back to Alaska?"

"Yes."

She looked right into him, past the blueness in his eyes and whatever hardware was in them. Lund broke away and shook her head. "No, Trey. That's the first time you've lied to me. You won't ever go back to Kodiak."

He lowered his head, perhaps realizing it for the first time himself. "Maybe you're right. Maybe I can't go back."

"Trey," she pleaded, "you can't let this control you! Whatever they've done, don't let it make you something less than you were."

He nodded resolutely. "I promise you this—once I've found the truth behind META, I will find you, Shannon. Do you believe me when I say that?"

To Lund's surprise, she rocked forward and kissed him.

DeBolt didn't seem surprised at all. He responded readily and they ended grasping one another, their bodies locked together in the basement's faint light.

He said, "When you called me two days ago . . . you said I had to trust someone. Now I'm saying it to you."

He reached into his pocket and removed two cell phones. One was hers, the other one of the prepaid devices he'd bought, both obviously returned by their captors. He reached around with his hand and slid hers into her back pocket, then theatrically put the other in his own. "They're going to take you away now. They'll drop you in a public place and turn you loose. When that happens, when you're certain you're safe, call me. The number is already loaded."

She nodded to say she would.

"There's one catch, though—they insisted on it." He held up the black hood.

Again she nodded, understanding. Lund had so far seen none of these men, and it made sense they would want to keep it that way. It also reinforced the prospect that they would hold up their end of the bargain—a no-strings-attached release.

DeBolt lifted the hood, and in the moment before sliding it over her head he paused and beamed a confident smile at her. Lund did her best to mirror it. Then her world again went black.

38

One hour later Lund was counting, just as they'd instructed. When she reached a hundred, she pulled the hood from her head.

She found herself in the parking lot of the Hilton Hotel, almost the very spot where she'd been standing this morning when they'd abducted her. She looked all around, but saw no sign of the silent man who'd ushered her here, nor the car she'd heard pull away. Lund had played by their rules, and she was glad for it. She was free again.

Now she was going to do her damnedest to return the favor to DeBolt.

She breathed deeply on the chill night air—after a full day of captivity she allowed herself that much. Lund turned on her phone. It booted up, and she poised her finger over the screen, ready to tap on DeBolt's number. Before she could do so, her phone chimed a handful of times as it collected the business of the day. Three voice mails, two texts, and a half-dozen emails. *Back to the old captivity,* she thought.

Lund made the call, and as the connection ran she began walking. She was almost to the lobby entrance when DeBolt answered.

"You okay, Shannon?"

"Yeah, I'm fine. Right back where we started."

"No issues?"

"Don't worry. I'm back in the hotel lobby and there are people all over the place. I'm safe. What about you?"

"I'm good, but I can't talk for long. Listen closely—there's a flight on American, it leaves at nine fifteen, connects in Chicago. It'll have you back in Anchorage by noon tomorrow. From there you can catch the C-130 and be back to Kodiak in time for dinner. There's plenty of room on all the flights."

"How do you know all . . . oh, right."

"Yeah, I know. It takes some getting used to."

"Are you going to keep the phone you're using?" she asked.

"No, I'll have to ditch it. But I've got your number. I'll call if I need anything."

She didn't respond. The contrast between their situations could not have been more stark. She would be home for dinner tomorrow. He had no idea where he would be in a day or a week. Didn't know if he would ever be able to reclaim the life of PO2 Trey DeBolt.

"I can still help," she said. "I have access to information too, things you might not be able to find."

"I know, and I appreciate that. But for now the risk is too high, Shannon. I don't want you involved."

Instead of arguing, she said, "Take care of yourself, Trey. I mean it."

"You too."

The connection ended, and Lund lowered her handset. She stared at the hotel's front desk, and it dawned on her that she'd only booked the room for one night. She wondered how they handled it when a guest disappeared but left their things in a room. *Guess I'm about to find out.*

She nearly pocketed her phone before remembering the messages. Lund checked them one by one. The texts were from friends wondering where she'd gone. The emails were all work related and none pertained to DeBolt. The second voice mail sent her finger straight to the call back button. Jim Kalata answered right away.

"Hey, Shannon. Did you get my message?"

"Yes. You said you made some headway on the William Simmons case."

"I did. First of all, Matt Doran came in and showed me the pictures he took on the scene. There was definitely somebody else up there, maybe even signs of a scuffle. I also checked Simmons' home laptop and found some pretty heated email exchanges. He was getting sideways with some kind of patient advocate over at the big hospital in Anchorage. Simmons was upset that nobody there would admit to knowing anything about Trey's case."

"So he was ruffling feathers."

"Big-time. Along with what Matt came up with, it bugged me, and it seemed to go beyond the island. So I did one of your arrival searches."

Lund had devised the procedure. Most crimes in Kodiak, like any place, were local in nature—victims and perpetrators were residents. But occasionally the involvement of outsiders had to be considered. Kodiak being an island, and a small and remote one at that, there were few avenues by which anyone could arrive and depart. If a date could be approximated, it was a simple task to go over the manifests for the few scheduled flights and see if any names stood out.

Kalata said, "I threw in as many discriminators as I could. I looked for a male who arrived and departed within two days either side of Sunday, the day of the accident. I screened out anybody less than twenty years old, and because Matt said that path up the mountain was really challenging, I also tossed anybody over fifty."

"And?"

"Honestly, it's a reach. But I really busted my butt on this, so you're gonna owe me."

"Dammit, Jim—"

"A beer—I just want a beer. Maybe two." He let her stew a moment longer, then, "My best find was a guy who flew in Sunday morning, then left that same night. He wasn't here more than eight hours. Never booked a room or rented a car, nothing. And get this—he flew in all the way from Vienna, Austria. That's four flights each way, like thirty hours of travel. Does that make sense to you? A guy flies halfway around the world to spend eight hours in Kodiak—as far as I can tell, to do nothing."

"There could be a lot of explanations, Jim. He might have been closing on a house or visiting a sick parent."

"I know, it's not much. I cross-checked his last name with the local phone directory—no matches. Same with county arrest and property records. I even called the hospital here. As you know, it's not a big place. There were only nine logged visitors that day—none were our guy."

Lund put some thoughtfulness in her voice. "You *have* been busy. Thanks for going the distance with me on this, Jim." She immediately regretted her choice of words, and before he could respond, she asked, "What's his name?"

"Douglas Wilson. The airline had an address for him in Missoula,

Montana. I tried to look it up, but drew blanks—I'm pretty sure the street address doesn't exist. Oh, and there was one other thing. According to Doran, the second set of footprints on the mountain were really deep."

"Meaning what?"

"Meaning this guy was nimble enough to get up a mountain, but he's one large individual. Altogether, it wasn't much to go on, but since I knew the flight times I went to the airport and looked over their surveillance video. One fuzzy image stood out—I'll send it to you now from my iPad."

Lund took the phone from her ear, and twenty seconds later it arrived. She opened the image and pinched it wider. When she did, the resolution suffered. There were three people in the frame, but she had no doubt which one Kalata was talking about: bald, unsmiling, massive build. His head was down as he parted the thin crowd. The human equivalent of an icebreaker.

Kalata's voice carried from the phone, "Ever seen him before?"

She put the handset back to her ear. "Never. You?"

"Not in my life." When she didn't say anything, he added, "Look, Shannon, you're right—this might be nothing. But I knew it was important to you, so I tried."

"Thanks, Jim. You did good. If anything else comes up please give me a call."

"How's your dad?"

The question caught Lund off guard. "Oh . . . he's—"

She was cut off by his chuckle. "Good luck, Shannon."

The call ended.

Standing in the hotel lobby, Lund whispered the name to herself. "Douglas Wilson." Hearing it aloud was no help. It meant nothing to her.

It was well after midnight in Vienna, and Patel had been on the phone with the technician in D.C. for nearly an hour. His name was Nelson Chadli, and he was the man Patel had chosen specifically to manage META on the server end. He and Chadli had studied together at Caltech, so Patel knew he was smart. He also knew he was timid by nature and prone to indecisiveness. On the scale of malleability, Chadli was a rock-solid nine.

"You've finished the sequence?" Patel asked.

There was a slight delay as the call ran across the ocean. "Yes, it is done now. I'm getting a response. There we are . . . the command algorithm is running."

"How long will the sweep take to confirm?" Patel asked.

"Well, things have been busy. Our real-time restricted databases, the ones with tailored access operations—they don't often get modified using an alpha-priority clearance."

Patel was happy the phone connection could not convey his grin. So lost in a technical haze was Chadli, he had no idea what was about to happen. The changes he was making would on appearances erase META from the primary server. They would in fact do quite the opposite. Once finished, Patel's software would be fully embedded, his Trojan horse complete. Although it wasn't a classic Trojan horse play. He intended no damage to the government's host system, nor was it meant to attack other databases. It would simply exist, working in the background, feeding and extracting like the parasite it was from the most labyrinthine network on earth. Aside from Patel, no one knew of its existence, not even Chadli, who at that moment was making META's intrusion permanent. The software was now operationally proven. In five years or ten, it might be discovered—if the overseeing agency restructured its servers to an entirely new architecture, or if a very, *very* clever auditor stumbled upon it. But Patel doubted any of that would happen. For the foreseeable future, he had private access to, the most powerful information gathering network on earth. Then Patel amended this thought. In truth, *he* wasn't the end user—Delta was.

But Delta was his.

He said, "Yes, I've discussed this at length with the supervisory team. The alpha-priority clearance was authorized far above our level—that's the point of the entire exercise, but I can't divulge details, and certainly not on an open line."

Chadli said, "I understand. While we're waiting for confirmation I'll run a usage scan."

"No!" said Patel quickly. "That's not nec—"

"Oh, it's not a problem. It only takes a few seconds." A pause, then, "I see there has been some use."

"Yes, those are authorized test inputs," Patel said quickly, which was true in the strictest sense. "Most were from here, in Vienna, followed by a few in Alaska. We were assessing geographic coverage and measuring response intervals." Then he added, "You may also see activity in New York City."

"Ah," said Chadli, "here we are. Yes, Vienna for the past month, and Alaska. New York today. Also up in New England for the last few days."

On hearing this Patel went rigid. *The last few days?* He sat upright behind the desk in his hotel room, and tried to keep a level tone. "Where in New England?"

"All across Maine, from top to bottom. Then New Hampshire briefly and Boston."

For the second time in twenty-four hours Patel was stunned. He knew Delta's schedule precisely—he had been nowhere near New England until a few hours ago. Then he was struck by an outrageous possibility.

Bravo?

He knew DeBolt had survived the surgery—that was a surprise to everyone—but could he possibly have gone active?

Patel tried to think clearly. He had specifically enabled Delta months ago, the final links made. Yet those instructions had pertained specifically to him. How could Bravo possibly be using them? Was there a weakness in the code he'd written, a back door that had somehow allowed access? Then a greater worry flooded into his head—the man had so far escaped Benefield's vaunted team of killers. Had Bravo gained an advantage over them by leveraging META?

"Dr. Patel? Are you still there?" came the reedy voice from across the ocean.

Patel reacquired his focus. "Yes, of course. My connection is a bit dodgy. Tell me one thing . . . where is the most recent activity?"

"I show usage in Boston right now . . . actually hits on two nodes. They're separated by about a mile. How could that—"

"*No,* that's fine," said Patel in a rush, "exactly as it should be. I have another call I must take. Let me know when the uninstall sequence has finalized."

"Yes, I'll—"

Patel cut the man off. Dozens of worries rushed into his mind, any of which might threaten his control of the situation. *But if it's true . . .*

He quickly went to his texting app, selected the contact he wanted, and typed a frantic message.

USE EXTREME CAUTION: BRAVO MAY ALSO BE ACTIVE.

39

Baumann and Stevens pulled into the unlit driveway at 3443 Saddle Lane, splashing into a days-old puddle. The two Navy SEALs had buddied up, as they usually did, to deliver the Coast Guard investigator back to where they'd found her. Things had gone smoothly, largely because she'd cooperated.

As Baumann parked and killed the engine on the SUV—a Homeland Security–supplied Ford Explorer—Stevens paused in the backseat with his hand on the door, and said, "What do you think about this guy, DeBolt? Is it possible? You really think he's like . . . connected somehow?"

"Has to be. You heard all that stuff he told the colonel."

Stevens whistled. "You know what you and I could do with something like that? What it would do for our unit effectiveness? It would be, like, exponential . . . or whatever the word is."

"No doubt about it," said Baumann, pocketing the keys. "I was thinking what you could do with it on the outside too."

"But you'd have to have all that stuff put in your head. Circuits or antennae, whatever the hell—a lot could go wrong there."

"True. But the things you could find out about people. Imagine it. I mean, any girl—you could get her address and phone number, find out if she has a boyfriend."

Stevens laughed. "Listen to you. Give you the keys to an information kingdom, and all you'd use it for is to get laid."

"What would you do? Rob a bank or something?"

"Maybe so."

Stevens was still laughing at his partner when they stepped out of the vehicle. It was in those next seconds, distracted as they were, that the two SEALs made the slightest of tactical mistakes. Baumann had been driving, and Stevens was in the backseat, the way they'd been situated to shepherd their prisoner on the outbound ride. Now back at the safe house, in the suburbs and feeling confident, they made an almost imperceptible error. Both got out of the same side of the truck.

Stevens started walking straight toward the house, his back to his partner. He only turned around when he heard the slightest of sounds—by some basal instinct, a sound that sent a shot of adrenaline through his system. That was because he'd heard it before, although always from a different perspective. A muffled gurgling noise.

In the span of a few milliseconds, highlighted by a spill of stray light from the house, Stevens saw three things in sequence: Baumann falling toward him with a look of total surprise on his face. A wide dark figure behind him. And finally the blade.

If he hadn't reached out instinctively to catch his friend, who was already dead, he might have been able to block, or at least blunt, the arriving knife. But his geometry was all wrong, and the blade arrived full force, just below his ribs and thrusting upward. As Stevens fell right next to his longtime partner, his last living sight was that of a hulking shadow moving toward the house.

"Do you think she'll do it?" asked Freeman. "Go back to Alaska?"

"I don't know," replied DeBolt, "maybe. But I know she'll try to help me."

They were in the kitchen, the colonel boiling a pot of water to make instant coffee. They all needed a lift. "How much did you tell her?" he asked.

"Most of what I told you. She knows about the META Project. Knows you guys were tracking me."

"But you didn't give her any specifics on us?"

"Didn't see a need for it."

Freeman nodded, and said, "Thanks for that." He searched through a cabinet, and pulled out a handful of sweetener packets, all either red or blue.

"Damned feds—doesn't anybody use real sugar anymore?" He pulled two coffee cups out of a different cupboard, and winced slightly as he set them down. Freeman flexed his hand open and closed, and looked accusingly at DeBolt. "My arm is still sore from when you whacked me with that damned fencepost."

"It was a rail from the staircase—and if I hadn't done it you would have shot me."

"I still might if you piss me off."

"So you don't know anything about META?" DeBolt asked.

"Never heard of it. Our only contact was Benefield, and like I told you, the mission brief he gave us was about a terrorist plot involving biological agents."

"But he never told you who was behind it?"

"He said it was domestic, not Middle Eastern. Looking back, he'd have to say that, wouldn't he? You'd never pass for a Paki or a Saudi. Nobody working on this project would have."

DeBolt nodded. "So you didn't even know our names?"

"No. We were given the locations of the strikes, and a photograph of each target. There should have been more—*I* should have demanded it. Now the whole thing has been shuttered the hard way, Benefield included."

"And you guys had nothing to do with that?"

The two exchanged a hard look.

"Benefield?" Freeman replied. "You're accusing me of murdering my commanding officer?"

DeBolt shook his head. "Sorry—I guess I'm a little desperate. But if not you, then—" He was cut off when the lights suddenly went out.

The room fell to a frozen silence, until Freeman said, "Did you—"

"No!" DeBolt cut in. "It wasn't me!"

A muffled thump sounded from the living room.

"Trigger?" Freeman called out.

There was no response. The darkness wasn't absolute—an emergency floodlight, obviously battery powered, sputtered to life somewhere out back. It cast in through the windows, channels of light amid shadowed voids. A glow from a distant streetlight shone pale through the front windows, creating a no-man's-land of illumination in the adjacent dining room. DeBolt saw Freeman glide silently toward the dining room, a gun materializing in his hand. "Randy!" he barked.

Nothing.

Freeman backed up to one side of the wall at the dining room entrance, and with rapid hand motions he pointed to the opposite side. DeBolt rushed over and put a shoulder to the wall.

The colonel peered around the corner, and whispered, "Shit!"

DeBolt ventured a look. In the living room he saw one of the other men—he couldn't say who—splayed motionless across the couch. The sheen that glistened over his face and upper body was colorless in the dim light, but he knew it could only be red.

Freeman looked again at DeBolt, and was raising his hand for another command when all hell broke loose. The wall near Freeman exploded in a hail of gunfire. The colonel fell back, clattering to the floor, then scrambled onto his knees, still gripping the handgun. He was moving low in the doorway when a massive figure lunged through. Freeman was sent flying, and the two men slammed into a dinette, chairs and table legs splintering under their combined weight.

They began grappling in close quarters, and DeBolt dove into the fray, trying to disable the bigger man's arms. A shot rang out, but nothing seemed to change. DeBolt had one of the attacker's arms barred, but it was like trying to hold back a lever in some immense machine. Freeman suddenly rolled clear, and the assailant turned his attention to DeBolt, lifting him completely off the ground in a wrestler's move and throwing him across the room. DeBolt slammed into a row of cabinets and fell to the floor stunned.

Another shot rang out, and this time DeBolt looked up to see the big man holding a gun and Freeman sinking to his knees. Clutching his chest, the colonel toppled face-first onto the tile and went still. The killer stood rigid and alert, his chest heaving like a steel-mill bellows. He was broad and powerful, his bald head glistening in a channel of light.

Freeman remained motionless, and DeBolt saw no sign of the other team members. That quickly, he was again alone. The attacker had his gun raised, fixed on DeBolt's chest with only the narrow kitchen island between them. The man knew he was physically superior, and that DeBolt would have drawn a weapon if he had one. He had every advantage. So DeBolt did the only thing he could in that instant. He stood perfectly still. Anyone who didn't know him would have viewed it as surrender. He waited for the gun to waver, for the man's stance to relax. Neither happened.

With the lights already out, DeBolt could think of no electronic trick, no distraction he could manufacture using META. Without shifting his gaze, he tried to be aware of what was around him. He saw one possibility—on the front burner of the stove, the pot of water that had been on a rolling boil seconds ago, before the power had been cut. With his eyes locked on his attacker, DeBolt searched for the pot's handle in his peripheral vision—which way was it facing? Such a simple thing two minutes ago. Now his life depended on it. He caught a glimpse—the handle was at the pot's four-o'clock position from where he stood. Good. Not perfect, but good. All he needed was an opening.

"Who the hell are you?" DeBolt asked.

The man's lips seem to quiver, as if he might speak, but nothing came. He raised a finger, telling DeBolt to wait. *I'll be with you in a minute.*

Was he mad?

No. He was too determined, too efficient. DeBolt saw what he'd done to Freeman, and the man in the living room. He knew why no other team members had responded to the melee. This assassin had single-handedly defeated five of the most lethal soldiers on earth. DeBolt stood waiting, willing the man to come just a bit closer. Then the most incredible thing happened.

In the heat of battle, amid the killing and the blood, DeBolt had ignored the screen in his head. Now, for no apparent reason, it flickered to life with three words that stunned him to the core. He looked at the monster five steps away, then again at the message.

The man seemed to understand. He knew. DeBolt's obvious bewilderment made his victory complete. And maybe it was.

Then out of nowhere, an unexpected intervention. Freeman, who'd gone still on the floor, whipped out his arm. It was a feeble blow, striking the killer in the leg and imparting no damage. But it served its purpose. The big man reacted instinctively, arcing his gun low toward the downed Green Beret colonel.

DeBolt didn't hesitate.

He grabbed the pot, took one step toward his adversary, and flung the scalding water. It splattered across the killer's face and he screamed—only it wasn't a scream at all, but rather a massive exhalation of air, surprise and pain venting from his body in a surreal hissing sound. His hand went to his face, and temporarily blinded he let loose a wild shot.

DeBolt was already moving. He swung the cast-iron pot with all his might, a blow that glanced off the killer's shooting arm. This time he grunted in pain, but his movements soon organized, and he shoved DeBolt away with his other arm.

DeBolt stumbled as shots splintered cabinets above his head. He ran for the dining room, turned the corner, and dove straight at the big window with his arms outstretched. He was in midair when more shots came, grouped in pairs, and the window shattered the instant before he struck it. Crystalline shards exploded all around him. He landed in a heap outside, tumbling through dirt. DeBolt scrambled to his feet, pushed through shrubs, and ran for the road.

He passed the Explorer and saw Baumann and Stevens on the ground, blood pooled beneath their lifeless bodies. He looked back and saw the big man vaulting through the window. DeBolt had a fifty-foot head start—not much, but a difficult shot with a handgun against a moving target. He cut randomly left and right, like a halfback juking linebackers, hoping to make himself even harder to track. It seemed to work. No more shots came.

He ventured another look back and saw the man giving chase. His next glance, a hundred yards later, was more satisfying. The gap was increasing. The killer had every advantage but one—speed. DeBolt didn't let up, his stride steady, his lungs heaving. Something splashed into his eye, and he looked down and saw his right arm covered in blood. He kept going, made a few turns, and soon the killer was no longer in sight. His pace slowed, but only slightly, survival instinct driving him forward. He considered whether Colonel Freeman might still be still alive. Doubtful, to be sure, but he had to help if he could. Then DeBolt heard a siren approaching, and he realized the colonel's fate, for better or worse, was out of his hands.

He was a mile clear when his thoughts regained order. Only then did he realize that the message, the one that had set him reeling, was still fixed in his visual field. It was there because nothing had taken its place, but might as well have been branded for eternity. It was an answer to the question he'd spoken to the killer, a query intended as nothing more than a distraction: *Who the hell are you?*

Out of nowhere, a three-word reply had arrived. An answer so startling, so outlandish in *how* it had arrived, that it displaced the world around him. Delivered by META, three words DeBolt could never have imagined:

I AM DELTA.

40

DeBolt had no idea how long he'd been running. *Fifteen minutes? Twenty?* He kept moving in the same general direction, twisting through a labyrinth of neighborhood streets until he reached a dated commercial district. His pace was slowing, his body beginning to protest. Still, he couldn't stop looking over his shoulder.

His left arm was covered in blood, and as adrenaline wore off the pain sank in. His arm, a battered shin, his ribs on one side—all had taken a beating somewhere in the melee. His lungs were straining, heaving, magnifying the ache in his rib cage. DeBolt at least took solace in the fact that he'd been here before, at the limits of physical endurance: in both training and real-world ops, he had pushed himself to the edge countless times. He knew his body and its signals. That being the case, when one leg began cramping, he knew it was time to let up.

He stopped in the shadow of a high wall, slumping against the stone and feeling the cold on his back. He closed his eyes, allowing his mind the same chance to reset. He had to think, had to recover. After a few minutes, with the world coming right, he opened his eyes. DeBolt took one cautious scan all around. He saw no sign of Delta.

Even better, he saw exactly what he needed a hundred yards up the street.

It was a typical convenience store, an older building with broad plate-glass windows across the front, crass advertisements for beer and lottery tickets displayed in every one. Best of all, a sign above the entrance attested that the store was OPEN ALL NIGHT.

DeBolt approached slowly, trying to time his arrival. Through the windows he saw the restroom sign, and he waited outside until the clerk had a line at the register. He wanted a straight shot down an aisle where there were no other customers. DeBolt wasn't going to do anything illegal, but his appearance was bound to draw attention, and he didn't want anyone calling the police.

When he saw three people in line, he made his move, keeping his back to the checkout stand and cradling his injured arm close to his chest as he made his way to the men's room. Once inside, he locked the door and leaned over the washbasin. He paused there, once again allowing shock to run its course.

In the harsh fluorescent light he saw the wound, a deep gash on his left forearm. There was no way around it this time—he was going to need stitches. Was there a 24/7 clinic nearby? A place that wouldn't ask questions? Possibly, if he paid in cash up front and created a plausible excuse. *A broken window,* he thought. When Freeman had returned his burner phone, he'd also given back the wad of cash they'd confiscated—done it without so much as a questioning look. DeBolt decided the colonel and his team were probably accustomed to working with rolls of cash. Or *had* been. Five experienced operators, all dispatched by Delta. DeBolt pushed that thought away, discomforting as it was. He tried to be glad for his foresight—since leaving the Calais Lodge he'd made a point of keeping cash in his pockets.

The lessons I'm learning.

He cleaned the wound at the sink using water and paper towels. When he was done, he looked into a blood-soaked trash bin and fleetingly wondered how much of it was Shannon Lund's. He scrubbed his shirtsleeve until it was no longer red, but simply wet, and finally took stock: a few other cuts and abrasions, but nothing worrisome. He tested his injured arm, flexing and grimacing, but knowing it would heal.

DeBolt leaned into the basin and splashed cold water on his face. For the first time he looked in the scratched mirror. He looked haggard and stressed, which wasn't altogether unfamiliar—it was how he usually looked after a long helo mission. The difference, of course, was that helo ops were finite, limited on any given day by fuel supply. The duration of his new assignment was measured in a far more fundamental way—how long could he stay alive? DeBolt recalled friends kidding him about being an adrenaline junkie. Backcountry skiing, rescue missions, big wave surfing. That all seemed laughable now, child's play compared to being hunted.

He dried his face, finger-combed his choppy postoperative haircut as best he could. DeBolt then input a command: *Emergency clinic nearby.*

The answer came quickly, mercifully, and Delta's unsettling three-word response was finally supplanted by something useful. An address and a map came into view. Six blocks east.

He unlocked the bathroom door and walked outside into a deepening night.

DeBolt was right about the walk-in clinic. He gave them a name but didn't have ID. He admitted to a few beers before he'd broken the damned window. He got questions and hard stares, but the spirit of Hippocrates carried the day, and they stitched him up and took his cash, and half an hour later he was back on the street with his arm properly bandaged.

His next stop was an all-night chain pharmacy where he purchased extra gauze and tape, along with a pullover hoodie to cover his filthy shirt. That done, he looked presentable, and he diverted to the Starbucks next door because he wanted to think and get out of the cold. And because a shot of caffeine never hurt. He found himself wondering loosely how that might interact with META. Would a double shot of espresso send his mind into hyperdrive?

He settled at a table with a simple cup of hot coffee. It felt warm between his hands, and the aroma was soothing. DeBolt tried to design a plan, tried to think forward. He always ended up in the same cul-de-sac. The META Project. There was a peculiar comfort in knowing he was not alone: Delta too had survived the surgery. If the kitchen hadn't been so dark, DeBolt knew he would have seen the telltale scars on the man's bald head. A vicious killer, no doubt with a military background, who had the same abilities he possessed.

Were there others? he wondered. Alpha and Charlie? Zulu, for God's sake? Was there an army of men like Delta roaming the world? DeBolt saw countless divergences between Delta and himself. He was trained to rescue,

Delta to kill. There was but one overriding commonality: META. A project whose creators were seemingly being eliminated en masse, the only residue being its product—at least two highly altered individuals.

He considered the manner in which Delta had communicated with him, some direct, inter-META link that DeBolt knew nothing about. He might be able to figure it out, but did he want to? And what else didn't he know? Did his requests for information compromise his position? Could he be tracked like a cell phone, his position triangulated? He looked around the coffeehouse, then out into the darkness beyond. How much more did Delta know? Where was he now? The uncertainty was demoralizing, dark, and confining. Like a box closing in from all sides.

There was only one place to get answers. If any of META's designers remained alive, DeBolt had to find them. He tried to consolidate his thoughts into one desperate request. After considerable deliberation, he settled on: *Need information on META. Are there any surviving creators?*

He waited for a reply.

Nothing came.

The first threads of despair began to envelop him. DeBolt was accustomed to physical challenges. He knew how to recover a lost line in the sea. How to stay warm in subzero temperatures. How to bring back a human heartbeat. But this—the interminable waiting, relying on the whims of some unseen computer before taking action. It was counter to everything he had ever done. Everything he had ever been. He needed META more than ever, and he hated it for that reason.

He finished his coffee, and still nothing came. DeBolt went back to the counter for a refill, this time adding a pastry. He should have been hungry, yet his appetite was nonexistent, quelled by the trauma and fatigue of the last days. He was wiping a blob of sugar from his lip when, quite literally out of thin air, an answer struck into view:

META CHIEF PROGRAMMER, DR. ATIF PATEL
CURRENT LOCATION: VIENNA, AUSTRIA

41

Lund was on an airplane, but she wasn't heading west. She'd bought a ticket on the last southbound shuttle to Washington, D.C., and first thing tomorrow morning she would visit the Coast Guard's national headquarters, the St. Elizabeths campus on the southeast side of town.

As she sat in a middle seat deep in coach, Lund finished off a much-needed beer and mentally mapped out how she could best help DeBolt. There seemed only one good lead—the suspect Jim Kalata had uncovered while investigating William Simmons' climbing accident. Douglas Wilson of Missoula, Montana. Was he one of the men who'd abducted her and DeBolt that morning? Possibly. Kalata thought Wilson might have traveled from Vienna to Alaska, intent on killing a man who'd been asking too many questions about DeBolt. Lund thought her partner might have that much right.

But she needed more. Fortunately, there was no better place to get it than Coast Guard headquarters. The Coast Guard was attached to the Department of Homeland Security, the best source of information in the world when it came to suspicious characters and air travel. Yet it wouldn't be easy. Lund was not traveling on official orders, nor had she opened any investigation relating to Trey DeBolt. She figured she could handle all that with a few phone calls, and perhaps some half-truths. But she would have to tread carefully. Only hours ago she'd been abducted by a shadowed entity of the United States military, then held in a government building. The very fact that they'd released her only reinforced the legal ambiguities that seemed to swirl around the META Project.

A flight attendant picked up her empty can. "Can I get you another?"

Lund almost said yes, but shook her head. "I could use a cigarette when we land though. Do you know if there's a smoking lounge in the airport?"

"Sorry, I'm not sure about Reagan National. Outside on the curb is usually best."

Lund had the feeling the woman would just as soon have told her to light up in the traffic lane, but she smiled her flight attendant's smile all the same and walked off. As she did so, Lund's gaze was caught by the screen of her seatmate's iPad. The airplane apparently had Wi-Fi, and CNN was running on his screen. Lund saw a nighttime backdrop of rolling blue and red lights, and a headline crawled across the bottom: SHOOTING IN WATERTOWN, MA. FIVE FATALITIES CONFRIMED.

"Getting as bad as D.C.," said the iPad's owner, who'd clearly caught her looking. He appeared to be a businessman, well dressed, although Lund had watched him put his jacket in the overhead bin, and his tie was now tugged loose. The man's tone was friendly, if a bit weary. Weighed down by either a long day at work or more senseless big-city violence—she couldn't say which.

"Yeah, it's a shame," she managed. "Tell me, I'm not familiar with Massachusetts—is Watertown near Boston?"

"Yeah, I've been there once or twice—maybe twenty minutes from downtown."

Twenty minutes, she thought. Roughly the length of the car ride she'd taken today. She looked again at the news feed, and saw a man and a woman in matching dark jackets that were emblazoned with big yellow letters: FBI.

Lund had a very bad feeling. Right then, she decided to skip the cigarette when she arrived and go straight to headquarters.

DeBolt found the Buick right where he'd left it, in a parking garage near Logan airport. He drove south, checking the mirror continuously, and took off-ramps to try to distinguish if anyone was following him. It was probably pointless—he was a complete amateur. Delta, on the other hand, was not. *Is this how it's going to be?* he wondered. *Running scared for the rest of my life?* His rhetorical thought actually found an answer—a resounding no. Either Delta would find him, or DeBolt would somehow bring his association with the META to an end. And the only way to do that: reach the last man alive who could explain it.

Dr. Atif Patel.

The name meant nothing to him. He repeated it aloud, hoping for some association. DeBolt drew a blank. He went to his connection to find more, but there was little available. He learned that Patel was not much older than he was. A graduate of Caltech, he was now a professor at Cal Berkeley and attached to a number of research projects there, all relating to computer software and systems architecture. He was a geek's geek, which DeBolt found encouraging—perhaps Patel was the Oz behind the machine that was META.

Yet there were also worrying voids in his search on Patel. No tax records, which he'd been able to gather on others, nor any address of record or phone number. He found no social media accounts or bank records. He couldn't even find an image of the man—at least not the *right* Atif Patel—which in this digital age seemed remarkable. It was as if his background had been sanitized, scrubbed from the information world. As if he'd gone into electronic hiding. It made sense in a way—if Patel was indeed an architect of META, might he not exclude himself from its otherwise universal grasp? Then a disturbing corollary came to mind: Might Patel have gone into hiding in order to escape the likes of Delta?

DeBolt did uncover one glaring inconsistency. If information on Patel was limited, one fact proved widely available, even advertised—he was attending an academic gathering in Vienna this week, and scheduled to give two presentations, the second in two days' time. After that DeBolt could find no indication of where Patel would be. Would he return to California? Attend another conference? Tour Europe? There was no way to tell, and this gave DeBolt a deadline—he had two days in which to reach Vienna.

The more DeBolt thought about it, the more he realized how challenging that might be. His only option was to take a commercial flight, but he had no identification. He also knew that paying cash for a one-way ticket was a surefire way to get the attention of authorities. Still, there had to be a way. He immediately discarded Boston's Logan airport as an option. The threat there would be extreme. Delta too close. So he continued driving south, knowing in a loose way where I-95 would take him.

He drove deep into the night. The road became a blur, and the stream of oncoming headlights thinned into the early morning hours. He turned on the Buick's radio, found an alternative rock channel, and cranked up the volume. He opened his window to be stunned by the inrushing air, New England autumn at seventy miles an hour.

DeBolt could barely keep his eyes open when he finally took an exit in New London, Connecticut. Less than a mile after turning off the interstate, he found himself at gates with a familiar emblem: the United States Coast Guard Academy. He'd never attended the school, but worked with many officers who had, men and women who seemed universally happy to be *from* the institution. Nearing two o'clock in the morning, he knew he would never get past security at the gate—probably not even if he still had his old identity card. So DeBolt navigated across the street instead, and pulled into a spot beside a Dumpster in the half-full parking lot of something called Connecticut College.

He locked the doors and turned off the engine, knowing the cold would seep in quickly. DeBolt did his best to ignore the screen in his head and let his mind roam. He thought about Joan Chandler. He thought about Shannon Lund, and hoped she was on her way back to Alaska. He thought about his crew from the helo crash, and wished he could remember something about the accident. Had he made a mistake that night, something that contributed to the death of his friends? Had those they'd been trying to rescue been lost as well?

And what if he *could* remember what happened on that doomed night? Would it replace the other mission so long entrenched in his memory? A vision came to DeBolt—not on META's tiny screen, but on the more intimate and familiar canvas of his memory. He recalled what had become the signature event of his duty in Alaska. The mission he remembered above all others. Every AST had a story like it—the one rescue, for better or worse, that you could never shake. If it ended well, it was the tale you'd someday tell your grandchildren. If not, it was the one you took to your grave.

His had involved three survivors, a couple and their teenage daughter, who'd been set adrift when their sailboat pitchpoled—careening down the backside of a five-story wave on a following sea, the boat's nose had dug into the trough, instigating a violent cartwheel. In a minor miracle, all three made it to a life raft, and from there they'd sent an SOS. An EPIRB signal gave an accurate position, but by the time the helo arrived all three were back in the water, the raft drifting away on a howling wind.

The storm that night had certainly been given a name, but DeBolt could never remember it. He only remembered dropping into the cold sea and finding three severely hypothermic individuals. One by one, he began lifting them to the safety of the helo. He remembered having to make the decision to leave the young girl in the water longest, despite the passionate protests of her parents. DeBolt had done it that way because in his opinion the parents were in worse shape—it was the only chance to save all three. His call. So at the end he was with the girl in waves that looked like buildings, in a wind that was gale force, and he had held on to her while they'd waited for the final lift. He held her close to be ready for the basket, but also to give her warmth. And God how she had held him back. His own strength was ebbing at that point, sapped by thirty frantic minutes in the Bering Sea.

And then—an ethereal moment like nothing DeBolt had ever experienced.

Tossed by ferocious winds, the helo had to abort its approach and reposition. In those desperate, vital minutes, as DeBolt himself became weaker and weaker, the tiny young girl whose body was pressed against his actually became stronger. She'd clung to him like a barnacle, her thin limbs and frozen fingers viselike in their grip. She had been in the water three times as long as he had, and didn't have the luxury of a dry suit. None of that mattered to her. Never had DeBolt witnessed a power like that one young girl's desperation to live. Even more surprising was what it instilled in him—an absolute resolve to make it happen.

Together, on that dark night over a year ago, they had both reached safety.

These were DeBolt's fading thoughts as he fell fast asleep in the backseat of the Buick.

The will to live.

Absolute resolve.

42

He had no identity documents. No way to procure real ones. No clue how to acquire something counterfeit. He had plenty of cash, but no credit card. In his favor: DeBolt had all the information in the world.

The business of traveling across an ocean—so ordinary this day and age—was greatly complicated by his circumstances. Most problematic of all: he was squarely in the sights of a killer, a man with the same cyber capabilities he possessed. *No,* he corrected, *Delta is better than I am, because he knows how to use it.*

How to get to Vienna? It was essentially an operational problem, yet unlike anything he'd encountered on a ship or a helo. DeBolt tried to be methodical, beginning before he even arrived at the airport. At a big box store he purchased an inexpensive leather attaché, a jacket that might have been business casual, and a notepad and pen to fill the attaché. He added an electric razor with a grooming attachment, and two pairs of off-the-shelf reading glasses, one with thick frames and the other thin, both with minimal refractive correction—his vision was just fine.

Arriving at New York's JKF airport he left the Buick in long-term parking, the doors unlocked and the keys under the front seat. DeBolt didn't know why he did it that way, but perhaps there was an intrinsic message . . . *No going back.*

At Terminal 4, the primary international gateway, he scouted the departure level for thirty minutes while his plan evolved. It was an ever-changing thing, with portions that remained a blank—like a half-finished sculpture in the hands of an amateur. He ignored the flight information boards, save for one quick study to verify that his options were bundled in a narrow time frame: flights to Europe from the East Coast departed almost exclusively in the late afternoon and early evening. While Vienna was his destination, he didn't particularly care how he got there, and he presumed that any identity that could get him across the Atlantic would continue to work throughout the European Union.

Yet DeBolt did have one concern. His advantage to this point, indeed the only reason he was alive, was his new capacity to acquire information. Would that connection work in Europe? In Austria? On his lone visit to Europe, a late-teen summer pilgrimage nine years ago with two friends from high school, he remembered that his mobile phone had been useless. Would his new connection be any better? Would he still be able to access limitless, sensitive information from whatever servers he was leveraging?

With hours remaining to refine his plan, DeBolt settled into a café in the departures lobby, and set up watch at a table overlooking the check-in lines. His central idea was a simple one—he would identify someone who bore a reasonable resemblance to him, steal his passport and travel documents, then create a reason for his victim to ignore his travel plans. The scheme would require considerable patience, no small demand given his situation. Necessarily, he needed a mark who would either not recognize the deception, or if he did, not be willing to report it. It would be counterproductive for DeBolt to reach Europe only to have the authorities there waiting for him. He allowed that it might take more than one day to find a viable situation, which was acceptable since Patel was not due to appear at the conference until the day after tomorrow.

To make it all work, he began with the server in in his head.

For thirty minutes he researched passport security measures, and got his best information from a classified FBI report—how META gained access to that he had no idea—which convinced him that he should concentrate on citizens of the United States. The gold standard for passports involved chip technology that recorded biometric data on the holder—digitized facial photos and fingerprints were the most common. European Union countries used varied criteria, but on balance their designs were considerably more stringent than those of the U.S. In particular, the United States did not yet encode fingerprint information within passports—something DeBolt certainly could not defeat—and while a computerized system of facial recognition was on the drawing board, it had so far not been fielded. His overall take—while the groundwork for greater security was being laid in the United States, the reality was much as it had been before 9/11: one photograph against the discerning eye of an immigration official.

The biggest hurdle in his plan was obvious—he had to find someone whose appearance very closely matched his own. Facial similarity aside, the age had to be close, plus or minus five years he decided. Height and weight, while listed on applications, were not included on the actual passport, nor was hair or eye color—a benefit to DeBolt, whose eyes were a sharp blue.

By two o'clock he'd made trial runs on three individuals, all of whom, given the time of day, were predictably bound for domestic destinations. He had particular trouble identifying one young man, and realized that META's facial-recognition technology was not infallible—the man was wearing eyeglasses, had a week's growth of beard, and was wearing a Yankees baseball cap. It took six uploaded images for DeBolt to get a result. But once he did, information began to flow, and he soon had a better profile on the man than did any customs official in the building.

At that point, batting practice was over. With two hours remaining before the first bank of transatlantic flights was to depart, DeBolt began his search in earnest.

The first serious candidate appeared fifteen minutes later. On first glance DeBolt thought the man might be younger, and when he stopped and waited for something or someone near a plastic plant, DeBolt got a good look at his face. Within five minutes he knew all he needed to know: Gregory White was a grad student at Columbia working on a master's in theology, and originally from Allentown, Pennsylvania. He bore a decent resemblance to DeBolt, and at six foot two—this from his Pennsylvania driver's license—was an inch taller and visibly thinner. His hair was similar in color and length, albeit a more stylish cut than DeBolt's postoperative chop. Altogether, a strong candidate save for one problem—he was ticketed on the El Al nonstop to Tel Aviv. Probably on his way to do research in the Holy Land.

DeBolt kept looking, and it was an hour before he made a second inquiry. Edward Jernigan, a fastener salesman from Dubuque, was close on height and build, his hair a bit darker. The problem was the face—the one characteristic that could not be overcome. It was close, but try as he might, DeBolt wasn't comfortable with the match.

Another hour passed without a contestant in his cyber lineup, and doubts about his scheme were beginning to creep in when a third option appeared. The facial features were encouraging, reasonably close to his own, but before even trying to capture an image for a profile, DeBolt waited to assess an obvious complication—the man was not alone.

She stood at his side, big blond hair and puffy lips. Her impossible curves seemed painted in white cotton. Both were smiling, all touches and laughs, like kids at the junior prom. She in Jimmy Choos, he in L.L.Bean. From fifty feet away DeBolt saw no wedding band on his left hand as it brushed across the woman's bottom. Nor did she wear one. He imagined a host of possibilities, and decided to narrow things down by starting with the woman. He got a good look at her, sent a request, and was rewarded thirty seconds later with her name. Not long after, he got her NYPD mug shot. For sixty rapid-fire seconds DeBolt sent one request after another and had no trouble getting results. He narrowed them to the most pertinent:

MARTA NATALYA KAMINSKI
ALIAS SUMMER DEAN
BORN 5-25-89
THREE ARRESTS PROSTITUTION/CLASS B MISDE-
MEANOR
CURRENT EMPLOYER: ELEGANT ESCORTS, NEW
YORK, NY

Having settled that half of the equation, DeBolt moved on. The pair were nuzzling now, and intermittently looking at photographs on her mobile phone. He elected not to peep into that slideshow, thinking for the first time in days, *Too much information.*

DeBolt concentrated on the man, and assembled the deepest profile of anyone he had so far investigated. Ronald Anderson was thirty years old, a partner in a small Chicago investment house. He'd been married for five years, and had two young children at home, suggesting a busy and certainly fatigued wife. He was on his way to Amsterdam for a business meeting, the day after tomorrow, to facilitate the buyout of a small software company—information DeBolt acquired by viewing email on Anderson's phone. He was booked home on a return flight two days after the meeting. Based on what he'd seen so far, DeBolt could only imagine how Ronald Anderson might amuse himself for the balance of four days in certain districts of Amsterdam. The situation was a virtual cliché, the kind of minor drama that played out every day in every city. For DeBolt, however, one detail was most compelling: Anderson was booked on today's 5:45 P.M. KLM flight to Amsterdam.

He watched the man jab a thumb over his shoulder, in the direction of the TSA security area. His flight was scheduled to depart in fifty minutes. DeBolt's interest peaked when the man pulled a passport and what looked like an airline boarding pass from a pocket of the roller bag he'd been dragging. He slid one inside the other, and tucked them into the breast pocket of his casual jacket—dark in color, but otherwise similar to the one DeBolt was wearing.

A plan began to take shape, and DeBolt sent two new commands: *Mobile phone numbers for Ronald Anderson, Marta Kaminski.*

As he waited for a response, it occurred to him that there were certainly dozens, if not hundreds, of people with the same names—just as any Google search would produce multiple Trey DeBolts. Yet moments ago he'd been gathering information on these specific individuals, and he suspected it would carry forward—the software or technician doing the heavy lifting, whoever and wherever they were, would make the association. Slowly, painstakingly, he was learning how META worked.

Two phone numbers arrived. He touched the burner phone inside his pocket, calculating how to create the geometry he wanted. More critically, how to do it without raising complications on the other side of the Atlantic. DeBolt needed Ronald Anderson's passport. He needed him to miss his flight, and not realize his passport had been stolen. *Or . . .*

DeBolt left his phone in his pocket and checked the terminal clock. He input a third command tentatively, not sure if it was even possible: *Capture 555-321-5728 at 5:02 Eastern Standard Time.*

As he waited, DeBolt saw the provisional lovers lock in a long kiss. A parting kiss. *Come on . . .*

Then:

555-321-5728 FOUND
DATA AND MOBILE DISCONNECT SET 5:02 EST
PROXY ENABLED

Marta Kaminski turned away and walked toward the exit, her extraordinarily round behind the center of Ronald Anderson's world. She did so unaware that in precisely two minutes her phone would be hijacked.

43

Lund had spent the entire day, and most of the previous night, at the St. Elizabeths campus, headquarters of the United States Coast Guard. Until now she'd known the place as no more than an address for emails and a hub for conference calls. Like most Coast Guardsmen, she'd never actually set foot inside. She was glad the complex was situated where it was, physically removed from the Pentagon and the greater D.C. establishment. Until she learned what she and DeBolt were up against, or more precisely *who*, she was determined to tread carefully.

Unfortunately, as was often the case, treading carefully produced nothing. Lund had one close friend in the building, Lieutenant Commander Sarah Wells, whom she'd worked with in San Diego. Wells had made the move to headquarters six months ago, and was happy to help Lund when she'd shown up this morning. That was nine hours ago, and Wells had been sidestepping meetings all day to help Lund mine information.

"I'm sorry, Shannon," Wells said, looking over the latest search results on her desktop monitor, "but I'm just not seeing anything on this META Project. If it exists, it's got to be black, something really deep. Does that make sense?"

"Yeah," Lund replied, "actually it might. What about my suspect, the guy who flew into Kodiak?"

"Douglas Wilson of Missoula, Montana. I tried to pull up the airline manifests for that day, like Petty Officer Kalata did. Problem is, the records seem to have fallen out of the system. I even double-checked with Homeland Security. Nobody can find them."

"But they *were* there—Jim found them. And he tracked down that picture I gave you this morning."

"I know. I've never seen data disappear like that—but for whatever reason, it's gone. I uploaded the photo and searched for a match, but it came up blank. Either the resolution wasn't good enough, or there simply wasn't a match on file. Wish I could be more help. Did you get anything more on this case up in Boston?"

While Wells had attacked the issues of META and Douglas Wilson, an increasingly distressed Lund had followed up on the murders.

"I know five men were killed in a house in Watertown. The initial reports filed by the investigators don't ask for help in identifying victims, which tells me they know who they are. Unfortunately, the names haven't been released, not even through law enforcement channels."

"Is there a particular name you're looking for?"

Actually one I'm hoping isn't on the list, thought Lund. She said, "Well . . . maybe this Douglas Wilson guy." She shuffled through a report she'd printed out. "I'd like your opinion on something, Sarah. The primary point of contact here is an Army CID special agent with an address in Boston."

"Army? I thought the FBI was running it."

"So did I. Last night I saw FBI-jacketed investigators on the news. Could the Army have taken this over—booted the feds off the case?"

"Not an easy thing to do, but I guess it's possible. Let see if Army CID has put anything out." Wells banged away at her computer. The results didn't take long. "Voilà! Not much else, but they did put out a list of the victims."

Lund inhaled sharply as Wells rotated the monitor to give her a better look. One by one she read off five names and ranks. Two Army, two Navy, one Air Force. None named Trey DeBolt.

"You all right?" Wells asked. "You look, like, a little pale."

"Yeah . . . I'm good. I had a long night."

Wells got up. "Well, sorry, but I've got to get to a staff meeting. If you're still around in the morning we can have another go at this. Maybe the Army will have put out a progress report by then."

"Yeah, okay. And thanks for your help, Sarah, I really appreciate it."

The two shook hands in the hall outside Wells' office. Lund walked toward the exit wondering where to go from here. There was no doubt in her mind that the house in Boston was the one where she'd been held yesterday.

Learning that Trey was not among the victims was an incredible relief, and the idea that he could have been responsible for the carnage didn't warrant consideration. So what had happened then? Had a different group of commandos arrived? Was a competing service or another country involved? Could Trey have fallen into someone else's hands? Whatever the case, she knew it had to do with META.

Lund had just reached the main entrance when her phone trilled. She looked at the screen hoping to see the number she'd seen last night—Trey's burner phone. It was different. But maybe the next best thing.

"Hi, Jim. Did you find—"

"*You bitch! You cheating, lying—*"

Lund jerked the phone away from her ear, both the words and volume ringing in her head. She said to the distant microphone, "Who . . . who is this?"

She heard a rattle over the line, like the phone was getting jostled, followed by a hushed conversation. A new voice came on the line, one she recognized immediately. "Shannon . . . it's Frank Detorie. Look, I'm sorry about that—"

"Who was that?" Lund cut in. "And why is she calling me on Jim's phone?"

A hesitation. "It was his wife, Shannon. We're at the morgue, and she got hold of Jim's phone and—"

"Morgue? Why are you at the morgue?"

An even longer pause, then in a muted tone, "I brought her here to identify Jim's body."

Lund felt as though she'd taken a punch, the air expelling from her chest. "What happened?"

"I wish I didn't have to tell you this way. His wife found his damned phone among his possessions, and she saw a string of texts that—"

"Texts? Frank, what the *hell* happened?"

"Hang on." She heard more hushed conversation. Soon it turned heated, and at the end she caught, ". . . you need to wait outside!" Detorie came back on the line. "Jim was killed this morning, Shannon."

Lund leaned into the portico's concrete-block wall.

"I can only say enough to make you understand the situation I'm facing. Jim Kalata was found in your apartment."

"*My* apartment?"

"Actually, he was in your bed, naked. His neck was broken, and there was a very clean gunshot wound to his forehead."

Lund felt suddenly cold, as though the tendrils of something distant and unnatural were wrapping around her. She couldn't move, couldn't speak.

Detorie covered her silence with, "Your service firearm was found on the floor next to the bed. We're still securing the scene, so there's been no time for ballistics or anything like that, but one round appears to have been fired from your gun."

"Frank," she managed, "if you're implying—"

"No, Shannon. I know you didn't do this. You were in D.C. last night when this happened. Half the damned night shift at Coast Guard headquarters can put you there."

"So you've already checked on that."

"Just like you would have done. But I've got to tell you, your commander in Seattle, Special Agent in Charge Wheeley, is more than a little upset. He had no idea you were on leave or TDY, or whatever the hell it is you're doing."

"Texts," she said, starting to regain function.

"What?"

"Texts. You said his phone had a string of texts, something that upset his wife."

"I can't go into that," said Detorie.

"You don't have to. She called me a cheating bitch. Clear enough. But I'm telling you right now that there was nothing between Jim Kalata and me."

"If that's what you say, I believe it. But I need you to tell me these things officially and on the record. I need you to get back here right away and clear this up. Your commander sent out the word—I'm surprised CGIS hasn't already shown up to escort you to the airport. Wheeley is on his way up from Seattle as we speak to oversee things—Kodiak CGIS is pretty much staffed at zero right now. Come back and we'll straighten everything out. This happened off station, so it's my turf. You know I'll do right by you."

"Yeah . . . I know, Frank. Thanks. I'll head to the airport right now."

Lund ended the call, but she didn't put her phone away. She gripped it gingerly, as if it held some kind of plague, and navigated to her text messages. Sure enough, they were there. Interspersed among the last three months of work-related texts she'd exchanged with Kalata, a handful of flirtatious messages. Wholly fabricated messages she had never sent. Never seen before.

Lund felt a shiver, and she flicked down to find her last true contact with Kalata—the photograph he'd sent her yesterday, a grainy picture of a hulking man. She had uploaded the picture for Wells only hours ago. She moved her finger left and right on the screen, back and forth. For the third time in a matter of minutes, Lund felt the web of META wrapping around her.

The photograph was no longer on her phone.

It had somehow been deleted.

Ronald Anderson watched Summer walk all the way out to the curb, and when she got into a cab he smiled inwardly. Perhaps on his way home he could reschedule his flight, include another layover in New York. He was on the company dime, after all. She'd been fun, enthusiastic. Then again, after four days in Amsterdam he might need a breather. He was reaching for his roller bag when his phone chimed a text.

He looked down and saw a message from Summer: I miss you already.

Anderson looked out at the cab she'd gotten into. It was stuck in traffic. He pecked out a response: Miss you too.

Summer: Want one last look?

He smiled and typed: Sure.

Anderson watched the cab.

Summer: I have to be a little discreet. Come closer.

He walked up to the big plate-glass window.

Summer: Take off your jacket. I want to see more of you.

Anderson smiled broadly. She really was playful. He shrugged off his jacket and hung it on the handle of his roller bag.

Summer: Come closer, outside. This is only for you.

His eyes were padlocked on the cab's darkened rear window, his breath quickening. He liked the idea of public places. Which view would it be? As he passed through the glass doors, he saw perhaps a flash of movement in the backseat. Anderson was five steps away when the cab pulled into the river of traffic and merged away at speed.

"Hey!" he shouted, his hands palm-up in a *what gives* gesture.

He watched for a few seconds longer, but soon the cab was lost in a sea of yellow. He snorted once, headed back inside, and retrieved his roller bag. Anderson was halfway to the security checkpoint when he realized his jacket was missing.

He looked back where his bag had been, but didn't see it on the floor. He'd only left it unattended for thirty seconds, and it had never been out of his sight—although his attention *had* been diverted. He looked around for anyone suspicious, anybody moving faster than they should have been, but it was an airport and everyone was in a hurry. In his pocket he felt a vibration: another text. He pulled out his phone and saw a message in the same thread.

Summer: This passport photo doesn't do you justice.

Anderson stiffened. He thumbed out a reply, misspelling nearly every word once: I need that back NOW!!!

Her maddening reply: Sorry. Let's make it tomorrow. It'll cost you $10,000. Details in the morning.

Anderson spun a circle on a square of polished tile, his face going crimson. He'd watched her get into the cab. *She must have had help,* he thought. He looked around and saw people moving in every direction, a lotto tumbler of humanity. He cursed aloud. *How did I get into this freakin' mess?*

Anderson was contemplating his options when Summer preempted them with: Considering calling the cops? Not a good idea for a john in NYC. BTW, your wife's phone number is 555-255-6242. And I took one pic you never saw.

Anderson's anger went to panic. How had she found out Charlotte's number? She must have accessed his phone in the room. He didn't even want to think about the picture. Another text from Summer. *Christ . . . Summer.* He didn't even know her real name.

He read: Her father's number is even easier to get—it's on half the bus benches in Chicago. Goldstein and Mahr, divorce and family practice. Ten grand is a bargain against what that phone call would cost you.

He found a bench and sat down, tried to think logically. Maybe he could bargain with her, get the passport back now, and write a check for five grand. If that didn't work, he'd try his damnedest for intimidation. No *way* was he going to get scammed. He knew where she worked. He could threaten to stalk her and make her life miserable. He called Summer's number and waited, steel ready in his voice. After two rings an automated voice picked up. *"The number you have reached is no longer in service."*

Anderson slapped his palm on the back of the bench. An elderly woman on the next bench over looked at him suspiciously. He checked the time: 5:17. He wasn't going to make his flight. He decided he could punch out an email to his office later, say the airline had screwed up, and tell them to re-book him on tomorrow's flight. His meeting was still two days out. It would be a short night tomorrow, but he could make it work. He began to think more positively. He had a day to get his passport back, one way or another. Everything would be fine. He just had to get it back.

Anderson went to his phone's web browser and looked up the number for Elegant Escorts. *I can handle this . . .*

44

While Ronald Anderson was having trouble contacting Elegant Escorts, a man similar in appearance took his assigned seat on KLM Flight 23. Everything so far had worked according to plan. Security had been a breeze. A weary TSA agent, no doubt at the end of his shift, had taken one look at the passport followed by a vacant glance at DeBolt's face. The KLM boarding agent showed even less interest. And here he was.

The big jet began backing away from the gate, and a flight attendant made an announcement about placing electronic devices in airplane mode. This caused DeBolt to wonder. His burner phone was not an issue—he'd already discarded it in a restroom trash bin. But what about the link in his head? Was there a way to suspend it? None that he knew of. He supposed he could ignore the ever-present screen and make no new requests. In truth, he liked the idea of it—eight hours off the grid after the madness of recent days.

Anderson had booked a seat in business class, a luxury DeBolt had never before experienced. The wide leather berth seemed to hold him with a custom fit, and he'd already been offered a drink, but politely declined, smiling inwardly at the thought. Drinking and driving was dangerous enough—but to combine drunkenness with META? On the lighter side, he supposed it would open up a whole new world of bar tricks. Hopefully he'd survive long enough to come up with a few.

The smell of brewing coffee filled the air, and he hoped that would be the next thing put on offer. The flight would be a long one, sleep a necessity, but before he drifted off, DeBolt wanted to set a plan for his arrival in Amsterdam. He'd so far sensed no complications from his theft of Ronald Anderson's identity. *Nine hours—that's all I need.* Since the last flurry of text exchanges through Marta Kaminski's hijacked phone number—voice was of course out of the question—the adulterous investment banker had gone silent. He was likely feeling used and powerless. A nice turn of justice, in DeBolt's view.

The jet began its takeoff roll, and soon the city fell away, a tapestry of glass and concrete designed by ten thousand architects, built by a million hands. Vast as it was, DeBolt thought the city seemed inconsequential against the cyber realm in which he now lived—a boundless universe that had barely existed when he was born. Quite accidentally, he found himself at the pinnacle of a shadowed new world: Trey DeBolt, end user of all that was. He considered Dr. Atif Patel. Was he truly one of META's creators? Could he explain to DeBolt what had been done to him? Did the man realize he was the last survivor of a government project gone mad?

"Coffee, Mr. Anderson?"

DeBolt looked up and saw a flight attendant: tall, blond, and certainly Dutch, eye-catching in a sharply pressed uniform. "Yes, please." As she set a cup on his table—china, not Styrofoam—he said, "Will Wi-Fi be available on the flight?"

"Normally, yes," she said, "but unfortunately this particular airplane is having a technical issue. I'm afraid you will have to disconnect for a few hours."

He grinned widely. "Not such a bad thing. I almost wish I could make it permanent." She smiled understandingly, then put cream in his coffee and was gone.

The city slipped away and a dark ocean took its place. The intimately familiar seascape below put DeBolt further at ease. By some strange pull, he tried for a connection, and managed one for a time. He used it to plot the position of Shannon Lund's cell phone—and presumably Lund herself. She was somewhere south of Washington, D.C., which implied she wasn't on her way back to Kodiak after all. He guessed she was continuing her search on META in some faceless government office. Maybe she'd even found something useful. His thoughts then turned tangential, to the safe house in Boston that wasn't safe at all, and he remembered Lund reaching up and kissing him. Remembered being glad that she had.

He conjured up her cell phone number on the monitor in his head. De-
Bolt composed a simple text message: *All is well. Stay safe, Shannon. Trey.*
He launched it into cyberspace, and a response came immediately.

INTERMITTENT SIGNAL

He tried to send it once more. DeBolt couldn't tell if it went through.

"I'm standing at the United Airlines counter right now," said Lund. She was
talking to her commander, Special Agent Jonathan Wheeley.

"How long will it take you to get here?" he asked.

"It looks like tomorrow afternoon. I checked Reagan National, but that
would have taken longer. Dulles has the best options, but it takes at least
three flights."

"All right. And would you like to explain why you're in D.C. right now?"

Lund shut her eyes reflexively. She didn't want to lie, but the truth was
hardly an option. That would only put Trey further at risk—either that or
get her an appointment with a Coast Guard–appointed psychiatrist. "It's a
long story," she said.

Wheeley remained silent.

"Boss, look . . . you've always been straight with me, and I appreciate
that. But there are a lot of complications here."

"Do any of them involve what happened to Jim?"

"Yes . . . but not directly . . . I mean, it's just too hard to explain."

"All right, Shannon. But I'll tell you one thing right now—if you didn't
have a rock-solid alibi, you would not be flying home commercial and unes-
corted."

For the first time she heard coldness in Wheeley's voice, a tone that said
he wasn't going to venture out on any long limbs to save her career. With a
strange feeling of liberation, Lund realized she didn't care. "I understand.
I'll be in touch as soon as I land in Kodiak."

"You do that."

A click, and she was free.

Lund slid her phone in the back pocket of her pants, and then looked at the ticketing line. It was relatively short, and the flight she needed didn't leave for three hours. She went outside to the departures curb, lit up a cigarette, and took a long draw. It was wonderful. Traffic swirled all around, engines humming and horns blaring. Her phone vibrated in her pocket. Lund pulled it out expecting a follow-up from Jon Wheeley. She saw instead a text message: All is well. Stay safe, Shannon. On way to Vienna to track down Dr. Atif Patel regarding META. Trey.

Her heart seemed to stutter, and she stood stock-still. Relief, joy, fear—all of it hit at the same time. Trey *had* gotten clear of the bloodshed in Boston. He was not only alive, but free. Dr. Atif Patel? She had no idea who he was, or what connection he had to META. She only knew that Trey was going to Vienna to seek him out.

Lund nearly responded, but as soon as her thumbs touched the keypad she hesitated. The text had come from a number she'd never seen. She was positive her phone had been tampered with—the photo of Douglas Wilson had vaporized. Was it safe to respond? Or would doing so only highlight Trey's position? Was this new message even from Trey?

More than ever, she understood what he was going through. She was trapped in a cyber corner, not sure how things worked. In this glorious new age of information, Lund found herself in a digital house of mirrors, every bit of information, every revelation descending into the realm of virtual reality. She had seen photos disappear, seen her text threads altered. What was real? What was manufactured?

She took a long look at the message, feeling helpless, increasingly adrift. META seemed everywhere, and now its vortex was pulling her in—as inexorably as it had Trey. Her thumbs came off the screen and she rushed inside. Lund checked the big departures board. Sixty seconds later she was in the United Airlines ticketing line. She stared impatiently at her watch.

45

KLM Flight 23 landed smoothly in Amsterdam at 8:09 the next morning, twin puffs of blue smoke whirling from its main landing gear on touchdown. DeBolt looked through his window, the glass peppered with condensation, and saw a brooding day in the making, steady rain and mist obscuring a milky sky. He'd slept well on the overnight flight, but as the massive jet lumbered toward the terminal, anxiety made its own landing.

Two questions governed his thoughts, and the first was answered immediately. On the screen in his mind he entered and sent the words: *Amsterdam Schiphol METAR.*

The response was almost immediate. It felt like a benediction.

METAR EHAM: 11240755Z 06008 1BR 2OVC 10/08 Q1009

METAR was the international format for aviation weather—as a helicopter crew member, DeBolt knew how to decipher it. Cool, wet, misty, fifty degrees—it was a lousy day in Amsterdam. Far more relevant—his private telecom network seemed operable in Europe. There had been no way to know if META would reach this far, so DeBolt was immensely relieved. He was sure the system had been birthed, at some level, inside the United States Department of Defense. But that gave no guarantee it would work worldwide. Then again, if META truly was some type of military program, wouldn't that be the point? He imagined a unit of men like Delta, all able to access unlimited data from any place in the world. How lethal a force multiplier would that be?

DeBolt's musings were cut short when the airplane reached the terminal. There his second concern rose to the forefront. Would Ronald Anderson's identity get him through Dutch immigration? That question ran headlong to an answer. He was one of the first passengers to disembark, and found no line whatsoever at the customs and immigration queues—another perk of business class—where a stern-faced blond man took his passport.

The irony of that moment was not lost on DeBolt. He had been born in Colorado, yet his parents were both Dutch, as was his surname. Standing at the immigration booth as Ronald Anderson, DeBolt looked at a man who one generation ago would have been his countryman, the same light hair and blue eyes, the same open facial features. There was a fleeting moment of panic that one Dutchman might recognize another, some primal ethnic connection. Then the passport came back through the window and DeBolt heard, "Have a nice stay in Holland, Mr. Anderson."

It was over that quickly. With no luggage, DeBolt walked outside to the curb and ran headlong into the cacophony of cars and busses that ringed every big airport. There he stood and tried to work out his next problem: how best to cover the last five hundred miles to Vienna.

Two hours after DeBolt reached Amsterdam, Lund arrived in Vienna on the nonstop United flight from Dulles. She was arrested immediately.

They were waiting in the gate area, two uniformed policemen and a plainclothes officer with a photograph in his hand.

"Shannon Lund?" the man with the photo asked as she emerged from the jetway amid a single-file crowd.

It was an ominous introduction, and one that left no room for denial. "Yes."

"I am Oberkommissar Dieter Strauss of the Bundespolizei. You must come with us." The man's accent was hard on the consonants. As a law enforcement officer, Lund realized he was not making a request.

"What is this about?" she asked.

"The United States has formally requested your detention. It relates to a criminal matter, but I can say no more here."

Lund wasn't surprised. Not really. Wheeley, or someone higher in the chain, had flagged her passport. Not soon enough to keep her from leaving the United States, but a ten-hour flight had allowed them to play catch-up. She was now a demonstrated flight risk, which wouldn't make her situation back home any easier. Worst of all—it brought her efforts to help Trey to a skidding halt.

She said the only thing that came to mind. "I'd like to talk to someone from the embassy."

The policeman grinned with one side of his mouth. "And someone from the embassy wants very much to talk to you. You will meet them at Bundespolizei headquarters."

"I checked a bag."

"One of my men is retrieving it now. Oh, and I must ask you for your mobile." He held out an empty hand.

Reluctantly, Lund reached into her purse and handed over her Samsung. The inspector seemed to study the device, then found the correct button to turn it off.

"Anything else?" she said with undisguised annoyance—even if she would have handled things precisely as Oberkommissar Strauss had if their places were reversed.

"No," said the policeman.

"Okay, then let's get on with it."

Everyone played their roles with staid civility. There were no cuffs, and they guided Lund to an unmarked government car which, twenty minutes later, delivered them to the side entrance of a building marked simply POLIZEI.

She was escorted through a long hall, rose three floors in an elevator, to be finally deposited in a very secure-looking interrogation room with a cipher lock on the door. Lund was given a water bottle, denied a cigarette, and asked very politely to wait.

As if she had a choice.

46

With the bulk of his journey behind him, DeBolt decided a train was the least-risk option for the remainder. Rail to Vienna would take twelve hours, even on high-speed ICE trains, but now that he was established in the E.U., it seemed the most likely way to travel without further testing the passport of Ronald Anderson.

He exchanged dollars for euros at a station currency kiosk. He had enjoyed the business class transatlantic flight, but with limited cash going forward, DeBolt opted for an economy seat on the train. The first leg to Cologne was relatively short, a two-hour blur on a high-speed route. He spent an hour at the station in Cologne where he exchanged the remainder of his dollars for euros, and took an espresso and a sweet roll at a track-side teashop. He also continued to test META's network.

Since arriving in Europe he'd had no trouble getting a connection using his internal wiring. As far as he knew, the only way tell if things were working was to make a request. He found himself wishing he had a status bar above his screen to display the current signal strength. *If I ever meet the designer,* he thought, *maybe I'll mention it.*

Even with a connection, DeBolt was unsure what META could do on this side of the Atlantic. Were there differences, limitations? Slower response times? He began with the facial-recognition application, and was mildly disappointed by the results—roughly half of his inputs came back with positive IDs, many of these proving to be Americans. He guessed that certain European countries, and probably much of the rest of the world, didn't register driver's license or passport photos in whatever database he was accessing. Or perhaps META was restricted from breaching the servers of particular countries.

He tried for identities on a number of people who he thought might be recent immigrants from the Middle East and Africa—DeBolt knew Europe was awash in refugees, and train stations were ground zero. Not a single one registered. The reason seemed apparent. Without a known image on file for comparison, it didn't matter how good your correlation software was. DeBolt also noted that many responses seemed to take longer, perhaps because his information had to funnel through fiber-optic cables miles under the Atlantic Ocean.

He noticed a security camera near the teashop entrance, and wondered if he might be able to get a feed, much as he'd done at the embezzler's house outside Calais. Camera networks, from what he remembered, were everywhere in Europe, and the idea of accessing them seemed unthinkable. He experimented with a few commands, but nothing seemed to work. As he did, DeBolt watched a constant stream of people come and go through the doorway, and he imagined what it would be like to track them through the indifferent eyes of so many black-and-white feeds. Everyone going about their business, not realizing they were being watched, or perhaps not caring. If he could gain that power? It would be intoxicating and voyeuristic, like being night watchman to the world.

He was considering whether to explore the concept further, outside the station, when reality intervened. So engrossed was DeBolt in this new idea, he nearly missed his train. He scrambled aboard with two minutes to spare, took a seat by the window, and marveled at META: there had to be hundreds of possibilities he hadn't even considered yet.

DeBolt settled in for an afternoon spent traversing the Rhine Valley and Bavaria. He set aside the what-ifs and committed to more practical research, even if he undertook it in a way that few people on earth could imagine—he closed his eyes and envisioned what he wanted.

He learned nothing more about Dr. Atif Patel, deepening his suspicions that the man had specifically blocked searches. More alarmingly, he learned that Shannon Lund's reservation on a United Airlines flight from Dulles to Kodiak had been canceled. DeBolt searched from every angle he could think of—airline reservations, TSA records, mobile phone tracking, credit card usage—but found nothing on Lund's current whereabouts. Had she taken some obscure route home, perhaps on a military transport? Or was she still on the East Coast digging for information? Either way, he decided she was safe. Safe because she was nowhere near him.

He slept intermittently, fitfully, until 5:42 that evening when, under a driving November rain, the train drew smoothly and punctually into Vienna's Wien Westbahnhof.

Late that same afternoon, another jet landed at Vienna International Airport. The A330 taxied home, was umbilicaled to its jetway, and passengers began to disembark. Among them was a large bald man who, weary after forty-eight hours of travel, was relieved to reach an end point.

Delta did not consider Austria home, but he'd come to like the place. He liked the food, the beer, and most of all the fact that because so many languages were spoken here—and inversely, so many *not* spoken—people didn't find it peculiar when he failed to respond to their questions or reply to conversational openers. He simply answered with a shrug, and nobody seemed to mind.

He slipped uneventfully through immigration using a new identity, the pretext of Douglas Wilson having exceeded its shelf life. He'd kept that one longer than he should have, a mistake that had necessitated his second trip to Alaska. Lesson learned. For years the Marine Corps had dispatched him across the world to do its own brand of violence, but those travels had typically been undertaken on military transports, or occasionally commercial flights, under his real name. He'd dabbled in clandestine work, but it was not his forte. Delta was a killer, no more and no less, an asset built for sand dunes and ditches and jungles, for urban assault in third-world hovels. Give him a door to breach, an MP4, maybe a few grenades, and he could sanitize a room with what bordered on artistry.

He *was* getting better at these new missions, the secrets and duplicity. And he would continue to do so. Delta had only begun to explore what his new abilities allowed. The more he learned, the more lethal he would become. There was already no soldier on earth like him. Not the prima donna squad he'd eliminated in Boston. Certainly not Bravo. *A Coastie,* he thought derisively. A man whose only training involved *saving* lives. Still, Bravo had been enabled with META, so he couldn't be underestimated. He wasn't a threat, but if he learned how to leverage his powers he could prove very elusive.

Delta initiated communications as soon as he reached the line of taxis outside. His instructions were waiting:

DONAUKANAL

He knew it well enough, a place they had met before. He went to the first cab in line and slid into the backseat. The driver turned and said, *"Wohin gehst du?"*

Delta took out one of his cards, along with the pen he always carried, and wrote an address on the back. The driver, a thickset Bavarian with a day's growth of stubble, made an upside-down U with his mouth and nodded to imply that he understood.

As they struck away from the curb, it occurred to Delta that communicating with the cards carried a degree of operational risk. He was leaving a written record of his destination with the driver. Of course, the man knew where they were going anyway, and could relay it after the fact to the police or any adversary. Still, it was yet another complication brought on by his condition. A small problem, but a problem all the same. The card also confirmed his inability to speak, and the fact that he was a United States Marine who'd been injured in combat. All true. He was proud of his service, but in light of his new trajectory in life, he supposed it was unwise to offer information unnecessarily. Any of it might be traceable, perhaps in ways he didn't even understand. Fingerprints or DNA on the card itself. There were some clever people in this world. Very clever indeed. He was on his way to meet one of them right now.

47

Delta paid the cab at the base of a bridge whose name he didn't know. He could have found out easily enough, but he'd long ago committed to not squandering his abilities on the trivial. His connectivity was an awesome weapon, and that was how he treated it, like a gun kept clean and oiled to be ready on a moment's notice.

It was nearly seven o'clock when he found Patel standing near the Badeschiff, or bathing boat, a barge moored along the river that had been ridiculously converted into a swimming pool. The diminutive Patel did not see him approaching, and when he finally sensed Delta's presence he turned with a start.

"Oh . . . good. I hope your travels went well."

Delta did not nod or shrug. Even if he could speak, he would have ignored Patel's small talk. It was one of the few positives of his condition—the expectation of silence without appearing rude. The two had once tried to sustain a back-and-forth dialogue, Patel speaking and Delta responding with text messages to his phone. Varying delays in transmission had made the process unwieldy, even confusing, and so they'd agreed to keep things simple. Whenever possible, Patel framed questions for direct yes or no answers, and Delta would either nod or shake his head. If a more detailed response was necessary, or if he had a question, he simply wrote it on one of his cards.

"Our second problem in Alaska has been dealt with?"

Delta nodded.

"Well done. We are gaining ground."

They began to walk the riverside promenade, meandering toward a well-lit strip where bars and restaurants predominated, and where an old warehouse was being upgraded into a chic new block of condos. The others strolling the riverside path fell into one of two broad categories: pairs of men and women moving slowly on their way to dinner, and younger packs, threes and fives, full of energy and anticipation for a night in the clubs. No one gave a second glance to the two incongruous men engrossed in a peculiarly one-sided conversation.

"Only two remain then—Bravo, of course, and this Coast Guard investigator. You went through her emails and phone history?"

Delta nodded.

"Did you find any link between them prior to the call that brought her to Boston?"

A shake of the head.

"What about her apartment? Was there anything to suggest that she and Bravo had a relationship? Pictures, birthday cards, clothes in the closet that were his size?"

Delta again shook his head.

Patel went silent as he considered it. "Why?" he said rhetorically. "I don't understand why she's become involved. There must have been some personal association before Bravo's accident. It's the only answer."

Delta waited until Patel was looking at him, then put his palms forward obviously as if to say, *So what?*

"Yes, I suppose you're right. It hardly matters." Patel pulled a small sheaf of paper from beneath his light jacket. Delta took it and saw the usual thirty-page printout bound with a standard office clip. It was yet another oddity—he was the most cyber-centric individual in the world, yet when it came to learning he was more comfortable with paper and ink.

"Lesson nine," said Patel. "It covers third-party access and availability. Certain servers are tied knowingly to your network—phone companies, social media, every state and federal agency in the United States with a law enforcement arm. That includes IRS, SEC, FBI—even the Library of Congress has an inspector general whose data is readily available. You'll find a list of foreign governments and private corporations who are unaware of their cooperation—all have been penetrated, some for continuous use, while the others can be accessed on demand if the need arises. The final category consists of organizations, companies, and foreign entities that either have very secure architecture, or whose data has been deemed not worth the trouble of acquiring."

Delta paused, pulled out a card, and wrote: *Can this last group be breached if necessary?*

"Any network can be breached given enough time and effort. Because you operate with Priority Alpha status, any request you make will bring an immediate attack on the holding servers. But keep in mind that the time to get results from this final class will vary. Minutes, hours, even weeks. I suggest exhausting every other option in your network before going that route."

Not for the first time, Delta was struck by the way Patel said it: *your network.* As though the entire system had been created for his benefit. He knew better, of course. He was here today, with all the world's information available, only because he had run over an IED on a dirt bike and gotten his skull shattered in just the right way. One more broken blood vessel in his head and they would have pulled his plug. One less and he might be back in the Corps. As it was, he had fallen in precisely the right notch of helplessness to become a pioneer in a new era of warfare. A circumstance, he supposed, that held loosely with his creed: *Semper fi.*

For twenty more minutes Patel gave what was essentially a lecture, points of learning that would be reinforced by the sheaf of papers. He then turned to more immediate business. "Have you been able to locate Bravo?"

Delta shook his head. It was an essential feature of META that those enabled could not be tracked.

"What about the woman?"

Delta nodded. Not a lie, but also not the truth. To begin, he realized he'd made mistakes. He should never have deepened Lund's involvement by leaving her associate's body in her Kodiak apartment. It had been clumsy and theatrical. But his efforts to flush her out had worked, meaning a third trip to the Aleutian Islands wouldn't be necessary—not only a time-consuming sideshow, but increasingly risky. He was certain Lund had arrived in Vienna. The problem—he didn't know *exactly* where she was.

"All right," said Patel. "Do what you do best."

When Patel turned to go, Delta put a heavy hand on his shoulder. He pulled out a card and scrawled one last question: *When will I be able to talk?*

He showed it to Patel, who said, "We've been over this. Your dysfunction can be repaired, but we first have to identify the source of the problem. It likely involves one of the implants, or there might be errors in the software code. I've been working on it in every spare moment, but you must understand—there are over four million lines of code embedded in the chips in your head. Alternately, the anomaly could be a result of scar tissue from the surgery. Any of these problems are correctable in time. Our priority must be to eliminate these last two loose ends to ensure META's permanence." They began walking again, and Patel added, "That *is* what you want, isn't it? To retain your new abilities forever?"

Their gazes met. Delta nodded once, and was surprised by the strength he saw in the scientist's eyes. He had spent most of his life around physically powerful men, thriving in a hierarchy governed by who could bench-press the most or run the fastest, who had the sharpest eye on the shooting range. Patel was one of the most feeble specimens of manhood he'd ever seen, yet he exuded self-assurance.

Why does he not fear me? Delta wondered.

The two parted, taking opposite courses along the river. Delta trundled the path with his usual directness, and he soon encountered a pair of young girls, both a bit overweight and tipsy on high heels. As they passed one seemed to throw a glance his way, then said something to her friend. He kept going without pause. He was used to it. People had long reacted to his physical appearance, an imposing presence that generally put people off— even before his total alopecia. His rough look had been further amplified by META, the back of his bald head stitched with scar tissue, and now blisters on his face and neck evidenced his meeting with Bravo—the bastard had thrown a pot of boiling water on him.

For as long as Delta could remember, his appearance had intimidated people. Those not frightened were acutely aware of his presence. Yet there had been a few women—just a few—who seemed attracted to him, some peculiar synthesis of fear and sympathy. Like a three-legged pit bull getting adopted from a shelter. A year ago he might have responded to the glance, might have uttered some vague opener to see if the girl would stop. He'd never been good at talking to women, so it rarely worked. Today it was no longer even an option.

He mulled what Patel had said: his speech problem was no more than a technical malfunction. That was good, he thought. Technical malfunctions could be repaired. Like a gun with jam or a Hummer with a flat tire. Fixable. He decided Patel would work faster without the distraction of the two Coasties. The sooner he eliminated them, the sooner his voice would be restored. In that moment, as he advanced along the south shoulder of the Donaukanal into a gathering night, Delta redoubled his commitment to make it so.

48

When she'd decided to come to Vienna, Lund hadn't known what to expect. She reckoned she might have a hard time finding either DeBolt or Dr. Atif Patel, whoever he was. A degree of frustration seemed a given, as was the prospect of fencing with authorities. The one thing she hadn't foreseen was boredom.

She'd been in the holding room for eight hours, the only visits being from a junior officer who asked occasionally if she needed a bottle of water or a sandwich. She'd taken him up on both three hours ago. Lund decided she'd underestimated the reach and efficiency of the Coast Guard, or TSA, or whoever had recognized her departure from the U.S. She'd wanted to slip into Europe quietly, before anyone realized she was a no-show in Kodiak. Special Agent in Charge Wheeley was the most likely culprit. He was under a microscope right now, his Kodiak CGIS outpost in tatters with one agent found dead in the other's bed. Regardless of how it had reached this point, Lund hated where she was now. Locked in a holding room, she could do nothing to help Trey. So it was, when a new face came through the door, she was encouraged. At least *something* was happening.

The man was average in height and build, with brown hair and—she had to say—a certain softness about him. Rounded edges, indoor complexion. He smiled mechanically, and said, "Hello, Miss Lund. I'm Blake Winston, with the U.S. State Department here in Vienna."

His words were clipped and pretentious, the Ivy League of four genera-tions ago. Put him in a striped sweater and an ascot, and he'd show you the way to Newport. She stood and got a fleshy handshake. "State Department?" she asked.

"Yes. Were you expecting someone else?" He had a briefcase in hand, and set it next to the empty water bottle on the room's only table.

"I guess I didn't know what to expect. I've never been in a situation like this before."

Winston put on a pair of glasses as he opened his briefcase. Lund thought he looked a bit young for readers. "Yes . . . about your situation." He referred to a document. "You are a civilian employee of the United States Coast Guard."

"That's right, Coast Guard Investigative Service."

"And you were given instructions by your unit commander to return to Kodiak for questioning regarding a homicide investigation."

Lund sighed. "Yes."

Winston looked at her as if expecting more. When she didn't offer it, he said, "So then . . . *why* did you come to Austria?"

It was the question Lund knew she would face, and she'd had all day to think of a good answer. What she'd settled on was weak and evasive, but really the only option. "I will address that with my superior once I'm back in Alaska."

Winston frowned, but didn't press the matter. "Very well. My instructions are to arrange your transport to Ramstein Air Force Base in Germany. We have a small jet departing later tonight—you and your escort will be on it."

"Escort?"

"An officer from our embassy security detail."

"Is that necessary?"

"Apparently, yes." Winston grinned at his cleverness.

"That seems like a lot of trouble to go to for—"

"Actually, it's no trouble at all. It's a U.S. Air Force jet, and the flight was already on the books. Your escort to Ramstein will be a Marine captain from the embassy detachment—he was traveling home on leave anyway."

"And when I get to Ramstein?"

"We're to hand you over to the Air Force Security Police. They will coordinate the rest of your trip home. According to this message"—he fluttered the paper in his hand—"you can expect three more military transports, with changes of aircraft in Dover and Anchorage."

"That'll take about a week. And more escorts?"

Winston shrugged. "You don't appear to be dangerous, but it's not my bailiwick."

Bailiwick? Lund sank back in her chair. "Okay, when do we leave?"

"There's some paperwork being run right now—the Austrians are funny that way. I think it's already gone through a magistrate—let's hope, because this late in the day we'd have a hard time finding one. Once that's all done, and when your escort arrives, we can head straight to the airport."

Lund thought, but didn't say, *It's probably good that you'll have some help, Mr. Winston. Otherwise I'd kick your ass right now and make for the hills.*

The senior constable in the Bundespolizei evidence room made a terrible mistake, although at the time he couldn't have known it.

"Two items to check," said Oberkommissar Strauss as he came through the door. He was carrying a small roller suitcase and a woman's purse.

The evidence man, who was lesser in rank, said, "Whose are they?"

Strauss handed over a form with the owner's name and an inventory. "A young American woman. We detained her this morning at the airport for the Americans, but the dummkopf from their embassy who was supposed to act as her escort still hasn't shown up. We're working it out, but in the meantime I'm going off duty."

The evidence man understood. Since the inspector of record was going off premises, the possessions could not be left unattended upstairs. In strict adherence to Bundespolizei procedure, Strauss would deposit everything in the evidence room for safekeeping.

Strauss filled out two adhesive tags and applied them, one to each the purse and the suitcase. The evidence room manager, who was more of a file clerk really, took possession as the inspector lifted the items over the counter.

"Shouldn't be more than an hour or two," said Strauss. "As long as it takes to push through the paperwork."

Once the inspector was gone, the evidence man input a locator number on his computer, and then turned toward the rows of shelves with both articles in hand. In spite of having no more than twenty steps to cover, he walked slowly, and eventually paused near the junction of two sets of shelves.

There he regarded each bag in turn. He was alone in the big room—always was except during shift change—yet he knew cameras watched the place continuously. The front desk, where each bit of evidence was signed in and out, was doubly monitored. Yet there *was* one dead zone, the very corner where he was standing, where no lens, human or otherwise, penetrated.

He parted the folds of the purse and saw a wallet and a phone inside, along with the usual sundries: hairbrush, lip gloss, a small mirror. A pack of cigarettes and a lighter. He pulled out the phone. It was an inspection he'd performed many times, and there was really no policy for or against it. He justified it by telling himself that he might one day break a big case, uncover some vital message or image that could be forwarded to the detectives upstairs. He never worried about whether such a search would hold up in court, nor did he dwell on what was closer to the truth: he was a nosy person, and rather liked looking at other people's pictures.

The phone was not powered, so he turned it on.

The device took thirty seconds to spring to life, and he immediately saw badges on the main screen that signified new text messages. He began there and saw a series of photos, but nothing very scintillating. They were actually rather strange, five photographs of what looked like footprints in mud. He didn't know what to make of it at first, not until the last image, which was embellished with text: Here are the pics for the Simmons case. Hope it helps your investigation.

The evidence technician fumbled the phone, nearly dropping it. Shannon Lund, in spite of whatever trouble she might have found, was also a detective of some kind. Unnerved, he quickly hit the button to turn the phone off, stuffed it in the woman's purse, and set that on the correct shelf.

The technician scurried back to the front counter wholly unaware of his mistake. In his haste to shut the phone down, he had hit the wrong button. Glowing ever so silently on a high shelf, the phone remained powered up.

49

Through halls where emperors had dined, and in the ballrooms where the Congress of Vienna had once gathered and danced, a lone Coast Guard rescue swimmer wandered, lamenting his past and in search of a future.

So close, yet so far.

That was the thought resounding in DeBolt's reengineered brain as he wandered through the Hofburg Vienna. He had crossed an ocean, spanned a continent, zeroed in as best he could. But here, amid an endless expanse of gilded halls and crystalline fixtures, he had hit a cold and hard stop.

All around him was his only lead on how to find Dr. Atif Patel: the World Conference on Cyber Security. DeBolt had come here straight from the train station, and in a trash bin near the conference entrance he'd found a discarded lanyard like the one real conference attendees wore. He had put it around his neck with only a glance at the printed name and corporate affiliation. No one gave him a second look.

He'd checked the events calendar for the conference before arriving—it was available online, and fortunately had not yet been taken down by a hacker with a sense of humor. Patel's only remaining appearance was scheduled for tomorrow morning. DeBolt didn't want to wait that long. The problem was, he had not been able to uncover where Patel was staying, where his credit cards had been used, or what his mobile number was. Those things DeBolt could ascertain on virtually anyone in the world drew a blank when it came to META's lone surviving creator—if that was truly what he was.

So he roamed the palatial complex and scanned nametags, particularly

those worn by men who appeared to be of Indian ethnicity—an assumption
on DeBolt's part, but he had no description of Patel to work from. He came
across an evening session in one of the large conference rooms, and through
the open doorway he saw a florid, professorial man at a podium prattling
about network solutions. It occurred to him that if for some reason he couldn't
locate Patel, he'd probably landed in the best place on earth to find *someone*
who could help him understand META. Even if the others here had no
direct knowledge of the project, he was literally surrounded by experts on
wireless networks and information systems. A demonstration of his abilities,
as he'd done for Lund and Colonel Freeman, would unquestionably turn him
into an overnight sensation. Instant celebrity. The downside to that, of course,
was that he would effectively be highlighting his position to the other man
like him. And Delta, DeBolt was sure, was not seeking celebrity.

He returned to the reception area where clusters of men and women
stood with cocktails. DeBolt picked a small group and studied each face.
Two men and a woman. He did his research, and was happy to get results
from facial recognition inputs. By the time he made his approach there was
no need to look at nametags.

"Annette Chu?" he said. "Stanford?"

A petite Asian woman in her forties pulled a glass of white wine away
from her lips. "Yes, that's right. Have we met?"

"Yes, years ago. My name's Trey Smith. I was a grad student at UCLA
when you were teaching there."

She smiled, put out her hand for a tentative shake. DeBolt could see her
trying valiantly to make an association.

"I'm sure you don't remember me," he said. "I finished the year after you
moved to Palo Alto."

"What did you study?" she asked politely.

"Network architecture." DeBolt shifted his gaze to the two men and introduced himself, before saying, "I went on to work at Cal under Dr. Patel. I
understand he's here at the conference, but I haven't been able to find him."
He let that hang.

"I haven't seen him," Chu said.

One of the men offered, "I went to his talk on day two. Very good—Patel's
at the forefront of wireless integration."

"I think I may have him beat," said DeBolt with a smile.

"You should come tomorrow morning," the man continued, "he's the featured speaker."

"I'd like to look him up tonight—I wish I knew where he was staying." This was met with blank looks all around.

And so it went. DeBolt worked the room nonstop. He talked to dozens of professors and PhD candidates, took a pocketful of business cards from corporate sales reps. Most had seen Dr. Atif Patel at some point during the conference. Many had attended his first presentation, and there was universal anticipation for his second talk tomorrow. Yet no one knew where he was at that moment. Indeed, no one had seen him all day. A former student of Patel's thought he might he staying at the InterContinental Wien. A Google rep swore she'd seen him walk into the Hotel Sans Souci. DeBolt took the time to investigate each claim. The InterContinental's electronic guest book was apparently easily breached, and he discovered in less than a minute that Dr. Atif Patel was not among its registered guests. The Sans Souci took nearly ten minutes, but the result was the same.

Try as he might, DeBolt could not locate the one man who he hoped could set him free.

Delta drove his rented car through the heart of Vienna, more a quest for inspiration than a means of conveyance. The evening rush was fast approaching, the bustling arteries below the Danube building to their daily crest. As he regarded the sea of blinking brake lights around him, it struck him that he might be the only driver on Martinstraße not annoyed by the traffic. When it came to handling a vehicle, Delta had long been subjected to different levels of concern, having spent too many years in places where roadbeds were inlaid with explosives, where overpasses spoke of snipers, and where every oncoming car had to be thought of as a bomb. The throng of urban mechanization around him now? It was practically soothing.

He rather enjoyed driving, a vestige he supposed of his first, and very brief, posting in the Corps with a logistics battalion. Even the recent accident in Iraq, which had nearly taken his life, had done nothing to dampen his enthusiasm. Delta liked the vibration of an engine, the feedback of steering in his hands. The paradoxical sensations of freedom and control. He'd often thought that driving was the nearest he came to relaxation.

In that moment, however, it simply allowed him to think.

It had been a frustrating day—this too a reminder of his years in the Corps. He remembered on one occasion waiting five hours for an ammo shipment, only to see the truck arrive empty. He remembered standing in a chow line for an hour to find nothing left but MREs—beef stroganoff, his most despised—because a herd of Air Force weenies had cleaned out the serving trays. Frustration. It was to be expected, a part of any mission.

His bad day had begun long before he'd arrived in Vienna, but now that he was here it was time for damage control. In the most literal sense, he had been honest with Patel—he didn't know where Bravo was at that moment. Almost certainly the Coastie had come to Vienna, and if so, Delta was sure he could find him. Lund was proving the more difficult target to track, and so she became his priority.

She'd readily taken the bait he had put out, deciding, based on his fraudulent text, to travel to Vienna in search of DeBolt. Unfortunately, she'd surprised him by being quick enough to get on *last night's* flight. Lund had arrived a full day earlier than planned—hours before Delta himself was scheduled to reach Vienna. With that one cock-up, his strategy to tail her from the airport tomorrow morning was shot full of holes.

Having at least been forewarned, he'd tried to be proactive. While tracking her United Airlines flight across the ocean, he had sent a tip to the U.S. Coast Guard, ostensibly from the Department of Homeland Security, regarding the international departure of a civilian employee who was wanted as a witness in a homicide investigation in Kodiak. Using Wi-Fi during the course of his own flight, Delta had sat back and monitored the situation via META. In the early hours this morning, he'd watched a stream of back-and-forth messages between the Coast Guard, U.S. State Department, and ultimately the Austrian government. It worked just as he'd hoped—Lund had been detained the moment she landed in Vienna. In effect, the Bundespolizei were holding her in custody for him.

Then a new problem arose—once Delta landed, he couldn't figure out where she'd been taken.

His improvised scheme was further undone by a series of misfortunes. Lund's phone had briefly come to life when she arrived at the airport, but within minutes it was turned off, probably by the police when they arrested her. Then came the truly maddening breakdown. META, for all its technological wizardry, had been stymied by the most ordinary of afflictions—the Bundespolizei computer system that tracked inmates and detainees had crashed. Delta was furious, but left with little recourse. He simply had to buy time in order to locate Lund.

He knew from message traffic that she was to be handed over to U.S. embassy staff, and subsequently transported back to Alaska under military escort. Not wanting that exchange to take place, he'd inserted a number of disruptions on the State Department end regarding the escort's authorizing paperwork. A chain of phone calls ensued between the escort officer, Marine Captain Jose Morales, and the local police. Soon the embassy and the State Department became involved, further levels of bureaucracy crosshatched. The channels of communication, and resultant confusion, grew exponentially.

Altogether, Delta knew he had created a window, albeit a very narrow one. His inspired idea of bringing Lund to Vienna was on the verge of going down in flames. Like so many ops, a promising blueprint had been defeated by the most common of enemies—complexity.

Driving wasn't giving Delta the clarity he needed. He sat rigid and seething, gripping the wheel hard as he weaved amid traffic and circled the same city blocks. He tried to think tactically, bending to the facts as he knew them. He considered going to the airport, waiting near the Air Force jet that was to transport Lund to Germany. When she arrived, he could kill her on the spot, although it would likely entail removing her escort as well. Delta had reservations about killing another Marine—even if he was an officer.

He tried to compose his thoughts. *Where would they take her?*

Given the circumstances—police involvement, immigration, and diplomatic channels—a large city like Vienna presented any number of possibilities. Was she being held at one of the many police stations? In a secure government ministry building? Had she already been transferred to the U.S. embassy? He tried to leverage META, but the responses came at a glacial pace. Embassy information—daily sign-in logs, message traffic, personnel files—all arrived as if through quicksand. Austrian government data welled up from an even thicker bog, a delay that he suspected was due to the translation from German to English. Or perhaps the delays were only a reflection of his outlook—his frustration level peaking.

He drove aimless circles around Alsergrund, the ninth district in central Vienna. He cruised streets once frequented by Freud, never giving a thought to how the father of psychoanalysis might have marveled over the processes of his META-Marine mind. At one point Delta was so distracted in composing a mental inquiry that he nearly caused an accident outside Schwarz-spanierstraße 15, the apartment in which Ludwig van Beethoven had died. It was soon after this near miss, with a taxi driver raising his fist in Delta's rearview mirror, that the distant voice of a drill sergeant from basic training invaded his thoughts. *When things go to hell, simplify.*

And that was what he did. He ignored everything that had happened that day, all the hunting gone wrong. Delta backtracked, past the Vienna airport, over an ocean, and settled on something far more basic—his last solid point of orientation. He had discounted the prospect for hours now, but decided it was worth another try. From the window in his eye, he dispatched a request to locate Shannon Lund's mobile phone.

50

Lund was slumped forward with her head on the folding table. She was nearly asleep. They'd brought her dinner an hour ago, a nice wienerschnitzel with potatoes and a salad that convinced her the Golden Anchor's cook could learn a lot from a prison chef in Austria. The heavy meal, not to mention a day of unadulterated boredom, had made her nearly catatonic.

She was stirred to consciousness when the door opened abruptly. It was Blake Winston.

"All right, I think everything is in order. We'll be leaving for the airport shortly."

Lund stood up and stretched. "What about my stuff?"

"We'll stop by the evidence room on our way out to collect it."

Lund gave a sigh of resignation. She'd come to Austria to help Trey, and now her failure was all but complete. Ahead of her was a two-day trek involving airplanes and escorts, followed by a grilling from her boss—at least she had two days to come up with a story that would sound more believable than the truth. She realized at that moment how little she cared about any of it.

"All right," she said. "Let's get this over with."

They were met in the hallway by a female police officer who led them two floors down to an evidence storage facility. At least that was what Lund took it for—the sign on the door was labeled with a German compound at least twenty letters long. The policewoman escorting them said in thickly accented English, "Neither of you are permitted inside. Stay here, please." She pushed a button on a cipher lock near the door, then looked up at an overhead camera.

There were three lights on the lock, and the bottom one turned green. She walked inside.

Lund said to Winston, "You don't smoke, do you?"

He frowned.

"Never mind. So is my escort here?"

"Yes, he and I arrived together. As I mentioned earlier, Captain Morales will take you as far as—"

A huge crash reverberated from inside the evidence room. Lund looked at Winston, then they both looked at the door. It was a solid item in a metal frame, no inset window. The light on the cipher lock was red.

"That didn't sound good," said Lund. "Maybe we should have a look."

Winston said uncertainly, "No, she told us to stay here. Besides, the door is locked."

Lund reached for the call button on the lock pad, but before she could sink it the bottom light went green.

She reached for the door handle, but Winston shouldered in front of her. "Wait . . . let me." He opened the door and started to go inside. He paused at the threshold. "What the hell . . ."

Lund looked past him into the evidence room and saw a giant set of shelves resting against a wall at a forty-five-degree angle. Between the wall and the heavy shelf was the body of a man in a police uniform—he was crushed and clearly dead. Lund noticed the look of horror on Winston's face, and she followed his gaze to the right. There she saw another body—the woman who'd escorted them here, lying glass-eyed across the counter.

Lund instinctively grabbed a fistful of Winston's finely tailored jacket, and in the next instant, as she began to pull, her eyes were drawn to a flash of motion. She made sense of it milliseconds later, as she was dropping to the floor—a hulking figure in a shooting stance, a silenced weapon extended. Two sounds seemed to arrive simultaneously—the spit from a silenced gun, and a muted slap. Lund hit the floor amid a spray of blood and tissue, and yelled, *"Gun! Gun! Gun!"* wishing she knew the German word.

She took one look at Winston, then wished she hadn't. His face was unrecognizable. Lund knew she could only save herself. She skated to her feet on the polished floor and ran down the hall, searching for an open door or a stairwell—any kind of cover from the open door behind her. Her heart soared when she saw a policeman emerge from a side office with his hand on a holstered sidearm.

It might have been the look on her face, or that she'd called out a gun. Maybe it was the desperate way she was running toward him. Whatever the source, his expression was stone serious, his eyes alert. Then the officer's gaze locked on something behind her, and he began to draw his weapon. She never heard the spits of the silencer, but the policeman's gun blasted a round into the floor as he went down. Lund threw herself toward the opening as the hallway behind her exploded in a shower of plaster and chipped wood. She careened off a wall and got to her feet. What she saw in the room was wonderful—six, maybe eight officers in uniform, every one tugging at a holster or reaching into a drawer for a weapon.

"To the left down the hall!" she shouted. "Officers down!"

There was shouting in German among the policemen, and the one with the most stripes on his shoulders apparently decided Lund was not part of the problem. He asked in English, "How many attackers?"

"I only saw one!"

More commands in German.

Lund kept moving, and someone shoved her toward the back of the room where two doors connected to a parallel hallway. She kept moving as shouting echoed all around. None of the words made sense to her, but she recognized the tones: commands, urgency, distress. An alarm sounded, and she saw a man shrugging on body armor, a shotgun in his hands. The cavalry was arriving.

Ahead she saw a green sign labeled: NOTAUSGANG. More intuitively, next to it was a pictogram of a person running and an arrow. *Exit.*

A young woman in civilian clothes was in front of her, head ducked low as she ran in the direction of the arrow. She disappeared into an alcove, and Lund followed. Two fire doors later, she burst out onto the streets of Vienna. She turned right because there were more people in that direction, and ran at top speed. Her head was on a swivel checking every door and sidewalk. The brooding Bundespolizei building soon fell behind, and she eased to a purposeful walk, her heart racing and her lungs heaving. Lund checked the sidewalks at every intersection, searching for the big bald man, listening for the sounds of World War III behind her. She didn't see or hear either.

Night was falling, the temperature dropping. Lund wasn't cold at all. She'd brought a light jacket. It was in her roller bag. Which was in an evidence room littered with bodies. How many? Winston, the female officer who'd gone inside, the evidence room clerk. The officer who'd put his head into the hallway.

Four victims.

Four at least.

But that was only here, only tonight. Lund knew there were more. She knew because two images now stood side by side in her mind, pinned there like twin Polaroids. Pictures that would stay with her forever. One was the massive man she had just seen holding a silenced gun. The other was the captured CCTV photo Jim Kalata had sent. The latter image had disappeared from her phone's memory, but it was permanently etched in her own. Two portraits of the same lethal subject, a man who'd been spanning the globe. He'd killed in Alaska, killed in Boston. Now he'd come to Vienna.

And he had come for her.

The body count at the Bundespolizei station grew quickly. The duty corporal in the evidence storeroom was obvious enough, as was the much-liked female deputy inspector. Both had broken necks. The American embassy official had suffered one catastrophic round to the face, while the sergeant in the hallway had taken two bullets, one to his neck and one to the chest, either of which would have been singularly fatal. It took thirty minutes to discover the final victim, who was stuffed into the trunk of a car in the parking garage. That casualty wore the uniform of a United States Marine Corps captain, and the car belonged to the motor pool of the American embassy in Vienna.

The station was locked down in a posture of highest internal alert, and the "all clear" took nearly an hour as every room, air duct, and closet was searched thoroughly. Strangely, amid an entire precinct of policemen, no one seemed to have seen the shooter. An administrative clerk thought she might have seen a stranger momentarily—a very wide, bald man who turned the corner down a hallway—as she emerged from the second-floor ladies' room. Detectives also soon realized that, amid the chaos, the American woman who'd been in custody, awaiting transfer on an expedited diplomatic request, had also gone missing. They were forced to consider, given the death of the American soldier who was to have been her escort, that the armed assailant had come to facilitate her escape.

With the police facing five murders, not to mention the escape of a detainee right under their noses, the mood fell decidedly grim. An all-out effort was made to secure evidence, and it was here that the final professional indignity was imparted. In the building's security center, a flummoxed technician reported to the chief inspector that all surveillance video for that day had somehow disappeared.

"What do you mean, 'disappeared'?" said the incredulous chief inspector.

"I . . . I don't know," replied the woman behind the monitor. "I've never seen anything like it." Her fingers rattled over her keyboard, stepping from one channel to the next. "We have forty cameras in the building, and the footage from every single one has been wiped clean. It must be some kind of system-wide failure . . . but we never got a warning that it was down. We're supposed to get a *warning*."

A despondent chief inspector took the only course available. He ordered the widest possible dissemination of the passport photo of an American Coast Guard investigator named Shannon Lund, adding that extreme caution was to be taken if she were discovered in the company of a large bald man. The chief dispatched every available detective into the surrounding neighborhood to search and ask questions, and sent an urgent request to city authorities to acquire CCTV footage from the immediate area. Vienna, like most European capitals, was wired for video, although not as extensively as the likes of London or Paris. Municipal surveillance here was largely targeted on areas prone to vandalism and graffiti. The chief knew there was also a vast constellation of corporate and residential video systems, yet these could not be accessed without the approval of a magistrate—an option, to be sure, but something that would take time.

So the Bundespolizei did what they could within the given constraints. The man put in charge of the investigation, a senior chief inspector, went through the motions of his inquiry with increasing frustration, stunned that their newly upgraded technology had failed in the most important hour. *What are the chances of that?* he thought idly.

51

DeBolt sipped a large caffè Americano as he fine-tuned yet another newfound skill. On the screen in his right eye was the face of a college-aged girl who seemed to stare right through him. He watched in amazement as she bit her lower lip in concentration. Completely innocent, completely unaware.

It was nearly ten o'clock, the conference at the Hofburg Vienna having ended over an hour ago. DeBolt had seen nothing of Dr. Patel at the conference, and had drawn a blank among his peers—no one knew where the professor from Cal was staying. He kept trying up to the last possible moment, until he was finally ushered outside by conference staff amid a group of IBM researchers, a well-lubricated bunch who were heading out on the town. They'd invited DeBolt to join them, but he had politely declined.

Disappointed and frustrated by what seemed a wasted evening, he'd crossed the cobblestone square, and on the far side DeBolt had taken up the inviting paths of the Volksgarten where the night tried unsuccessfully to conceal rows of finely sculpted hedges and a disparate array of fountains. Within ten minutes he'd come across Café Wien, a classic Viennese coffeehouse, and taken a seat outside at a shadowed corner table, feeling somehow safer in the open.

He'd been waiting for his coffee when the idea came to him, and now, twenty minutes on, yet another new world had been unlocked. The concept was born from a selfie stick—an Asian couple taking a self-portrait at a nearby table. Realizing he might be captured in the background, DeBolt was able to identity the man, and subsequently capture his phone number.

He tried to search the phone for the picture they'd just taken, and to his surprise was soon flicking through images as easily as if his finger was on the device's screen. It was, after all, only data, the merest of hurdles being where it was stored and who had access. To his surprise, he found he could also activate the phone's camera—actually either one, front or back—and if he were so inclined, turn the device into a remote surveillance tool.

Applications for this newfound utility had rushed through his head. He'd watched the Asian couple smile through four more snapshots. At that point, DeBolt was subjected to a stagnant view of the awning overhead after the man set his phone on the table and the two began talking. Bored with that, he ran with the concept, and inside ten minutes had pirated an IP address for a nearby laptop computer. The young girl behind it was taking advantage of the café's Wi-Fi network. DeBolt could easily have looked over his shoulder to discover that she was working on a document of some kind. A school project perhaps, or a letter—he hardly cared. DeBolt was more intrigued by the laptop's camera.

This took longer, but the end product was essentially the same. In a near real-time stream, he watched a shamelessly voyeuristic video of the girl's face as she typed, her brow furrowed in concentration no more than two feet from the lens. He considered going further, exploring the files on the machine to see what was available to him, but decency intervened.

A week ago he would have been astounded, but curiously DeBolt felt only numbness at the prospect of being able to hijack the camera on virtually anyone's phone or computer. He knew there would be more, other electronic muggings he'd not even dreamt of. *It's only data after all.*

He considered what else was on the horizon, and hoped that many of his questions might be answered tomorrow. He was eager to meet Patel. The man *had* to show up for his presentation, and when he did, DeBolt would be in the front row. Was he aware that the META Project had imploded? Did he realize he was the lone survivor among those who'd built it? DeBolt wondered what the scientist knew about him. Had he been informed that Bravo was a success? If so, did he also know about Delta?

DeBolt's musings were suddenly sideswiped by a more unsettling question: Why was Delta pursuing him?

He knew Colonel Freeman and his team had been acting through a chain of command, executing a kill order against what they'd been told was a terrorist cell. Then Delta had arrived on the scene. DeBolt remembered the message he'd received through some private channel they shared: *I am Delta.* The very concept of such communication was profound—a kind of web-enabled telepathy.

He had heard nothing from Delta since Boston, yet assumed the killer was still pursuing him. But to what end? Then a new worry intervened. Besides Bravo and Delta, there appeared to be but one remaining survivor of the META Project—Dr. Atif Patel. Might Delta try to hunt him down as well? If so, Delta was probably hitting the same information roadblocks De-Bolt had—the only thing available on Patel was that he would present at tomorrow's conference.

Taken together: DeBolt realized he might not be the only one in the front row.

Feeling a sudden urge to start moving again, he left five euros on the table and was soon on the sidewalk outside Café Wien. There he paused and, after a mental coin flip, turned right. He began to study the streets around him. If he were a spy he would look for surveillance teams or unmarked vans or whatever spies looked for. As it was, DeBolt scanned for his only known threat—the distinctively large frame of Delta.

He typically liked being outdoors—hiking mountain passes, swimming in the ocean, bicycling through canyons. Here, however, swathed in the crisp autumn air of Vienna, he was suddenly uncomfortable. He felt exposed and vulnerable, like a deer that had ventured too far from the forest. It wasn't just a matter of being seen—given what he'd learned in recent days, the idea of being identified by line of sight seemed utterly nostalgic. Might META broadcast his position? Could Delta intercept his communications, then use them to acquire his location? *If so, then I can theoretically do the same in return.* Unfortunately, DeBolt knew the two of them were not on level ground: Delta understood how the system operated.

It gave harsh new meaning to the phrase, "Getting in your head."

He walked cautiously up Burggasse, not sure whether to steer toward shadows or light. He was confident he would get his answers tomorrow morning—assuming he could survive that long.

Twelve hours.

It was a long time to be alone with such despondent thoughts.

Lund's heart leapt.

It was after ten o'clock, and even thought most shops were closed, the crowds were thick on the wide boulevard of Graben, a well-heeled shopping area in Vienna's first district. What had Lund's attention, however, was not Chanel or Hermès, but something far more useful. On the far sidewalk, a hundred yards ahead—a familiar profile. Tall and athletic, moving confidently under faux gaslights on the busy sidewalk. Walking away with an easy long stride.

"Trey!" she said under her breath. Lund began to trot.

He disappeared around a corner, moving quickly, and she ran as fast as she could. Closing ground, she rounded the corner and spotted him again, light jacket and dark pants. "Trey!" she shouted.

He didn't respond. She was twenty steps behind him, and about to shout again, when he turned ninety degrees and drew to a stop. Under a wash of light from a busy gelato shop Lund saw his face for the first time as he bent down to kiss a pretty woman on both cheeks. Her spirits foundered.

She ground to a halt, her feet suddenly leaden. Lund sank a shoulder against a stone wall and tried to catch her breath, watching as the couple sat together at a table and began an animated discussion. They might have been deciding which nightclub to visit later, or reminiscing about the rain shower they'd been caught in the last time they were here. Subjects of amusement, of no consequence whatsoever. The kinds of things most people talked about. And if it *had* been Trey, what would the two of them be discussing? *Why is this man trying to kill us? How can we stay out of jail? What's Austria's policy on extraditing Americans?*

She looked all around and saw happy people in a tidy city. "Foreign" was not a strong enough word. She didn't speak the language here. Didn't have identity documents or money. Had Trey even reached Vienna? If so, was he still alive, or had the assassin finished that half of his job?

She saw but one hope. Lund had earlier found a public library and accessed a computer. Having arrived minutes before closing time, she'd typed as fast as she could. With great restraint, she avoided the online version of the *Kodiak Daily Mirror*. Whatever was happening in the murder cases there—William

Simmons *and* Jim Kalata—it was a distraction she couldn't permit. Vienna was the here and now, and she flew from web page to web page searching of direction. It was the name Trey had sent—Dr. Atif Patel, whom he'd somehow linked to the META Project—that hit sevens. Patel would present a lecture at ten o'clock tomorrow morning at the World Conference on Cyber Security, which was taking place at the Hofburg Vienna. The same article explained that Patel was an expert on computer systems and software, which she took as further proof of his ties to META.

By the time she was ushered out of the library, three minutes after closing, Lund had settled on two possible scenarios. First, Trey might already have made contact with Patel, in which case the scientist would know where he was. If not? Then Trey would also be at the auditorium tomorrow. Either way, it gave her a destination—a time and a place from which to start reclaiming her life.

She began walking again, mixing into the crowds amid Graben's charmless palette of designer neon. The sky above was a milky white, low clouds absorbing the lights like a great blanket. As if insulating and protecting the city. Lund remembered having the same impression when she had first arrived in Kodiak. She'd seen a small town holding fast against the sea and the winter, a safe harbor where the rest of the world was kept at a distance. She began to feel more confident, thinking perhaps there was a future after all.

Then she saw a picture behind a broad window that froze her to the sidewalk.

It was on the wall of a bar, on the middle of three televisions. Framed by mirrors with scripted writing and liquor bottles in neat formation. Left and right were a pair of soccer games, but the central screen was tuned to a news channel, presumably Austrian because the captions on the footer were in German. She saw her passport photo in full-bloom color, her name right below. Shannon Ruth Lund. She knew *why* it was there, of course, confirmed by the follow-on shots: blue lights rolling in front of the decimated Bundespolizei station, a body beneath a blanket rolling past on a gurney. Being a cop herself, she recognized the entire production. Her picture front and center, widest possible dissemination. The backdrop of a tragedy.

The police wanted very much to talk to her.

Lund watched for any other pictures, any headlines she could decipher. She saw nothing to further her understanding of things, and more disappointingly, nothing to suggest that the brute who'd launched the attack was either deceased or in custody.

Lund realized she was gawking at the screen from the sidewalk. Was the barman staring at her? Possibly. But maybe only as an invitation. Maybe he needed another female to help balance his cast of regulars. She set out quickly, like any woman would who was underdressed for a chilly night in Vienna. She took a turn at the first side street.

Two blocks farther on, she took another.

Lund knew what she had to do—stay out of sight until morning. Either that, or think of a way to find Trey before Patel's presentation. Of course that would be the better option.

But how?

52

Budget. Cash. Hostel.

These were the words DeBolt concentrated on as he searched for a place to spend the night. The results came quickly.

Certain quarters of Vienna were inarguably historic, steeped in the culture of Europe's great periods. Others leaned toward finance, districts where money was kept behind great walls, and prosperity itself seemed etched in the air. The neighborhood of Schottenfeld was neither of those. It was boxy and constrained, crammed with angular buildings of no particular era. The residents also seemed an uneasy mix. He saw groups of restless teenagers, impatient to move on, and the old and indifferent who weren't going anywhere. DeBolt counted more backpacks than briefcases, and he saw bike racks at every building. Yet for all Schottenfeld's ambiguity, it did hold one particularly endearing trait: it was a place where budget hostels gladly took cash in advance.

The night was winding down, dinners at an end and the streets falling empty. DeBolt picked up his pace, knowing where Schottenfeld was headed. In a few more hours only three factions would remain on the sidewalks: the drunk, the criminally inclined, and the police. He wanted nothing to do with any of them, nor their unavoidable interactions.

More than anything, DeBolt needed rest. His body was drained by travel, his mind dulled by hours of experimenting with maps and phone cameras and computers. He was so tired, in fact, that when a message popped into his head, absent any input from him, he initially attached little importance to it. He ignored it as one would an unknown caller on a phone. Then, as if through a fog, he remembered receiving the plot on Joan Chandler's phone ten hours after his request. He studied the message, and its very uniqueness brought him back to his senses.

REPLY IF POSSIBLE.

He blinked, unable to make sense of it. DeBolt nearly responded with, *Who the hell is this?* but then paused on the sidewalk. Confused, he sat down on a knee wall fronting the brooding façade of a minor museum. He pinched the bridge of his nose and tried to think clearly. He finally sent: *Source of last communication.*

A quick response.

00 1 907 873 3483
SHANNON LUND
SMS TEXT MESSAGE SOURCED VIENNA, AUSTRIA

DeBolt's foot slipped and he nearly tumbled off the wall. "You're here?" he whispered to himself. He immediately formulated a reply: *You're here in Vienna?*

YES. HAVE TO SEE YOU REGARDING META/PATEL.

DeBolt was overwhelmed. Happy. Fearful. Confused. There could be only one reply: *Meet me at 84 Kandlgasse.*

CAN'T COME TO YOU. LOOK AT NEWS.

He didn't take the time to find out what she meant: *Where then?*

RIESENRAD.
PLEASE HURRY.

DeBolt: *I'm on my way.*
He immediately conjured a map, then pushed and scaled it to fit his

needs. The Riesenrad, he discovered, was a giant Ferris wheel at the Prater amusement park. Lund was two miles north of where he stood. DeBolt had wits enough to avoid running, a residual of his previous thought—*drunks, criminals, and the police.* He set out at a measured pace, and with his navigation set and his weary legs responding, he did what she'd suggested and searched the local news. It took a few tries, but he hit the mark with: *Vienna, headlines, American, woman.*

Three options were presented, and he selected an online news article, the late edition of something called *The Local.* DeBolt scanned an article recounting a disaster this evening at a local Bundespolizei precinct. The headline summarized that five people had been killed. He found Lund's name in the third paragraph:

> *Bundespolizei have undertaken a nationwide hunt for the suspect in the killings, an unidentified male, large build and clean-shaven head, and also an American woman, Shannon Ruth Lund, who escaped from police custody during the attack.*

A light drizzle began to fall, the tops of buildings going hazy in the uplit swirls. The sweet smell of rain cleansed stagnant urban air. DeBolt quickened his pace, knowing what it all meant. There could be no mistake, no illusions. Delta had come to Vienna, as single-minded as ever. In Boston he'd assaulted a safe house and killed an entire team of Special Forces operators. A district police station in a peaceful quarter of Vienna? That would be child's play. Five more bodies in the wake of his destruction.

But there *was* one strand of hope.

Shannon had escaped. The Bundespolizei were scouring the country for her, but DeBolt knew where she was, less than two miles away. Unfortunately, he also knew who else might be searching for her. The distant Riesenrad had just come into view when he skidded to a stop on the sidewalk in the gathering rain.

His hair was matted and his breath came in slow gasps. *What was it? Something terribly wrong.* Then he understood. He knew what it *might* be.

How can I be sure?

DeBolt considered a way to prove or disprove his frightful new idea. Options came and went until he settled on one. It required little composition: *Quick stop for smokes. What was your brand?*

The reply was immediate.

MARLBORO.

DeBolt breathed a sigh of relief and set out again, full-on rain pelting his face in a cold rush of wind.

53

Like most storied parks, the Prater was not without its ghosts. Over a century ago, in 1913, the lives of a remarkably disparate group of young men intersected in Vienna. There were four, and they came from all points of the compass, each bursting with the vigor and idealism for which youth is known. None could have imagined then, in the halcyon days of that verdant summer, how their respective revolutions would transform the world: Stalin, Trotsky, Tito, Hitler. All roamed the Vienna park called the Prater in that year of ill-omened serenity.

The rain was coming in sheets by the time DeBolt reached the Hauptallee, the pedestrian boulevard that ran centrally through the Prater. Chestnut trees arched over the path, skeletal and fading, their spent foliage lining the shoulders and sweeping into drifts against a burdened wrought-iron fence.

DeBolt passed a carriage drawn by a muscled draft horse, its wet coat glistening, a man and woman huddled under the awning behind the driver. He saw his destination looming to his left, the brazen Riesenrad wheel that rose high above the city. He rounded a planetarium, and on entering the amusement park encountered the usual assortment of carnival rides and bumper cars. According to a sign, the park was open until midnight for a special weekend celebration, but the rain had clearly thinned the crowds, and a number of rides appeared to have packed in early. Altogether, the place looked sodden and weary, ready for a good night's rest. An ice cream vendor leaning on his cart looked hopefully at DeBolt, and a barker in the distance seemed to beckon him personally to a show, although it was hard to say since De-

Bolt didn't speak a word of German. He imagined he could translate what the man was saying if he were so inclined—yet another function of META on his list to be explored.

He approached the Riesenrad cautiously. The ride was still, and he saw no one in line—only a two-hundred-foot-tall wheel suspended in a deluge. The operator sat under a tarp, his legs propped indifferently on a crate as if not caring whether he found another customer.

DeBolt stopped twenty paces from the entrance. He turned a full circle searching for Lund. There was a young couple on the sidewalk, elbows locked and smiling as they rushed through the rain. A mother and father prodded two young girls along, everyone looking edgy after a long day of fun. DeBolt didn't see Lund, and he began to feel uneasy.

It came out of nowhere—a message flashing to the display in his eye.

BEHIND YOU.

DeBolt spun and saw him instantly. A huge figure in a heavy coat, a long-barreled gun hanging casually in his hand. He was standing under the overhang of a closed ticket booth, partially hidden but in plain view to DeBolt. Fifty feet away, he was at the edge of the useful range for a hand-gun.

DeBolt took one step back. Fifty-three feet.

Oddly, Delta didn't move. He simply stood there waiting, his bald head glistening in the rain, his broad face a blank.

DeBolt knew he had only one chance—he ran.

He kept to the main thoroughfare, hoping for more people to add confusion, and perhaps a better chance of encountering a policeman. He sprinted past rides with names like Autodrom and Boomerang, and didn't venture a look back for a hundred yards. When he finally did look over his shoulder, Delta was nowhere in sight. He sprinted onward, certain the killer was following. He wondered why Delta hadn't taken a shot when he had one. Had it been too public? Was he not an expert marksman? Whatever the case, DeBolt relied on his one advantage, proven already on the streets of Boston. In a pure footrace, he would win every time.

How could Delta not know that?

DeBolt kept running, but his uncertainty began to grow.

The amusement park seemed endless, but finally gave way to something different—pathways lined with cafés and beer halls. The patios were all empty, but inside he saw warm lights and thick crowds. There wasn't a policeman in sight, and DeBolt guessed they were all elsewhere—searching the city in vain for the killer who was right behind him.

He made a series of turns, then finally stopped to evaluate things. He was breathless, his lungs sucking air, his heart pounding in his chest. Delta could never have kept pace with his sprint. DeBolt envisioned him blocks away, bent over with his hands on his knees. Trying to recoup enough wind to check a hundred alleys and alcoves.

How long had he been running? Five minutes? Ten? DeBolt knew from rescue missions that time was difficult to gauge once adrenaline kicked in. He decided to keep moving in the same general direction, toward the Danube and away from the park's entrance. He hadn't gone ten steps when a great figure appeared in front of him.

In front . . .

Delta was closer this time, emerging from behind a sculpted hedge at the entrance of a faux British pub. He walked straight toward DeBolt at a casual pace. He didn't look winded at all.

This time he raised his gun and fired.

54

The silenced gun had a surprisingly loud report. It was nothing compared to the resulting crash when the window behind DeBolt, which fronted a closed souvenir shop, shattered and rained to the ground. He dove to his right, tumbling behind a freestanding restroom, as two more shots laced the rain-shrouded night. He scrambled to his feet, and using the building for cover DeBolt reached a narrow alleyway. He burst through the first doorway he encountered, and found himself in a kitchen facing two surprised young men. Both wore cooking aprons.

"Wo gehst du hin?" one asked.

DeBolt didn't even try to decipher it. At a glance he saw a grill and an oven, kegs of beer stacked against the far wall. Beyond the two men he saw a passageway leading to a crowded bar. The air smelled of fryer oil and chlorine.

"Call the police!" DeBolt shouted as he rushed past the cooks.

Neither tried to stop him as he dashed into the bar. There everyone's eyes were glued to a soccer game—the same one on all four televisions—and a raucous cheer rose as something happened in the game.

"Polizei!" DeBolt yelled. "Call the *Polizei!"*

The revelry died in an instant. The place went quiet except for the game's televised commentary.

"Polizei!" he shouted again. "The killer from the police station—the man they're searching for! He's outside!"

He saw a woman put a mobile phone to her ear. That was good. DeBolt needed help. He needed people and fear and confusion.

"What did you say?" said one of the barkeepers, his Austrian accent thick.

"The killer from the police station! He's outside!"

"I heard about it," someone said from the crowd. "They are looking for a man."

Erring on the side of caution, the barkeeper extracted his own mobile from under the counter. DeBolt looked out the pub's front window and saw a reasonably well-lit sidewalk. A lone couple was walking by casually. He glanced back toward the kitchen, expecting Delta to appear any second. Nothing happened.

The mood in the pub began to split. Some of the patrons looked warily at the door he'd just come through. Others were looking at him. DeBolt shouldered through the crowd, toward the front door. Then he stopped suddenly, something holding him back. *Nothing is making sense.* He had a ten-second lead on Delta, no more. The man should have arrived by now, crashing through the kitchen, killing anyone who tried to stop him. Might he have circled out front?

DeBolt sensed something very wrong. He of all people should have seen it coming. When Delta reappeared a minute ago, he'd shown no signs of exertion. DeBolt felt like he'd run a four-minute mile.

He's hunting me, he thought. *He's using META.*

But how?

He edged closer to the window and scanned outside. He saw a pair of young women walking arm in arm. A girl on a bicycle, her head down against the rain. There was no sign of Delta. His caution went to fear.

How are you doing it?

He glanced a second time at the girl on the bicycle. Could that be it? Did Delta have transportation? Possibly, but that wouldn't work alone.

How are you tracking me?

Delta was the lion chasing a gazelle, slower on foot but wearing his prey down, technology taking the place of a companion pride. DeBolt didn't think his position was being linked in real time—he was increasingly convinced it only transmitted when necessary to support certain applications. If not that, then what?

Then a recent memory flashed, partial and disjointed: 98 Mill Street in Calais, Maine. A tiny red light. Staring up at himself and waving. He remembered the train station in Cologne, studying his surroundings while he'd sipped an espresso.

What had worked in Maine hadn't in Holland.

So let's try Austria.

DeBolt searched outside and saw them right away. One was mounted on a pole, another wedged under the eave of a T-shirt shop. Closed-circuit cameras.

He immediately went to work: *CCTV near present position.*

STAND BY FOR AVAILABLE FEEDS.

DeBolt stood waiting, still breathing in ragged gasps. Everyone was watching him. A map lit in his visual field. According to the scale, it covered a one-hundred-meter radius. He saw twelve, perhaps fourteen cameras, most on established roads and pathways, a few inside buildings. There was a color code—red, yellow, and green. The colors meant nothing to him, but seemed intuitive enough. He highlighted the nearest green, and the reply took fifteen seconds. The video came streaming in, but certainly with a short delay, just as with the monitor he'd annexed at the embezzler's front door in Maine. Like the college girl's laptop he'd invaded earlier tonight.

Yet for all intents and purposes, he was looking at a live video feed.

He saw the front of the restaurant he was standing in. It was called Schweizerhaus. He saw the crowds inside, but felt no urge to zoom in and wave. DeBolt knew it was accurate. He switched to other cameras, got feeds from nearby pathways, including the courtyard behind Schweizerhaus where Delta had been minutes earlier. None gave him what he wanted.

Where are you?

The fourth feed, with a red symbol, was inoperative. The nearest yellow camera got the result:

STAND BY ENCRYPTION BREAK
ESTIMATED WAIT 15–90 MINUTES

Not an option. He shifted to another feed, and when it came through he stood transfixed. On a tree-lined path he saw a large man atop a motorcycle. It was a medium-sized bike, but beneath Delta it looked like something from a circus act. DeBolt watched him dismount, then followed along as he walked the motorcycle toward a bush and left it there. Delta stood waiting in a deep shadow.

DeBolt referenced the map. The spot was perhaps two hundred yards away—the direction in which he'd been running. The most obvious path of escape.

A hand suddenly grabbed his shoulder. DeBolt turned with a start, his arm cocking back for a punch.

The bartender, who'd clearly seen such moves before, leaned away.

"You are okay?" asked the Austrian.

DeBolt stood down. "Yeah, sorry. I'm on edge after . . ." He didn't know how to complete the thought. Didn't know how to raise an instantaneous lie.

"The police, they are coming. You wait here for them."

DeBolt sensed another shift in atmosphere. Most of the clientele were watching him now. He'd been wholly absorbed by the images in his head, and DeBolt wondered how he must appear to others when engaged in his private exchanges with META. Did he look disconnected from his surroundings, a cell phone stare without the external device? Did he appear simply distracted, or more like a madman hearing voices?

He said, "I'll wait outside." It was the most convenient answer for everyone.

He went through the front door, passed beyond the welcoming awning. The rain had eased, but only slightly, and he kept his head angled downward. The vision remained in his eye, a camera feeding its constant view. He saw Delta standing in the open, much as he was—not scanning the sidewalk for his target, but holding fast with a thousand-yard stare. DeBolt turned toward the nearest camera, the one mounted on the closed T-shirt shop. He stood and looked right at it, steady and unblinking. On the screen in his eye Delta straightened ever so slightly. Then he quarter-turned to his right and did the same in response—he stared straight at the camera DeBolt was using to watch *him*.

And there they stood. A surreal impasse in the rain, transmitted across miles of wire and routers and sky, opposing images fixed in coarse shades of gray. Two hundred meters apart, each man knew exactly where the other was. Each could track any movement. A *High Noon* standoff, twenty-first-century version. DeBolt stood tall and straight, but it was a false ease. He had broken Delta's advantage, but for how long? Could the man disable his feed? Could he ruin the camera network, or even spoof looped images while he repositioned? DeBolt thought not.

I'm learning, he thought. Then more purposefully: *Delta . . . I'm catching up with you.*

On his screen he saw the man suddenly cock his blocklike head. DeBolt's eyes narrowed, and he tensed slightly as Delta began to move. He watched cautiously as the killer walked toward his motorcycle. Watched him swing a leg over the seat and kick it to life. DeBolt was poised, ready to move. But then he saw Delta turn away and ride east, leaving the Schweizerhaus and the Prater behind.

DeBolt referenced the map and stepped through four different cameras, tracking the assassin until he disappeared in a tree-lined dead zone. He was at least a mile gone, headed away, when DeBolt finally lost track of him. So there *was* an internal network, he thought. Delta had gotten his message, but not replied. Did that imply there were risks in using it? Would such an application give up his position? Another facet of META left to explore.

Sirens rose in the distance, and DeBolt looked over his shoulder. Someone in the bar was pointing at him and talking. He imagined what was being said. *That one there. He rushed in shouting for the police. Next he was staring at the walls. Claims someone is following him.*

DeBolt began walking, and on his network map of CCTV cameras he identified a gap in coverage running through a nearby woodland. How easy . . . once you knew how it all worked. He ducked into the trees and disappeared. Newly confident. Newly empowered. For a week now he had been hunted. He'd been shot and assaulted, constantly running for his life. But now he sensed a divergence to that narrative. He was getting stronger, more capable.

As he trod through the woods, pushing aside wet branches and slogging through puddles, DeBolt very deliberately reiterated his earlier thought: *Yes, Delta . . . I'm gaining on you.*

55

Lund spent the night in a homeless shelter three blocks north of the Imperial Palace. With no money, no identity, and wanting to keep a low profile, she played the part of a marooned American tourist who'd been parted from her passport, baggage, and friends—all true in the strictest sense.

She was taken in without question, Austrians being a forgiving lot, and given a place in a church-run dormitory. For the price of a desperate smile she got a roof over her head, a smelly cot, and in the morning two surplus sausages with hot cereal, all capped by a spontaneous blessing from a roaming Catholic priest. She took it all in the spirit in which it was provided, which was to say, with gracious humility.

She was told by a shelter worker, a college-aged girl with flaxen hair, that during the recent flood of immigration many such houses had been established. The girl also mentioned that Lund was the only passer-through she'd ever met who had arrived from the West. Syrians, Pakistanis, Ethiopians, Afghanis—they were the dominant lot, with an atmosphere of compassion prevailing, and Lund learned that any smile was quickly returned.

It did not escape her how far removed she was from her old life. In the matter of a few days, she'd gone from being a CGIS investigator in Alaska to impersonating a homeless person in Austria. For Lund, it was perhaps the most profound manifestation of META's insanity. All the same, that maelstrom had also brought Trey into her life, and for that she was grateful.

She had just finished breakfast when she noticed a dark-skinned young man reading an English-language newspaper. With his face buried in the central pages, Lund went closer, and on the front page she saw a picture of the Bundespolizei station where last night's tragedy had unfolded. Thankfully, her own picture was not splashed next to it.

She peered around the paper to see the man's face, and realized he was very young—seventeen or eighteen, she guessed.

"Excuse me," she said.

The young man looked at her.

"May I see that when you're done?"

"American?" he replied.

She nodded.

"My English no much good."

The rising question of why he was reading an English-language paper was answered when he slipped one page clear—the football news, which included a number of action photos. He handed her the rest.

"Thank you," she said.

He gestured to a team photo on the page he'd retained. "Manchester United!" he said, and with no less enthusiasm than a lifelong season-ticket holder.

"Yay!" Lund replied, adding an exaggerated smile.

She backed away, settled on a nearby chair, and began studying the newspaper. Two articles covered the station shooting. One delivered the facts, and the second was an editorial on the woeful state of the Bundespolizei—according to the writer, a direct result of the right-leaning government's penny-pinching ways. Lund concentrated on the fact-based article and learned that, as of press time, little headway had been made in the case. The suspect in the shootings, described only as a heavily built man with a clean-shaven head, was still at large. An American woman wanted for questioning had also not been found. One anonymous police source floated the idea that the two might be in cahoots. Alternately, a government spokesman speculated that the woman might well turn up as victim number six.

For Lund it changed nothing. She discarded the paper and began walking through a room where fifty other refugees were milling about—people with whom she felt a surprising degree of camaraderie. She quickly found what she needed. A man with a wristwatch.

"Can you tell me what time it is?"

A fifty-something cross between George Clooney and a train hobo looked at her blankly.

She pointed to his watch, and his face brightened. He cocked his wrist toward her. It was 11:03.

"Dammit!"

Patel had been due to speak at ten. Lund had no idea she'd slept so long. She rushed for the exit, and burst outside into a cold wind and a blinding sun. After taking a moment to get her bearings, she hurried off in the direction of the Hofburg Vienna.

Back in the shelter, the man with the watch wondered what all the fuss was about. He was Armenian, a taxi driver before his car had been confiscated by Turkish soldiers when his Chinese-made GPS receiver had led him astray near a disputed border area—another incidental casualty of globalization. He looked away from the door, checked his watch, and perhaps saw the problem. His watch was still set to Armenian time—the thing had five buttons, and he really didn't know how to work them.

He shrugged it off.

Technology, he thought. *It will be the death of us all.*

With the specter of Delta lurking at every corner, DeBolt kept his movements to a minimum. After catching a few hours of sleep in the mail alcove of an apartment building, he had risen shortly after first light and worked his way cautiously toward the Hofburg Vienna. He'd skirted major roads, keeping to alleys wherever possible. In the gloom of dawn he'd regarded the backsides of buildings that appeared rough-hewn and weathered, the stains of centuries like scars on a battle-weary soldier.

He used the map in his head to avoid areas where green—readily available—CCTV coverage existed. He walked under a raised section of highway for a time, and where that ended he followed a polluted ditch overgrown with vegetation. Next came a dirt path that edged the backyards of a row of brownstone homes. At one he saw a clothesline near the back fence, a pair of pants and a shirt, roughly his size, fluttering in the early breeze. The clothes he was wearing were hopelessly soiled, doomed by last night's rain-sodden getaway and a night spent on a concrete floor. DeBolt made the switch. The pants were a marginal fit, but his belt made them work, and the shirt was two sizes too large. He left a hundred-dollar bill on a clothespin.

His approach became more cautious when the Imperial Palace came into view. He moved from alley to alcove, and imagined Delta doing the same. At the very least, he found comfort on that one point—when it came to CCTV monitoring, he and the assassin had found level ground. *But what am I missing?* DeBolt wondered. *What tricks does Delta know that I don't?*

Steps away from the palace commons, he paused to study the grounds. Between him and the conference entrance were a busy road, walking paths, and rows of overmanaged topiary clinging to the green of summer. Beyond that he faced a fifty-yard expanse of stone terrace. It was all open and vulnerable, and from a security standpoint probably the most heavily monitored acre in all of Austria. If Delta was surveilling any single place, this would be it.

DeBolt wondered if there was some way he could remain outside and intercept Patel, catch him on his way in. As far as he knew, there was only one entrance. Appealing as it was, the idea had one critical flaw—he had no idea what the man looked like.

But might there be a way?

He considered his new skill set, desperate for a fresh approach. The answer came out of nowhere on the sidewalk in front of him. It was wearing a lanyard.

"Excuse me!"

Matthias Schulze turned around and saw a young man with a bad haircut approaching him on a jog. His hand was raised in the air like a cop holding up traffic.

"Yes?" Schulze said.

The man pulled to a stop a few steps away. "Are you attending the cyber security conference?"

Schulze's conference badge was hanging from his neck on a lanyard. He smiled, and said, "I think there is no denying it." He was proud of his English, even if the occasional word got crushed under his Hamburg accent.

"I was wondering . . . do you have a conference brochure? The one that lists the schedule?"

Schulze was carrying his leather organizer—he was German, after all. "Yes, I think I have it here."

282 · WARD LARSEN

"I'm sorry to bother you, but I left mine in my hotel room, and I'm not sure about the schedule today. I traveled here all the way from the University of Alaska, in Anchorage. There are some interesting topics I don't want to miss."

Schulze smiled. "Then let me help—you have come a very long way."

He dug into a pocket of his portfolio and quickly found it. He handed the guide over, saying, "I am a professor at the University of Hamburg. I recommend Albrecht's talk this afternoon on parallel processing."

The American took the conference guide and began flipping through it. "Yes, parallel processing."

An encouraged Schulze said, "I have recently authored a paper myself, 'Idle Time Processing Across Networks.' You have heard of it maybe?"

"Maybe . . ." The blue eyes seemed to pause on one page in the guide and concentrate keenly.

"Did you find what you were looking for?"

"Yes, this is exactly what I needed." The man from Anchorage handed back the guide. "I know how to schedule my day now. Thank you so much."

"Perhaps I will see you later. Remember," he called out as the American walked away, "Albrecht at two o'clock!"

"I'll come if I can, Matthias!"

Schulze smiled, slightly surprised that the man knew his name. He looked down at his lanyard only to realize that his nametag wasn't showing. He'd taken it out earlier to find a breakfast coupon, and must have reinserted it the wrong way—only the blank backside of the card was now displayed. *So how had he . . . ?*

56

The sun rose higher, cutting the chill morning air. DeBolt had taken up a bench in the Burggarten, half a mile from the Hofburg Palace. He'd selected the seat carefully, concealed between a pair of mature willow trees. In front of him an algae-laden pond stretched across the garden, a physical barrier to the busy avenues beyond. Reluctantly, he was learning.

DeBolt had reached one conclusion: simply showing up at Patel's presentation was a last-ditch option. Delta *would* be there. Aside from presenting himself as a target, it might also endanger Patel, who, as far as DeBolt knew, was the only person alive who could explain what had been done to him. His goal, therefore, became clear: he had to find Patel *before* he arrived at the conference.

His original idea had been to hack into hotel registries. Unfortunately, there were a vast number to cover, and a comprehensive search might take hours. It also occurred to him that Patel could be staying in a group of rooms blocked off for convention participants, meaning his name might not be clearly listed. Then DeBolt had struck on a new plan. If he could locate Patel by CCTV, he might be able to intercept him before he reached the Hofburg.

To make it work, he combined two previous-used processes. He had uncovered a few basic facts on Patel, but still had no idea what the man looked like. To carry through on his scheme, he needed to find out. To that end, he'd flipped through the pages of the borrowed conference agenda to find the list of presenters. There, as hoped, he found a biography, and more importantly a photograph, of Dr. Atif Patel. While Matthias Schulze looked on curiously, DeBolt had concentrated intently on the photo in the brochure.

Once he'd captured the image, and sent the helpful German on his way, DeBolt was ready for the real work. He looked out across the placid garden, and phrased his request carefully, making every effort to avoid extraneous words—something he increasingly viewed as necessary to achieve timely and accurate results. The sparse prose of one computer talking to another: *Recall image, Dr. Atif Patel.*

The picture he'd seen in the brochure was reproduced on the screen embedded in his vision. It was a head shot, with reasonably good resolution. With some effort, DeBolt found he could manipulate the image, enlarging and cropping. Patel was clearly of Indian heritage, which was in line with his name.

Finally: *Upload for facial-recognition analysis.*

Less than ten seconds later, a minor victory.

UPLOAD SUCCESFUL.
STANDBY ANALYSIS.

The wait seemed interminable. DeBolt sat watching a pair of swans cruise the far side of the pond. Their white bodies were almost still, balanced and effortless, yet beneath the surface their webbed feet had to be motoring furiously. The unseen means of propulsion. He wondered where his request was being dissembled at that moment. Washington? Langley? The Pentagon? Some giant, anonymous data center in Utah? Were humans involved at all or was it a strictly automated process? He had so many questions. Today, perhaps, he would finally get answers.

He wasn't even sure if this part of his plan was viable. Could he create, from a photograph in a conference brochure, a facial-recognition signature for Atif Patel, a man he'd never seen in person? Even if it worked, the second part of his scheme seemed an even greater reach. DeBolt was no expert on urban surveillance or metadata analysis . . . all the same, he knew what he had managed last night.

The cameras.

The genesis of his idea had been cued from a vague memory. Something he'd once read—although he couldn't say where—describing how law enforcement agencies used software to match facial profiles to CCTV footage.

It was a way of leveraging computers to crunch massive amounts of data, plucking a specific terrorist's face from throngs of travelers in an airport or a train terminal. It seemed like a useful application, the kind of thing that *would* be developed because there was a practical need.

A message arrived.

FACIAL PROFILE COMPLETE
NO IDENTITY MATCH
LOGGED AS UNKNOWN #1

DeBolt was not surprised by the lack of a match. Like everything else about Patel, his official record was a blank. But that wasn't what he was after. He input: *CCTV within one-mile radius of present position. Search facial profiles for unknown #1.*

STANDBY

DeBolt did exactly that.

57

Through the waking of a dull and lusterless morning, DeBolt waited and watched a pond whose water was like glass. He felt a distinct urge to move to a new location—having just sent his position into cyberspace, he couldn't discount the chance that it might be digitally hijacked by Delta. He forced himself to stay on the bench, refusing to succumb to paranoia.

He realized his plan had weaknesses. To begin, it made a number of assumptions. Would Patel even walk to the conference? What if he took a taxi or a bus? Would the server to which DeBolt was connected have enough capacity, enough raw processing power to scour thousands of faces in near real time? Once again, he imagined mainframes in some distant, dark room churning through terabytes of information.

He remained still on the bench.

After ten minutes there was no response.

After fifteen doubts began to weigh in. With each passing second it seemed more of a long shot. Time was not on his side. If no reply came soon, he would have to find a way to approach Patel inside the well-monitored confines of the Hofburg. All while keeping a wary eye out for Delta.

DeBolt decided to give it five more minutes. When that passed, he decided to wait five more.

Three hundred yards from where DeBolt sat on a bench, an out-of-breath Lund rushed toward the main entrance of the Hofburg Vienna. Once she was inside, her first reaction was one of surprise. She was taken aback that a gathering of cyber specialists and software vendors would be held against the backdrop of a gilded European palace. Lund found her attention diverted by ornate columns, copper domes gone green, and the vast field of statues dressing the cornices and anterooms.

She saw a series of signs directing attendees of the World Conference on Cyber Security to the official access point. Hoping she wasn't too late, she followed the signs past a series of columns, and then up a staircase sided by a statue depicting Hercules or Neptune, or perhaps some Germanic mythological figure—art had never been her strong suit. Classical music drifted from unseen speakers, soft and soothing.

She arrived at a bustling reception area and found a pedestal where a schedule of the day's events was posted: Dr. Patel's ten o'clock presentation was set in a room called Festsaal. There was also a map to guide her to the right corridor. Lund had been to her share of conferences, and while hers had related to law enforcement, she supposed they were all similar in one respect— oversight would be lax. She took the direct route, falling into a role. She gave the occasional nod to strangers, glanced at a few merchant poster boards, but kept moving in one direction. Her confidence was rewarded when she drifted past the sign-in table without a glance from the two busy women behind it.

She found the Festsaal room quickly, and on turning inside was immediately struck by two things. First was the overt grandeur of the hall. With mural-covered ceilings, carved stone, and chandeliers the size of cars, it had to be as beautifully appointed as any room in Vienna. The second impression was far more worrying—the place was nearly empty.

Had she missed the presentation?

"Dammit!" she muttered under her breath.

At the back of the room Lund saw two men engaged in casual conversation, and she caught a few words of English. She hurried over.

"Excuse me—"

The man she'd interrupted broke off, and both looked at her.

"I missed Dr. Patel's talk. Did either of you see him leave?"

"Dr. Patel?" said the taller of the two, in what sounded like a Scandinavian accent. "He is not here until ten o'clock."

"Ten?" Lund repeated. "But . . . what time is it?"

The other man checked his watch. "Nine twenty."

Lund stared at him stupidly, recalling the man with the watch in the homeless shelter. She sighed heavily. "I'm sorry, I forgot my phone . . . I'm lost without it."

The distress on her face must have been pronounced, because the taller man said, "Don't worry. We too have been waiting a long time to hear Patel." He winked conspiratorially. "We will have the best seats, no?"

With forty minutes to spare, Lund thanked the men.

They watched her curiously as she took a seat in the back row, deep in a corner and partially hidden behind a column. Without a doubt, the worst seat in the house.

A simple misunderstanding, she thought, sinking back into a padded metal chair. It occurred to her that this had been the sequence of her life in recent days. Meandering through a grocery store one moment, flying off to Maine the next. Waiting in a police holding room, then dashing away from a killer. It was a distressing pattern—hours of boredom interspersed by moments of sheer terror. Once more, she found herself in the waiting cycle.

Which didn't bode well for what was to come.

"Only two bags?" asked the bellman.

"Yes," Patel replied, watching the young man carry his suitcases toward the door of his room. "They will be taken straight to the airport?"

"Of course, sir. Our concierge has made arrangements with the delivery service."

Patel slipped the man five dollars, and watched him disappear. He checked his watch: thirty minutes remained until his scheduled presentation. He collected his speaking notes from the writing desk, an undeniably thin stack for a one-hour presentation. In truth, he'd not put much thought into the effort, deciding to stick with one of his stock lectures: "The Art of Systems Architecture." Patel cared little if he engaged the crowd—today would be his final performance behind a lectern, his life in academia having reached its predestined end. He had not yet purchased his outbound airline ticket, but Patel's preliminary feelers had identified three interested parties, all predictably to the east: Russia, China, and India.

All that would have to wait just a few hours longer.

Patel opened his leather portfolio and stuffed his notes inside carelessly. They hung up momentarily on the only other item in the attaché, a loaded 9mm Beretta Nano. Delta had provided it, Patel having no idea how to procure such a thing in a foreign country. He could use it in the most basic sense, but doubted it would come to that. Not if Delta did his job.

Either way, he was prepared.

Patel left the room, and when he shut the door it was perhaps with a flash of reflection. He thought he might return to Vienna someday under more casual circumstances. Stay for a time and relax in the very room where the marriage of META to its host had been consummated.

Having already settled his account, Patel bypassed the front desk and headed outside into a bland morning. He took his usual route to the Hofburg—through the Stadtpark, past the pigeon-laden statue of Schubert, and then the vacant Kursalon. He navigated Walfischgasse as if he were a local, and had just rounded the Albertina art museum, with its sculpture of what looked like a giant diving board, when someone called, "Excuse me, Dr. Patel?"

He stopped and turned, and encountered a man he'd never seen before. He was slightly younger than Patel himself, keen and athletic. Of course he knew who it was. Patel's grip on his attaché tightened ever so slightly as he said, "Do I know you?"

"I very much hope so."

With the benefit of forewarning, Patel managed things well—his face remained a blank. "I don't understand."

"The META Project, Dr. Patel. I'm what came from it."

"You mean—"

"Yes," the man interrupted. "I'm Option Bravo."

58

DeBolt watched the man closely as he said it. *I'm Option Bravo.*

Patel appeared stunned, and looked him up and down. "You're saying . . . ," he hesitated mightily, "they actually *went forward* with the surgeries?"

"I think there may be a lot you don't know. I need some questions answered. We should talk." He looked across the crowded sidewalk, then at the busy Albertina Museum entrance. "Somewhere more private, I think."

"Yes," Patel agreed, "I know just the place."

Patel waited for a break in traffic, then set out across the street. DeBolt almost balked, realizing Patel had no understanding of the threat from Delta. He fell in behind, but as soon as they reached the other side, he said, "Tell me where we're going. I'll get us there."

Patel almost replied, but then stopped on the sidewalk and stared at him. Ever so slowly, like a rising sun, a look of astonishment washed across his distinctly Indian features. "You're not . . . not *active*, are you?"

DeBolt of course knew what he meant, and he felt a peculiar sense of relief. Patel was the one person on earth to whom he would not have to prove his abilities. There would be no laborious fact-finding or clever tricks. "I'm active," he said. "Now, tell me where we're going."

Patel studied him carefully, in the way an art aficionado might view an intricate sculpture in the museum behind them. He finally said, "The Winter Riding School. I was given a private tour yesterday, but it's been closed to the public recently for renovations. There should be no one there on a Sunday morning, and I think the service entrance might be open."

DeBolt input the Riding School, and found it situated inside the Hofburg Palace, directly under one of the great domes. "Follow me."

Patel hesitated. "But . . . you used it? Just now, to find the Riding School?"

"Yes."

Patel smiled in wonder. "How incredible that must be."

Five minutes later, after a long and circuitous route, they arrived at the service entrance of the Winter Riding School. A disinterested museum worker stood near the door—not security, but a custodian pushing a cleaning cart—and Patel dropped the name of the official who'd given him a tour the previous day. It seemed to work, and they walked into the great hall.

Inside was a towering gallery like nothing DeBolt had ever seen. Central was a rectangular riding area, the brown dirt floor hoof-beaten and emanating a distinctly earthen odor. DeBolt saw a poster advertising an equine show, the featured act being Lipizzaner stallions. The performance arena was surrounded by two high floors of box seating and observation balconies, giving the impression of a Roman arena. He and Patel were on the top level amid ornate columns and balustrades and statues—why should it differ from any other part of the Hofburg? It all seemed from another age, and DeBolt imagined gallant horses strutting, soldiers in riding coats and silken breeches. Altogether, it could not have been more incongruous to an age of smartphones and cyber conferences.

To an age of META.

Scaffolding dominated one wall, and on the framework were cross-planks holding half-used buckets of paint and plaster. Repairs of the chipped stone columns and sculpted cornices had obviously taken pause for the weekend. There were no workers in sight, nor any tour groups, and the custodian had pushed his cart elsewhere. They were alone—just as DeBolt had wanted.

He checked for cameras, with both his eyes and his connection, and as far as he could tell there were none in the high cornices. He uploaded a diagram of the place to learn the path to every exit—he *was* learning. Only then did DeBolt allow himself to relax. His journey from Alaska, through Maine and New England, was finally at an end. He had what he wanted—the undivided attention of META's last surviving architect.

They stood along a heavy balustrade, two levels above the brown-dirt arena.

"Bravo," Patel said, regarding him as a father might look at a long-lost son. "I knew live tests were inevitable. But the initial subjects were never expected to—"

"Survive?" DeBolt cut in, surprised by a rush of anger welling inside him. "Well, here I am! What the *hell* were you people thinking? Playing God with human life?"

Patel seemed suddenly nervous. "Yes, I know. I was never comfortable with that. But for you, the first group of four—the criteria were very specific. Alpha through Delta were supposed to be terminal cases, individuals with neural activity but no chance of recovering. We *had* to test the viability of the surgery, the implant procedures. I—" He pulled his phone from his pocket, studied the screen, then began thumbing out a message.

"What are you doing?" DeBolt asked.

"My presentation. It begins in a few minutes. They are wondering where I am."

"Tell them you're going to be late."

Break her neck.

Delta reasoned that was his best chance to kill the woman and not be noticed. It struck him how thin and white her neck was—considerably more delicate than that of her colleague in Alaska. He'd used both hands on that man—but then, there had been no tactical reason to do otherwise. Here he would have to finish Lund with one hand, leaving the other free to support her body when it went limp. It was, after all, a very public place.

He'd been watching her for fifteen minutes, which seemed an interminable wait. He would have done it by now if there weren't so many damned people around. He'd seen guards in the halls behind him, but they were only museum police, and none too alert. Men and women trained to look for thieves and pickpockets. Not trained assassins.

All the same, he'd entered the Hofburg cautiously. No photos had arisen from his attack last night on the Bundespolizei outpost—META's cleansing of the police video files had been meticulous. Unfortunately, it wasn't so easy to erase the memories of the handful of policemen who'd glimpsed him. A general description had been circulated of a muscular bald man. To confuse the issue, Delta had bought a long, loose overcoat, and tied two sweaters around his waist. It made him appear simply overweight, and he'd topped everything off with a cheap felt trilby to cover his bald head. Taken together, more the profile of a soft banker than a hardened killer.

He was situated at the back of the meeting room called Festsaal. He thought it was a stupid name. Delta had rarely found himself in conference rooms over the years, and when he did they typically had names like Iwo Jima and Guadalcanal. He stood partially hidden in a small alcove, ten steps behind the last row of chairs. That was where Lund was sitting. It was an amateur move, but then she *was* nothing more than a detective. She had opted to hide in a shadow, which in this scenario was the worst possible choice. In a more central seat, surrounded by a crowd, she would have been far more difficult to spot, and harder yet to attack. As it was . . . *ten steps.*

Yes, definitely the neck. It would be quick and clean, and if he released her carefully she would remain in a sitting position. Pull her eyes closed, Delta thought, and she might be a conference attendee who had stayed out too late, or one who'd gone catatonic from a tedious presentation. His plan also allowed a simple egress to the back doors. Yet there was one problem: a man had taken a seat immediately to Lund's left, a middle-aged matchstick in a knitted scarf. There were three empty seats in every other direction.

Delta grew impatient. He decided to snap the matchstick as well.

It all came down to timing. Patel's presentation was due to begin in two minutes. Only there wasn't going to be a presentation. Delta had received two text messages from Patel, the first fifteen minutes ago: Have DeBolt with me. Then, moments ago: Come quickly. I think he suspects something.

Delta wondered if Patel was carrying the gun he'd provided. Probably, he decided. But would he know what do with it?

Ten steps.

His frustration peaked. At that moment he was frozen by the crowds. There was a constant stream of attendees at the entrance, double doors only a few steps to his left. Some were arriving late for a talk that wasn't going to happen. A handful of others were leaving, already seeing the writing on the wall. He wished Patel had shown up—everyone's attention would then be predictable, focused on the lectern at the front of the room.

Delta felt tension knotting in his arms and shoulders. He didn't want to lose Lund—not when she was this close. In the end, he did what he was trained to do. He settled back on his heels and waited ever so patiently. The little programmer would have to take care of himself just a little bit longer.

DeBolt let Patel send the text to explain he would be late. Then he made him start from the beginning.

"It was my concept," Patel admitted. "I had been talking with DARPA for years about a project to give high-level systems management a more operational focus. DARPA, of course, is a DOD asset, and I finally gained a proponent for the idea in the Pentagon."

"General Benefield?"

"Yes. He and I had many meetings, and I convinced him that with enough support, with access to certain high-level servers, we could develop a system to harness virtually limitless cyber capabilities and funnel them in near real-time to select individuals. 'Cyber-soldier' was his preferred term. The Army has been researching such concepts for years. I explained that I could write software to link with a neural interface—it would create a direct pathway between the brain and available communications networks."

"That's what's in my head?" DeBolt asked. "Some kind of antenna to connect through Wi-Fi or cell networks?"

"Essentially, although it's much more complex. Other networks exist—military and government grids. The system prioritizes available channels and chooses the best and most secure method. It's all transparent to the user."

"User? Is that what I am? You make it sound like I got new cable service."

Patel acquired a tone of remorse. "Please . . . I realize you were not a volunteer for META. I had no say in the selection process for subjects. But now that it's been done, and gone active . . . I'm naturally curious as to what functionality you've acquired."

DeBolt explained some of what he'd learned to do, and Patel seemed pleased.

"The problem all along," Patel explained, "has been the neuroscience. The human brain exhibits amazing plasticity—it adapts to injury and dysfunction. For years researchers have been closing in on a true web-neural interface, permitting communication between the brain and external devices. Think of it as using a computer without the mouse or keyboard, or a smartphone without the touchscreen. This is not science fiction—it's long existed in bits and pieces. Cochlear implants are common. Retinal implants have been in clinical trials for years. META only joined all these elements a decade ahead of what might have been. The fact that you are standing before me, as Bravo, fully capable—you are the proof."

"I don't want to be your proof. I want my life back."

Patel seemed disappointed. "Do you not realize what you're capable of? You have abilities no human has ever had."

"Trust me, it's a curse. Ever since this operation, I've had a target on my back. Anyone who gets near me is either killed or kidnapped. And you should know something else . . . I'm not alone."

Patel eyed him cautiously. "What do you mean?"

"Another of META's experiments survived, and he also went—as you say—*active*."

"Which one?"

"Delta."

Patel's gaze sank to the floor. "Delta? He is alive?" The professor's hand went to his pocket and again retrieved his phone. He read a message before asking, "How do you know this?"

Suddenly DeBolt sensed something wrong. Patel's reaction to Delta being alive. His phone play. He was too calm, too much in control. DeBolt said, "Are you aware of what happened to General Benefield?"

"The general? Yes, I know about that. A few days ago he came to Vienna to see me and . . . he was murdered."

"He was executed. Delta has gone mad . . . or maybe he was already that way, even before you gave him the keys to your cyber-universe."

A symphony of church bells rang outside, their notice reaching into the Winter Riding School and echoing between its walls. Ten o'clock.

Patel pocketed his phone.

Something is very wrong, DeBolt thought. He had to see what was on Patel's phone. Should he invade the handset using META? *No*, he thought. Unlike his battles against Delta, here DeBolt was physically superior. It would be quicker to simply take it.

Yes, take it! Get the phone now!

DeBolt was three paces away. As soon as he took his first step toward Patel, the scientist backed away. His hand went into a pocket.

A different pocket, DeBolt realized too late.

It came back out with a gun.

59

"You knew about Delta," said DeBolt as he looked down the barrel of a stubby semiautomatic. The weapon appeared steady in Patel's hand, yet he took another step back to put more ground between them. A sign of confidence in his marksmanship? Or discomfort in the tactical situation? DeBolt suspected the latter. He estimated they were separated by eight feet—too far to go for the gun, regardless of Patel's skill level.

"I *created* Delta!" said Patel. "Just as I created you."

DeBolt shook his head, trying to make sense of it. "But . . . surely you realize every remnant of META has been destroyed. The surgery clinic in Maine burned to the ground, Benefield is dead."

"There was also the unfortunate DARPA software team in Virginia," Patel added. "You never knew about them. I could never have managed the project alone—the system architecture and coding were extensive. We hired a group of programmers, a few support personnel. Thirteen men and women altogether."

"*Thirteen?*" DeBolt said, as much to himself as Patel. Yet another rise in the body count. By now he should have been numb to such a revelation, but it struck a blow all the same. "Were there other subjects?"

"Alpha and Charlie . . . but they never had a chance. One was an Army sergeant, the other a Navy corpsman. Neither could possibly have recovered from their injuries."

"You've killed a lot of people."

"It wasn't me—I am only a technician, a computer engineer. Although, one might say I programmed the demise of META. The wet work, as they say, was done by Colonel Freeman and his Special Forces team. And of course Delta."

"But META was your idea, your creation . . . why destroy it now?"

"You still don't understand, do you. I *haven't* destroyed it. I've taken ownership. META is mine alone now, and it can't be reversed. The software you so blithely use to make amazing discoveries is deeply embedded at its source—it won't be discovered for years, if ever."

"What *is* the source?" DeBolt asked. It had always loomed as his biggest question.

"It won't hurt to tell you. Not given your immediate prospects. But you should have figured it out. Think about it, Bravo. You don't merely see maps and websites. You can access military intelligence and satellite imagery, obtain data on any individual in the world who has a profile on a server. You can hack into corporate databases, activate a cell phone camera in China, map the electrical grid in Bulgaria. What little you've stumbled upon so far—it only touches the surface."

DeBolt stood still listening, hanging on every word.

Patel smiled. "Yes, there it is. I can see it in your expression—just like Delta. At first you don't want any of it. You feel used, as if you've been turned into some kind of cyborg, half human and half machine. You're overwhelmed and burdened by your new abilities. But slowly you begin to realize what you have. What you *might* do with it. Can you deny it? The feeling of supremacy, of having virtually all knowledge available for the asking?"

DeBolt wanted to deny it . . . but Patel wasn't completely off the mark. He *had* felt it, a confidence, even an ascendancy. He had been given an intoxicating power others could scarcely imagine.

"Of course you know where it comes from," the scientist continued. "Tell me—what is the most capable agency in the world when it comes to sorting data and signals intelligence? Who can hack at will into virtually any network— friend or foe, corporate or government? Who can monitor anyone's phone traffic and track their commutes? What agency coined the term 'yottabyte'—that's ten to the twenty-fourth power—because 'zettabyte' wasn't enough? Think, Bravo. You know."

DeBolt didn't want to admit it, but Patel was right again. There was but one possible source.

He *had* known all along.

Lund watched the conference spokesman trundle up the center aisle. He was beefy and wore an ill-fitting business suit—put him in leather suspenders and lederhosen, and he would have looked right at home in a beer hall. He approached the lectern at the head of the Festsaal gallery, played with the microphone for a moment, and said in thickly accented English, "My apologies for the inconvenience. Dr. Patel has obviously been delayed. We are trying to reach him and discover the nature of the difficulty. When we get any information, an update will be provided. As we wait, refreshments are available in the main hall."

There was a flourish of hushed conversation, and what had been a trickle of defectors became a flood. The central aisle filled shoulder to shoulder. The place would be empty within minutes. Lund considered joining the crowd, but saw little point. If Patel was going to show up, this was where it would be. Anyway, where else did she have to go?

She settled deeper into her chair.

If nothing else, she thought, *I'm safe here.*

The rail-thin man sitting next to her got up to leave.

60

The National Security Agency was born in 1952 as a child of the Cold War, tasked by none other than Harry S. Truman to crack the communications codes of hostile nations, in particular those in the Communist Bloc. Its very existence was classified for years, leading to the running jest that its acronym stood for "No Such Agency."

By turn of fate, the end of the Cold War coincided perfectly with the rise of the information age, and seeing its primary mission fading, the NSA did what government agencies always did when survival became an issue—it morphed into something its creators could never have imagined.

Today's NSA operates on a budget of no less than forty billion dollars a year, the exact amount being highly classified. It is run by forty thousand employees, and the headquarters building alone contains seventy acres of floor space. Dozens of subsidiary data centers lay scattered across the country like seeds on the wind, a cyber network whose collective electric bill is north of a billion dollars a year. Yet if any one fact could cement its reputation, it is found amid the personnel rosters: The NSA is the world's largest employer of mathematicians. By their efforts, and without question, the National Security Agency is caretaker to the greatest pyramid of knowledge ever assembled. And Trey DeBolt, by no choice of his own, found himself at the apex.

"NSA," he said.

"Naturally," said a pleased Patel.

"So META is run by the government."

"The government," Patel spat. "Our government is nothing but a behemoth, a beast that feeds and grows, and becomes so large it cannot even see itself. META is but a lost grain of sand, a program canceled before the people who paid for it even realized what was in their grasp. As of today, the program is officially dead, along with nearly everyone who had knowledge of it."

"So my abilities are going to shut down soon?"

Patel smiled broadly. "Quite the opposite," he said, "and therein lies the elegance of what I've created. You must understand, the NSA processes fifty petabytes of information every day . . . *fifty petabytes*. That's an amount of data few people can grasp, save for the armies of analysts who do the sorting. What I have given you and Delta is unique. Not only do you have a connection to NSA, you have the highest priority access for cyber, on par with only a handful of people. The president, the director of national intelligence. The heads of CIA and NSA. In recent years great efforts have been made to expedite high-level requests, to hack into servers and get near-instantaneous results. It's called tailored access operations. I was granted permission to install META under the guise of a DOD experiment, to explore the feasibility of bringing such near real-time access to Special Forces operatives in the field—it would be the greatest advance in weaponry since gunpowder."

"A weapon," said DeBolt. "That's how you envision META?"

"Not at all. That was how General Benefield saw it, and the reason I was granted access. On paper, the project has ended, and by all appearances it has. Even I no longer have the ability to manipulate the software—it is now air-gapped, completely out of my hands. But deep within the NSA's tailored access architecture, inside the most capable servers on earth, the code I implanted endures in utter silence."

"And on the outside?"

"You and Delta are the only benefactors."

DeBolt looked obviously at Patel's weapon. "So what's the point of that?"

Patel sighed forlornly. "I never expected two successes from our first four trials. Honestly, I predicted that META's next phase, which was another year away, would be the first chance for a subject to survive the surgery. I wish I could work with you, study your abilities. But it's simply not possible. Given what you know . . . the risk is far too great."

A metallic clatter sounded somewhere down a hallway, the noise reverberating under the high ceilings. Patel's eyes never wavered.

DeBolt said, "So you'll eliminate me—like all the others. But what about Delta? He's a killer, a madman. Why choose *him* as the test subject for your perverse experiments?"

"For one good reason—he will always do as I say."

DeBolt was baffled by Patel's answer, yet he sensed an opening. He closed his eyes for a brief moment, then said, "Tell me about Delta. How could anyone control him?"

His patience finally paid off.

Delta watched the thinning crowd in the aisle. Another minute, two at the most, he could finish what he'd come to do. The woman was still there, alone now in the last row. She'd glanced over her shoulder a minute earlier, her eyes actually passing over him. But there had been no recognition. Like any good predator, Delta could tell when his prey had been alerted.

He began edging away from the alcove, closing in. His hands lifted out of the pockets of his overcoat.

Then the most peculiar thing happened.

Patel lowered the gun ever so slightly, but DeBolt was still too far away to cross the divide and wrestle it away. So he waited. He listened.

"Delta?" Patel said derisively. "He is my idiot savant. A thug born in a uniform who now takes his orders from me. Right now he has Miss Lund cornered not a hundred yards from where we stand."

DeBolt shuddered inwardly. "Shannon . . . she's *here*?"

"Of course. We brought her here, in very much the same way we brought you."

DeBolt remembered the message as if it were still in his visual field:

META CHIEF PROGRAMMER, DR. ATIF PATEL
CURRENT LOCATION: VIENNA, AUSTRIA

"You manipulated what I saw."

"Not me. META is embedded now, so I no longer have access. Delta took care of it—he does everything I tell him to do."

"But why? What hold do you have over him?"

"You haven't spoken to him, have you?"

"We've crossed paths twice, but they weren't exactly social encounters. He did send me a message directly through META."

Patel smiled with satisfaction. "Another success—intranetwork messaging. You see, Delta is no longer on speaking terms with anyone. He has lost his ability for speech—a complete mute."

"Because of the META surgery? What was implanted in his head?"

"That's what he believes. I've told him his loss is reversible, and that in time I can find a surgeon who will repair the damage. It gives him great hope."

"But it's not true."

"Not at all. The implantation procedures were performed by Dr. Abel Badenhorst, a very capable surgeon—he also did your work. He assured me that Delta's speech loss was entirely the result of the accident that brought him to us. It was an explosion, a combat injury that nearly killed him. The damage to his frontal lobe was significant, and it robbed him of his ability to communicate. It can never be repaired. 'Complete verbal apraxia,' I think was the term Badenhorst used. Yet Delta believes in me. He is amazed by what I've given him, and each day I teach him more about operating META to its full effect. He will do what I ask—my army of one, connected to the most capable, intrusive computer servers on earth."

"Aren't you worried he'll learn that you're lying to him?" DeBolt asked.

"How could he? I tell him I am coordinating with great surgeons, devising a plan to reverse the damage. But such things take time. A year, maybe two. At that point I won't need him any longer."

"Why not?"

"Because I will have transferred META to its new owner."

"New owner?"

"Of course. I've known from the outset that META's prospects in the U.S. were limited. The surgery is extensive, revising multiple lobes of a subject's brain to permit both visual and aural signals, not to mention subvocalization—that's the ability to transfer your thoughts to the screen in your right eye. It involves circuitry in your head, and a biologically sourced power supply. All very invasive, and entailing considerable risk."

"Alpha and Charlie are proof of that."

"There, you see? Moral outrage. Most Americans would shudder at the concept, call it human experimentation. Fortunately, I ran across General Benefield, a man with the right connections, and whose ambition outweighed his sense of ethics. He procured the window I needed into NSA. Mind you, it could never be permanent. Five years, perhaps ten, and someone will uncover my architecture and remove it. It doesn't matter. Years ago, as I formulated the concept, I sent inquiries to colleagues in a select group of nations, asking if their governments might have an interest in pursuing such work. The NSA's networks would no longer be at my disposal, but Russia and China have parallel, if somewhat less effective agencies. Their responses were enthusiastic to say the least. And now I have Delta to prove the concept—my living, breathing, technology demonstrator."

"Russia and China? You're going to sell this madness to the highest bidder?"

"Certainly. Delta—and by some accident, you—are merely the beginning. You are the beta-test versions, as we might say at Cal. In two, perhaps three years, I'll have a veritable army of operatives like you in development elsewhere."

DeBolt held steady. As Patel talked, he let his eyes wander across the entrances of the great hall. He had to keep the man talking. "So this is all about money. You would sell out your country? Perform experiments on others like you did on me? On Delta?"

"Your patriotism falls hollow on me, Bravo. I was born in the United States, but what does that mean for a man whose skin is as dark as mine? My parents came from India, and worked day and night to give me an education. I played by all the rules, worked and studied hard, but I still heard the whispers behind my back, heard so-called friends laughing at me. America might be my homeland, but I have always felt like an outcast . . . so if it is harmed by my work, I will suffer no remorse."

"An outcast? Just like Delta will be for the rest of his life? The difference, I suppose, is that he doesn't know it." DeBolt then very deliberately repeated his earlier words. "He *will* learn that you're lying to him."

Patel was silent for a moment. His gaze went taut as he analyzed what DeBolt had just said. *How* he had said it.

Both men heard a door burst open somewhere in the great hall.

61

Lund could breathe again. The big man behind her had abruptly turned and left.

Had he been waiting for Patel's speech like the rest? She had noticed him a few minutes ago when she'd turned around. Even half hidden behind a wall he was hard to miss—broad chested in a full-length coat, his face and head obscured by a hat tilted low. Was it the man from the station? She'd caught only a glimpse of him then, little more than a meaty face behind an outstretched gun. There was also the grainy picture Jim Kalata had sent, the one that had mysteriously been wiped from her phone.

Was it him, or am I only seeing ghosts?

She'd been worried enough to keep watching the man—on the column in front of her seat was a polished steel chair rail, and in its reflection she'd watched him closely. It was imprecise, like surveillance using a funhouse mirror, but if the man moved she would know it. And move he had.

She'd watched him shoulder away from the alcove and step slightly closer. Lund had no weapon, but she knew there was an exit at the other end of the room. She was seconds from bolting when the man had gone still. He didn't move for nearly a minute, then rushed away in a flurry of coattails and felt. He was surprisingly quick for a big man, and left the room with a purpose. She'd caught but one direct glimpse as he disappeared out the door, the back of his coat and hat, an amorphous dark mass turning left into the outer hallway.

That had been two minutes ago.

Lund got up slowly, no longer concerned about the appearance of Dr. Patel. She went to the entrance, leaned carefully out into the corridor, and looked left.

She saw no sign of the man in the overcoat.

DeBolt and Patel spotted him at the same time.

Delta.

The two remained a few paces apart along the high balustrade, a grand seating box from which emperors and queens had watched the Riding School's stallions parade through routines.

Delta had emerged from a side entrance, and he was coming at them now. Slowly and deliberately, like a machine building steam. He took an angle that stranded them, penning Patel and DeBolt between two ornate walls and the gilded balcony railing. Effectively blocking the only way out. Delta came to a stop, and for the first time DeBolt saw expressiveness in the killer's face. But what was it? Pain? Anger? Whatever the source, it was hateful and murderous . . . and fixed very clearly on Patel.

"What is wrong?" Patel asked. He looked at DeBolt. "What have you done?"

"You should know," said DeBolt. "*You* gave me the ability to transmit audio in real time. How does it work? The cochlear implant you mentioned? I actually researched that. It's essentially a microphone, and using META I can upload sounds for analysis—words to be translated or voiceprinted. A very useful function."

Patel's gaze switched back to Delta.

"He heard everything you said," DeBolt assured him. "He deserves to know the truth."

Delta took a step toward Patel.

"No! It's not like that at all! I can repair your speech . . . if *anyone* can, it's me! I promise you, I will never stop working until you are made whole."

Delta kept coming, and soon the three men formed a perfect triangle. All at once, Patel seemed to remember the gun in his hand. Synapses connected, and signals were sent through his unaltered brain. He lifted the gun until it was level on the assassin's chest. "Stop!"

Delta kept coming.

Patel fired, the sound of the shot thundering through the great hall.

DeBolt saw a tiny explosion on Delta's chest, smoke and a confetti-like burst of fabric. The killer only moved faster. Patel got off three more rounds, all striking Delta in the torso, before the two men met chest to chest. Delta wrapped his massive arms around Patel and began to squeeze. The engineer flapped his arms and legs as he was lifted completely off the ground. He gave a visceral scream, desperation echoing through the hall, and then all the air seemed to go out of him. His mouth remained wide in agony, but no further sounds came. DeBolt heard a terrible crackling sound, like a dozen tiny balloons popping, and Patel seemed to fold in half, his head bending back toward his heels.

The assassin's face was red with rage, his mouth open in a soundless scream as he lifted the lifeless engineer over his head and threw him over the rail. Patel's body thumped onto the dirt floor three floors below, his spine creased at an impossible angle.

DeBolt quickly spotted the gun on the floor nearby. With one step, it was directly at his feet, yet he made no attempt to bend down and retrieve it. Strangely, Delta didn't try to intercept him. Instead, he moved back to where he'd been moments ago—a position to block any escape. With the gun at his feet, DeBolt kept his eyes on Delta. Patel had struck the killer with multiple rounds—DeBolt had seen the bullets strike home—yet he appeared uninjured. But he wasn't invulnerable.

Body armor, thought DeBolt. It was the only explanation. If DeBolt took a shot, he would have to aim for the head. But that wasn't what he wanted. He ignored the weapon and tried to read Delta. Whatever frenzy had possessed him was gone, and DeBolt was again looking at an expressionless mask. "There's no need for us to be against each other," he said. "Patel was the enemy. You and I . . . we didn't ask for any of this."

He waited. Delta didn't respond. No nod, no shoulder shrug. No transmission through META.

"We both served our country," said DeBolt. "We're on the same side."

The big man looked at him thoughtfully, as if weighing what DeBolt was saying.

"You and I are casualties of META—none of this was for our benefit. I only want it to end, and I think you do too. No one else on earth can appreciate what you've been through—not like I do. *I understand!*"

Finally, Delta opened his mouth, and without making a sound he mouthed three words DeBolt could easily read: *No, you don't.*

DeBolt saw the big man tense, saw his body lower slightly, like a massive cat ready to lunge. DeBolt looked down at the weapon, and when he did his spirits sank. The gun's slide had locked back. Which meant it was empty.

62

Delta came at him fast.

Without a weapon, DeBolt knew he had little chance against the assassin in close quarters combat. He took the only way out. With one great stride back, he vaulted over the rail behind him.

Delta's hand swiped at his shoulder as DeBolt launched into the air. He dropped twenty feet, his arms outstretched for balance as he tried to set for a landing: legs together, knees bent, ready to roll onto a hip. Thankfully the dirt was soft, but he hit hard and his right knee buckled in a bad way.

The pain was excruciating, and DeBolt instinctively grabbed his leg. He looked up and saw Delta leaning over the rail. For a moment he thought the killer might follow, but then he seemed to realize DeBolt was injured. He disappeared, his heavy boots stomping across marble.

With Patel's body right next to him, DeBolt rolled away and tried to get to his feet. His first attempt failed as a bolt of pain shot through his leg. The sound of Delta's footsteps thundering down a staircase made him try again. He managed to stand, and at a glance saw only one exit from the dirt riding floor. DeBolt hobbled toward it and fell shoulder-first into what looked like a barn door.

He burst out into daylight.

Lund was cautious as she canvassed the halls of the Hofburg Vienna, increasingly convinced that she was right—the man who'd been standing behind her in the conference room was the killer. The assassin she'd seen for an instant at the Bundespolizei station. Could he really be responsible for Boston as well? Kodiak? Her cautionary detective's instincts told her it was improbable that one man could have managed it all. *Almost as improbable as human minds networking with computers.*

Strangely she wasn't fearful. He had left hurriedly, and Lund could think of only one reason for him to do so—a more important target had arisen. *Trey?* she wondered. *Or perhaps Dr. Patel?*

She moved more quickly down a long hallway, and rounded the castle chapel. She went through doors that led nowhere, and apologized to two Hofburg employees when she interrupted a meeting in an office. Her pace quickened as her conviction hardened. Trey, Patel, the killer. They were all here, somewhere.

Lund was nearly on a dead run when she entered the National Library. Thinking this had to be wrong, she backtracked. That was when the first *crack* rang down the hall. Lund froze, immediately recognizing the sound as gunfire. After a pause, a volley of three more rounds came in quick succession. She spun a circle at the intersection of four hallways as the report of the shots bounded amid walls and arched ceilings. Which direction had it come from? Finding the source inside these cavernous halls was like trying to trace a lone spark in a burst of fireworks.

She opted for what looked like the least-used path—an entrance to something called the Winter Riding School that had been barricaded off for construction. Two minutes later, she rounded a warning sign, slipped through an unlocked door, and found herself in a great sunlight-splashed hall. Squarely in the middle, on a floor of churned dirt beneath a giant chandelier, was a body so severely crumpled it could not possibly sustain life. The face was turned toward Lund, and she discerned a male with Indian features. Behind a shattered pair of glasses his face was twisted into a mask of pain, the last expression he would ever wear. Lund knew who it had to be—the man who was twenty minutes late for a presentation in the Festsaal Gallery.

Dr. Atif Patel.

She saw no one else in the cavernous hall, but her gaze latched quickly on one other anomaly.

A big door at the back of the riding floor had been left ajar.

DeBolt tried to keep moving. Keep functioning. His right leg was useless, deadweight dragging beneath him. The sidewalks were busy, the boulevards behind the Hofburg bursting with the commotion of a thriving city. He tried to keep as normal a gait as possible, knowing a pronounced limp would act as a beacon, highlighting him to Delta.

DeBolt kept to the flow of crowds, tried to lose himself in small groups. His knee was swelling, tightening with each step like a fast-rusting hinge. Fleetness of foot, the one advantage he'd had over Delta, was now lost. He considered hiding, but knew it was hopeless—no one could hide from META. His only chance was to get away, to create distance. Which meant he had to find a quicker way to move.

He found it just in time, red and boxy, gliding up the street a hundred yards behind him. A city tram. He searched ahead for the next stop and easily spotted it—a sign with a tram symbol next to sheltered benches. He hobbled as fast as he could, not caring how conspicuous he was, desperate to reach the stop before the car arrived.

The tram passed him effortlessly, then drew to a stop. DeBolt nearly fell trying to catch up, but reached the door just in time. He hauled himself up into the car—there was only one step, but his right leg was carrying almost no weight. He collapsed into an empty front seat as the tram started moving. His breathing was ragged, the cold air dry on his throat. He ventured a look back, and for a moment there was nothing, only the buzz of Vienna on midday. Then he saw the unmistakable shape, a wide overcoat bulling through the crowds.

The track was angling closer—it would take the tram to within fifty feet of Delta. The killer's eyes were scanning, searching, and when they paused on the tram car DeBolt hunched down instinctively in his seat. Had he been seen? He ventured another look and saw the bald head pointed loosely toward the tram. Delta was no longer searching, his features lost to an empty gaze—the same one that was on his own face, DeBolt supposed, when he employed META. What function was he using? Was he commandeering feeds from cameras? Intercepting police communications? If Delta *had* spotted him on the tram, DeBolt was sure there was a computer network or application that could be used to track individual cars.

He suddenly realized his own screen seemed to be failing, the video intermittently going to snow. *What now?* Had the hard landing from his jump dislodged something in his head? DeBolt pushed away the ridiculous thought. Striving for logic, he looked outside and saw the problem—the tram was electric, and high-voltage wires were strung above the track. It was no more than signal interference, the same as when he'd gone near the electrical substation in Maine.

The tram rocked from side to side as it made its way up the street. He tried for a map in his head to see where it was taking him, but the feed kept getting interrupted. The same electricity that was taking him away from Delta was also blocking META. He guessed they were running north, toward the Danube.

Soon the tram slowed for its next stop, and DeBolt ventured another look back. His heart skipped when he saw someone running to catch up on the far side of the street.

It nearly stopped beating altogether when he realized who it was.

"I saw you get on the tram," Lund said breathlessly, "but I didn't think I could catch up! I've never run so fast in my life!"

She was in his arms, her chest heaving into his with the rhythm of a heartbeat. DeBolt kept holding her, his cheek buried in her soft hair while he looked warily out the window behind. He saw no sign of Delta, and wished it were otherwise. A few minutes ago he'd at least *known* where the man was. He was ecstatic to see Lund, but terrified she was so near the killer.

She pushed away and looked at him, her expression an awkward mesh of relief and desperation. "I got your message about Patel, so I came as fast as—"

"No," he cut in. "That message wasn't from me." They passed through three stops while DeBolt explained everything he'd learned since they'd last talked in Boston. He covered how everyone associated with META had been killed, Patel's oversight of the project, and its link to the NSA. He told her about Patel's plans to sell the technology to the highest bidder. Finally DeBolt told her how he'd gotten Delta to turn against his creator.

"That's why he left the gallery," Lund said.

"What?"

"I saw him, the killer—he was right behind me in the room where Patel was going to speak, only a few feet away. It was a very public place, so he must have been waiting for the right time."

DeBolt felt a shudder rise through her shoulders and translate into his hands. He said, "But then I got Patel to confess, and I transmitted it to Delta. When he learned the truth, he ignored you and came after Patel in a rage."

"I saw what he did—the body in the dirt."

"He went berserk. I tried to reason with him after he killed Patel. I tried to explain that I was no threat to him. I told him we were both victims of META. He came after me anyway. I jumped over the top-level balcony, landed in the dirt."

"I saw you limping."

"Right knee and lower leg."

"Is it broken?"

"I don't think so, but I can barely walk."

She looked outside. "We need to get out of town. Can you get a car, the way you told me you did at that diner in the States?"

"Like OnStar, some European version? I don't know. Right now I can't do anything." He pointed up. "Those high-voltage lines screw up my connection—I've noticed it before."

"Then we have to get off the tram."

He considered it. "If Delta saw either of us get on this car, he'll find a way to track it."

DeBolt looked outside and saw a great basilica-style church. Beyond that the Danube stretched out before them, rolling lazily under a wide double-stacked bridge. The tram came to a stop called Mexikoplatz, and after a careful look outside they got off. DeBolt leaned heavily on Lund as they walked toward the river.

He said, "There's a big parking lot near the base of the bridge. We can find a car there."

Progress was slow, and ground they would normally have covered in two minutes took five. They paused together at a deep set of stairs, five flights leading down to a parking lot where at least a hundred vehicles stood in wait. "There's got to be something we can use down there," he said. "We'll start with the luxury brands. I think they're more likely to have a system I can—" DeBolt's voice cut off abruptly.

Lund looked at him, saw his distress. She looked all around. "What is it?" she asked. "Do you see him?"

He stood frozen on the sidewalk.

"What's wrong, Trey?"

He hesitated, then said, "The stairs. It'll take me forever to climb down with my bad leg. You go down and do some research. I'll need makes and models, license plate numbers with the country of origin. I'm not sure which will be the easiest for META to hack, so we have to expect some trial and error."

"But Trey, I can help you down the stairs and—"

"No, go now! Do not question me on this!"

Lund hesitated, taken aback by his sharpness. She said nothing, but started down the long stone staircase.

DeBolt waited until she was halfway down before following the instruction in his right eye.

TURN AROUND, BRAVO.

He saw Delta step from behind a stone column. He was across the street near the church, no more than fifty yards away. It left only one way out for DeBolt. He limped away from the stairs and headed toward the bridge.

63

All too late, DeBolt realized how perfectly Delta had orchestrated things. Only two people now stood in the way of his private ownership of META. Using his abilities, Delta had easily lured him to Vienna, and so too Lund. The man had tracked them both through the city, and even though they'd managed to escape him, DeBolt twice, the final outcome was never in question—it was only a matter of time.

At that moment, the killer had DeBolt in a nearly perfect situation—isolated, injured, and alone. If there was any consolation for DeBolt, it was that his snap decision had been the right one. He might have given Lund a chance. Once he'd split from her and moved toward the bridge, Delta had followed him. *Bravo is the greater threat.* That would be his guiding thought. DeBolt only wished he could live up to it.

The bridge was a modern and busy thoroughfare, two levels of traffic stacked on top of one another. The sidewalk fed into a pedestrian bridge on the outside of the lower level. It ran straight and true, a wide concrete path spanning a quarter of a mile to the far shore.

DeBolt saw a few other pedestrians and one bicyclist on the path. He was sure Delta noticed them as well, and was no doubt calculating how to do his work without drawing notice. The answer seemed obvious: on DeBolt's right was a metal rail that ran the length of the bridge, and beyond that was a thirty-foot drop into the Danube. He remembered how Delta had killed Patel, and adapted those mechanics to fit what a police detective might think later this afternoon when the body of a young man was collected from a bank downstream: *Broken neck, poor bastard. That's what happens when they go off the big bridge.*

DeBolt hobbled as fast as he could, his right leg screaming in pain. Thankfully, the four-foot-high guardrail was on his right side, and he used it as a crutch, trying to gain a rhythm. It would never be enough. The far end of the bridge seemed miles away, and with a look over his shoulder he saw Delta closing in. The man wasn't even running, just keeping a methodical pace thirty steps behind him.

DeBolt was so focused on moving, he hadn't realized the screen in his eye was again blank. The static was stronger than ever, crackling on the screen, buzzing in his ear. He passed a service door that was set into the concrete wall that separated the path from the enclosed lanes of traffic, and on it he saw a warning sign—the words were in German, but DeBolt recognized the high-voltage symbol. The bridge, he realized, had embedded utility tunnels. Water and sewer, heavy-duty power lines. It meant META was disabled for both him and Delta. Was there some way to take advantage of that briefly level playing field? Nothing came to mind. Delta seemed to hold every advantage.

DeBolt heard the killer's footsteps behind him, heavy and relentless, like pistons in a great engine. He heard the cyclic exhaust of his breath. At the dead center of the bridge the handrail bowed outward, the path going to double width for a twenty-yard stretch. It created an observation deck of sorts, a platform from which one could drink in the beauty of Vienna. Realizing he had to do something, *anything* to change the situation, DeBolt veered toward the widest part of the platform. On reaching the outer rail, he came to an abrupt stop at the edge.

He looked down at the river and saw a dark body of water, swirls and eddies flowing smoothly past. He gauged the surface to be forty feet beneath the walkway. *Forty feet, a good estimate.* He was, after all, something of an expert when it came to judging height above water. In that instant, DeBolt sensed a slight but distinct swing. However slim, he'd found a remnant of what he once was. A trace of familiar ground.

All at once he knew what he had to do . . . but to make it work, his timing would have to be perfect. He looked over his shoulder and saw Delta closing in. He was slowing down, looking up and down the pedestrian walkway. DeBolt tried to read his thoughts—not using META, but by putting himself in the man's position. There was no longer any hurry, so he wanted to choose his moment. Or perhaps he was only being cautious—with his prey cornered, he had to expect a fight. Delta had dispatched Patel with ease, but this time he was facing a man who was young and strong, and who had some measure of training. A man who'd scalded him with boiling water the last time they'd engaged.

DeBolt reached the rail and backed against it.

Delta stopped where he was, ten steps away. He looked once more up and down the walkway.

DeBolt did the same.

There was no one in sight.

DeBolt made his move.

Defying the pain in his leg, he half rolled, half vaulted over the steel rail. The move surprised Delta, who rushed to close the gap. DeBolt could have jumped right then—and maybe he should have. But to escape like that would change nothing.

In the space of two seconds, DeBolt found a lip of concrete and set his feet. He gripped the hip-high rail with both hands. Then he leaned back as far he could, his body reclined steeply over the chasm below. It was a vantage point he was intimately familiar with, even if the Danube below looked warm and serene compared to the Bering Sea. A veritable swimming pool.

DeBolt concentrated on one thing—his good left leg. He twisted that foot sideways to gain solid contact with the bridge, and bent his knee slightly. The movements strained his damaged right knee, but in the end he was poised precisely where he wanted to be—hanging precipitously from the rail, a fall imminent.

Delta arrived like a train, the impact of his body shaking the thick metal rail. The killer's hands went straight for DeBolt's throat. DeBolt actually allowed him to get a good grip. Then, in the instant before pressure could be applied, he released his hands from the bridge rail. The effect was subtle against all the other forces involved—most prominent being the strength of Delta's upper body—but there was a shift in their combined momentum. DeBolt then did the unexpected. He reached out for Delta's own neck. He didn't grasp flesh, but rather the collar of his heavy coat, and as soon as he had two tight fistfuls, DeBolt jammed his left leg straight with every ounce of strength.

DeBolt's body angled back, away from the bridge and toward the abyss. Delta recognized what was happening, but all too late. Their combined center of gravity was too far from the rail, moving too fast. DeBolt's grip was too tight. Delta's hips were dragged over the rail, and there was a terrible hesitation. Then both men tumbled outward, spinning like blades of a broken propeller into the cold Viennese air.

Falling from great heights is an unnatural event for most humans. Striking the water at forty miles an hour even more so. That was the speed they would reach after dropping forty feet, a number DeBolt knew precisely. He also knew they would sink ten feet as their descents were arrested by the water. There was nothing to be done about any of that. It was physics, pure and simple. He was confident the center of the Danube River was deep enough. Like a smart kid jumping into a new swimming hole, he'd worked through that ahead of time.

The two men released their grip on one another in midair, a perfectly natural reaction. At that point any commonality ended. Delta began wheeling his arms in an attempt to combat the fall, a basic instinct that was quite useless. He wasn't traveling fast enough for appreciable wind resistance, so trying to arrest his rate of fall or stabilize by flailing was all but impossible. Gravity and momentum were going to have their way.

DeBolt, on the other hand, was an expert when it came to falling. To begin, he knew he had precisely 1.58 seconds to work with. He pulled his legs together, from thigh to injured knee to toe, and crossed his arms and tucked them tight into his chest. He sucked in a deep breath and closed his mouth, keeping a board-straight spine and neck. He did it all in less than a second.

DeBolt hit the water, and after the shock of impact he felt the familiar, rapid deceleration. He opened his eyes and looked for the bubbles to tell him which way was up. He was able to orient himself quickly, even discerning the light of day playing on the river's surface. Then he looked for Delta. He was predictably an arm's length away, limbs flailing in a froth of bubbles made effervescent by the midday light. His legs kicked mightily, but only one arm was moving, the other hanging limp at his side. He was obviously injured—possibly a broken arm, but more likely a dislocated joint. Delta was also looking up at the surface, and pulling mightily toward it. Only it wasn't working.

DeBolt knew why, a hopeful calculation he'd made moments ago on the pedestrian bridge. Delta was wearing body armor. And body armor, by definition, was extremely heavy. The man was effectively wearing an anchor.

DeBolt floated motionless, neutrally buoyant, his body quiet in the water.

Barely using oxygen. He watched Delta pull a mighty one-armed stroke, then sink a little deeper. *Pull and sink. Pull and sink.* He finally realized his predicament and began tearing apart his wardrobe. He ripped off his overcoat, followed by a heavy sweater, both ghosting out amorphously in the steady current. He was struggling and kicking, working hard, his thick muscles burning oxygen at a prodigious rate. The armored vest—the real problem— had plastic snaps that had to be unlatched one by one. His meaty fingers fumbled in desperation.

Still sinking.

Delta's movements began to slow.

DeBolt couldn't take it any longer. It wasn't in his DNA to watch an injured man drown. He kicked downward, wishing he had fins, and approached Delta in the way he would approach any drowning victim—from behind. He got a hand under one armpit, but as soon as he did Delta twisted in the water to face him. In a fit of rage he grabbed DeBolt's throat with his good hand. It was an ill-considered move on any number of levels. DeBolt wasn't breathing to begin with, so shutting down his airway accomplished nothing. More critically, it meant Delta was ignoring the vest that was dragging him to the bottom of the river. DeBolt had a hand underneath Delta's good arm, which gave him plenty of leverage. With a twist of his body he was free.

Delta continued downward, and DeBolt kicked away a final grasp at his legs. Now he too was feeling the demand for air. He hesitated for one last look, and saw a fading and motionless Delta, his arms stretched upward almost as if in supplication. DeBolt began stroking upward, his own lungs becoming insistent. Uncharacteristically desperate. His vision began to blank and he wondered if he'd waited too long. Wondered if he was pulling in the right direction.

But he never stopped.

DeBolt kept kicking, kept battling. Just as he had not long ago in frigid waters off the coast of Maine. And before that with a tiny young girl in the wind-whipped Bering Sea.

Absolute resolve.

64

Two days later

The United States Ambassador to Austria, Charles Emerson, arrived at his destination by limousine, and at the curb he instructed his security detail to wait—an escort for the remaining hundred feet, he explained, wouldn't be necessary. Grudgingly, the two burly State Department men in front complied.

Emerson set out at a businesslike pace across the gray-stone commons. He looked down to check his watch only to realize he hadn't put it on. The call had come very early, waking him more than an hour before his alarm was set to go off. Not the kind of thing he'd envisioned when he'd accepted the chief diplomatic post to Vienna.

It had seemed a good idea at the time. His father-in-law was the newly elected president's onetime Yale roommate, and over the years a steadfast contributor to his campaigns. That being the case, the ambassadorship to Austria had been Emerson's for the taking. He'd been tempted right off, given the uninspiring course of recent years. Emerson had long endured tiresome stints on corporate boards, and he served as director for a number of charitable organizations, but those affiliations were largely coming to a sunset. Not surprisingly, his wife, whose family pedigree went back to the days of Newport and railroads, was effervescent at the prospect of hostessing state dinners in the heart of old Europe. So take the posting Emerson had.

The job of ambassador was rather different from what he'd expected, more work and less play. He could not deny that, over the course of the last year, he and Marylyn had shared some prize moments. On the other hand, when the phone call had come two hours ago, well before dawn, his wife had barely stirred.

The wind caught Emerson's hair, and he looked up at a foreboding sky—the Viennese weather had proven an unforeseen irritant. As he reached the head of the terrace, Emerson found himself wondering what other storm might be brewing at this hour. Looming before him was an oft-visited destination, Minoritenplatz 8, or more formally, the Austrian Ministry for Europe, Integration, and Foreign Affairs. The "Integration" part was a recent addition to the letterhead, a feeble response, Emerson knew, to the intractable immigration crisis.

He was met at the entrance by a familiar face, the foreign minister's personal secretary, a statuesque blonde who was as professional as she was attractive, and who unfailingly slayed any attempt at small talk with her blue Teutonic gaze. In faultless English she offered a crisp, "Good morning," and Emerson muttered something in reply about the lovely weather. Minutes later he was being ushered into the top-floor office of the Austrian foreign minister.

Sebastian Landau stood and walked briskly around his desk.

"Good morning, Charles. Thank you for coming."

Emerson took a professional handshake, and was guided to a pair of settees where coffee was waiting. Landau was an exceptionally young man, Emerson had always thought, for such a vital government post. Before arriving in Austria, Emerson had envisioned himself dealing with old-school Prussian types with broad mustaches, boorish and predictable men who would carry on for hours about riding and hunting fowl, and who capped every meeting with a splash of good port. Seb Landau—that was what he went by, Seb—trained for bicycle races, knew a lot about sushi, and was prone to wearing colorful scarves. Emerson had a loose suspicion he might be homosexual, not that he cared about that sort of thing. Landau seemed competent, intelligent, and was generally chipper. That last trait, however, had gone missing this morning.

The two men seated themselves to be separated by the coffee tray, and Landau took the initiative to pour two steaming cups. Emerson had taken up the Vienna post one year ago, and in that time the two had crossed paths regularly, although more often than not on the diplomatic cocktail circuit. Regardless of venue, they'd both kept largely to business, and no personal relationship had yet evolved between them. In the haze of the early hour, Emerson actually considered whether today's summons might be a bit of social rapprochement. Then reason prevailed—message traffic had been flying between their respective camps in recent days.

"I know it's early," said Landau, "but something has come up we must address immediately."

"Does this involve Captain Morales?" Emerson asked cautiously. This had been their most pressing recent business—the U.S. Marine who'd been found, three days earlier, murdered in the trunk of an embassy car in a Bundespolizei parking garage. One casualty of a madman's rampage.

"Indirectly, yes." Landau steepled his hands under his chin thoughtfully, as if lining up what to say. "As you know," he began, "this shooting incident a few days ago . . . it remains very much at the forefront for us."

"A terrible tragedy. I haven't heard anything new on our end, but I did pass along your request for assistance to the State Department. I can tell you it's been given highest priority. The last update I saw arrived yesterday afternoon—we still haven't found anything to help identify this man you dredged out of the Danube."

"Nor have we, and I imagine we're hitting the same roadblocks. We took pictures and fingerprints, but there are no matches in any of our databases. A number of people saw this attacker, but no one remembered hearing him speak, which means we can't even narrow things down using language or accents. We know he entered Austria last week using a false identity, but our efforts to source his U.S. passport have gone nowhere."

"I fear we've come to the same conclusion," said Emerson. "It was an elegant forgery."

Landau sipped his coffee, then said, "We have no idea where he stayed while he was in Vienna, who he saw, or what his motive was for going on such a tear."

Emerson had in fact gotten two classified briefings from Foggy Bottom on the affair, but they'd offered no more than what was in the local newspapers. The day after the attack on the police station, the killer had murdered a scientist, then drowned as he struggled with another man after the two fell from a bridge into the Danube. Police divers had quickly found the suspect's body right where he'd gone in—well anchored by the armored vest he was wearing.

324 · WARD LARSEN

"Has there been any progress on finding the second man who fell off the bridge?" Emerson asked.

A somber Landau shook his head. "No. At least twelve people saw it happen, but there's no trace of him. The police are still dragging the river, but at this point it seems a pointless exercise."

"I understand your frustration. I've been told the currents *are* strong in certain areas."

Landau frowned, his youthful face adding ten years. "I'm no detective," he argued, "but I think it defies logic that his body hasn't been found. One witness claims to have seen him swimming away, but then he disappeared under the span. Another attested to some splashing under the bridge's southern bastion shortly after the incident."

"So whoever he was . . . you're suggesting he might have pulled himself out?"

"It's possible, although the climb up the embankment is quite steep. I suppose if he'd had some help . . ." The foreign minister let that thought drift, then said, "About this woman who was involved, Miss Lund. She also remains unaccounted for, and we'd very much like to talk to her. Have you come up with any information on her whereabouts?"

Lund's identity had never been in question, but no one could say why she'd come to Austria. The Bundespolizei thought it highly suspicious that the attack on the station had occurred as she was being released from detention, and that the Marine guard sent to retrieve her had been targeted by the killer.

Emerson kept to the facts as he knew them. "We haven't been able to locate her, but I can confirm that a murder took place in her apartment in Alaska. Lund was proven to be elsewhere when the crime occurred—a rock-solid alibi. By all accounts, until a week ago she was a Coast Guard investigator with a spotless record. I agree that we should talk to her, but her association in all of this seems quite tangential. The prevailing thought is that she was pursuing an investigation of her own, perhaps even tracking this man who did so much damage. Our first concern is for her well-being, given that she's disappeared under such grim circumstances."

"Yes, we did place her at the Hofburg that morning. The very gallery where Dr. Patel was scheduled to speak."

"Yes, Dr. Patel," said Emerson, "the professor from California. Does the Bundespolizei still consider him a bystander who got caught up in all this?"

Landau didn't respond right away. With a pensive look he stood and walked toward his window, which Emerson knew from previous visits presented Minoritenplatz—a scene today held hostage by the profound morning gloom. "A bystander," he finally said. "Yes, that *was* our original thinking. Unfortunately, certain curiosities have arisen regarding Dr. Patel."

To this point, Emerson had heard nothing that wasn't in yesterday's briefing. He now sensed a shift in Landau's course, and correspondingly, he suspected, the reason he'd been summoned at such an unseemly hour. "What kind of curiosities?"

"We studied the phone Patel was carrying when he was killed. There was also a laptop computer in a suitcase he'd sent to the airport. Oddly, both had been scrubbed."

"Scrubbed?" Emerson repeated.

"Cleansed. Erased. Somehow all information on both devices has been very professionally wiped clean."

"How could that be?"

Instead of answering, Landau turned back to face him and shifted course yet again. "With so little evidence to go on, the Bundespolizei were relying heavily on what the postmortem on our assassin would tell us."

"I see," said an increasingly cautious Emerson. "Was there something in particular they were looking for?"

"The body was taken to the morgue at our main hospital, and during the preliminary examination the medical examiner noted some highly unusual scarring on the killer's scalp—indicative, perhaps, of recent cranial surgery. The work was quite extensive—in fact, no one in our medical examiner's office had ever seen anything like it. They were convinced that a thorough postmortem would determine what kind of operation had been performed. In fact, due to the unique nature of the work, they thought they might even find indicators of *where* it had been done. A comprehensive autopsy was scheduled to have taken place yesterday. Our investigators saw it as the best hope for obtaining an identification."

Emerson was lost. "Are you saying the postmortem *didn't* take place?"

"That's correct."

"Why not?"

"Because the body has gone missing."

Emerson sat stunned. He realized Landau was watching him closely, gauging his reaction. "How on earth did that happen?"

A reticent foreign minister diverted from the sullen panorama of his window to a bookcase that ran the length of one wall. "I'd like to show you something."

Emerson stood and went closer as Landau used a remote control to activate a video monitor that was built into the bookcase. A video began to play, and the foreign minister provided commentary. "This is closed-circuit footage of the morgue where the body was kept. It's a very secure facility, and due to heightened interest in this case, the Bundespolizei took the added precaution of placing a guard at the entrance. The video we're watching is from two nights ago."

Emerson watched the video run, and saw a morgue like any other—not that he was an expert. Large drawers lined one wall, and there were a few stainless-steel examination tables, all of it cast in severe industrial lighting. He saw the occasional technician come and go, but for the most part the scene was one of stillness, the only evidence of time's progression being a clock in one corner of the screen. Then, quite abruptly, the video went to snow.

"What happened?" he asked.

Landau ran back to one of the last useful frames. "At 2:31 A.M. the video signal is lost. Our technicians have gone over the system and determined there was an interruption in the camera feed. In other words, it's not a problem on the data storage end—the camera simply stopped sending images for thirty minutes. We can't recover the information because there's nothing to recover." Landau kept working the remote, and said, "The video is reinstated at 3:02. Notice anything different?"

Emerson saw a scene much like the first video, but with one glaring exception—one of the big steel drawers was partially open. "You're saying someone stole the body—and manipulated this security system to cover their tracks?"

"Without a doubt."

"But you said there was a guard."

"Yes, at the main entrance. There is, however, a service entrance. It is almost never used—only to transfer heavy equipment in and out—and is secured by a very capable cipher lock. At 2:34 that morning someone breached the system, inputting an access code to the door. This is a ten-digit code that changes every week, and is known to only two administrators. Both have been put in the clear."

"So . . . how then?"

Landau stopped the video. "The service entrance I mentioned connects to a receiving dock where the hospital's supplies are brought in. It wasn't in use, of course, at that time of night, and the door was locked securely. Interestingly, there's a camera outside this entrance as well, part of a completely different network. That system also malfunctioned at precisely the same time."

The foreign minister retreated to his desk and took a seat.

Emerson said, "You're suggesting that someone hacked into two separate security systems in order to remove the suspect's body?"

"Three, actually. There is also a bank directly across the street from the hospital's service entrance, and we thought it was worth checking. Same result. Then there is the matter of the defeated cipher lock at the morgue, and a second on the receiving dock. And of course Dr. Patel's phone and laptop. I've been told by our cyber technicians that permanently erasing data from such devices is tricky—very hard to do without having them physically in hand."

Landau reached into his top drawer and pulled out a sealed envelope. He pushed it across the desk toward a sinking Emerson, who asked, "What's this?"

"Ambassador Emerson, the Republic of Austria hereby lodges a formal complaint against the United States of America. Serious crimes have been committed on Austrian soil, and a number of American citizens are involved, both as victims and, perhaps, as perpetrators. More damningly, the investigation of these crimes has been impeded and evidence destroyed by electronic means, the likes of which are available to only a few countries on earth. I dare say that neither China nor Russia would have any interest in disrupting our investigation. That being the case, the Republic of Austria hereby makes the following demands. First, all intrusions are to halt immediately. Second, the United States government will give every assistance to get to the bottom of this matter, including the return of any appropriated evidence to the Federal Police Forces of Austria."

Emerson stood rigid in front of Landau's desk. He looked at the foreign minister, then took the envelope, and said, "You have my word, sir. I will look into this immediately."

Emerson did precisely that.

The formal complaint was routed directly to State Department headquarters, and within the hour it arrived squarely on the desk of a flummoxed secretary of state. There was no getting around it—the facts *were* damning. Someone was interfering with a police investigation in Austria, and there seemed only one nation with both the necessary technical prowess and a motive. That being the case, the secretary of state, a seasoned and long-tenured veteran, saw things in much the same light as the government of Austria. Someone was culpable, and he would do his damnedest to find out who.

He envisioned three primary suspects: CIA, NSA, and NRO. Even so, he decided a comprehensive inquest would be best, and so he included on his list the FBI, U.S. Cyber Command, all military intelligence agencies, and a little-known and near-black cyber initiative that fell under Homeland Security's purview.

A clipped message was sent to each agency asking for information regarding American involvement in the goings-on in Austria. The secretary of state made a point of putting his name at the bottom, leaving no doubt as to the seriousness of the inquiry. The results arrived sporadically over the next forty-eight hours and, while essentially the same, were best encapsulated by the curt reply from the director of the CIA: *We know nothing about this.*

65

The hilltop was in Styria, somewhere north of Graz but not yet to the mountains. It wasn't the biggest hill, nor the smallest, only a middling swale that would show wide contours on any map. It certainly wasn't worth a name, and neither of the two people who stood near the crest made any effort to record where they were or how they'd gotten there. No effort at all.

For autumn in Austria, it could not have been a more ordinary day. The skies were partly cloudy, the temperature moderate, and the wind stirred occasionally from no particular direction. Altogether, hesitant conditions that gave away nothing about what would come in the following days.

DeBolt stood back from his job. He was shirtless, and his exposed skin gleamed with sweat from his exertions. He limped toward the rock where Lund was sitting and put down the shovel.

"Leg holding up?" she asked.

"More or less. The knee's pretty swollen, black and blue both above and below . . . but it'll be fine."

"I think you tore ligaments."

"Maybe." He sat down next to her.

She chinned toward his work. "I could have helped with that."

"No, I wanted to do it."

Neither spoke for a time, and they sat in silence staring at the freshly turned plot of earth.

"Should we say something?" he asked. "Maybe put a marker on it or a cross?"

330 · WARD LARSEN

"I don't think he was anything. Thomas Alan Heithusen, Marine Corps gunnery sergeant. I found out that much."

Lund didn't ask how. "Sounds Christian," she said. "But from what little we know . . . I think bringing him here was enough."

DeBolt nodded.

"I wonder," she said in contemplation, "what makes a man like that?"

DeBolt didn't have to ask what she meant. He looked out over the hills, and said, "What makes any of us like we are." He recognized the bleakness of his tone, and how it reflected the mood he'd been in for far too long. Would there ever be an upswing? he wondered. He remembered better days, before the crash, before Alaska, but they'd somehow been rendered vague and distant. Almost untouchable.

Lund said, "I have to go back to Kodiak. I've got a lot to face up to there. Not sure how long it will take, or if I'll have a job when I'm done."

He nodded. "Yeah . . . I'm sorry about that. That you might lose your job because of me."

"Not your fault, DeBolt."

"I liked Kodiak."

"Me too," she said. "Civilized isolation."

He stood, took the camping shovel in hand, and with a big arcing swing heaved it far out into the forest. There was a rustle as it landed in the distant brush, then silence returned. DeBolt regarded the forest around them. "This isn't a bad place. It's peaceful."

"I wonder where Patel will end up."

"Don't know. He was a smart man with big ideas. But he never considered what META would cost others. He only saw what it could do for him. Same with Delta, I suppose . . . in the end it got the better of them both."

"And now you're the only one left. What will you do with it? Use META to get rich?"

He turned and looked at her, saw the smile. "I guess going back to the Coast Guard is out of the question. But I have prospects."

"Like?"

"Given what I'm capable of . . . there are a lot of possibilities. I could become a scientist or a journalist."

"A detective," she offered.

He laughed out loud, his gloom lifting in a flash.

"What's so funny? CGIS could use someone like you."

"Sure. And what happens when I tell them in the interview that the NSA has put radio waves in my head? People who say stuff like that end up in straitjackets."

"Not if it's true."

He took a seat on the rock next to her. "I was already working on a degree, majoring in biology. I thought I might try to go to med school."

"There's an entrance exam for med school, right?"

"The MCAT."

"Bet you'd score pretty high."

He smiled. "Maybe. But who knows how long I'll have META. Someone could flip a switch tomorrow and turn it off forever."

"But if they don't?"

"Right now, I need some rest. Honestly, if I had to do something tomorrow . . . I think I'd go to Fiji and surf."

After a long pause, she said, "That's it? You've got the most amazing gift a human has ever known . . . and you want to go surfing?"

"Not just surfing—*Fiji.* The best waves on the planet."

"It's not much of a long-term plan, DeBolt."

"I need time to think things through. Maybe I'll get a job, something simple. Something that doesn't involve information at all. A lifeguard or a bartender. I can make a few bucks and get by, deal with people without having to learn anything about them."

"Bartenders learn about people—they just do it the old-fashioned way. Can you mix a Manhattan?"

"No."

"Then lifeguard it is."

He was silent for a time, and his good nature faded as quickly as it had come. The darkness closing in again. He said reflectively, "I see things differently now."

"How's that?"

"I don't know. I guess you could say I'm more . . . cynical."

"About what?"

"Everything."

"Trey, you're not old enough to be jaded."

"Age has nothing to do with it. I've had more near-death experiences in the last month than in a career of rescue swimming. I've seen people do horrendous things to one another. If that's what META brings, I want no part of it."

"But you can't turn it off. It's there in your head, connected, whether you like it or not."

"I can ignore it."

She looked at him questioningly. "Can you?"

He fell quiet.

Lund dug a heel into the wet grass. "Computers, information . . . where does it all end? I mean, compare technology a generation ago to what exists today. Smartphones, Google Glass, Wi-Fi everywhere. Now you've got META. What will it be like in fifty years?"

"I don't know. But I'm convinced of one thing—merely designing a technology doesn't make it a good idea. As far as META goes, I'd like to toss the whole concept into the deep end of the ocean."

"Even given what it might do for you?"

DeBolt picked up a handful of smooth stones and stood. He walked to a ledge and whipped a rock sidearm over the hillside. He did it a half-dozen more times before saying, "When I was in high school my grandfather died. He was a great guy, took me hiking and skiing a lot when I was a kid. He was never rich, but he did okay. He and my grandmother had an average house, with the usual stuff—big TV for watching games, a 'sixty-nine Camaro in the garage he always wanted to restore but never got around to. They lived in the same house for forty years. Then she died, and he started to go downhill. My mom was getting bad by that time, early-onset dementia, so I was pretty busy with her. There was no way I could handle him too, so we moved him into a nursing home. It was actually all right, they took good care of him. I got the job of selling my grandparents' house, getting rid of all their stuff. And let me tell you, after forty years in the same place—people accumulate a lot. He died two years later, more or less peacefully. His wife was gone, he was tired, and he let go because it was time. A few days after he passed, I stopped by the nursing home to thank a few people for all they'd done. As I was leaving, a nurse gave me a small box. Inside were a pair of glasses, a cheap watch, an electric razor, and a framed picture of Grandma. That was it—all his worldly possessions."

He threw one last rock, then looked at Lund, and said, "You come into this world with nothing. You leave with what can fit in a shoebox. Everything in between . . . it really doesn't amount to much. It's the experiences that count. The places you go. The people you meet and what effect you have on them. That's all anybody ever leaves behind."

She looked at the fresh grave. "And what did *he* leave behind?"

DeBolt was silent for a long time. He turned back toward the hills, and said, "I've never killed anybody before."

"You've saved a lot of lives."

"It's not the kind of thing you can add and subtract, come up with a net zero."

"You had no control over what happened, Trey. Delta forced the issue. It was his life or yours . . . and probably mine," she added.

He thought about it, then nodded. "Thanks for putting it like that."

Lund stood and walked slowly to DeBolt's side. She reached up and kissed him on the cheek. "So there you have it," she said. "I'm heading to Alaska, and you're going to Fiji. Any idea how we get there?"

"For you it's easy. You walk into the nearest Bundespolizei precinct. I'll find my own way. But I was thinking . . . maybe we could put it off for a day or two."

"Stay on the run? They'll be looking for the car."

"We'll ditch it."

"Where do we stay?" she asked.

"I still have enough cash for a couple of sleeping bags, some food, maybe a tent. Sleep out under the stars. Nobody can track that, can they?"

"Not even you."

They hiked back slowly to their stolen Mercedes. Neither addressed what would happen after Kodiak and police interviews, after Fiji and falling off the grid. Perhaps because they didn't know. Or perhaps because they did.

When they reached the car it was still running. The main road was only a mile away, and DeBolt knew he would soon have a connection with a macrocell GSM antenna—yesterday he'd discovered how to differentiate source signals.

Lund paused before getting in the passenger seat. She looked out over a nearby lake, the low sun reflecting on its glassy surface.

"Might be nice camping over there," she said.

"Maybe we can get back before dark."

"I wonder what time the sun sets tonight."

DeBolt thought about it. But only for a moment.

He said, "I have no idea."

ACKNOWLEDGMENTS

With deepest gratitude I would like to thank those who helped with *Cutting Edge*.

To begin, much appreciation to everyone at Tor for supporting a book that falls outside my traditional wheelhouse. In particular, thanks to my editor, Bob Gleason, for your encouragement, not to mention the faith you've shown in me over the years. Also to Elayne Becker for your keen eye and attention to detail. A special thanks to Linda Quinton, whose support has been essential. And of course, to Tom Doherty, for the incomparable house you've built.

With respect to my agent, Susan Gleason, I can say something few authors can: I have never felt disappointed after ending one of our calls.

Finally, thanks as ever to my family: your support has never wavered.

Claire and Present Danger

By Gillian Roberts
Published by Ballantine Books

CAUGHT DEAD IN PHILADELPHIA
PHILLY STAKES
I'D RATHER BE IN PHILADELPHIA
WITH FRIENDS LIKE THESE . . .
HOW I SPENT MY SUMMER VACATION
IN THE DEAD OF SUMMER
THE MUMMERS' CURSE
THE BLUEST BLOOD
ADAM AND EVIL
HELEN HATH NO FURY
CLAIRE AND PRESENT DANGER

Claire and Present Danger

Gillian Roberts

Ballantine Books • New York

A Ballantine Book
Published by The Random House Ballantine Publishing Group

www.ballantinebooks.com

Library of Congress Cataloging-in-Publication Data

Roberts, Gillian, 1939–
Claire and present danger / by Gillian Roberts.—1st ed.
p.   cm.
ISBN 0-345-45490-1
1. Pepper, Amanda (Fictitious character)—Fiction. 2. Preparatory school teachers—Fiction.
3. Philadelphia (Pa.)—Fiction. 4. Women teachers—Fiction. I. Title.
PS3557.R356C58 2003
813'.54—dc21   2002043654

Manufactured in the United States of America

First Edition: June 2003

2   4   6   8   10   9   7   5   3   1

This is for Ferne and Steve Kuhn—
despite the puns!

Acknowledgments

Special thanks and gratitude to Jon Keroes, who generously and repeatedly shared his considerable professional expertise. Any errors are mine, as is the fact that I took the information and twisted it to suit my criminal purposes.

And to my longtime partners in crime, estimable agent Jean Naggar, and amazing editor Joe Blades—thanks, as well, for making work a pleasure.

Claire and Present Danger

One

"ALWAYS thought it was kids who were reluctant to go back to school, not teachers." Mackenzie sat on the side of the bed, tying the laces of his running shoes.

"Another popular myth shot to hell," I muttered. "The big thrill was getting new notebooks, lunch boxes, and backpacks."

"An' I was too insensitive to think of buyin' them for you. Guess I'm not a New Age kind of guy, after all."

"I didn't get so much as an unused gum eraser."

"But you aren't actually re-entering. You did that two days ago."

He meant prep time. A duo of days designed to quash whatever optimism had built during summer. Days of listening to a lazy end-of-summer fly halfheartedly circling the room while Maurice Havermeyer, Philly Prep's pathetic headmaster, droned along with them. The difference was this: The fly's noises were interesting.

Our headmaster's spiel was stale from the get-go with the same meaningless jargon-infested exhortations to be ever more creative, innovative, and effective. I fought to keep from putting my head on the desk and falling asleep, and wondered if I could peddle copies of his talks as cures for insomnia.

He reassured us he'd be there to offer all the help and resources he could, but he was careful to never define precisely where "there" might be. Maybe he didn't have to. Anyone who'd worked with him knew it would be as far away as possible from the problem or question.

Two days of sprucing up classrooms, filing lesson plans with the office, checking bookroom stores against class lists, and creating colorful bulletin boards nobody except our own selves would appreciate. And all of it surrounded by the loud silence of a school without students, which was not, to my definition, a school at all.

But now, here we were. The real stuff. Back to school.

"Thought you loved teachin'," Mackenzie said.

I do, although what love affair isn't a roller-coaster ride? "It isn't that," I said, looking at a to-do list I'd prepared the night before. "It's everything converging at once." I felt stupid even saying that. It wasn't as if anything came as a shock, and it wasn't as if there were that many *everythings*. What was exceptional was how daunted I felt by my list of obligations.

I had to teach. No surprise.

I had a part-time job after school to help our personal homeland security, but I'd been working there along with Mackenzie all summer, so that wasn't out of the ordinary, either.

Starting to push things over the edge, however, was an obligatory appearance at a ninetieth birthday party for a former neighbor. Given her advanced age, I couldn't rationally beg off and promise to be at her next big bash, even though the only living creature to whom old Mrs. Russell had shown kindness was Macavity, my cat. Her house had served as his summer camp and spa, and it would have been more logical for him to attend the festivities, but I didn't see how to swing that, either.

But to really make the day require at least forty hours, I had Beth. My event-planner of a sister was thrilled by my engagement, which she and my mother saw as a victory for their side, capitulation and unconditional surrender on mine. Beth was so delighted and relieved, she was doing her damnedest to absorb me into the world of wives before I was one. At the moment, this translated into attendance at a dinner she had orchestrated and produced, a fund-raiser for an abused-women's shelter. "You'll love these women. They're the movers and shakers of the whole area," she said. She wisely left off the "even if they are married," although her point was that life went on after a wedding ceremony, and that I'd better set a date soon.

"Half my reason to be there," she continued, "is to network. There are nonprofit consultants, foundation heads, and corporate executives." People who could help build her business. Plus, it was all for a good cause and one I subscribe to—but dressing up and eating dinner as a way of helping the less fortunate has never made sense to me. Not being able to afford to go to such events is one of the few perks of living on a shoestring.

This time, I couldn't use poverty as my excuse, because Beth had comped my ticket. Besides, she was doing me an enormous favor in a few days, and being cheering section, back-up, and support for her networking attempts was a form of prepayment for what I metaphorically owed her.

Before it even began, the day cost me hours deciding what I could wear that would see me through my four lives. I settled on an outfit that wasn't great for any of them, a gray suit I'd had for years that I hoped was so unremarkable, it belonged nowhere and anywhere. The bed was piled high with my rejects.

And that's why, at 7:30 A.M., instead of being exhilarated by a new school term, I was worn out.

"If it's too much, skip Ozzie's." Mackenzie came over to where I was packing up my briefcase and kissed me in the center of my forehead.

"Ozzie's not the problem." I was moonlighting. Actually, both of us were moonlighting. After years of deliberation, Mackenzie had taken the plunge, leaving the police force so as to attack crime from a different perspective. He was now a Ph.D. candidate in criminology at Penn. Despite his partial fellowship, moonlighting was going to be necessary for at least the next four years.

Need I say that my mother's hysterical delight in my engagement had been tempered by this switch in careers? "He had a good, steady job," she said. "Why on earth . . ."

"This is what he's wanted for a long time, and it's fascinating, Mom. He'll study sociology and criminology and law and biology—it's a great course. And then he can go into research, or teach, or—lots of things."

"It takes so long!"

Translation: How could you marry a man with no income for the next how long?

Further translation: Your biological clock is going to strike midnight before you'll be able to afford children.

"But Mom," I said. "When he's done, he'll be a doctor. Your son-in-law, the doctor."

". . . . ."

Translation: A Ph.D. in a cockamamie field is not a *doctor*.

Nonetheless, she was not that far off track. Poor R Us, and when we did the math on paying the mortgage plus luxuries like food, it seemed a good idea to bring in whatever extra cash we could. Philly Prep did not pay its teachers a living wage, unless you were living in a pup tent in Fairmount Park.

That's why Mackenzie had gotten his P.I. license and was working whatever hours he could manage out of the office of Ozzie

Bright, retired cop and current private investigator, and I was working for C. K. Mackenzie. *With* him, I liked to say and think, but the truth was, *for*. I wasn't licensed, and so was more or less his apprentice, and he, my supervisor, although I'm not fond of thinking in those terms. I like to consider us a partnership, not boss and employee, or pro and peon, which is closer to reality.

Over the course of the summer, C. K. let me try my wings at everything from interviewing witnesses and new clients to clerical chores like handling the nonstop flow of papers for discovery. The words *private eye* prompted images of shady gents in fedoras and platinum-blonde dames in teeter-totter high heels. Of cracking wise and trapping bad guys.

The job wasn't exactly that. Mostly, I sat in front of a computer, or filed papers. Solo. Since our schedules seldom overlapped—I was at school while he was working, and at the office while he was in school—the "working together" part was as fictional as the fedoras, but we were definitely partners at trying to help our communal bottom line.

Besides, most of the time I enjoyed the work, and Ozzie Bright, as idiosyncratic a man as he was, was several flights of steps up from Maurice Havermeyer.

"A regular Nick and Nora, you two," Ozzie had said when we entered his lair, and who could resist that idea, either? What's better than having fun and being in love while simultaneously squelching crime? So what if N&N were stinking rich all the time and stinking drunk most of the time? And then there was their adorable dog.

On our side we had unpaid bills, sobriety, and an overstuffed dust mop of a cat.

And mostly unimaginative cases. Nick and Nora messed with big-time baddies. Our clients were mild, straightforward, and their crimes white-collar, when there were any crimes at all.

For example, finding a long-lost high school love didn't, in our case, lead to revelations that she was a serial killer we could cleverly snare. Instead, when we found her, happy, bland, and the grand-mother of five, the drama was that our client threatened not to pay because after thirty-seven years, she wasn't the way he remem-bered her.

We'd done background searches on two prospective corporate hires, and only one turned out to have all the credentials he claimed. We'd done interviews for the defense of a man accused of sexual harassment and, to my surprise, it appeared that the case had no basis and he'd be acquitted. Mackenzie was getting a good reputation in the biz, but in truth, not quite with Nick and Nora pizzazz.

But on this particular Monday morning, neither the pressures of back to school, the duties of my part-time job, nor the pileup of unappetizing parties made my nerve ends twang. It was the other thing. "Plus, there's . . ." I couldn't finish the thought honestly. In-stead, I said, "Too much."

"I haven't seen you like this before. You don't seem . . ." He stopped midsentence and laughed out loud.

"What?"

"I know about posttraumatic shock—but pretraumatic shock? You're so efficient, not wastin' time waitin' till the actual trauma happens."

"I cannot imagine what you mean." Lying again.

"There's no trauma in store, Amanda. I can't fathom why you're so worried. If we were kids, askin' their permission," he said. "If there was some big objection anywhere to our gettin' married—maybe I'd understand. We're even spared worry over whether Daddy's gonna disapprove and disinherit me, 'cause there never was a thing to inherit except my good looks and charm."

In a few short days, I was going to meet Mackenzie's parents for the first time. I'd spoken with them on the phone. We'd exchanged notes and birthday cards and Christmas gifts, and in every instance they sounded warm, welcoming, and delighted with the prospect of my joining their family. I couldn't have identified or quantified what worried me about meeting them, but worried I was. I constantly felt as if I had overdosed on caffeine, my blood hoppity-skipping through my veins and my skull expanding and contracting as if I were pumping up a leaky basketball.

"It's stage fright," I muttered. "That's a pretraumatic shock." And as close to the feeling as I could get. Would my performance be adequate? Would I get flowers and curtain calls, or be splattered with rotten tomatoes?

Their impending arrival had stirred the muck of memory, so that I recalled fleeting anecdotes, funny stories told over glasses of wine a year or two ago—anything that had to do with my beloved and other women. Now, with painful clarity, I remembered being told about a girl in C. K.'s hometown who Gabrielle, a.k.a. Gabby, Mackenzie had believed the "perfect match" for her son despite said son's total lack of interest. That part was not exceptional, but I'd heard about her because Gabby Mackenzie continued to tout the virtues of the girl back home even after her son and I were living together. C. K. thought it was funny. I might have at the time, too. Now I didn't.

I remembered everything I was supposed to have long forgotten. Every casual aside made in the past years. Every response, however terse and reluctant, to every question I'd asked. Stories such as the one about the girl back home that had been told as a funny example of how silly his mother could be.

The original context no longer mattered. I'd sifted everything out until I was left with the facts, which I examined and analyzed with the zeal of a scientist.

I remembered the girl he'd actually been engaged to, years ago. Miss Bayou High—something like that. The prettiest and most popular girl in school. In town. And rich, he'd said, treating it all as a joke. "But you've got to know, our standards were so far down, they were subterranean. Her father was a partner in a not overly successful body shop, but compared with us—she was an heiress. And a nightmare. As soon as she had a ring on her finger, she dropped the sweetness and light and turned into a harridan and as interesting and deep as the paint jobs they did on pickups."

At the time he told me this, I'd laughed and said her mistake was dropping the act with the engagement ring. As for me, I'd wait till I had a wedding band before I showed my true and ugly colors.

All in jest, and said in that phase of dating when you tell a carefully edited "all" to the new interest in your life. Now, with my new perspective on life, I think we should present ourselves as tabula rasa and never, ever write on our slates. No past, no first love, early loves, puppy loves, and no mistakes. Information has a toxic, delayed-release afterlife.

The thing was, I remembered the minor footnote to Miss Bayou High's story as well. She was ancient history to C. K. and to her three former husbands—but he'd found it entertaining that his mother still exchanged Christmas cards and occasional visits with her. That, of course, was the portion upon which I fixated, giving me further reason to fear Gabby Mackenzie. It was painfully obvious that I was not her daughter-in-law of choice, and her sweet long-distance welcomes were simply good, insincere, Southern manners.

Mackenzie had delivered his reassurances while standing in the middle of the loft, doing that peculiar side-to-side jounce in place. My in-law angst was delaying his run and doing harm to his heart and day. I had to admire him for staying around to convince me, again, that his parents were not coming north to blow this damn Yankee girl away. "Amanda, honey," he said, shifting left to right to left to right, "they're excited about meetin' you. It's no big deal to them. They've been through this kind of thing lots of times."

"I thought you were only engaged once before."

"I meant," he said, bouncing as if he were waiting for a traffic light to change, "my vast collection of siblings, most of whom are already married, some for the second time and one for the third.

I'm the last holdout, except Lutie, who is between husbands rather than never married."

That didn't help. Maybe they resented dragging themselves north for a redundant daughter-in-law, and not even the right one, at that.

"It'll be fun. You'll see. We'll show 'em the Liberty Bell and Independence Hall and take a buggy ride through Society Hill and they will not only fall in love with you, but with Philadelphia, too. It's all taken care of, so relax. You've got enough on your plate today without worryin' about them, too."

"Thanks," I said. "I know you're right." That wasn't exactly true, but I couldn't bear talking about in-law worries any longer.

With another kiss, he was at the door, opening it as the phone rang. I took a deep breath, then lifted the receiver. A call at this hour could only mean disaster. Or—

My mother. "Mom," I said, and Mackenzie relaxed his vigil, waved, and closed the door behind him. "Mom," I said again. "You caught me about to leave. First day of—"

"I know. That's why I called now. I just spoke to Beth—"

We'd bought my mother a cell phone for her birthday. The sort with low-rate long-distance perks. We'd explained that she could now wait until we were awake to phone, and it wouldn't cost her any more. "I get up so early," she said in response. "There's nothing else to do at that hour."

And so she phoned. I geared up for a recital of what the day held for her between her clubs and charities, her card games and shopping expeditions. This was a woman who could devote an entire day to finding the right drain-stopper, and consider the time well-spent when she found it. Further, she loved to relive the hunt and the triumph by reciting it in detail to her daughters.

"I've got a surprise for you." Her voice had lowered to a mischievous chuckle.

I was now officially engaged, so she'd stopped sending me clippings and books about ways to meet men. Nowadays, I received domestic trivia: a soap-holder she'd discovered in her daily rounds, a subscription to a decorating magazine, a sleek vegetable-peeler, clippings about perfect weddings. I wondered what today's discovery might be.

"I spoke with Beth," she said again.

"Uh-huh." She was primed to re-create her conversation with Beth, thus doubling the pleasure of whatever tale she had to tell. I carried the phone around the loft, checking that I had the necessary supplies for the day and evening. Roll book. Lesson plans for all five classes. My annotated copies of the novels I was teaching. The key to Ozzie's office. The wrapped and beribboned gift for old Mrs. Russell, a set of Pavarotti CDs. Pavarotti was second only to my cat on her shortlist of loves. And thinking of Macavity, I checked that his dish of kibble was full. Ticket for Beth's fund-raiser.

"She said Chuck's parents are coming up."

It was my fault she called him Chuck, which wasn't his name at all. Early on, when I didn't know that C. K. stood only for itself, when I was sure they were the initials of names he wouldn't share with me, I assigned him "C" names at will. Unfortunately, during one of those guessing-game sessions, I identified my new gentleman caller to my mother as "Chuck." It was a joke, but I delayed setting my mother straight because, unlike C. K.'s parents, she wouldn't consider a set of initials a proper name.

My fault, too, for telling my sister anything about my life without considering the ways my loving mother could mess with the information when she found it out, which she always did.

Of course, this time, I'd had no choice but to tell Beth, because I wanted her involved. She was Good Family, and she'd make a great impression with her weathered stone palazzo on the Main Line, and her talents as a hostess. She was making dinner for the Mackenzies the night they arrived. That was the favor I was prepaying by going to her event tonight.

But still my fault because I'd failed to tell her to keep the entire business a secret from our mother.

"So I thought—what could be a better time than now? It's almost an omen, don't you think? It's so awfully hot here in Florida now, and this way, we'll all meet each other! Bingo! Won't that be fun? We're flying up Thursday in plenty of time for dinner, so don't worry—staying at Bethie's and . . ."

I'd missed something—the moment when I'd be asked whether this was a good idea.

Let me make it clear that I love my parents dearly. They are kind, decent people. And that includes my mother.

But when I thought of what currently occupied her mind—C. K.'s decision to turn away from his "nice, steady" job, concern that we hadn't set a wedding date, upset that the Mackenzies had produced eight children without considering what it would do to Bea and Gilbert Pepper's daughter's wedding budget—and then I thought of Gabby Mackenzie's easygoing, soft voice on the phone and her laissez-faire attitude . . .

I broke out in a cold sweat. My mind boggled. My imagination envisioned tossing these incompatible sets of people together in Beth's living room and I cringed.

For starters, my mother's relief and joy at the prospect of *finally*!—that word was always there, always with loud punctuation, as if my shelf-life expiration date was years past—marrying me off would terrify any sane person, which I dearly hoped included Gabby Mackenzie. And my father barely spoke. He knew how, of course, but to date, he hadn't found much worth mentioning.

Mackenzie claimed his parents would be sanguine, even casual about our status and plans or lack of same, but my mother could drive anyone crazy. I envisioned her arriving with a clipboard, shaking their hands, then moving on to her itinerary.

When was The Event going to be?

Where?

What sort?

Color scheme?

Who'd marry us?

Who'd—

Pit that against the Louisiana contingent, the laissez-faire let the good times roll side—

"I know you have to run, honey, so I'll say goodbye now, and we'll call when we get to Beth's. I'm so excited! Love to you and Chuck!

I said that an early morning call was either news of a disaster or my mother. I hadn't fully realized it could be both.

Two

'M willing to bet my students think that at term's end, I'm taken to the basement of the school, deflated via a secret valve in my foot, and stored on a hanger until school starts again.

And I'm willing to bet they accepted and believed my happy-faced expression all during this first day back to school. My real life had begun again!

They might even think I believed their feeble expressions of pleasure, or at least acceptance, at being back in harness for another full school year, spending time with me, rather than the beach, camp, mountains, videos, CDs, or computer games.

We all pretended we'd missed each other terribly, and the day flowed on, busy with book distribution, my contracts with each class, and the assignments I'd prepared. My theory is to slam them into the school mode so quickly, they're not sure what hit them. Homework the first day and no turning back.

In a school like Philly Prep, where the majority of our students couldn't—or wouldn't—perform elsewhere, it's better to be whispered about with hushed horror ("she's so *hard*!") than taken for a teacher they can easily dupe. You always can—I always do—ease up and relax the standards, but you can't tighten them once they've discovered the joy of tromping all over you.

This seemed particularly important on an enervating hot and humid day like today. We used to call it Indian summer, but in fact, it's all-ethnicities and origins summer. It is, in fact and reality, still *summer*. We invented this premature, back-to-school autumn. We fill magazines with cute woolen sweaters and bright-colored scarves when, in fact, it was a day designed to sit on a porch and sip lemonade or, better still, go to the shore. Surely not a day to find yourself back behind a desk. But while I saw children looking groggy from the heat, and I felt beads of perspiration on my own forehead by midday, nobody complained or made a case for starting school when the weather improved. That's the first-day glow.

Today was also the day to get a handle on the feel of each class, what a business would call its culture. Every class is a new and unpredictable chemistry experiment. I wish I knew the secret formula, because when the personality elements combine the right way, teaching is one long high.

This is a rare situation.

Even when it doesn't work, I remain fascinated by the mismatches, and by how nothing really changes in the basic politics of school. On this first day, the class hasn't jelled into what it will become, but the players are there, ready to adopt roles that remain the same, year after year.

I could spot the potential queen bee in each group, the future

Miss Bayou High. Just as when I was in high school, she was the girl who looked closest to how girls have been told they should look. She always had great hair, however that translated this year; a slender build; clean, even though not necessarily gorgeous, features; and a self-assurance she hid under an elaborate dance of self-deprecation. If a girl is too obviously secure about her appearance, it counts against her, sets the rest of the girls against her. This is not a good situation, but it is how it is.

Boys aren't taught to be modest and self-effacing. Their king—or perhaps duke, if The King is in another section—can acknowledge his divine rights. Then there are the imitators, the hangers-on, the king's and queen's courtiers, and somewhere on the fringes, the serfs, the unaccepted. The outsiders, the ones who don't fit the precut ready-made puzzle pieces, are the most interesting. They'll someday spin being different—another word for *unique*—into gold or dross. They're the future inventors of obscure cyber components, the performers and poets—and the highway snipers.

"You're choosing the grade you want to receive," I told my seniors. "Here are ten points you can or cannot cover in your discussion of the book you choose." The list included a dozen analytical approaches to fiction, such as *types of conflict*; *point of view, with examples*; and *the significance of the setting*—each with specific directions as to what the student would need to do about explaining that aspect of his book. They could choose to include six of the points and earn an A, four of the points and earn a B, or three of the points for a C. We didn't discuss anything less than that.

While I handed out the sheets and spoke, the alpha determined how her group should react. Would my assignment and I live or die? Thumbs up or down?

They weren't drones, and she wasn't a dictator. But she was *popular*, that most significant word in the school vocabulary, and she was the arbiter of what was appropriate dress, behavior, and attitude.

A new transfer who'd obviously decided not to attempt to belong to the popular group—she of the blue lipstick, two rings threaded through her upper lip, and a spitting-cat tattoo on her bicep—studied the list, deciding what she'd do on her own, not so much as glancing at her classmates.

The alpha male, of course, rolled his eyes and pushed the paper to the side as if disinterested. The assignment wasn't fair—I was forcing them to abandon cool nonchalance and actively work for a given grade level.

I gave myself a metaphorical pat on the back. My reputation for being hard, possibly even mean, was being strengthened. The first and best advice my student-teaching supervisor gave me was, "Don't smile till Christmas." I still haven't managed that, nor did she mean it to be taken literally, but it's advice I've passed along more than once.

The day meandered on. In many ways—most?—I am as beguiled and naïve as my students and I view back-to-school with an optimism close to insanity. This year, I swear, I'm going to be completely and consistently prepared. This year, I'm going to mark every single paper the night after it's handed in. This year, every nuance of the classroom will be in service of some greater philosophical purpose.

Isn't denial a wonderful thing?

Every autumn I harbor such thoughts even though I know that within minutes, my energy and efficiency will dissipate under the inexorable pressures of time and reality. Simply learning who everybody is becomes exhausting. It's sad but true that you most quickly learn the names of the troublemakers, which might be the entire point of their troublemaking. By the end of first period I knew that Bo Michaels, a big, good-looking dimwit, was going to be a thorn in my side as he burned up excess energy by being class clown.

By the end of third period, I had two more names carved on my heart, Butch and Sundance wanna-bes, buddies who had long ago perfected their two-against-the-world act. Unfortunately, there weren't any banks to rob in sophomore English, so they contented themselves with high fives, secret signals, and unsecret ogling of the girls.

The day progressed until finally, it was last period with the newest Philly Prep students, the ninth graders.

I didn't love having them at the end of the day, but I didn't have a vote in the scheduling. By this point, kids are either ready for naptime or antsy and overeager to get out of the building. But this early in the term, and this painfully new to the building, ninth graders tread softly, adjusting themselves to being low men on the new totem pole, and to finding allies among the other young'uns.

"Let's try something," I said after distributing *Lord of the Flies* and asking them to put their chairs in a circle.

"Does this count?" an intense-looking girl asked.

I spared her the near-obligatory pedagogical explanation that everything counted as a learning experience. She meant grades, and I knew how *she*—Jessica, another name immediately memorized—was going to be straight through till June.

"It doesn't count," I said, wishing I could say that in the real world when I was at risk for doing something stupid. "The book we're going to read is about a group of young people stranded on an island, and I thought it would be fun to see how you think you'd handle the situation before you see how they did. So imagine yourselves on a desert island without a single adult around."

Predictably, they looked guilty as they laughed with pleasure. "Your dream situation," I said. "Paradise. But the snake in paradise is that there's no way off the island, and all you've got is the clothing you're wearing and whatever's in your pockets. No food, no beds. The island is partly sandy beach, partly forest, partly a mountain, and partly a lagoon. How would you organize yourselves to survive?"

I gave them twenty minutes to work out a plan while I sat

outside the circle, acting as secretary, taking notes on what they decided they'd do.

For a long time they looked at each other, waiting for someone to take the lead and tell the rest of them what to do. Finally, a red-haired boy broke the silence. "If nobody else is going to do anything, I will," he announced.

"What are you," another boy asked, "the chief?"

The redhead—Mike—nodded. "And here's what we have to do."

At least five boys protested. It wasn't fair. Just because he'd spoken first didn't give him the right to . . .

The girls, to my dismay, said nothing. Along with them, I listened to polite male jousting for position, until they finally decided there wasn't going to be a chief. Instead, an untitled somebody would check the chores and rules, and that role would shift every day. For the moment, however, Mike could be in charge.

Mike assigned jobs. "Who can hunt for food?" he asked, and I tried to imagine which of these city boys knew a thing about stalking prey—and if any did, why? We recorded the names of the hunters. "Who can fish?" This produced another male squabble about whether fishing should be separate from hunting and whether the same people could do both.

The females played mute until a pale, undersized girl raised her hand (unlike the boys, who shouted out their suggestions) and said, "Can't we—I mean the girls—can't we do something, too?"

A girl on the other side of the circle who'd been whispering to her neighbors gave the girl who'd spoken The Look. I have seen it my entire life. Fashions and slang change, but The Look remains the ultimate feminine, passive-aggressive weapon.

The Look shows no emotions except, if possible, a negative one so powerful, it's like a suction pump. It's a black hole in the emotions, a blank stare, almost as if the girl doling it out were removing from its recipient both air and the possibility of human feelings.

I am sure the fabled Evil Eye was a version of The Look.

What a pity *Lord of the Flies* was exclusively masculine and these girls wouldn't necessarily see themselves reflected in it. I'd have to make sure they did.

After a moment's pause, Mike responded with Darwinian theory as he saw it. "We're more fit, is all," he said. "We're the hunters and we're the ones who will have to tend the fire and watch out for wild animals and things. It's how it is. Survival of the fittest." He held up an arm and flexed his bicep for emphasis.

So much for my new-school-year optimism.

The girl who'd given The Look, a pretty girl with sun-streaked hair—Melanie, when I checked—giggled. "Oh, but really," she said, looking on the verge of a blush, "but really, what about us, Mike? You know, the unfit ones?" She rolled her eyes and giggled again. It was the same question the undersized girl had asked, but the first speaker had forgotten the self-deprecating part, the flirting part, the accepting that the boys were the leaders part.

Weren't things like that supposed to have changed a few decades ago?

"You'll do the cooking and cleaning," Mike said. "And, of course, if there are babies . . ."

All the boys—because not a single pimply, gawky, undersized oddly constructed one of them would dare appear not to get the implications of Mike's line—laughed self-consciously while the girl who'd asked the question made yipping noises of feeble protest and covered her face with her hands.

They eventually had a plan, sloppy and incomplete, but they'd organized their anarchistic, adult-free society with provisions, laws, and punishments.

It was a nice preface to *Lord of the Flies*, a nice sense that they could run things and no sense yet of the disasters built into their Darwinian fantasy world.

And worse, no sense that they'd already seen Darwin in action. *Been* Darwin in action, fighting for airspace and the means of surviving high school, which was its own desert island with no help in sight. I had to hope that a slender, but great novel would help them deal more benignly with the process.

And now, the school day was done. Time to whip off my English-teacher disguise and become: Amanda Pepper, After-School P.I. Today promised to be quiet, more like Amanda Pepper, After-School Clerk; but I was tired, not yet re-acclimated to the unceasing state of alert teaching required, so I wasn't upset to be facing nothing more taxing than filing papers.

I stopped to check my mailbox before heading out. There wasn't much except Philly Prep's homemade junk mail. I glanced at items as I removed them, and tossed them into the nearby trash can until I realized that the new secretary looked stricken by my callous disregard for her hard work. If she hadn't authored the pieces, she'd been the one to put them in the cubbies. I saved the rest for a later, secret disposal and, as a secretarial kindness, I read through a straight-faced, dead serious reminder that the next faculty meeting's focus was "Our Mandate Is Striving for Excellence." Faculty was urged to bring suggestions. The only suggestion I had, if we really wanted excellence, was to replace the entire student population, a great portion of the faculty, and, specifically, the headmaster who'd written the bulletin. The mandate might be striving for excellence, and good for it!—but if so, it was the only thing around that was. Havermeyer claimed he was upgrading the academic aspirations of the school, but so far, if you had the tuition and your kid's I.Q. was the equal of his resting pulse rate—he was in.

At the bottom of the detritus I spotted a pink While You Were Out slip that said, in a loopy handwriting with an open o dotting the i: *Ntervu nr U 2-day? Call 4 d-tails.* Signed with a smiley-face. I had to intuit the rest of it: that it probably was a message from Mackenzie; that it might have to do with work; and that it should have been delivered to me a good while back, before all those other notices were piled on top of it.

"Sunshine?" I walked toward the new secretary. She was here on an interim position, if we were to believe the official P.R. Helga, the office witch, was on indefinite sick leave. Apparently, being found in flagrante delicto with the headmaster had made Helga gravely ill. It had certainly had that effect upon me.

Havermeyer's immune system—at least when it confronted his own offensiveness—was iron-clad. He was still around, although since the day I discovered them, he badgered me less often and seldom met my glance directly. I hoped Helga had a record-breaking sexual harassment case going, suing the pants off the man—much more fun, I'd have to believe, than removing them for any other purpose—and that she'd make so much money, she'd never return to Philly Prep to darken my days and hoard my supplies.

In the meantime, we had a sweet, though dim, replacement for the Witch: Sunshine Horowitz. ("That's not my real name," she'd trilled, making me think perhaps her name was actually Sunshine Jones, "but it's what everybody's called me since I was a teensy-weensy baby!")

"Miz Pepper!" she chirped. At the end of her first student-filled, undoubtedly chaotic day on the job, she didn't appear frayed or fatigued. "How can I help you?"

I was so unaccustomed to that kind of response from behind that desk, I was momentarily speechless. "This note?" I finally said.

She glanced at it, then winked at me. "You like Sunshine-Brand Shorthand? I invented it all on my lonesome, and it's real easy to read, and fun, right?"

I tried to strike a casual, nonthreatening pose, but there was no place to rest an elbow or forearm. Sunshine collected tiny metal animals, all polished to a blinding gleam and heavy on unicorns. She made her office "homey," she said, by lining them up on the center divide.

"Ah," I'd said upon first encountering them. "The *brass* menagerie. By Tennessee's cousin Pennsylvania, perhaps?"

Her eyes were the pale blue of empty sky, and my quip produced as much comprehension as a cloudless vista, despite her valiant smile. "States are related?" she asked. "Or is that some kind of joke?" Her smile remained wide and hopeful. Made me feel bad for confusing her.

21

"Some kind of bad joke," I'd said. "An English teacher sort of joke."

"Ahhh." She nodded and gave a conspiratorial wink. Obviously, lots of incomprehensible jokes and comments had been made in her company, but I wasn't going to add to them ever again if I could help it. She was too innocently, blankly happy, and it would be cruel, like hurting a kitten.

The cure for Sunshine's saccharine self was the memory of Helga scowling, refusing to allow me a new red pencil because it would deplete her stock of them. Sunshine didn't scowl. Not ever.

She was further confirmation of the wise saying "Be careful what you wish for." If anybody ever asked for further confirmation.

"There's no name on the message," I said.

"No?" She wrinkled her nose and put a fake pout on her face. "Why is that?"

I didn't think I was really supposed to come up with an answer.

"I know! I remember! I wasn't given a name, that's why!" And she giggled.

"Maybe you were given initials?" I asked quietly.

"Could be." She shrugged and smiled. I let it go and, instead, pointed at the time on the message. The call had come in an hour and a half ago.

Sunshine beamed that smile at me and nodded, proud, perhaps, to have written down what each line on the little form required.

"It says 'While You Were Out,' but I was here the entire time," I said.

"They come from the store with that already written on it," she said. "Should I have crossed it out?"

"No, no. I meant . . . the messengers—those children who are here during the day, one or two per hour?—it's sort of a tradition to have them carry messages. Bring messages up to the teachers. It doesn't interrupt class or anything, and sometimes messages can be urgent."

She looked as if I'd given her a gift. "Thank you!" she said. "I had no idea, but now I do! Thanks again. People here are so incredibly kind!"

I walked a few steps away and turned on my cell phone. Mackenzie had a class in an hour and was probably en route, but he also had a phone, so there was a chance he could explain what he'd meant—or what he'd actually said. And maybe after that, I'd try to help Sunshine understand that she had to include information even if she couldn't turn every word into a rebus puzzle.

"I told it all to that—who was that?" C. K. said.

"I suspected as much," I murmured.

"Except the client's address and name. Didn't want to entrust anything serious."

He's a wise man.

"The woman's a block from where you are. Other side of the square." He'd upped the tempo of his sentences. I imagined him checking his watch, driving faster. "If you could do the interview, get all the information she has, a photo if you can—and more important, get a sense why she wants it. I need a feel for her."

"Fine. What's it about?" I loved the unspoken words, that Mackenzie trusted me, was ready to rely on my take on the situation, and my evaluation of what I'd see and hear.

"Need to make sure this isn't a stalker case. She wasn't all that forthcoming."

"Hasn't she seen old movies? She's supposed to swagger in, sit on the edge of your desk, cross her legs, and spill her guts or con you."

"She's got physical problems. Incapable of swaggering."

I didn't want to break the collegial mood by suggesting that a physically challenged stalker was, possibly, an oxymoron, although the concept of a stalker on a walker was almost entertaining enough to make it a worthwhile risk. "Do you think she didn't want to meet up with you in person?"

"That's what you'll find out."

I liked everything about this. About us. And about a stalker who wouldn't leave home. Must be frustrating, to say the least.

"Name's Claire Fairchild," he said. "Wants a background check."

Even better.

"On her future daughter-in-law."

End of the investigative fantasy honeymoon. I was indignant on behalf of this unknown future daughter-in-law. The back of my neck heated in vicarious outrage as I imagined how I'd feel if I found out that Gabby Mackenzie had hired someone to check me out.

"You there?"

"Yes, but I hate the idea of—"

"Of not being objective? Of taking only clients whose interests and activities dovetail with our worldview?"

Nice of him to use the word *our* while he kindly reminded me that I'd vowed to be less judgmental and to understand that few investigators were nominated for the Nobel Prize, and that the Pennsylvania P.I.'s code of ethics doesn't include "refusing to work with people whose behavior doesn't appeal to you." For some reason, they'd also left *Honing to Amanda Pepper's Personal Sense of What Is Right* off the list of licensing prerequisites. A P.I. license was a business license, not a higher degree in philosophy.

I'm familiar with all of this because more than once we'd discussed my likely need to dismount my high horse. But it had been theoretical then, and mostly a joke.

"You have time for it?" Mackenzie asked with an edge of impatience. "Sorry to be rushed, but my class—"

Of course I agreed, and I scribbled down the woman's name and address.

After I hung up, I was still thinking about pros and cons and ethics and investigating your son's beloved, and my expression must have shown my disdain.

"Everything's all *right*, isn't it?" Sunshine asked. This time, her smile was small, filled with hope, but not quite ready to commit.

I hated frightening her, casting a shadow on her golden world. I envisioned the landscape of her mind with Disney-style super-natural sunbeams crisscrossing one another and, on each, a blue-bird, warbling.

"Everything's perfect," I said. "In fact, I just got some good news."
The good news was: This mother-in-law from hell wasn't mine.

Three

'D passed this solid old building countless times, and many of
those times, I'd stopped to admire its concrete ornamentation—
cornucopias and wreaths, stone grape clusters, bouquets of
roses—an unabashed stony hosanna to abundance and pleasure.

This afternoon, I didn't pause for a long examination. It was
still too hot to willingly dawdle outside. The air trembled and lay
low, vibrating with hidden electrical charges in the dark clouds.
But even if I hadn't been hoping there'd be air-conditioned relief
inside, I was eager to see Mrs. Fairchild's home, having long speculated what the pre–WW II apartments looked like.

For starters, how lush to have the elevator stop at one's front door instead of open onto a long corridor. This was Claire Fair-child's floor, every parqueted inch of it, including the blue and ruby Oriental rug outside a door that looked newly lacquered with layers of a shimmering cream. The brass NO SMOKING plaque next to the buzzer seemed anachronistic in these lush, prewar surrounds.

When the cream door was opened, Mrs. Fairchild's condo proved one of the few things that turned out to be exactly as I'd fantasized it. High ceilings, carved crown moldings, mellow wood paneling, herringboned inlay floors with more jewel-toned Persian rugs. And that was only the foyer.

"Lovely," I couldn't help but say to the housekeeper, even though I wasn't sure whether my private eyes were supposed to notice architectural niceties.

The housekeeper was the roundest woman I'd ever seen. She was tiny and apparently pregnant with someone huge, and her unborn child occupied all the space available from her chin to her thighs. "Mrs. Fairchild, she waits for you in living room," she said. "You see no smoke sign, yes? You wear perfume?"

It took a while to sort out her unmatched facts and questions. "I don't smoke, no," I said. "I do wear perfume, but I'm not wearing it now."

"Perfume make Mrs. Fairchild sick." She turned away from me.

I followed her, amazed she could walk this briskly, or, in fact, move at all. It looked as if it would be easier for her to roll.

I wondered if Claire Fairchild had environmental allergies, although this carpeted and draped home was anything but the stark-surfaced clean room I thought such sufferers required.

The living room's street-side wall was almost entirely tall French windows that, on a nicer day, would probably have been open onto a balcony edged with a filigreed, art deco railing. Despite the gunmetal light this afternoon, the room sparked and glowed with carved and polished surfaces.

And it was air-conditioned. I took a deep breath and relaxed into it.

A sandy-haired man in his forties wearing jeans and a plaid shirt sat in a wing chair near the French windows. He looked pleasantly worn out and faded, like much-used leather, but that could have been the light. Across from him, in a matching chair, a woman, shiny dark hair framing her face, smiled at me. She was more elegantly turned out than the man, dressed in a long-sleeved blouse with ruffled lace cuffs and collar, close-fitting black slacks, and soft boots, giving her the appearance of a nineteenth-century poet. I wondered if the two people had arrived together, as they looked as if they'd set out for separate destinations.

Only then did I notice the older woman in a chair turned away from me, toward the windows and the couple. She leaned sideways, nodding and smiling a welcome. I walked over and shook her hand.

Claire Fairchild was a delicately made white-haired woman in an ethereal blue dress that looked knitted of fibers so fine, they might sigh and melt away. Her earrings matched a long strand of pearls, and both echoed the tones of her hair, and she wore dainty, impractical blue shoes meant for a night on the town, dancing.

She seemed a suitable accessory for her environment's gracious elegance. The only discordant note in the entire room was the portable oxygen tank that stood at the ready next to her chair.

"Forgive me for not getting up," she said. "I save my air for talk. Hot day like this—tried to go outside . . ." She shook her head slowly side to side. "Delighted to . . ." She paused, deciding, too obviously, how to address and present me. ". . . see you again, Miss Pepper," she finally said. "I'd like you to meet my son, Leo."

The fair-haired man half-rose and put out his hand, which I shook. "Pleasure," he said rapidly, ducking his head in a shy bow. A man apparently not overly comfortable in social situations.

"And I'm Emmie," the girl dressed like a Romantic poet said. "Glad to meet you. I'm Leo's fiancée." She didn't seem to mind that no one had remembered to introduce her.

I shook her hand. "I'm Amanda," I said. "Glad to meet you."

Her smile was so all-encompassing and warm, it felt like a hug of greeting.

"Sit," the housekeeper said, not unpleasantly, pointing at a love seat across from Mrs. Fairchild, who, in turn, gestured at the table between us, which had a French press filled with coffee. "You can go now, Batya."

The housekeeper waddled out. Claire Fairchild redirected her attention to me. Her movements were slow, and she spoke with deliberation, possibly weighing how much breath any given word required. "Coffee?" she asked, and I nodded and watched her pour.

She passed me the cup. "My son and Emma—"

"Emmie," the young woman said softly.

"Emmie, then, came to tell me they've set a wedding date."

"Congratulations." I glanced again at the poet with the radiant smile, she who I was supposed to investigate. *Poor baby.* "I wish you all the best."

Silence followed. We all knew what was missing: an explanation for who I was and why I was there.

"Miss Pepper," Claire Fairchild said, "is my reader."

"Your what?" Her son's eyebrows and general level of interest both rose.

"Reader. You know how tired I can get. She suggested reading to me, so I could close my eyes and—"

Bad choice, I thought. Bad, bad choice. Hadn't she heard of books on tape? And why would she have hired a reader this afternoon when she didn't seem tired and was handling the coffee service without stress. She could hold a book if she could fill my coffee cup.

Nevertheless, I nodded and smiled agreement. Her son and future daughter-in-law returned my smile with visible reservations, and I didn't blame them.

"We met in the Square." Claire Fairchild gazed proudly at me as if I were a precocious child or a puppy she'd discovered.

"Have you two done this before?" Leo asked his mother.

"Many times."

"I never knew you had secrets, " he said with a smile that he probably intended to indicate humor, but didn't, quite. "I never took you for a reader, least of all for someone who loved it so much, you'd hire somebody to help with it. What other secrets are you keeping behind our backs?"

I could have told him a whopper of one.

Mrs. Fairchild almost laughed, as if his words had been funny, but ridiculous, but controlled the impulse, looking as if laughing hurt her lungs. I considered what a sad lot in life that would be.

"Is that your line of work, then, Miss Pepper?" Leo Fairchild asked. "You're a professional . . . reader?"

"Oh, no. Wish I could be, but it's simply auxiliary funds. We, uh, met by chance, but it's a business of sorts. I advertise in that local paper—the throwaway you get? Amazing how many grown-ups still love to be read to." I was being a bad liar, saying way too much, embellishing the lie in ways that could be exposed.

"What a clever idea, though," the fiancée said. "And what a luxurious, delicious way to spend an afternoon."

"Quite different, I think, from tape-recorded books," I said. "This is personal." Even I didn't know what I meant. I drank more coffee to keep me from more verbal nonsense.

"Then what else is it you said you do?" Leo Fairchild was awkward, but smart, and not easily put off track. His concern on behalf of his mother was obvious and sincere.

"I teach school, and you know how poorly teachers are paid, and I like reading, so—"

"What is it you teach?" He'd seemed faded and pale when I first saw him, but now I thought he'd simply been withdrawn for some reason. Now, his forcefulness and will were obvious. He even looked younger. He didn't trust me. He probably thought I was here to scam his mother, and he didn't care if I knew it.

"English." I try to lie by telling as much truth as possible.

"Where?" he demanded.

"Right—other side of the Square. Philly Prep."

"An English teacher! No wonder you like to read, then," the Poet said. "What a nice thing to do, too. Like having a friend visit, I'd think. You must love it, Mother Fairchild." She was going out of her way to put me at ease, and of the three of them, I liked her best so far, and realized I was building a grudge against the woman who wanted this sweet woman investigated. My client.

Leo stood up, and his bride-to-be followed suit. "I hope you don't think us rude to rush off," he said in a tone that suggested he really didn't care what I thought, "but we were about to leave right before you arrived, and given that you and Mother have this . . . well . . . appointment, we'll say goodbye now."

I wished them well again, and watched as they kissed the white-haired woman farewell. Nothing more was said until we heard the front door click.

"The coffee's still hot," Claire Fairchild then said. "You could use a refill." She leaned forward to pour me a cup.

"I could serve my—" I said.

"So can I," she said carefully, continuing to pour.

I studied her, and although she was paying attention to the coffee, I knew she was giving me the same careful dissection. "Sorry about that lame excuse," she said. "But you didn't seem to have any cover story of your own."

"I didn't know what to cover," I answered honestly. "I hadn't known I'd need to cover."

"But you did well, once you knew the situation. I like that. Your story about teaching—that was a clever thing to come up with on the spot. Do you think they believed it?"

"Not really."

"Not Leo," she agreed. "Such bad timing for them to show up this afternoon, of all times. Especially with that news. Sugar?"

I declined.

"Still, maybe good you saw them. Emphysema, if you're wondering what my problem is." She passed me the cup and saucer. "A muggy day like today . . . I get out of breath." She was quiet for a while, and I adjusted down to her rhythm of speech and waited in silence, as unnatural as that felt.

"I thought this disease was a big nothing when I was warned." Her breathing was audibly labored. She pulled hard and paused between sentences to refill her lungs. "I was wrong. It's a big something."

I was having coffee with a woman being slowly asphyxiated, and I didn't know how to respond. Yes, it was a big something, a huge, deadly something. But how could I say that without sounding fatuous? I nodded, and opened my mouth in the hopes that appropriate words would swim into it. They didn't, so I shut it again, hoping instead that my dropped jaw had not signified my stupidity, but instead, sympathy and horror on her behalf.

"I'm not dying, in case you think that."

"No. I . . . That's good . . . I'm glad." I wished I could rewind the tape and go back to standing outside her creamy front door. I wanted this first meeting not to count, as my students would put it. Second time through, I'd have a ready explanation for my presence, and wise words about bad lungs. And maybe even a handle on what I was doing here.

She sipped coffee, then put down the cup. "I expected a man," she said. "I spoke with a man." She sounded as if we'd pulled a fast one, swapping an inferior product for the real thing.

That didn't endear me to her, but I wasn't about to be sidetracked. I fired up my speech center again, and strengthened my backbone. "I work with Mr. Mackenzie," I said. "We're partners."

I was glad she had challenged me, because I get a kick saying things like that out loud.

The soft noise of her breathing filled the room while she decided whether I was telling the truth, and even if so, whether she found me acceptable. "I suppose you'll do," she finally said.

The incapacitated fragility, while real, barely covered a will of steel and a temperament to match it, and it was so forcible, I could almost see the metal shimmer through her skin, like an undercoat of armor.

She cleared her throat. It seemed a major production number. Then she spoke again. "The problem is, my son is getting married."

I was sorely tempted to ask whether her son also considered his impending marriage a problem. He certainly hadn't looked that way, taking his future bride's hand, speaking in the plural about leaving. But Claire Fairchild had hired us, so I used my mouth to sip coffee, not speak. Java in the mouth, in lieu of foot.

"Let me restate that. The problem is not the *idea* of marriage." She paused, breathed in and out, and continued. In a way, it was nice. There was time to consider each sentence already spoken, and to plan the following one. It made for efficient, thoughtful and, most of all, meaningful, communication—or should have. "The problem is his fiancée," she said.

I nodded, waited, then had to prompt her because she apparently considered that enough. "And why is she a problem?"

Claire Fairchild planted a blue-eyed permafrost stare on me. It was more efficient than the air-conditioning in lowering the temperature. "I don't know who she is. Appeared from nowhere. Nobody knows her."

I was appalled, but not entirely surprised. This was traditional Philadelphia, the city of Who Are Your Parents? For the benefit of non-Philadelphians, the translation of Claire Fairchild's so-called problem would be: Nobody in Philadelphia—nobody in the right echelons of Philadelphia families—knew this woman's family. Therefore, nobody knew how to rank her, and nobody knew whether she could be given her social green card.

But that attitude was an infamous part of the Philadelphia of long ago, when your ancestry mattered more than who you yourself were. Do not ask for whom the Liberty Bell rang. Those people were tone deaf.

This was the twenty-first century. Claire Fairchild's words and attitude lowered her score on my estimation-o-meter. I worked at keeping my expression neutral, but I felt sorry for that sweet-faced woman in her deliberately Romantic clothing. She'd so obviously wanted to please.

"I know what you think." Ordinary words, but she made them so forceful, I almost believed those icy eyes had, in fact, penetrated my skull and seen my guilty ideas. "You think I'm a snob." Pause to breathe. "That I'm talking about social status."

"I wasn't—I didn't—" But of course, I was. I did.

"Understandable. I might have taken it that way myself."

I am a talkative woman, often too much so, and seldom tongue-tied, but the nearly palpable force field surrounding this woman had the power to freeze my lips together and to turn off the pilot light in my brain. I waited for her to clarify what she meant.

"I might have," she repeated, "but it would be ridiculous. I'm not that sort of woman."

When I didn't respond, she sighed. "I've never wanted for comfort," she said. "Not socialites, however. Not from a famous family. No pedigree. Leo made the real money."

I avoided her laser stare and kept my gaze on an invisible spot between her head and the wall behind her.

"You're surprised."

I was going to deny that, but then I wondered why I should.

"This place? It would have been beyond my means, but Leo bought it for me. Always kind to me, Leo. He takes good care of me." She sat regarding her patrician hands and long fingers before she spoke again. "Not good to leap to conclusions. I'm not the stereotype you've decided I am." She looked at me, the eyes still frostbitten, but a small, nontaxing smile on her face as well.

"I assure you—" I began.

She shook her head slightly and wagged her index finger, dismissing whatever protests I contemplated.

So she was a smart woman and she'd read my mind, and I'd been wrong. But in that case, I had a new and equally nasty motive for investigating that young woman. Claire Fairchild's son had made the big time, and the only woman in his life till now had been Mama, who wasn't ready to become the second-best woman in his life.

She sighed, as if she'd again read my mind. Time, then, to switch gears. Tackling straight-on questions and answers might dispel some of the tension. The room had become as charged as the storm-awaiting air outside. "Why don't we—"

"Are you clear on my motives?"

I looked at her directly. "To be honest, not at all. You told me what wasn't your reason for calling me in, but you haven't said what was, or what you do want."

"Because you jump to conclusions. Make assumptions." She lifted a hand and indicated the room, the world in which she lived. "It's not about money, either. . . . I have everything . . . more than I need."

"Good, then. But . . ." And I waited, finishing off the coffee.

She seemed hellbent on outlasting my silence, and she won.

"Why don't you tell me what this is about," I finally said. "Unless you really want me to read you a book."

"Seems nice, doesn't she?"

"Emmie? Very much so."

She nodded. "She is nice . . . always. . . . Leo's a brilliant mathematician and electrical engineer. Socially?" She shook her head. Her physical motions were minimal, energy saving, but her concern for her son was nonetheless clear. "Naïve . . . gullible . . . late-bloomer . . . an innocent in many ways."

I already knew that, simply by meeting them for a few minutes. I wanted her to get to the point. I had seen that Leo Fairchild wasn't Mr. Sophistication. What I hadn't seen was what was wrong with beautiful Emmie—or why Claire Fairchild was on the warpath. But people reveal themselves when they ramble, even when they require frequent pit stops for ingathering breath, so I stayed silent, professional, I hoped, and worked to maintain bland approval on my face. I wanted to register, not react, like movie P.I.s, which, along with mystery novels and a word or two from Mackenzie, comprised my training manuals.

"Why are you silent? Ask me things."

Maybe I was wrong. Maybe it was shrinks who weren't supposed to approve or disapprove of anything. Still, you wouldn't think somebody who could barely breathe could be so belligerent. "I did ask," I said. "You haven't answered."

"You think I'm a meddling old crone."

"Of course not! I—"

"Where's your handle on reality, girl?"

"What?"

"Pay attention! I *am* meddling."

I couldn't help a small smile. She was honest, I'll give her that. I admire self-awareness, even when what you're aware of is that you're dreadful.

She was a miserable troublemaker—and, yes, a major-league meddler—and I liked her, which was frightening.

"The problem is, I'm a chronically ill meddler," she said. "That's why I'm hiring you to meddle for me."

I no longer liked her, and I wasn't overly fond of me, either. I'd sold out to the enemy, was doing its dirty work. Was betraying my entire species: quaking fiancées facing malevolent mothers-in-law.

My emotions rode the seesaw, and I didn't know where they'd come down—except that on this first day back to school, I'd have to give myself an F for remaining professional and uninvolved.

Four

"OKAY," I finally said, pulling on my invisible private-eye cloak that would make me tough and strong-jawed. "What's up? Why am I here?"

Mrs. Fairchild raised her eyebrows.

"I'm not asking you a metaphysical question."

She grinned. In another setting, at another time, she probably could be fun. But now, the grin flattened, and vertical creases—canyons, really, they were so deep—appeared between her eyebrows. Frowning was not a recently acquired or unfamiliar expression. "I need to know who she is." She leaned forward in her chair, examining me as best as she could, and avoided the point yet again. "You look too young for this kind of work."

It was a statement, not a question, so I let it ride. Besides, I wasn't all that young. Thirty-two is old enough to have this job. Any kind of job, in fact, except president of the U.S. But given that Mrs. Fairchild was treating her fortysomething son as if he were a helpless, innocent boy-child, it followed that she probably thought of me as being in the late fetal stage. "A first question, then. What's Emmie's full name?"

She raised her eyebrows this time. "When I introduced—didn't I say?"

"She introduced herself, and only said 'Emmie.' "

"Well, then. That's part of the problem. You see?"

I did not. I tried to imagine how the nickname and/or the omitted last name could so offend this woman that she'd call in private investigators, especially since Leo had also been introduced with only a first name. Since the only theories I could envision involved more bigotry than I could manage, I stopped imagining.

"Cade," she finally said. She looked as if she was waiting for a reaction so she could spring. "Calls herself Cade."

Calls herself? As I called myself Pepper, and she, Fairchild? I ignored the slur and moved on. "I know she said *Emmie*, but is that officially Emma?"

She shrugged and simultaneously shook her head. A halfhearted body language "who knows anything at all?"

But we were discussing a first name, not something generally subject to interpretation and misconstruction. "Ms. Cade's name seems to distress you," I said. "Why is that?" I could have recited amazing names I have seen on the Philly Prep list of students, names that would highlight Emmie Cade's ordinariness. Offhand, I remembered students named for geographical sites including Morocco, Paris, and Verona, semiprecious gems (I was particularly fond of Lapis Lazuli O'Brien), climactic conditions including a Hurricane Waters, and Sirocco something or other; and one name that was not only odd but included punctuation: X-tra Stein. I always wanted to know the story behind the poor girl's naming, and I had to believe that despite the fancy spelling and having a dash of her own, the Steins were not overconcerned with X-tra's self-esteem.

Mrs. Fairchild would have appreciated the names, but I wanted her to keep believing that my story of a day job teaching was a clever ruse and, in real life, I was her full-time investigator. She appeared to be a woman who would not be happy with someone who was not only female, but who had to stop sleuthing in order to grade spelling exams.

I cut to the chase. "What troubles you about her? What do you want us to look for?"

She lifted both hands, palms out, as if to defend herself. "Who is she? That's the trouble." She seemed eager to make herself clear no matter how many sentences and pauses it took. "That's what you have to find out. She's sweet. Friendly. Fine first impression."

Did I have to point out that I needed a problem, and she was giving me an endorsement?

Then, after another long pause: "But—out of nowhere."

And we were back to the starting line. I drained my coffee cup on that one because otherwise, I'd have had too much to say. The "nowhere" business grated on my nerves. Where was someone supposed to appear out of? Was it necessary to send trumpeters and heralds in advance? Courtiers to inform the court of where you've been, so it won't be labeled *nowhere*?

"Do you mean she's a recent newcomer to Philadelphia?" I finally asked.

"A year. Less."

That was the sin. Of course. An outlander. An alien. I could see the movie marquee now: *She Came from Somewhere Else!* Thousands of tiny Claire Fairchilds fleeing in horror.

"Rented a house in Villanova. Joined the cricket club. Charitable groups. Right circles right away. Met Leo at a party. Moved here, into this building. Engaged to my son."

"She lives here?"

She pointed her index finger upward. "Upstairs." She lifted her eyebrows. "She said the suburbs were no place to be single and childless."

Moving to Leo's mother's building, lovely and unique a place as it was, did seem a rather obvious positioning of the troops for the major assault.

Nonetheless, she was right about living as a single in the suburbs. And even if she moved to the city so as to be more visible to Leo, so what? All's fair, they say, and so far, this newcomer sounded pleasantly—dully—ordinary. Maybe a little tawdry—a gold digger. But Claire Fairchild had said this wasn't about money. And in any case, while it might be more interesting for her to have put her energy into ending world hunger, if her goal was marriage to a wealthy man, then she'd demonstrated expertise and wisdom, and had been out front and honest about it. My mother would have revered her, wished she'd been her daughter, and before I had attached myself to my significantly unwealthy man—would have wanted me to make Emmie Cade my guru and life guide. Maybe I didn't want her as my new best friend, but, so far, she sounded as unworthy of investigation as it was possible to be.

Maybe we were having a semantic problem. I tried to figure out what Claire Fairchild actually meant, to force out specifics about the *nowhere* business. "Has she told you where she lived before she moved here?"

"In her way."

"Meaning?"

Mrs. Fairchild required several deep breaths before continuing, and then her words were spaced with pauses. "Emmie talks. Chatters. Smiles. Answers. Laughs. Very merry. Open-seeming."

The significant word, apparently, was *seeming*.

This time, Claire Fairchild leaned over and lifted her coffee cup and sipped at what had to now be a lukewarm brew. She carefully returned the cup to the table before speaking, and I wondered if she had a repertoire of distracting actions to take her listener's—and her own—mind off what a strain it was to keep up a conversation.

She looked at me directly. "Later, you realize, she didn't say anything."

"I think I understand."

She pursed her mouth, but decided to be clearer. "Where she grew up? She says . . . father was executive. Changed companies. Moved a lot. Lived in Atlanta."

Something tangible at last. "That's a start." I wrote it down.

"And Bridgeport. Austin. Fargo."

I looked up. Mrs. Fairchild's mouth had tightened. "Gotcha," she was saying, as if I were her enemy, as if we weren't supposedly working in tandem. "Chicago," she said. "Los Angeles. Cleveland." She tapped her index finger on the arm of the wing chair. "Many schools, too. Talk. More talk. Funny stories, but . . ."

"You mean that ultimately you realize she never mentioned what companies her father worked for?" I asked, hoping to spare Mrs. Fairchild a bit of air. "Or a specific school?"

She nodded. "Or dates. Or neighborhoods. Los Angeles!" Both of her hands rose and spread apart to show the daunting size of L.A., the meaninglessness of not being more specific about origins.

I thought about the beautiful woman in the poet's blouse, her graceful gestures, that flash of high-wattage smile, her free-flowing compliments about my supposed job. I could imagine her speaking at length and saying very little, but saying it in a warm and delicious manner. Was she accidentally or deliberately offering conversational cotton candy?

A woman could babble out of nervousness when confronted with the formidable Claire Fairchild. Or she could have a conversational style based on the idea that nothing about herself was all that interesting or important, so above all, she shouldn't bother listeners with specifics. Instead, she'd aim to entertain, amuse, and turn the conversation to other topics and other people. What, in fact, could be a more traditionally feminine philosophy than to feel that her purpose was to make the listener happy? Maybe she'd been taught to behave that way.

Nothing Claire Fairchild said necessarily triggered suspicion. I'd

41

had friends—short-timers passing through Philadelphia—whose fathers worked for I.B.M., and they'd referred to the initials as standing for "I've been moved." Things might have changed by now, but that's how it was for a large segment of the nation's children, and for a long time.

Plus, I knew people who were congenitally vague, avoiding specifics as if they were tainted. They intended to be clear, they thought they'd been clear, but I nevertheless had to ask, "Do you mean . . . ?" Poor communication skills, not anything malicious.

"Did she say where she lived right before she moved here?" I asked.

"Near San Francisco."

I must have frowned, thinking what *near* might mean in researching a person's tracks.

"Yes," Claire Fairchild said. "Vague. I ask, 'where?' She says . . . 'Gosh! You know Indian Cliffs? Little town, a way out? I was near there.' Always places nobody's heard of."

I wondered whether Claire Fairchild had ever traveled, whether "places nobody's heard of" was accurate, or a reflection of a stay-at-home, unsophisticated woman. Not that I knew where any "Indian Cliffs" was in the Bay Area, either, but I was the perfect example of someone who hadn't—yet—gotten to travel.

"Then she talks about the baby deer by the front door, and the fox that ran by." She paused and bit at her bottom lip, remembering.

I nodded encouragement.

"The story's charming. And over. Nothing . . . definite. Ever." She looked up toward the scrolls on the crown-molding and sighed. Then she looked at me, and her expression was solemn.

"So you called us." I still didn't get it. Emmie Cade sounded ditsy. Besides, one look at Claire Fairchild's unforgiving eyes, and a woman in love with her son had good reason to blur what might be a less than stellar, educated, or straight-and-narrow past. I'm sure I'm not the only adult female who has adventures and experiments in my past that I'd prefer be kept quietly away from prospective in-laws.

And there was the issue of how powerful Claire's hold was on her boy, how much her opinion would matter. As witness her having hired me.

"I could use more information," I said. "All I've got at this point is her name and a last address somewhere near San Francisco."

Claire Fairchild rolled her eyes. I had no idea why.

"For example," I asked, ignoring the theatrics, "has she mentioned a college?"

She shook her head. "Here's what I know: Her birthday is August first. Same as Leo's."

That was cute.

"Or so she says."

"And her age?"

A slow head shake this time. " 'Much younger than Leo!' she said. Seemed wrong to press her on it. On anything. Finally found out she's thirty. Widowed. College?" She shook her head in her abbreviated, energy-saving manner—one turn left, one turn right—and continued in her telegraphic stop-and-start manner. "Parents died. Small plane crash. No siblings."

Fortune was not smiling upon me. My first solo flight and I, too, were going to crash. So far, I had found no visible inroads to Emmie Cade's background. "Did you talk about the wedding?" I asked.

She looked miffed. An intrusion into her personal life, I suppose, as if inviting me here weren't precisely that. "They only announced it today. That's why they were here. I told you," she said with mild indignation. "*Two weeks* from now."

"So you said. Not much time. That's why I thought you might have discussed a guest list. Bridesmaids? Maid of honor? Out-of-town friends or—"

"Only the date. Small, of course. Tiny. No attendants I know of. No list."

I took a deep breath and considered. "Did she ever say what brought her to Philadelphia?"

Mrs. Fairchild was silent, considering. Then she shook her head. "Her friend, I think. Victoria. Nice girl."

"You've met her?"

She nodded. "Knew her before Emmie. Leo's friend. Knew Emmie back when. Bumped into each other again in San Francisco last year."

Good—an actual way to wiggle into Emmie Cade's past. "Do you remember Victoria's last name?"

"Baer, but Emmie sometimes calls her Smitty. Maiden name Smith, I guess. Victoria's divorced."

"You said school friend. Is Victoria Baer perhaps a college friend?"

She raised her shoulders in a gentle shrug. Her expression was worth a thousand words, or at least thirteen: *Did you expect anything more concrete than that? Didn't I say she's vague?* Then she returned to spoken language. "Emmie called her a school friend. But . . ." She sighed and lifted her shoulders, reverting to world-weary body language. "Emmie's vague about college. She quit, anyway. No degree."

Another easy source moved back into the shadows.

"Got sick, she says. That—whatever you call it. Students get it. My day, called 'the kissing disease.' " Her mouth curdled again. She knew how Emmie had contracted her illness.

"Mononucleosis," I said. "A virus." Not that it would be okay in Claire Fairchild's cosmos if her son's intended had gotten an illness that involved the transmission of bodily fluids.

"Didn't go back. Talks about getting a degree now. Why not? She doesn't work."

"You said she's widowed. Is her income from her dead husband?"

Claire Fairchild lowered her eyelids and almost subliminally raised her shoulders.

Maybe Victoria Baer would be less vague. Or at least tell me the name of her alma mater.

"That ring." Claire Fairchild tilted her head and nodded toward my hand on the arm of my chair. "Are you engaged?"

I nodded.

"Pretty."

"It was my fiancé's grandmother's." The small sapphire encircled by tiny diamonds didn't particularly look like an engagement ring, which was one of many reasons I loved it, but apparently Mrs. Fairchild was ever on alert for signs of impending matrimony.

"Will it affect your attitude?"

"Toward what?"

"My . . . this investigation."

"Why would it?" Though I'd never admit it, I knew the answer, and, I suspect, so did she. And the answer was yes, definitely—it already had prejudiced me against her. She'd notched up all the dreadful mother-in-law clichés by calling in auxiliary troops with which to persecute a girl. She'd have frightened and repulsed me even if I myself were not engaged.

"You know his parents?"

"I'm about to meet them. They live out of state." *They're going to appear out of nowhere,* I wanted to add, *and how about that?*

"Do they know you?"

She wasn't making sense. "As I said, we haven't met."

"Do they know normal things? Your name—"

"You know that about your son's fiancée."

She shook her head.

So that was the problem with the name. She didn't believe it was real.

Not that she said so. She aimed her iceberg eyes at me and said nothing.

"Mrs. Fairchild?"

She seemed to pull herself back from the far horizon. "I didn't decide to investigate out of the blue."

"Of course not." The velocity and emphasis with which I lied were improving with practice.

"But that's what you think."

My lies were fast and loud and failures.

"I don't do things like hire private investigators."

Need I mention what a rush that sentence gave me? Forget her imperial attitude. She believed I was what I said I was, even though

I barely believed it. She'd handed me my credentials. I felt knighted by the queen.

"I don't care what you think."

The thrill was gone. "It's your dime, Mrs. Fairchild, but if I'm on the wrong track—or if you think I am—maybe you could be more helpful about rerouting me. More precise about why you decided to hire me—"

"I didn't."

"Us, then. Hire us."

She had a wide variety of lip-poses. This time, she pushed her chin forward and pulled her mouth tight, regarding me again with her freezing gaze.

I'd about had it, especially if *it* meant coffee, in which case I'd had about too much of it. "While you're thinking," I said as I stood up, "could you direct me to a powder room?"

She pointed toward the entry and to the right. Even though I'd asked to leave the room, I felt dismissed.

The apartment was spacious, with a hall leading off the entry. I passed a full dining room, its long table ready to seat ten, and then I saw the door she'd mentioned and opened it.

Except she hadn't meant this door, because I found myself in a narrow room lined to its high ceiling with shelves heavy with china and glasses on one side, and boxes and bags of rice and grains on the other. Traditionally, a butler's pantry, I believed, but at the moment, a housekeeper's refuge. I'd nearly tripped over Batya, the super-pregnant dumpling, who sat on a low step stool, crying.

She looked up at me, a tissue pressed to her nose, her eyes swollen and red-rimmed.

"I'm sorry," I said. "I thought this was the—" What did it matter what I'd thought?

Batya clutched her belly and looked away.

"Are you all right?"

She flashed a bitter look at me. Okay, it had been a stupid question. People who are all right don't huddle, crying, in a butler's pantry. "Is it—is everything okay about the baby?"

She looked down at her pregnant belly, as if surprised by it. "Yes, why . . ." She shook her head and retreated into herself again.

We were in a social situation that might be described as awkward. Having intruded, discretion—backing off and making an exit—seemed polite. It also seemed inhumane. Was I to behave as if I'd noticed nothing? "Can I do something for you?" I asked.

She shook her head back and forth, vigorously. "No," she whispered. "No. Please. I handle this."

I heard fear, but also a real plea for me to leave her alone. "Okay, I'll—"

She put up a hand. "Wait—please, miss—don't say to Mrs. Fairchild."

"Say that I—" I didn't know how to finish that sentence. Somehow mentioning out loud that she was crying in the butler's pantry made it worse. "—saw you?"

"Yes. You did not see me, yes? Please, is important."

"Sure," I said after a pause. "But are you positive there isn't something I could do?"

"Nobody can help me. Nobody on the earth."

"I could try." I knew I should back out of that pantry and remove this scene from my mind. This really was none of my business. Or was it—in the way it was everybody's business. There are no parables of the Half-Assed Samaritan who asked politely, then backed off.

"If you say to her I tell you anything, it makes worse. That you saw me cry? That makes worse." She drilled her words into my skull with her eyes and intensity. "*She* makes worse."

She. My client. She who gets upset about women's names and intimidates the investigator she hired.

"Two years I work for her," Batya said softly. "Two years, day and night. I live here. She says, 'Batya you are best. Stay with me.' My aunt, she watches my baby."

My surprise must have shown, because Batya's baby was inescapably, hugely here.

"Other baby," she said. "He is two years, but he needs medicine." She shook her head, as if forbidding that child's sickness to be true. "I see him Sunday only. She feeds me, gives me room, I buy his medicine, but . . ." She grimaced and shook her head.

"Money?" I whispered. "She pays you, doesn't she?"

She didn't look at me now. She shrugged, and looked away, and I had to lean close to hear her say, "Not so I can live somewhere else. Not so I can live with him. She say that is all she can pay. She is widow on—how you say—always the same money."

"A fixed income?"

"Fixed. Yes. She says someday, when she dies, she is leaving me money. Is all big lie. Mr. Leo, he's rich. He gives her everything. She gives me nothing."

I looked at her, an eggplant-shaped woman, face wet with tears. "And now this," I said softly. "Are you crying because of this baby?"

She looked up at me and sniffled. "For both babies. I ask Mrs. Fairchild for more money. Only what other people get. Is fair, what I ask. I work hard for her. I cook, shop, clean, help with the sickness. I take good care." She put her hands protectively around her belly.

I thought of how many positions there were like this one, how many ill and elderly people could have used Batya's services. It would be easy enough for her to quit, to find a new job or accept public assistance. Unless . . . "Are you a legal alien, Batya? Do you have a green card?"

She looked up at me, her mouth open and her eyes wide and wild. Her worst fears had been realized.

"I'm not going to tell anybody. I wanted to know what she . . . Is that it?" The threat of deportation is a powerful form of blackmail and, apparently, of keeping virtual slaves from fleeing.

"My husband left. Disappeared. Mrs. Fairchild, she says it doesn't matter. Is my fault." She clutched her belly and rocked.

"Don't panic," I said. "Let me find out what can be done. Just take care of yourself and your baby and don't panic—and I won't say a word to Mrs. Fairchild."

"Or to—"

"To anybody. I promise."

"But she—she—" She shook her head and was silent.

I tiptoed out, the echo of that *she* hissing through my brain.

ive

WHEN I returned to the living room, Claire Fairchild
looked as if she'd fallen asleep. I stood near the
entry and cleared my throat by way of announcement. Her eyes opened and she adjusted her torso to a more upright position. I suspected that once, before parts of her went bad,
she'd had ramrod posture.

"Don't sit down," she said.

Fired? Like that? I formulated a protest, feeling as humiliated as
the frightened housekeeper had been, except my emotions immediately steamed and mutated into anger. Enough of this woman's
imperial attitude!

"The desk." She pointed. "Bottom drawer."

As almost always, I was glad I'd held my temper. I didn't hear arrogance in her voice. I heard exhaustion. It had probably been a busier than normal day already, with her son's visit and, as added psychic strain, his announcement of a wedding date to a woman she wanted investigated. Me. And, from the appearance of it, earlier on, a confrontation with her housekeeper.

I went to the small desk—what was called a *lady's* desk because it's easier to say *lady's* than *useless, undersized, and intended for trivial, inconsequential tasks.* It was narrow and delicately formed of pale wood inlay. I opened the lower of its two shallow drawers.

"On top," she said. I extracted a plain manila envelope and held it up. She lowered her head in a nod of acknowledgment, then, wiggling her index finger again, indicated that I should bring it over.

I handed it to her and sat down on my assigned love seat.

"I thought I was being too . . . careful . . . putting it there. He drops over. Lucky today."

So there was more to this than a snit about inadequate storytelling skills, and we were finally getting to the point.

She slowly unclipped the envelope and extracted sheets of paper and photographs, all of which she let sit on her lap. "I worried," she said. "Not right, how she says nothing. How determined she is. Moving here. But I called because of this." She checked one of the papers on her lap, then passed it to me.

The top of the page was dominated by a drawing of a skinny-necked insect with huge eyes and saw-edged front legs, an unreal creature from an inept science-fiction film. Below was a message written in a collage of different-sized print from what looked like newspapers and magazines. I had the sense of being back in an old movie. Given computers and clip art, nobody had to cut up newspapers to remain anonymous. This was the *Antiques Roadshow* of crime. I read the message:

> the PRAYING man TIS! lookS devout but LOOKS lie! sHE eats
> its mate when sex is done.

"Did this come in the mail?"

She nodded.

"Do you have the envelope?"

She shook her head and frowned. At herself this time, I trusted. "I remember. From New Jersey, somewhere."

"You couldn't have known," I said, wondering why I was trying to spare her feelings. "In any case, this could mean anything, about anybody or nobody. Most likely, it's a prank. I don't think it should worry you. Somebody plucked your name from the phone book—"

"Not listed."

"You know what I mean. Somebody found your name and address. For starters, it's on the wall downstairs, next to the buzzers. This isn't necessarily anything, and its meaning—it doesn't make sense."

"Then this came." She passed a second sheet that was again crudely fashioned out of snippets of print, some words pasted on letter by letter. Letters were clipped from shiny magazine stock, others from newspaper headlines or advertisements.

Would not YOU Feel More InFORMed IF! you Could read THE Independent Journal?

I looked up at Mrs. Fairchild. "Sent from Altoona," she said. "I remember."

"What's it mean? What's this *Journal*? The sender doesn't sound bright, to put it mildly."

She shook her head and passed me a third page that had only a date, about fifteen months ago. "From Chicago." The envelope was clipped to a page dominated by an illustration of a praying mantis.

It made me sad that the detailed drawing had been hacked out of a library or textbook, just for the sake of this ill-intended mailing. I knew that defacing books was not the problem I was supposed to be considering, but all the same . . .

The message read:

PRAY NOW! Don't wait UNTIL It's TOO late & YOU are tHE prey!

I was ashamed of myself for noticing—and worse, being pleased by—the fact that we were dealing with a literate crank, because *it's* and *too* were properly spelled. I guess you can take the English teacher out of the classroom, but et cetera. "Is this the end of it?" I asked.

She shook her head. "Six so far. Every three–four days."

"Since . . . ?"

"Last two weeks." She passed me the fourth:

Nothing is free xcept some murderers.

Dollar signs of various sizes dotted the page, and the name *Independent Journal* was repeated, accompanied by a date.

"Mailed from Baltimore," Mrs. Fairchild said.

"Did you check out that newspaper? Find out where it is?"

"Went to library." She made a small gesture toward the window. I understood. She meant the library snuggled at the edge of the Square. She could walk there, though judging her strength, it would occupy the major part of the day. "Batya helped me."

"Does she know about the threats, then?"

"Batya knows everything. I can't do . . ." She sighed. "Batya knows."

Then pay her a living wage, I wanted to shout. Stop blackmailing her, threatening to have her deported.

"Librarian found the paper. Outside San Francisco."

Where Emmie Cade last lived.

"Librarian said it has no . . ." Her brow wrinkled as she tried to remember something. "Archives!" She nodded. "No online archives." Her voice was weak, and she paused more often, but seemed determined to get everything out and onto the table. "But—"

I thought I knew what she wanted to say. "They have them on file, and we can request articles."

She nodded. "You'll find them."

That seemed an easy-enough task. "Did you report these notes to the police?"

"What would I say?" I had put the pages on the small table beside the love seat, and she glanced at them. "Looks like kid stuff." She stopped and breathed quietly, silently, for a minute, her eyes lowered. Then she looked up at me. "Wouldn't have called you, except . . ." For the first time, she seemed unsure of herself.

"There's more, isn't there?"

Her face contorted, and she looked near tears as she handed me another page with a copy of the newspaper article the earlier mailing had referred to.

To my surprise, the article had nothing to do with Emma Cade. "Who is Stacy?" I asked, because that was the name below a blurred picture—a copy-machine copy of a mediocre newspaper photo.

"Emmie. Stacy. King. Cade. Who knows what else?"

I looked at the shot of a woman, a mourner obviously taken by surprise. Her face was misted behind a veil, and one arm blurred as it rose to shield part of her face. She wore black. Only a brooch—a twisted, abstract outline of a heart—broke its severity. The woman was identified as Stacy King, widow of noted sailor Jake King.

The text was unsettling. It managed to make clear, in oblique and nonlitigious ways, the confusion and suspicion surrounding Jake King's death. Apparently, he'd been everybody's favorite regular rich guy. He'd been a dot-com entrepreneur when the going was good, smart enough to pull out reams of money in time. But being a land-animal was only his day job. His soul lived on the water. Many fellow members of his yacht club were quoted as being incredulous that he'd had any accident, let alone a fatal one. According to them, Jake was practically drown-proof. He'd been exceptional, an avid sailboat racer and all-around expert seafarer, and nobody could understand why, on a calm spring day, he'd pitched over the side of his boat, half naked, not wearing the life vest he always wore, and drowned.

"It was the heat," the widow was quoted as saying. "The wine. I warned him, but he loved fine wines, and it was his party." Her take on the accident sounded weak and unconvincing.

"Jake was lots of things, but not a reckless sailor," his ex-wife, Geraldine Fiori King, also an expert sailor, was quoted. The article semi-obliquely referred to a long and nasty divorce that followed Jake King's meeting the lovely young Stacy. "He respected the ocean and bay," the first Mrs. King said, "and the only time he took his vest off—well . . . you know . . . let's say to go to sleep, okay?"

An investigation was underway. I thought of the lithe young poet-woman I'd seen within the hour. "Are you positive this story and this Stacy has anything to do with your son's fiancée?"

She passed over the two photos she'd earlier pulled out of the manila envelope. One showed two young women, smiling into the sun. One, in a broad-brimmed hat trimmed with daisies, wore a halter top and a softly patterned long skirt that showed the outline of her legs through its translucent material. Her feet were bare. The hat was good for her skin, but bad for recognition purposes, as it shadowed her features. Her companion held her hand up as a visor, almost as if she were saluting the photographer. She wore a man-tailored shirt, sleeves rolled up, and tails tucked into a pair of belted, tailored slacks and deck shoes. She reminded me of my sister and all my sister's friends.

"That's her, too. This past summer. The halter girl. The other is a proof."

"The other woman? Proof of what?"

She shook her head.

I understood. Not the other girl, but the other photo, and not evidence of anything, but a photographer's proof.

"Leo thought maybe an engagement announcement." She took a few slow breaths before starting again. "She didn't like any of the shots. So, nothing in the paper, but . . . I still have proofs. Must return." Finally, a clear image of the young woman I'd met today. Emmie Cade, a.k.a. Stacy King. I didn't know why she hadn't liked the portrait unless she truly didn't want a clear image of her-self anywhere. The photographer had captured her delicate beauty and the exceptionally warm smile. She didn't look as if she were posing. She didn't look capable of artifice of any sort. Instead, she looked as if she were transparent and the viewer had a view straight into her pure heart, catching her in a moment of joy.

I would have pressed my case that this woman wasn't related to the one in the news story, except that Emmie Cade wore the iden-tical, unusual brooch of metal that had been hammered and twisted into a semiabstract image of a heart.

"You know," I said, "despite whatever initial confusion there was at the time of that news story, and despite these anonymous messages, the law found her innocent or she wouldn't be here. This feels like maliciousness. Somebody who's furious that she's finding happiness again. Or somebody without any real reason, just a desire to make trouble."

"I hope so." She looked at me, head slightly tilted, challenging me to say she was lying. Oddly, I believed her. I couldn't remem-ber anyone else about whom I'd had such a mix of positive and negative emotions, all at the same time.

"That's why Leo isn't to know about this," she said.

"What if—they're probably just an evil-minded prank, but if there's any real threat—"

"Not till he's married, I think. No point before. No money till then."

"And that marriage is taking place in two weeks?"

"I can't let it. Not until you"—she gestured toward the pages—"What I'll do is get sick. Today. Near death. Delay wedding until you . . ." She squinted at me, as if close-reading my expression. "I'm pretending sickness," she said. "I look worse than I am," she said. "People think—they'll believe, but I'll be around for years."

"Of course." If force of will had anything to do with longevity, she'd outlast me.

"When we know what's true, I'll recover. Up to you."

I nodded, painfully aware of how many people's happiness, and perhaps lives, now depended on my nonexistent investigative expertise.

"Until then . . ." She put her finger to her mouth.

She was being remarkably considerate. She was suspicious with cause and worried on behalf of her son, but unwilling to taint his relationships—with his fiancée and with her—with her fears.

"He's happy," she whispered, underlining and emphasizing my thoughts.

She was a complicated woman: a considerate and worried parent, a meddling, autocratic harridan; a woman with a sly wit and an imperious attitude, Batya's inhumane slave-keeper. All of the above and who knew how much else?

Her daughter-in-law-to-be was all charm and grace, mildly ditsy and vague and/or a conniving gold digger and murderer. So far.

This wasn't what I wanted. When I read fiction, I wanted characters as complicated as they are in real life. In real life, however, particularly in this real-life new job, I wanted no ambiguity. I wanted a comic book world, with 100 percent bad villains and my good guys spotless. And while I was at it, I wanted X-ray vision and the knowledge, flat out, whether to like or trust somebody or not.

I put the studio portrait of Emmie Cade into my briefcase along with the anonymous notes. I paused as I added the snapshot of the two women smiling into the sun. "Do you know who the second woman is in this picture?"

"Victoria. Victoria Baer."

"Does she live in the city?" I would have staked my day's income that she did not. Given that Emmie's first rental was in Villanova, my bet was that her one friend in the area lived nearby in the suburbs. Besides, she looked Main Line. She had that classic look, so understated as to be barely audible, reflecting the utter fear of flashiness or trend-following.

She looked like my sister Beth's wardrobe.

"Bryn Mawr," Claire Fairchild said.

I'd find Victoria Smith Baer in a flash. Even though she and Emmie Cade would be younger than Beth, I was willing to bet I'd get a leg up via the suburban matron's six degrees of separation. The hardest boiled gumshoes relied on confidantes, pipelines, and snitches. Those are guy words for gossips. I knew gossips.

"Then that's it for now." I briefly outlined whatever I could think of as to when we'd report back to her, and while I spoke, I tidied the pages she'd given me and the photographs. She passed me the manila envelope and I was ready to refill it when I remembered something. "Didn't you say you've received half a dozen of these notes?"

She nodded.

"I have five." I recounted to be sure.

She pulled back in surprised confusion and shook her head.

I looked around and didn't see any more pages. Then I looked inside the manila envelope and saw it. "It got itself stuck."

She watched as I pulled it out, then put her hand to her mouth and nodded.

This page was different, red construction paper, onto which black bold oversized letters spelled out:

AND THERE'S MORE DEAD!!!!!

That was all. The letters looked clipped from happy ads. This one got to me viscerally. I looked up and was startled to see a smirk on Claire Fairchild's face.

"Hate that, don't you?" she said.

"What's that?"

"Having to change your mind." She squinched up her mouth, but couldn't control the slightly malevolent grin.

"About what?"

"Witches and crones and meddlers. Evil mothers-in-law."

"I have no idea what you're talking about, ma'am." I stood up. "I'll let myself out." I didn't want to summon sobbing Batya.

Mrs. Fairchild's moment of triumph passed along with the mild smirk. She looked more delicate than ever and she'd aged during the visit. "I'm afraid," she whispered. "Afraid of what that means. That there's more dead. Is that in the past or—"

"Please try not to worry," I said as I made my exit. "From now on, we'll take care of this."

I could say that—and almost believe that—because at the time, I had no idea of what any of this meant.

Six

ACK outside Mrs. Fairchild's building, bidding adieu to the ornate scrolls, cryptic gargoyles, and the vaguely antebellum swirls of balcony rails, I understood that I wasn't going to be the next centerfold for the Sleuth-of-the-Month Club. Other than that, I knew nothing. Hadn't a clue. Literally.

I walked toward the office in a deep funk. This wasn't what I'd anticipated. All summer long I'd worked under Mackenzie's supervision, and had done well, he said. But this was my true maiden voyage, my test flight. I'd expected to interview the client and leave bursting with ideas as to what to do next, but at the moment, all I drew was a blank.

Background searches can be routine, and I'm sure that's what C. K. thought this one would be. Unfortuately, that assumes the investigator has a few salient facts about the person being investigated—beginning, perhaps, with her actual name.

Instead, I'd been given a blank wall and told to read the writing on it, and in this case, the moving finger had moved on so quickly, not even fingerprints were left.

Maybe being a private eye, even a part-time one, wasn't such a hot idea. Much as I loathed the idea of admitting my incompetence, much as I loved the idea of our partnership, push had now come to shove, and look who was falling down. Perhaps it was time to restrict myself to dangling participles and pronoun case. It was possible my mission on earth was not solving crimes, but disabusing people from saying, "He invited John and myself." Or, "Between you and I."

Surely preserving the Mother Tongue was as important a public service as doing background checks.

On the other hand, we needed additional income, and pronoun usage wasn't going to generate it. The question remained: How could I track this creature of murky past, floating names, vague antecedents, no relatives, and no known jobs or schools? And how to do it subtly so her fiancé is never made aware of my investigation?

I stopped, mid-Square, and considered what I did have.

A birth date, August 1, thirty years ago. If, in fact, I believed that cute coincidence that she'd been born on the same day as Leo.

I didn't have her Social Security number, nor did I have her last address, but I could get a place-name, now. Surely a town would be named somewhere in the records of Jake King's death, and I could work from there.

I had a news story, a possibly fake birth date, and a studio photograph. What I didn't have was an idea of how best to proceed. I wasn't eager to ask Ozzie, who was gruff at best, if he'd deign to speak to me, nor did it seem adult to go home and await Mackenzie's wisdom like a pitiable, helpless flower of a girl—the hothouse variety that isn't native to Philadelphia.

"You all right, young woman?"

Bad sign when the person offering to help you is a bent-over old woman at least fifty years your senior. "You look dazed," she said, her gray eyes circled by worry-wrinkles. "Something hurting? You need a doctor?"

I assured her I was fine, thanked her, took a deep breath, and reminded myself that I had resources. I had my brains and, for once and probably the last time till June, I didn't have a paper to mark or a lesson to prepare. That's about as free as this woman gets.

I passed Philly Prep across the way and thought about the abominable Sunshine and her ability to look on the bright side even when there wasn't one. Hard as it was to swallow, I had to be more like her and focus on the positives.

I had the name of Emmie's local friend and former classmate and she most likely could give me a lead into Emmie's origins. Where she'd gone to school at some point. Her actual maiden name. And I had the newspaper story, the newspaper's archives. If the death of Jake King was as big a mystery as that article made it out to be, there'd be other stories, more information, especially about the widow. A coroner's inquest. Perhaps a trial.

For now, I'd assume that after all the fuss over Jake King's death, Emmie had opted to take back her maiden name. That didn't explain the Stacy-Emmie switch, but I didn't need her first name for the Social Security death index. I was looking for her father's name, and Cade didn't seem that common a surname.

I wasn't down for the count yet. By the time I reached the office, I was reinvigorated. I needed to be, because Ozzie Bright—whose name did not reflect truth in advertising—was never overjoyed to see me, and was always less than helpful. He'd welcomed Mackenzie, on any basis, because Mackenzie could walk and chew gum at the same time, plus, he understood computers. Ozzie could make neither of these claims.

He wasn't a misogynist; he was more of what was called "a guy's guy," comfortable working with men. I'm sure that in his secret heart, he referred to me as "that dame." And dames had no place in his office, except as clients.

Ozzie was tolerated, however—more than tolerated, accepted fully, and recommended by his former associates on the force—because while he was still wearing a uniform, he'd suffered an "unfortunate accident," the details of which were never discussed, except that they involved a weapon and a never-to-be-disclosed part of his anatomy. The silence surrounding Ozzie's condition was a prime example of male bonding, but a female couldn't help but notice that whenever it was obliquely referred to, all the men in the room murmured, "Poor bastard."

His cranky and stubborn ways, his frustration and ineptitude with electronics, the basic tool of today's private investigator—all that was greeted with the slow, sad shake of the head and an almost saintly level of tolerance. I didn't expect much of Ozzie, except that he'd let me do my thing without interference.

Which is what I did. "I'm only here for"—I checked my watch and estimated the time I had between now, the party at my former neighbor's, and arrival at the Bellevue—"a half hour," I told him. He didn't bother to hide his relief.

Not everyone's listed on the Social Security death lists. Some people belonged to private pension plans, a group that included lots of teachers, in fact. But it was highly probable that a corporate executive—if Emmie Cade had been telling the truth about that—would have paid in.

I looked up Cade.

First big surprise: There were over two thousand. I suppose that did, in fact, mean it wasn't an overly common last name, but the numbers were nonetheless daunting. Still, I hoped that among all those names, I'd narrow it down to logical dates and find the woman and man with the same place and date of death. Her parents, my plane-crash victims.

The list was alphabetical. I had to pick a letter and click on it, which meant I couldn't do a visual check through the alphabet, and I couldn't retain whole lists in my head waiting to find a date-mate elsewhere. Ninety-five names and I was still in the A's.

Two hundred and still counting and I was still in the B's.

This wasn't a great plan.

Maybe Emmie was named for one of her parents. Six hundred names in, I reached names starting with "Em." Emmas and Emmetts, Emmers and Emogenes, Emersons and Emorys.

This was no help.

I realized at some point that Mrs. Cade—still assuming that was Emmie/Stacey's actual maiden name—might have been a school-teacher, or unemployed and not on the list at all.

For too long, I nonetheless doggedly continued, eliminating Cades who'd died before the seventies—before they'd have had a chance to father Emmie. And then, I realized I was still looking at too wide a selection, since if she'd moved around through high school on her father's corporate track, that meant he had to have lived into her teens. I pushed my cut-date into the mid-1980s.

If I lucked into a set of names, I'd know where they died, and when, and I could check a local newspaper. A plane crash would make the news, or there'd be at least an obituary, but I had to be lucky. Some entries didn't even list a last residence or place of final benefits.

I was not lucky. I wound up out of time, with only a headache.

I quickly packed my things, and bid adieu to Ozzie, who grunted back. Feeling ever more frayed and sweaty, wilting in the oppressive humidity, I made my way through the streets, up to my former neighborhood. I was struck by a tidal wave of nostalgia for the row of tiny homes on the narrow cobbled street. Nothing much had changed since I'd moved. In fact, nothing much had changed since Benjamin Franklin probably rode a horse down this street.

My old house had been rebuilt, maintaining its Colonial façade. It looked to be in the hands of loving tenants, with its cherry-red window box overflowing with geraniums. The hitching post on the curb had been painted to match the flower box and the front door.

The street was still too narrow for easy passage of cars, impossible for parking. All was as it always had been: houses intended for servants, people who walked, not for cars, which had to be parked on a more modern street or rented garage.

There it was in all its glory. Cute, photogenic, inconvenient, and cramped—and I really missed it and all the people who'd been my neighbors.

I entered the crowded home of my friend Nancy Russell and her mother, a woman whose first name, as far as I could tell was *Mrs.* I had never called her anything else, except behind her back, when she was *Old Mrs. Russell* or *Nasty Old Mrs. Russell*. Or worse.

She has been a longtime burden for Nancy, who, luckily, has a strong back and a sufficiently strong income to hire caretakers much of the time.

In all her ninety years, Mrs. Russell has never had time for most of humanity or even for domestic animals. She believes both species scheme behind her back and exist only to spread disease and plan her downfall.

Except for my cat, Macavity. She adores him and believes him the exception to all her rules. Until she grew truly enfeebled, she was—at her request—the proprietor of Old Mrs. Russell's Cat Camp for Macavity Pepper.

I would have brought him were it not for this crazy day's schedule, I explained to both Nancy and her mother. Given that Mrs. Russell is deaf and refuses to wear her hearing aid, explaining anything to her is strenuous. Aside from arthritic knees and hips that now kept her in a wheelchair, and the hearing loss, she was still forceful, emphatic, and tyrannical, and she made it clear that if it didn't involve Macavity, she wasn't overexcited about my presence.

I gave her the Pavarotti CDs. She'd put on her hearing aids for him. I knew she adored him, and I knew she wouldn't admit it. And then I made my way through the crowd.

In truth, I, and probably everyone there, had stopped off en route to our real lives on behalf of Nancy, not her mother. We were here to salute and celebrate her dutifulness and goodness of heart. And also, to secretly, or at least privately, commiserate. Her mother had been a mean-spirited dictator her entire life, and had only moved in with—or on—Nancy when her health was, in theory, failing. But that had been fifteen long years ago. Apparently, Old Mrs. was going for the longevity gold.

It was fun to catch up with local gossip about squabbles among my former and new neighbors. As always, wars began over anything, from one homeowner's decision to paint his shutters screaming chartreuse to a raid on another's illegal backyard crop. The people who'd bought the house I'd once rented had paid a fortune, Harvey Weiss said, escalating everybody's real estate appraisals and taxes. Nobody paid him much heed, not even his petite, preternaturally calm wife, who, as always, stood beside him, rolling her eyes at his utterances and saying nothing except, "Oh, Harvey."

"But the thing is," Carlie Hopper added, "they turned it into a showplace. Every nook and cranny just so, with the right hue of paint—they used color consultants—and the perfect piece of furniture. And the day the last accent piece was put in place, they split up."

All this and more was presented like an ongoing chorale—the neighborhood news vendors, cranks, complainers, and gigglers singing their predictable parts. Carlie Hopper found the marijuana bust the funniest thing, while Harvey Weiss found it further proof of the decline of Western Civilization as he did the very idea of chartreuse shutters. His wife rolled her eyes. "Oh, Harvey," she murmured.

Nothing much had changed. Everything set off Harvey, especially me. When you live on the same block as an obsessive-compulsive who thinks the world's already too messy, and who also is slightly paranoid and in love with conspiracy theories—and then your house explodes, you've definitely crossed his bottom line. Not that it was my fault—no chemistry sets in my basement—but that didn't matter. I'd made a mess on his street, and worse, I'd picked up my cat and left the mess behind.

I smiled and listened, learning that Peggy O'Neil's fifth-grade daughter was now bald because she'd wanted to bleach her hair but, not quite getting the concept, had used laundry bleach.

A young man at the other end of the block—this was told sotto voce and we all leaned close—had pierced places you didn't even want to think about, but which he, most definitely, wanted to discuss.

Someone's son had gone off to study hideous contagious diseases in Africa, causing everyone to shudder at the dangers he faced. Harvey, of course, demanded that he be quarantined far from the street before he was allowed back on it. "No telling what he'll be carrying on him, or in him," he said with customary emphasis.

"Oh, Harvey," his wife said. I wish for once she'd say what she meant by that, because I really couldn't tell, which, of course, was her intent. Was she expressing awe or disdain? Was the end of the sentence really "—get lost!" or variations thereof? Was she asking him to pipe down, or praising his worldview?

"Amanda, you didn't hear the news, did you?"

The speaker was Pris Shoemaker, an astoundingly dull drama queen I tried to avoid because that's the way she spoke. You could almost hear kettledrums in her background, insisting that she carried dire news. And she didn't want to lessen the impact of her message by actually saying it. Instead, you had to do the Pris Shoemaker dance.

"Hear what?" I was supposed to say.

"I nearly fainted when I heard," she'd then say.

"Heard what?" I'd say . . . and so forth and so on ad nauseam.

She delighted in, wallowed in, the shock and degree of emotion she could produce—even if it turned out to be irritation and anger. I vowed to show no emotion now, no matter her news.

But this time, she was among people who knew her style, so the woman next to her jumped in and said, "About Lily? She's—"

Pris rushed to the point without requiring prompts. "—in the hospital. She"—Pris lowered her voice, although everyone else in the circle already knew what she would say—"tried to kill herself."

"Oh, no!" The rocket of feeling that shot through me negated any promise to show no emotions. I adored the appealing Lily. She looked like one of those girls who grow up to be supermodels, the girls nobody believes were ever less than stunning. Right now, aside from the dark-rimmed glasses she always wore, she was all arms, elbows, and wild auburn curls. Someday she'd be willowy. Right now, she was skinny. And funny, and smart in school. What on earth had possessed her?

"Gave everybody quite a scare, but I think she'll be okay. She's in treatment. The whole family is."

"She always seemed a happy kid," I said. "What happened?"

"Who knows?" Pris said. "They say she left a note that said she wasn't popular. That nobody liked her. She's in sixth grade, for heaven's sake!"

Despite the generalized murmur of concern, Harvey saw one little girl's breakdown as another crusade for America. "Don't anybody tell me that it isn't proof we're not going right to hell," Harvey said. "If they don't grab guns and mow each other down, then it's like this—kids driving each other to kill themselves. And adults are no better. It's like—it's like—why don't you talk about the Feders and the Washburns? I'm sure seeing them as a daily example didn't help Lily."

"Oh, Harvey," his wife said.

"For Pete's sake—don't act as if—"

I didn't need to ask what Harvey meant, ridiculous as it was as a motive for a child to try to destroy herself. The Feders and the Washburns were our street's Hatfields and McCoys. Nobody knew the origin of their feud, only that it never ended, and given that they lived on a narrow street of homes with common walls, and went to work in suits, the fighting took on subtle guises. Window-box plants wilted and died and the demise was blamed on the other side. Halloween pranks went out of bounds and involved spray paint on front doors. Windows broke. Phones rang in the night.

And one or the other side complained to whomever would listen. If either of those families was in the house right now, I was sure they were complaining to someone.

"Feder killed Washburn's sapling," Harvey said.

I shook my head. "Come on. Everything that happens is blamed on the other one. Hurricanes and heat spells. Stuff happens, that's all."

"Sure, but grudges like they've got—they never die. People are meaner than ever. It's a fact!"

Things Harvey felt always became facts. If he said so, then the fact was, people were holding more grudges today than they did fifty years ago. I also knew what the next step in his reasoning would be. It was always the same.

"It's the pollution," he said right on cue. "It's the stuff we're poisoning ourselves with. Makes us crazy."

"Romeo and Juliet's families managed to keep a feud going in unpolluted air. And how about Cain and Abel?"

Harvey snorted disdain and waved my comments away. "You shoot industrial waste up into our—"

I looked at my watch, said, "Oops!" and backed away.

Harvey and Pris and eternal feuds had cured my nostalgia for neighborhoods lost. I made my way to Nancy, who knew I couldn't stay long, and we made a date to get together soon. She was a good human being who'd built a career importing tribal artifacts and jewelry. It had involved lots of adventures and opportunities to be away from her mother. But on the domestic scene, she'd spent way too long with the wrong man—a married wrong man who, after fifteen years, was still promising to leave his wife any minute now.

It's fairly awesome what stupid things smart women do about the opposite sex. What lies we listen to and tell ourselves. Nancy could drive a hard bargain with an Indonesian hill tribesman and she could argue price with someone in the markets of Morocco without knowing either one of their languages, but she never once understood Mr. Wrong's lies. She had her part-time man, her full-time mother, and a few good trips a year. Maybe that made her more contented than she chose to let on.

As for me, I was feeling overblessed with lives and people. The day already seemed at least a week long, and I could barely remember its beginnings. But I had miles to go before I could rest. Still ahead: Beth and an evening of eating for a good cause.

It almost made me want to hang around Harvey a little longer.

Seven

I HEARD the excited din while I was still in the elevator, and I admit to a frisson of terror before embarking, a reversion to a nearly forgotten childhood shyness. It didn't feel easy facing a roomful of women I didn't know, women with cash reserves and a sense of privilege I didn't have. I immediately credited the unseen crowd with a sophistication I in no way shared, and to make matters worse, that gloss suddenly became the only important quality a woman needed. It was a variation on the showing-up-naked-onstage nightmare. I had shown up unpolished.

I knew my all-purpose suit was grossly wrong, my shoes impossibly out of fashion, my haircut inferior. Not a one of these things

GILLIAN ROBERTS

had mattered to me twenty minutes ago when, in fact, I was feeling pretty fine, nor would they in a few hours or the rest of my life, but they did right now.

Maybe this was an aftereffect of hearing about Lily's attempted suicide, because it was a very junior high sort of anxiety.

I took a deep breath and stepped out of the elevator.

The women were attractive, well-groomed, affluent looking, and animated. They were undoubtedly lovely people I'd like to have met one at a time, but wedging my way into a crowded party of strangers is not my favorite leisure-time activity. What conversations I manage taste like Styrofoam bonbons—light, bland, and indigestible. With all the generalized good-natured cocktail chatter and glitter of dress up, enormous parties seem more about maintaining the appearance of having a good time than actually having one. I often wonder about the faces on the society pages, the people who make merry nonstop, sometimes for a cause and sometimes simply to overcelebrate an opening, a birthday, a launching or just their own wealth—night after night with the same people. Only the outfits change. Do they love one another that much? Find one another endlessly fascinating?

Another of life's mysteries I never expect to unravel. But it wasn't a mystery why I was here. I'd escaped such events most of my life, but I hadn't escaped family obligations or sisterly affection. Along with two of her friends, my sister Beth had followed her bliss, turning her homemaking and entertaining organizational and creative skills into a package called As Needed: Event Planning and Coordination for Individuals and Corporations.

The business had been slowly building, but tonight's event was its biggest coup, not only because of the event itself, but, Beth had explained, because of the contacts it could provide.

None of that would have dragged me here. Nor would Beth's assumption that these events were part of "growing up" and facing my future as a serious—i.e., married—woman. That attitude would normally get her nowhere except in trouble with me, but this time, she'd followed that imperious declaration with one that did touch me.

She was nervous. A lot was at stake. I wasn't sure if my role was as her groupie, nursemaid, cheerleader, or witness, but here I was because Beth matters to me.

The cause was worthy. The funds raised tonight and at other events would build and maintain a battered-women's shelter and counseling for its inhabitants. I not-so-secretly believed everybody would be better off if we each wrote a check, stayed home, and read a good book, but for reasons I cannot fathom, I am not the boss of the world.

So here I was, feeling very much the peasant at the palace. Everyone else seemed hyper-happy—waving, greeting, kissing both cheeks, and chattering away in small groups. Most of the people I know don't travel in Beth's circles because the tab is too high for our paychecks. Beth likes to pretend that our differences boil down to her *Mrs.* versus my *Ms.*, but they go deeper than that, way down into our wallets. That wasn't going to change at whatever point Mackenzie and I set a date and were wed.

I hadn't a clue as to how I could mingle my way into the circles. I was regressing even more, back to about fourth grade now, watching the popular clique at recess. I couldn't stand this for too long.

I didn't have to. Within seconds, as if she'd been waiting for me—and, given her nervousness, maybe she had—Beth, the world's best hostess, was at my elbow, practically thrumming with tension as she steered me toward women dressed in chic ensembles and shoes that hadn't had to get them from dawn to this point. "So far, so good," she said, her eyes on the room, not on me. "Marilyn even got me—us, I mean, you and me—at the table I wanted."

"Of course she would. You guys arranged this shindig. Why wouldn't you sit wherever—"

"We don't do the seating chart. How could we? She used gentle suggestions after she tested the waters."

"What are you talking about?"

"The politics. Where you put people is all-important for their egos, their wallets, their friendships, their enmities—it would be like my arranging the seating for your wedding."

That wasn't anything I'd thought about till now, but considering how readily relatives who didn't speak to each other came to mind, quickly followed by friends who had once been coupled with other friends' current mates, I decided not to pursue this thought, which didn't even include the hordes otherwise known as the Mackenzie family. "Actually," I said, "it might be nice, if ever we need to do that, of course, to have you do it."

"Huh?"

"Never mind. I'm happy you're sitting where you want to be." Not that I understood why it mattered. She'd be next to me, and wasn't that the entire reason I was here?

I wondered if amphetamines could be made airborne and pumped through air-conditioning, because not only Beth, but everybody here seemed overly delighted with everything: ecstatic to see one another, enraptured to be in this room, all but twirling with anticipation of this lovely evening. Bottom line was: They were women who probably knew one another, saw one another elsewhere, and were gathered together tonight to eat and listen to a talk about the problem of spousal abuse. Was that really the stuff of the ear-piercing level of merriment—and that included Beth's controlled hysteria at being seated at a specific table. "Who is it you're near?" I asked. "The guest speaker?"

Beth's expression suggested that I ran my knuckles on the carpeting while I spoke. "Of course not!" she said. "She's at the head table."

"Then who—"

"This woman who consults to nonprofits. What is there to consult about with groups like that except how to get more money? She's very successful and the absolutely perfect contact. You're sitting next to her because it would be too obvious if I were."

Her transformation from carpool mom to business magnate was

nothing short of amazing, even though Business Beth's skills had been obvious during her stay-at-home phase.

"If you're obliquely warning me to behave, so that I don't mess up your prospect, I'll try my best," I said. "I remember about not making rude noises, not eating with my hands, not talking about politics or my sex life or yours—but I can't remember the rest. Tell me."

She made a big-sister fake pout and fake-elbowed me in the side. "It's good for you to meet these people," she said, switching out of her tycoon mode.

Luckily, I didn't have to endure the cocktail hour for long. I'd arrived late and had about ten minutes to meet a sprinkling of women and discuss how great the weather had been until today, how wretched it was today, how hard it must be to teach what with how bad kids were and how bad the world was.

All predictable, impersonal, and quickly finished, but even in that short period, my smile muscles were going for the burn.

"I'm so glad you came," Beth said as we went to our table.

I felt a pang. She'd implied that I'd had a choice.

"It's great having you as a sister," she went on. "Your life is so exciting. I feel as if I get vicarious points 'cause I'm related to you."

Since, as far as I knew, where Beth and my mother were concerned, the most exciting (and only significant) thing I'd done in the last thirty-two years was become engaged, I was astounded by her remark. Then I realized she meant my after-school job and that she, too, had been brainwashed by Hollywood. When we had more time, I had to find out what she envisioned me doing. It would probably be along the lines of what I'd imagined—back-alley crime and fast-talking men, not a wheezing old woman with a sobbing servant, or long lists of deceased Cades. And that was an exciting day, as compared with the ones where I simply organized papers and entered data on the computer.

We reached a table draped in celadon cloth sparked by cobalt blue napkins and white dishes. Each table had a bonsai tree as a centerpiece. "Is that symbolic?" I asked Beth. "You know, like how we stunt the growth of those we beat up?"

She laughed. "It's pretty, and short enough to see over."

"Well, whatever . . . those battered women sure know how to throw a party."

Beth closed her eyes in exaggerated disgust with me. But I continue to have my problems with these events, so that I considered the beautiful table furnishings and wondered how much Beth had paid to rent them, and how much furniture or counseling that might have bought a battered woman.

I wanted parties to be about having fun with people you already or might grow to enjoy, dinners to be about eating and socializing—and charity to be from the heart, and about the recipient, not the donor.

The table slowly filled, and my sister introduced herself, and me, to each newcomer. Two women walked over together and settled down. "She's Kay, I'm Fay. We rhyme," the one in violet silk announced, insisting on shaking hands clear across the table, which made for a long, painful experience and a new appreciation for the diminutive bonsai. Her friend Kay opted to nod and smile instead.

Millicent somebody joined us and said she worked for the sponsoring charity, and a Dorothy also sat down, barely got out her name, then folded her hands and looked away from us all, as if completely disinterested.

"I'm Vicky Baer," the well-tailored newest of the newcomers said as she sat down beside me.

I missed a beat before I managed what felt like a normal smile and nod, but inside, I was all gasps and exclamation points to the point where I was afraid to look at her directly.

I was as hyperastounded by being seated next to this woman as Beth had been at being placed at her table, and I couldn't believe that we'd both been intent on finding the same person. I tried to keep my jaw from dropping.

She was the woman in the photograph, the one in tailored slacks and shirt. The one who'd dressed like Beth. The one I'd planned to find via Beth's Main Line tendrils. And here she was among her peers, in her natural habitat. Not all that remarkable—and yet, completely astounding. It took my innards a while to stop turning cartwheels.

"Glad to meet you," I said, after identifying myself and hoping the time lag between Beth's introduction and my response hadn't actually been months, the way it felt.

"I think we've met before." Beth said to Victoria Baer across me. And she went on, charting where their paths had crossed, friends they had in common. In short, establishing her credentials as a part, however remote, of the same social circle. I barely heard the specifics because I was too busy concentrating on what I'd say and how I'd say it when I had the chance. I reviewed the great empty page I had on Emmie Cade and where her old pal could fill in the blanks. I debated how much I could ask, and considered the downside of asking too much.

I thought about what I already knew. They'd met at school, though at what stage in their schooling, at what school, I didn't know. I had to steer the conversation around to matters educational.

And at that point, I realized Vicky was saying that she was a consultant to nonprofits, and my sister, possibly afraid of showing her business hand and seating plan by responding with her own profession, chose that moment to include me in the conversation.

"I'm so sorry," she said to me with exaggerated party manners. "Didn't mean to talk right across you. Everybody—this is my sister, Amanda." Only Vicky Baer and the pale, smiling, silent creature on her other side could hear. The silent woman was also nameless. She'd whispered something inaudible as she'd seated herself, and since then, she'd nodded—silently—at anything anyone said. She nodded now, her smile implying that of all the names Beth's sister could have had, mine was the best, pure music to her ears.

Beth rolled on, possibly believing that her duties that evening included emceeing the event itself. I relaxed. This was going to work out amazingly well, and I was delighted that I'd come. "Amanda's keeping quiet like this because—" Beth said.

End of relaxing. I tensed up, hoping against hope that she wasn't headed where I feared.

She was. "—she's a *sleuth*. Be careful what you say or do!"

And like that, my sister had taken my amazing, serendipitous proximity to Victoria Baer—my incredible good fortune—and blown it to smithereens.

Did she think P.I. stood for Public Investigator? I kicked her under the table.

She looked at me in honest surprise, then moved her feet, as if that had been her fault. Then, her humor restored, she winked. "She's entirely too modest," she told the table in general.

"Excuse me?" Victoria Baer said. "It's so noisy in here. What was that? What did you say you did?"

"Fact is, I didn't say—"

"A private investigator. Isn't that a hoot?" Beth's voice had climbed to new eager-anxious hostess heights. "You know, like Miss Marple."

"She wasn't a—"

"Okay, like Columbo."

"He was a cop." Not that I cared about her imagery. I cared about how she'd wrecked my stroke of good fortune, and I wanted to throttle her.

Violence wasn't going to get me anywhere. Surely I could re-think the situation, turn this to my advantage or at least neutralize the damage. Sure, the bad news was that Vicky Baer would now be suspicious if I moved beyond table-talk pleasantries to anything specific. But given bad news, wasn't it a cosmic necessity, then, for balance's sake that there be good news, too? I was hard-pressed to think of what it could be, until I reminded myself that Beth hadn't told Victoria the precise facts I needed to know.

Of course, that was because Beth didn't know them, but all the same, I clung to that. Victoria Baer didn't know me, and the odds of bumping into her again were slim, so I could return to plan A and ask away.

Most of all, Vicky Baer didn't know that her friend was being investigated and would have no reason to imagine such a thing unless I stuck both my foot and leg into my mouth.

"She's modest about it," Beth said, still replying to Victoria Baer's question, which, I was sure, had been polite conversation that didn't warrant a dissertation. "I don't know why." She smiled, or at least bared her teeth, waiting for a response I truly couldn't muster. The things I could think of would have broken my promise to mind my manners.

"Truly," I finally said. "I help out in an office a few hours a week. I file papers, but Beth has me confused with Sam Spade." Ha-ha, laugh it off, forget about it, please, Ms. Baer.

"Or Emma Peel in *The Avengers*," Fay—or Kay—said from across the table. "I always loved the way she dressed."

"That's precisely how it is. And how I dress, too," I agreed.

"It sounds exciting and . . . dangerous," Victoria Baer said.

"Filing? The only dangers are paper cuts and being bored to death."

She smiled politely and, as two more women joined us, completing the table, the conversation turned to them, much to my relief. Except, of course, that at the next lull, Beth again felt the need to introduce me to them as her sister, the shamus. Time to either gag my sibling or take over the conversation myself for damage control. "Beth doesn't want you to know that my actual job is quite ordinary and seldom glamorized by Hollywood productions. I teach high school English. Now you know the dull truth, and please don't think less of Beth because of how boring I am."

"Teaching's probably more dangerous than we thought your other job was. Kids today." The speaker was one of the newcomers, an elderly woman with unnaturally black hair through which her scalp showed. I wonder when "kids today" became shorthand for how drastically the human race was in decline. I suspected that the phrase was one of the first the Neanderthals expressed.

"They're not that bad," I said.

"Everything I hear, I read . . . where do you teach, then?"

I told them.

"A private school," the black-haired woman said. "No wonder."

I took that as the perfect cue. I sat further back in my chair, withdrawing from the table-wide conversation, and turned my attention to my left. "To tell the truth, I sometimes dread saying where I work, because so many people are hostile to the very idea of private schools, and I understand their point of view. I do. Free education and public libraries—access to information and knowledge, how to use it—that's the basis of democracy, if you'll forgive my getting on the soapbox."

Ms. Baer raised her eyebrows and shrugged a "what can you do with people who don't like whatever—but don't take my sympathy to mean I'm wildly interested in this topic, either" sort of gesture.

"I gather you're not one of the people in the antiprivate schools camp," I said as a salad was placed in front of me. The greens gave me something to poke and cut so that I didn't look too eager for information.

"It would be hypocritical to attack private schools, because I attended them from kindergarten on," Vicky Baer said. "And I deal with them professionally now. I consult to nonprofits that need to find ways to raise funds."

"Really? That would certainly include the private schools I know," I said. "Your work sounds like fun. Or at least, if it's not, you're not stuck in that school forever."

She'd been toying with her fork, but I could almost see through her skull as she recategorized me from ignorable dinner partner to: Contact. She put the fork down and reached under the table. "Here," she said. "Let me give you my card. And I have a brochure that explains more of what I do. In case your school ever . . ."

I wonder what percentage of cards exchanged in this random, optimistic, and hopeful way ever result in a sale or a job, or even a phone call. I certainly had no clout with either Havermeyer or the trustees about how or through whom they should raise money. And yet turning down a card seems a deliberate insult, like blatantly saying, "I am not interested in you and I have no desire to know how to reach you."

She groped under the table and, at one point, grabbed my ankle. "Sorry," she said. "It's gotten wedged—" And then she pulled out a pocketbook that might have been a briefcase, or was both things. It had pockets and flaps and zipper compartments, but nonetheless, as she lifted it, the contents spilled onto the table, the floor, and me.

Vicky Baer looked crestfallen. Her façade of professionalism wasn't quite as smooth at the moment, and she seemed profoundly stunned. I, on the other hand, am so used to my mask of competency shattering that I can almost take it in my stride, apply emotional bandages, and put myself back together. Vicky, however, lowered her lids, shutting out the sight of her possessions, then she opened her eyes up again and, lips tight, carefully replaced a lipstick, a small bottle of aspirin, a telephone, electronic calendar, and compact, while I transferred a miniature staple gun, a roll of quarters, a vaporizer, a tin of breath mints, a small unopened packet of tissues, a black felt-tip pen, and an unused packet of plastic file tabs.

"There are times you're really relieved that no men are around, aren't there?" Beth asked from the other side of me.

"I didn't want to carry an actual briefcase tonight," Vicky Baer mumbled. "I thought this would hold it all, but I forgot to zip the top when I sat down."

I wanted to tell her that it was all right. That everybody on earth had upended a purse, and nobody cared.

"Oh, God, even this. How did this get in there?" She lifted a rawhide dog chew—used—off the floor and, frowning, dropped it back into her purse along with a white plastic square I recognized as containing floss. Then she smoothed her skirt and sat up straight. "My dog," she said, glancing at her watch. "That was a good reminder, I guess. I'll have to go see to him in a few minutes."

I looked around and she shook her head. "Poor Bruno's in the car," she said. "All safe, windows open, in case you're worrying. His joy in life is the car, and he's a well-behaved creature, so, since he needs regular medication, it's easiest to take him with me when possible."

Beth made sympathetic noises.

And then, Vicky Baer remembered her original mission and unsnapped a comparment of the bag and handed me one of her cards, satiny and impressively embossed V. S. BAER, INC., IDEAS UNLIMITED, and underneath, ECONOMIC CONSULTATION TO NONPROFIT INSTITUTIONS. The card was clipped to an equally lush, heavy-stock brochure.

"I'll pass this on," I said. "My school's fund-raising efforts are pretty lame."

"Could I see your brochure?" Beth asked, and Vicky Baer, recovered from her faux pas and, recognizing interest, perked up. "Here, have your own. You don't have to share."

Then I, too, remembered my original purpose. "That private school you attended—was it one of ours? I mean here, in the city?"

"Eventually. I lived in Ohio," she said. "Till eleventh grade, and then I was here, at Shipley."

A prestigious school on the Main Line, but Emmie Cade hadn't lived in these parts till now, as far as we knew. Cleveland, however, had been a stop along the corporate route. "Good school," I said. "A lucky move, although I suppose that's provincial of me. Your Ohio school might have been just as good."

She shrugged and nibbled a leaf of frisée.

"Did your family move around a lot? I've had students whose parents relocate almost every year, and sometimes it creates problems. Any advice?"

The salad was crisp and deliciously dressed, and after a moment, when Ms. Baer appeared to have decided against speaking again, I turned to Beth to congratulate her. "This is terrific," I said. "Pretty room and tables and great salad."

Beth beamed when Vicky came out of her silence to agree that this was indeed a fine event. She'd decided to speak, after all, but just as she began to talk about her schooling again, Beth decided it was appropriate to admit that she had organized tonight's fine event, and that yes, that was her business and she had a card, too, and would Vicky want one?

I started to kick her again under the table, but she wouldn't know why I was doing so, so I controlled myself while the two women smiled and nodded and calculated how much business the other might generate for her.

Finally, Vicky Baer remembered my question. "The thing is," she said, "I have no wisdom to impart because *we* never moved. I did. My family stayed in Ohio. I lived with a cousin here till I graduated, then went off to Cornell. It was all my decision." She returned to her salad, and I to mine.

I had what I'd needed. Emmie Cade had never lived in the area before. Cornell had not been mentioned, but Ohio had. I could find out what school Emmie had attended in Ohio through Vicky's transfer records and then, her parents' names, her address, and her former and possibly next address as well. I had a friend who taught at Shipley and I was betting she could help me out with the innocuous but meaningful information.

"Did you study fund-raising? Is there such a major?" I asked.

"Not that I know of. I majored in biology, believe it or not. I thought maybe I wanted to be a doctor, but . . ." She shook her head. "Other options seemed more appealing, at least at the time." She smiled at the memory of her young and presumably naïve self. "You know, the whole shebang—husband, white picket fence, and two kids." She flashed another, possibly insincere smile, then looked down at what was left of her salad. "Unfortunately, almost the same day as I was married, I realized that none of those things appealed to me. Now, I'm single and in love with my job and my dog, and that suits me fine, and I still don't want to be a doctor. How about you? Why did your sister say you were an investigator if you're an English teacher?"

"I am both, but truly, the so-called investigation work is part-time, and almost one hundred percent clerical work. I'm helping someone out, and it's nothing like in the movies. Beth likes to tease me about it, and she was including you in the joke this time." I busied myself spearing a reluctant piece of roasted red pepper. "Was it difficult, moving to Philadelphia?" I asked. "I met a woman who told me this is a tough place to be a newcomer."

"The City of Brotherly Love isn't?"

"Apparently, you have to be here a few generations before the love turns on. Or so I hear."

"It wasn't particularly hard on me," she said. "Probably because when you move into a school situation . . . And I was living at my cousin's, so I was a part of an established family. And my ex's family's been here for eons, so when I married and moved back here, there wasn't a problem."

"Guess that's it," I said. "That woman who said it was a tough city is grown and our age, and I don't think she has children—they sometimes make it easier. You can always join the PTA."

Vicky Baer wasn't interested, but until the speaker got up on the podium, her options were pathetically limited. She had the nodding silent woman on her left, and she had me and, sporadically, my sister, who was working hard to appear disinterested. So mostly, Vicky Baer had me, and she listened, and even if she didn't pretend interest, she didn't dump her salad remnants on my head and tell me to shut up.

"I always feel personally responsible," I said. "As if this is *my* city—in more than a symbolic way, and I'm in charge of making it nice for new and old-timers. I wonder if there are newcomer groups to help people like her along."

"Where does she live?" That was Beth, jumping in—meaning she was monitoring our every word no matter what else she seemed to be doing—and, as always, eager to be helpful. Or maybe this time, simply eager to be in further conversation with the consultant without seeming as if that was her intention. Every sentence she uttered, despite its actual vocabulary, could be translated as: "I'm not blatantly soliciting your business, though you could be of incredible help to me, and I hope you've noticed the exquisite discretion and tact that I bring to the jobs I am assigned."

"Not far from you," I told my sister. "In Villanova, I think."

Vicky shifted in her seat to allow the waiter to remove her salad plate. He was as good an excuse as any for letting me know how little she cared for my chatter.

But there was Beth, bless her. Beth, who could not seem to stop talking. "I know really nice people near her in St. David's—and a lovely book group in Radnor. Book clubs are a wonderful way to meet new, bright people. Give me her name and maybe I can help. I don't want to give her the wrong idea of this city."

"I think I wrote it down," I said. "My memory . . ." I began to reach under the table, then sat back up. "I remember—Emma Cade." I didn't want to say her silly-sounding nickname.

Beth had taken out a small notebook and now, she wrote the name down. "I hope she's in the book," she murmured.

I turned to include Vicky Baer in the conversation, or to look as if I were. I wanted to check her expression, and I was gratified. She looked like Macavity when he thinks he's heard something crawling in the walls. If her ears could have become erect or swiveled, they would have. "You look as if you were about to say something," I said.

"It's Emmie, not Emma. I know her. And she's not in Villanova. Not anymore. She's in Center City. Right off the Square."

"Really? I must have missed . . ."

"Good, then." Beth snapped shut her red-leather-covered-notebook. "You were worried about something that isn't a problem at all."

"You know her," I said. "Amazing. Cliché or not, it really is a small world."

"Six degrees of separation and all that," Vicky said. "The Main Line isn't that big, then you break it down into age groups, it approaches tiny. How'd you meet her?"

I decided it was okay to have met Claire Fairchild. "At her future mother-in-law's place," I said. "How about you?"

"I knew her back in high school."

"Shipley? I thought she said she was new to—"

"In Ohio. She arrived in tenth grade. She called herself Mary Elizabeth then. M. E. Her initials, not Emma."

I couldn't help but think of all the Emma-related names I'd scanned this afternoon, of all the time I'd wasted.

"I didn't see her again till college—"

"Two schools, then. Cornell, you said."

She nodded. "—she called herself Betsey in those days. Then she dropped out and we completely lost touch until a year ago, when I bumped into her in San Francisco. She was calling herself something else again. I don't know why. She somehow needs . . . disguises. Anyway, now she's here, so we see each other sometimes."

"You know, now I'm remembering more, and the fact is, she said she moved here because she knew someone—that must be you."

Vicky Baer frowned. "Me? Moved here because of me? Like I said, I knew her, but not like that. That'd be frightening, to be responsible for somebody's cross-country move. She must mean somebody else." She looked at me. "It's like with her names. She's got an imagination. Take everything she says with a grain—or a bushel—of salt."

Two things were apparent. First, Vicky Baer didn't sound like much of a friend to Emmie Cade. She seemed, in fact, barely interested in her. Second, I hadn't thought my pitch all the way through. I should have come up with a better hook than the lonely newcomer angle, because now we were out of material and prompts.

I ate chicken and tried to avoid its fanciful packaging. The chef, in a fit of insanity, or misogyny, had created a chicken something or other, dripping butter and cream and wrapped in puff pastry. It was a given that two out of three—if not three out of three— women in this room were on diets and every one of us picked at the concoction, protesting politely, pretending not to eat the forbidden parts and failing utterly because they tasted so good. This time, when I looked over at Beth, my expression was, at best, quizzical.

"I did not make up the specifics of the menu," she said. "The woman who did looks like she has a metabolic problem, and kept saying that everybody had paid so much for this dinner, she wanted it to be special. So live it up—tomorrow, we diet."

Given all the food that was going to be returned to the kitchen, I was relieved that we weren't raising funds for the homeless or the starving. I turned back toward Vicky. She was a disciplined woman, and her dinner was largely untouched, but she wasn't a subtle woman. She showed her displeasure and abstinence from fattening food and, possibly, from further conversation, by folding her hands in her lap.

I couldn't let my font of information dry up this way. I turned to Beth and whispered. "Ask me something—anything—about the newcomer I met. Or newcomers, or—"

"Why?" she whispered back.

I shook my head. "Just ask—I'll explain some other time."

"But I . . ." And then she got it—or thought she had, and unfortunately, it was the same thing in the end. "Ooooh," she said. "You're—" her eyes darted toward Vicky "—but you can't—*her?*—I can't believe she—"

"Not her. No. But—ask, okay?"

She nodded, and I turned back to Vicky Baer, who looked abstracted until she noticed I was angled toward her and became alert again. "Sorry—I was lost in thought," she said. "And it wasn't worth a penny, so don't try to bribe me."

"I never would."

"Amanda," my sister began.

"That woman, Emmie," Vicky said at the same time. "Why would she tell you she was—"

"—is there a Center City version of a Newcomers Club?" Beth continued. "Do you think—"

I put my hand on Beth's knee and squeezed.

"But you—"

I pressed her knee again. She winced. But she also stopped talking.

"—lonely, or having problems?" Vicky finished her question. "She's engaged. Leo knows lots of people."

"You know what," I said. "She hasn't been here long, and she's engaged, so she probably knew her fiancé before she moved here. I'll bet *he's* the one person she knew and that's what she meant."

Vicky shook her head. "She was married, you know. Widowed not that long ago, in California, right before she moved here." She laughed, though it wasn't a particularly happy sound. "Besides, I introduced her to Leo. At a party at my house, so I fear, by default, I must be the person she meant. And you're right. It's been a whirlwind affair, but you know, when a man's ready, he's ready. And it was certainly high time for Leo. It's nonetheless amazing that Emmie Cade so quickly got herself through the poisoned brambles."

"Meaning?"

She looked at me as if deciding what to say, how honest to be. "His mother," she said. "I hope I'm not out of line—you said you met Emmie at Mrs. Fairchild's, and I don't mean to say anything against the woman, but . . ." She shook her head and grew quiet, poking her fork into the puff-pastry crust around the chicken.

"I don't really know her," I said, stepping carefully, hoping an explanation for how I do and don't know Mrs. Fairchild would form as I spoke. "We . . . the school is having a 'good-neighbor' campaign. You know, heading off at the pass the kind of complaints you get from people who live nearby, so . . ." I let it go at that, and hoped Vicky Baer's need to express her opinion was stronger than my ability to come up with a reason I needed to hear it.

She raised an eyebrow, and put down her fork. "Claire Fairchild is nice enough—unless she thinks you want a piece of what is hers. That applies to her possessions, which includes her things, of course, her money, and most of all, her son. She's destroyed every relationship Leo ever had, and I know this from personal experience."

"You and Leo?"

She made a mock pout. "Let's just say she wasn't exactly a help. My point is, there's no reason to think the old lady won't destroy this one, too. Poor Emmie. You'd think it was time for her luck to change."

"She's had a bad mother-in-law before?"

"Just a virulent variety of bad luck. Her last husband drowned. That was horrible. And I understand that her first husband was a general rotter. Of course, Emmie was pretty wild herself. Ran off during her freshman year with a guy . . ." She seemed a little lost, remembering.

"Her first husband?"

She shook her head. "Just a passing fancy. Then I lost touch. The rest I only learned later on, when I bumped into her out west."

Two marriages behind her, then, not one. And a third waiting in the wings, and she was younger than I was. A prodigy.

Vicky gave in to hunger and pulled apart a dinner roll, slowly eating a segment of it.

"Bad luck indeed," I murmured, noticing that somehow, my chicken en croute was nearly gone. "She's awfully young to be marrying for the third time."

"There was a near fourth," Vicky said. "An engagement. But he died in a motorcycle accident two weeks before they were supposed to be married."

Two husbands, a third pending, two violent accidental deaths, one by motorcycle, one by drowning. I couldn't help but remember that red paper with AND THERE'S MORE DEAD!!! on it.

"The fates seem lined up against poor Emmie," she said. "She's a bad luck girl. I don't know how else to describe it."

We both sat in silence, Vicky chewing her single bite of dinner roll, when we heard a tinkly version of the opening of Beethoven's *Fifth*.

"My phone," she said. "Sorry. I forgot to shut it off. I'll take it outside." She checked her watch. "Be back in ten minutes," she said. "Might as well go water, walk, and medicate Bruno."

I sat there thinking about what she'd said. I agreed there was bad luck aplenty in the story I'd heard, but I wasn't sure whether it was aimed at Emmie Cade or whether she held the franchise for bad luck, and she was the one doling it out to the hapless men who crossed her path.

Eight

"**G**OOD work," Mackenzie said when I told him all I'd found out within a few hours of meeting Mrs. Fairchild. "Especially with next to nothing to go on. But don't count on coincidence striking twice. Or ever again in this lifetime."

I knew that, but I tried explaining why the evening's find had been lucky, but not exceptionally coincidental. It had been more like finding a bird in its expected roosting spot. "As soon as I saw her photograph, I was going to get Beth's Main Line tom-toms in action. The surprise was that it went from thought to actuality without any action in between. A miracle."

His nod of acknowledgment slid toward nodding off, his head lowering toward his open text for Quantitative Methods in Sociology, his hand still holding his pen, resting on his notebook. I had glanced at the book and found it largely unintelligible, and all through our mutual descriptions of our varied days—his classes and his work with Ozzie, my classes and ditto—he'd rubbed his eyes, stifled yawns, and insisted he wasn't tired. Now he snapped back up, cleared his throat, and said, "What's next?"

"Check with Shipley and find out Vicky's Ohio school, call there, see when Emmie—who I think was Betsey then, but I'll check—attended, her address, parents' names, if she transferred in or out, then from and to where—whatever else I can find out. Forwarding address, I suppose. Maybe something will lead to the first husband—the rotter. Or the fiancé who was killed. Can I say I'm considering hiring her and doing due diligence on her résumé?"

He shrugged. "Most people don't check back to high school."

"They might, since she didn't finish college. I don't want grades or anything personal, just her stats. Would Cornell have records of however long she was there?"

He nodded again, though he was so tired, that was a dangerous bit of body language, too tempting on the downward motion. "Don' forget the San Francisco stuff."

Embarrassing not to have already mentioned it. It was so obvious as, possibly, the real smear on what's-her-name's record. I appreciated the gentle, nonsuperior way he'd mentioned it, as if anybody would have needed prodding about it.

"—the marriage records," he was saying. "Maybe mention of how that first marriage ended. An' the transcripts of the inquest. I'll start that in the mornin', before class." He leaned back and stretched his arms. "I am beat," he said, standing up. "So—what's your take on Ms. Cade?"

"In person? Absolutely charming. It's only all this . . . confusion surrounding her."

"Con men—and women—have to be charmin'. It's part of their basic equipment kit."

I nodded acknowledgment. "Creepy, too. First of all, she said Victoria Baer was her great good friend, or that's the impression I got from Claire Fairchild. But that seems a gross exaggeration. Makes me wonder how stable Emmie Cade is, how tight her grip on reality is. She said she moved here because of Vicky, but Vicky acts appalled by the idea that she had anything to do with it. At best, she acts as if they are casual acquaintances from way back—a year of high school, a year of college, a surprise encounter in San Francisco, and no more than that."

He yawned and opened his eyes close to bug-eyed wide, trying to appear alert.

I pretended his ruse had fooled me, so I could justify continuing. "Mostly, I don't get it about the name changes, not to mention two dead guys. She's been awfully busy on the romantic and death front for one young woman."

"Or she's a total flake with amazingly bad luck," Mackenzie said.

"I don't much believe in luck. Except when it seats me next to the person I'm looking for."

THE NEXT MORNING, before I was fully dressed, let alone en route to school, the phone rang.

"Has to be your mother," Mackenzie said from across the room. He'd been up for at least an hour and was already studying. What a good student he was. Wish I had him in my class.

"That didn't take deductive powers," I answered.

"Maybe they're calling off school because of the rain," he said amiably. Above us, the skylight drummed with water and had been since a massive electrical storm around midnight.

"Maybe they've changed their minds and aren't coming," I said.

"Let us hope."

I took a deep breath and lifted the receiver. "You said you'd explain," the voice said by way of greeting.

"Beth?" She really was mutating into our mother at an ever-accelerating speed.

Mackenzie returned to his coffee and studies.

"Explain what? When did I say . . ." I could only find one of my favorite black shoes, and I looked at Macavity suspiciously, though he was far too indolent to drag a shoe under the bed. I held the phone between my shoulder and cheek and got onto the floor to search. The cat stood next to me, peering in the same direction. I wondered what he thought he was looking for. It's pathetic and loveable when cats pretend to know what's going on. Then he gave up, lay down on his back, figuring that since I was in the neighborhood, maybe it was for a belly rub.

"Don't act naïve," Beth said. "I'm your sister—not a spy—and you know what I'm talking about: Vicky Baer. You asked me to keep her talking last night about newcomers, or that newcomer. You said you'd explain. Were you or weren't you investigating her?"

"I told you I wasn't." I'd spotted the shoe in the absolute mid-point under the bed. The impossible-to-reach point. I stood up and went in search of a broom with which to snag it. "Am not."

"Then why did you ask me to ask about that newcomer when we'd finished talking about newcomers?"

I kept quiet because the only honest answer was that I'd asked because I was an inept idiot, who behaved as if Beth had no brain or sense of curiosity.

"You owe it to me." This wasn't a familiar Beth. Perhaps this hard-edged tone was part of Business Beth's new wardrobe. "I'm hoping to do business with her, so if there's some dark secret I should know about, then . . . then—I should know about it!"

Macavity saw the broom and took off for the other side of the loft. I got back down and poked at the shoe with the handle until it was out the other side, and said only, "There's no secret—network her like crazy. You're safe."

Beth was silent for a moment, digesting this and not giving up. "Then it has to be because she knew that newcomer you met," she said. "That Emmie Cade."

"Apparently." I'd forgotten that Beth had written down the

name. And then I heard what I'd dreaded—that nearly silent *oh!* where Beth figured something out, most likely that I hadn't met any newcomer who babbled about her life to me. I was about to say something to hold her off at the pass—as soon as I thought of what it was, when she dropped the entire matter. Maybe I'd been wrong about her powers of intuition.

"You don't have to tell me a single thing more—I understand. But don't act like your job's so unglamorous, like you're a clerk and nothing more," she said, making me wonder what she thought she understood. "And, since I have you on the phone, what do you think of the Emory mansion?"

"Excuse me? I've never heard of them, let alone visited their home."

"The family died out years ago, and their house is used for events. It's beyond gorgeous, and it'd be perfect. I'm going out there this morning, to check it out for a corporate party. Anyway, it's about thirty minutes outside—"

"Nice, Beth, but I have to get to work. Good luck with the Averys."

"Emorys! Aren't you even interested?"

"Of course I am. I love hearing how you put things together, but right now, I haven't even had coffee and—"

"I mean for you! For your wedding."

"What wedding?"

"Aren't you ever going to set a date? What's wrong with you? And then you're going to let me help you with it, aren't you? It's what I do, and you have to think ahead, way ahead. This place gets booked—"

This was way too weird for a dark, rainy morning, but since she was already scratchy about Victoria Baer, I had to tiptoe around this. It took another solid five minutes to extricate myself from the conversation and to extract a promise that she'd say nothing further about this mansion or my wedding date until so requested. But for fear of making something more important to her than it already was, I didn't extract a similar promise about last night's dinner conversation. The less said, the better, I felt. I wanted her to forget about it, and mentioning it would only make it seem still more important. I could only hope for the best. After all, she didn't know Emmie Cade, so I couldn't envision any problems ahead.

A learning experience, I told myself. That's all it was. A lesson in the perils of speaking before I thought through all the possible consequences.

WE WERE INTO THE SECOND-DAY SLUMP, or they were.

American ingenuity and business sense has made sure there are numerous perks about back-to-school. Kids get new clothing, new supplies with delicious designs and covers. Even assignment books, designed to list the hated work they'll have to do—even those are cleverly packaged. First day back, everything from head to foot is new or newly washed. Back to school is filled as well with nonconsumer benefits, like seeing people after a long summer's absence.

Twenty-four hours later, the student body's collective expressions reflect a sense of having been duped, as in some primitive cartoon series. Fooled again, though they aren't sure how it happened this time. They can't blame this one on the teacher. They were party to it, but now, it's the second day of forever, and their shoes have scuffs and no matter what teen idol is on the cover of the assignment book, its blank pages are all waiting to be filled with things they don't want to, but have to do.

A lot of heavy lifting ahead.

Perhaps they even remember that they didn't see those other kids all summer because they didn't particularly want to.

They looked at me with inarticulate desperation, as if I could help them, or at least explain what had happened, but of course, I was a part of the problem and not its solution. Anyway, I knew it would get better, and I also knew that they'd probably felt just as robbed and cheated by summer, which was never the two-month dream of bliss they'd envisioned.

To balance things out, my back-to-school malaise was gone, and I felt glad to have shifted gears and to be in my element again. We all have our own ways to delude ourselves, and mine was to believe—again—like my own variation on that hapless cartoon character: this year would be different. I had three preparations for my five classes, had planned out the year, and was positive, despite all past evidence, that not only would the students enjoy the challenges ahead, but so would I. And of course I'd work efficiently, gladly, and promptly, papers returned almost before the students handed them to me. And when they looked at their compositions and my comments—they'd get it. They'd change. They'd think coherently, make clear points, learn new words, and thank me for my incisive advice. And while we were at it, they'd fall in love with books and reading and ideas and self-expression.

I was basking so comfortably in this pedagogical hallucination that I smiled back first thing in the morning when I arrived, dripping wet despite my umbrella, which had turned inside out, and Sunshine said, "And aren't we glad that heat wave's over!" It wasn't a question—it was a command to be joyous. "And isn't this just the most perfect day for studying?" she continued. "Mother Nature herself is saying, now kiddies, forget about that lazy summertime you had—it's back-to-work time!"

It was still pouring, the skies so low and menacing, I anticipated forty days and forty nights. My umbrella was ruined, and I was drenched, but so what? I borrowed a smidge of Sunshine's attitude and added it to my dizzy belief in the new school year. I'd dry out. Life would go on.

And I didn't particularly mind, though I wasn't overly amused, either, when Bo Michaels avoided committing to any book at all for his report by falling off his chair and pretending to have a heart attack. I had tagged him as class clown the day before, but today, drenched in the milk of human kindness and teacher-blindness, I tried to avoid classifying him, labeling him in any negative way. Instead, I determined to focus on why he needed to make a fool of himself.

And third period, I was able to ignore the still-subtle shenanigans of Butch and Sundance. I knew, even in this strangely manic mood of mine, that they'd soon be problems needing attention, but for right now, they were simply vaguely amusing, testosterone-poisoned adolescents.

Gilding my benign-teacher float was the afterglow of having done well with my first assignment for C. K. I loved the day. I loved my capabilities. I loved my students. I loved Mr. Mackenzie.

I should have known that every calm precedes a storm, and giddiness during a storm precedes God only knows what. At noon, while I was checking that all the seniors, including Bo the Clown, had indeed chosen books, a messenger arrived. That did not, however, seem bad news. In fact, it was good news, proving that Sunshine was educable. She now understood the relationship between messengers and messages.

Apparently, her deciphered message meant that one of my ninth-grade parents was downstairs, wanting to meet her daughter's English teacher. *1ts 2CU* Sunshine wrote. I struggled with the *1ts* until *wants* became clear. Little Office Sunshine had signed her note with an oversized smiley-face with an exclamation point for a nose. A *really* smiley-face. I had my first tremor of less-than-joy, but it had nothing to do with the message, only the person who'd written it out. Ten months of unsolicited, inept rebus puzzles and jolliness lay ahead. I had to find a way to depress her.

But aside from that, I took the note and the visiting parent as a sign that things were indeed improving. Perhaps our standards were rising, as Havermeyer claimed. This woman could have waited until parents' night and I could have gotten more work done, but I wasn't ready to object to an overinterested parent after years of complaining about the other sort, the ones who dumped their screwed-up children on us as if we were an all-purpose repair service. While we patched in literature and history, we were expected to also toss in ethics, etiquette, and psychological soundness.

So I walked downstairs to meet Mrs. Lawrence, expecting a pleasantly nervous mother who wanted to tell me something special about her child. A talent with words, a shyness she'd like me to notice. Problems at home.

And I tried to remember her daughter, one of the new students in ninth grade. I thought she was the pretty girl with streaked blonde hair and an aura of confidence, and wondered what her mother's special worry would be.

Sonia Lawrence was a striking woman, dressed in a navy silk blouse and a fawn-colored suit with shoes to die for. She carried her raincoat on one arm, and held a folded umbrella, and neither the sky nor either of those items had allowed one drip on her. Her hair was the same sun-streaked blonde as the student I'd picked, so I thought I'd been right.

"I hope you don't mind this unannounced intrusion," she said, "but my office is nearby, and I had an unexpected break. The school told me you had a prep period now, so I hoped I could have five minutes of your time."

Nobody on earth has ever braved a storm to make a five-minute optional personal trip. I should have gone on alert, but why? It was the second day of school. I hadn't had time to commit grave offenses. "Why don't we sit on the benches in the entry," I suggested.

"But I'll only take—"

"It's more comfortable," I said, and she followed me to the carved wooden bench near the front entry.

"My daughter Melanie is in your last-period class," she said once she'd settled herself.

I nodded and smiled, waiting for her to define what was special about Melanie, aside from her striking good looks and what seemed inherited self-confidence.

"She brought home *Lord of the Flies* last evening."

I nodded again.

"I realize that it's something of a classic."

I was getting tired of nodding.

"The author's famous."

"He won the Nobel Prize." I had to hope that if it was good enough for the Swedish Academy, it was good enough for Mrs. Lawrence.

"In these times," she said, "do you think you're being sensitive to the traumas the children have been through—the entire nation has been through?"

I waited for her to continue, to make sense, and when she didn't, I sighed, then spoke. "Mrs. Lawrence, I honestly don't know where you're headed. It's a rich, complex book that's also approachable, a wonderful study of many things the students come to understand—mass hysteria, mob psychology, various approaches to life, civilization and what it might mean, the potential for evil in—"

"That's precisely what I mean. Why present our children with more evidence of human evil? Do you think that's sensitive in these times?"

The second *sensitive* in one minute.

"I understand that the term *lord of the flies* is a translation of the word *Beelzebub*—the devil himself." She looked triumphant, convinced she'd scored a point.

I still wasn't sure of the game.

"Don't be mistaken—I'm not a religious fanatic. I'm not a book burner. I am nonetheless quite upset at the idea of my daughter being forced to read about young boys who wind up committing murder. Perhaps in years gone by, Miss Pepper, but in these times, I find this book to be in poor taste."

"I appreciate your input, but I think it's more important than ever to encourage thought about how we behave, and why. And about violence and hatred—"

She put one well-manicured hand on mine. "They've had enough.

Haven't you read about the traumatized children? You're standing by with a whip, to inflict further pain."

"Don't you want Melanie to learn to think? Isn't that what keeps democracy alive—citizens who think? It isn't so much the specific content of any given book as it is what she's going to take from it, and the unit plan has them learning—"

"I don't like what they're learning. They're learning that people can revert to savagery in the blink of an eye. To murder. That they can choose a scapegoat and destroy him. Is that who you're saying we are?"

"Excuse me—I didn't write the novel. And the author isn't saying anybody in particular is any particular—"

"I know how that novel ends. The rescuers are at war, too. The adults are just as cruel, aren't they? That's his point, isn't it?"

"Perhaps one of many points."

"The adults are just as capable of moral relativism and violence, aren't they. He's saying—and you're saying by teaching that book—that everyone is basically rotten. We're animals under a thin veneer of civilization."

"No. Not so. Not everybody in the book—"

"Thank you for hearing me out. I don't want my daughter reading this, so perhaps you'd better think about this some more. In these times—we're at war, Miss Pepper. You have heard the president, haven't you? We're at war against evil—and you're teaching your students that everyone is evil."

"No. If we don't think things through—"

"Even children."

"—people are *capable* of evil, out of fear, out of mass hysteria, and—"

"It's not only insensitive and an incorrect view of mankind, it's unpatriotic at a time like this. I'll get back to you on this."

She stood up, smiled, took my hand to shake, and said, "Thank you for taking time with me."

And that was it. She was out the door. This was an entirely new line of attack and criticism, and she wasn't finished with me. But what frightened me most about Sonia Lawrence was her efficiency. She'd delivered her message, her warning—or threat—her reasons for her feelings. The frightening part was that she'd done it in precisely five minutes.

This was a woman who meant every word she said.

Now I, too, was into the second-day slump.

Nine

"INSENSITIVE! She said it more than once! Someday, every single book ever written will be on a forbidden list," I fumed. "It's either sex, or historically accurate but nowadays-offensive racial words, or the hint of subversive political leanings—or—or—well, now, *insensitivity!* She all but accused me of being a traitor to my country!"

Mackenzie looked mildly sympathetic. Ozzie, over in his corner cubicle, didn't even look up. I wasn't sure that Ozzie had ever heard the word *book*, let alone read one. He was the man for whom TV and beer were invented.

Not that I'm insensitive to TV-watching beer drinkers. Some of my best fiancés are to be found in that group now and then.

And in truth, even Ozzie has another great passion, and that's for speed. In others. He himself is slow-moving, except, I gather, when he's on his motorcycle. He loves it, and anyone or anything that physically taxes itself to the limit. "I like fast," he's said repeatedly, explaining himself in typically terse fashion. And the office illustrates that in a style that would confuse most viewers who didn't understand the theme and mistook his lair for old-fashioned sloppy.

The portion of wall I'm near at my desk is layered with pictures of champion racehorses, the Concorde, an ad for a Jet Ski, photos of Lance Armstrong, drawings of greyhounds, and motorcycle-related icons. Ozzie does not discriminate—if it's fast, he likes it, pinning up posters and magazine pages as they appear and appeal to him.

To the best of my knowledge, this is the one place on earth that defies the laws of gravity and here, what goes up never comes down. I suspect that small, blind life-forms breed between the images, but I'm not going to check it out.

"You ask me," Ozzie suddenly said, though nobody had, "you have two choices. Either tell her to go to hell—"

"An appealing idea," I said, "but it then involves my finding another job."

"—or change the book. It's school, it's work, and does any kid care what the book's called they have to read? In fact, does anybody care?"

"I care. I know it's not the best school in town, but I care. These kids aren't stupid. They—including her daughter—are capable of thinking about the potential for evil, about choices, about mob violence—about the book I've assigned. How can they vote and be part of this country—she pretty much called me *unpatriotic!*—if they don't learn how to reason things through?"

"Jeez," Ozzie said. "It was only a suggestion." He turned back to his computer, more convinced than ever, I feared, that talking to women wasn't worth the breath it took.

"I should have taught math," I said. "Math teachers don't get harassed. Nobody tells them that algebra is insensitive, or calculus unpatriotic."

"There's the small issue that you aren't fond of mathematics," Mackenzie said softly. "In that case, you'd be miserable because nobody was tryin' to stop you."

"Then history," I muttered.

"Subject to interpretation and reinterpretation," he reminded me. "But speakin' of history, both political and personal, reminds me. You sufficiently decompressed now to consider Emmie Cade?"

"I've been working on it." Mackenzie had been out checking real estate records—another thing I'd have to learn about. And while he was gone, I'd been finding out what I could about Jake King and his widow, holding on to my anger about Sonia Lawrence and all the well-dressed ignoramuses with whom I had to deal. Then Mackenzie appeared, and I exploded. Because I could. If for no other reason—though there are many other reasons—I'd marry the man because he knows when it's time to stand back and let me release my steam valves.

I was calm again now, and grateful. "I've called my friend at Shipley, and she's going to check out Vicky Baer's school records, find out the name of the Ohio school. The records are archived somewhere, and she needs to contact the person in charge. Plus, I've been reading through the *San Francisco Chronicle*'s archives for last year. I typed in *Jake King* and last year's January through December dates and came up with seven hundred and forty-two mentions. Much of it concerning royalty and sports teams. I never realized what a popular surname it was."

Mackenzie nodded. I felt let down. I'd expected more recognition of my labors, although I couldn't have said what: a gold star? Roses flung at my feet?

"Forget to put a plus between the words?" he asked softly.

That didn't deserve an answer. Of course I'd forgotten. Of course the slogging labors were due to my forgetting. But I had gotten information about Jake King, ace sailor who "could read water," according to friends who'd sailed with him.

He had been a champion racer in half a dozen Pacific contests, and from what I read, everybody loved him except his ex-wife, who didn't consider Jake's death any reason to lessen her fury toward him.

And reading between the lines, noting what wasn't on the page, nobody was overly fond of Jake's actual widow. People were quoted—without attribution—as having been at the funeral and memorial service "for Jake" or because they "loved Jake." Some expected quotes were notable for their omission. Nobody remembered to express sorrow for the bride-widow.

The article said that the widow King was the former Stacy Collins, and that as Stacy Williams, she'd been an actor. I wondered, then, whether there was a Mr. Collins, or a Mr. Williams? Mary Elizabeth. Betsey in college. M. E. or Emmie now. Stacy. Cade Collins Williams King. Who else? It felt more like games with lights and shadows than actual name changes.

"I did some stuff today, too." He didn't have class on Tuesdays, but had been home studying most of the day, I'd thought. "Got you a stack of faxes from the *Chron*."

"You know somebody in San Francisco?"

"More a six degrees of separation thing, like your sister and the Main Line matrons would have been. Guy I know left the force, went out to do security work, mostly with Silicon Valley people. But he knew somebody in the city, who knew somebody at the *Chron* an'—lots about your lady. And the guy's ready to put together all the legal records if you want them."

"Like that?" I couldn't believe it. Yesterday, finding anything out about the woman calling herself Emmie Cade seemed daunting. Today, even if I'd spent all the intervening time polishing my nails, we'd have her background, thanks to Mackenzie's contacts.

"Bottom line is, the lady never has been arrested, let alone gone to prison. A lot of smoke, but no fire."

"Meaning?"

"After—what shall I call her? She's got half a dozen names."

"Emmie. Live in the moment. That's who she currently is."

"Okay. After Emmie moved here and was gone from Marin, the *IJ*—that paper that had the big article about Jake King's death—ran a feature on her. A reporter there—spoke to him today—spent a few months gathering background. Apparently, maybe because of rumors started by Jake's ex-wife, who didn't get any money when he died, people were convinced Emmie killed him and got off scot-free, and then somebody knew somebody else in Austin, where she was engaged to the motorcycle man and knew that there was talk about her in Texas, too. It prompted this guy to dig into her past."

He passed me five pages of faxed news story. The photo at the top of the page showed the same sweet face and smile I'd met yesterday. This time, future-Emmie wore an abbreviated wedding veil that poufed around her head but didn't cover her face.

The headline said, "Out of a murky past—and gone again?"

"She disappeared from there?" I asked.

"No forwarding address, apparently." Mackenzie leaned back, satisfied with himself. "That motorcycle accident bothered folks. It was somewhat weird and thought to be a suicide, which nobody could prove, but that didn't stop them from blamin' it on her. This fellow, Collins—"

"One of her names. But they weren't married, right?"

"Right. But he bought a house with her, jointly, with survivor's rights, and he'd rewritten his will so that Emmie—who was Stacy Williams then—got his estate. Not vast, mind you, nothin' like Jake King's, but vast enough to use as a jumping-off place for the next husband-hunt."

"I am so confused. When was Collins? Before or after her other marriage?"

"After it. Husband number one was—is—he survived her—William Stacey. Most people take their husband's name when they marry. His last name. She did that, but changed her first name to Maribeth."

"Which is really only a variation on her given names."

He shrugged. "Still, who takes her husband's name after a divorce? She was Betsey before she married him, Maribeth Stacey durin' the marriage, and Stacy Williams—his name backward—afterward."

"And Stacy Collins by the time she met up with Jake. I wonder how she ever remembered who she was."

He grinned. "An', may I say, according to the gossips who consulted with that writer, she walked away from William Stacey with a handsome bundle as well, and that despite rumors that she was having entirely too much fun on the side durin' the marriage with another rich guy who loved giving expensive gifts. A married rich guy. The woman has a talent for other people's money. Then she comes here and snares another one."

"It could all be gossip," I said, glancing through the long article.

"Far as I know, nobody sued about that article," Mackenzie murmured. "I asked."

"She might not have ever known about it." I skimmed over comments about Betsey's—or Stacy's—or Maribeth's flirtatiousness, and what you'd call the step beyond flirtatiousness. Open approaches to "men of substance," as the writer put it. Between marriages she'd made requests for loans while she was getting started with acting, for start-up money for a business that never materialized, for short-term help while she had a cash-flow problem with vague "trusts." I looked up at Mackenzie. "Nobody I'd want my son to marry."

"Well, as I hope to co-create any son of yours, let me go on record sayin' me, neither. But—here's the point: When you strip away the innuendos and the theories of, and the suspicions, what do you have? A woman with a bad rep, whose morals are less rigid than we like. A woman whose love of money might be greater than her love of men, but that's not for sure. Remember—our question was only: Who is she?"

I took a few minutes to go through the articles, making notes to which I added what now felt like the pathetic crumbs I'd gotten from the computer today and dinner the night before, and then I was ready to read off the list to Mackenzie.

"According to this article, and to Vicky Baer, she was born Mary Elizabeth Cade, daughter of Michael and Patricia. Born in Chicago, moved all over the place. Attended a series of schools. I know that one of them was in Ohio, where she met Vicky Smith, now Baer."

"Do you think Mrs. Fairchild needs quite all that?"

I had no idea what or how much a client wanted. If I'd hired me, I'd want every single thing I could dig up. "She was still Mary Elizabeth then, and their paths crossed again at Cornell, where she called herself Betsey and stayed only a short while. In Mrs. Fairchild's version, she got mono and didn't come back. In Vicky Baer's version, she ran off with a guy. Might be that both are true. Anyway, she never graduated from any college. She married William—Billy—Stacey when she was twenty-one, moved to Atlanta, where she called herself Maribeth Stacey. They had an ugly divorce, many rumors of an extramarital affair or two—on her part—and she walked away with money."

"And unpaid loans."

"Then she moved to Austin and Geoffrey Collins, motorcycle man." I considered his name. "I don't think of Geoffreys with a G as Harley types."

At that, Ozzie turned his head, and I nodded. "He died in an accident, Ozzie," I said.

"That proves she's no good, then," he said. I wasn't sure if he meant Emmie of the many names or Geoffrey's motorcycle, but I plugged on.

"Geoffrey had a car dealership."

"He should have driven what he was sellin' other people to drive," Mackenzie said.

"Are you saying nobody has accidents in cars?" Ozzie snorted his derision of slow-moving four-wheeled vehicles before he returned to his work. A chemical corporation paid him a small annual stipend to do background checks as needed, mostly for job applicants, who apparently lied alarmingly about their academic and work backgrounds. Emmie might be vague about her past, but as far as I could tell, she hadn't lied. Except, perhaps, about killing a person or two along the way.

"You were sayin'," Mackenzie prompted.

"The car dealership. Right. Guess who inherited it, then sold it? And guess when that legal document had been worked out?"

"Ten minutes before his accident?" Mackenzie suggested.

"Close. Two weeks. Guess she didn't want it to look suspicious. By now, she was trying to act, and called herself Stacy Williams— her ex-husband's name in reverse. You wonder how she managed her I.D. cards and drivers' licenses. Acting didn't work out, and I guess she figured new name, new chance, so she took Geoffrey's last name, even though they'd never married. Now she was Stacy Collins, and she moved to the Bay Area, met and married Jake King. They were married as soon as he could divorce his wife. He apparently got sole custody of his ketch—a seventy-five-foot ocean-going aluminum yacht."

Ozzie turned at the words and nodded his approval. "You have any idea how much a thing like that would cost?" he said softly. "This is a well-off widow indeed."

They were married aboard the boat and then sailed off to Tahiti. Six months after their return, during an anniversary celebration aboard the boat, the man who could sail the Pacific, continent to continent, drowned on a sunny, calm spring day. Despite a boatful of people, no one had seen the accident, nor could anyone explain it. Repeatedly, mention was made of his expertise. "He could have been in the Olympics if he'd wanted to," one person had said. And there endeth the western newspapers' report because their trail got cold. She was gone."

The article said she'd told people she was going away for a short while to "heal" after Jake's death, and it wasn't until the Kings' home was put on the market, six months later, that people realized she was gone for good. No forwarding address, no further contact with former neighbors and acquaintances.

No close friends, apparently. A few who said they'd felt close to her—until she came on to their husbands.

"At which time she drops Jake's name and appears here as M. E.—or Emmie—Cade, with, once again, the cash to rent or buy the right place in the right neighborhood, meet the right people at the right clubs and charities, and catch her a new one. Did she ever hold an actual job, or try running the businesses she borrowed money for?"

"The article didn't mention any occupation except home-wrecker and fortune-seeker. She said she'd been an actress for a while."

"Great. One of the untraceable jobs, unless she's listed with Equity. And she won't be."

"Odds are against it," I agreed.

"She'd have a story for it. Never made it that far, didn't get the parts that would qualify. Waited tables, waited for a break. Moved on."

"Which could be exactly what happened. It certainly wouldn't be unique—and might further the desire to find money instead." I looked at my notes from the day before. "She did interior design in Austin, too."

"Again, nearly impossible to prove or disprove. Given that we have no evidence of her being trained for that, you have to hope she paid her dues to a professional organization. A lady has a sense of style, good taste, a retail sales number, and affluent friends she'll shop for, and sometimes, like that, she's got a new title. How do you trace her through that? Besides, once she had her first nest egg, she probably didn't need an actual job."

"It looks good to seem to be living off a trust fund," I said. "It's attractive—literally. Money goes to money. If it's obvious you don't need it—you're given full access to it." I took a breath and considered the woman's sketchy past and the reason Mrs. Fairchild had hired us. "I wonder why the person who sent those warnings about the praying mantis didn't send this story instead. This is so much more damning."

C. K. pulled at his right earlobe. That unconscious gesture seems to pull a switch in his brain. Someday, when we're both in rocking chairs, and he's had so many good ideas, one of his earlobes will rest on his shoulder blade. "Maybe that person didn't know about this article," he finally said. "Somebody who doesn't live in Marin County, who never knew the paper wrote about Ms. Cade."

"Somebody with a never-ending hate for her? Like the person who told the reporter the rumors in the first place?"

He nodded. "A Texan, wasn't it? Remember, that story came out six months after Jake King died, when the house was sold and Emmie Cade—or Stacy King, as she'd been—was long gone to places unknown."

"And we'll never find out who that person was, right?"

"Doubt it. Newspaper confidentiality about sources."

"But none of the postmarks were from Texas."

"A mystery," C. K. murmured. He didn't seem that concerned, though it remained significant to me.

"So what next?" I asked.

He looked at me without saying anything, as if he was waiting for me to say something more. It's always a pleasure to contemplate his fine features and shocking blue eyes. They are such an acute blue, you want to search for bluer words—azure, cerulean, cobalt—except they aren't cobalt, they're lighter and brighter. They're so blue, you'd notice them from around the corner.

But at the moment, I wanted him to teach me this business, and he wasn't, so his eyes were simply blue, and annoyingly amused, and I wasn't into gazing upon them much longer. "Manda," he said softly after too long a pause, "it's okay."

"Meaning what?"

"C'mon. You don't have to play the ingénue, the apt pupil, the disciple. My ego can handle your charging forward on your own. I'm countin' on it and proud of you for it."

"I don't understand a thing you're saying. In plain English, what would an experienced investigator do next?"

"No need to ask me that. Suppose you gave an assignment to research a question about *Lord of the Flies*, and your smartest student finds the stuff she needs and writes it up. What should she do next?"

Oh. That.

No. "I can't call her up and tell her this," I said. "Not now!"

"Why not? It says who Emmie Cade is and was. That was the assignment. If she wants more, she tells us so, and we continue."

"She hired me twenty-four hours ago, and I barely did a thing—you did it."

"The newspaper in California did it, and that's called research. How different is it from the databases online? You thought it would all be nosing around with a magnifying glass?"

"I thought it would be—different."

"Sometimes it is, but the thing is, this is now. What else does Claire Fairchild need to know before she decides to tell her son about his intended? Do you think she needs more?"

"What about the identity of the letter-sender?"

"That wasn't what the client requested. Ms. Cade has no arrests, no records. I checked. A speeding ticket outside Austin, but that's about it. What's left to find out?"

It seemed hasty, unprofessional, slipshod. Too easy.

Mackenzie laughed out loud, a sound I usually relish and savor, but not when I'm the butt of the joke, and I knew I was this time. "Had a mechanic like you once. Every job, no matter how small, took a couple of days. Finally, I said, 'If I pay you the same exorbitant rate you charge for three days, could you have my car back in an hour?' He could and did, and said he didn't want me to think what he did so well and quickly was easy, was all, so he kept the car in his garage those needless extra days. That's what you think we should do. Hold back on the information so she thinks it was harder to get."

It sounded shabby when he said it that way, but indeed, that was not far from the feeling I had.

"Instead, dazzle her with our incredible professionalism."

"Your professionalism."

"We're a team," he said softly, the blue eyes back to their indescribable color. "A little dumb to be competitive on this, isn't it?"

"I'll write the report," I said. "Leo Fairchild is going to be furious. Vicky Baer said his mother had ruined all his previous romances. And now this one, most likely, as well."

Mackenzie shrugged. "I don't know that this will ruin anything. This is all—"

"I know. Rumor, speculation, and ever-increasing assets." I turned to face my computer, but Mackenzie put a hand on my arm.

"Claire Fairchild's worried. Her son set a wedding date. She's playin' sick to stop his plans until she hears from you. Talk with her. Today. Now. Phone her, tell her the facts, and that you'll send a written version and copies of the news stories, and so forth, later—if she wants anything around where Leo might find it."

"She wanted—wants—him to be happy," I whispered. "I think this information is going to make her very sad."

"Gonna make a lot of people sad," he said.

For reasons I couldn't have fully explained, except for the nonstop barrage of bad-mouthing Mary Elizabeth Betsey Maribeth Stacy Emmie Williams Stacy Collins King Cade had received, I thought about sixth grade, when for a few months, I was labeled a slut. It was a laughable, pitiable choice of insults, because puberty was taking its good old time with me, and while I can't say I'd never noticed boys, or suspected that someday they'd interest me, they didn't yet matter much, and I am not sure I even knew what the word *slut* meant—except that it was a bad thing to be. But somebody, for some reason, decided I was too something that annoyed them, and stories circulated, took hold, and grew. A time of torment, of prepubescent hell.

Luckily, the next year we moved into a neighboring district and, like that, my bad reputation evaporated to the point where I sometimes missed it.

But since then, I try to question labels. C. K. was right. Everything we'd read could be angry, hurt, or jealous rumors that had calcified over time, taking on weight and solidity and mistaken for historical truth. Of course, the woman had fed the negative fires with her inappropriate flirting and unpaid loans. Maybe she lacked character and was in fact a bad bet for Leo Fairchild. Or maybe she was too pretty, too delicate, too attractive to too many men, and she was the designated *slut* the way I had been in sixth grade, with as little basis.

"Look at you," Mackenzie said. "Frozen to the spot."

"No, I'm going to—"

"Tell you what. I'm starving and I have a lot of reading tonight. Why don't we both call it quits here for today and head home?"

I was all for delaying contact with the Fairchilds. "Great. I'll tell her tomorrow, I promise."

He shook his head. "We can stop off and tell her in person on the way. She's a worried woman. Deserves to know. And the rain's stopped. It'll be nice—we'll take a walk."

"Both of us?"

"Like I said, *we.*"

"That'll make her happy, even if the report doesn't. She was disappointed when I showed up, because she'd talked to you—to a man. She'll feel she's getting her money's worth."

"Even though we did it in twenty-four hours," he said.

Our office is on Market Street, close to where the cityscape begins to slide off whatever downtown pretenses rule elsewhere. Almost nobody comes to us. We deliver, instead, and often, it's completely a matter of phone calls and e-mails without any face-to-face. But if anyone did visit the office, they'd feel right at home in the old detective movie of their choice as they'd climb to the second-floor space Ozzie rented. The glass-paned office door felt like a window into the past. We were next to a dance studio—social dancing, not ballet. When business was good, the walls reverberated with Latin and swing rhythms. The proprietors, an angry couple in their fifties, often chose to bicker at the top of the stairs. They wore formal wear day in and day out, she in ridiculously high strappy shoes, and he in a tuxedo bought when he was at least two sizes smaller. The shoulder seams tended to split, and facing material popped out until his wife noticed, glared, and used one dagger-nailed finger to push the stuffing back inside. This evening, we had to circle around them. His stuffing was showing again.

The rain, finally over, had cleansed the air, and we had a pleasant, relaxed walk to Claire Fairchild's solid fortress of a home.

Batya opened the cream-colored front door to the condo, her eyes once again, or still, swollen and red. She held her hands under her gigantic belly, as if to keep it from falling onto the floor.

"Do you remember me?" I asked. She didn't react quickly, but she finally nodded.

"This is Mr. Mackenzie, who spoke with Mrs. Fairchild on the phone. We'd like to talk with her now."

"No, no." And in case we didn't understand those words, Batya shook her head.

"I know she's under the weather, but she's expecting us."

"She is not. No. She can't—"

"Honestly, it's okay. She won't get mad." The pathetic housekeeper was still terrified of her employer. I tried to calm her fears without telling her too much about why we were here. "Actually," I said, "she's waiting for us. She expects us. She may not have told you, because she thought we'd take longer, but—"

Batya shook her head to the point where I feared it might wobble off its moorings. "Stop. No. She isn't—can't—"

"Five minutes is all," Mackenzie said. I was sure that would do it. He has a way of wrapping his words in Southern gauze that makes them acceptable, but no less strong. It always works.

Obviously, distraught Eastern Europeans do not comprehend how attractive that accent is supposed to be. *"No minutes!"* Batya said. "Mrs. Fairchild can't see you, can't hear you—not you, not nobody. Mrs. Fairchild—she's dead!"

Ten

BATYA'S announcement left me breathless.

"Steady there," Mackenzie said.

I was astonished, but not faint. Nonetheless, "Water," he said to Batya. "And she'd better sit down." Before the house-keeper could respond, he steered me in, his arm around me, bracing me.

"I'm fine! What are you doing?" I whispered, my back to the watching Batya.

"Indulging my curiosity." Mackenzie seated me in the same love seat I'd occupied the day before. I tried to look dizzy.

Mackenzie shook his head. "You'd better sit down, too," he told

Batya. "In your condition. Rest, please. You've already had a bad shock. I'll get you both water."

"Yes," she said, propelling herself into a hard-backed chair against the wall. Once on it, her feet barely touched the carpet. She'd need help getting off without tumbling forward, and I wondered how she managed when she was alone. "Is awful," she said, eyes wild. But once he'd left the room, she had no conversational bon mots to offer, so we sat in an awkward silence until I put my head back and closed my eyes, opening them only when I heard the slosh of water.

C. K. held two glasses. I sipped mine and mimed calming myself down.

"I'm sorry we've intruded at a time like this," he said softly.

Batya fanned the air with her hand. "You okay now?" she asked me, and I nodded. "I was afraid. Maybe I have two heart attacks here."

"Is that what happened?" Mackenzie asked. "Mrs. Fairchild had a heart attack?"

She nodded and sniffled, arched back until she could reach a pocket, and extracted a crumpled lump of overused tissue, then blew her nose. "Like that." She snapped her fingers.

"I thought her problems were with her lungs," Mackenzie said.

"Mister," Batya said. "I am not doctor. I wake up when emergency comes pounding and they say looks like heart, and later, that's what Mr. Leo tells me. That's what doctors tell him."

"Wait—paramedics arrived when you were asleep?"

"Wakes me up, yes. Pounding, banging—they would break door if I didn't let them in. Scared me. Like secret police, like—my own heart—" She forgot she was holding a glass, and she pressed her hand and the glass to her chest and spilled a goodly portion of it onto herself.

"Was someone else here, too?"

"Nobody. Me. Only me."

"You think Mrs. Fairchild called the paramedics, then?"

"Who else? Except she is unconscious when they get here. They say for some time. Hour, more. Makes no sense, but is how it is. Maybe rescuers come slow, like take an hour?"

"What time did they get here?"

She blinked her swollen eyes, looked worried by the question, then silently debated it before nodding. "Midnight?"

"And was she still alive?" Mackenzie asked.

She shook her head.

"Near the phone when she . . ."

Batya winced.

Mackenzie opted for euphemism. ". . . passed on?"

Batya shook her head and looked down at her belly, not as if she wanted to gaze upon her unborn child, but as if she didn't want to meet our eyes. "She was on bed, but half off, too."

Trying to reach the phone? I was over the initial shock, and now I felt her death as a great pressure on my own heart. What an ironic pity, to think you were pretending to be sick, when unbeknownst to you, you were, in fact, fatally ill.

After a beat too long of silence, Batya looked up at us. "She said she felt bad, but I didn't know so bad!"

"Nobody's blaming you," Mackenzie said softly.

Batya didn't look convinced of that.

"People have heart attacks without warning."

"Is not my fault," she said. "Mr. Leo, he tells me to go to bed. He says everything is fine. Later—I can't hear so much in my room, way back there. She has buzzer to get me." She shook her head. "What am I doing now? No job, and Mr. Leo, he says I was supposed to take care of her! He says this to me today, after she is dead."

"Let's back up a bit. He told you to go to bed. That was last night, correct? He was here?"

"Everybody is here. Was train station. They come, they go . . . I don't feel so good now and so much back and forth and Mrs. Fairchild sick like that is too much. Not my fault. Mr. Leo, he saw how tired I was and he say, go to bed, Batya. I lock up."

"Everybody?" I asked.

She nodded. "Mr. Leo, two times. First, he comes himself. Later, he comes again with the lady."

"Emmie? The woman he's engaged to?"

"Her." She blew her nose and sat still for a while. "But the other lady, the friend, she comes, too. After him. Before them. I am good housekeeper, but with the baby and my worries right now—"

"What other lady, Batya?" Mackenzie asked gently.

"Miss Cade's friend, Mr. Leo's friend. She's here before." She looked at us. "With the animal name."

Mackenzie glanced at me. "Ms. Baer?" I asked. "Here? Last night?" The same night I had dinner with her?

She nodded.

"Do you know why?"

She sighed. "I say Mrs. Fairchild is sick. Is late. She says not so late—is maybe nine-thirty. A minute only. Needs name. She wants make rain. Crazy."

Mackenzie raised an eyebrow and checked to see if I knew how women affected precipitation.

"A shower," I said. "She wanted to give Emmie a shower." Nice. Odd, too, because she'd said they weren't that close. On the other hand, the timing suggested that she'd known about the wedding date and it had only been set that day. Emmie must have phoned her—maybe the call Vicky got at dinner, the one she took outside, when she gave her dog a potty break. Maybe my fabricated tale of the newcomer with no friends had prompted the desire to be kinder toward bad-luck Emmie.

I was getting lost on a side trip, and I pulled myself back to the present, in which Mackenzie was asking questions, almost as if he were still a homicide cop. Batya, perhaps used to being questioned by strangers in her homeland, didn't seem to realize we had no right to be in the apartment, let alone to interrogate her.

"What time was Mr. Leo here?" Mackenzie asked. "The visit when he told you to go to bed."

She shook her head, held up her wrist. "No watch. Too swollen. Maybe nine-thirty?"

"Was Ms. Baer still here?"

She shook her head. "Maybe ten. Too late, yes? Kills his own mother coming here middle of night."

"And you went to sleep, yes?"

"I go to my room."

"So you don't know when he left."

"You have baby. See how you sleep near end of the pregnant. This is why I am tired."

"Are you saying you heard them leave?"

"I leave my door open a while. I don't sleep at all."

I wanted to ask how that was so when she'd already said she couldn't hear a thing from her room "back there."

I knew Mackenzie had caught the discrepancy as well, but he was incredibly polite. He smiled and looked concerned for Batya's welfare, and for all I know, he was. He has a way of asking a question that almost makes the words invisible, almost makes the person he's addressing think they've thought them up themselves, that the topic is precisely what they want to talk about. Even when he has to ask the question several times. "Do you know what time you heard him leave?"

"I hear door. I hear them in hallway, talking, then door. Not so long after, he tells me go to bed."

"Ten o'clock, then?"

"Something like. A little later, sure. Yes, sure, because now I remember. My show ended, so I turn off TV."

"And his fiancée was with him the whole time."

"This time, yes. This his second time here last night. Third time here for day. He comes first with her in day, then alone after dinner, then later, with her again. Then they leave. I didn't trust about door. He was angry, maybe he forgets to lock. So I check. And I check her, too."

I was glad I hadn't asked. Her door had been open and she'd

been actively listening until she knew the door was locked and her employer was safe for the night.

"Mrs. Fairchild?"

She nodded. "She was okay. Sitting in bed, says she's going to sleep. I thought she would cry, he is so mean to her, but no. American children . . ." She pursed her mouth with distaste. It was hard for me to think of fortysomething Leo as a child.

"How was he mean, Batya?" I liked the way Mackenzie pulled her name in, often enough—but not too often—softening its edges so that it was a gentle and friendly tap on the shoulder.

"His own mother is sick in bed, but still, they shout. No—*he* shouts. Never her. It hurts too much." She tapped her chest, showing us where it hurt Claire Fairchild. Then she tried to lean forward, toward us, as if to confide, but only her head jutted out while the rest of her stayed in place behind the belly. "I not listening. Understand? I not do the . . ." She cupped her hand to her ear. "Never. But Mr. Leo is so loud."

"Could you hear what they were saying?"

She shrugged. "Noise. Angry. Words that don't make sense."

"Like what?"

"About wedding. And something—crazy. I don't know. First he asks about *reader*. I think he says 'reader,' but my English . . ."

Me. They were arguing about me, about my transparent excuse for being there. The temperature dropped precipitously, and I shuddered.

"She say something I don't hear because I never—" Again, the cupped hand to the ear.

"Of course not," Mackenzie said. "But sometimes, people are so loud, you can't help but hear. Even in a big apartment like this one."

She nodded. "I have work, always work. I don't listen behind door. And she talks soft. Normal. But he's so angry then, so loud, and he says 'you'—he means his mother—'hire' or 'fire,' I can't make out, 'the pie.' Fire the pie? Maybe should be bake the pie?

Hurts my head, crazy talk, so I stop listening, finish dishes, he leaves. Then, I think I sit down, have tea—but the Rain Lady comes. The wolf."

"Baer. Did she stay long?"

"Not very. I am so tired then from carrying trays, opening doors . . ."

"How did Mrs. Fairchild seem then?"

"She say sick. Maybe her heart hurts, she doesn't tell me such things. I am servant."

"Did everything seem normal about her? Did she eat much dinner?"

Batya looked at us both as if we were dangerous, as if a wrong answer might trap her. "She never eat much. I carry that heavy tray and . . . no. Not much."

"More or less than usual last night?"

"Same."

Either the answer was one she considered safe, or the simple truth, since Claire Fairchild had not truly been any sicker than was normal. Except: She died.

"How long do you think Ms. Baer stayed?"

"I have no watch," Batya repeated. "Who knows? All I think is why so many people this one night when she is sick? And me—I can't lay down until they go. My back always hurt now."

"Did she stay a long time, or not long?"

"Maybe not so long. But then Mr. Leo is back, and Miss Emmie. And she brings flowers!" Batya slapped her forehead as if that was mind-boggling news. "Big yellow and red flowers."

I could picture Emmie Cade in a lace-trimmed blouse and layered chiffon skirt, nearly hidden behind a huge bouquet. Flowers signaling peace, a truce, an end to mother–future-daughter-in-law hostilities.

"Flowers make Mrs. Fairchild sick!" Batya said indignantly. "No perfume—no flowers. She knows!"

But so did Leo. Why, then, did he allow Emmie to bring them? I almost asked, but Mackenzie did something with the muscles around his eyes. Not exactly a squint, but a clear cease-and-desist message. I wondered how he did that, and whether I could successfully imitate the expression.

"I put them in kitchen, where Mrs. Fairchild never goes. Should have put outside, in trash, but my back . . ." She pulled and twisted the fabric of her sleeve and sighed. "Maybe their smell kills her?" She snuffled, but her eyes stayed on us, deciding how we felt about her guilt.

"I doubt that," Mackenzie said. "Too far away." He spoke with great scientific assurance, as if the potentially lethal impact of floral perfumes had been the first subject in his doctoral program, and he'd gotten an A on the final. "You did the right thing, making sure Ms. Cade went in without her flowers."

Batya looked at him sideways, checking for expression, then at me. "I did right thing," she repeated. "Yes."

"And when you took the flowers, what did she do?"

She raised her eyebrows and opened her eyes till there was white all around the pupils, and put her hand to her mouth. When she was convinced we understood the gesture, she relaxed again. "Like that. *Sorry,* she says. *Forgot.* Then she goes in."

"To Mrs. Fairchild's bedroom," Mackenzie prompted.

Batya nodded. "By self. Soon, he goes in, too. Both in there now. Wear her out. Too much company for sick woman. I go in and tell them no, she not well, and they say, 'Just a minute. I be there just one minute.' Everybody says it and nobody is just a minute except his girlfriend—"

"Emmie Cade."

"Yes. Her. She is still upset about flowers, and when I say must leave, she does. She waits in living room. He says I should go to bed, but I listen because they make Mrs. Fairchild sicker. Then they leave and later, people bang on door and she is dead." She wiped at her eyes again with the exhausted lump of tissue.

I sat holding my water glass, listening to them, admiring how Mackenzie had finessed our way into the condo and into Batya's confidences. I remembered what he'd told me about successful con artists. He, too, could have had a lucrative life of crime because he had the ability to adopt a guileless, completely convincing persona while he lied through his teeth. I wasn't sure that was a great trait in a prospective husband. He also made it easy to forget to question his presence, and I think that would be true even with a more sophisticated person than Batya, a person aware of niceties such as civil rights.

They spoke, but a voice inside of me did as well, and it wouldn't stop. Claire Fairchild was nowhere near death, it said. Something is rotten here. She told me she could fool them all, and she was right. Somebody believed she was that sick, or believed everyone else would believe it, and killed her.

I heard as well a counter-voice, challenging my assumptions, asking the simple question: How? Nobody was there when she died, and there were apparently no signs of violence, or they would have been noted. How could it be anything but a natural death in that case?

Certainly, death arrived with a snap of the finger, and people keeled over taking everyone by surprise. But until proven otherwise, I was sure that a woman doesn't investigate a shady future daughter-in-law, a possible killer, fight with people who are outraged and threatened by the investigation, intimidate and threaten her servant, then abruptly die of natural causes without provoking suspicion.

"Is there something I can do for you?" Mackenzie asked Batya. "Are you here alone?"

"Batya is alone in this world."

But not quite as desperately so as she'd been a day earlier. Batya was now free. Nobody was blackmailing her anymore.

Mackenzie didn't have to prod this time. Batya answered the question. "I cannot leave house alone. No. And Mrs. Fairchild, she says . . ." She looked at us, one at a time, and bit at her bottom lip.

"Go on," I prompted. "It's okay. Whatever it is, it's okay."

"She say if she die, she leave me money. Because I take good care of her. I am poor woman . . ." She had run out of tissue and, this time, she lifted her shoulder in an attempt to blot her tears. "Two babies, one sick, please God new one should be okay, and what? What then? My husband is disappeared and now Mrs. Fairchild, too." Mackenzie fished around in his pockets, found a handkerchief, and passed it over to her. She looked at it, and then at him, as if he'd offered her an annuity for life instead of a piece of cloth. "I wash and clean it for you later," she whispered.

He shook his head.

"Because," she said, "life. I look at my life and ask, what is life, anyway, and I think, Batya, life is tissue paper. Strong, ha! Like tissue, I am protected by tissue paper."

I imagined long nights in a smoky Serbo-Croatian café, arguing what life was. Or long days in a Center City condo.

"Thin, like tissue. Over, like this," and once again she snapped her fingers. "My sainted mother is one minute frying breakfast and next . . ." She lifted one hand, as if to snap her fingers one more time, then she sighed, and put the hand back down.

Both Mackenzie and I nodded sagely. We agreed. Life was tissue paper, but now she had genuine cotton in her hand. Make of it what she would.

Apparently, the baby was also voting with its feet—whether on the tissue or cotton side of life, we couldn't tell. Batya looked startled, then put her hand on her belly. "Jumping all the time. The shock . . ." Then she looked at us. "Is not right, he shouts at his mama. My baby never will shout at me. Not allowed where I come from. Child respects."

We both maintained our solemn expressions of agreement, but I wondered if Mackenzie, too, was considering how carefully Batya cast the shadow of suspicion on Leo Fairchild and, as an alternate, the bride-to-be who had brought the death flowers. If, indeed, there was anything suspicious about Claire Fairchild's death, the housekeeper was making sure she was in the clear.

And why not? Her mental ledger sheet had no downside to Claire Fairchild's demise. It was all plusses: no I.N.S., no deportation. Plus, a legacy. Death had all the advantages.

"Help me," Batya said, pushing forward in the chair. Mackenzie all but catapulted out of his chair and took her arms. "I mean with problem." She nonetheless accepted the hoist. Once she was standing, she brushed off her belly and faced us.

She reminded me of the *Venus of Willendorf*, that Paleolithic carving that supposedly represents the first woman, or at least, the first work of art of an idealized naked woman. The exaggerated, enormous breasts resting on a very pregnant belly, and the rest of the body nearly inconsequential, mere methods of moving around that enormous fertility.

The Venus of Philadelphia spoke. "Help tell me what I do now."

"Do you have family here?" Mackenzie asked.

Batya bit at her bottom lip. "Aunt. She watches my baby, but is no room there. I sleep on floor when I go. Still, better than here, with ghosts."

Perhaps Claire Fairchild had been telling the truth and she'd posthumously reward the woman's years of loyal service. I hoped so. Unless, of course, Batya had arranged the woman's end.

Batya pointed toward the back of the condo. "I mean help me with that. What I do about that?"

"About what?" I asked, just to prove I was also in the room.

"Come," she said, leading us down the hallway to a bedroom. "Mrs. Fairchild's room is mess. Is all right if I clean? Looks bad for housekeeper to leave mess."

The bedclothes were pulled back with a sense of rush and emergency, but that seemed all that was amiss. Otherwise, it looked like a chronically ill elderly person's room. Apparatus, bottles, and comforting aids, like special pillows.

The bed was like a hospital bed in that the back portion could be angled up, and it was in that position now. She must have had it that way to talk with her visitors.

The hospital theme spilled onto her night table, which looked like a pharmacy display, overflowing with pill bottles and pill dis-

CLAIRE AND PRESENT DANGER

pensers. I saw a large segmented one that had the days of the week on it, and it wasn't the only pill holder. The tabletop was crowded with her medications, but also with small vanities—a lipstick, a hairbrush, a compact, plus predictable necessities like a tissue dispenser and water carafe, and the telephone that hadn't been used but nonetheless summoned the paramedics. A water glass lay on the floor, a still-wet spot showing around it. It must have been standing on the night table, en route to the telephone.

"What's this?" Mackenzie asked.

"Her compact," I said. "For face powder."

"No!" Batya raised her arms. Hands off, she was saying without words. "This thing, Mrs. Fairchild, she breathes in it so doctor knows how she is."

"How? Does he come visit for checkups?"

She shook her head. "No. She does it a lot, and the telephone, she says, it goes through telephone to him."

Mackenzie stared at it for a long while, as if whatever had happened was recorded on it. "I'd like to know. . . ," he said. "I wonder if . . ."

Batya looked worried. "Is important thing. Scientific. I never touch."

He nodded, then smiled at her and looked around. The oxygen tank idled on the floor near a basket filled with magazines. As Leo had unfortunately noted, she didn't seem much of a reader. I didn't see a single book in the room, but a TV set on the far wall faced the bed. The remote control was still on the spread, and Batya pointed at it and waited until Mackenzie said it was fine to remove it.

"Was she using oxygen when the paramedics came?" Mackenzie asked in the lightest of voices.

Batya looked stumped and shook her head. Then she spoke slowly. "I . . . no. No," said more emphatically. "Strange. Should be on her face at night. Night is worst for her breath, when she sleeps."

"That is strange," Mackenzie said in that agreeable voice that made Batya and C. K. part of a team.

I didn't find it strange that she hadn't been on oxygen. Claire Fairchild had died before she settled in for the night.

"Mrs. Fairchild would be angry at mess like this."

My definition of a mess had a lot more slack built into it than Batya's did. But I wasn't the housekeeper, still afraid of what the late Mrs. Fairchild would think of the scene, and my ego did not ride on such things.

"People think lazy housekeeper, such mess. But the TV, they say all the time don't touch anything."

"That's at the scene of a crime," Mackenzie said, as always making the word have no hard edges. When he says it, *crahm* sounds nearly edible, and not at all frightening. "Police weren't here, were they?"

"Men came to take her away."

"Paramedics took her to the hospital."

"She is dead already when they come."

"Yes, but . . . they weren't the police. Still," he said, "it's okay to leave things alone for a bit. Take a rest. Relax."

"Is okay I make the bed? Mrs. Fairchild, she—"

"Why not? But don't touch anything else yet."

She nodded gravely and moved, slowly, toward the bed, obviously eager to smooth the covers. "Nothing else," she said. "Nothing else, then Mr. Leo, he cannot say I take his mother's things."

"Good idea. Everything will take care of itself in a while," Mackenzie said kindly. "You have other, happier things to think about, like your baby."

She blinked and looked down at her beach-ball body and I thought she might cry, but instead, she took another deep breath and nodded while she fussed and pulled and straightened and smoothed the sheets and covers.

I felt sorry for the life that had driven her out of her home and homeland, sorry she was now so alone in this new world. Sorry that her job and husband were both gone and, along with them, whatever safety she'd envisioned for herself and her children.

Nonetheless, while Batya smoothed the last inch of cover, I tried to memorize everything I could see, to burn a mental image of where things were placed and what things they were. To be the camera.

As if it were a crime scene, because I was positive it was.

Eleven

"**W**ELCOME to the ranks of the unemployed," C. K. said as we left the late Mrs. Fairchild's building. "Well, except that you're not, teach."

"Unemployed? Are you saying that just because—"

"She's dead? You weren't going to say that, were you? Just because she's dead doesn't mean she isn't still employing us? Who is she, Elvis? She's gone, the investigation's gone, and we're outta there. As is, it's going to be harder 'n hell to get paid for what we already did. Leo doesn't sound like the easiest guy on earth, and he obviously wasn't happy with his mother's decision to hire us."

"Can you walk away from the whole thing like that?"

"What else am I supposed to do? The woman is finished with problems and questions, unless the afterlife is a much more anxious spot than we've been led to believe. An' she definitely can't write checks anymore." He stopped in front of a hole-in-the-wall restaurant and read the menu posted in the storefront window. "Are you as hungry as I am?" he asked.

"Look here, Mackenzie. She's gone, but we're still here."

He stood up straight again. "Indeed. Here and alive and hungry as hell."

"About our budget? Our carefully worked out mutually agreed-upon eating plan? And today of all times—right after you tell me we aren't going to be paid for the job we just did."

"What say? Just this once? Even though this menu's Greek to me. Place smells good."

I glanced at the menu. "This is Greek to everybody." We had gone over our new finances a dozen times, and had come up with the current income and outgo plan. Due to Mackenzie's more regular hours, now that he was no longer chasing crazed killers around on their time schedules, dinner together was a predictable almost-daily event, and somebody had to think about it. We took turns being responsible for producing something edible.

The new budget did not allow for lots of meals away from home or even cooked by other hands and brought into the home. In exchange for these additional domestic duties, we agreed to drop our standards of cuisine to anything that didn't cause permanent damage to the central nervous system.

Truth is, I'd come to enjoy both my turns and Mackenzie's, though most times, we split the chopping and broiling or whatever needed to be done. It was a good time of day, close to my favorite, when we'd gone our separate ways and were back together to talk about where our travels had taken us.

"Pretty inexpensive," Mackenzie said. "The prices are in English."

Tonight was officially my turn. Was it my ethical responsibility to remind him of that, or of our promises to be fiscally wise at all times?

I decided it was not. He was an exceptionally smart man, and surely he'd considered those factors already and didn't need my input. Besides, I had a hunger headache and was still upset about Claire Fairchild, and not a little upset, too, with the way Mackenzie had blithely dismissed the entire matter.

We went into the small room, fragrant with olive and lamb-scented steam, and my stomach and I realized the encounter with Sonia Lawrence had detoured me from lunch and I hadn't had a chance to eat anything since half a bagel at breakfast, except the pretzels that were a constant at Ozzie's office.

Ambience was not this restaurant's forte. Once, this had been a living room, which should have made it homey, but it was bleak, with the look of a newly deserted home. I had the feeling the owner had blown all of his decorating funds on a few pints of paint.

We sat at a table covered with a white cloth with a square of white paper atop it. That was festooned with a small vase with a droopy rose, the one that bloomed after the last rose of summer. We were the only customers, and the restaurant appeared a one-man show. The owner/host/waiter/chef practically danced over to us and presented us with menus, and I was glad we'd brought a little action and cash into his life.

I was tempted to order everything listed, but contented myself with pastitsio, that lovely confection of ground lamb, pasta, and many fat calories posing as a sauce.

Mackenzie ordered fish in a garlic sauce, and once we'd been served bread and a dish of olives and feta and neither of us seemed likely to keel over from starvation, I cleared my throat.

"You aren't, are you?" he immediately asked.

"I have to."

"You won't give it up?"

"It isn't right."

"You've got to understand that most times, you aren't going to know the end of the story. It's an important idea to get hold of. Most times, you do your piece of investigatin', turn it in, and then you're on to a new question. You don't know how it's used, who was found guilty or set free, or whether the wife actually divorced the guy who's been hidin' his money away. We're only chapters in somebody else's story."

"Something isn't kosher back there, Mackenzie," I said. "That's all I could think while we were there, and that's all I can think now."

He examined the pathetic rose, not meeting my eyes. "No reason to assume that." His breath denuded the flower of two of its remaining petals. In an act of botanic kindness, he looked at me directly and spared it further damage. "It's a job. Was a job. It's over."

"The woman was healthy—except of course for the emphysema, but people last decades with that. She was faking illness. I don't believe in coincidence."

He drank a hearty gulp of his water. "Should have ordered ouzo, if I didn't have to study later on. You know, sometimes I think about all the studyin' ahead, the years of it, an'—"

"We at least have to tell the police about . . . her. The fiancée." There was absolutely nobody in the place except the two of us. The proprietor, who was reading a newspaper at the far end of the room, had spoken only broken English, but I still couldn't bring myself to be indiscreet and say her name. "Isn't it the law or something?"

"The law for us is the same as for anybody else. Nothing special granted to us, so the decision is based on what you think a right-thinkin' citizen should do."

"Okay, then, as citizens, shouldn't we—"

"Manda? Listen up. If you boiled all those things we found about the woman down, we'd still only have hearsay, speculation, and gossip. The accidents? Maybe she's attracted to men who push too hard—riding the motorcycle, sailing around the world."

"Leo Fairchild is certainly not a—"

"Maybe she's ready for a change. An' maybe she's shown some less than totally honorable behavior. Or maybe she really did try to start a business, or try to repay loans, even if she failed. But a beautiful woman gifted by admirers is as old as history. Not your feminist ideal? Okay. Not mine—but not illegal, either."

"There's something shabby about her ethics. All the playing around with her name, and the trail of dead bodies—"

"Like I said, accidents. Suicide, maybe. Not murder, or she'd be locked up now."

"Unless she's too damn pretty and clever."

"My mama used to talk about girls who had 'bad reputations.' She used to warn my sisters how once you had a bad rep, it was yours forever, and what could be worse?"

I knew that refrain, and in fact, it was the first common bond I'd heard of between our sets of parents.

"You're buyin' into it, is that it? And you want to tell the police—before there's evidence of any crime whatsoever—that Emmie Cade has a bad rep?"

"You make it sound so . . ."

"Don't get swept along by a whole lot of bad-mouthin'. Didn't you tell me some story about your bein' a slut?"

I nodded again.

"It made me so hopeful, too," he said with the shadow of a grin. "Who knew it was all a figment of somebody's imagination?"

Emmie Cade's story was different. Years and years of bad behavior.

"You want to toss suspicion on her for no good reason? Why not wait till we find out what happened? Why not wait till after the autopsy and the pathologist's report? Then—if—sure."

"Will there be one? If the doctor said heart attack—"

"He wasn't in attendance and she didn't have a history of heart disease particularly, so yes. I believe so. Why not wait?"

I nodded.

"I mean more than a few minutes."

"Not too many minutes," I said. "Enough of them and Leo Fairchild will be married to that woman."

"And?"

"Isn't it obvious? Besides, I more or less made a promise to help

Claire Fairchild about this marriage. To help her stop it if it put her son in danger."

He moved the small silver vase from between us and leaned forward, smiling. "Interesting way of looking at it. Ozzie would have a good laugh at that interpretation of our roles. But tell me: Why are you so sure she was killed?"

"Because I came to see her, and Leo got suspicious, and somebody's secret was going to be exposed."

"Ah," he said softly, leaning back in his chair. "You've managed to feel personally responsible. Consider this: If you believe you triggered events, how did that happen?"

"The way I said."

He shook his head. "Too vague. What I'm askin' is, who knew we were hired, aside from Mrs. Fairchild and the two of us?"

Even before he'd finished that sentence I realized where he was headed, and I wasn't willing to travel that road with him. It'd only make me feel worse. "You can't think Beth . . ."

"I have to think Beth, because who else is there? If she didn't tell Vicky Baer, for whatever reason, then how did the information make its transit around?"

"It didn't necessarily start with Vicky Baer. She came to talk about giving a shower for Emmie. Obviously, Emmie herself told her that she was getting married in two weeks." The awful thing was, I could envision Beth telling Vicky Baer because she thought what I did was "cute" and might make her own subtle sales pitch that much more engaging. I can arrange everything, she'd be saying in essence—even a sister who's sleuthing around the Main Line. She would never do anything that she perceived as potentially harmful, but why would bragging about your sister's job be a bad thing? She'd undoubtedly said something, and Ms. Baer thought back to all my remarks about her old friend, and put two and two together. Those excellent schools she'd attended insisted you knew that much math.

And then, likely as not, indignant on her friend's behalf, she told her, and Emmie told Leo.

I must have looked still more depressed, because Mackenzie changed tracks and tried to make me feel better. "The most logical explanation is that Claire Fairchild told Leo when he confronted her about—"

"Me," I said. "My fault. I should have had a better cover story, but I didn't know I'd need a story, and of course, I had no way of knowing the woman didn't read."

"Doesn't matter now. So maybe she told him, he told Emmie, and she did or didn't tell her old friend. Or it started the other way."

"But if Leo was the one who found out, in that fight with his mother, he probably wouldn't be stupid enough to tell his fiancée. I mean, I assume he didn't want the two women in a permanent state of war."

"Unless his mother told him about what happened in San Francisco and he got scared, too. Wanted her to know he was on to her."

That produced an olive-eating silence until finally, only a small container of pits remained. The feta and bread had long since disappeared. I couldn't think of any logical response, and all I wanted to say, again and again, was: It wasn't right.

"Here it is and it's beautiful, is it not? My two best, best dishes! Enjoy!" The owner chuckled as he presented us with enormous platters. The aroma of nutmeg drifted up from mine, and Mackenzie smiled and inhaled deeply over his garlicky entrée.

"There's Batya, too," I said. "She overheard everything."

"But she wasn't being investigated, so your theory—"

"Maybe her motives had nothing to do with me."

"Gets you off the guilt-hook, then, right?"

"Well . . . I'm bothered about who called the paramedics, aren't you? She's the only possibility."

"Why would she lie and say she didn't, then?"

"So she could lie and say she didn't know Claire Fairchild was dying."

The chef-owner hovered nearby, waiting.

We complimented him on the aroma, then tasted, and recomplimented as he continued to stand there. He poured more wine into my already-full glass, convinced Mackenzie—not a difficult job—that one glass of wine wouldn't prevent studying later on, and again awaited a verdict, which was again positive.

The food was delicious, but if he insisted on being an active part of every dining experience, I could understand why the place wasn't thriving.

Finally, he left us alone.

"Something rotten happened there," I said. "You know how to find things out. You were a homicide cop all those years."

"I'm not one now. I have no legal—"

"You're clever."

"You have an idea, don't you?"

"More a gut feeling somebody did that woman in."

He stopped, a fork filled with flaky white fish doused with the stinking rose—I could smell the garlic from across the table—midway to his mouth. "How?" he asked quietly. "She was alive after everybody left. So how?"

"I don't know. Something slow. A poison?"

"There are symptoms with poisons. Symptoms not meant for the dinner table."

"Something biological warfarish. Something the government's afraid terrorists will use."

"Like what?" He didn't even look up from his food when he asked that. He didn't care.

"There must be those things—look at the anthrax deaths—or what are we all worried about protecting ourselves against? Claire Fairchild went from relative health to zap, dead—"

He sighed. He over-sighed, so that if there were a far balcony, the theatergoers would know he was tired, possibly peeved, and definitely not interested. "Forgive me," he said. "I love you dearly, and among the things I love about you is your mind, which comes up with surprise after surprise, as now. But for the rest of dinner, could we shelve this and talk about reality?"

"As if—"

"Reword that. Let's talk about urgent matters."

"Those matters are two days away," I said. "Claire Fairchild is dead now." It was much easier thinking about a dead near-stranger than contemplating the visitors ahead.

Ever since they'd announced their "All-U.S.A.-Scattered-Offspring Visitation, I'd felt like one of those metal hunters at the shore, poking in the sand and sifting out the worthless from the treasures. Not only did every remark about past affairs of the heart resurface, but so did odd bits and pieces, descriptions and explanations of his family from which I built an image of parents who seemed an acquired taste, like cigars or octopus sushi. Mackenzie called them *eccentric* and *colorful*, but anyone who's read books by Southern authors knows to duck when those adjectives are in the vicinity. *Eccentricity* mutates into *lunacy* when it crosses the Mason-Dixon, and *colorful* families are genetically suspect and dourly *dysfunctional* in Yankee-land. We grow eccentrics in this climate, too, but then we lock them up.

For starters, C. K.'s parents, who hadn't even given him a first name, were themselves named Boy and Gabby. More properly, Boyd and Gabrielle, but nobody called them that. I frankly cannot imagine a grown man in Philadelphia being called—allowing people to call him—Boy.

Perpetual Boy or not, Mackenzie Père sounded less dotty than Gabby, and their couplehood was always described in the most glowing of terms. C. K. forever referred to his happily mismatched parents when I'd get nervous about our differences. To him, they were the gold standard of how opposites can attract and keep on attracting.

Boy was described as an outdoorsy sort of man, fond of hunting and fishing, bad jokes, and lamentably conservative politics that Gabby in no way shared.

I wasn't apprehensive about their eccentricities on my own behalf. It was how those interesting deviations from the norm were going to mesh with my parents' familiar yet strange ways. My father was shy, taciturn, an observer, a city boy who considered stamp collecting a sport. He'd never hunted and never wanted to. His politics were liberal, thoughtful, and soft-spoken. He loved his family passionately, but was not a demonstrative man.

My mother was listed as an Independent, and her political philosophy mutated according to whatever annoyed her at any given moment. She wasn't shy about sharing her views—or changing them fifteen minutes later. She was also an inveterate toucher and hugger, and even normal Northerners had been known to step back and be astounded by one of her unprovoked hugs.

My mother was coming north to crack the whip and get us in line—and that meant the line down the aisle. None of this shilly-shallying and delaying. Bea Pepper was on her way.

My father was coming north because my mother was, and when the word *wedding* floated through the ether, what he thought about—but was too polite and quiet to say—was the enormous Mackenzie clan and what it would cost to manage such a guest list. He was not a wealthy man and he was all for taking things as slowly as possible.

Mackenzie's mother had never even hinted that she'd like things to move more swiftly—at least not with me—and who knew what Boy Mackenzie wanted, aside from a shotgun and a fishing rod?

The fathers didn't seem likely to get along, and the mothers seemed even less so. But their arrivals were forty-eight hours away. Somehow, it would all work out. That had become my new mantra, but at the moment, my mantra's batteries had run out.

"You look so worried," Mackenzie said. "Shouldn't be. They'll love you to death. They're all for having fun and celebrating whatever's around to celebrate. That's undoubtedly how they wound up with eight children." He reached over and put one of his hands atop mine, the one that had his grandmother's ring on it. "No reason to be concerned," he said softly. "Everything's going to be fine."

But his words were southerning up, which is to say, mushing down, spun and liquified in the blender of his own apprehensions.

And why shouldn't he be nervous? Why shouldn't we both be? Why on earth were we supposed to believe that stupid mantra—It Will All Work Out—when nothing whatsoever had, so far?

Mackenzie was wrong. Dead wrong. It was easier and more productive to think about Claire Fairchild. There was nothing I could do about the Parents' Visits. That would be its own disaster, or it would not.

But Claire Fairchild had suffered the ultimate disaster, and I could do something about that.

I smiled at my fiancé, my love, my partner. I smiled and realized how easily looks—including mine—could deceive. Because I wasn't going to let go of whatever Claire Fairchild's death might mean, or my part in causing it, no matter what Mackenzie thought.

Yes, I was his partner, in life and in work, but neither relationship meant I was supposed to be indistinguishable from him. I was myself, and I'd do whatever I thought was right.

He smiled back, his face full of love and trust.

I wasn't sure I liked me at the moment.

Twelve

ONE of the often-overlooked good things about teaching is that it's very Zen, an ongoing lesson in living in the minute. To do even a mediocre job, and to avoid all hell breaking out, a teacher has to be present in mind as well as body.

That sounds easy, but if taken seriously, it's anything but. Being on, being alert, being aware of what's happening in twenty to thirty separate bodies and minds makes for an incredibly difficult job even without the mandate of wedging culturally important information between the audience's ears. Imagine what pay and benefits Actors Equity would demand if their member performers had to hold the stage, being alert and on for five to six hours per performance. *Hamlet* each and every school day.

But the good side of this is that it means the teacher's mind can't wander and obsess, even if really important nonclassroom matters loom, like planning how to prepare for meeting the senior Mackenzies. Making A Good Impression. This translates into the mundane quandary of what to wear. Certainly not the otherwise perfect white silk blouse the teacher currently has on, not tomorrow and not perhaps ever again, because ten minutes earlier, her pen leaked navy blue ballpoint gorp, a splat the size of a cat's head over its right sleeve.

And this particular teacher could not, at the moment, think of a single other item in her wardrobe.

She might have thought about how messy the loft was and how much scrubbing and tidying she'd have to do tonight, and she knew her mother certainly wished she would. But luckily, there was no opportunity to think about such concerns. She had to Be Here Now And Always.

I was also too busy paying attention to the classroom to ponder the meaning of the note in my mailbox this morning, complete with smiley-face, of course. *Dr. H.,* it said. Sunshine had reverted to plain English for The Supreme Boss of Us. That *Dr.* part was an ongoing mystery. Nobody knew in what field that doctorate had been pursued, or what offshore diploma mill had produced it, because he showed no special learning—not even basic smarts—in any area yet plumbed. But no surprise, Sunshine believed in it and accorded it the full dignity of a normal abbreviation. After that, the note degenerated into pure Sunshinelish. *1ts 2CU—f2f b43@ bk. OK?*

Sunshine's notes forced me to sound them out the way a kindergartener might. "Onets—*wants*—two—to—Oh, C.U. To see you. Face-to-face be . . . no. Before three, about book." The effort exhausted me and only the *OK?* didn't require effort. Hers was the longest, least efficient, shorthand I'd ever seen.

It had to be about Sonia Lawrence's difficulties with *Lord of the Flies.* If I needed further proof of Havermeyer's lack of a brain, and

I did not, here it was. Any half-wit could have told her that even if we were at war with evil, understanding the enemy, recognizing the impulse toward it would be a good thing, the equivalent of arming our side.

Couldn't he have simply said thinking was a good thing? On second thought, how could Havermeyer, who'd never dared to entertain an original thought, say that? I'd have to do battle, senselessly. I'd win. Havermeyer was wary of me, ever since I'd caught him playing doctor instead of behaving like the one he claimed to be. But the idea of having to waste breath and energy on something this stupid exhausted me in advance.

Not that I could really think about that, either. I owned nothing suitable in which to meet my future in-laws tomorrow. I had a mess of a loft that would tell the world, or at least the senior Mackenzies, all that I didn't want them to know about me, at least not until my wonderful qualities put my less-wonderful aspects into perspective, and I needed a haircut and didn't know if I could get an appointment during tomorrow's lunch hour.

And my parents were flying in to make sure there was a clash of cultures.

Not that I was thinking about them, either. I was a teacher. I had to be alert and on throughout the day.

We were dealing with antonyms, and that's what was on my mind. What is the opposite of looking forward to meeting your in-laws?

To give a hypothetical example of what a conscientious teacher simply cannot consider while she is in front of a classroom: If a woman is about to meet her future mother-in-law who—have I mentioned this?—designs and makes her own clothing, even, sometimes, to the point of dyeing the fabric and/or weaving it—then what should that hypothetical young woman wear? Should she be tailored and professional looking when she knows said future mother-in-law is fond of a former Miss Swamp who undoubtedly wears bangles, bustiers, and white patent go-go boots? Or should she instead try to anticipate and echo her colorful mother-in-law to-be? Make the older woman feel comfortable, the way a good hostess might by dressing so her visitors think they've picked the perfect outfit themselves. Should she worry about the workmanship and check all seams and feel really, really bad that she has no idea how to work a sewing machine?

Because if she did let such thoughts creep into even a sliver of her brain, her class might seize the advantage and win their case against learning any vocabulary at all. The S.A.T.s were under fire—that was probably the single current event my students recognized—and for all they knew, they said, the tests might be history and irrelevant by the time they'd apply to colleges. And they'd have wasted all this time learning words!

"It isn't like nobody understands me," a cute young thing said. "I mean, I've been talking my whole life and if I don't know *ambidextrous*, who will care?"

"Yeah," the boy the next row over said. I checked the chart. Brad. I had to memorize their names, forget about Boy and Gabby and focus on the classroom. Brad obviously had the hots for the cute young thing, even if winning her involved talking about vocabulary. "It's not like I have these big blank spots when I talk, you know. Like I'd have to shut up because I didn't have that vocabulary lesson."

There's a dark part of me that loves to watch them rally their forces and shape logical arguments, even when their defense is ignorant nonsense. But sooner or later, you have to stop it, even if you aren't obsessively thinking about all the things you haven't done or taken care of that's going to cost you points with your future in-laws. "We're learning how to think," I said. "We're also talking about analogies, about seeing the relationships between words and ideas. . . . There will still be S.A.T.s, but with more emphasis on your writing. So how about learning a few words with which to express yourself?"

They regarded me with compassion and pity. I was so far removed from their concept of sane behavior and ideas, they looked as if they were planning an intervention to get me the help I so desperately required.

Meanwhile, my inner couturier had gone over the edge and was screaming in many languages, pacing in tight circles inside my brain. How about that linen outfit? Needs ironing. Tonight, then, after I clean and polish and straighten. Won't wear it to school, because by the time they arrive late tomorrow, it'll look as if I'd slept in it.

Or maybe I would indeed sleep in it and have a head start and an excuse.

Is black better? Is black always safe? Or too . . . New York. They're from Louisiana. They won't get it. But my black slacks didn't need ironing the way the beige linen ones did.

"Who's ever going to even say *ambidextrous*? And why would they if they can say 'I can write with both my hands,' " the boy—I checked the seating chart—Daniel—on the other side of the cutie pie—I checked the chart again—Allison—said. Dueling hormones for the fair Allison's hand. If they'd only learn the word *ambidextrous*, they'd know they could each have one of her hands.

When would I have their names memorized? It had never taken this long, had it? "Either hand," I murmured.

The other good news is that even as you're failing to be a decent teacher, and you aren't really there, the sheer force of adolescent will and obstinacy drives the hour on, heaves it through the slow lurches of the classroom clock until this session's over. Either they'd learned *ambidextrous* or they hadn't, and I'd settled on ironing the linen outfit because then I could wear a celadon summer sweater Mackenzie had given me for my birthday. He said it matched my eyes, which it doesn't, but his mother would have to approve of something her son had chosen. Maybe that would include me, too.

THE MORNING SEEMED INTERMINABLE. Actually, it wasn't an illusion. It just barely terminated itself after about five years. When

I'd exhausted my patience with my inner-wardrobe mistress, my attention again ran sideways, into a pit called Havermeyer Is On My Case Again.

I should probably be ashamed to say that this item fired fewer brain cells than my choice of clothing had. But then, I'd been coping with Havermeyer for years, and I was completely new at the daughter-in-law thing.

Experience pays. What I've learned about the headmaster and perhaps all truly stupid people in power is that somewhere in the center of their bombastic hearts, they know they're dumb. They deserve a bit of sympathy, because it must feel rotten to be in constant danger of being shown for the fool and fake they are.

It should be against the law—against the Constitution—for an idiot to be in charge of innocent children's destinies. But given the situation, and the tenuous state of our jobs and the economy, we protect and defend our young by using guerrilla tactics against Our Leader.

I've learned that my best defense is an offense, and I bamboozle him by using his own methodology, i.e., emphatic stupidity.

I don't question or await his answer. Instead, I agree with him, right from the get-go. I behave as if I know what he's about to say, which is, amazingly enough, precisely what I wish he'd say, and nine times out of ten, he silently retreats and changes his position so that he can agree and even, perhaps, believe that's what he meant all along. Why not? It isn't as if there's any bedrock of conviction or philosophy for him to tap into, test ideas against.

And so at noon, finding him idling away the time in his office, I decided to get the meeting over. "Thanks for grabbing this problem by the horns," I said as I entered his office. It's an odd room, decorated with Latinate diplomas from unrecognizable institutions. I wish there were time to study them, but he's made sure they're out of clear-reading range. Besides, I had to stay aggressive. "That woman means well, as we both know, but really . . . can you imagine?"

He'd gestured for me to sit, and had taken his seat again, behind his massive, empty desk. I considered how warm he must be on this balmy September day. He wore a vest no matter the season, and I was convinced it was only so that he could dangle his pseudo Phi Beta Kappa Key across his shirtfront. Now, he cleared his throat.

I rushed in before he could. "She's so worried about adolescents reading about evil that she's going to leave them unable to recognize it. And where would we be if we censored young minds that way? The author's a Nobel Prize winner—isn't that a sufficient credential? He's part of the canon, now."

I was pretty sure my principal thought I was now talking about artillery. That war on evil, perhaps.

"It's a good thing this happened early in the year," I rattled on. "This way, a tone and precedent—especially in the light of the higher standards you're implementing here—is set for the future." He waited a few moments, then nodded very slowly, as if he were still learning how to lower and raise his head. "And I hope it's not out of line to say how impressed I am with your swift and efficient handling of the entire situation."

The hook had been set. I could almost see it in the fleshy part of his cheek. It was safe to pause for breath now.

"Mrs. Lawrence is concerned about her daughter's—"

"Feel free to reassure her that you've alerted me to that and I'll take special care of—pay special attention to—her daughter. And again—thanks so much for handling this. I'm positive that with your reassurance, she's already calmed down." I was halfway out of my chair by the last words.

Havermeyer looked more and more troubled, but he, too, stood, and nodded in his slow, heavy-headed manner.

I put my hand out to shake his, and he nodded again, shook my hand, then pulled back. "Did you know you have a—" He pointed at the ink blot. I was tempted to do a Rorschach with it, but before he could remember that this wasn't how he'd intended the meeting to go, I looked at the mess on my sleeve with exaggerated horror. "Oh, no! I'd best take care of that. Maybe it's not too late! Thanks for pointing it out," and I was out of there.

Except I was buzzing—my cell phone, bought for the after-school life, was buzzing.

"You are sooo popular!" Sunshine chirruped as I fled into the hallway. "But did you know you have a boo-boo on your—"

"Please," a female voice on the phone said. "I need to talk to you."

I covered my free ear with my hand and began the ascent to my room, where, perhaps, I'd find quiet. Most lunches—except mine—had been eaten, and now, kids were everywhere.

"I know you probably don't want to—or don't care, but I have this horrible feeling—"

"Who is this?"

"Emmie Cade. We met the day before yesterday. I need to talk to you."

I was midway up the staircase and I paused, nearly causing a major collision with a young man racing up behind me. "But, I . . . but we—how did you find me?"

"You told us where you taught school. And she—Mrs. Fairchild—told us—told Leo, really. He was so worried about who you might be that she told him what she'd done, why you were really there."

I had no idea what to say. Was I even supposed to talk to her? According to C. K., our business with the Fairchild family—current and future members—was finished. Our client was finished, too. There was nothing further we could do for her and nothing to discuss.

But when I didn't say anything, she rushed back in. "He thought—forgive him, but Leo thought you were suspicious. He knew his mother didn't care for books, so he didn't believe your story and he thought maybe you were a con man—a con person. That's why she finally told him the truth. About your investigating me. And he told me."

And now she was telling me. Why?

"I thought he must be wrong—and then I checked today, and here you are, really a teacher. So even though she said—and Leo said he checked, because she told him the company you work with—I don't see how you can teach school and actually investigate anything—"

"Surely you didn't phone me to discuss time management, did you?"

Her voice lowered almost to a whisper. I was in my room now, and I closed the door, though I couldn't have said what I thought I was keeping out. "I have to talk to you. Otherwise—please?"

"With Mrs. Fairchild dead, I'm—we're—no longer involved, so I don't see why—"

"No, please."

"If you have something important to say, say it now. I'm really busy—"

"It isn't something that feels right on the phone. And to be honest, it'll take a few minutes. I could meet you anywhere, anytime. Please? My life's at stake here."

She was ridiculous. Dramatic, silly, and preposterous. She was taking her Romantic Poet image too seriously, but playing the damsel in distress didn't suit her. She was the one to fear. She was the one who left casualties in her wake.

And I was the one with the Mackenzies barreling toward me tomorrow, and much more than one after-school session's worth of preparations and stocking up ahead of me. "This is not a good day," I said. "I don't have any free time whatsoever."

"I wouldn't ask, honestly." She had a lovely, melodic voice, even when she insisted it was under strain. I amazed myself by feeling sorry for her—then felt sure that's what she wanted. "But if I don't see you before the police—"

"What police?"

"*The* police."

"What do the police have to do with anything?"

"The *police!*" As if repeating the word with ever-more emphasis would give it context. "I'm sure they'll want to talk to you, and I need to talk to you first, because she hired you and I don't know what all—"

"Stop. I don't understand what you're saying, and you're saying it too fast. Why are the police going to talk to me?"

"Because—because—" She sounded near tears, or perhaps in them already. "I thought you'd know, you being on this investigation, and—"

"Ms. Cade. In about five minutes, my classroom will fill up with twenty teenagers. Try hard to make yourself clearer. The police are going to talk to me because . . . ?"

"They—the somebody, whoever it is who does things like that—"

"Like what?"

"Test. Do things to—to dead people."

"A pathologist?"

"Yes. I think so. That's it, I think. They—he—said something's wrong in her bloodstream. In her."

"Like what?" Something slow-acting that allowed those hours to elapse? I hadn't been serious when I'd said it.

"Barbiturates."

A medication. Not a poison. An accident, not a murder. The woman had prescription bottles filling the top of her nightstand. She must have grabbed the wrong one. "Too much of one of her medicines?"

"It didn't sound that way. Besides, she had that box with the dates and little places for morning pills and noon pills and night-time pills. They were all counted out in advance. Help me." She sounded as if she were calling out from the bottom of a well.

I realized I had pulled my head away from the phone, and I was shaking it, as if to quell the urge to reach out and rescue her. Her defenseless "help me" echoed, and I understood how good she'd be at seducing me over to her camp. I didn't want to be there.

I didn't want to know what she wanted of me, why she had to see me. You don't have to meet and plan things out if you're going to tell the truth. That's one of honesty's main advantages: It saves time.

I wanted to tell her she deserved whatever she got, and I was not going to be her next comrade in crime, or a stepping-stone to her next victim.

I looked forward to talking with the police and turning over the flyers and the news story from California, and whatever else had been faxed to Ozzie's office yesterday after we left. I wished I could tell her that I knew enough about her already to want to stay miles away, but all I actually said was, "I'm too busy to meet with you."

"But—you can't do this to me! I won't let you—"

Let me! I didn't wait to hear what she wouldn't let me do, what she might threaten. I said goodbye.

It took me a while to shut off the phone. It's hard when your hand is shaking.

Thirteen

I HADN'T been lying—I did keep a special eye out for Melanie Lawrence. Judging by the maternal concern for her sensibilities, I thought she might be somebody I'd missed, an introverted, shy, socially backward child who'd been dangerously overprotected and monitored, and I was ready to help her maneuver her way through this brave new high school world. The important thing was not to blame the sins of the mother on the child.

But I hadn't missed her, and if ever a girl looked as if she didn't need my help—or anyone's—it was Melanie. She was the amazingly self-assured creature I'd noticed the first day. The leader of the pack. The girl and the mother's worries didn't mesh, mainly because the girl was so much of a diamond chip off the maternal block, a petite blonde with features so regular and pleasing, they were just this side of computer-generated. She sat through class surrounded by friends, attentive herself, smiling and nodding acknowledgment of points made in the discussion of the opening segment of *Lord of the Flies*, and adding a few well-spoken comments of her own. She was going to grow up and run the world, or at least a megacorporation.

Lord of the Flies was, as always, a great book for discussion, both rich and unintimidating. "What do we know at this point about these boys?" I asked. "What do we know about Ralph?"

"Strong."

"Good looking," a girl said, and when the boys laughed derisively, she sat up straight and said, "It says so! It says that's one reason they picked him as leader."

"Not that smart," a boy said. "Piggy's the one who figures out what to do."

I kept checking my seating chart. Had to learn names more quickly. I wished kids came in more colors and patterns. It would be so easy to remember who went with a paisley face or plaid hair.

"Mean!" a tiny girl—Olivia—said softly. "That whole thing of calling him Piggy when he asked not to be."

"Then is everybody mean?" I asked. "Didn't everybody laugh when Ralph called him Piggy?"

A moment's silence, people looking side to side, checking out one another until a boy—Tony—shrugged and said, "You know how it is. Going along with the group."

Good. Whether or not Sonia Lawrence approved, we were moving toward a discussion of group psychology, and her daughter didn't seem in danger of toppling over from the weight of the topic. "Any other signs of these boys being ready to go along with the group?"

They were right there with me, having made note of the choir in its matching uniforms and their obligatory voting for their leader. "And Jack," I said. "What do we already know about him?"

"He's dangerous," Melanie said. "He has a knife. I was wondering why he had one. But he's ready to use it, too."

I decided to stop worrying about Melanie.

"He'll use it," a girl nearby added. "Because he lost face when he didn't kill the pig."

"He said so," one of the boys added. "He said, 'Next time.' "

"Have you thought about how you know these things?" I asked. "How the author made you know that without telling you directly?" No response, but they weren't rolling their eyes, which was a plus. "Have you ever heard the term *foreshadowing*?" They didn't groan the way kids do when they're asked to look at the craft behind the story captivating them.

I felt something akin to a tickle in the heart. This was going to be a good class. We'd have fun and learn a few things along the way—and that *we* included me.

This was all the more remarkable because it was the last period of the day. Post-lunch for them. I'd again missed my own. Pre-freedom for all of us. This hour is generally subject to both impatience and torpor, which is not a great combo, but here they were, working together as a group, and their sparks of intelligence ignited an active discussion that lasted until the bell interrupted, announcing the end of day.

As though the bell tolled for me—my mind instantly switched to the next hurdle: getting ready. I envisioned a marathon race, a movie in fast-forward as I cleaned and ironed and manicured and even marked papers and made up a quiz for Friday, so that I'd be ahead of the game and have time for Gabby and Boy. I'd had such a good time last period that I'd barely had time to think about the impending visit, which was high testimony to the quality of my ninth graders. But now, the Mackenzies' road-weary car—it had already visited four others of their scattered offspring—crashed into my classroom and my brain.

The room emptied. A few boys nodded discreetly as they made their exits. I took that as high praise, a thumbs-up. I was going to be allowed to live. "This was fun, Miss Pepper," Melanie said as she left. "But—" she leaned closer.

I felt a shudder of worry. She was going to mention evil. She was going to echo her mother.

"I think you'd want to know that you have this big ink stain on your sleeve," she said. "It's a real shame. It's a pretty blouse."

I was most assuredly not going to worry about her anymore.

And then the room was empty, except for Olivia, still placing her book in her backpack. I watched with mild amazement, because no able-bodied living human, aside from a mime, moves that slowly. I knew she spoke normally, she'd participated in class, and I wondered if she had a neurological problem. "Olivia?"

She looked up—slowly. "Sorry," she said. "You can go. I . . ."

"Need some help?"

She looked startled, inappropriately frightened by my question, then silently shook her head.

"Are you all right?"

She switched her head shakes to nods.

"Then I have to lock up, so—"

"Could I stay a while? I won't touch anything."

How could I explain that this was not the day to deal with idiosyncratic desires—or serious mental problems, except for my own. She was tiny and she looked windblown, inside the room, as if a secret storm had set her quaking. Much as I hate admitting it, it's never a great sign, and surely not a normal sign, if a student isn't eager to leave my room.

"Wish I could let you, but I'd be in big trouble if I did that," I said. "What is it? Are you well?"

She nodded.

"Then is something frightening you—something out there? Somebody?"

She sighed and shook her head, then she stood up abruptly. She was small and boyish, almost hidden—or hiding—inside her baggy clothing. "I'm sorry. I'll leave now."

"Tell you what," I said. "Would it be all right if I walked out with you? How do you get home?"

"The bus. On the corner."

"Would you keep me company? You're on the way to my car."

She blinked, then shrugged. "Okay, I guess."

She'd be safe and save face, because everyone would assume she was in some kind of trouble—with me. Why else would anyone be near a teacher when she didn't have to be?

I steeled myself against all manner of real and imagined Olivia-demons, but absolutely nothing threatened or seemed out of place. No stalkers, no cars idling, no derogatory calls, not even an embarrassing whistle or insult, and finally, the bus arrived and Olivia climbed on.

I turned away, glad for the anticlimax, and nearly smacked into a petite woman it took me a moment to recognize.

"Oh, no," I said. "I told you on the phone—I'm in a rush. Not today. There's nothing to say, anyway."

"Please. I'm desperate!"

I believed that she'd once been an actress. A good one, too—and she still was. "Maybe some other time."

"There isn't any other time. I'm sure I'll be—they're going to—please. I feel as if . . . my whole life—you have to help me."

"Help you?" I didn't know what to say. Help her? What was wrong with this picture? Claire Fairchild was dead. Emmie Cade's husband was dead. A former fiancé was dead, too. The people who got close to her needed help, not her.

"You think I'm evil."

Evil. Such an old-fashioned word, a pre-Freudian word, but obviously back in popularity. This was the second person in as many days to present me with the idea of evil. "I have no opinion of you," I lied. "I don't even know you."

"You were investigating me. Maybe you still are. I'm sure you've heard bad things, but they aren't true." She spoke softly, but *they aren't true* sounded strained, as if she wanted to scream them. "I have to convince somebody that they aren't true." Her calm façade crumbled as she spoke, and she waved her hands, pushing off her phantom "bad things."

I was painfully aware that we were standing on the corner, smack on the busy sidewalk of a midtown street, and students who passed stared openly. "This isn't the best place," I said softly.

"Where is, then?" she said. "I waited outside here for you. I only—I feel as if—"

Her stammering felt fake and annoying. In fact, I couldn't stand the entire situation. I had things to do, a life of my own and no time to be segmented and pulled apart.

"It has to be now." Her voice had regained calm and a new solidity. "Now."

"No, it doesn't. I'm sure you have your reasons, but I honestly cannot—"

"If somebody was poisoned, and you could save them, but you were really busy right now—and I don't doubt that you are—all the same, would you wait until it was convenient for you to see them? They could be dead by then!"

But the nonhypothetical person was already dead. Odd she should pick the poison analogy.

And maybe this business was not for me. Could you imagine either Nick or Nora ignoring the damsel in distress—or the femme fatale—whatever this shape-shifting woman was—because they had to prepare for their in-laws? I sighed, reconsidered, and admitted that my priorities were slightly skewed. "Can you be quick, please?" I finally asked. "I wish I were exaggerating about how pressed for time I am, but I'm not."

"I'd like to think that I'm as important as any other case you're investigating," she said quietly.

I was flattered. In her eyes, once I left the schoolhouse, zap, I was instant P.I.-woman. "You are, of course," I said, "but the truth is, this isn't my case anymore. Our investigation is over. The client died."

"That's just it! It isn't over. Can't be, with that—what they said, and you never had time to find out who I really am. You only heard bad things."

I pulled back a step.

"Didn't you?"

"Tell me what's on your mind. I don't have time for games, and I'm going to my car in five minutes." I checked my watch and made sure she saw me doing it. It also reminded me that I truly meant what I was saying. Ready, set, go.

She looked around, clearly wishing for a more intimate spot and for time to present her case. "If we could find a—"

"Can't. Here and now, or not at all. Five minutes—less the time we're wasting."

"It's that I don't know how to say it because I don't know what's going on."

"You need to talk to me but you don't know what to say?"

"How to."

"Try. One word, then another. The way you usually would."

She blinked, then she looked down, at the tips of her chic, polished shoes. "People don't like me," she said, head still lowered.

I might have expected this of a teenager. Or the poor child Lily, who'd tried to kill herself because of perceived unpopularity. Or from me, those months in sixth grade, but not from an adult, and a near-stranger. "I'm not a mental health worker. I can't help your personal problems."

"You're proving my point. You don't like me, either. Do you? And you don't even know me. I'm not talking about not being invited to the prom. People like me that way—but then something happens. Like it did with Leo's mother. People—for no reason—get bad ideas about me."

"Hey, Miss Pepper! Don't you ever go home?" a student called out as a gaggle of girls walked by. I waved and returned my attention to Emmie Cade's poor, pitiable-me routine.

She hadn't turned to see who'd spoken and didn't react to the mild interruption. She was completely engrossed in her own woes.

"Why are you telling me this?" I asked, although I had a working theory of what she was up to. She knew we'd found out about her various and sundry dead consorts, the mystery surrounding her recent and untimely widowhood, and this was damage control. A helpless, girlie variety of same.

"Mrs. Fairchild told Leo she'd heard bad things she wanted to check out. Bad things about me. But what? Why? Who said them? I'm an ordinary person, trying my best. Bad things happen *to* me, but that can't be what she meant. I've had bad luck with men, but now, with Leo, I thought—" She tilted her head and looked at me, her expression pure needy appeal.

That was probably the method she'd used so effectively several times already. Maybe with guys, she threw in more eye-batting and perhaps even a tear.

She read my face—or, at least, my lack of response—and her expression melted down into resignation. Despair. "I'm afraid you heard something damaging to me," she said, her voice soft and tremulous. "I'm afraid that since Mrs. Fairchild died so unexpectedly—"

"When a person's killed, it's generally unexpected." It was mean to say that, to watch fear return to her face, but I hated what she was trying to do with me.

"And I'm so afraid! What will the police think when they know she suspected me of . . . I don't even know what. But that she was investigating me—and then this happens." She blinked fast, as if holding back tears, and shook her head briskly, telling her own self not to cry. "The worst part is—I don't know why this keeps happening. Why don't people like me? Why do they think such awful things?"

I had no answer. Or, more accurately, I thought the answer was lodged in a cliché somewhere—where there's smoke, et cetera. When she was always the last person standing—and when so many had fallen—one had to worry. But even I, Amanda Cruella, wouldn't say that out loud. She looked so fragile now, and even though I knew it was a practiced pose, part of her repertoire of endearing stances, I was sure a harsh word could shatter her.

"What should I do?" she asked. "How do I stop this? How do I set the record straight?"

"I honestly don't think there is a *record*, but I guess if I were you, I'd wait until somebody, somewhere said something directly to you. And then I'd be honest."

"Can't I hire you? You could find out why this keeps happening to me."

"I'm sure there's a serious conflict of interest there," I said, sure of nothing of the sort. It felt as if there should be a conflict—but with whom? On what basis?

She accepted the idea. "Then could you help me just because—because I'm a decent human being and I'm in trouble?"

"Calm down. You aren't making sense."

"Why did she suspect me? What did she suspect me of?"

"Who?"

"Mrs. Fairchild—your employer. What were you investigating?"

"You."

"I know that. Leo told me. But why? What did she think? What bad things did she hear? From whom? How?"

"It doesn't matter now."

"It does! Who else heard whatever it was? And why is this happening? I left San Francisco because it had started back there. There was this . . . buzzing. That I'm a . . . that I did horrible things. I ran as far as I could get, but three thousand miles away—it's happening again. This behind-my-back—but as fast as I turn around, nobody's there." She looked wide-eyed and terrified, even though her words were fairly well organized. I didn't trust her or her claims of being afraid.

"I'm sorry you're going through this, but I do believe that ultimately, the truth, whatever it is, will out."

It was her turn, after pressing almost too close to me the whole time, to step back now, and turn herself into a vaguely amused sophisticate. "You believe that," she said slowly.

I nodded.

"It's so naïve. I'm surprised. I thought you were savvier. Understood more about the world."

"Look, whatever it is—" I felt awful sounding as if I didn't know about the rumors. She might be guilty of a multitude of crimes, but somebody else was, in fact, spreading the word. Somebody, or several somebodies—the post offices had been scattered—had mailed damning notes to Claire Fairchild. Had worked to craft them, to find the information, to post them. Emmie Cade's suspicions were grounded in reality. What I didn't know for sure was whether the accusations were grounded in reality as well. "It's only rumor, you say. Sticks and stones and all that. Ignore it."

"How can I?" Her voice rising, she reached out as she spoke, as if to grab my hand, to literally pull me over to her side. I stepped back and she caught herself, and clasped her hands together. "Mrs. Fairchild is dead." She sounded slightly out of breath, as if she were exercising. "She took medicine that killed her. She doesn't go out much. She doesn't shop. Somebody had to give it to her, then, right? I was there that night, and if they think I already . . ."

I waited.

"In San Francisco, my husband drowned. All the papers kept saying was what an expert yachtsman and sailor he was, and that's true. But they didn't say he was also an expert drinker. Not a drunk, not an alcoholic, I think, though I'm not sure, but a man who binged socially. It's easy to keep that under wraps when you have money and own your own company, even though it was pulling that down, too. I didn't really understand about it until after we were married, but I had hopes we'd get it more under control. We didn't.

"Instead, we got better at keeping it a secret. He'd get tipsy at parties, but then we'd leave. I'd drive or we'd take a taxi, or hire a limo service, and maybe he'd finish his drinking at home, where nobody except me would see it. He didn't always go into his office, even when he was around, and things there were sliding, so when I suggested that he was drunk that day . . ." She shuddered. "Why would I lie? His friends knew. Nobody suspected anything terrible then. It was sad—but not that much of a shock, even. They knew what had happened—and then it all turned around. His first wife, I think. She hates me. I understand. His kids hate me, too. Somebody, anyway, started these rumors, and suddenly the papers quoted people as saying—even people who'd been drunk with him lots of times—that he was a great guy, a regular pal—fun to be with, which he was, and that they were shocked about the drowning because he was such a good sailor."

"You're saying he fell overboard drunk?"

"Of course. And that's what the law thought—thinks—too. He wasn't wearing a life vest, and that's presented as highly suspicious— if you saw those news stories, or maybe you actually did, if you were checking out my past."

I didn't respond.

"Why is that suspicious? It's embarrassing, but not evil. He was—we were—I was in the . . . in our bedroom. I was below. He wanted to get another bottle of wine. He was . . . amorous. People don't wear life vests then."

"There were all those people—"

"Nobody around us. Just me and Jake in our own room. And that's taken to be suspicious, but if you understand the situation . . ."

I was listening to her as skeptically as I could manage, but also wondering whether listening at all was a good or stupid thing. Would Mackenzie compliment me for gathering additional information or would he say he couldn't believe I'd wasted so much time? Much more than five minutes had passed. He'd made it clear that we'd be lucky to be paid for what we'd already done—I had to remember that this semi-career was all about money—and we surely wouldn't be recompensed for standing on the corner talking with the prime suspect.

"I'm not a bad person," Emmie said. "I'm not saying I've been the most careful, or . . . or—" She waved her arms again, as if one of them might catch the missing word. "Sensible woman. I was . . . I don't know. Wild. And I made dumb choices. And sometimes I took the . . . easier way. If somebody offered to help me out . . . maybe I shouldn't have, but it was never really bad stuff. I liked the wrong guys. Except for Leo, now. He's different. He's solid. And, okay, I've done things that weren't . . . I was not a perfect little good girl. Or big girl. But none of that means I did the kinds of thing they're saying."

"Maybe they aren't saying anything. Or more likely, maybe nobody is listening to whatever somebody's saying."

"Mrs. Fairchild was."

"She was hoping I'd find nothing. She liked how happy her son was."

Emmie looked at me sideways, her mouth curled. "She hired you to check me out. That's not what I consider real friendly."

That reminded me of my own future mother-in-law, and I checked my watch.

"It's making me ill," she said. "I can't sleep without drugs—I can't eat—it's making me crazy and sick. That woman—that Batya—she says I killed Claire Fairchild with this little bunch of flowers I brought for her. Poor woman—I think she's snapped."

"I'm sorry," I said softly, and I meant it. I didn't know how people tied their lives up in knots this way.

"Can I talk with you again? Will you help me? Is there some way you could find out who's spreading these rumors?"

I knew they were more than rumors. They were newspaper reports, her actual track record. "I'll—I'll think about what's appropriate," I said. "And now I absolutely—"

"Thank you! Thank you for listening."

No matter how many doubts I had about whether she was a liar and a murderer, there was something undeniably winning and sympathetic about her. Mackenzie had reminded me that even the newspaper story was innuendo and supposition. "The Truth" as an absolute was nowhere to be seen, so maybe she was being victimized on a grand scale.

Or maybe she was an experienced—almost a professional—manipulator. Actress, seasoned fortune-hunter, experienced seductress. A siren, and I was a sucker. I made my way to my car, thinking only, now, of Gabby and Boy, Bea and Gilbert, and how I was going to handle the next few days. Countdown had begun, and I had enough to do to fill every one of those twenty-four hours.

Mackenzie should be home by now, cramming as much reading and classwork in as possible tonight so that he wouldn't feel pressured when his parents arrived.

We'd have time to talk while we cleaned together, later, but I wasn't sure I could wait that long to tell him about Claire Fairchild's unnatural death, and Emmie Cade's bizarre curbside appearance. In fact, I knew I couldn't. I unlocked the door to our loft and called out, "Study break time! Drop the books because you won't believe what—"

Three tall people stood up.

Impossible. Mackenzie had hired actors to scare me out of my wits. This was Wednesday. They were coming tomorrow. *Thursday.*

The two tall strangers grinned at me. They stood in the middle of the mess and chaos of my household, smiling. Or perhaps silently laughing at the pathetic situation.

I blinked.

They were still there.

"Noah's girl—" the balding one said.

"Clarissa," the Technicolor one added.

"Clarissa was invited to visit a friend, and Noah and Angela were driving her upstate, so we left a day early. No traffic, either."

"Besides, we were so excited about meeting you, honey! Come over and give a hug." She wore a shiny scarlet peasant-style blouse and dangling green and scarlet sparkling earrings, and she opened her arms wide. Her nails matched her earrings. Including the sparkles.

When he'd called his mother "colorful," I hadn't realized he meant it literally.

"Poor baby," she said. "You've got this huge blotch on your sleeve, did you know?"

"Meet the folks," Mackenzie said.

Fourteen

EITHER his parents called ahead from the road, or Mackenzie had suddenly become prescient. It was not in either of our natures to rush home from school and shop, straighten and polish, and yet, once my vision stopped flashing and crackling and my synapses returned to their usual connections, the tidiness of the loft registered.

I tried to not look surprised by anything. Not the untimely arrival of the senior Macks, at the passable condition of the gigantic room, or at the miraculous apparition of tortilla chips and salsa dip on the table.

C. K. Mackenzie's stock shot through the roof, rose so high, the entire world economy snapped back into high gear.

"She's just as pretty as you said she was," Boy Mackenzie told his son, giving him a congratulatory whomp on the shoulder. Boy's boy had found a good 'un.

I knew it was a compliment, and I knew I had to look pleased, but I really didn't love being talked about—in fact, being weighed and measured and judged—in the third person while I stood there, still encircled by Gabby Mackenzie's arms.

The woman was a world-class hugger. I could barely find the breath to smile in response to Boy's appraisal of me. She finally released her grip, but held on to my arms. "She certainly is that," she said. "Pretty as can be."

I wondered where they thought I actually was and when they'd decide to speak directly to me. "Thank you," I said softly, absolutely hating this. Visions of Miss Swamp filled my head, with me next to her as the "before" image. My lipstick had worn off hours ago, and I hadn't combed my hair since lunchtime. It didn't bear thought. At least I could blame the ink stain on fate, not bad grooming. "And now if you'll excuse me, I'll change into something clean and—"

"Nonsense!" C. K.'s mother said, leaning back—still holding me—and smiling broadly. "You look fine."

I did not look fine. Or *fahn*. They were Southern. Of course they'd say I looked wonderful. I had to ask Mackenzie what they said when they were alone, what proportion of any conversation was close to sincere and how much was automatic pilot. Of course, despite his rapid acclimation to Philadelphia, he was still a Southerner, too. He'd lie graciously along with his folks.

Meanwhile, he was looking at me with controlled eye signals that I interpreted to mean, "What did you mean when you came in the door, babbling?" while I was trying to blink, in code and eye squeezes, "Claire Fairchild was murdered!"

Good thing nobody tried our codes in wartime. Didn't work. We looked like people with eye disease.

I took a deep breath and filed Emmie Cade and Claire Fairchild away until appropriate, and focused on my future family members. I let go of trivialities like murder and murderers, and made room for my hitherto unsuspected inner Southerner. At once, sharp edges softened, the light in the loft grew golden and life simpler. I gestured for everyone to sit down again, settled myself near Gabby Mackenzie, smiled, said, "Help yourself to this lovely looking salsa"—said it more than once, to tell the truth—and then said, "Tell me about your trip! You've gone so far and done so much, you must have had all sorts of adventures!" The exclamation points that dotted each sentence's end came from a surprising and inexhaustible wellspring of acute hostessing and, to my amazement, each little ! sparked smiles and conversation, so we were off and running.

Gabby was well nicknamed, but unlike my father, Boy was an equal partner in storytelling. They finished each other's sentences, interrupted, corrected, laughed, and continued on, so that their combined narrative of far-flung children, grandchildren, homes, pets, and picnics broke the ice and, by some sleight of hand, pulled me into the great swarming mass of Mackenzies where, to my surprise, I almost felt comfortable.

But Claire Fairchild's death intruded, despite my best wishes. And Emmie Cade's paranoia. Murder will out, or at least seep its vivid stain into an otherwise pastel, pleasant conversation. What had happened to Mrs. Fairchild in the middle of the night? Who had happened?

And when I forced myself away from them again, back into the present and the warm family glow—my parents intruded themselves. This was not a mix that was going to work. Not even if Gabby and Boy spoke nonstop, which, apparently, was pretty much what they did. My mother would know they needed to catch their breath sometimes, and she'd be ready to pounce with her two cents.

She wasn't mean-spirited, and she meant well, but without knowing her specific agenda (though I feared it involved Handel, bouquets, and the phrase "I do"), I knew that introducing her would be like putting a tree limb into the spokes of a moving bicycle. Trees and their limbs are nice. There are, nonetheless, situations they don't help.

"You've got to hear this, Manda," Boy said, pulling my focus back into the room. I hoped my expression hadn't been too remote. "Porter's boys have these dogs, these dogs that—"

Gabby burst out laughing. "Stop, stop immediately, you terrible man! I can't bear—they are the worst behaved, most adorable things—"

I should make it clear hereabouts that I have, from time to time, thought Mackenzie's accent rendered him nearly unintelligible. But he tries. And he's been in Philadelphia long enough to have clipped off some of those open-ended vowel sounds that once clouded his words. For my part, I'd retrained my ears and I can make out what he's saying most of the time, although the more emotional he gets, the blurrier his syllables become. Most of the time, that doesn't matter. As long as I'm sharing the emotion, who cares what he's saying?

But his parents were another matter. I had to assume everything they said—and they said so very much—mattered. I would only seem intelligent if I understood why they laughed so often, and it was in my best interests to comprehend what they were telling me about this family I was joining.

Given my years of training with their son, I could understand them, but only by puzzling it through, which left me a beat behind. I felt as if I were running after phrases, grappling them to the ground, pulling off all the fuzz and sugarcoating and only belatedly saying, "Aha! Gotcha." And then, leaping up to gallop after the next batch that had gone sliding by.

Word-wrangling was exhausting. The good side was that it left me precious little time to think about Claire Fairchild and to appreciate my mother, whose words, however infuriating they could be, were spoken in my Yankee mother tongue.

"You would think," Boy said, "that they had enough on their

hands with two sets of twins, so that they'd make sure their dogs behaved, because those kids surely don't. . . ." He smiled the whole time he said it, obviously enjoying his grandchildren's mischief. Perhaps, even the dogs'.

"Made me miss my babies, though," Gabby said.

This time when I captured the words, I did a mental double take. Babies? The woman was a veritable goddess of fertility, but her eight babies were strapping adults now. And if she meant her grandchildren, why miss them when she'd been visiting them? Maybe she missed the dozens back in Louisiana?

Mackenzie saw my expression. "These days, Mama calls her dogs her babies," he said. "Speakin' of lummoxy ill-behaved creatures."

Boy laughed again. "That's so they'll remind her of her real babies. Besides, the dogs mean well. Can't say that for the kids. On the other hand, the kids were pretty smart, and Gabby's babies—frankly, this might not be politically correct—"

"I'm not sure dogs are into that yet, Dad," C. K. said.

"Well, our two—they are mentally challenged, I swear."

Gabby waved her spangled fingers at him. "The poor dears."

"The poor stupid dears," Boy said.

"What are their names?" I asked, to make conversation. I was already deluged with names. Eight kids, six current spouses, three or four formers, and nine million grandchildren. Enough. But names were easier to follow than narratives.

"Cary Grant and Katharine Hepburn," Gabby said.

Of course.

"Finally named something for the actors themselves, not the roles they played," C. K. said.

His parents—or his mother, most likely—enraptured by the actors, had named C. K. and his siblings after the roles and personas they had played. They were always good people and, most often, super-rich, imaginary wealthy relatives with whom she gifted her children. My poor guy, named for C. K. Dexter Haven, the loveable wastrel in *The Philadelphia Story*, didn't even get a full name. I must say, however, I'm glad she opted for the C. K. part rather than the Dexter.

With the dogs, however, she'd finally gone for the real thing.

"Poor Cary needs his medication twice a day, and I'm so worried that dizzy little girl will forget."

"He's epileptic," Boy said.

"Really? I didn't know dogs had epilepsy," I said.

"Not uncommon," Boy said.

"Poor baby," Gabby repeated. "I worry all the time Lizzie will forget the medicine and he'll have another seizure."

"Now, Gabby," Boy said. "Lizzie's taken care of your babies before, and she always does a good job."

"But we've been gone so long this time." She sighed.

"They'll be fine, Mom," C. K. said, and the talk drifted back to human Mackenzies.

I was running so hard after their words that it took me longer than it should have to realize that neither Gabby nor Boy ever gave a sign of passing judgment on their large clan, except to laugh at their antics. Not a flick of a mouth, a squint of the eye, an inflection in the words. They were amused by, or surprised by, or confused by, people—related to them or not—but I didn't see a frown of disapproval, or the heavy silences of disappointment. I didn't even feel the prodding finger of expectation.

I didn't dare think about this in contrast to my mother—but I couldn't help myself. She didn't precisely disapprove—but she always had an agenda, a next step, and was eager to move you on to it. So if she'd been here, and in fact, when she did arrive, instead of happily spinning wheels as we were now doing, instead of enjoying the fact of the engagement and the new relationships, she'd be pushing and pulling, tugging and entreating. Move on! Move on! Most likely, at such time as I actually do feel ready to marry C. K., immediately after he kisses the bride, my mother will step up with her imaginary clipboard and say, "Okay, now you're married. Time for children. How many? When?"

Maybe Gabrielle Mackenzie would be able to change the tempo, keep it easy the way it was now. I watched with pleasure as she used the whole of her arms to animate her sentences, and each time I was amazed by her dazzling, glitter-dusted fingernails. The woman had never had money, and without it and the help and comforts it could have provided, she raised eight children of her own, plus numerous strays and, according to her son, did it with laughter and few complaints. I hadn't believed him about the non-complaints, but I was a believer now. She was a hardworking, kind-hearted woman with a comic vision of life.

Even her fingernails were laughing, in their own way. Those hands that had scrubbed and nursed and tied shoelaces and brushed hair and ironed and mended—those hands had been given their Emancipation Proclamation by their owner. Each red and green and silver nail celebrated its accomplishments and, at the same time, waved as flags of freedom, announcing that these hands were on vacation from soapy dishwater and scrub brushes.

I decided then and there that I liked her and, more than that, I admired her.

This was going to work out. At least when my mother wasn't around.

Gabby took a two-inch-thick packet of snapshots out of her pocketbook. "Meet the family," she said, passing them to me. She leaned close and pointed a spangled nail at a face and named it, one after the other. I tried memorizing what Noah looked like and what color hair Phoebe had, and which child belonged to which adults, but there were too many, and none of them looked related to the other. I tried the same method I used in the classroom, matching names with hair color, nose size, freckles, height, jug-ears and buck teeth—anything that marked a person's face as his own and none other. So Noah was dark-haired and relatively short and married to Angela, a woman who looked as if she ran miles every day; and Porter was a strawberry blonde—going bald—and tall and married, for the second time to the same woman, Myra, who was sharp-featured and dark-haired, and they had two sets of twin boys and two badly behaved dogs; and Lutie was slender and elfin and had surely been told lots of times that she resembled Audrey Hepburn, and had been married three times already, and was on the verge of a fourth merger, most likely also doomed, they calmly acknowledged. The marriages had been worth it, Gabby said, because they produced three equally elfin and exquisite grandbabies. "Her new beau is handsome. I'll say that for him. So who knows what kind of adorable baby they'll produce?"

I'm not saying it was a great attitude, or even a sane one. I'm simply saying it was refreshing and easy to be around.

I didn't even try for any of the dozens of children's names. They lived all over the country and weren't likely to drop in, so that could wait.

I murmured my admiration of each and every shot.

"A motley bunch, aren't they?" Gabby said. "Never could figure out why they all look as if we spotted them sitting by the side of the road and snapped them up and took them home."

And in truth, except for his rangy height, I couldn't see any resemblance between Mackenzie and his parents, or between him and his siblings as a group. I liked the idea of a tight clan of people who looked as if they should barely know each other.

Boy took a small notebook out of his pocket. "So here's the tally," he said with great satisfaction. "Two thousand, nine hundred fifty-four miles so far this trip. Decent mileage, too. Twenty-four on the highways—"

"Zero to five all the times he refused to ask directions and we spent hours and hours lost—you would not believe how many times," Gabby said, and then she laughed. If he was from Mars and she was from Venus, they'd found an intermediate planet where they could cohabit and enjoy the view all around them.

C. K. took his father's detour into driving adventures as a signal it was time to move on. Literally. "What shall we do about dinner?" he asked politely. "What tickles your fancy? I'm sure you noticed that we live in a trendy, cutting-edge neighborhood."

His animated parents went blank. Reading body language and

facial expressions was easier than deciphering their speech, so I knew instantly they had donned polite Southern masks to hide the fact that they knew their son was protecting them from the ugly truth: This neighborhood, their faces said, was pathetic, but how brave of you to pretend otherwise.

We live in Old City, which was, along with Society Hill, where Philadelphia began on the banks of the Delaware River. In the nineteenth century it grew to be the center of manufacturing. When that moved on, people like us moved in, converted the warehouses, put in and supported galleries, cafés, and excellent restaurants. Our loft had once been the top floor of an Oriental rug warehouse. Today, an art gallery occupied the ground floor.

But I realized how provincial I was about it. I knew its value, and its place in the city's geography and history, but C. K.'s parents might see it otherwise. Their poor children lived in one room in an abandoned warehouse. They couldn't even afford the normal amount of interior walls. The neighborhood was sadly deficient in greenery, just like everything they'd heard about Northern slums. There was no front porch or garden, only skylights and oversized windows that viewed other former factories.

"There's a Spanish restaurant, a Turkish, sushi, seafood—what would you like?" C. K. asked.

"We did our research," Boy said. "Went to the Automobile Association, found out everything about this city. And, we read all about it on the Internet. So if it's all right, we'd like to go a little more native than your ideas."

"You want Pepper Pot Soup," C. K. said, "in honor of Ms. Pepper here. And an old Philadelphia tradition dating back to when General George Washington and the Continental Army were out in Valley Forge and near starvation. The cook only had scraps of tripe and some peppercorns, but he made a good enough soup to keep them going till they won the war."

A two-second and definitely suspect culinary-based explanation of the Revolution. "Pure tripe," I said.

He took that as verification, not as an insult. "Tripe was what saved the day," he said. "Everybody knows an army travels on its stomach."

Meanwhile, Gabby stepped back, as if horrified that she'd offended me. "We didn't make the Pepper connection, honey."

"No, no," I said. "It isn't my—"

"Hell, we didn't know about it at all," Boy added. "It wasn't on those Web sites. What is it?"

"Do you think the fact that it's made of an ox's stomach lining has anything to do with being left off the list of must-eats?" I asked. "We aren't known for our cuisine."

"Scrapple, then," Mackenzie said.

"Named for my aunt, Gladys Scrapple," I said. "Just joking. And that isn't what you want, either. First of all, it's a breakfast dish. And second—there is no second. No."

"Philadelphia is famous for good eats," Mackenzie said.

"You're—that's not nice," I said. "Just because you were raised in the land of fabulous foods."

"And you, in the land of—"

"Scrapple. As in scraps." I said. "The pieces of meat nobody wants, like ears and feet and gums and—"

"Oh, my, how . . ." Gabby was trying to be polite and gracious about eating animal noses, but she nonetheless waved away the idea with a flash of green and red fingernails.

"And—then it's spiced up and held together by lard," I said. "Are you really suggesting that isn't more yummy than beignets?"

"Crawfish étoufée?" Mackenzie said, grinning.

"Bananas Foster?" Boy added.

"Oysters Louisiana?" Gabby said.

"*Hoagies,*" Boy said. "That's what we read about and that's what we came for tonight. Is there a restaurant like that in this neighborhood?"

Sometimes, there is a little extra-Manda sitting in the corner, laughing hysterically at the parallel life she intended to take. I'd wanted so to appear competent in front of my beloved's parents. We'd made extensive plans for their arrival. Beth was even at this

177

moment orchestrating and prepping for an exquisitely designed meal for the next evening. I had intended at the very least to have clean and organized hair, and no stain on my blouse.

I suppose all that translates into a need to feel in charge of my destiny, or at least in control of something. But here I was, stained, mussed, and taken by surprise. I gave in to it. I accepted reality.

Gabby and Boy—and C. K.—were from the land of laissez-faire. I decided to let go and enjoy the evening. Be Southern and thank you, Scarlett. Tomorrow would be time enough to be hyper-aware of what I wasn't thinking about, but should be.

Hoagies would be fine. Different colors of cholesterol sliced and oiled and stuffed into a roll. What's not to like?

"Great, then," Gabby said. "We're off to the races, and darlin' "— she gave my shoulder a friendly, nonpainful pinch—"while we munch, you and I can talk about dates."

"Dates?" I was engaged, I didn't date anymore, and surely she— no. Couldn't be.

"Here's what I was thinking," she said. "Lutie's having her wedding back home, so why not combine the two? I know it's her fourth and your first, but that shouldn't matter, should it? It's still a wedding, and that way, everybody's already gathered together. His family's rowdy, I hear, but you know, ours can get that way, too. And with your parents in Florida, almost next door, and the savings of a double wedding . . ."

I barely heard the rest of the details, and there were lots. Gabby Mackenzie had figured it all out. My audio portion returned when I heard her say, "I already have my dress—the cutest thing. Made it myself and did a fine job, if I say so myself. I hope stripes are all right. You like chartreuse or fuchsia? You're not going to get all fussy about color schemes and things like that? You know, when— who was it, Boy? The first of our boys to marry—"

"Noah," he said.

"Right. When Noah was getting married, I read that the mother of the groom is supposed to do two things: Keep her mouth shut, and wear beige. But darlin', do I have to tell you I do not fit that pattern?"

I thought maybe I'd just curl up inside my head and stay there.

". . . how about it?" she said.

I looked up through the skylight, wishing to lodge a formal complaint with whoever was in charge up there. The one who was laughing himself silly. I know I'd said I'd relinquish control, but I only meant about my hair and my blouse. Not my wedding—an event I wasn't ready for, in any case.

I half turned, and caught Mackenzie's expression. He's good at hiding his feelings, which served him well as a homicide detective, but either he'd changed with his new life as student, or his mother had the power to melt his adult traits the way my mother could with me. In any case, he was watching us, his mouth half open, its shape somewhere between a smile and a cry for help.

"It sounds wonderful," I heard myself say. "And so thoughtful of you, too! But the fact is—"

What's the fact? Quick, quick!

"My sister—you'll meet her tomorrow—is already planning the wedding. That's her profession, you see. It's all set."

Mackenzie's mouth was now three-quarters open. "Wanted to surprise you all," I said. "Didn't we, darlin'?"

He nodded. "We were goin' to tell all of you, Amanda's parents as well. Tomorrow."

"Well, that's wonderful, then. When's the big date, then?" Gabby Mackenzie said, completely happy about everything.

"Christmas," Mackenzie said.

My turn to stare, mouth hanging open.

"We're both on vacation from school then."

"Christmastime." I nodded, amazed I could still move my head, because it felt as if a brick had just been tossed against it.

Not only had I started actually marching down the aisle, but worse: I'd given myself the push. I'd been intent on manning the barricades through my mother's visit. I'd planned to spend every minute in active, alert resistance, explaining why marriage was im-possible at this time. I was ready and able to defend my right to refuse, to establish my own timetable for major life steps, to hold my ground till she retreated.

I might as well phone and tell her to cancel her trip.

She'd already visited. She was already here.

I had become my mother.

Fifteen

C. K.'s parents apparently had boundless energy, and our hoagie and Italian ice fiesta lasted too late for a working day. By the time we bid adieu and Gabby and Boy headed off for their hotel, C. K.'s voice was strained as he muttered calculations about when he could fit in the missed reading he'd intended to do this afternoon.

I had great pity for him, but an equally urgent need to tell him about Claire Fairchild and Emmie Cade. I'd worried earlier about whether he'd be upset about the time I'd spent with Emmie. Instead, he was upset about the time I was going to take telling him about it. But through his yawns and despite his loving looks toward

181

his books, he made a phone call to a buddy he'd worked with in homicide.

I heard him talking softly for a long while, with lots of half-laughs and many names, some of which I recognized, and then he said, "I'll be here. Yeah, till late. Thanks," and hung up.

"Tom's checking," he said. Then he yawned and settled in at the oak table that serves as an auxiliary desk. It has the best light in the house with its overhead lamp, and it's closest to the coffeepot, so it's his main post, and at this hour and this level of exhaustion, he was going to need all the help bright light and caffeine offered.

He tried to study while we waited, and I tried to allow him to do so, but I didn't succeed, and therefore, neither did he. Just because we couldn't yet talk about Claire Fairchild's death with any assurance didn't mean there was nothing left to discuss.

"Do you think your parents liked me?" I asked.

He looked unduly surprised by my question, then he pulled out all the stops and flowed with fulsome Southern praise and reassurance. "Of *course* they did. Wasn't it obvious? What about all that laughing, and hugging, and literally clutching you to their bosoms? How about all that talk about your bein' their new daughter and all? Those welcome-to-the-family lines?"

He was so emphatic that I didn't believe a word, which meant I had to ask for lots more words. I had to ask about how "truth" was defined in the former Confederacy, and what percentage of a Southern smile could be considered sincere.

He finally drew a deep breath that might have also been a profound sigh, and once the air had circulated through him down to his feet and back up and out again, he said, "And should Southerners trust Middle Atlantic sincerity?"

"We're not as nice, Mackenzie. So sure."

"Like about dates? Like about weddin' dates?"

"Oh. That."

"How's that? I could barely hear you."

And I could barely muster up a complete voice. I sounded like a mouse in an animated cartoon. "You think your mother took it seriously?"

"You kiddin'? She marked the date and, like she said, she already has the dress, so I think we're gettin' married during winter break. An' she absolutely cannot wait to talk with your mother."

Despite the warmth still clinging from the day, I felt chilled. I looked at the man under the hanging lamp and knew that I loved him, and that he was the person I wanted to be with.

Everything up to this point felt familiar. Meeting, dating, dating more, living together. Even being engaged was more or less part of the continuum—a sort of intensified going steady.

But marriage! Terra incognita. I had wanted to wait until I'd thought the word through long enough to fray it, make it a comfortable fit, and I would have, except for my big mouth.

"I think it's a great idea," Mackenzie said. "An' why not? I mean what I'm saying, despite my roots in the South." Even so, he looked enormously relieved when the phone interrupted further discussion of our impending nuptials, and he answered it before it completed its first full ring. This time he mostly listened, nodding, making um-hmm noises, saying things like, "An' I thank you for that," "Who could have heard?" and "Interestin'." And then, after a pause, a chuckle, he said, "We'll be even. No, I mean it this time," and he clicked off the phone.

"Yes?" I asked. "That took forever. Is the poison's name the longest word in the English language? Or was that your mother telling you how much she really didn't like me?"

"It was phenobarbital."

"Who?"

"It was Tom, tellin' me the drug in the bloodstream was phenobarbital. A pretty common, legal drug."

"She took so many different pills—did she simply overdose on that one?" I remembered about the box and the premeasured amounts going into every cubby, but despite such aids, people get confused, disoriented, and accidentally overdose.

Mackenzie shook his head. "Not possible. It's used for a lot of things—including as a downer for overcharged speed freaks, amphetamine junkies. So it's on the street, and anybody could have gotten some without going through a doctor. Officially, it's used, short-term, for things like insomnia or anxiety—kind of a tranquilizing sedative—but it depresses the respiration, so somebody who already has respiratory problems—well, it's obvious. It'd never be prescribed, because it does what it did to Claire Fairchild. Slowly stops the breathing altogether and permanently."

"So, it truly was murder, not a heart attack and not an accident."

"And not missed this time," Mackenzie said.

"What does that mean?"

"The obvious. Lots of deaths like this get missed. The doctor decides it's natural and nobody checks. Person's buried, end of story. Pathologists love to say: 'If there was a light burning on every grave of a murder victim, our cemeteries would be illuminated brightly at night.' "

I was chilled by the image and its meaning.

"Okay, now?" he asked, and with great show, he pulled the text closer to him and picked up a highlighter.

But it wasn't okay yet. I replayed what he'd said and found myself stuck on something he'd skipped right over. "Insomnia."

"I could use some insomnia," he said. "Maybe then I'd get this reading done."

"Emmie told me she can't sleep. She takes something."

"Manda, there are so many sleeping pills . . . half the world can't sleep when they want to. Now me? I could. I could right now within ten seconds, but I have to study instead. 'Sides, think about it. Would she tell you outright she was on a drug to sleep if she'd poisoned somebody with it?"

"Have you met her?" I asked.

He looked puzzled, and shook his head. "Why?"

"Just wondering." I'd been sure he was so blinded by her sweet and innocent façade that he couldn't believe any wrong of her. I was determined not to be, but now I wondered whether my refusal to judge her on face value was pushing me in the opposite direction.

"Tom said it's used for kids with seizures, and far as I know, we don't have a kid on our list of suspects. Fact is, we don't have a list. Further fact is, whatever happened and how is none of our business. An' Tom said he'd let me know if and when anything significant comes up. This," he waved toward his textbook, "this, however, is now my business."

"Wait," I said. "One second more is all. Something you said . . ." My tired brain tried to sift through piles and mismatched scraps, but levers and gears felt rusted out, or perhaps buried under hoagie layers, and I pawed through my mental archives at less than warp speed.

"I really need to—"

"There's something I should be remembering."

"About phenobarb?"

"Maybe. No. About who takes it—wait—"

"You keep saying *wait* and I do, I am, but nothing happens."

"That's what *wait* means." I controlled the urge to say *wait* again, because it was so close, almost there—and then it was— "Batya's child is sick."

"She had that baby today?"

"There's an older one. A sick one. Her aunt takes care of him. She told us, remember?"

"What does bein' sick mean? Kids get sick. He could have a head cold. He could have an allergy to seafood. He could have a harelip or typhoid fever. Listen, Manda, I've done my bit—against my better judgment. I found out what there is to know, and now, I can't talk anymore. I either read this stuff now, or skip dinner with the folks tomorrow."

I ignored the threat. It was hollow, anyway. "She kept saying sick baby, or the like. It sounded more serious and chronic than a head cold."

"An' Batya struck me as a hysteric."

"She's got big-time problems. She's a virtual prisoner there."

"Was. But about her child? Did she say he has seizures?"

I shook my head. "She said something about the cost of his medicine."

"It could be nothin' more than chicken pox."

"She had motive, Mackenzie. Mrs. Fairchild said she was leaving her money in her will but pretty much giving her nothing while she was alive."

"Stupid tactic," he muttered.

Batya put the pills in their proper cubbies. It would be so easy to substitute the murderous medication for a regular prescription.

It would be easy for anyone to do so. I was back to square one. And speaking of that, "Who called 9-1-1?" I asked. "Did you ask? They have records, right? They always know who called it in."

He blinked and looked up at me, frowned, and seemed to reel in my words, as if they'd missed their mark but were still hovering in the ether, awaiting delayed entry to his consciousness. "Oh, right," he finally said. "The doctor called it in." He put his elbows on the table and his attention on the page of his text, looking excited and challenged, like a champion swimmer about to make the plunge.

I stood up as an act of good faith. "I promise to shut up in a minute, but you need to explain, because there wasn't any doctor there."

He looked at me with distant recognition, then once again seemed to climb out of the book and rejoin me. "This is it, then?"

I nodded. I even meant it this time.

"There's this gizmo people with chronic lung disease use. Circular gizmo connected to the phone line. We saw it next to the bed, remember? You thought it was a lady's compact."

"She breathes into it, Batya said."

"She opens it up and breathes into one side of it and, through the miracle of modern medicine, the person monitoring it on the other end can analyze the velocity of her breath and know how her lungs are doing and what she needs in the way of medication."

"That's amazing. I mean that seriously. It tests how well her lungs are working through the phone lines?"

"Far as I understand these things. She has to do this a few times a day, and if the results are confusing, they'd ask her to try again, and that night, apparently the test breaths showed a downward spiral—less and less velocity."

"So it took a while. It took a long while for that drug to slowly stop her breathing."

"Guess so."

"And she probably didn't fully recognize what was going on, so it wasn't as if she called for help."

"But the doctor did," he said. "When the tests come back that way, they retest, and then they call the patient, they phone, because the medication needs adjustment, but, of course, nobody answered the phone."

"She was probably unconscious by then."

"Or dead."

"But where was Batya? Why didn't she answer the phone?"

He tilted his head. "You're really set on her, aren't you? Tom said there isn't a phone in the maid's room. Apparently, Mrs. Fairchild was afraid she'd call Romania, or wherever she's from. Plus, Batya says she was asleep by that hour."

"Or awake, but not interested in saving Claire Fairchild's life."

He ignored that. "And Claire Fairchild always kept the ringer turned down low. She could hear it, but it didn't carry. When the doctor got no response, he phoned 9-1-1. Now you know everything I know and pretty much everything the police know at this point and when they know more, you'll know, too. But that'll be it. Tom said if I cared all this much about a homicide, why'd I leave? I've used up my bargaining chips for a while." With great deliberation, he put his finger on a line of text and leaned forward to read it. But he looked up for one moment and said in a serious, weighted voice, "Let go of it. It's a police matter now, and we don't have any other option." He didn't wait for me to agree or promise or say I understood. He returned to his textbook with a relieved sigh.

I kept my thoughts to myself, but they kept me up even after I'd said goodnight. I registered the barb about our not needing further information about Claire Fairchild, but I couldn't understand how Mackenzie could just turn off interest in something like this, could be content to be that chapter in somebody else's story.

Maybe it was because I'd met everyone involved and he hadn't. Or maybe I was too new at investigating, becoming intimately involved in someone's life and concerns and then, at some externally determined signal, stepping back. Way back—out of sight and out of mind.

I wasn't built that way. Instead, I lay in bed staring at the high ceiling, thinking about Batya, Emmie, and Leo's stack of grievances against one ill elderly woman, trying not to think how easily any one of them could have killed her, and trying as well to ignore all that and build a case for what I wanted to believe, irrationally or not, which was that none of them had done this.

It was a long time before I could stop seeing brightly lit cemeteries and fall asleep.

Sixteen

I WAS exhausted the next day, and nagged by trivia such as the realization that I'd never ironed my linen suit. Even as I thought it, I also thought "who cares?" I'd already made a bad first impression. More importantly, I was surrounded by matters of life and death and love and marriage—and adolescent educations— and my wardrobe choice was a shameful concern.

And yet it was stuck in my mind, like a yellowing reminder on a corkboard.

I entered Philly Prep with one unworthy goal: to leave it as quickly as possible. Perhaps I could manage a brief nap at home before I faced the dual-family nightmare evening.

"Oh, you!" Sunshine called out. I'd gathered my meaningless notices and flyers, relieved to see there seemed no follow-up or second chapter to Mrs. Lawrence's flap about *Lord of the Flies*. "You popular thing, you!"

I looked around to see who she could mean, and she giggled. No other teachers were in the office at the moment. "You, silly! The word on the street is that there's a blogger or five saying good things about you!"

"Blogger?" Was this the verbal equivalent of her appalling shorthand?

She waved an *oh, go on with you* gesture, as if I'd committed a witticism. "*You* know. They think you're sharp, so you must know about Weblogs."

"Who thinks . . . no. I'm confused."

She giggled again. I was an endless source of amusement to Sunshine, and I wondered why it annoyed me so much to be the generator of such joy. "Can't say who," she said. "I promised. So let's just say—"

I knew she was going to invoke a small avian creature. She didn't care how shopworn her clichés were. Blogger might be new, or at least new to me, but it would soon be old and she'd still be cherishing it. And now—

"A little bird told me. They think you're cute, too." And she giggled again. "You could be Miss Blogg of the year! If there only were one!"

"When you say 'they,' who do you mean? I don't want names, but are we talking about students?"

She nodded emphatically. "Lots of them have these Internet sites, you see, kinds of journals where they write their opinions of things and people—like you. Back to school and all, that's what they wrote about, and they like you."

"So far," I said. "We're four days into this semester."

"First impressions count!" she trilled.

"What else do they put on these sites?"

She shrugged. "Anything they want to. Just like any other diary."

"A diary everybody can read."

"And doesn't that make it fun?"

I thought that made it not a diary, but never mind.

"They talk about themselves, what they like . . . I had one for a while about my kitties because they're so dear. And each day I'd say cute things they did. And about my unicorn collection and when I found new ones and all, and I'd list links with other really good unicorn sites or blogs I really enjoyed. Things like that." She looked lovingly at the line of tiny creatures on the divider. "I put photos of them up and all . . . but then I got this job and, well, you know, I wouldn't say it to them, but I . . . kind of outgrew it, I guess."

"Blogging," I murmured. "Live and learn."

"Absolutely!" she said as if that was the newest, smartest phrase she'd ever heard.

I was popular! Finally! Blogs and bloggers liked me. I guessed that was nice news and I used it to keep me skating over the surface of the day. I had no intention of getting involved with my classes, as I was saving my emotions for the evening ahead.

The entire morning I accomplished this unworthy goal, ending with the juniors, who were about to embark on a research paper. I've done the "do not plagiarize" spiel so often, I went onto automatic pilot.

"News alert," I said. This part was indeed new, and I had to pay attention to what I was saying. "There's a spiffy program I can and will use that checks the entire Internet to see whether any sentence of your paper that makes me suspicious was copied. New technology for an old problem."

They looked stunned and disheartened. I wondered if my fans were in this class, and how soon I'd be voted out as a favorite of the gods. Favorite of the blogs, I should say.

"High tech or low, the penalty's the same. If you don't acknowledge the original source, you fail. So let's go over how to take notes and to give credit where credit is due." I heard a collective sigh, but I didn't feel a moment's qualms about making it hard and even painful to steal someone else's ideas. "If people don't footnote and attribute quotes and ideas, there's no way to check whether what you're being told is true or not. And this applies to the miracle of the Internet as well. Check their references before you accept whatever is written there as gospel truth. It's too often rumors or one person's opinion. Check the source."

And after a familiar demonstration of note taking and record keeping, it was lunchtime.

I decided to spend the hour out of doors, in the park across the way. I'd find a sandwich or the pretzel vendor. The day was sunny and crisp, with the sweet tang of impending autumn. A day to cherish and press into a keepsake book, and I wanted to be part of it. My need to leave had nothing whatsoever to do with the Square's proximity to Claire Fairchild's condo.

I was obviously not the only person heading for the great out of doors, and it took a while to merge with the lunchtime exodus. The stop-and-start human traffic and, perhaps, the clusters of whispering and giggling girls gave me time to remember that it was imperative that I speak with my sister.

Once outside, I stood near the school building at a polite distance from the students pouring out, and I made my call. As annoying as they are, I was once again grateful for the invention of the cell phone, which kept me from making my personal calls in front of the office staff. Even though Sunshine would never scowl, tap her foot, and check her watch the way our former secretary, or warden, had, I did not want her privy to my web of lies.

Even before I spoke a single word, I felt winded, as if I'd already jumped hurdles. Beth was sweet and serene. She'd pick our parents up at the airport in two more hours and, in the interim, she'd whipped up delicacies that would earn her toque at Le Cordon Bleu. "They'll love, love, love it all," I said. "Just the way they adored their hoagies last night."

"Where? Who? You said they were arriving today. Why were they here last night?"

"It had to do with Noah's daughter's sleepover, so don't ask." I told her the entire sordid tale, starting with my surprise introduction and rushing as quickly as I could toward and over my amazing, damning gaffe.

Beth squealed, and I knew she'd be applauding if she weren't holding the phone. Actually, I realized, those peeps, squeals, chuckles, and whoops were, indeed, the sound of one hand clapping.

"Would you tell Mom and Dad, then?" I asked. "I mean, before we all get there? So it looks as if you're breaking a brand-new secret?"

She agreed. "But Christmastime? Why then? Places are booked solidly and—"

"Beth, I don't care if it's in that mansion. Maybe it can even be postponed, or forgotten. And if not, it can be in our loft, which is not booked for the holidays. Or City Hall. I don't want to go to Louisiana and be half of Lutie Mackenzie's fourth wedding into a, quote, *rowdy*, unquote, family."

"Have you told Sasha yet?"

My friend Sasha was still partying her way through Great Britain. "You're the only person, aside from his parents who—"

"Better tell her soon. It's hard to get decent flights during the holidays."

"I cannot believe you're already working on the guest list," I said.

"Okay, okay. Just trying to make things easier on you."

"I realize that." I didn't mean my sigh to be as loud as it was.

"Don't worry about it," Beth said. "Let me see what I can do. I'll work on it this very afternoon."

I had no doubt she would. They would. I imagined my mother hurling her bag onto Beth's guest room bed, rolling up her sleeves, and digging in to Beth's library of sites for overblown events while my father asked, dolefully, "How much does that one charge?"

"They have an enormous family," I reminded her. "Eight kids, six—no, there's Lutie's intended—seven spouses, thirty-seven grandkids, uncles, aunts, cousins . . ."

"You might want to reconsider their offer. I wouldn't mind a trip to New Orleans."

"Then go. You don't need a family wedding as an excuse. And Bethie? Tonight? Expect a Technicolor explosion. Gabby Mackenzie has never heard the word *neutral*, not in colors or opinions or temperament."

"Sounds like I'll like her."

She would. I did. That didn't ease my growing discomfort.

I headed across the street to the Square, thinking about anything and everything except the idea of being married four months from now. And thinking about weddings, how could I not wonder about Emmie Cade and Leo Fairchild's? Was it still scheduled? Were they being sidetracked by being suspects?

I walked through the crowds of students and citizens soaking up the September sunshine, and headed toward the farthest corner from the school. I told myself it would be the least populated. It was mere coincidence that my goal was only thirty-five steps away from the Fairchild building—I could, in fact, see its balconies from where I stood. The objective was a quiet, only partially occupied bench. Olivia didn't seem to take up even the space a small person might.

"Mind if I share?" I asked through the pops and bursts of sound and laughter filling the rest of the park.

Olivia didn't look up. She shrugged. Not precisely a warm welcome. One of her hands held her lunch, still in its plastic Baggie. She looked like inert matter, as privately desolate as she'd appeared at the end of school yesterday. I settled for the shrug, and sat at the far end of the bench.

She took out her copy of *Lord of the Flies*, put it on her knees and, using only one hand, carefully found a page. Then she held it open with that hand while the other continued to cradle the untouched sandwich bag.

I felt pulled into her bubble of silence. It was more than a stillness. The withholding of sound and the effort to keep something bottled up thinned and charged the air surrounding us.

She stared at her book. I was positive the show of needing to finish her assignment was a pretense. Olivia's entire being announced that she was the kind of girl who'd always have taken care of her homework. And in fact, when I really looked at the open book, I realized she was almost at the end of the novel, well ahead of where assignments would have put her. But her message was clear: Company was not welcome. I thought about finding the pretzel man, but talking with Beth about the evening ahead and wedding ceremonies had quelled my hunger. In fact, I felt as if food might make me ill.

That meant I had nowhere to go except, perhaps, to that building steps away. I tried to remember whether I'd actually promised not to, then laughed at my attempt to be legalistic. I didn't have to have promised. Claire Fairchild's death was now officially a homicide and out of our hands.

But during the course of the long night before, I'd wondered what Batya was going to do, or had done, and how she'd now support herself and her children. More than that, I wondered whether Leo Fairchild was privy or partner to his mother's supposed bequest and/or to the I.N.S. threat she'd held over the housekeeper's head.

"Thanks for the rest," I said. "I just needed to sit a moment." I saw a splat on the book, and Olivia slammed it shut, then reached up to fiercely brush her index finger across her right eye.

She was wearing a delicate yellow T-shirt and flower-sprigged short skirt, and all the same, she felt dark, something with the power to absorb even the brightness of this day. Her ache was almost palpable over here, on the other side of the bench.

I felt an impotent rage, knowing I couldn't fix whatever made Olivia's life feel so frightening and hard to bear. I was only her teacher. I crossed her life's path five of the hundred and sixty-eight hours in a week. Something much more significant than I weighed her slight body down. However, maybe knowing somebody wished they could work miracles would help. "Olivia?" I whispered.

She looked at me for a slice of a second, then back down at her closed book, speaking so softly, I had to work to make out her hesitant words. "I . . . don't . . . understand . . . why people are so . . . mean."

"Do you want to talk about it?"

She looked at me again, her eyes wider, and shook her head. "No. No. I meant—I mean—the *book*." She looked away again.

As an English teacher, I should have been thrilled that assigned reading was having such a powerful effect. It was a magnificent, rich book, and its message heartbreaking, especially in this dangerous new world. For one frightening moment, I thought perhaps Sonia Lawrence had been right and this book was too much for these students in these times.

Then logic returned, and I could in no way buy the idea that William Golding had driven Olivia to stay in my classroom after school, and to sit alone during lunch, crying.

That, however, was what she wanted me to believe, so I sat weighing respect for her privacy and need to mourn whatever it was in her own way against my concept of responsible adulthood. "The book," I finally said, "is thought-provoking. Yes, people can be cruel. We all have the potential to be that way. To be uncivilized. But we also have the potential to be kind. To think things through. To not act out of blind fear. It would be heartbreaking if we didn't have the ability to keep an eye on what's right and wrong, to choose not to go along with the crowd, not to bend under mob rule." I leaned forward, to try to really see her.

She didn't move, except for her eyes, which glanced at me, as if to make sure I was real. "I sound like a jerk," I said. "Sorry."

She didn't say anything, didn't deny my jerkdom. At a time like this I almost missed Sunshine—or my future mother-in-law—both of whom, with profound insincerity, would have pooh-poohed, told me I was anything but a jerk, and insisted that, in fact, my platitudes had been enormously helpful. "Can I help you in any way?" I asked. "I would really like to."

She shook her head rapidly, her eyes wide with fear that I might do something, anything.

"Okay, then. But take that as a permanent offer. At any time, if you change your mind and think of something I could do—or if you want to talk . . ." She sat impassively, a plaster statue depicting resignation, loss, capitulation. "Okay?"

She finally nodded with great insincerity.

I had no choice but to move on through my day, although I no longer envisioned myself as skating on the surface of anything. I felt like someone who'd stumbled badly and had one leg through the ice.

The lunch hour was barely underway, I was not welcome on my park bench, I was practically face-to-face with Claire Fairchild's building and I didn't think I'd actually taken a vow to have my curiosity surgically amputated. I worried about Batya, too, about her impending delivery date, about her illegal status, and about whether Leo would honor his mother's financial promises. I couldn't see what would be hurt if I simply stopped by. A friendly, innocuous courtesy call.

There. I'd successfully argued my case with me and I'd won. Guilt-free, I made my way to the lovely old building, where I was greeted with yellow crime-scene tape across Claire Fairchild's once elegantly austere front door. If Batya was in there, she was now truly imprisoned, but of course, she couldn't be, and wouldn't have been, ever since the tape went up yesterday, when the dead woman's blood showed traces of barbiturate.

C. K. was supposed to have been told of any new information, and this seemed new enough. I pulled out my cell phone and called the man.

"Mackenzie here," he said softly.

"The door's taped up."

"Manda? We're at Carpenter's Hall, listenin' to a talk about the First Continental Congress. I mean, they are, my parents. I'm outside to take this call. But this is where it started. This is where they talked about splitting with Britain. Can't this wait?"

"I don't think so. Claire Fairchild's apartment is a crime scene now."

"It was always a crime scene," he said. "Ever since a crime was committed there."

Sometimes his wit eludes me. "But, Batya—she was staying here."

"Tom called," he said. "Cell phones are a mixed blessin'. Gets harder to escape work—and that isn't even my work anymore."

"Tom called and you didn't tell me?"

"I didn't want to talk to that ditz secretary, an' I know she doesn't interrupt your teachin', so I thought it could wait while I played tour director."

I understood that his attention and interests were elsewhere. I didn't care. "What did he say?"

"Tom?"

"Who else would I mean?"

"We've been hearing about and from Ben Franklin and Thomas Jefferson and John Adams, who had a lot to say."

"*Tom.*"

"There's an A.P.B. out for Batya. She's disappeared."

It took me a moment to process that. "Batya?"

"Right. Once again, the butler, more or less, did it."

"But disappearing doesn't necessarily have anything to do with what happened to—for all we know, she's in labor somewhere."

"Her aunt says she doesn't know where she went. Took the little boy, too."

"But her aunt would never tell—she's illegal. She'd be deported."

"And turns out you were right. Her little boy has seizures and takes phenobarb."

"That still doesn't mean she'd—"

"You're suddenly her defender? Yesterday, you were giving me reasons why it had to be her. So you were right. Why change positions now?"

I couldn't have rationally said why, except that Batya was no longer an academic puzzle, something to be figured out. She was a woman whose motives were based on grave problems, and life in prison would only increase the weight of problems on the next generation. "Still and all," I said, knowing how weak I sounded, "she in no way seemed—she was so concerned about keeping the bedroom untouched—"

"Odd that she knew it was a crime scene, wasn't it?"

"That was a language problem. A TV-watching problem. Not proof of anything."

"I have to get back to my parents. I should tell you this: Before she disappeared, Batya tried to refill a prescription that didn't have any refills left."

"Not—" I gave up on blanket denial. "Phenobarb?"

"She said her aunt had lost the last batch."

I was silent long enough for Mackenzie to ask if I was still there. "So that's it," I finally said.

"Pretty much. She can't get far with a toddler and ultimately a newborn. I'll see you later."

The image was horrifying and bizarre, but I thought she could get far. Women had children at home, or with midwives. Women like her would shelter and hide her.

I wondered why I found it comforting to envision her evading justice.

I made my way back toward the school, through clusters of students, nannies, toddlers, and a scattering of the elderly, most of whom normally wait until the Square clears of teens. Midway through the park, a blur on the far periphery of my vision spun around and came toward me at a near run.

I didn't want to see her. I'd already struck out, dramatically, in my attempts to help Olivia, and then, to offer help to Batya.

I didn't want to see a person I didn't want to help in the first place, but there she was. Emmie Cade.

Seventeen

"I WAS going to come to your school later on—after school—to ask if you were going to, but look—bumping into you now. Great! Saves time, I guess."

I unspooled the sentence, looking in vain for its core. I felt suddenly and totally exhausted, physically burdened, as if heavy weights had been strapped across my shoulders.

"So can you?" she asked.

I shook my head.

"No? You can't?"

"I don't even know what—"

"Help me! Take me on as your client. You said you'd find out if it was allowed."

I'd forgotten all about that, and with great apologies, I told her so. She looked like a child told that Santa was a myth.

"It doesn't matter now, anyway," I said.

"But it does. They're already—the police, I mean—everybody's being questioned and even Leo—even he's acting as if I . . ." She didn't look poetic today. She was wearing clothes, not a costume. In place of long lace sleeves, a blue denim shirt, and jeans. Her skin, especially around her eyes, looked strained.

She leaned closer, her voice now a hoarse whisper. "I can't let this ruin my relationship with Leo. I won't. I need your help—I need to find out why I keep being—why—" She seemed unable to complete the thought, to say out loud what pressed so painfully on her mind.

"Say whatever it is. Putting it into words won't make you guilty of something you're not."

She straightened her posture, inhaled, and said in one long breath, "I don't know why people think I'm such a bad person when I'm not." She exhaled again. "When I never was."

I couldn't help but notice that while her mouth had managed to brave saying it without breaking, her eyes were moist by the end of the sentence. What a tear-filled, no-lunch hour I was having. "Please—you know what I mean," she said. "Don't you?"

I nodded, even though I wasn't sure, and the only thing in my mind was that old joke: "Just because you're paranoid doesn't mean somebody isn't out to get you." Is it also possible that where there's smoke, there's really only fairy dust or fog?

"And it's your business to find things out."

I was about to tell her about Batya, and then I reconsidered. I didn't care what the police believed or how obviously everything pointed toward the housekeeper—I still wanted to know about the anonymous notes. Why, in fact, people did seem to hate Emmie, suspect her of multiple crimes. That would be a new case, a brand-new investigation having nothing to do with the murder. "The police haven't been bothering you, have they?"

She shrugged, nodded, shook her head, and completely confused me. "Everybody," she said. "They haven't said anything to me in particular, but they did ask me a lot about poor Jake. And even about . . ." She lowered her eyes, looked down at her hands. Her eyelashes were amazingly lush and long, throwing shadows on her cheekbones. "About a man I was once engaged to. I can't imagine how they did that much background on me hours after Mrs. Fairchild died—" She blinked, fighting back tears.

I knew how they knew so much so quickly. We'd turned over everything we had: the news stories, the anonymous notes. This presented a new ethical question. Could I accept her as a client if I was the one who'd gotten her into trouble by providing information the police would otherwise have no ready way to know?

Awkward did not begin to describe how I felt. Another situation in which A. Pepper not only failed to help but actively made everything worse.

"I apologize," I said. "I meant to find out about this situation, but something urgent came up. I promise I'll check into this. Are you all right meantime?"

Her laugh was closer to a quick, hard bark. "I can't sleep or eat, Leo barely looks at me directly because"—she shrugged, ready to foolishly trust me with whatever she knew—"because the medicine they found in her bloodstream . . . I had pills like it for insomnia. Leo knew it. We'd been . . . I've been staying with him. Now, it's so awkward . . . I mean, if there's no trust, if a man thinks maybe I killed his mother!—I'm going back to my place for a while." She hoisted the tote bag straps up higher on her shoulder. "A little space between us. Maybe for the best."

Leo was her perceived problem. Leo's lack of faith. She had a powerful innocence—or fabulous acting skills. Whichever it was forced me to acknowledge that the police were probably right, and Batya was guilty. Which also meant that not only had Emmie not harmed Claire Fairchild, but that it was possible she hadn't ever deliberately harmed anyone.

I noticed a generalized movement of the students across the way, as if they were swaying, en masse, toward the school building. I checked my watch. The bell would ring in three minutes. "I have to run," I said.

She shook her head. "I still don't get it how you can do two jobs, but I guess it's obvious you can." She sounded wistful, perhaps because of her own spotty work history. "You'll call me, then?" She fumbled around in her bag and found a pen and a piece of paper and wrote down a number. "That's my place," she said softly.

I nodded.

She looked down at her toes, today shod in utilitarian running shoes. "I'll probably be there a while." Head still lowered, she walked away.

I turned to go, then reconsidered and ran a few steps to tap her on her back. "I have a question."

She pivoted, eyes wide.

"What's with the names?"

"I don't—"

"Your names."

"My *names*?"

"There are so many of them. Why is that?"

She looked surprised, then, stymied. Her pretty brow wrinkled above her nose. "I guess, if you're going to help me, you need to know whatever you need to know, but the names don't have much meaning. I mean, I could explain each switch, but it's so boring, starting with never liking Mary Elizabeth." She closed her eyes and did a mock shiver. "It wasn't ever me. It's a Goody Two-shoes kind of name."

"Bore me. Lots of people dislike their names—but you've disliked a whole series of them."

"All I did, mostly, was play with the name itself, use nicknames, so I was Maribeth at one point, and Betsey at another, and I think Liz for a short time, but that didn't fit, either."

"Emmie, there are—"

"Oh, yes. M. E., the initials, too. I nearly forgot."

"But how about Stacy? Weren't you Stacy Williams for a while?"

She grimaced, and nodded. "I dropped out of college and got married to a guy named Billy—William Stacey—and so I was Betsey Stacey then. I'd always dreamed about going on the stage, or being in movies, but that wasn't the right kind of name, and Billy didn't want his surname used that way, so I turned his name around. Stacy Williams. That sounded right but, in the end, it was the only 'right' thing going on in my life. I didn't get anywhere with the acting—of course, we were in Atlanta, not exactly the center of the world of drama, and then, the marriage ended, too."

She looked at me as if I now understood some arcane secret, as if she'd said enough. She hadn't.

"You were going to explain all the names."

She lowered her head. The word "woeful" snaked through my brain. "When Billy walked out—"

I was surprised to hear that her husband had ended the marriage. I'd assumed that those choices—that everything—had always been in her control. The new understanding troubled me and suggested other untested assumptions on my part, and that idea, potentially upending everything I took for granted, was dizzying.

"I was pretty much of a mess. Not my favorite time," she said, trying for a small smile that, instead, upped her "woeful" quotient. "And I certainly didn't want either my actual married name, last name Stacey, or that stage name that was his name in reverse. I moved to Austin and changed back to my maiden name—lots of women do that, so I was Stacy Cade. Then I fell in love with a great guy named Geoff Collins. We were engaged and then . . . then his motorcycle turned over and . . ." She sighed, and shook her head. "It wasn't legal. We weren't married, but I didn't know what to do, how to show how much I cared, and so I used his last name when I came to California, and I was trying to act again. Stacy Collins, and after a year or so, I met Jake and I became Stacy King. After Jake . . . after him, I felt as if all the names had been . . . part of my string of horrible luck, so I dropped Stacy and King and went back to being Mary Elizabeth Cade, except . . . I still can't stand that name, so M. E. is a nickname, do you see? I told you it was boring."

Interesting how history is seen by its various players. Her story rang true, but all the same, every suspicious overtone had been wiped away along with mention of repeated survivor's inheritances. If she believed that version of her past, let alone if it actually was accurate, I could understand why she'd be confused by her bad reputation and the dark cloud of suspicion that had relocated with her.

"And now," she said. "Now, with Mrs. Fairchild dead and Leo so worried and . . . I have no idea what all his mother said to him that evening, about me, what she heard, or thought, but he looks at me as if . . . as if—"

The bell rang. I don't know if we were saved by it, but I was relieved. My tidy mental household, where facts and truths had all been hammered into place and I knew the territory blindfolded, was abruptly being renovated, leaving me dizzy and tripping over certainties. I needed to think. I quickly made my farewells.

Unfortunately, a classroom is about the last place on earth to enjoy peaceful contemplation. Emmie Cade's sad trek to Claire Fairchild's condo faded from my mind as the classroom filled. This group was starting the semester with a writing unit, and I was trying to make playing with words as enjoyable as possible.

"I want you to write an argument," I said. "That doesn't mean a quarrel, it means I want you to take a side on an issue, and write something that would convince your reader of your point of view." We'd counted out, and now I said, "Everybody who was a *one* is on the *it's a good thing* side, and all the *twos* are on the *it's a bad thing* side. And here's the idea you're arguing: Would it be a good or a bad thing for a sophomore to win the lottery and wind up with one hundred million dollars."

"Good!" the sophomores said in unison.

"No fair if I have to say it's a bad thing," said a boy who was made mostly of freckles.

"Why should we have to pretend to believe one way when we don't?" a sulky girl in the back asked, so we talked about thinking about what our opponents might believe, and thereby being able to anticipate and answer their statements. "It gives you an advantage and stretches your mind—and makes you wilier in the future. Consider it mind reading. And I promise, even if you're on the side that says winning all that money would be a bad thing, and then you go out and win a hundred million dollars—you'll be allowed to keep it."

They divided into groups of yays and nays and collectively brainstormed for the next fifteen minutes. "See how many points are made and with which ones you agree. Take notes. Then you'll organize your thoughts and write up your own argument, based on those points."

I knew I could relax when I heard the "it's a bad thing" group generate ideas. In fact, they sounded like Cotton Mather—anything enjoyable was inherently bad. The "it's a good thing" group was having a heavy debate about whether a person that rich needed to complete high school and how many pairs of shoes any female had a right to own.

While they debated, laughed, protested, and made notes, woeful Emmie Cade pushed back into consciousness and I tried to unassume, to see her as she was, to base my view only on facts, not opinions or loaded words I'd read.

It was nearly impossible, which was a frightening truth in itself.

The good news—and I sorely needed some—was that when the bell sounded again and the class ended, I realized that for the past few hours, I hadn't had time to obsess about the evening ahead.

The ninth graders settled down with enough chatter to make

me think they were forming a community. They'd come from several feeder schools, so the speed with which they seemed to have cohered was heartening.

Unless, of course, this was its own little *Lord of the Flies* community in the making.

I wondered where that thought had come from—and then I saw Olivia, who suggested that while no man is an island, perhaps an undersized adolescent girl might be. She looked as isolated as she had out in the park, but a thin veneer of fear had been added.

It was too soon in the school year to be this concerned about a child. Too soon in the story, as if we'd skipped the introduction and the buildup, ruined the tension, and leaped directly to the nail-biting climax.

I wished I could approach Olivia, waggle my finger, and say, "You know the rules forbid grave emotional distress the first two weeks of school. There are too many other things to attend to at that time, Missy, so reset your mental state to the 'normal' setting immediately."

Things were degenerating on the fictional island of boys as well, but that was according to plan. I broached the meaning of the bespectacled character of Piggy, carefully never saying words like *symbolic*. "Where does he fit in with the boys?" I asked. "What do you think is his role in the group?"

And after a minimum of searching, they suggested that he was civilization. He knew the rules; he advocated proceeding logically, taking things a step at a time, preserving themselves by building shelters, by taking a census of who was there.

"Then given that they're so proud of being English, of being civilized—why is Piggy having such a hard time?"

"Because he isn't attractive," Melanie said. "He doesn't look like a leader. I'm not saying that's right," she quickly added, "but all the same, I think that's a part of it. And he doesn't fit in." She said this last line with great assurance. Melanie had the look of a girl who would fit in—or make the rest of her peers fit themselves to her mold.

"Anything else?" I asked.

"What he wants, what he says they should do isn't as . . . exciting or fun as what, say, Jack wants."

"Good point, David." I'd had no trouble memorizing his name. Few eyes actually twinkle, no matter what poets say, and few are actually turquoise, but David's did and were. He was also observant and intelligent and it would be tempting to call on him all the time, to hear his opinions, of course, but also so see the turquoise twinkle trick. "It's more fun to be wild, to give in to impulses."

"For a while, at least," someone else added, and the discussion flowed on about the meaning of the names, the specifically named Jack and Ralph, the derogatory nickname for Piggy, the merged names of Samneric, and the generically named "littluns," about the fire that's set and burns out of control.

It went so well that I believed Havermeyer's hyperbole. Our standards were rising. This was probably the best and surely the most enjoyable class I'd ever had.

Olivia remained conspicuously silent, although she listened and watched and had read more of the book than most of the class. And then, a few minutes before the end of the hour, we got to the beast. "What is it, do you think?" I asked. "Will the hunters find it?"

And then, Olivia, her posture abruptly ramrod straight, her hands flat on her desktop, spoke out clearly and forcibly. "There's nothing to find. There's no beast. They're the beast. It's whatever they don't understand. Whatever they're afraid of. That's what they turn into a beast."

And having said her piece, she sat back in her seat and, without showing any sign I could have defined, seemed to once again withdraw into the position of a distant observer.

The class rhythm of easy, rapid-flowing conversation halted. Some of the children looked surprised, as if in the course of the hour they'd accepted Olivia as a mute, and they'd just witnessed a miracle.

No one, perhaps with good cause, seemed able to pick up on her idea and run with it. "That's a good observation," I finally said. "Do you think it's true off that island, too? Do we turn what we fear into monsters and beasts?"

And once again, I fell in love with my ninth graders. I hoped this lasted, that when their hormones fully kicked in and they felt more familiar that they didn't try hard to "fit in" by imitating the older classes' studied apathy. I hoped they'd always be eager to discuss ideas, even painful ones that questioned their own prejudices.

I wondered what Melanie Lawrence's mother would say if she had been in the room. Would she have understood why it was not only good, but important, for our children to grow up able to think, and to consider ideas that were possibly foreign, or threatening? That if they did that, perhaps they wouldn't turn those fears into their own beasts, to be hunted and killed?

Probably not.

At the thought of her mother, I glanced at Melanie herself, and caught her smiling pleasantly at Olivia and yet somehow projecting a forceful negativity—a deliberate nothingness. As if poison came out from that smile. I couldn't understand how she was creating that impression, but I could feel its result, and I knew I'd have to find language for it because I didn't like it and wouldn't tolerate it. Olivia, meanwhile, studied her fingernails, purposely or inadvertently missing the stare-down.

And then the bell rang, and the class looked like so many jack-in-the-boxes, tops off. Even Olivia gathered her things and would have left with the rest of her class, albeit at the back of the pack, had I not put a hand out to stop her. "Could we talk a moment?" I asked.

She drew a deep breath, as if I presented a challenge, or a trial. "If it's about . . . how I was, I'm okay now."

"That was an exceptionally insightful comment you made, about fear and how we handle it."

She looked at me directly for the first time. "Miss Pepper, I'm okay now. Thanks, but—there's nothing to talk about. I'm transferring out. I decided today, and talked to my mother during last period, and she says I can."

"No! Why would you? The semester's barely begun and—"

"I know how it'll be. It'll be just how it is. Nobody will talk to me."

"But why?"

"Because . . ." She shook her head. "It just is, and it won't stop."

"How can you know something like that? There are new people here, new friends to be made—"

"It was this way all summer. I thought it might stop. We used to be friends. I helped her a lot with her math homework."

"You and . . . ?"

"Melanie."

Perfect Melanie? Always smiling, popular, protected by her mama? If I hadn't seen that blank nothing of a stare this afternoon, I wouldn't have believed Olivia at all. I shuddered at what was going on and what I miss and what I didn't know how to fix.

"We went to the same camp in July, and this boy—this boy she liked, he liked me, and from then on, she said we weren't friends anymore, and she got all the other girls to not talk to me and—" She blinked furiously, her unnatural calm gone. "Everybody likes her. I thought maybe when I came here, it would be different, but . . ." She shook her head. "She told the math teacher she thought she saw me cheating on a test this morning. Nothing's different."

"Couldn't we talk this through? Get both of you together and—"

"It's worse now," she continued, as if I hadn't spoken at all. "As soon as she got home, she blogged me. She's still doing it. People who didn't know me, even, they read her log and . . ." She shrugged.

"Does she tell lies about you?" Maybe we could stop it, then.

She looked as if she was deciding, as if she didn't quite know. "Not lies, really. No. Things like . . . I'm stuck-up. I think I'm too smart. I guess that's because I helped with her math homework. I dress bad. I'm not loyal. I steal boyfriends . . ." She shook her head again, this time with an expression of amazement. I thought of her and then of Melanie, and understood why she'd have trouble believing she could "steal" someone away, but I could also see how appealing she would be when her face wasn't creased with worry lines, her posture not bent into a slump.

"I still think that surely, there's something we could do to make things better. We can't let someone drive you away—we can work things out. We're civilized people!" I heard myself echo the pathetic claims of the soon to be savage, murderous English boys in *Lord of the Flies*.

She looked at me directly, as if she, too, had heard the echo, and in a quiet voice, said, "Melanie is like Jack, the hunter, the wild boy people want to follow. I'm Piggy."

"That's fiction. We can learn from that—we're supposed to learn from that—"

"There isn't anything anybody can do, except what I'm doing. I'm going to go to the public school near me. It's big. She's not there. It'll be better."

There are societies and religions that consider being excluded the ultimate punishment. The loss of community is basically a death penalty.

Young girls were experts in the trade. Boys might go out and fight, but girls were probably the ones who'd thought of shunning as a penalty in the first place. We could protest and protect, we could teach sensitivity—but I wasn't convinced it would change much, because the process was subtle and below the radar of most adult eyes. So there was no way I could tell this diminutive girl that her ninth-grade worries were trivial or meaningless. I could still feel aftershocks of the year my enemy labeled me a slut, and remember how relieved I'd been to enter a different junior high from the one my tormentor attended.

"I'm so sorry," I said. "It's cruel and stupid."

She put her copy of *Lord of the Flies* on my desk. "I finished it," she said. "I wanted to know how it turned out, but now I'm sorry I do." She looked at me directly for the first time, I thought, and she seemed to grow an inch or two. "I hoped I was wrong about how I thought it would turn out. I hoped Piggy would get out of there alive. But that isn't how things work out, is it? Hoping is worthless, and it doesn't save anybody."

I took her hand and held it. I wanted to hold on to her, keep her, fight her battles for her, and knowing I couldn't do any of those things didn't lessen the wanting.

"The difference between fiction and life, Miss Pepper, is that Piggy couldn't escape to another island. I can."

I watched her go, and this time, it was my eyes that were damp.

Eighteen

THIS was far from the first time I found myself yearning for a mentor—a wise headmaster to whom I could turn for advice and counsel—but at Philly Prep, such an idea was ludicrous. Maurice Havermeyer was going to see Olivia's sad trajectory out of our school only as an entry on the debit side of his ledger, and therefore, a major failing on the part of a faculty that should have strapped her down and kept her paying tuition.

I sought instead the wisdom and companionship of Rachel Leary, the school counselor who was once again large with child. Children, actually. She'd been told she was having twins. "Tell me you're here to give me a back rub," she said as she packed up files.

She'd bid us all—except Dr. Havermeyer—adieu last June, sure she was going to be a full-time mother for a while, but the economy had slumped right down on her household, and her husband was looking for work, so she was back. At least until maternity leave kicked in.

"Did you come here with a problem?" She sounded fearful.

"I came here to steer you out of the building." The problem had been resolved, for better or for worse. "But how about an issue to mull?"

"An issue that doesn't have to do with Stan finding work and the mortgage getting paid and what we'll do about child care with three kids under three—or anything related to that?"

I promised.

"Or about college applications and interviews?" The nightmare season for high school counselors.

I promised again.

"Or—"

"This isn't about Havermeyer, either."

She chuckled. "How did you guess the third side of my grief triumverate?"

As we carefully made our way down the staircase, I told her about Olivia.

"I don't know," Rachel said when we reached the empty entry lobby. "That's a horrible situation that's unfortunately not exactly rare. We can try sensitivity training."

"Her class is reading *Lord of the Flies*. It's almost a blueprint for ostracism and ganging up on somebody—but it hasn't stopped anything from happening. Although, of course, we haven't finished it yet."

"It won't, nor will the sensitivity training, if you ask me. It's hard to change behavior when it's intentional. It's not like being unintentionally or stupidly sexist or racist—it isn't as if her tormentor doesn't know and delight in the fact that she's making life miserable for that girl. But I can help set up a program, at least get them talking about it. It's subterranean, though."

"I thought Melanie was the sweetest thing. Actually, she is sweet, and smart and good in class."

"See what I mean? It takes deliberate action on their part for us to even see what's going on—and then, intervention, likely as not, makes it worse."

"That's what Olivia said."

"Smart girl," Rachel said as we left the building. "And much as I hate to say it because it's ethically and morally and every way wrong and it shows a huge failing on our part—but I think she's made the right decision. Sometimes, if there's poison in the air, the best idea is to head to where you can breathe."

Piggy's other island. I suspected she was right, but that didn't make Olivia's departure less depressing.

"Did you know the students are making book on when I deliver these guys?" she said. "The high flyers are going for an unscheduled in-school delivery. A sort of live action you-are-there sex ed class."

"And an effective way to encourage safe sex."

She chuckled. "Havermeyer would love it."

"Finally. Something no other school can boast, besides absolute mediocrity."

I HAD SHOWERED and shampooed and was lining my eyes when the phone rang across the room. Macavity pricked his ears, as if finally, somebody was calling him. "It's not for you, dear cat," I said. His eternal optimism was touching. Who was it he thought might phone? "Relax."

And I relaxed, too, once I realized it wasn't either my parents or my future in-laws on the other end. Then I grew tense again.

"Hey, Amanda," the voice said. "Joan here."

"Hey yourself, Joan. How's everything?" We speak a few times a year, so—why now, when I was wearing panty hose, wet hair, eyeliner, and precious else? And why hadn't I found the portable phone instead of this one, which had me chained to the kitchen wall? I didn't want to be rude, so I ran through "I-can't-talk-right-now-but-I-do-love-you" exits, like making a lunch date, or calling her back tomorrow.

"I apologize for the delay, but I got it," she said.

I had no idea what she meant.

"You forgot?" Her voice rose a full octave on that final syllable. My failing memory was a huge and audible disappointment—*I* was a huge disappointment and I'd also probably hurt her feelings. And then I realized what this was about. Joan worked at Shipley. I'd asked her to investigate Vicky Smith Baer's transfer, mostly so I could find out where she'd come from, and then I'd know a school Emmie Cade had attended.

I also realized that what had seemed important three days ago no longer mattered. Mackenzie's contacts had come through speedily and, in any case, Claire Fairchild was dead and the investigation over.

"Of course I didn't forget!" I lied. "I'm astounded that you were able to find the material so quickly!"

"I wanted it to be faster, but the woman who's in charge of the archived files was out with the flu and when she returned, she was overwhelmed with accumulated work—and she's the kind of administrative assistant you do not want to tangle with."

"I know the type."

"Finally, this morning, she found the files. Then it took me all day to call Ohio Cliff, to get a little clarification."

"It's okay, really." I would never tell her it didn't matter anymore. She'd tried so hard.

"No, I know things must be urgent in your new line of work."

"Honestly, Joanie, I'm delighted you were able—" This could go on forever, and even though I had time—an hour, in fact—this particular back-and-forth wasn't overly interesting. "What was it you found out? And why did you have to call the school in Ohio?"

"I thought—I hope it was okay, Manda. It's just that I checked Victoria Smith's file. She transferred to Shipley in November." She paused, for dramatic effect, I thought.

CLAIRE AND PRESENT DANGER

I gave her the prompt she so audibly yearned for. "November."

"Well, that's it. Juniors who are getting ready to apply to colleges and take S.A.T.s and just . . . be juniors don't switch midsemester when there's no emergency. And there wasn't any note about a problem, except one note saying that her current grades were not to be taken as the norm. That she'd gone from being an A student, on the hockey team, and all-round epitome of prep school girl—it didn't use those words, of course—to a pretty bad student. She had C's and one D. And I noticed that her parents didn't move with her, and that there hadn't been a death in the family, so I snooped further, and there was a note from the admissions director saying she should be admitted at this unorthodox time because she was in an unusual situation and a change of scene was all that was required. So that's when I remembered a woman at Ohio Cliff I met at the conference, and I—I hope it's okay and it didn't foul anything up for you—I phoned her."

"And?" I was getting chilly, wished I'd snagged a shirt or robe en route to the phone. Also, I thought Joan had already made her point, but I listened on.

"I failed miserably. When I asked about what that message meant, she wouldn't tell me. She said it was confidential material and she couldn't see the relevance to anything all these years later. I just wanted you to know I tried."

"And succeeded. Completely. You found everything I needed."

"I guess I thought you wanted more. I know I did, after I saw that note. I mean the girl went to class, so it wasn't that she was pregnant, which is one reason to leave your old school midyear. I think they're just covering their behinds. Not that anybody would sue a dozen years later, but who actually knows? She said it had nothing to do with the school or faculty or administration, and in her opinion, everyone acted precipitously. 'Time would have taken care of it,' she said. As if that means anything. But I kept talking and hoping she'd get more specific. All I got in the end was that 'girls will be girls.' It was something about popularity and cliques and not belonging. Nothing that should have produced flight. I'm sure it was just what we see here—and you probably see at your school, too "

Joanie was sweet, and a dear friend, but once you pushed the "on" button, it was difficult stopping her. "Teenage girls," she said. "Moody, unpredictable. So she exercised her woman's—young woman's—prerogative to change her mind. Probably angry with her family because they wouldn't let her stay out late. Who even knows? I am constantly amazed here, and you must be, too."

"Yes," I said. "Certainly. About boys, too."

"Right. Of course. Our boys astound me, too. But I suppose I can understand Ohio Cliff's reticence, because you never know what's going to turn itself into an accusation that the school somehow failed the child. In any case, I'm happy to say, I couldn't find any evidence of any more problems once she was here with us. She was a good student, in fact."

Her voice had become pleasant background buzz to me, like crickets on a summer's night. I wasn't sure about that woman's prerogative, or pure moodiness.

Then I realized that Joanie's pace had slowed. Stopped. She'd been waiting for a response. "So I'm sorry I couldn't get any more," she said, wrongly interpreting my missed cue as disappointment.

And once again, I told her not to apologize at all. And then I swung the conversation over to how she was doing with the new school year underway, and finally to why I couldn't talk as long as I wanted to, what with the big dinner tonight. "Mackenzie's going to pick me up in . . . a few minutes," I said, lying about the time for expediency's sake. I actually had almost an hour till we sallied forth to pick up his parents at their hotel, but for once, I wanted to dress and dry my hair at leisure.

"I'm so sorry. I didn't mean to keep you. Your in-laws! You're getting *married*!"

And that, of course, is not an item to be lightly dropped into the end of a conversation, so we spoke on. She offered unsolicited old-married advice about mothers-in-law ("Beware!" being the condensed version), and I asked about the exploits and achievements of her three children, and how the new term was going at her school.

And at mine. "I think it's going to be all right. I like a lot of the new kids and they seem—for the time being—actually interested and motivated. And I was told that I'm getting good notices on their blogs."

I was showing off, demonstrating not only my reported popularity, but my up-to-the-minute mastery of contemporary adolescent technology. Joanie was suitably impressed—and confused, so then I had to explain what little I knew about Weblogs. I was, however, truly intrigued by them because they seemed important—the next thing after telephones for keeping up nonstop teen communications. And that was, given Olivia's experience with them—and mine—a good and a bad thing.

Finally we reached the psychologically apt time for a polite farewell. Once again, I thanked her for her help, and then, after we made a date for an after-school cup of coffee two weeks hence, on a day she didn't have to carpool, I could graciously, politely, hang up.

It's conversational etiquette that makes Mackenzie roll his eyes and mutter—till I object—about how long it takes women to say goodbye. It's one of the few aspects of his personality that depresses me, because it means he doesn't understand part of the basic rules of civilization. If it were up to him, telephone exchanges would be about information and nothing more. Over and out with military precision, and that of course wasn't the half of it. Anyone who works with teens knows that.

But even having completed the call according to my inner rhythms of social interaction, I didn't feel finished with it. I stood near the phone, thinking I now knew something, but I couldn't access it. If I stood still, I might catch it. So I stood a minute in my sheer-toes panty hose, hair drying in berserk patterns, trying to pinpoint that thing, that something that was so close—and then almost into consciousness and then it was there—it was *that* close—

And the door opened. "Hey, Manda?"

I needed one minute more to get that thought into range, so I put up my finger in the universal signal of "hold it," and C. K. stopped talking.

But not everyone did. "Our feet are killing us, so we thought we'd save time and come directly here instead of—whoops!"

Although her greetings had begun before she was visible, now, Gabby Mackenzie was inside the loft, which is, after all, one large cube, with only bedroom and bathroom partitions. And there we stood for a painfully long second, both of us wide-eyed with disbelief.

"Oh, my," I heard from a male voice that was not my beloved's.

My beloved, in fact, laughed out loud, which might be grounds for removing him from the category of "beloved" altogether. But I couldn't give much thought to that, because I had turned my back and was running, hands clapped on my rear end, toward the sanctuary of the partitioned-off bedroom.

One thing about the experience was that it cured me of all concerns about what I'd wear when with my in-laws. As long as I wore something, I'd be ahead of where I was now.

Nineteen

BY the time we were en route to Gladwynne and dinner, I'd gained proper attire and hairstyle, but had long since lost or abandoned the thread of the idea I'd been pursuing. No matter, I decided. If I have questions, Emmie herself will answer them.

And then my niece and nephew, sister and brother-in-law were hugging me, and Horse the dog was bumping his head against my knees for attention and my parents and Boy and Gabby were cheek-kissing, hand-shaking and hugging, and round and round in every possible combination people demonstrated that an impending marriage trumps everything.

I relaxed into the confused merriment. Why not? We were an island of loveliness filled with happy cooking smells, the beautiful surrounds of Beth and Sam's house, their adorable children, and almost equally adorable dog. It was, in fact, close to the picture of comfortable domesticity that's always supposed to be either a bore or a sham, but certainly wasn't in this case. I knew this from careful and cynical long-term observation. And like a delighted audience at this performance of marital possibilities, the two sets of parents cheered.

I didn't think I'd ever seen my mother this happy, and it made me the slightest bit sad for all the times I'd been annoyed by her matrimonial nagging. Her hints and prods had been irritating, infuriating, and often ludicrous, but they were from her heart, part of a sincere belief, however antiquated and ridiculous, that to be married was to be safe in some way she passionately desired for her daughters.

Now, thanks to my unintentional announcement of a marriage date, she considered me safe. Her work was done, and on this, the seventh day, she rested.

And though I'd promised myself not to think about it this evening, my mother's contentment inevitably contrasted with my memory of Claire Fairchild, who also only wanted her child to be safe. A wave of sadness took the edge off the bright evening.

But not for anyone else. By blundering into a wedding date, I'd defused the potential tension of this evening, and the two sets of parents, so dramatically dissimilar, were united and excited about seeing this through in style. I thought I'd be building conversational bridges all night long, but there was no need. I could have left the building and the party would have raged on.

I looked at my mother in her little black dress, the one she insisted be a part of every woman's wardrobe, her proper patent pumps, and her mother's marcasite initial pin. She'd have looked like a Puritan preaching to a lady of the evening, had both she and Gabby not looked so delighted with each other's company. Gabby, towering over her, was laughing at something my mother had said.

She looked like a tropical bird in the emerald brilliance of her dress—scoop neck, bouffant sleeves, skirts flouncing with blue and red embroidered tracery—the sort of thing Marie Antoinette wore when pretending to be a milkmaid, except for the strappy red high heels.

Even the fathers, Mackenzie, and Sam had found common ground, and all four were nodding in agreement with a topic I couldn't begin to guess.

My sister, supervising her own daughter who was carrying a tray of endive piped with what appeared to be crème fraîche and caviar, caught my eye and gave the thumbs-up sign. And then Sam poured champagne all around, and Mackenzie and I were toasted with only one minor glitch when my mother called the groom-to-be "Chuck" and Gabby did a double-take.

Joy reigned in Gladwynne. Poor Olivia and dead Claire Fairchild and mixed-up Emmie Cade faded into the distance till they disappeared altogether.

Dinner was a fine medley of barbecued lamb and crisp green beans and more wine and much laughter with Gabby, mother of seven married children who'd had thirteen weddings amongst them, regaling the table with tales of outrageous mishaps and mismatches. My mother looked worried by the stories at first, and then gave up and laughed along with everyone else.

Even the children, sipping apple juice in wineglasses, behaved, and when they started to fade, I took them upstairs. My longstanding role as spinster aunt included reading them bedtime stories when I was around, a perk I intended to keep. Now that Alexander was of an age to have favorites, each session followed a long negotiation. "Not the poop book again," Karen insisted. "Or else I get my own story."

I didn't have time for two books, and finally, they agreed on *Best Friends for Frances*, which seemed appropriately about siblings finding out they could be friends. I hadn't realized or remembered that the book was concerned with Frances's response to being excluded, but reading about it brought Olivia back into the room, the awareness of how much less aggressive and successful she'd been than a fictional badger.

Of course, badgers didn't have to go to high school. That made their lives easier.

Beth, afraid I was being trapped by her children, came upstairs, and together, we finished the story and tucked them in.

And ultimately, it was a traditional ladies-cleaning-up scene, with all of us vying for the "most helpful" award, but thanks to Beth's superpreparedness and modern conveniences like dishwashers, there was little washing, and no drying, and four women circling the kitchen until we divvied up the few chores. I was delegated to rescue the leftovers from Horse, which I did while we continued to talk about families, weddings, Beth's event-planning skills, and how cute the children were.

The senior generation was in the dining room, clearing the tablecloth and protective pads while I put leftover mint sauce in the refrigerator.

"I like your in-laws," Beth said. "They're fun."

"That they are. I can't believe how it's defused Mom. She's kind of rolling with whatever anybody says."

Beth raised her eyebrows. "Gabby is a bit . . . overwhelming," she whispered. "But in a good way."

"She's such a happy person," I whispered back, although the two mothers were talking at such a feverish pace in the next room, they couldn't have heard us even if we were louder. "As if life's a super game, and she's on a perpetual winning streak."

I wondered if I could adopt some of Gabby Mackenzie's resolute joy, and then I accepted the fact that I was not made of the same material, and I closed the refrigerator, checking what new shots of the children or invitations Beth's refrigerator sported. Snooping, to be blunt. I saw a mildly familiar item. Vicky Baer's brochure. "What is she doing up here?" I asked. "The refrigerator is hallowed home ground."

Beth laughed. "I haven't actually had a chance to read it yet, but I want to check out whether there's any crossover on there."

"Meaning?"

"You know. She consults all over the place, to all sorts of non-profits, and I'm putting together a little dinner party . . ."

"May I suggest that subtlety isn't your strong point?"

"Come down from your ivory tower," she said, and that made me laugh.

"What's the opposite of an ivory tower?" I asked. "A mud trench? That's more like Philly Prep."

"I realized I know somebody at a foundation she works with," she said, "and I thought it might be nice, since they already know each other, to invite them both. In fact, I called her—Vicky—right before you got here, but she was out. A woman who barely spoke English answered. I do wish people who have trouble with the language would simply leave an answering machine on."

I made sure the wrap was tight around the last of the lamb and returned to the crammed refrigerator in search of a place for it. "So is she coming to your gala?"

Beth shrugged. "I only spoke—if you can call it that—to this woman, who said 'the lady is with the friend who is feeling bad.' It took me so long to get that, that I didn't have the energy to try to leave a message. I'll call her tomorrow. Check out the brochure. She's got an impressive business going."

I had zero interest in it. Besides, Vicky had given me one as well and it must still be wherever I'd shoved it, should I ever want to check it out. But Beth seemed to want me to acknowledge what a trophy she'd snared and how clever she'd been, to officially approve of her networking savvy, so I obliged her, opening and skimming through it.

Vicky Baer had indeed developed an impressive business. Or a sufficiency of people willing to lie and give her nice little endorsements. There were tributes about increased endowments, a revised and three-times-more-profitable fund-raising plan, good service that didn't end with the contract, et cetera. I didn't personally recognize any of the sources, except Shipley School, but there were lots of them with the quotes, and then a sidebar list of still more.

This was a career I'd never have thought of, almost an oxymoron, helping nonprofits make money. Helping herself as well, I had to believe. And sampling just a few names, she'd pleased the boards of the KBS Foundation in Philly, and One Hundred Percent for the Children in D.C. I had a brief and nasty moment thinking that nobody would know if she'd made these places up. A King Henry School, that should have been in England, but found itself in Chicago; another, a more plainly named Prep school in Baltimore; and two in upstate New Jersey, right outside New York; The Family Foundation in Altoona; and The Learning Project in San Francisco for starters.

That's right—she'd bumped into Emmie while on business in San Francisco.

"I hope her success now extends to you," I said, returning the brochure to its refrigerator magnet.

I meant it. I was impressed. But I was also . . . I don't know what. Irritated by it. Something prickled, though I couldn't identify it. I wondered if I was jealous of her remarkable success, and hoped not. But I couldn't think why else her credentials annoyed me this way.

"One thing," Beth said softly. "You were honest with me the other night, weren't you?"

"About what? Of course I was. I always am, but what do you mean?"

"About Vicky. That she wasn't the one you were investigating."

"Absolutely not the one."

"Because you'd tell me, right? I mean, even if it's part of your job, and if you found out I was walking into something bad—there's no code forbidding you to tell me, is there?"

"My code of honor would absolutely make me keep you safe."

She exhaled loudly, as if she'd been holding her breath on this all evening.

I went back into the dining room to be certain that nothing edible was left in sight.

"You're amazing," my mother said as Gabby slid a drawer

226

closed. "How did you know where that went? And before? How did you know where the table pads went, too?"

Gabby winked at me. "Magic?" she said.

"Beth's magic, probably," I said. "She's the most logical person I've ever met, so everything is in—"

"He didn't tell you, huh?" Gabby's mouth curled in a tight, lop-sided smile.

"Who? Tell me what?"

"My son," she said in the most matter-of-fact way. "Tell you that I'm a witch." Her smile expanded till it half-covered her face, and she laughed and pointed at me, at my expression. "Guess not!"

"What—what do you mean?" My mother had her hands raised, cupping the top of her head, all but drawing a pointed hat up there.

"No, no," Gabby said, the half smile still on her face. We amused her. "Nothing special. Ordinary witchy things. I see things, commune with things."

We all saw things unless we were blind. And communed, I had to assume, with something. But we didn't see through solid cherry breakfronts, or commune with table pads as to where they belong.

"I'm not like an Orthodox witch," she said. "I'm a sole practitioner. No coven, no big rituals, and most of all," she said, looking around to make sure her work was done, "not that stupid bad-spell stuff in fairy tales. That's not real. That's just evil propaganda."

"Of course it is!" my mother said, eager as ever to be prejudice-free. "But then . . . when? What?"

Gabby raised her shoulders and inhaled, then let out the air and relaxed. "I just have . . . powers, but I can't truly say when it comes on me. It's erratic. And between us girls, since the change, I think I'm mostly losing it. My grandmother said the same thing happened to her. I mean, look—it's down to knowing where table pads go." She shook her head, then smiled again. "Easy come, easy go," she said. "And now, let us get our poor hostess out of the kitchen, and join our gentlemen friends."

My mother glanced at me warily, quickly, then away. She obviously didn't dare to say a word or think it. Gabby might have one of her rare postmenopausal second-sight bursts and read her mind. Besides, for all her marital advice and warnings, she'd never once told me to avoid men whose mothers were witches.

We reconvened in the living room, where the conversation rolled back and forth between the out-of-towners about their mutual visits. My mother almost visibly took herself in hand and rose above her reluctance to play with witches, and mentioned possible outings. I moved still closer to my Mackenzie, who put an arm around me and smiled. He was one happy man.

"Your mother just said she's a witch," I whispered.

His smile faded, and he closed his eyes for a second. Then he sighed and fixed his blue gaze on me. "I was hopin' she'd skip that."

"It's not news to you?"

He shook his head.

"And you never felt the need to mention it?" It is hard to shout in a whisper, and my throat ached doing so, but I had no choice. There was suddenly an arid desert between us, littered with important things unsaid, secrets kept. I didn't dare guess what else lay there. The fact that he'd kept it to himself was much more serious than Gabby's beliefs. I was up on things. I knew that Wiccan was a feminist religion, a goddess religion, that it really didn't have anything to do with the dreadful stereotypes fear had created through the ages.

Although I wasn't sure anything much I knew applied to Gabby's iconoclastic witchhood that seemed to depend on a ready supply of hormones.

"You were complainin' this very week that you wished I'd never told you a thing about my past."

"This is a little different, don't you think? This would be like being frank with me about a genetic problem, or a history of . . . of—"

"Horse thieves?"

"Okay, not exactly, but—"

"She's an entertaining, loving lady, isn't she?"

"Is witchcraft what you meant when you always added 'but eccentric'?"

He raised one eyebrow.

"Okay. *One* of the traits you meant."

"She's Acadian. They're different, you know. Named for the great doomed lovers in Longfellow's poem, Gabriel Lajeunesse and Evangeline Bellefontaine."

"They're fictional. She didn't inherit this from them."

"They were family ideals. And do you remember the lovers' story? How they found each other again in Philadelphia?" He smiled, as if that made everything all right.

"Found each other in Philadelphia and promptly died," I said.

He looked at me solemnly. "My sisters do not have the gift."

"Let me be clear on this. Your sisters are not witches."

"Correct."

"And you? Men can be witches."

He shook his head again. "Apparently, the Mackenzie DNA includes antiwitch matter."

I couldn't help but wonder what other family secrets lay in store and whether I was at all eager to enter that store. I just hated not knowing something that central about his family, and worried now that Mackenzie had carefully censored his words, as if he needed to protect me from the truth, or protect the truth from me.

I didn't like either option.

I wondered if the surprise introduction of a witch in the family gave one an out from a wedding. I'd bet even my mother would accept that as an excused absence.

Twenty

"WHAT a good time I'm having," Gabby said as the four of us walked to the car. It was still early. The dinner hour had been arranged for small children—and the originally planned arrival of the Mackenzies. The evening out here in the suburbs was lovely, with a faint whisper of autumn, a brisk edge to the soft night and, all around us, that wistful scent of the end of growing, of roses blooming for the last time.

"What a grand evening," Gabby said. "Lovely day."

"Evening's still young," Boy said. "Tell me it isn't true about this city rolling up the streets and let us take you out for a nightcap."

C. K. was grinning, contentment on every feature. He looked over at me. Apparently, he no longer cared about the stack of books he was supposed to be reading for school. He was definitely ready for more, but was letting me decide whether the good times kept rolling.

He was being a gentleman. A happy one.

Is there anything on earth more infuriating than being incensed with a man who's oblivious to it? "Sure," I said, because that postponed the argument I knew awaited us. I didn't want to spoil his parents' time, either. And it was early, just past eight P.M. "Anywhere. Your call."

"In that case," C. K. said, "there's a bar in South Philly that will provide not only drinks, but local color of a sort that will make you know you're not in Lafayette, Louisiana, anymore, folks."

We drove the Expressway in silence. Mackenzie turned on the radio and searched for the easy-listening station, the instant background noise because there wasn't any foreground. We seemed to have used up our chatter.

Gabby's need for polite sociability broke the silence. "What a darling family you have," she said.

"Thanks," I responded. "They thought the same of you." And then I set my hearing to "pleasantries," and let whatever was said blur into the background music becoming, if not white noise, then at best, pale, pale beige.

"Food delicious, too," Boy said, or something like it. "That lamb . . ."

"House beautiful . . ."

"Lovely . . ."

"Adorable . . . clever . . ."

"Even a lovely dog." That, of course, from Gabby.

Everything was perfect at Beth's. She had standards. She didn't get a mother-in-law who dressed like Merlin and recited chants.

"What dog have you ever met that you didn't think was lovely?" Boy seemed eternally amused by his wife. "This woman is a dog's best friend. Any dog. All dogs."

"Good creatures," she said.

And here I'd thought that cats were witch's familiars. Macavity had certainly taken to her immediately, but I'd ascribed it to his adoration of all things Mackenzie. Now I knew better.

"Do you think so, Manda?"

"Sorry," I said. "My mind was wandering."

"We could make a picnic Saturday? Everybody, includin' those adorable children of your sister's."

Saturday. Their last day. "Sounds great. I don't know Beth and Sam's schedule, but I'm sure they'd love it."

"How about Valley Forge?" Mackenzie said. "Toss in a little history." He had a future as a tour guide. Bars, picnics, you name it, he'd find the local angle.

"And their dog, too," Gabby said. "The park would allow him."

"Oh, Gabby," Boy said. "You're too much."

"I'm so homesick for the babies," she said. "And so worried Lizzie isn't going to remember to give Cary Grant his phenobarb both times. You know how she forgets things—and by the time we get home, he'll be having those fits again."

I sat up straight. "Excuse me?"

Mackenzie wasn't listening to me. He was into tour guiding. "Look," he said. "This is South Philly. See the row houses? All the same?"

"Like apartment buildings on their side," Boy said.

"Phenobarbital? For dogs?" I asked.

"New York's an island and had nowhere to go but up, but Philly could stretch out, and here you see it," C. K. said.

"Poor Cary's been takin' it for a while," Gabby said. "I just haven't been away all this long since then, and Lizzie's sweet but absentminded—"

"Her mind is pretty absent most of the time," Boy admitted.

"—and if Cary doesn't take it twice a day . . ."

I felt as if an electric prod had been applied to my brain. It zigged and zagged and pointed fingers and ran in circles shouting for attention.

Slow down, I told myself, as if I were back teaching the sophomores. Organize your thoughts.

Dogs. Medication. Vicky Baer's dog.

The ideas spun, chasing their tails.

Joan's call about Vicky Baer, nee Smith. Grade slump. Nothing the school did . . .

Olivia. Leaving school because of another girl.

Organize your thoughts!

The brochure.

Why the brochure? Why had it upset me? Her triumphant list of schools and foundations. Verbal bouquets from impressive clients all over the map. D.C., Baltimore, Altoona, Chicago, San Francisco . . .

"Cary will be fine," Boy said. "Not like you to worry this much."

"Mackenzie," I said, before he could point out other landmarks. "Humor me. Word-association time. What's the significance of these three cities: Baltimore, Altoona, Chicago."

"They all have an a and an o in their name."

I don't know how he does things like that so quickly, but I did know that wasn't the answer I needed. I sighed and folded my arms across my chest and even shook my head a bit to loosen up my thoughts, shake them out of the ruts they were in, get them organized.

I had it. "The *notes*!" I spoke as softly as I could, but I couldn't contain my excitement. "I knew there was something about that brochure—the anonymous notes came from the places Vicky Baer travels to!"

"Lovely. Except . . . so what?"

"So what? She sent those notes. That's what!"

"And? Mean-spirited, I'll grant you, but . . . I repeat, so what? Legally, what is that? Abuse of the postal service? Claire Fairchild might have been interested in that—if it's true—but she's beyond caring. Batya murdered her. Case closed."

No. It wasn't. Even if I didn't yet know why, I knew it wasn't over. And it felt urgently important that I line up the wild and unrelated messages flashing neon in my brain. Find the words to explain the electrical charges in my nervous system.

High school! Olivia. Leaving. Vicky leaving. Not the school's fault.

Sick dogs! Vicky left the dinner to take care of one.

No. Wait. My brain buzzed, the signs flashed randomly, all together, separately and I still couldn't make them out.

Phone call! She was going to take care of the dog after she took her phone call.

Emmie Cade had announced a wedding date that day. Was that the call?

Leo had already quarreled with his mother that day. Had found out about her hiring us. Told Emmie. Was that the call?

Pretending! Nobody knew Claire Fairchild was faking her illness then.

Shower! Something made Vicky visit Claire Fairchild that night. Was the idea of a bridal shower that urgent? Especially after she'd told me she wasn't all that close with Emmie, though they were old acquaintances, more than real friends.

Friend! Vicky's visiting a friend who was feeling bad. Right now. "Mackenzie." I put a hand on his arm.

"And here we are," he answered. "At the corner." I saw a beer's name lit up on a red brick wall. Accurate as ever, he'd found us a Typical South Philly Bar. It could occupy a display at the Smithsonian.

"No," I said.

He pulled into a spot a few houses up.

"No," I said again. "Turn around. We're wrong—everything we thought is wrong. The whole way we looked at this was wrong."

"This is it. I'm right," he said, looking confused.

"I mean about Claire Fairchild. Batya didn't do it, Mackenzie."

"Please," he said. "The police are—you know that. I told you—"

"They're all wrong, too! I know what happened now. Trust me. Turn around. We have to go to Emmie's right now." I looked at my watch. "And hope it's not too late."

"Actually, you're not making sense," he said, not unkindly. "My folks—we all agreed to a nightcap." He turned off the ignition.

"No! Turn it back on—I was wrong. I can't mess this up, too—she asked me to help her!"

"Who?"

"Emmie Cade!"

"No need to raise your—when? What about?"

"That isn't the point!"

"What *is* the point?"

"That you have to leave here right now and get to her—she's in danger!"

"Phone her if you're worried."

"What difference would that make? We have to go!"

"You're lettin' your imagination—"

"Ooooh, noooo," Gabby suddenly said, or moaned. She pressed both the heels of her hands to her temples. "I can't believe—I'm havin' the most terrifyin'—painful—vision—a girl—cryin'—something bad—somebody needs me. Quick. Somebody . . ." Her voice faded off.

"Oh, for Pete's—" Mackenzie said.

"Hits her like this," Boy said with audible admiration.

"She cries, she dies. . . ," she whispered rhythmically.

"Mother, please. It's not funny anymore."

The neon in my brain buzzed and flashed, all the words turning into danger signs.

"She needs, she—"

"Mother, those rhymes are—"

"Son," Boy said. That was all. Apparently, it was enough.

"This is craziness," Mackenzie muttered, but he started the car, turned the corner, then turned again, back into the direction of Center City and Emmie Cade. "Why, when all logic—" He gave up on the idea of logic. "You're going to be humiliated," he said. "This is about the least professional . . ."

I didn't answer. Neither did my ally, the witch, who sat muttering her pathetic rhymes, her hands still pressed to her temples. "Hurry," I said. "She's counting on our misreading everything. Don't play into her hands."

"Hurry, scurry," Gabby muttered.

Traffic was miraculously light—almost as if a witch were in control—and within fifteen minutes, we were in front of Claire Fairchild and Emmie Cade's building.

Way in front. We couldn't find a parking space.

"Tell you what. I'll wait in the car with my folks," Mackenzie said. "You can go up and check things out. Take your cell phone. Call if there's a problem."

What had happened to our partnership? What if something as wrong as I feared was going on and I was already inside the apartment? "At what stage in the problem should I call?" I asked, keeping my voice calm.

"I have to go with her. I have to see the girl in pain. Touch her—touch something of hers." Gabby Mackenzie still pressed her temples as if holding on to a vision, and her voice sounded as if it came out of an empty vase.

Mackenzie punched the steering wheel. "There aren't any parking spaces," he said.

"I'll make one happen," Gabby said, just as—right before?—slightly after?—a man walked out of the building jiggling keys.

"Damn," Mackenzie said as the man pulled an SUV out of a prize spot.

Damn was right. I looked at Gabby in amazement, then, in the two of us went, top speed, while C. K., still trying to save face and avoid going anywhere, pretended to be occupied with locking up the car and talking to his father.

Gabby and I entered the outer lobby. I found M. E. Cade's apartment number on a neatly printed list behind glass, and pressed the buzzer.

"They don't listen, do they?" Gabby said.

"Excuse me?"

"Like father, like son. Good as it gets, but—that tiny flaw. Don't take us seriously. Humor us, gentle us—and do what they think's right."

"Are you saying what I think you're—"

"Takes special powers now and then to get through to them."

"You *are* saying what I think you're—"

The men arrived. She didn't have to tell me to drop that conversational thread. We were buzzed in, and rode to Emmie's floor in silence, though Mackenzie's expression spoke volumes.

The future Mrs. Fairchild didn't occupy an entire floor the way the late Mrs. Fairchild had, and since the visiting clairvoyant apparently didn't do doors, I managed to go in the wrong direction twice, which was difficult, before determining on which door to knock. Only then did I allow myself to consider precisely what I was going to do with or about any of this.

Or admit, despite my supernatural backup, that I could be humiliatingly wrong.

The hallway was silent except for Mackenzie's whistle-hum, a faint and unpleasant sound he's apt to produce between his teeth, all unawares, when he would rather be anywhere but where he finds himself. "Nobody home," he said after a too-long wait.

"I know she's here. I'll prove it." Gabby pounded on the door, then nodded smartly.

And the door opened.

"That the girl in trouble?" Gabby asked me out of the side of her mouth.

I shook my head. "That's trouble itself."

"What's this?" Vicky Baer said. "Who are all of you?" She put a finger up to her mouth. "She's ill. Can't see anybody, certainly not a huge group of people."

Without a signal, without a word, Gabby and I pushed forward, moved Vicky to one side, and ran into the apartment.

"Hey!" Vicky screamed from right behind us. "Where do you think you're—"

"Emmie!" Like the panicked fool I was, I shouted her name even though I was sure she was already dead.

The living room was nearly empty. Little furniture and no body. Nobody. I ran through an archway, toward the bedroom, I assumed.

"Wait!" Gabby called, and I turned and saw her zoom through the open French windows, her arms held wide, and then, closed tight around a small figure leaning on, and half over, the balcony railing, like something dropped and abandoned there.

She looked smaller than ever, diminished. Boneless and liable to sink to the ground if Gabby let go, but Gabby didn't. Instead, she whispered something while gentling Emmie onto a wrought-iron chair next to a small table holding a bottle of wine and two glasses.

I flooded with relief to the point where I thought I might slide to the ground myself. She was alive. The terrible thing hadn't happened.

"Emmie's had too much." Vicky stood at the open doorway, hands on hips, Mackenzie and Boy behind her. Her voice so disapproved of what she saw, it felt curled down at its edges.

Gabby stood above Emmie, emerald sleeves billowing in the evening's breeze.

"I don't think so," I said to Vicky. "Claire Fairchild had too much, but Emmie hasn't had quite enough. What was next on the schedule? She was going to have a sudden impulse to jump? It wouldn't take much of a push. She's pretty small."

"You're out of—she's been drinking and ranting—"

I held up the bottle. "Nearly full. And neither glass really touched." Pity, I thought. It was good wine, going to waste.

Below us, a car honked and brakes squealed.

"I'm callin' paramedics." Mackenzie opened his cell and cursed softly. "Phone's dead."

"She's drunk!" Vicky insisted, but C. K. was gone, into the apartment in search of a live phone.

We were on the same side again. Partners.

Emmie showed signs of life. "Sorry," she said. "Sorry. Cliffffffff . . ." She sounded like a tire going flat. "Long time ago . . ."

"Who?" I asked, wondering where this man fit into her biography, but remembering, then, Joan's call. The school in Ohio from which Vicky Smith had fled.

"Says I ruined . . . sorry . . . teen . . ."

"Too drunk to make sense," Vicky said. "I'm going home."

"No, wait," I said. She wouldn't have, but Boy stood behind her like a closed gate. "What's your poor dog doing for medication these days?"

"Dog?" Gabby'd been idling, hovering over Emmie like a guardian angel, or mere mortal of the kind-and-concerned variety, not a proper witch at all. Of course, there'd been no need for magic. Emmie was alive. The word *dog* piqued the first sign of interest in the happenings.

"Why?" I asked Vicky. "Why Claire Fairchild? What did she ever do to you?"

Vicky eyed me blankly, her face a mask, and I knew. It had never been about Claire Fairchild. She'd been nothing more than a war casualty, *collateral damage*, that dehumanizing term that was easier to say than human beings killed by a war they weren't waging.

A woman treated as no more than a bump en route to a more important goal. A life dispassionately trashed as a device to frame someone else, a bullet to remove a rival. It hurt to believe it. "And Emmie takes the fall. Literally," I said. "That was your plan."

"I don't know what you're talking about. There's nothing mysterious about Mrs. Fairchild's death."

I hated that she referred politely, remotely to the woman she'd killed.

"She was dying," Vicky said. "No secret. She died. I don't see what you—"

"You don't die of pretending to be ill. You die when somebody substitutes her pet's medicine for your real pills."

"Your *dog's* medicine?" Gabby's voice again came out of empty tubing, echoing somehow on its own, and she was all action, her normal laissez-faire gone. She raised her arms toward the sky, her sleeves billowing, her nails twinkling in reflected light.

"Who are you?" Vicky shielded her face with her hands, as if Gabby physically threatened her.

"A witch," Gabby said in that inhuman hollow-pipe voice. "And I don't like you one bit."

"There's no such thing as a—" Vicky swallowed hard, and curled her mouth, but she didn't take her eyes off Gabby for a second, and when Gabby made two sets of claws of her spangled nails—that's all, not a word or a curse or a spell—I thought Vicky might faint. "You're insane!" She didn't sound convinced.

"Sorry, sorry, sorrrrr . . ." Emmie said in a whisper. "So long ago, shouldn't—"

"Shut up!" Vicky screamed, still keeping her eyes on Gabby, who made a sound suspiciously like a hiss.

"High school," I said. "And then what? Cornell? The boy she ran away with?"

"Nothing. Who cared?"

"You did. And then San Francisco—what? Bygones will be bygones, so you're polite to the widow and then what? Leo?"

"Din' know . . . Leeeeeee . . ." Emmie couldn't finish the name. Her head dropped further forward, and she was silent.

"Hang in there. Help's coming. Damn phone was in the bedroom—under the bed." Mackenzie was back. He went to Emmie, and I edged over and back to give him room and watch him try to keep her awake.

Below us, in the distance, I heard the whine of an ambulance. "Hang in there," he said. "Hear that? It's for you. It's help."

She flopped forward. Mackenzie bent to lift her.

"I'll let them in," Boy said. "She looks bad. Can you save her, Gabby?"

Gabby? The hissing spectator? Nonetheless, she looked at her husband whose I.Q. I was beginning to question, and nodded. An arrogant witch, or maybe they all were. Came with the territory.

"Stop acting as if she's a—"

"I can't read you your rights anymore," Mackenzie told Vicky, "but you'd better think about them, because the police are on their way, too." He got Emmie to her feet. "Don't give up yet," he said. "C'mon," and he walked her, slowly, toward the apartment.

"Police?" Vicky put her hands back up to her face. "You can't—I didn't do—" His back was to her, and she stopped, her mouth half open, her eyes suddenly tearing, and her words increasingly garbled. "You have to tell them I never meant for her to die! I only wanted—I only—you can't—it wasn't right—*again! She's* the witch. She ruins my life over and over again!"

"Don't you badmouth witches," Gabby said.

"Doesn't matter what you wanted," Mackenzie said, his back to her as he softly spoke to Emmie, and patted her cheeks. "Murder's what you got."

"What'll I do?" she wailed.

"Spend a long time in prison," I said, but just then, I saw Emmie Cade trip as she crossed the threshold into the apartment. "Watch out!" I called. "She's—" Gabby began, and both Mackenzie and Boy bent to catch her, bumped heads, then managed nonetheless to save Emmie from collapse before they stood up and rubbed their sore spots.

And all of us heard a terrifying squeal of tires and, from nowhere, down below, shouts.

I think I knew before I turned and saw the empty balcony that Vicky Baer was no longer with us.

IT WAS OVER. Pretty much like that. The paramedics were delayed because of Vicky's leap, but they arrived in time, and there we were, locking up someone else's apartment.

No fireworks, no dark alleys, no punches, chases, gunshots, merely a witch and a zombie and, for me, a subtle shaking that wouldn't stop, and a terrible confusion about who, truly, the victim had been and when a crime actually begins. What do we do with hurts that started a lifetime ago?

I was glad Olivia refused to be cowed, that she'd move on, live her life. But what if Melanie kept showing up, kept removing what she held dear?

If you're Gabby Mackenzie, you say it doesn't bear thinking about right now. "It's all confusion, honey. All you can do right now is go through the motions of normal. Then, someday, things fall into place of their own accord."

That more or less made sense.

And if you're Gabby, you say that maybe it was all for the best, perhaps the least painful end for Vicky Baer, and you adopt her dog.

That made sense, too.

And, later on, when we were having a drink, silently and still in shock, and the men chose to recuperate in a guy way, walking over to the TV, where the Phillies were involved in extra innings, you take a deep breath and say, "So we did it, didn't we? A little witchcraft comes in handy."

That made no sense.

For starters, what had we done? Vicky Baer had jumped to her death, still feeling pursued by a fury named Emmie Cade. Did we pat ourselves on the back for that?

And Gabby's part of the *we* hadn't done a thing except stretch her hands toward the sky.

When I didn't respond, she prompted me. "Didn't we save the good one?" she asked.

I wasn't sure anymore who'd been the good one. "We saved the one who hadn't murdered Claire Fairchild. Who only hurt people unintentionally. Or because it was easier, or more lucrative."

"You said she was the good one."

"Since you mention that, I'm confused why I had to tell you."

"You care that I didn't know which girl was which? Big deal."

I also thought her incantations were pathetic rhymes, but she was going to be my mother-in-law, so I kept my mouth shut.

"Would you like it better if I called it women's intuition, which is just another name for paying good attention?" She shook her head. Tendrils of her snow-colored hair had pulled loose from the ornate updo and looked like punctuation marks around her face. "Men don't like that better. They ignore it. Puff up, pat your head, and say, There, there little lady."

True enough. I'd never invoke *intuition*.

"Like, say, that parking spot I made happen. It is possible that while you all blathered away about who was going where, I saw the man come out holding his keys. But maybe not. Maybe it was magic, and what does it matter? It worked out. I mean, God knows I'm sorry for that girl, but she killed a woman and didn't seem to give a damn. Not even now. She was going to kill another one. And—"

I knew what was coming, her priorities, what really got to her.

"—she endangered her doggie's life taking away his medicine. She had the last word this way. Played judge and jury and doled out her own punishment."

I hadn't thought of it that way, and now I did, while I sipped scotch. It helped. I was no longer as conscious of every nerve end in my body.

"So what do you think?" Gabby asked, breaking into my reverie. "Want to be a witch, too?"

"They don't do well in these parts. Think Salem."

"Oh, right," she said. "A pity what they did, wasn't it?"

"Plus, I think your son's onto your game."

She winked at me. "His father, too. Doesn't matter, though. It's like a middle ground where they can agree and still save face. And speaking of them, it's high time they paid attention to us, don't you think? I mean, you aren't even married yet and he's ignoring you. Can't have that." She clapped her hands, twice.

And damned if that instant a huge male cheer didn't rise up from the bar. "Home run!" the TV announcer shouted out. "And

243

GILLIAN ROBERTS

that's the game, folks, a nail-biter with the Phillies in eleven with—"

I looked at Gabby with new amazement.

She winked at me, and then at the men, whose mood had lightened considerably. "We won," Mackenzie said.

I looked at him. "We did indeed," I said. We had.

My partner, my fiancé, my love. My one-of-a-kind son-of-a-witch.